Richard Laymon wrote over thirty novels and seventy short stories. In May 2001, *The Travelling Vampire Show* w... Best Horror Novel, a prize for which I shortlisted with *Flesh, Funland, A Good,* and *A Writer's Tale* (Best Non-fiction). books of the Beast House Chronicles: *Th The Midnight Tour.* Some of his recent n *Lonesome October, No Sanctuary* and *Amara.*

A native of Chicago, Laymon attended Willamette University in Salem, Oregon, and took an MA in English Literature from Loyola University, Los Angeles. In 2000, he was elected President of the Horror Writers' Association. He died in February 2001.

Laymon's fiction is published in the United Kingdom by Headline, and in the United States by Leisure Books and Cemetery Dance Publications. To learn more, visit the Laymon website at: http://rlk.cjb.net

'A gut-crunching writer' *Time Out*

'In Laymon's books, blood doesn't so much as drip as explode, splatter and coagulate' *Independent*

'This author knows how to sock it to the reader' *The Times*

'No one writes like Laymon and you're going to have a good time with anything he writes' Dean Koontz

'A brilliant writer' *Sunday Express*

'Stephen King without a conscience' Dan Marlowe

'This is an author that does not pull his punches . . . A gripping, and at times genuinely shocking, read' *SFX Magazine*

'Incapable of writing a disappointing book' *New York Review of Science Fiction*

'One of the best, and most underrated, writers working in the genre today' *Cemetery Dance*

Also in the Richard Laymon Collection published by Headline

The Beast House Trilogy:
The Cellar
The Beast House
The Midnight Tour

Beware!
Dark Mountain*
The Woods are Dark
Out are the Lights
Night Show
Allhallow's Eve
Flesh
Resurrection Dreams
Darkness, Tell Us
One Rainy Night
Alarums
Blood Games
Endless Night
Midnight's Lair*
Savage
In the Dark
Island
Quake
Body Rides
Bite
Fiends
After Midnight
Among the Missing
Come Out Tonight
Night in the Lonesome October
No Sanctuary
Amara
The Lake
The Glory Bus
Funland
The Stake

*previously published under the pseudonym of Richard Kelly

The Travelling Vampire Show

and

Dreadful Tales

headline

THE TRAVELLING VAMPIRE SHOW
first published in Great Britain in 2000
by HEADLINE PUBLISHING GROUP

DREADFUL TALES first published in Great Britain in 2000
by HEADLINE PUBLISHING GROUP

First published in this omnibus edition in 2007
by HEADLINE PUBLISHING GROUP

A HEADLINE paperback

3

ISBN 978 0 7553 3182 6

Typeset in Janson by Avon DataSet Ltd, Bidford on Avon, Warwickshire

Printed and bound in Great Britain by
CPI Antony Rowe, Chippenham and Eastbourne

Headline's policy is to use papers that are natural, renewable and recyclable
products and made from wood grown in sustainable forests. The logging and
manufacturing processes are expected to conform to the environmental
regulations of the country of origin.

HEADLINE PUBLISHING GROUP
A division of Hachette Livre UK Ltd
338 Euston Road
London NW1 3BH

www.headline.co.uk
www.hodderheadline.com

The Travelling
Vampire Show

This book is dedicated

to

Richard Chizmar

owner, manager and coach
of the CD team.

You took us to the show.

Chapter One

The summer I was sixteen, the Travelling Vampire Show came to town.

I heard about it first from my two best friends, Rusty and Slim.

Rusty's real name was Russell, which he pretty much hated.

Slim's real name was Frances. She had to put up with it from her parents and teachers, but not from other kids. She'd tell them, 'Frances is a talking mule.' Asked what she *wanted* to be called, her answer pretty much depended on what book she happened to be reading. She'd say, 'Nancy' or 'Holmes' or 'Scout' or 'Zock' or 'Phoebe.' All last summer, she wanted to be called Dagny. Now, it was Slim. A name like that, I figured maybe she'd started reading westerns. But I didn't ask.

My name is Dwight, by the way. Named after the Commander of the Allied Expeditionary Forces in Europe. He didn't get elected President until after I'd already been born and named.

Anyway, it was a hot August morning, school wouldn't be starting again for another month, and I was out in front of our house mowing the lawn with a push mower. We must've been the only family in Grandville that didn't have a power mower. Not that we couldn't afford one. Dad was the town's chief of police and Mom taught English at the high school. So we had the money for a power mower, or even a *riding* mower, but not the inclination.

Not Dad, anyway. Long before anyone ever heard of

language like 'noise pollution', Dad was doing everything in his power to prevent this or that 'godawful racket'.

Also, he was opposed to any sort of device that might make life easier on me or my two brothers. He wanted us to work hard, sweat and suffer. He'd lived through the Great Depression and World War Two, so he knew all about suffering. According to him, 'Kids these days've got it too easy.' So he did what he could to make life tougher on us.

That's why I was out there pushing the mower, sweating my ass off, when along came Rusty and Slim.

It was one of those gray mornings when the sun is just a dim glow through the clouds and you know by the smell that rain's on the way and you wish it would hurry up and get here because the day is so damn hot and muggy.

My T-shirt was off. When I saw Rusty and Slim coming toward me, I suddenly felt a little embarrassed about being without it. Which was sort of strange, considering how much time we'd spent together in our swimming suits. I had an urge to run and snag it off the porch rail and put it on. But I stayed where I was, instead, and waited for them in just my jeans and sneakers.

'Hi, guys,' I called.

'What's up?' Rusty greeted me. He meant it, of course, as a sexual innuendo. It was the sort of lame stuff he cherished.

'Not much,' I said.

'Are you working hard, or hardly working?'

Slim and I both wrinkled our noses.

Then Slim looked at my sweaty bare torso and said, 'It's too hot to be mowing your lawn.'

'Tell that to my dad.'

'Let me at him.'

'He's at work.'

'He's getting off lucky,' Slim said.

We were all smiling, knowing she was kidding around.

She liked my dad – liked both my parents a whole lot, though she wasn't crazy about my brothers.

'So how long'll it take you to finish the yard?' Rusty asked.

'I can quit for a while. I've just gotta have it done by the time Dad gets home from work.'

'Come on with us,' Slim said.

I gave a quick nod and ran across the grass. Nobody else was home: Dad at work, Mom away on her weekly shopping trip to the grocery store and my brothers (one single and one married) no longer living at our house.

As I charged up the porch stairs, I called over my shoulder, 'Right back.' I whipped my T-shirt off the railing, rushed into the house and raced upstairs to my bedroom.

With the T-shirt, I wiped the sweat off my face and chest. Then I stepped up to the mirror and grabbed my comb. Thanks to Dad, my hair was too short. *No son of mine's gonna go around looking like a girl*. I wasn't allowed to have much in the way of sideburns, either. *No son of mine's gonna traipse around looking like a hood.* Thanks to him, I hardly had enough hair to bother combing. But it was mussed and matted down with sweat, so I combed it anyway – making sure my 'part' was straight as a razor, then giving the front a little curly flip.

After that, I grabbed my wallet off the dresser, shoved it into a back pocket of my jeans, hurried to the closet and pulled a short-sleeved shirt off its hanger. I put it on as I hurried downstairs.

Rusty and Slim were waiting on the porch.

I finished fastening my buttons, then opened the screen door.

'Where we going?' I asked.

'You'll see,' Slim said.

I shut the door and followed my friends down the porch stairs.

Rusty was wearing an old shirt and blue jeans. That's

pretty much what we *all* wore when we weren't dressed up for school or church. You hardly ever caught guys our age wearing shorts. Shorts were for little kids, old farts, and girls.

Slim *was* wearing shorts. They were cut-off blue jeans, so faded they were almost white, with frayed denim dangling and swaying like a fringe around her thighs. She also wore a white T-shirt. It was big and loose and untucked, so it hung over her butt in the back. Her white swimsuit top showed through the thin fabric. It was a skimpy, bikini-type thing that tied behind her back and at the nape of her neck. She was wearing it instead of a bra. It was probably more comfortable than a bra, and definitely more practical.

Mostly, in the summer, we all wore swimsuits instead of underwear. You never knew when you might end up at the municipal pool or at the river . . . or even when you might get caught in a downpour.

I had my trunks on under my jeans that morning. They were sort of soggy with sweat from mowing the lawn, and they clinged to my butt as I walked down the street with Rusty and Slim.

'So what's the plan?' I asked after a while.

Slim looked at me and hoisted an eyebrow. 'Stage one's already been executed.'

'Huh?' I asked.

'We freed you from the chains of oppression.'

'Can't be mowing the *yard* on a day like this,' Rusty explained.

'Well, thanks for liberating me.'

'Think nothing of it,' Rusty said.

'Our pleasure,' Slim said, and patted me on the back.

It was just a buddy-pat, but it gave me a sickish excited lonely feeling. I'd been getting that way a lot, that summer, when I was around Slim. It didn't necessarily involve

4

touching, either. Sometimes, I could just be *looking* at her and start to feel funny.

I kept it to myself, though.

'Stage two,' Slim said, 'we see what's going on at Janks Field.'

I felt a little chill crawl up my back.

'Scared?' Rusty asked.

'Oh, yeah. Ooooo, I'm shaking.'

I *was*, but not so much that it showed. I hoped.

'We don't *have* to go there,' Slim said.

'*I'm* going,' said Rusty. 'If you guys are chicken, I'll go by myself.'

'What's the big deal about Janks Field?' I asked.

'This,' said Rusty.

The three of us had been walking abreast with Slim in the middle. Now, Rusty hustled around behind us and came over to my side. He pulled a piece of paper out of the back pocket of his jeans. Unfolding it, he said, 'These're all over town.'

The way he held the paper open in front of me, I knew I wasn't supposed to touch it. It seemed to be a poster or flier, but it was bouncing around too much for me to read it. So I stopped walking. We all stopped.

Slim came in close so she could look at the paper, too. It had four torn corners. Apparently, Rusty had ripped the poster off a wall or tree or something.

It looked like this:

THE TRAVELLING VAMPIRE SHOW

COME AND SEE THE ONE AND ONLY
KNOWN VAMPIRE IN CAPTIVITY

VALERIA

GORGEOUS! BEGUILING! LETHAL!

THIS STUNNING BEAUTY, BORN IN
THE WILDS OF TRANSYLVANIA,
SLEEPS BY DAY IN HER COFFIN.
BY NIGHT, SHE FEEDS ON
THE BLOOD OF STRANGERS.

SEE VALERIA RISE FROM THE DEAD!
WATCH AS SHE STALKS VOLUNTEERS
FROM THE AUDIENCE!
TREMBLE AS SHE SINKS HER TEETH
INTO THEIR NECKS!
SCREAM AS SHE SUPS ON THEIR BLOOD!!!

WHERE: Janks Field 2 miles South of Grandville on Route 3
WHEN: One Show Only – Friday, midnight
HOW MUCH: $10
(NOBODY UNDER AGE 18 ALLOWED)

Amazed and excited, I shook my head and murmured 'Wow' a time or two while I read the poster.

But things changed when I got toward the bottom.

I felt a surge of alarm, followed by a mixture of relief and disappointment.

Mostly relief.

'Oh, man,' I muttered, trying to sound dismayed. 'What a bummer.'

Chapter Two

'A bummer?' Rusty asked. 'You outa your mind, man? We've got us a travelling *vampire* show! A real live *female* vampire, right here in Grandville! And it says she's *gorgeous*! See that? Gorgeous! Beguiling! A stunning beauty! And she's a *vampire*! Look what it says! She stalks volunteers from the audience and bites their necks! She *sups* on their blood!'

'Bitchin',' Slim said.

'Might be bitchin' if we could *see* her,' I said, trying to seem gloomy about the situation. 'But there's no way we can get into a show like that.'

Eyes narrow, Rusty shook his head. 'That's how come we're going over there now.'

'Oh,' I said.

Sometimes, when Rusty came out with stuff like that, 'Oh' was about the best I could do.

'You know?' he asked.

'I guess so.' I had no idea.

'We'll look the place over,' Slim said. 'Just see what we can see.'

'Maybe we'll get to see *her*,' Rusty said. He seemed pretty excited.

'Don't get your hopes up,' Slim told him.

'We *might*,' he insisted. 'I mean, she's gotta be around. *Somebody* put all those posters up, you know? And the show is *tonight*. They're probably over at Janks Field getting things ready right now.'

'*That's* probably true,' Slim said. 'But don't count on feasting your eyes on the gorgeous and stunning Valeria.'

He blinked at Slim, disappointment and vague confusion

on his face. Then he turned his eyes to me, apparently seeking an ally.

I looked at Slim.

She raised both eyebrows and one corner of her mouth.

The goofy expression made me ache and laugh at the same time. Forcing my eyes away from her, I said to Rusty, 'The gal's a vampire, moron.'

'Huh?'

'Valeria. She's supposed to be a vampire.'

'Yeah, so?' he asked, as if impatient for the punch line.

'So you think we're gonna maybe sneak up on Janks Field and catch her *sunbathing*?'

'Oh!'

He got it.

Slim and I laughed. Rusty stood there, red in the face but bobbing his head and chuckling. Then he said, 'She's gotta be in her *casket*, right?'

'*Right!*' Slim and I said in unison.

Rusty laughed pretty hard about that. And we joined in. Then we resumed our journey.

After a while, Rusty drew out in front by a stride or two, turned his head to look back at us, and said, 'But seriously, maybe we *will* catch her sunbathing.'

'Are you nuts?' Slim asked.

'In the *nude!*'

'Oh, you'd like that.'

'You bet.'

Scowling, I shook my head. 'All you'd see is a little pile of ashes. And the first breeze that comes along . . .'

Slim started to sing like Peter, Paul and Mary, 'The vammmmpire, my friend, is blowwwwing in the wind . . .'

'And even if she *didn't* burn to a crisp at the first touch of sunlight,' I said, 'she'd sure as hell know better than to put on her vampire show with a *suntan*.'

'Good point,' Slim said. 'She's gotta look pale.'

'She could cover her tan with makeup,' Rusty explained.

'That's a point,' Slim agreed. 'She probably uses a ton of makeup, anyway, to give her a convincing palor of undeadness. So why *not* a tan underneath it?'

'An *all-over* tan,' Rusty said, leering.

'We've gotta find you a girl,' Slim said.

I suddenly wondered how *Slim* would look sunbathing in the nude, stretched out on her back with her hands folded under her head, her eyes shut, her skin slick and golden all the way down. It excited me to imagine her that way, but it made me feel guilty, too.

To push it out of my mind, I said, 'How about Valeria?'

'There ya go,' Slim said. 'I hear she's stunning.'

'I'll take her,' Rusty said.

'You haven't even seen her yet,' I pointed out.

'I don't care.'

'Don't believe everything you read,' Slim told him. 'Valeria might turn out to be a pug-ugly, hideous hag.'

'I bet she's incredible,' Rusty said. 'She *has* to be.'

'Wishful thinking,' I said.

Smiling as if he knew a secret, he asked, 'Wanta put your money where your mouth is?'

'Five bucks says she's *not* gorgeous.'

'I haven't got five bucks,' Rusty said.

Which came as no surprise. His parents gave him an allowance of two bucks a week, which he was always quick to spend. I did better, myself, getting paid per chore and also doing some part-time yard work for a couple of neighbors.

'How much?' I asked.

'Don't bet, you guys,' Slim said. 'Somebody'll end up losing . . .'

'Yeah,' Rusty said. '*He* will. You wanta go in with me?'

'You've gotta be kidding,' Slim said.

9

'Come on. You're always loaded.'

'That's 'cause I don't squander my money foolishly.'

'But this is a sure thing.'

'How do you figure that?' Slim asked.

'Easy. This Travelling Vampire Show? Valeria's the main attraction, right?'

'Sounds like she's the *only* attraction,' I threw in.

'And we all know it's bullshit, right? I mean, she's no more a vampire than *I* am. So she *has* to be gorgeous or you'd end up without any customers. I mean, you might be able to get away with having her be a fake *vampire*. Nobody's gonna expect a real one of those, anyway. But . . .'

'Some people might,' I broke in.

'Nobody with half a brain,' he said.

'I'm not so sure of that,' Slim said.

We both stared at her.

'Maybe vampires *do* exist,' she said, a sparkle of mischief in her eyes.

'Get real,' Rusty said.

'Can you prove they don't?'

'Why would I *wanta* prove that? Everybody knows they don't exist.'

'Not me,' said Slim.

'Bullshit.' He turned to me. 'What about you, Dwight?'

'I'm with Slim.'

'Big surprise.'

'She's smarter than both of us put together,' I said. Then I blushed because of the way she looked at me. 'Well, you are.'

'Nah. I just read a lot. And I like to keep my mind open.' Smiling at Rusty, she added, 'It's easy to have an open mind since I've only got half a brain.'

'I didn't mean you,' he said. 'But I'm starting to wonder.'

'To set *your* mind at ease, I doubt very much that Valeria *is* a vampire. I suppose there's a remote possibility, but it seems highly unlikely.'

'Now you're talking.'

'I also agree that, since she probably isn't a vampire, she'd *better* be beautiful.'

Rusty beamed. 'So, you want to back my bet?'

'Can't. You'll need someone to take a good, objective look at her and decide who wins. That'd better be me. I'll decide the winner.'

'Fine with me,' I said.

'I guess that'll be okay,' said Rusty.

'Don't look so worried,' Slim told him.

'Well, you always take Dwight's side about everything.'

'Only when his side is the "right" side. And I have a feeling that *you* might win this one.'

'Thanks a lot,' I told her.

'But I promise to be fair.'

'I know,' I said.

'So what're we gonna wager?' Rusty asked me.

'How much money do you want to lose?' I asked him.

I wasn't very confident about winning, anymore. He'd made a pretty good argument; if Valeria isn't a vampire, she *has* to be beautiful or there'd be no show. But I saw a hole in his case.

Valeria didn't have to be a real vampire for the show to work. She didn't need to be incredibly gorgeous, either. The Travelling Vampire Show might be successful anyway . . . if it was really and truly exciting or scary.

'Let's leave money out of the wager,' Slim suggested. 'Suppose the loser has to do something gross?'

Rusty grinned. 'Like kiss the winner's ass?'

'Something along those lines.'

I frowned at Rusty. 'I'm not kissing your ass.'

'It doesn't have to be that,' Slim said.

11

'How about the loser kisses *hers?*' He nodded at Slim.

Her ass? The loser?

Slim's face went red. 'Nobody's kissing *my* ass. Or my anything else, for that matter.'

'There goes my *next* idea,' Rusty said, and laughed. He could be a pretty crude guy.

'Why don't we just forget the whole thing?' I suggested.

'Chicken,' Rusty said. 'You just know you're gonna lose.'

'We might not even get to *see* her.'

'If we can't see her,' Slim said, 'the wager's off.'

'We don't even *have* a wager.'

'I've got it!' Rusty said. 'The winner gets to spit in the loser's mouth.'

Slim's mouth fell open and she blinked at him. 'Are you brain-damaged?' she asked.

'You got a better idea?'

'*Any* idea would be better than that.'

'Like what?' he asked. 'Let's hear *you* come up with something?'

'All right.'

'Let's hear it.'

Frowning as if deep in thought, Slim glanced from Rusty to me a few times. Then she said, 'Okay. The loser gets his hair shaved off.'

In that regard, Rusty had a lot more to lose than I did. He had a head of hair that would've put Elvis Presely to shame, and he was mighty proud of it.

Nose wrinkled, he muttered, 'I don't know.'

'You said it's a sure thing,' I reminded him.

'Yeah, but . . . I don't know, man. My hair.' He reached up and stroked it. 'I don't wanta go around looking like a dork.'

'It'll grow back,' I said.

'Eventually,' added Slim.

'Anyway, I'm not gonna let Dwight anywhere *near* me with a razor.'

'I'll do the shaving,' Slim said.

Hearing that, I suddenly didn't want to win this wager. I hoped Valeria would be the most amazingly beautiful woman in the world.

'How about it?' Slim asked.

'Count me in,' I said.

I could tell by the look on Rusty's face that he wanted to back out. But honor was at stake, so he sighed and said, 'All right. It's a bet.'

Chapter Three

The dirt road leading through the forest to Janks Field was usually unmarked. Today, though, posters for The Travelling Vampire Show were nailed to trees on both sides of the turn-off. And a large sign – the side of a cardboard box nailed to a tree – pointed the way with a red-painted arrow. Above the arrow, somebody had painted, VAMPIRE SHOW in big, drippy red letters. Below the arrow, in smaller drippy letters, was written, MIDNITE.

'Nice, professional job,' Slim commented.

'We probably aren't dealing with mental giants,' I said.

'WHY ARE YOU TALKING SO QUIET?' Rusty boomed out, making us both jump.

We whirled around and watched him laugh.

'Good one,' Slim said, looking peeved.

13

'A riot,' I said.

'YOU TWO AREN'T *NERVOUS*, ARE YOU?'

Slim grimaced. 'Would you pipe down?'

'WHAT'RE YOU SCARED OF?'

I wanted to bash him one in the face, but I held back. I don't think I've mentioned it yet, but Rusty wasn't exactly in the best of shape. Not a total lardass, but pudgy and soft and not exactly capable of fighting back.

Which might seem like an advantage if you want to slug a guy in the puss. But I knew it would make me feel lousy. And he was my best friend, after all – other than Slim.

Grinning, he boomed, 'CAT GOT YOUR TONGUE?'

Slim pinched his side.

He gasped, 'OW!' and twisted away. 'That *hurt!*'

'Keep it down,' Slim said.

'Jeez.'

'We're gonna have to be sneaky going in,' she explained, 'or they'll toss our butts out and we'll never get a chance to see Valeria.'

'Or don't you *want* to see her?' I asked Rusty.

'Jeez, guys, I was just screwing around.'

'Let's hope nobody heard you,' Slim said.

'Nobody heard me. We're *miles* from Janks Field.'

'More like a few hundred yards,' I told him.

'And sound really carries around here,' Slim added.

'Okay, okay, I get the point.'

The dirt road wasn't as wide as Route 3, so we didn't walk abreast. Slim took the lead. Rusty and I stayed pretty much beside each other.

There was no sunlight. Of course, there hadn't been any sunlight *before* we entered the woods – just a gray gloom. But now, with trees all around and above us, the gloom was deeper, darker. Things looked the way they do when you're out after supper on a summer night and you can see just fine, so far, but you've only got maybe half an hour before it'll be too dark for playing ball.

'If it gets much darker,' I said, 'Valeria won't *need* her casket.'

Rusty put a finger to his lips and went, 'Shhhhh.'

I gave him the finger.

He smirked.

After that, I kept my mouth shut.

Our shoes were almost silent on the dirt road except when one of us stepped on a twig. Rusty was breathing fairly hard. Every so often, he muttered stuff under his breath.

A very quiet tune seemed to be coming from Slim. 'De dum, de doo, de do-doo . . .' It blended in with the sounds all around us of buzzing flies and mosquitos and bees, bird tweets, and the endless flutters and rustling scurries of unseen creaturs. 'De-dum, de do, de doo.'

Rusty made no attempt to shush her.

But suddenly he said, 'Wait up.'

Slim halted.

When we caught up to her, Rusty said in a hushed voice, 'I gotta take a leak.'

Slim nodded. 'Pick a tree,' she said.

He glanced from Slim to me. 'Don't go anywhere, okay?'

'We'll stay right here,' she told him.

I nodded.

'Okay,' he said. 'I'll be back in a minute.' He stepped off the dirt road and made his way into the trees.

'Do you have to go?' Slim asked me.

'Nah.'

'Me neither.' She pursed her lips and blew softly through them. Then she said, 'Sure is hot in here.'

'Yeah,' I muttered. I was broiled and drenched and itchy, my clothes sticking to me.

15

Slim's short blonde hair was matted down in coils against her scalp and forehead. Sweat ran down her face. As I watched, a drip gathered at the tip of her nose and fell. Her white T-shirt was clinging to her skin and I could see through it.

'This vampire better be worth it,' she said.

'Too bad we won't get to see her.'

Slim gave me half a smile. 'If she's in her casket, we'll have to bust her out of it. We're not gonna put ourselves through all this and not get a look at her.'

'I don't know,' I said.

'Don't know what?' she asked, and peeled her T-shirt off. In spite of her bikini top, she seemed to be mostly bare skin from the waist up. She wadded her T-shirt and mopped the sweat off her face.

I looked the other way.

'What don't you know?' she asked.

For a moment, I wasn't sure what we'd been talking about. Then I remembered. I said, 'She isn't gonna be by herself. I don't think so, anyway.'

'You're probably right.' Lowering the shirt away from her face, she smiled and said, 'She needs casket handlers.'

'Right.'

'Probably has a whole crew.' She wiped her chest, her arms.

'And they might not be model citizens,' I said.

Laughing softly, she lowered her head and began to wipe the sweat off her belly and sides. I sneaked a glance at her breasts. The thin pouches of her bikini top were stretched smooth with them. Around the edges of the fabric, I glimpsed pale slopes of skin.

'We'll have to be careful,' I said.

'Yeah. If they look *really* scurvy, we'd better forget the whole thing.'

Hearing footsteps, we both turned our heads and saw Rusty trudging toward us.

Slim continued to rub at herself with the balled shirt. I wanted her to put it back on, but I didn't say anything.

'All set,' Rusty said. I saw him check her out. 'What's going on?'

'Nothing much,' Slim told him. 'Just waiting for you.'

'We're thinking we'll have to be really careful,' I explained. 'Valeria's gonna have . . .'

'Casket keepers,' Slim threw in.

Rusty smiled and nodded.

'No telling how many people might be with the show,' I said.

'And it's likely a *scurrrrvy* lot,' added Slim with a bit of Long John Silver in her voice.

'They go around with a travelling vampire show,' Rusty said, 'they've gotta be at least a *little* strange.'

'And maybe dangerous,' I said.

Rusty suddenly frowned. 'You guys aren't gonna chicken out, are you?' Before either of us had a chance to answer, he said, ' 'Cause *I'm* going irregardless.'

'Irregardless ain't a word, Einstein,' Slim told him.

'Is too.'

She wasn't one to argue. She just gave him a funny smile, then pulled her T-shirt on. 'Let's go.'

After that, none of us said anything. We weren't that far from Janks Field, so I think we were starting to get more nervous.

Janks Field was the sort of place that made you nervous no matter what.

First off, nothing grows there. It's a big patch of hard bare dirt surrounded by thick, green woods. But it's not bare on purpose. Nobody *clears* the field. As far as anyone knows, it's always been that way.

I've heard people say the dirt there is poison. I think they're wrong about that, though. Janks Field has more than its share of wildlife – the sort that lives in holes in the ground – ants, spiders, snakes, and so on.

Some people say aliens landed there, and that's why nothing will grow.

Sure thing.

Others say the field is cursed. I might go along with that. You might, too, after you know more about it.

The reason they call the place Janks Field isn't because it belongs to anyone named Janks. It doesn't, and never did. It's called that because of Tommy Janks and what he did there in 1954.

I was just a little kid at the time, so nobody told me much. But I do remember people acting funny the summer it all happened. Dad, being chief of police, wasn't home very often. Mom, usually cheerful, seemed oddly nervous. And sometimes I overheard scattered talk about missing girls. This went on for most of the summer. Then something big happened and everyone went crazy. All the grown-ups were pale and whispering and I caught bits and pieces like, 'Some kind of monster . . .' and 'Dear God . . .' and 'their poor parents . . .' and 'always knew there was something *off* about him.'

As it turns out, some Boy Scouts had hiked into the field and found Tommy Janks sitting by a campfire. He was a deaf mute, so he never heard them coming. They caught him with a gob of meat on the end of a stick. He was roasting it over the fire. It turned out to be the heart of one of the missing girls.

Must've been awful, walking into a scene like that.

Those Boy Scouts became instant heroes. We envied them, hated them, and longed to be their friends. Not because they captured Tommy Janks (my dad did that), but because they got to *see* him cooking that heart over the fire. Those scouts were legends in their own time.

One of them, years later, ended up committing suicide and another . . .

That's another story. I'll stick to this one.

After my dad busted Tommy, he led a crew out to the field and they found the remains of twenty-three bodies buried there. Six belonged to the girls who'd disappeared that summer. The rest . . . they'd been there longer. Some, for maybe five years. Others, for more like twenty or thirty. I've heard that several of them might've been in the ground for a hundred years.

The field apparently hadn't been a cemetery, though; nobody found signs of any grave markers or caskets. There were just a bunch of bodies – a lot of them in pieces – tossed into holes.

Tommy Janks got himself fried in the electric chair.

The clearing got itself called Janks Field.

Chapter Four

There hadn't been a road to Janks Field, dirt or otherwise, at the time Tommy got caught cooking up the girl's heart. But Dad managed to drive in with his Jeep. He made the first tire tracks into that awful place. By the time the bodies and bones had been removed and all the investigations were over, the tracks were worn in. And people have been driving out to Janks Field ever since.

19

First, it was to gawk at where all those bodies had been found.

Before long, though, teens from Grandville and other nearby towns realized that the field was perfect for making out. At least if you and your girl had the guts to drive in there at night.

Not only did people go there to park, but some pretty wild parties went on sometimes. A lot of booze and fights and sex. That's what we heard, anyway.

We also heard rumors of witches and so on meeting at Janks Field to practice 'black magic.' They supposedly had naked orgies and performed sacrifices.

I sometimes thought it'd be pretty cool if they were sacrificing humans out there. I imagined bonfires, drums, nude and beautiful and sweaty girls leaping wildly around, chanting and waving knives. And a lovely, naked virgin tied to an altar, her body shiny with sweat, terror in her eyes as she waited to be sliced open in a blood sacrifice to the forces of darkness.

The whole notion really turned me on.

Turned Rusty on, too.

We used to talk about that sort of thing in hushed, excited voices. Not in front of Slim, though. I *couldn't* have said any of that stuff with Slim listening. But also we figured, being a girl herself, she might not want to hang out with us if she knew we had fantasies like that.

Whenever I imagined the Janks Field witch orgies, I always pictured Slim as the virgin tied to the altar. (I didn't mention that part to Rusty or anyone else.) Slim never got sacrificed because I came to her rescue in the nick of time and cut her free.

I don't know if any humans actually *were* sacrificed at Janks Field back in those days. It was fun to think about, though: sexy and romantic and exciting. Whereas the sacrifice of animals, which apparently *was* going on, just seemed plain disgusting to us.

The animal sacrifices disgusted and worried just about everyone. For one thing, pets were disappearing. For another, people going to Janks Field for make-out sessions or wild parties didn't appreciate tripping over the dismembered remains of Rover or Kitty. Also, they must've been worried that *they* might be next.

Something had to be done about Janks Field. Since it was outside the city limits of Grandville, the county council chose to deal with it. They tried to solve the problem by installing a chainlink fence around the field.

The fence remained intact for about a week.

But then a concerned citizen named Fargus Durge entered the picture. He said, 'You don't have orgies and pagan sacrifices going on in the town squares of Grandville or Bixton or Clarksburg, do you?' Everyone agreed on that. 'Well, what's the difference between the town squares and Janks Field? The *squares're* in the middle of town, that's what. Whereas Janks Field, it's all by itself out there in the middle of nowhere. It's *isolated*! That's how come it's a magnet for every teenage hoodlum, weirdo, malcontent, deviate, sadist, satanist and sex-fiend in the county.'

His solution?

Make Janks Field *less* isolated by improving access to it and making it a center of legitimate activity.

The council not only saw his point, but provided some funding and put Fargus in charge.

They threw enough money at the problem to bring in a bulldozer and lay a dirt road where there'd only been tire tracks before. They also provided funds for a modest 'stadium' in the middle of Janks Field.

The stadium, Fargus's brainchild, consisted of high bleachers on both sides of an arena.

A very *small* arena.

The county ran electricity in and put up banks of lights for 'night games.'

On a mild June night a little over two years ago, Fargus's stadium went into operation. It was open to the public unless otherwise booked for a special event. Anyone could use it day or night, because the lights were on a timer. They came on at sundown and stayed on all night, every night, as a deterrent to shenanigans.

Fargus's 'special events' took place every Friday and Saturday night that summer. Because the arena was so small, there couldn't be anything the size of basketball games, tennis matches, stage plays or band concerts.

The events had to be small enough to fit in.

So, Fargus brought to the stadium a series of spectacular duds: a ping-pong tournament, a barbershop quartet, a juggling show, a piano solo, a poetry reading, an old fart doing card tricks.

Even though the events were free, almost nobody showed up for them.

Which was a good thing, in a way, because Fargus's big plan for the stadium hadn't included a parking lot. This was a major oversight, since most people drove to the events. They ended up parking their cars every which way on Janks Field. Not a *big* problem if only twenty or thirty people showed up.

But then one night toward the end of that summer, Fargus charged a five-dollar admission and brought in a night of boxing and about two hundred people drove in for it.

Things were so tight in Janks Field that some of them had to climb over the tops of cars and pickup trucks in order to reach the arena. Not only did the field get jammed tight, but so did the dirt road leading in.

Regardless, just about everyone somehow made it into the stands in time to see most of the boxing matches.

They *loved* the boxing.

But when it came time to leave, all hell broke loose. From what I heard, and my dad was there trying to keep order (not on duty, but moonlighting), the logjam of cars was solid. Not only were there *way* too many cars in the first place, but some of them got flat tires from the broken bottles and such that always littered the field.

Feeling trapped, the drivers and passengers, in Dad's words, 'went bughouse.' It turned into a combination destruction derby/brawl/gang-bang.

By the time it was over, there were nineteen arrests, countless minor injuries, twelve people who needed to be hospitalized, eight rapes (multiple, in most cases), and four fatalities. One guy died of a heart attack, two were killed in knife-fights, and a six-month old baby, dropped to the ground by its mother during the melee, got its head run over by a Volkswagen bug.

After that, no more boxing matches at Janks Field.

No more 'special events' at all, duds or otherwise.

The stadium became known as Fargus's Folly.

Fargus vanished.

Though the 'night games' were over, the huge, bright stadium lights continued to remain on from sunset till dawn to deter lovers, orgies and sacrifices.

And the grandstands and arena remained in place.

The Travelling Vampire Show would be the first official event to take place in Janks Field in almost two years – since the night of the parking disaster.

I suddenly wondered if it *was* official. Had somebody taken over Fargus's old job and actually booked such a bizarre event?

Didn't seem likely.

As far as I knew, the county had abandoned Janks Field. Except for paying the electric bills, they wanted nothing at all to do with the scene of all that mayhem.

I doubted that they would even *allow* a show to take place there – much less one featuring a 'vampire.'

Unless maybe some palms got greased.

That's how carnies got their permits, I'd heard. Just bribed the right people and nobody gave them trouble. A show like this would probably operate the same way.

Or maybe they hadn't bothered.

Maybe they'd just *shown up*.

I must've let out a moan or something.

'What is it?' Slim asked, her voice little more than a whisper.

'What's a show like this doing at Janks Field?' I asked.

Looking puzzled, Rusty said, 'Why do you care?'

'I just think it's weird.'

'It's a great place for a vampire show,' Slim said.

'That's for sure,' said Rusty.

'But how did they even know about it?'

Grinning, Rusty said, 'Hey, maybe Valeria's been here before. Know what I mean?' He chuckled. 'Maybe she's done some prime sucking in these parts. Might even be the one who put some of those old stiffs in Janks Field.'

'And she likes to come back for old time's sake,' Slim added.

'But don't you think it's odd?' I persisted. 'Nobody just stumbles onto a place like Janks Field.'

'Well, if you trip in a snake hole . . .'

Rusty laughed.

'I mean it,' I said.

'Seriously?' Slim asked. 'Somebody came out in advance to set things up. Don't you think so? And he probably asked around in town and found out about the place. That's all. No big mystery.'

'I still think it's weird,' I said.

'Weird is what you want,' said Slim, 'when you run a Travelling Vampire Show.'

'I guess so.'

'The only thing that really counts,' Rusty said, 'is that they're here.'

But they weren't.

Or didn't seem to be.

We followed Slim out of the forest. The dirt road vanished and we found ourselves standing at the edge of Janks Field.

Way off to the right across the dry, gray plain stood the snack stand and bleachers. Overlooking them, gray against the gray sky, were the panels of stadium lights.

We saw no cars, no trucks, no vans.

We saw no people.

We saw no vampires.

Chapter Five

We started walking across the field.

'Guess we beat 'em here,' Slim said, her voice hushed.

'Looks that way,' said Rusty. He also spoke softly, the way you might talk late at night when sneaking through a graveyard. He looked at his wristwatch. 'It's only ten-thirty.'

'Still,' I said, 'you'd think they'd be here by now. Don't they have to set up for the show?'

'Who knows?' Rusty said.

'How do we know someone *isn't* here?' Slim asked, a look on her face as if she might be kidding around.

'I don't *see* anyone,' Rusty said.

'Let's just be ready to beat it,' I said.

They glanced at me so I would know they got *both* meanings. Usually, such a remark would inspire some wisecracks. Not this time, though.

'If anything happens,' Slim said, 'we stay together.'

Rusty and I nodded.

We walked slowly, expecting trouble. You *always* expected trouble at Janks Field, but you never knew what it might be or where it might come from.

The place was creepy enough just because it *looked* so desolate and because a lot of very bad stuff had happened there. Bad things *still* happened. Every time I went to Janks Field with Rusty and Slim, we ran into trouble. We'd been scared witless, had accidents, gotten ourselves banged up, bit, stung and chased by various forms of wildlife (human and otherwise).

Janks Field was just that way.

So we expected trouble. We wanted to see it coming, but we didn't know where to look.

We tried to look everywhere: at the grandstands ahead of us, at the mouth of the dirt road behind us, at the gloomy borders of the forest that surrounded the whole field, and at the gray, dusty ground.

We especially kept watch on the ground. Not because so many people had been found buried in it over the years, but because of its physical dangers. Though fairly flat and level, it was scattered with rocks and broken glass and holes.

The rocks were trecherous like icebergs. Just a small, sharp corner might be sticking up, but if your foot hits it, you find out that most of it is *buried*. The rock stays put and you go down.

You don't want to go down in Janks Field. (Forget the double meaning.) If you go down, you'll come up in much worse shape.

Even if you're lucky enough to escape bites from spiders or snakes, you'll probably land on jutting rocks and broken glass.

The field was carpeted with the smashed remains of bottles from countless solo drinking bouts, trysts, wild parties, orgies, satanic festivities and what have you. The pieces were hard to see on gray days like this but, whenever the sun was out, the sparkle and glare of the broken bottles was almost blinding.

Of course, you never walked barefoot on Janks Field. And you dreaded a fall.

But falls were almost impossible to avoid. If you didn't trip on a jutting rock, you would probably stumble in a hole. There were snake holes, gopher holes, spider holes, shallow depressions from old graves, and even shovel holes. Though all the corpses had supposedly been removed back in 1954, fresh, open holes kept turning up. God knows why. But every time we explored Janks Field, we discovered a couple of new ones.

Those are some of the reasons we watched the ground ahead of our feet.

We also watched the more distant ground to make sure we weren't about to get jumped. That sort of thing had happened to us a few times before in Janks Field. If it was going to happen again, we wanted to see it coming and haul ass.

Our heads swung from side to side as we made our way toward the stadium. Each of us, every so often, walked sideways and backward.

It was rough on the nerves.

And it suddenly got rougher when Slim, nodding her head to the left, said, 'Here comes a dog.'

Rusty and I looked.

Rusty said, 'Oh, shit.'

This was no Lassie, no Rin Tin Tin, no Lady or the Tramp. This was a knee-high bony yellow cur skulking toward us with an awkward sideways gait, its head low and its tail drooping.

'I don't like the look of this one,' I said.

Rusty said, 'Shit' again.

'No collar,' I pointed out.

'Gosh,' Rusty said, full of sarcasm. 'You think it might be a stray?'

'Up yours,' I told him.

'At least it isn't foaming at the mouth,' said Slim, who always looked on the bright side.

'What'll we do?' I asked.

'Ignore it and keep walking,' Slim said. 'Maybe it's just out here to enjoy a lovely stroll.'

'My ass,' Rusty said.

'*That's* what it's here to enjoy,' I pointed out.

'Shit.'

'That, too.'

'Ha ha,' Rusty said, unamused.

We picked up our pace slightly, knowing better than to run. Though we tried not to watch the dog, each of us glanced at it fairly often. It kept lurching closer.

'Oh, God, this ain't good,' Rusty said.

We weren't far from the stadium. In a race, we might beat the dog to it. But there was no fence, nothing to keep the dog out if we *did* get there first.

The bleachers wouldn't be much help; the dog could probably climb them as well as we could.

We might escape by shinnying up one of the light poles, but the nearest of those was at least fifty feet away.

A lot closer than that was the snack stand. It used to

sell BEER-SNACKS-SOUVENIRS, as announced by the long wooden sign above the front edge of its roof. But it hadn't been open, far as I knew, since the night of the parking disaster.

We couldn't get into it, that was for sure (we'd tried on other occasions), but its roof must've been about eight feet off the ground. Up there, we'd be safe from the dog.

'Feel like climbing?' Slim asked. She must've been thinking the same as me.

'The snack stand?' I asked.

'Yeah.'

'How?' asked Rusty.

Slim and I glanced at each other. *We* could scurry up a wall of the shack and make it to the roof easily enough. We were fairly quick and agile and strong.

But not Rusty.

'Any ideas?' I asked Slim.

She shook her head and shrugged.

Suddenly, the dog lurched ahead of us, swung around and planted its feet. It lowered its head. Growling, it bared its upper teeth and drooled. It had a bulging, crazed left eye. And a black, gooey hole where its right eye should've been.

'Oh, shit,' Rusty muttered. 'We're screwed.'

'Take it easy,' Slim said. Her voice sounded calm. I didn't know whether she was talking to Rusty or the dog. Or maybe to both of them.

'We're dead,' Rusty said.

Glancing at him, Slim asked, 'Have you got anything to feed it?'

'Like what?'

'*Food?*'

He shook his head very slightly. A drop of sweat fell off the tip of his nose.

'Nothing?' Slim asked.

'You've *always* got food,' I told him.

'Do not.'

'Are you *sure?*' Slim asked.

'I ate it back in the woods.'

'Ate what?' I asked.

'My Snickers.'

'You ate a Snickers in the woods?'

'Yeah.'

'How come we didn't see you?' I asked.

'I ate it when I was taking my piss.'

'Great,' Slim muttered.

'I didn't have enough to share with you guys, so . . .'

'Could've saved some for the Hound of the goddamn Baskervilles,' Slim pointed out.

'Didn't know . . .'

The hound let out a fierce, rattling growl that sounded like it had a throat full of loose phlegm.

'*You* got anything, Dwight?' Slim asked.

'Huh-uh.'

'Me neither.'

'What're we gonna do?' Rusty asked, a whine in his voice. 'Man, if he bites us we're gonna have to get rabies shots. They stick like a foot-long needle right into your stomach and . . .'

Slim eased herself down into a crouch and reached her open hands toward the dog. Its ears flattened against the sides of its skull. It snarled and drooled.

'You sure you wanta do that?' I asked her.

Ignoring me, she spoke to the dog in a soft, sing-song voice. 'Hi there, boy. Hi, fella. You're a good boy, aren't you? You looking for some food? Huh? We'd give you some if we had any, wouldn't we?'

'It's gonna bite your hand off,' Rusty warned.

'No, he won't. He's a good doggie. Aren't you a good doggie, boy? Huh?'

The dog, hunkered down, kept growling and showing its teeth.

On the ground around us, I saw small pieces of broken glass, little stones, some cigarette butts, leaves and twigs that must've blown over from the woods, a pack of Lucky Strikes that was filthy and mashed flat, a few beer cans smashed as flat as the cigarette pack, a headless snake acrawl with ants, someone's old sock . . . a lot of stuff, but nothing much good for a weapon.

Slim, still squatting with her hands out and speaking in the same quiet sing-song, said 'You're a nice doggie, aren't you? Why don't you guys see if you can climb the nice snack stand, huh, doggie? Yeahhh. That's a good doggie. Maybe Dwight can give Rusty a nice little boost, and they can wait for me on top of the nice little snack stand? Is that a good idea? Huh, doggie? Yeah, I think so.'

Rusty and I looked at each other.

We were probably both thinking the same things.

We can't run off and leave Slim with the dog. But she TOLD us to. When she says stuff, she means it. And she's smarter than both of us put together, so maybe she has some sort of fabulous plan for dealing with the thing.

I rebelled enough to ask Slim, 'You sure?'

She sing-sang, 'I'm so sure, aren't I, doggie? Are you sure, too? You're such a good doggie. It'd be so nice if you two lame-brain dingleberries would do as I ask, wouldn't it, fella?'

With that, Rusty and I started easing ourselves backward and sideways.

The dog took its eye off Slim and swiveled its head to watch us. The threats in its growl told us to stay put, but we kept moving.

31

With only one eye, it couldn't watch both of us at once.

Ignoring Slim straight in front of it, the dog jerked its head from side to side like a frantic spectator at a tennis match. Its growl grew from threat to outrage, drowning out Slim's quiet voice.

She reached to her waist, grabbed her T-shirt and skinned it up over her head.

The dog fixed its eye on her.

'*Go, guys!*' she yelled.

Rusty and I dashed for the snack stand. I slammed my side into its front wall to stop myself fast. As I ducked and interlocked my fingers, I saw Slim in a tug-o-war with the dog. She had her right knee on the ground. Her left leg was out in front of her, knee up, foot firm on the ground to brace herself against the dog's pull.

Rusty planted a foot in my hands, stepped into them and leaped. I gave him a hard boost. Up he went. I half expected him to drop back down, but he didn't. I didn't bother to look. Instead, I kept my eyes on Slim and the dog.

The dog, teeth clamped on its end of her T-shirt, growled like a maniac, whipping its head from side to side and backpedaling with all four legs as if it wanted nothing more out of life than to rip the T-shirt out of Slim's hands.

On both feet now, she stood with her legs spread, her knees bent, her weight backward. The stance, her shiny wet skin and her skimpy white swimsuit top, almost made her look as if she were water-skiing. But if she fell here, she wouldn't be going into the nice cool river. And the dog would be on her in a flash, savaging her body instead of the T-shirt.

'Get up here,' Rusty called down to me.

Slim's arms and shoulders jerked hard as the dog tugged. She saw me watching. 'Get on the roof!' she yelled.

And as she yelled, the dog let go.

Slim gasped and stumbled backward, swinging her arms, the shirt flapping. Then she went down.

The dog attacked her.

Shouting like a madman, I ran at them. Slim was on her back. The dog stood on top of her, digging its hind paws into her hips while it fought to rip her apart with its claws and teeth. Slim, gasping and grunting, held on to its front legs and tried to keep the thing away from her neck and face.

I grabbed its tail with both hands.

I think I only meant to pull the dog off Slim and give her time to run for the shack. But, instead, I went slightly berserk.

As I jerked the dog away from her, I saw her scratches, her blood. That may be what did it.

Somehow I found myself *swinging* the dog by its tail. I was hanging on with both hands, spinning in circles. At first, the dog curled around and snapped at me. Its teeth couldn't quite reach me, though.

Pretty soon, it stopped trying and just howled as I twirled around and around and around.

While I swung the dog, Slim got to her feet.

I caught glimpses of her as I spun.

She was there, gone, there, gone . . .

Then she was on the move toward the snack stand. Closer. Closer. Around I went again and glimpsed her leaping. Around again and Rusty was pulling her up by one arm. Next time around, I glimpsed the faded seat of her cut-off jeans. Then I saw her standing on the roof beside Rusty.

Around and around I went. Glimpse after glimpse, I saw them shoulder to shoulder up there, staring down at me.

I saw them again. Again. They looked stunned and worried.

I was awfully dizzy by then and my arms were getting tired. I thought maybe I'd better end things soon – maybe by slamming the canine into a wall of the snack stand. So I started working my way in that direction.

Rusty yelled, 'Don't bring it *here!*'

'Just let it go!' Slim called.

So I did.

Waiting until it was pointed *away* from the snack stand, I released its tail. The weight suddenly gone, I stumbled sideways, trying to stay on my feet.

I didn't see the dog at first, but its howl climbed an octave or two.

Then, still staggering, I spotted it. Ears laid back, legs kicking, it flew headfirst, rolling through the air as if being turned on an invisible spit.

Far out across Janks Field, it slammed to the ground. Its howl ended with a cry of pain, and the dog vanished in a rising cloud of dust.

Slim's voice came from behind me. She said, 'My God, Dwight.'

And Rusty said, 'Jesus H. Christ on a rubber crutch.'

Then, growling like a pissed-off grizzly bear, the dog came racing out of the dust cloud.

Rusty yelled, 'Shit!'

Slim yelled, 'Run!'

I squealed a wordless outcry of disbelief and panic and sprinted for the shack.

Chapter Six

Leaping, I grabbed the edge of the roof. Rusty and Slim caught me by the wrists and hauled me up so fast I felt weightless. An instant later, the dog slammed against the wall.

I sprawled on the tarpaper, gasping for air, my heart whamming.

While I tried to recover, Slim sat cross-legged beside me and patted my chest and said things like, 'Wow,' and 'You saved my life,' and 'You were a wildman' and so on, all of which made me feel pretty good.

While that went on, Rusty stood near the edge of the roof, leaning over the big wooden BEER-SNACKS-SOUVENIRS sign to keep an eye on the dog. He said, 'It's still down there' and 'I don't think it's even *damaged* from all that,' and 'How the shit are we gonna get outa here?' And so on.

After a couple of minutes, I sat up and looked at Slim. There were scratches on her face, shoulders, chest, arms and on the backs of her hands. She even had claw marks on the top of her right breast, running down to the edge of her bikini top. Those weren't bleeding, though. A lot of her scratches hadn't gone in deeply enough to draw blood – but some had.

'It really got you,' I said.

'At least it didn't bite me. Thanks to you.'

Looking over his shoulder, Rusty said, 'You'll *still* have to get rabies shots.' He sounded almost pleased by the idea.

'Screw that,' Slim said.

'You *will*,' Rusty insisted.

'You want to take a look at my back?' Slim asked me.

I crawled around behind her and winced. Her back, bare to the waist except for the tied strings of her bikini, was dirty and running with blood from her fall on the ground. In at least five places, bits of broken glass were still embedded in her skin.

'Oh, man,' I muttered.

Rusty came around for a look and said, 'Good going.'

'I try my best,' said Slim, smiling.

I started picking the pieces of glass out of her.

'You're gonna need a *tetanus* shot, too,' Rusty told her.

'No way,' Slim said.

'Besides,' I said, 'she had a tetanus shot last year after that moron stabbed her.'

'That's right,' Slim said.

'And one shot lasts like five or ten years,' I added.

'Couldn't hurt to get another,' Rusty said. 'Just to be on the safe side. *And* the rabies shots.'

After I pulled the pieces of glass out of Slim's back, she was still bleeding. 'You'd better lie down,' I told her.

She stretched out flat on the roof, turned her head sideways and folded her arms under her face.

Her back looked as if it had been painted bright red. Blood was leaking from ten or twelve slits and gashes. Nowhere, however, was it *gushing* out.

'Does it hurt much?' I asked.

'I've felt better. But I've felt a lot worse, too.'

'I'll bet,' I said. I'd seen Slim get injured plenty of times and heard about other stuff – like some of things her father liked to do to her. Today's cuts and scratches seemed pretty minor compared to a lot of that.

'You're gonna need stitches,' Rusty informed her. 'A *lot* of stitches.'

'He's probably right,' I said.

'I'll be fine,' she said.

'Long as the bleeding stops,' I said, and started to unbutton my shirt.

'Unless infection sets in,' said Rusty.

'You're sure the life of the goddamn party,' Slim muttered.

'Just being realistic.'

'Why don't you make yourself useful,' I said, 'and hop down and go get a doctor.'

'Very funny.'

I took off my shirt, folded it a couple of times to make a pad, and pressed it gently against several of Slim's cuts. The blood soaked through it, turning the checkered fabric red.

'Your mom's gonna kill you,' Rusty said.

'It's an emergency.' Where the blood on my shirt seemed worst, I pressed down firmly. Slim stiffened under my hands.

Rusty bent over us and watched for a while. Then he took off his own shirt, folded it, knelt on the other side of Slim and worked on her other cuts.

'Applying pressure should make the bleeding stop,' I explained.

'I know that,' Rusty said. 'You weren't the only Boy Scout around here.'

'The only one with a first-aid merit badge.'

'Screw you.'

'Two Boy Scouts,' Slim said, 'and no first-aid kit. Very prepared.'

'We *used* to be Scouts,' Rusty explained.

'*Used* to be prepared.'

'Next time,' I said, 'we'll make sure and bring some bandages along.'

'The hell with that,' said Slim. 'Bring guns.'

Rusty and I laughed at that one.

After about five minutes, most of the bleeding seemed to

be over. We kept pressing down on the cuts for a while, anyway.

Then Rusty looked at me and asked, 'You were kidding when you said that about going for a doctor, right?'

'What do you think?' I said.

'Just wanted to make sure. I mean, I *figured* you must be kidding, you know? 'Cause I would've done it if I had to. I mean, if Slim really *had* to have a doctor. Like if it was life or death, I would've jumped on down and done it, dog or no dog.'

It seemed like a strange thing for him to say.

Strange and sort of nice.

Slim said, 'Thanks, Rusty.'

'Yeah, well. It's just the truth, that's all. I mean, I'd do *anything* for you. For *either* of you.'

'If you wanta do something for me,' I said, 'how about once in a while using underarm deodorant?'

Slim laughed and winced.

'Screw you, man! If anybody stinks around here, it's you.'

'Nobody stinks,' said Slim, the peacekeeper.

I checked underneath my bloody shirt again. Rusty looked under his, too. We both studied Slim's back for a while.

'Bleeding's stopped,' I announced.

'Good deal,' said Slim.

'But it'll probably start up again if you move around too much. You'd better just lay there for a while.'

'Not like we're going anyplace anyhow,' Rusty said.

I stood up, stepped to the front of the roof and leaned forward to see over the top of the sign. The dog, already staring up at me, bared its teeth and rumbled a growl. 'Get outa here!' I shouted.

It leaped at me. I flinched and my heart lurched, but I held my position as the dog hit the wall about four feet up and tried to scramble higher. It worked its legs furiously, claws scratching at the old wood for a second or two. Then it fell, tumbled onto its side, flipped over and regained its feet and barked at me.

I muttered, 'Up yours, bow-wow.' Then I turned away.

Rusty, sitting cross-legged beside Slim, gave me a worried look. 'What're we gonna do?' he asked.

'Stay right here,' I told him. 'At least for now. Give Slim's wounds a chance to dry up a little more. When we're ready to go, we'll figure out something about the dog.'

'Maybe it'll be gone by then,' Slim said.

'That's a good one,' Rusty said.

'God, I'm being *nice* to it and the thing tries to rip my face off.'

'Sometimes,' I said, 'being nice doesn't work.'

'You can say that again.'

'Sometimes, being nice—'

'Okay, okay,' Rusty said.

I sat down beside Slim and turned my hands over. They were rust-colored and sticky. I wiped them on the legs of my jeans, but not much came off.

Rusty looked at his hands, too. They were as stained as mine. Frowning slightly, he brought his right hand close to his face. He stared at it for a few seconds, then raised his eyebrows and licked his palm.

'Oh, that's cute.'

Lying on her stomach with her face toward me, Slim couldn't see Rusty. Rather than twisting around and maybe re-opening some of her cuts, she asked me, 'What's he doing?'

'Licking your blood off his hand,' I explained.

He did it again. Smiling, he said, 'Not bad.'

'Grade-A blood, buddy,' Slim informed him.

'I can tell.' He sucked his red-stained forefinger. 'Maybe

those vampires've *got* something. Tasty stuff. Try some, Dwighty.'

I shook my head. 'No thanks.'

'Scared?'

'I've got no problem with Slim's blood.'

'As well you shouldn't,' Slim pointed out.

'But I just got done swinging a filthy damn *cur* around by its tail.'

'Weenie,' Rusty said, grinning and lapping at his hand.

'Speaking of which,' I said, 'what've *you* been touching lately?'

Things dawned on him. He put his tongue back into his mouth and frowned at his hand. Looking a little sick, he shrugged his husky bare shoulders and said, 'No big deal.'

A smile on what I could see of her face, Slim said, 'I'm *sure* Rusty must've washed his hands after going to the bathroom.'

'I didn't piss on 'em, if that's what you mean.' Then he managed to blurt out, 'Not much, anyway,' before he burst into laughter.

Slim and I broke up, too, but she stopped laughing almost at once – either it hurt or she was afraid the rough movements might start her bleeding again.

After a minute or two of silence, Rusty asked Slim, 'Want me to lick your *back* clean?'

'*God* no!'

'Christ, Rusty,' I said.

'What's the big deal?' he asked me. 'I'm just offering to clean her up a little.'

'With *spit*,' Slim said. 'No thanks.'

'Get a grip,' I told him.

Meeting my eyes, he said, 'You can do it, too. You want to, don't you?'

'*No!*'

In fact, I did. Blood or no blood, the idea of sliding my tongue over the hot, smooth skin of Slim's back took my breath away and made my heart pound fast. Under the layers of my jeans and swimming trunks, I got hard.

Nobody knew it but me, though.

'You're out of your gourd,' I said. 'I'm not licking her and neither are you.'

'What'll it hurt?' Rusty asked.

'Forget it,' Slim told him.

'Okay, okay. Jeez. I was just trying to help.'

'Sure,' I said.

' 'Cause you know what? If we don't clean all that blood off Slim's back, it's gonna draw the vampire like a magnet.'

'*What?*' I gasped, amazed.

'Points for originality,' Slim said.

'You think it won't?' Rusty asked.

'I think there's no such things as vampires,' I said.

'Me, too,' said Rusty. 'But what if we're wrong? What if this Valeria *is* one? All this blood's gonna bring her to us like chum brings sharks.'

Though I didn't believe in vampires, I felt slightly nervous hearing him say those things. Because you never *really* know.

Do you?

Really?

Most of us *tell* ourselves we don't believe in that sort of stuff, but maybe that's because we're *afraid* to think they might exist. Vampires, werewolves, ghosts, aliens from outer space, black magic, the devil, hell . . . maybe even God.

If they do exist, they might *get* us.

So we say they don't.

'That's such bull,' I said.

'Maybe it is and maybe it isn't,' said Rusty.

'*Probably* it is,' Slim threw in.

So I said, 'If Valeria *is* a vampire, which she *isn't* ... A, she's not even here yet. And B, even if she *gets* here, she can't do squat to us till after dark. And we'll be long gone by then.'

'Think so?' Rusty asked.

'I know so.'

Sure I did.

Chapter Seven

I eased myself down on my back. The tarpaper felt grainy against my bare skin, but at least it wasn't scorching hot the way it might've been on a sunny day.

'What're you doing?' Rusty asked.

'What does it look like?'

'We've gotta get out of here.'

I shut my eyes, folded my hands across my belly, and said, 'What's the big hurry?'

'You wanta get caught up here when *they* show up?'

Slim asked, 'Why not? We came to see Valeria, didn't we?'

'To get a look at her – not to get *caught* at it.'

'I'd rather get caught at that,' Slim said, 'than get my butt chewed by Old Yeller.'

Rusty was silent for a while. Then he said with sort of a whine in his voice, 'We can't just *stay* up here.'

'It isn't just the dog,' I told him. 'The longer we wait, the less Slim'll bleed on the way home.'

'But *they're* gonna show up.'

'Maybe they'll have bandages,' Slim said.

'Very funny.'

'Let's give it an hour,' I suggested.

'If we're real quiet,' Slim said, 'maybe the dog'll go away.'

'Sure it will,' Rusty muttered.

Then I heard some scuffing sounds. Turning my head, I opened my eyes. On the other side of Slim, Rusty was lying down. He let out a loud sigh.

The way we were all stretched out reminded me of the diving raft at Donner's Cove. Whenever we swam at the Cove, we always ended up flopping for a while on the old, white-painted platform. We'd be in our swimsuits, out of breath, dripping and cold from the river. Soon, the sun would warm us. But we wouldn't get up. You felt like you *never* wanted to get up, it was so nice out there. The raft was rocking softly. You could hear the quiet lapping of the water against it, and the buzz of distant motorboats and all the usual bird sounds. You could feel the soft heat of the sun on one side, the hard slick painted boards on the other. And you had your best friends lying down beside you. Especially Slim in one of her bikinis, her skin golden and dripping.

Too bad we *weren't* on the diving raft at the Cove. Too bad we were stranded, instead, on the scratchy tarpaper roof of the BEER-SNACKS-SOUVENIRS shack. Not surrounded by chilly water but by the wasteland of Janks Field. Not waves lapping peacefully at the platform, but the damn dog growling and barking and every so often hurling itself at the shack.

This just wasn't the same.

Not quite. The raft was paradise and this was the pits.

And even if the dog should magically vanish, I *knew* Slim would start bleeding all over the place the minute we hit the ground.

She'd already lost a fair amount of blood.

She would lose a lot more on the way home.

What if she lost too much?

I turned my head. Blinking sweat out of my eyes, I looked at Slim. Her eyes were shut. Her face was cushioned on her crossed arms. It was speckled with tiny drops of sweat, and dribbles were running here and there. Her short hair, the color of bronze, was wet and coiled and clinging to her temple and forehead. She was marked from temple to jaw by three thin red stratches.

I found myself wanting to kiss those scratches.

And maybe also kiss the tiny soft curls of down above the left corner of her mouth.

While I was thinking about it, she opened her eyes. She blinked a few times, then raised her eyebrows. 'Time to go?' she asked.

'Hasn't been an hour!' Rusty protested from the other side of Slim.

'I've been thinking,' I said.

'Hurt yourself?' Rusty asked. Apparently, the rest period had improved his mood – if not his wit.

'I don't know about walking home from here,' I said.

'You and me both,' Rusty said. 'We try, the dog'll have us for lunch.'

'I'm not thinking about the dog.'

'You oughta be.'

'Dog or no dog, I don't like the idea of trying to walk home. Slim'll probably start bleeding again.'

'Big deal,' she said.

'It might be.'

'It's not like I'll bleed *that* much,' she said.

'What I was thinking, though, is that maybe one of us *better* go for help.'

'Oh, joy,' Rusty muttered.

'And what?' Slim asked. 'Send out an ambulance for me? Forget it. I've got a couple of little cuts . . .'

'More than a couple.'

'Even still, it's no big crisis. I don't want to have a goddamn *ambulance* coming for me.'

'What I thought was, I'll run to town and get somebody to drive me back here. Or I'll borrow a car and do it myself. Either way, we end up *driving* you home.'

Slim's upper lip twitched slightly. 'I don't know, Dwight.'

'You wanta *leave* us up here?' Rusty asked.

'I'd be back in an hour.'

'But shit, man, an *hour*. I don't want to be stuck up here for an hour.'

'Take a nap.'

'What if something *happens?*'

'I'll protect you, Rusty,' Slim said, speaking loudly because her face was turned away from him.

He tossed a scowl at her. Then he said, 'Anyway, what about the dog?'

'Long as you stay up here, it can't—'

'I know *that*, man. What about *you?* You think it'll just let you leave?'

I shrugged. 'I'll take care of it.'

'Oh, yeah? Good luck.'

He said it sarcastically, but I answered, 'Thanks,' and got to my feet. I stepped to the edge of the roof. Knees almost touching the back of the BEER-SNACKS-SOUVENIRS sign, I bent forward and looked down.

The dog, sitting, suddenly sprang at me and slammed against the shack.

'I think it's a moron,' I announced.

'Do you have a plan or something?' Slim asked.

'Not exactly.'

45

'I don't want you to get hurt.'

I looked around at her, feeling a nice warmth. 'Thanks,' I told her.

Sitting up, Rusty said, 'It's gonna have your ass, man.'

The dog threw itself at the shack again, bounced off and fell to the dust.

I gave the sign a nudge with my knee. Though it felt sturdy, it was nailed to the roof on wooden braces made of two-by-fours. With a little effort, I could probably kick one of the braces apart and have myself a club – maybe with a few nails sticking out.

Only one problem.

When you're my dad's son, you don't go around destroying other people's property. Not even a crummy sign on a closed snack stand in Janks Field.

It's not only wrong, it's illegal.

If Dad ever found out that a son of his had kicked apart someone else's sign in order to make himself a club in order to beat the crap out of a stray dog . . .

'What're you doing?' Rusty asked.

'Nothing.'

'Want help?' he asked.

A laugh flew out of Slim, but then she groaned.

'You okay?' I asked her.

'Been better.' She grimaced slightly, then added, 'Been worse, too.'

'Do you have any fond feelings for the dog?' I asked.

'You kidding?'

I shrugged. 'I mean, you're sort of an animal lover.'

'That has its limits,' she said.

'So . . . you won't be upset if something bad happens to this dog?'

'Like what?' she asked.

'Like something *really* bad?'

46

Looking me steadily in the eyes, she said, 'I don't think so.'

As I nodded, I saw Rusty giving me this very weird look. His eyebrows were rumpled in a frown, but his eyes looked frantic and his mouth seemed to be smiling.

'What?' I asked him.

'What're you gonna do?'

I shrugged, then walked over to where the sign ended. Down below, the dog watched me and followed. When I stopped, it stopped.

'Get outa here!' I shouted at it.

It barked and leaped, slammed the wall and tried to scurry up. Then it dropped. As it landed on its side in the dust in front of the shack, I jumped.

My plan was to land on the dog with both feet.

Cave it in.

On my way down, I heard it make a quick, alarmed whine as if it knew what was coming.

I braced myself for the feel of my sneakers smashing through its ribcage – and maybe for the sound of a wet *splot!* as its guts erupted.

But it had just enough time to scoot out of my way.

Almost.

Instead of busting through the dog, one of my feet pounded nothing but ground and the other stomped the end of its tail.

The dog howled.

I stumbled forward and almost fell, but managed to stay on my feet. As I regained my balance, I glanced back. The dog was racing off, howling and yelping, butt low, tail curled between its hind legs as if to hide from more harm.

Rusty, at the edge of the roof, called down, 'Got a piece of him!'

The dog sat down, curled around and studied its tail.

'I'll be back as soon as I can!' I yelled.

My voice must've gotten the dog's attention. It forgot its tail and turned its head and stared at me with its only eye.

I muttered, 'Uh-oh.'

It came at me like a sprinter out of the blocks.

'Shit!' Rusty yelled. 'Run! Go, man!'

I ran like hell.

Somewhere in the distance behind me, Rusty yelled, 'Hey, you fuckin' mangy piece of shit! Over here!'

I looked back.

The dog, gaining on me, turned its head for a glance toward the voice.

Rusty let fly with a sneaker.

The dog barked at him . . . or at the airborn shoe.

The sneaker hit the ground a couple of yards behind it and tumbled, throwing up dust. Not even a near miss. But the dog wheeled around and barked.

Rusty threw a second sneaker.

The dog glanced over its shoulder at me, snarled, then dodged the second sneaker (which would've missed it anyway by about five feet) and raced forward to renew its seige of the snack stand.

Chapter Eight

Afraid the dog might change its mind and come after me again, I ran for all I was worth until I reached the edge of the woods. Then I stopped and turned around.

The dog was sitting in front of the shack, barking and wagging its tail as if it had treed a pair of squirrels.

Up on the roof, Rusty waved at me, swinging his arm overhead like a big, dopey kid.

I waved back at him the same way.

Then Slim, apparently on her knees, raised herself up behind the sign. Holding onto it with one hand, she waved at me with the other.

My throat went thick and tight.

I waved back furiously and yelled, 'See ya later!'

And a voice in my head whispered, *Oh, yeah?*

But who pays attention to those voices? We get them all the time. *I* do, don't you? When someone you love is leaving the house, doesn't it occur to you, now and then, that you may never see him or her again? Flying places, don't you sometimes think *What if this one goes down?* Driving, don't you sometimes imagine an oncoming truck zipping across center lines and wiping out everyone in your car? Such thoughts give you a nasty sick feeling inside, but only for a few seconds. Then you tell yourself nothing's going to happen. And, turns out, nothing *does* happen.

Usually.

I lowered my arm, stared at my friends for a couple of seconds longer, then turned and hurried down the dirt road.

I ran, but not all-out. Not the way you run with a dog on your tail, but the way you do it when you've got a long distance to cover. A pretty good clip, but not a sprint.

Every so often, I had an urge to turn back.

But I told myself they'd be fine. Up on the roof, they were safe from the dog. And if strangers should come along – like some punks or a wino or the Travelling Vampire Show – Rusty and Slim could lie down flat and nobody would even know they were there.

Besides, if I returned, we'd all be on the roof again a couple of miles from home and no way to get there without Slim bleeding all over the place.

Going for a car was the only sensible thing to do.

That's what I told myself.

But the farther away from Janks Field I ran, the more I wished I'd stayed. A couple of times, I actually stopped, turned around and gazed up the dirt road to where it vanished in the woods.

And thought about running back.

Maybe I would've done it, too, except for the dog. I hated the idea of facing it again.

First, I felt sort of guilty about trying to kill it. Which made no sense. The damn thing had attacked Slim – it had *hurt* her and tried to rip her apart. For that, it deserved to die. Clearly. Without a doubt. But all that aside, I felt rotten about jumping off the roof to murder it. Part of me was glad it had scooted out of the way.

Second, the dog was sure to attack me if I returned to Janks Field on foot. It would try to maul me and I'd try to kill it again.

But I hope the dog wasn't the reason I decided to keep going. I hope it wasn't for anything selfish like that.

But you never know about these things.

The real whys.

And even if you could somehow sort out the whys and find the truth, maybe it's better if you don't.

Better to believe what you want to believe.

If you can.

Anyway, I didn't go back. I kept on running up the gloomy dirt road, huffing, sweating so hard that my jeans were sticking to my legs.

I met no one else. The road, all the way from Janks Field to Route 3, was empty except for me.

When I came to the highway, I stopped running. I needed to catch my breath and rest a little, but I also didn't want anyone driving by to get the wrong idea.

Or the right idea.

With Grandville only a couple of miles away, some of the people in cars going by were sure to recognize me. They might not pay much attention if I'm simply strolling along the roadside. But if they see me running, they'll figure something is wrong. They'll either stop to offer help or *tell* everyone what they saw.

Golly, Mavis, I was out on Route 3 this morning 'n' who should I see but Frank and Lacy's boy, Dwight, all by himself over near the Janks Field turn-off, running like he had the Devil itself chasing after him. Seemed real strange.

S'pose he was up to some sorta mischief?

Can't say, Mavis. He ain't never been in much trouble. Always a first time, though.

I wonder if you oughta tell his folks how you saw him out there.

I better. If he was my boy, I'd wanta know.

And so it would go. In Grandville, not only does everyone know everyone, but they figure your business is their business. Nowadays, you hear talk that 'It takes a village to raise a child.' You ask me, it takes a village to wreck a child for life.

In Grandville, you felt like you were living in a nest of

spies. One wrong move and everyone would know about it. Including your parents.

After giving the matter some thought, I decided I didn't want to be seen on Route 3 by *anyone*. So every time I heard a car coming, I hurried off and hid in the trees until it was out of sight.

I hid, but I kept my eyes on the road. If something that looked like a Travelling Vampire Show should go by, I wanted to know about it; I planned to call off my mission to town and run back to Janks Field.

When I wasn't busy dodging off to hide from cars, I wondered how best to get my hands on one.

My first thought had been to borrow Mom's car. But on second thought, she never let me take it without asking where I wanted to go. Janks Field was supposed to be off limits. She would be very angry (and disappointed in me) if I told her my true destination. Lying to her, however, would be even worse. 'Once people lie to you,' she'd told me, 'you can never really believe them again about anything.'

Very true. I knew it then and I know it now.

So I *couldn't* lie to her.

Which meant I couldn't borrow her car.

And forget about Dad's.

Both my brothers owned cars, but they loved to rat me out. No way could I go to either of them . . .

And then I thought of Lee, my brother Danny's wife.

Perfect!

She would let me use her old red Chevy pickup truck, and she wouldn't yap.

I'd learned how to drive in Lee's pickup with her as my teacher. If she hadn't taught me, I might never have learned how to drive. Mom had been useless as an instructor, squealing '*Watch out!*' every two seconds. Dad had snapped orders at me like a drill instructor. My brother Stu was a tailgating speed-demon; being taught how to drive by Stu would've been like taking gun safety lessons from Charlie Starkweather. Danny might've been all right, but Lee was in the kitchen when we started talking about it, and she volunteered.

That was the previous summer, when I'd been fifteen.

I spent plenty of time that summer hanging out with friends my own age: Rusty and Slim (calling herself Dagny) and a kid named Earl Grodin who had an outboard motorboat and wanted to take us fishing on the river every day. We *did* go fishing almost every day. Earl loved to fish. The strange thing was, he insisted on using worms for bait but he hated to touch them. So Rusty and Dagny and I took turns baiting his hook for him. And teasing him. You've never seen such a sissy about worms. Eventually, Dagny tossed a live one into her mouth. As she chewed it up, Earl gaped at her in horror. Then he gagged. Then he slapped her across the face as if to knock the worm out of her mouth, so I slugged him in the nose and knocked him overboard. After that, he didn't take us out fishing any more. But the summer was almost over by then, anyhow, so we didn't mind very much.

We sure had fun on his boat while it lasted, but I had even better fun on the roads with Lee.

Being a school teacher, she had the summers off. She told me to drop by the house whenever I wanted driving lessons, so that's what I did.

The first time out, she told me to get behind the wheel of her big old pickup truck. She sat in the passenger seat, gave me a few instructions, and off we went. Their house was near the edge of town, so we didn't need to worry much about traffic. Good thing, too. Even though the driving part of the operation turned out to be easy, I did have trouble keeping my eyes on the road.

That's because Lee was a knockout.

You take a lot of beautiful women, they're shits. But not Lee. She was down-to-earth, friendly and funny. I'd say that she was just a normal person, but she wasn't. She was *better* than normal people. Way better. She didn't seem to know it, though.

When we went driving, she usually wore shorts. Not cut-off jeans, but real shorts. They might be red or white or blue or yellow or pink, but they were always very short and tight. She had great legs. They were tanned and smooth and very hard to keep my eyes away from.

On top, she might wear a T-shirt or a knit pullover or a short-sleeved blouse. Sometimes, when she wore a regular blouse or shirt, I could look between the buttons and catch glimpses of her bra. I tried not to do it often, though.

Mostly, I just stole glances at her legs.

I *would've* tried to sneak looks at her face, too – it was a terrific face – but I could look at that without being sneaky about it.

The first afternoon out with Lee, I learned how to drive. I didn't really need any more lessons after that. She knew it and I knew it, but we kept it to ourselves. Two or three times a week, for the rest of the summer, I went over to he house and we took off in the truck.

While I drove us through towns and over back roads, we talked about all sorts of stuff. We shared secrets, complained about my parents, discussed our worries and our favorite movies, laughed. We laughed *a lot*.

It was almost like being on a fabulous date with the most beautiful girl in town. Almost. What made it different from a date was that I held no hope of ever having any sexual contact with her. I mean, you can't exactly fool around with your brother's wife. Also, she was ten years older than me. Also, she was out of my league entirely.

All I could do was look.

Lee *knew* I was sneaking glances at her while I drove, but it didn't seem to bother her. Usually, if she noticed, she didn't mention it. Sometimes, though, she said stuff like, 'Watch out, we're coming up on a curve,' or 'Don't forget about the road entirely.' She was always cheerful when she said such things, but I always blushed like crazy. I'd mutter, 'I'm sorry' and she would say, 'Don't worry about it. Just don't crash.'

Then one day I crashed.

For some reason, Lee wasn't wearing a bra that day. Maybe they were all in the wash. Maybe she was too hot. Who knows? Whatever the reason, I noticed it the moment she walked out of her house. Nothing showed through her bright red blouse, but her breasts seemed to be moving about more than usual. They were loose underneath the blouse, no doubt about it.

After noticing that, I tried to keep my eyes away from her chest as much as possible.

Maybe ten minutes later, I was driving along a narrow road through the woods, Lee in the passenger seat, when I finally just *had* to look.

I glanced over at her.

Between two buttons of her blouse, the fabric was pursed like vertical, parted lips. Looking in, I could see the side of her right breast. Her *bare* breast, smooth and pale in the shadows. Not very much of it actually showed – a crescent maybe half an inch wide, at most.

But much too much.

All of a sudden, I couldn't hear a word Lee was saying. I kept steering us along the road, smiling and nodding and turning my head to look at her – first at her face to make sure she wasn't watching me, then at the curve of her exposed breast.

I felt breathless and hard and guilty.

But I couldn't stop myself.

Suddenly, she yelled, '*Watch out!*' and flung her hands out to grab the dashboard.

My eyes jerked forward in time to see a deer straight ahead of us. I swerved and the deer bounded out of the way and I missed it just fine. But then I couldn't come out of the turn fast enough. I took out a speed limit sign.

We weren't hurt, though.

Next thing I knew, Lee and I were standing side by side in front of the truck, looking at its smashed headlight.

'I'm really sorry,' I said.

'That's okay, honey,' she said. 'These things happen.'

'Danny's gonna kill me.'

She patted me on the back and said, 'No, he won't. We'll just keep this between the two of us.'

'But he'll see the damage.'

'Let's you and I just forget you had a driving lesson today. Danny'll think I'm the one who crashed. That'll suit him just fine, anyway.' She smiled at me. 'You know how he loves to whine about "women drivers".'

'I can't let *you* take the blame,' I protested.

'I insist.'

'But . . .'

'If he finds out *you* did it, he'll tease you to death and he'll broadcast it to everyone he knows. You don't need that.' Then, giving my shoulder a friendly squeeze, she added 'Besides, it's my truck. If I say I was driving it, I was.'

Lee never told on me.

For the next week or so, Danny had a lot of fun at her expense. I was tempted to confess, but then everybody would've known Lee had lied. That would've made things worse all the way around.

Anyway, that's the kind of woman Lee was. I could count on her to help me retrieve Slim and Rusty, and she wouldn't blab about it.

I just hoped she'd be home.

Chapter Nine

I stayed fairly calm most of the way to Lee's house, but the sight of her pickup truck in the driveway turned me into a nervous wreck.

She's home!

I felt a lurch of panic.

Even under the best conditions, I sometimes chickened out about visiting Lee. That may seem strange, since we were such great friends. But you've got to understand how beautiful and special she was. As much as I liked being with her, I hated the idea of intruding on her. I *never* wanted her to think of me as a nuisance.

I didn't much want her to see me shirtless and sweaty and filthy, either.

All of a sudden, I changed my mind about asking for Lee's help. Instead of heading for her front door, I kept on walking.

Maybe I would just go home. If I told Mom the truth, she would take me out to Janks Field. Then she'd tell Dad all about it, and he . . .

'Dwight?'

My heart jumped. I turned my head and saw Lee in the doorway, holding the screen door open.

'Oh, hi,' I called as if surprised to find her in this neck of the woods.

'What're you walking away for?' she asked.

I stopped. 'I'm not.'

'How about a Coke?'

I shrugged. 'Okay. Thanks.' I hurried across her front lawn.

She stood there, holding the door and watching me, a look on her face as if she knew *everything* but considered it more fun to play ignorant.

Not dressed for company, she was wearing an old blue chambray shirt – probably one of Danny's. The sleeves were rolled halfway up her forearms and the top couple of buttons weren't fastened. Her shirt wasn't tucked into anything. (Maybe she wore nothing it *could* be tucked into.) Her legs were bare, and she didn't have on any shoes or socks.

As I trotted up the porch stairs, she asked, 'Where you been hiding yourself?'

I shrugged and blushed. 'Nowhere much,' I said.

In the doorway, she gave me a hug. I didn't often get hugs from Lee; only if we hadn't seen each other for a long time. I put my arms around her. As she kissed my cheek and I kissed hers, she gave me a good solid squeeze, mashing me against the front of her body. Her shirt was soft against my skin. By the feel of her breasts, I knew she wasn't wearing any bra.

It was just about the best hug ever.

But we broke it up after a couple of seconds. Lee turned away, saying, 'Come on, let's get those Cokes.'

I followed her toward the kitchen, watching the back of her shirt. It draped her rear end, then stopped. The tail fluttered slightly as she walked.

'So what've you been doing with yourself?' she asked.

I suddenly remembered.

'Oh, yeah,' I said.

That was all I needed to say.

About one stride into the kitchen, Lee stopped and turned around and raised her eyebrows.

'Maybe the Cokes better wait,' I told her.

'What is it?'

'I was sort of wondering if you'd let me borrow your truck for about half an hour.'

'Sure,' she said, not even hesitating to think about it.

'Thanks.'

I followed her through the kitchen. Her brown leather purse was on top of the table. She picked it up, reached inside, pulled out her keys and tossed them to me. I caught them.

'Thanks,' I said again.

As I started to turn around, she said, 'I've got nothing to do for a while. Want me to come along?'

I must've made a face.

'Guess not,' she said and shrugged.

'It's not *that*. If you *want* to come along, it's fine with me. I just don't want to . . . you know, *impose* on you.'

'When you're imposing, I'll let you know.'

'Okay.'

'And you're not.' She gave me a quick smile. 'Not yet, anyway.' The smile gone, she added, 'You *need* some help, don't you?'

'Well, I need a car. But it'd be great if you want to come along with me.'

'You sure?' she asked.

'Sure.'

'Where're we going?'

'Janks Field.'

She let out a laugh, throwing back her head, then shaking it. When the laugh was over, she said, 'That explains plenty.'

'Still want to come?'

'You bet. But what's the problem?'

'Slim got attacked by a dog.'

Lee grimaced. 'Slim being Frances?' she asked.

'Right. Anyway, it didn't hurt her much, but she fell down and got some cuts. I was afraid she'd bleed all over the place if she tried to walk home, so I left her there with Rusty. They're on top of that snack stand.'

'What about the dog?' Lee asked.

'It was still there when I left. But it can't get to them as long as they stay on the roof.'

'So the idea is to drive out and rescue them?'

'That's it,' I said.

'No problem. Just let me have a minute to get dressed. Go ahead and grab yourself a Coke. You look like you could use one.'

'Okay. Thanks.'

'If you want to wash up or something, feel free.'

I nodded, and she left the kitchen. When she was out of sight, I sighed.

Cheer up, I told myself. She'll be back.

But then she'd be 'dressed'.

Sighing again, I stepped over to the sink. I washed the dried blood off my hands, then splashed cold water onto my face. I used a wet paper towel to clean the sweat and grime off my arms and chest and belly. After that, I took a Coke bottle out of the refrigerator and pried its cap off.

I only managed a few swallows before Lee came in. She looked almost the same as before. Now, however, white shorts showed below the hanging front of her shirt. She wore white sneakers, but no socks.

'Ready to go?' she asked.

'All set.'

'Want me to drive?'

'Sure.' I tossed the keys to her. She caught them, then stepped past me and grabbed her purse off the table.

On our way to the front door, she said, 'We'll come straight back here unless Slim turns out to need a doctor or something.'

'Good idea.'

Outside, Lee held the screen door.

I reached for the main door, meaning to shut it behind me, but she said, 'Let's just leave it open. The more air gets in, the better.'

So I left it open and stepped outside.

The screen door banged shut as I followed Lee down the stairs.

Walking ahead of me, she reached behind herself and hitched up the tail of her pale blue shirt. Both the seat pockets of her shorts were bulging. From one, she removed a white tin of bandages. From the other, she took a squeeze bottle of Bactine antiseptic. She dropped them into her purse as she walked.

Over at the driveway, she pulled open the driver's door of her pickup truck. I ran around to the other side. Still hanging on to my Coke, I opened the passenger door with one hand and climbed up.

Lee's purse was on the seat between us.

Leaning forward slightly, she punched a key into the ignition. She gave it a twist and the engine chugged to life. Then she sped backward out of the driveway, swung into the street and started working the forward gears, picking up speed. 'We're off!' she proclaimed.

'Sure are.'

She grinned at me. 'How about a drink of that?' she asked.

'Sure.' I handed the Coke to her. She didn't wipe the bottle's lip at all, just raised it to her mouth, tilted it high, and took a couple of swallows. Through the pale green of the glass, the Coke was a rich brownish red color.

There was still an inch of pop in the bottle when she handed it back to me. 'Go ahead and finish it,' she said.

I nearly always wiped off the lip of a bottle before drinking after anyone. But not this time. I put it into my mouth, knowing her mouth had just been there. She wasn't wearing any lipstick, but I almost thought I could taste her lips.

'So what were you three doing out at Janks Field?' she asked. 'Looking for bones?'

'Looking for a vampire,' I said.

She turned her head and hoisted her eyebrows.

'I know. Vampires don't exist. But there's supposed to be a vampire show at Janks Field tonight. One night only. The Travelling Vampire Show. Rusty says they've got fliers for it all over town.'

'This is the first I've heard about it,' Lee said. 'I haven't been into town yet today. Danny's off on one of his trips, so I slept in.'

'Where'd he go?'

'Chicago. One of those sales conventions. So tell me more about the Travelling Vampire Show.'

'There's supposed to be a real vampire . . .'

'No kidding?' She looked at me and grinned. 'I've never seen one of those, myself.'

'Her name's Valeria. I guess she's supposed to go after volunteers from the audience.'

'Cool,' Lee said.

'Anyway, *we* can't go to the show. It doesn't even start till midnight and it's adults only and I'm never supposed to *go* to Janks Field at all.'

'So of course you went there anyway.'

'Yeah. You know, just for a look around. We thought we might get a chance to see Valeria.'

'In daylight? You kids need to brush up on your vampire lore.'

'Oh, we know all about *that*. We're not stupid.'

She grinned at me.

'We just wanted to see what was going on. We figured maybe it'd be like a carnival and we could watch them setting up for the show, something like that. And maybe we'd get a look at Valeria.'

Gorgeous! Beguiling!

I decided not to mention that Valeria was supposed to be a stunning beauty.

A blush suddenly spread over my skin.

Oh, God, don't let Lee find out about our wager!

'Thing is,' I said, 'we didn't seriously think she'd be spending all day in a *coffin*. You know? I mean, the whole thing's gotta be a fake-out. We figured we might actually see her wandering around in the daytime. Then we'd *know* she's a phony.'

'So, did you see her?' Lee asked.

'I guess we got to Janks Field ahead of the show. Nobody was there except us. And that dog.'

Chapter Ten

Lee drove down Route 3 at a safe speed just slightly over the limit, but after the turn-off, in the seclusion of the dirt road, she poured it on. This didn't surprise me. I'd ridden with her many times before and knew all about her reckless streak.

I couldn't complain, though. *She'd* never crashed.

So I held my peace – along with the dashboard and door handle – while she ripped over the narrow, twisty road. The force of her turns sometimes bumped me against the door sometimes threw me toward her.

I was tempted to let go and fall against Lee, not to punish her for the wild driving but to have the contact with her. It might've been embarrassing, though. And it might've made her crash into a tree or something. I didn't want to take the risk, so I held on tight.

We jerked from side to side, shook and bounced all the way to the far end of the road and burst out of the dense forest gloom into the open gray gloom of Janks Field. Lee almost sent me through the windshield the way she tromped on the brakes.

We skidded to a stop.

Parked near the shack where I'd left Slim and Rusty were three vehicles: a truck the size of a moving van, a large bus, and a hearse. All three were shiny black, and unmarked – no fancy signs announcing this was the Travelling Vampire Show, no paintings of bats or fangs or Valeria. Nothing at all like that. As if the show wanted to keep itself secret as it roamed the roads on its way from town to town.

Several people seemed to be unloading equipment from the truck.

'Looks like the show has arrived,' Lee said.

'Guess so. If that's what it is.'

'What else could it be?'

'I don't know,' I said.

'I don't see your friends, though.'

'Me neither.'

'Think they're still up there?'

'They might be. Maybe they're lying down flat behind the sign.'

'Let's find out,' Lee said. She started driving forward.

My mouth jumped open, but I managed not to gasp. Instead, trying to sound calm, I said, 'What're you doing?'

'We came to find Slim and Rusty. That's what we're going to do.'

'But these *people*!'

'We've got every right to be here.'

'Hope *they* see it that way.'

'No sweat,' she said, bravado in her smile but a flicker of worry in her eyes.

She drove slowly. Over the sound of the engine, I heard glass crunching under the tires.

'You sure about this?' I asked.

'Sure I'm sure.'

'What if we get a flat tire?'

'I don't get flats.' She gave me another one of those smiles. Then she added, 'And if I do, we'll just have a couple of these strapping young chaps change it for us.'

As she drove closer, a few of the workers stopped what they were doing and watched our approach. Others continued to go about their business. I counted twelve, in all. (There might've been more, unseen.) Though I saw a variety of trousers on them – blue jeans, black jeans, black leather –

they all seemed to be wearing shiny black shirts with long sleeves.

Studying their outfits, I noticed that all the workers weren't men. At least four seemed to be women.

I wondered if one of those might be Valeria herself.

Maybe they're *all* Valeria, I thought – and take turns playing the role. Or maybe the real Valeria is whiling away the afternoon in the bus.

Or in the hearse.

As Lee eased her pickup to a stop, I looked over at the hearse. I figured there might be a casket inside, but the rear windows were draped with red velvet. Lee shut off her engine.

A man was walking toward us.

Lee opened her door. It seemed like a bad idea.

'You getting out?' I asked.

'*You* don't have to,' she said.

'What about the dog?'

She looked back at me. 'Where is it?'

'I don't know, but it must be around here someplace.'

'Maybe it decided not to stick around when it saw what was coming.'

'Maybe that's what *we* oughta do,' I said.

'We're fine,' she told me, and climbed out.

I threw open my door, jumped to the ground and hurried around the truck. I came up behind Lee and halted by her side. The man stopped a few paces in front of us. He glanced at me, seemed to decide that I didn't matter, and turned his eyes to Lee.

He was so handsome he was creepy.

His long, flowing hair was black as ink, but he had pale blue eyes. The eyes might've looked wonderful on a woman; on him, they seemed unnatural and weird. So did his slim, curving lips. All his facial features were delicate, and he had smooth, softly tanned skin. Except for the slightest trace of beard stubble along his jaw and chin, he might've easily passed for a beautiful woman.

At least from the neck up. The rest of him was a different story. He had broad, heavy-looking shoulders and arm muscles that strained the sleeves of his shirt. The top few buttons were unfastened as if to make room for his massive chest. He had a flat stomach and narrow hips, and wore black leather trousers with a sheath knife on the belt.

After sliding his eyes up and down Lee a couple of times, he smiled. I've never seen such white teeth. Even though the vampire was supposed to be Valeria, I couldn't help but check this guy's canines. They looked no longer or more pointy than anyone else's.

Sounding friendly enough, he said, 'If you're here for tickets, I'm afraid we don't open the box office until an hour before show time.'

'I can't buy any in advance?' Lee asked.

'Not until eleven o'clock tonight.'

'But what if I come back tonight and you're sold out?'

'Oh, that won't happen. Not here. We sell out at some venues, but this arena isn't gonna fill up. Nice if it does, but it won't.' He glanced at me, then said to Lee, 'There is an age restriction, you know. The show's meant for adults, so no one under eighteen gets in. I think your brother's still a little on the young side.'

'But he's the one who wants to see it,' Lee protested.

The man flashed a grin at me. 'I'll *bet* he does.'

'A couple of his friends, too,' Lee added.

'Well, if they're no older than he is . . .'

'Maybe they're around here someplace. They came out ahead of us, so they should've been here by now. Teenagers? A husky boy and a slender blonde girl?'

67

The man frowned slightly and shook his head. 'Haven't seen 'em. Nobody's here but our crew.'

Turning her head in the general direction of the snack stand, Lee shouted, '*SLIM? RUSTY?*'

I watched the roof. Nobody popped a head up.

'If they do come along,' Lee said to the man, 'would you let them know we were already here?'

'I'd be glad to.'

'Thanks. I *told* them that they were too young for a show like this. But they're *so* fascinated by the whole subject of vampires . . .' She shook her head. 'You know, teenagers.'

'I know exactly,' the man said. 'I was one myself a few years ago. And fascinated by vampires.'

'They just *had* to come out here and see what it was all about. I'm sure they were hoping I'd somehow be able to work magic and buy tickets for them. They seem to think I can do anything.'

'I'd like to be able to help you . . .'

'Lee,' she said, and offered her hand.

'Lee,' he said. He took it gently in his long fingers. 'Pleased to meet you, Lee. I'm Julian.'

'And this is my brother, Dwight.'

Though I wished she hadn't used our real names, I smiled and held out my hand. Julian let go of Lee's hand and shook mine. His fingers felt warm and dry.

After releasing my hand, he faced Lee and asked, 'Are you aware of what happens in our show?'

'Not really.'

He performed a mock-embarrassed cringe and shrug. 'Well, there's always a certain amount of blood-letting. Generally, quite a lot. In fact, it can get *very* gory. It looks worse than it is, but it can be shocking for people who aren't used to it.'

'I see,' Lee said, nodding slightly, a concerned look on her face.

'Also, clothing often gets torn in the heat of battle. It's not unusual for private parts to . . . become exposed.'

Lee broke out a smile. 'Sounds more interesting all the time.'

Julian chuckled softly. 'Well, I just want you to understand why we try to keep kids away from the show.'

'I'm *almost* eighteen,' I said, almost telling the truth.

'How old *are* you?' Julian asked me.

'Seventeen.' I blushed as I said it. I hate lying.

'And your friends?'

'They're both seventeen, too,' I said, and blushed even hotter because Slim, though sixteen like me and Rusty, looked more like fourteen.

I'm sure Julian knew I was lying. But he turned to Lee anyway, and said, 'I might be able to make an exception for them if they'll be accompanied by an adult.'

'Oh, I'd be coming with them,' she said.

'Then I suppose it'll be all right.'

'Oh, that's wonderful. Thank you, Julian. Let me get my purse.' She ducked into her truck and snatched her purse off the seat.

This has to be some kind of fake-out, I thought. She's not *really* going to buy tickets.

Standing beside me again, she asked Julian, 'How much will that be for four tickets?'

'They're ten dollars each.'

'So forty dollars,' she said. She hung the purse from her shoulder, reached in and took out her wallet. Head down, she flipped through the bills.

I caught Julian staring at the front of her shirt.

He has the hots for her, I realized. That's why he's breaking the rules.

'Shoot,' Lee muttered. 'I don't seem to have forty in cash.'

So that's it, I thought. She never *did* plan to buy any tickets.

I felt relieved, but also a little disappointed.

But then she said, 'You wouldn't happen to take checks, would you?'

'From you,' said Julian, 'of course.'

So she hauled out her checkbook and a ballpoint pen. With a smile at me, she nudged my arm. I realized what she wanted, so I turned around and bent over slightly. She braced the checkbook against my back and began to write.

Pausing, she asked, 'Who should I make it out to?'

'Julian Stryker,' he said. 'That's Stryker with a y.'

'Not to the Travelling Vampire Show?' she asked.

'To me. That's fine.'

'You won't get in trouble?'

'I shouldn't think so. I'm the owner.'

'Ah.'

She stopped writing on my back. Straightening up, I watched her rip the check out of the book.

Her home address was printed on it, of course.

She handed it to Julian.

He held it open in front of him, studied it for a few moments, then slipped it into a pocket of his shiny black shirt. He patted it there and smiled at Lee. 'If it bounces, of course, we'll require your blood.'

She grinned. 'Of course.'

'Let me get your tickets,' he said. He turned away and walked briskly toward the open front door of the bus. Like the hearse, the bus's windows were draped on the inside with red curtains.

I waited for Julian to vanish inside. Then I whispered to Lee, 'That check has your *address* on it. Now he knows where you *live*.'

'No big deal,' she said. 'While he's gone, why don't you take a look at the roof?'

I scowled toward the snack stand. It was only about twenty feet away, and none of the workers seemed to be watching us any longer. So I walked over to it, jumped, caught hold of an edge of the roof and pulled myself up.

Slim and Rusty were gone.

They'd left behind nothing, not even my shirt.

I dropped to the ground. No sign of Julian yet. I strolled back to Lee and reported, 'They aren't there.'

'Probably ran off when they saw what was coming.'

'But what'd they do about the dog?'

Lee shook her head, shrugged, then smiled at Julian as he came out of the bus. In a quiet voice, she said to me, 'They're probably on their way home.'

'Sure hope so,' I muttered.

'Four tickets for tonight's performance,' Julian said, raising the tickets and smiling as he came toward us. With each stride, his black hair shook, his glossy shirt fluttered, and he *jingled*. The silvery, musical jingling sounded almost like Christmas bells, but not quite.

It sounded more like spurs.

I looked down at his boots. Sure enough, he wore a pair of spurs with big, silver rowels.

Had he been wearing them all along? Maybe, but I don't think so. Maybe he'd put them on while he was in the bus.

If so, why?

Why would he wear spurs at all?

I glanced around just to make sure there wasn't a horse nearby, and didn't see one. Of course, you could've fit half a dozen Clydesdales inside the truck and nobody'd be the wiser.

But I doubted there were any horses at all. More than

likely, Julian wore the spurs as fashion accessories to his costume.

Maybe part of him longed to be Paladin.

The jingling went silent when he halted in front of Lee. He presented the tickets to her.

'Thank you so much, Julian,' she said.

'My pleasure. We don't have reserved seating, so come early.' His smile flashed. 'And stay late. After the show, I'll introduce you to Valeria. You, your brother and his friends.' He cast his smile in my direction.

'That might be nice,' Lee said. 'Thank you.'

'Yeah, thanks,' I threw in.

'The pleasure is mine,' he said to Lee. 'I'll look forward to seeing you tonight. All of you.'

She blushed and said, 'All four of us.'

'Isn't that what I said?'

'Guess so.' Nodding, she said, 'Thanks again.' Then she turned away and climbed into her truck. I hurried around to the other side and hopped into the passenger seat.

As she backed up, Julian walked away.

She swung the truck around and we started bouncing our way across Janks Field.

'You didn't have to buy *tickets*,' I said.

'You want to see the show, don't you?'

'Well, yeah. I guess so. But Mom and Dad are never gonna *let* me.'

'Maybe not.' She tossed me a smile tinted with mischief. 'If they know about it.'

'Anyway, what about Slim and Rusty?'

'We've got *four* tickets and Danny's out of town. All four of us can go, just like I told Julian.'

Holding back a groan, I muttered, 'I don't know. I just hope they turn up. They were supposed to wait for me.'

'I'm sure they're all right.'

Chapter Eleven

As Lee steered us into the shadows of the dirt road, she said, 'If I'd been up on that roof, I would've jumped down and run for the woods . . . probably before the show even pulled into sight. A truck like that, it'd make a lot of noise coming through the woods.'

'The bus, too,' I added.

'They must've heard the engines in plenty of time to get away.'

'But what about the dog?' I asked.

She shook her head. 'Maybe it was gone by then.'

'What if it wasn't?'

'Might've been distracted by the new arrivals.'

'Yeah, maybe,' I said, but I pictured Slim and Rusty racing over Janks Field, the yellow dog chasing them and gaining on them and finally leaping onto Slim's back and burying its teeth in the nape of her neck and taking her down. Rusty looking back over his shoulder . . .

Wrong, I thought. Rusty's slower than Slim. He would be dragging behind and first to get nailed by the dog.

Unless Slim held back to protect him.

Which she might do.

Probably *did* do.

So then, though she was the faster of the two, she would've been the one to get attacked.

In my mind, I once again pictured Rusty looking over his shoulder. He watches Slim go down beneath the dog, then hesitates, knowing he should run back to help her.

But does he go back?

With Rusty, who knows?

I'm not saying he was a coward. He had guts, all right. I'd seen him do plenty of brave things – even *foolhardy* things, every so often. But he had a selfish streak that worried me.

Take for example how he snuck off, that morning, to eat his Snickers.

Or what he did last Halloween.

Rusty, Dagny (later to be known as Slim) and I figured Janks Field would be the best of all possible places to visit on the spookiest night of the year. Maybe, as a bonus, we'd get to spy on a satanic orgy, or even (if we *really* lucked out) a human sacrifice.

But what had seemed like a great idea during the last week or two of October turned suddenly into a *bad* idea at just after sundown on Halloween. Confronted with walking out to Janks Field in the dark, I think we all realized that the dangers were more real than make-believe.

We'd gathered on the sidewalk in front of Rusty's house and we were all set to go. We wore dark clothes. We carried flashlights. We were armed with hidden knives – just in case. At supper, I'd told Mom and Dad that I would be going over to Rusty's to 'goof around.'

Which was not exactly a lie.

As we left Rusty's house behind and started walking in the general direction of Route 3, Dagny said, 'I've been thinking.'

'Hope you didn't strain nothing,' Rusty said.

'Maybe we should do something *else* tonight.'

'What do you mean?' he asked.

'*Not* go to Janks Field.'

'You're kidding.'

'No, I mean it.'

'You wanta chicken out?'

'It's not chicken to be smart.'

'*Bwok-bwok-bwok-bwok-bwok.*'

'Hey, cut it out,' I said.

'You gonna chicken out, too?' Rusty asked me.

'Nobody's chickening out,' I said.

'Glad to hear it. I'd hate to think my two best friends are a couple of yellow-bellied cowards.'

'Up yours,' I said.

We kept on walking. Most of the houses in the neighborhood were well lighted and had jack-o'-lanterns glowing on their proches. On both sides of the street, small groups of kids were making the rounds, walking or running from house to house with bags for their goodies. Most of them were dressed up: some in those flimsy plastic store-bought costumes (witches, Huckleberry Hound, Superman, the Devil and so on); many in home-made outfits (pirates, gypsies, vampires, hobos, princesses etc.); and a few (who probably lacked imagination, enthusiasm or funds) pretty much wearing their regular clothes along with a mask. Whatever their costumes, many of them laughed and yelled. I heard people knocking on doors, heard doorbells dinging, heard chants of, 'Trick or treat!' We'd done that ourselves until that year. But when you get to be fifteen, trick or treating can seem like kid stuff.

And I guess it *is* kid stuff compared to a journey to Janks Field.

Walking along, seeing those kids on their quests for candy, I felt very adult and superior – but part of me wished I could be running from house to house the way I used to in my infamous Headless Phantom costume, a rubber-headed axe in one hand and a treat-heavy grocery sack swinging from the other.

Part of me wished we were hiking to anywhere *but* Janks Field.

Part of me couldn't wait to get there.

I have a feeling Dagny and Rusty might've felt the same way.

Regardless of how any of us felt, however, there was no more talk of quitting. Soon, we left town behind and walked along the dirt shoulder of Route 3. Though we had flash-lights, we didn't use them. The full moon lit the road for us.

Every so often, a car came along and we had to squint and look away from its headlights. Otherwise, we had the old, two-lane highway all to ourselves.

Or so we thought.

When we finally came to the dirt road that would lead us through the woods to Janks Field, Dagny stopped and said, 'Let's take five before we start in, okay?'

'Scared?' Rusty asked.

'Hungry.'

That got his attention. 'Huh?' he asked.

Dagny reached into a pocket of her jeans, saying, 'Anybody want some of my Three Musketeers?'

'Big enough to share with a friend!' Rusty proclaimed.

'Sure,' I said.

I took out my flashlight and shined it for Dagny as she bent over, pressed the candy bar against the thigh of her jeans, and used her pocket knife to cut it straight through the wrapper. Rusty took the first chunk, I took the next, Dagny kept the third.

Before starting to eat, she slipped the knife blade into her mouth to lick and suck it clean.

Rusty and I started to eat our sections of the Three Musketeers.

In the moonlight, Dagny drew the blade slowly out of her tight lips like the wooden stick of an ice-cream bar. Then she said, 'Somebody's coming.'

Those are words you don't want to hear, not on Halloween night at the side of a moonlit road, forest all around you, the town two miles away.

I suddenly lost all interest in the candy.

'Don't look,' Dagny whispered. 'Just stand still. Pretend everything's all right.'

'You're kidding, right?' Rusty whispered.

'You wish.'

Dagny stood motionless, gazing through the space between Rusty and me.

'Who is it?' I asked.

She shook her head.

'How many?'

'Just one. I think.'

'What's he doing?' Rusty asked.

'Coming down the road. Walking.'

'How big is he?' I asked.

'Big.'

'Shit,' Rusty muttered. Then he popped the last of his Three Musketeers bar into his mouth and chewed loudly, his mouth open, his teeth making wet sucky noises as they thrust into the thick, sticky candy and pulled out.

'What'll we do?' I asked Dagny.

'See who he is?' she suggested.

'Let's haul ass,' Rusty said through his mouthful.

'I don't know,' Dagny said. 'Running off into the woods doesn't seem like a brilliant plan. If we stay here, at least some cars might come by. Anyway, maybe this guy's harmless.'

'Three of us, one of him,' I pointed out.

Dagny nodded. 'And we've got knives.'

Still chewing, Rusty glanced over his shoulder to see who was coming. Then he turned his head forward and said, 'Double shit. I don't know about you guys, but I'm outa here.' He hustled for the darkness where the forest shrouded the dirt road. Looking back at us, he called, 'Come on, guys!'

Dagny stayed put.

Therefore, so did I.

'Come on!'

We didn't, so Rusty said, 'Your funerals.' Then he vanished into the darkness enclosing the dirt road.

'Great,' I muttered.

Dagny shrugged in the moonlight. '*Two* of us, one of him.'

I stuffed the remains of my Three Musketeers into a pocket of my jacket, then turned around.

And understood why Rusty had run away.

What I suddenly didn't understand is how Dagny could've remained so calm.

Gliding up the middle of Route 3 was a ghost. A very tall ghost. Actually, a very tall person covered from head to ankles by a white bedsheet. With each stride, a bare foot swept out from under the sheet. But that's all I could see of the person except for his general shape. On top of his head was a black bowler hat. Around his neck hung a hangman's noose which served as a weight to hold the sheet in place.

There wasn't much wind, but the sheet flowed and trembled around the stranger as he walked.

So far, he remained in the middle of the road.

'Maybe he'll just walk by,' I whispered.

'Who do you think it is?' Dagny asked.

'No idea.'

'Who's that tall?'

'Can't think of anybody.'

'Me neither.' Dagny was silent for a moment, then said, 'He doesn't seem to be looking at us.'

True. To see us standing at the mouth of the dirt road –

several feet beyond the edge of the highway – he would've needed to turn his head.

'Maybe he doesn't know we're here,' I whispered.

We both went silent, side by side, as the sheeted figure glided closer and closer.

It stayed on the center line, face forward.

But I *knew* its head would turn.

And then it would come for us.

My heart pounded like crazy. My legs were shaking.

Dagny took hold of my hand.

As she squeezed my hand, we looked at each other. Her teeth were bared, but I couldn't tell whether she was giving me a smile or a grimace.

Turning our heads, we faced the stranger.

He kept walking. And then he was past us.

Dagny loosened her grip on my hand.

I took a deep breath.

The man in the sheet kept walking, kept walking.

We didn't dare say anything. Nor did we dare look away from him for fear he might turn around and come back toward us.

Soon, he disappeared around a bend.

'What was *that*?' Dagny asked, her voice hushed, though the sheeted man was far beyond hearing range.

'I don't know,' I muttered.

'Jeezel peezel,' she said.

'Yeah.'

We both kept staring down the road.

'Is he gone?' Rusty called from somewhere among the trees.

'Yeah,' I said. 'You can come out now.'

Rusty tromped out of the darkness. The moonlight flashed on the blade of the knife in his right hand. 'What'd you wanta just *stand* here for?' he asked, sounding annoyed.

Dagny shrugged. 'Why run?' she asked. 'He didn't *do* anything.'

'I was ready for him,' Rusty said, raising his knife. 'Lucky for him he kept going.'

We all turned and stared at where the sheeted man had gone.

I really expected him to reappear, gliding toward us around the curve.

But the road was empty.

'Let's get out of here,' Dagny said.

'Janks Field?' asked Rusty. When he saw how we looked at him, he said, 'Just kidding.'

So we headed north on Route 3, walking back toward town. We walked more quickly than usual. We often looked behind us.

When at last we reached the sanctuary of well-lighted streets, porches with glowing jack-o'-lanterns and houses with bright windows, we slowed to our usual pace. And we didn't look behind us quite so often.

'You know what?' said Rusty. 'We should've gone after him.'

'Sure,' said Dagny.

'No, really. I mean it. Now we'll never find out who he was. And you know, he must not've been following us like we thought, so what *was* he doing? Where was he *going?* There isn't another town for twenty miles in that direction.'

'Nothing but more forest,' I added.

Shaking his head, Rusty said, 'Shit. We should've followed him or something.'

'Sure,' said Dagny.

'Wouldn't you *love* to know what he was up to?'

'I don't think I *want* to know,' Dagny said.

* * *

The thing about that night is that Rusty got scared and fled.

We could've gone with him, of course. It was our choice not to run off and hide. But after he knew that we were staying by the road, he didn't come back.

He didn't stick with us.

That's the point.

Rusty couldn't be completely trusted to watch out for Slim. In a bad situation, he might save his own hide and let Slim go down.

I never should've left them on the roof together.

Chapter Twelve

On our way back to Route 3, Lee drove down the dirt road very slowly. We both scanned the woods in hopes of seeing Slim and Rusty.

Three times, Lee stopped her truck and tooted the horn. I climbed out and called their names. Then we waited. Nobody yelled back. Nobody showed up. So she drove on.

When we reached the two-lane highway, I said, 'Maybe you'd better let me out.'

She shook her head, but she didn't drive on. Most adults would've just stepped on the gas and whisked me off, but not Lee. 'I don't think they're in the woods,' she said. 'By now, they're probably long gone.' She put her hand on my leg. 'Did you tell them where you'd be going?'

Blushing a little because of her hand, I said, 'Not really. Just that I wanted to get a car and come back for them.'

She patted my leg. 'You know what? I bet they're looking for *you*. They probably headed straight for town . . .'

'But we would've passed them.'

'A lot of ways we could've missed them. Depends on when they left. And maybe they took short cuts.'

'Maybe,' I muttered. I supposed Lee was right about missing them one way or another. It was sure possible. 'But I've got a feeling they're still out here,' I told her. 'I feel like something went wrong, you know? I mean, Slim already had all those cuts. What if she passed out? Or what if the dog attacked them? Or maybe Rusty broke his leg jumping off the shack. Or maybe they were captured by those people who run the vampire show. I thought they were a pretty creepy bunch. No telling *what* they might do if they caught someone like Slim.'

Lee didn't smirk or laugh at me. She looked concerned. 'You're right,' she said. 'Any of that stuff *might've* happened. Or something else, just as bad, that you haven't thought of.' A smile crept in. 'Though I think you've covered the bases fairly well.'

I almost smiled, myself.

'The deal is,' she continued, 'they're probably some-where in town by now – more than likely at *your* house, because they'd be needing to let you know what happened and your house would be about the best place to find you.'

Nodding, I said, 'I guess that's where they might go if they're okay.'

'So let's look there first.'

'Okay.'

'If we don't find them at your place, we'll keep looking till we *do* find them. That sound good to you?'

'Sounds fine.'

So then she pulled out onto Route 3, turned right, and

headed for town. 'We might even pass them along the way,' she said.

We didn't.

The first thing I noticed as we approached my house was the empty driveway. It puzzled me for a moment. Mom should've been back from the grocery store. Apparently, she'd had other errands to run.

A *lot* of errands, I hoped.

With a little luck, maybe she and Dad would never have to find out about any of this.

'Look who's here,' Lee said.

Her words gave me a moment of pure joy, but it faded when I saw Rusty leaning back against an elm tree in the front yard, shirtless, his arms crossed.

No Slim.

Rusty looked carefree, though. He smiled and waved as we pulled up to the curb. On his feet were the sneakers that he'd thrown at the dog. I took that for a good sign.

But why wasn't Slim with him?

Feeling squirmy inside, I climbed out of the truck. Lee got out, too. As we walked toward Rusty, he asked me, 'Where you been?'

'Out to Janks Field,' I said. 'Where's Slim?'

'She went home.'

'Is she all right?'

'Fine. Except for, you know, the cuts.' He smiled at Lee. 'Hi, Mrs Thompson.'

'Hi, Rusty.'

'So what happened?' I asked.

'Nothing much.'

'You were supposed to wait for me.'

'Yeah, well. We did. And then we thought we heard you coming ... a car, you know? You were supposed to come back with a car, so we figured it must be you. Only what came out of the woods was a *hearse*. Man, I nearly . . .' With a smile at Lee, he said, 'It scared the heck out of us. I mean, a *hearse*? Give me a break. So we figured it wasn't Dwight coming to the rescue.' Looking at me, he added, 'Where would *you* get a hearse, right?' To Lee, he said, 'Then a big black bus came out of the woods, and that's when we figured it must be the Vampire Show. So we beat it. We jumped down behind the shack and ran into the woods.' He shrugged his meaty, freckled shoulders. 'That's about it. When we got back into town, we split up. Slim went to her place and I came here so I could tell you what'd happened.'

'What about the dog?' I asked.

'Last I saw of that little . . . mutt . . . it was running toward the hearse like a madman, barking its tail off.'

'So it didn't chase you guys?'

He shook his head. 'Nope. We got off scot-free.'

All my worries had been for nothing. That's usually how it is with worrying. More often than not, we get ourselves all in a sweat over something that *might* happen, then everything turns out just fine.

'What about Slim's cuts?' I asked. 'Did they bleed much on the way home?'

'Nope. They were fine.'

'They didn't reopen?'

'Huh-uh.'

From what he said, I might just as well have stayed on the roof with them. It would've saved a lot of wear and tear on my nerves.

'Where did our shirts end up?' I asked.

'Slim has 'em. They're ruined anyway. She wore 'em home.'

'Where'd her T-shirt end up?'

'Still on the ground, I guess. Did you see it when you were there?'

I shook my head. I hadn't seen Slim's T-shirt or any sign of the dog or the sneakers . . .

'Wait,' I said.

He suddenly looked worried.

'How'd you get your sneakers back?' I asked.

'Huh?'

'What'd you do, run halfway across Janks Field when the hearse and bus were already there and . . .?'

'Heck no. We jumped off the *back* of the shack.'

'Then how'd you get your shoes?'

'My shoes?' He looked down at his sneakered feet. 'Oh!' He gave out a laugh and shook his head as if relieved. 'You thought I threw *my* shoes at the dog!'

'I *saw* you throw them.'

'Not *my* shoes. Those were Slim's.'

'*Slim's* shoes?'

'Sure.'

'Jeez, man. Why didn't you throw your own?'

'It was her idea.'

'Real nice.'

'Don't blame me, she tossed me hers and told me to throw 'em, so I did.'

'So then she had to go through the woods and all the way home barefoot?'

'No big deal. She was fine. Anyway, I offered her mine but she wouldn't take 'em.'

'Not that they'd fit her anyway,' I said, a little annoyed.

I had sure misjudged Rusty, giving him credit for what turned out to be mostly Slim's doing.

At least Rusty had done the throwing.

'Well,' said Lee, 'glad you both made it out of there all right. We had our doubts.'

'We got out fine,' Rusty said, smiling and bobbing his head. 'In fact,' he added, 'Slim's coming over here as soon as she's gotten herself all bandaged and cleaned up.'

'Good deal,' said Lee. Then she turned to me. 'I think I'll head on home, now. When Slim gets here, why don't the three of you talk things over and decide what to do about tonight?'

Rusty raised his eyebrows.

'Lee got us tickets for the show,' I explained.

'No shit?' he blurted. Then he quickly added, 'Excuse me, Mrs Thompson.'

'No problem, Rusty.'

'Just slipped out.'

'Tickets for all of us,' I explained.

'Oh, man, this is *too* cool.'

'I'll hang on to the tickets,' Lee said, 'drive us out there tonight.'

'Oh, wow. . .'

'But you'll have to work things out, yourselves, with your parents. Handle them however you want. I won't tell on you, but I don't want to have a hand in any deceptions you decide to use.'

'We'll figure something,' I said.

'If we're going,' Lee said, 'we should probably leave from my place by about ten-thirty. We'll want to get there early enough to beat the crowd – if there *is* a crowd. And find ourselves a parking place.'

'That'll be great,' I said. 'Your house by ten-thirty.'

'And you're welcome to come over earlier. Always better not to wait till the last moment.'

'We'll come over as early as we can make it,' I told her.

Then she nodded, said, 'See you later then,' and headed for her truck.

Rusty and I watched her drive away.

'Your brother,' he said, 'is one lucky son of a bitch.'

'You're telling me.'

'Shit. What I wouldn't give . . . ' He shook his head and sighed.

'Well, *we're* the ones going to the Vampire Show with her.'

'Yeah! Fantastic! She got four *tickets*?'

'Bought 'em,' I said. 'They cost her forty bucks.'

'She forked over *forty* bucks?'

'Well, not cash. She used a check.'

'Do we have to pay her back?'

'She didn't say anything about it. I think she's treating us.'

'Wow!'

'It didn't even matter that we're underage. The guy knew it, but he didn't care. Julian? He's the owner. He's the one we talked to when we went looking for you guys. He sort of warned Lee that it's an adults-only show...'

'What'd he say?'

'He said the show can be real gory. And *clothes* get ripped off.'

'Holy shit!'

'Yeah. But Lee didn't seem to mind. She said she wanted the tickets anyway, so the guy went ahead and sold them to her. But only on the condition that she goes to the show *with* us. We can't, like, go without her.'

'Ah. I bet he's got the hots for her.'

'You know what else? If we stick around after the show, he'll introduce us to Valeria.'

Rusty moaned almost as if in pain. 'We get to meet her face to face?'

'If Julian keeps his word.'

'Ohhhhh, man. This is gonna be *some night*, huh?'

'I'll say,' I said. 'If we can go.'

'We're going. Man, we're going – I don't care *what*.'

'Maybe I can finish mowing the lawn before Slim gets here.'

Chapter Thirteen

Rusty sat on the porch stairs of my house and watched me finish mowing the front lawn. Then he stood around while I did the back yard and both sides. I was sweaty and out of breath by the time I'd finished. He came with me when I put the mower away in the garage.

Just as we were leaving the garage, Mom drove up. She parked in the driveway and climbed out of her car. She was dressed in her tennis whites – a good clue as to where she'd been.

'I was afraid you'd given up on the yard,' she said.

'No. I just took a little break.'

'Hello, Russell.'

'Hi, Mrs Thompson.'

'How's everything?' she asked him.

'Just fine, thank you.'

After a quick glance around, she asked us, 'Where's d'Artagnan?'

She could only mean Slim.

'On her way over,' I said, though I was starting to wonder why she hadn't shown up yet.

'She had to stop by her house,' Rusty explained.

To deflect a possible interrogation, I asked Mom, 'How was the tennis?'

She beamed. 'I *trounced* Lucy.'

'Good going,' Rusty said.

'Shouldn't you have let her win?' I asked.

I asked that because Lucy Armstrong was the principal of Grandville High – where Mom taught English and where Rusty, Slim and I were students.

'She wins often enough with no help from me. It's high time I got the upper hand. I beat her in two straight sets and she had to pay for our lunch. Just wasn't her day, I guess.' Mom looked us over for a moment, then said, 'Have you fellows had lunch yet?'

'Not yet,' I said.

'Well, why don't you come inside the house and I'll make you some sandwiches?'

She trotted up the porch stairs ahead of us, her tiny white skirt flouncing. I guess she was in pretty good shape for a person her age, but personally I wished her skirt could've been a little longer – like maybe long enough to cover her underwear?

Not that Rusty seemed to mind the view.

Inside the house, I said, 'If you'd rather do something else, I can go ahead and make our sandwiches. No problem.'

'Sounds good. Any time I can get out of making a meal . . .' She smiled. 'I'll just go ahead and take my bath.'

Did she *have* to say that in front of Rusty? He was probably already imagining her in the tub. That's the kind of guy he was. I know, because that's also the kind of guy *I* was. Except not about my own mother. Not about Rusty's mother, either; you wouldn't *want* to imagine her naked. But Slim's mom was another matter. She looked a lot like Slim, only taller and curvier. Whenever she was around, I had a hard time taking my eyes off her. Slim noticed, too, and seemed to think it was funny.

Rusty watched my mother climb the stairs. If she'd been Slim's mom in a tiny skirt like that, I would've been doing the same thing, so I tried not to let it annoy me.

'We might take a walk into town or something after we eat,' I called up the stairs.

She stopped climbing, turned with one foot on the next stair, and looked down at me. I bet Rusty liked *that* view.

89

'So if we're not here . . . ' I said, and shrugged.

'Just be back in time for supper.'

'What're we having?' I asked.

'Hamburgers on the grill.' Smiling, she added, 'There'll be enough for your friends if they'd like to join us.'

'That might be neat,' I said.

Rusty, looking embarrassed, shrugged and said, 'Thank you. I'll have to check with my folks, though.'

'We can go over to your place and ask,' I threw in.

'Good idea,' Rusty said.

'I'll just go ahead and count on the three of you for burgers,' Mom said. 'If somebody doesn't show up, more for the rest of us.'

'Great,' I said.

'Thank you, Mrs Thompson,' Rusty said.

Around adults, he was always excessively polite. Not unlike Eddie Haskell on *Leave it to Beaver*, even though he looked more like a teenaged, overweight version of the Beave.

'Come on,' I told him, and led the way into our kitchen. I walked straight to the refrigerator. 'Lemonade or Pepsi?' I asked.

'You kidding me? Pepsi.'

I opened the door, pulled out a can and handed it to him.

'Aren't you having one?' he asked.

'I had a Coke over at Lee's house.'

He snapped off the ring-tab and dropped it into his Pepsi the way he always did. I figured someday he would swallow one of those ring-tabs and choke on it, but I didn't say anything. I'd already warned him about it often enough so that I suspected he kept on dropping the rings into his cans just to annoy me.

Acting as if I hadn't even seen him do it, I stepped over to the wall phone.

'What're you doing?'

'Gonna call Slim, see why she isn't here yet.'

'Good idea.'

I dialed her house.

As I listened to the ringing, Rusty took a drink of his Pepsi, then went over to the kitchen table and sat on a chair. He looked at me. He raised his eyebrows.

I shook my head.

So far, the phone had jangled seven or eight times. I let it continue to ring in case she was at the other end of her house, or something. I knew the ringing wouldn't disturb anyone, because nobody lived there except Slim and her mother. And the mother was probably away at work.

After about fifteen rings, I hung up.

'Not home,' I said.

'She's probably already on her way over . . .'

Just then came a thump of plumbing, followed by the *shhhhh* sound of water rushing through the pipes of the house. Mom had started to run her bath water.

Rusty lifted his gaze toward the ceiling – as if hoping to see her.

'Hey,' I said.

He grinned at me. 'Maybe Slim's taking a bath. Has the water running. Can't hear the phone.'

'Maybe.'

After gulping down some more Pepsi, he suggested, 'How about we give her five minutes, then try again?'

'If she's running bath water, she'll be in the tub five minutes from now.'

'But she'll hear the phone,' he explained.

'Not if she's taking a shower.'

'Girls don't take showers.'

'Sure they do.'

Leering, Rusty said, 'Nah. They just love to lounge in

a tub full of sudsy hot water. They do it for *hours*. By candle light. Sliding a bar of perfumed soap over their bodies.'

'Right,' I said.

'Hey! Just thought of something! How would you like to be *Slim's* bar of soap?'

'Get outa here,' I said.

'No, really. Think about it.'

'Shut up.'

'Or would you rather be *Lee's* soap? Sliding all over her. Just think of all the places . . .'

'Knock it off, okay?'

'You're blushing!'

I turned away from him, picked up the phone and dialed Slim's number again. This time, I only let it ring twelve times before hanging up.

'Let's go,' I said.

'Where to?'

'Slim's house.'

'Want to catch her in the tub?'

'I want to make sure she's all right.'

'She's fine.'

'She should've been here by now. She's not taking any bath, not with all those cuts on her back. Maybe a quick shower, but she would've been done with that a long time ago and it only takes five minutes to walk here. So where is she?'

'What about our sandwiches?'

'I'm not hungry,' I said. 'And you ate a Snickers in the woods.'

'That was *hours* ago.'

'We'll get something later. Come on.'

'Shit,' Rusty muttered. He polished off his Pepsi, then scooted back his chair and stood up.

On our way to the front door, I said, 'Slim *did* make it home, didn't she? You stuck with her the whole way?'

'Almost. We split up at the corner.'

'At the *corner*?'

'The corner of *her* block.'

'Great,' I muttered, throwing open the screen door.

Rusty followed me onto the porch and down the stairs.

'So you don't *really* know she made it home?'

'Her house was right there.'

'You should've walked her to the door.'

'Oh, sure.'

'And even if she made it *into* her house,' I said, 'nobody was there to take care of her. Maybe she got inside and passed out, or something.'

'What was I supposed to do, go in with her? Then you'd be riding my ass for being alone in the *house* with her.'

I guess he was right about that.

'You could've at least made sure she was all right,' I muttered. 'That's all.'

Speaking slowly, in a clipped voice that sounded as if he might be running short of patience, Rusty said, 'She told me she'd be fine. She said she didn't *want* any help. She told me to go over to your place and she'd be along as soon as she got done bandaging herself up.'

'How was she supposed to put bandages on?' I asked. 'The cuts are on her *back*.'

'Don't ask me. I'm just telling you what she said.'

I said, 'Damn it.' My throat felt tight and achy.

'Don't worry, Dwight.' He sounded a little concerned, himself. 'I'm sure she's fine.'

Chapter Fourteen

Even though Slim didn't have a father and her mother worked as a waitress at Steerman's Steak House, she lived in a better neighborhood than mine and in a better house.

That's because they inherited the house and some money from Slim's grandparents.

Slim's mother, Louise, had grown up in the house and continued to live there even after she got married. This was because she and her husband, a low-life shit named Jimmy Drake, couldn't afford to move out. At the time of the wedding, she was already pregnant with Frances (Slim), and Jimmy had a lousy job working as a clerk in a shoe store. After Slim was born, Jimmy wouldn't allow Louise to have a job.

Actually, this wasn't unusual. Back in those days, most men preferred for their wives to stay home and take care of the family instead of run off to work every day. A lot of women seemed to like it that way, too.

In this case, though, Louise *wanted* to work. She hated living in her parents' house. Not because she had problems with *them*, but because of Jimmy's behavior. He drank too much. He had a violent nature and a horny nature and he enjoyed having people watch.

Slim never told me *all* the stuff that went on, but she said enough to give me the general picture.

To make it fairly brief, when she was three years old (so *she'd* been told), her grandfather fell down the stairs (or was shoved by Jimmy) in the middle of the night, broke his neck and died. That left Jimmy with the three gals.

God only knows what he did to them.

I know some of it. I know he tormented and beat all of them. I know he had sex with all of them. Though Slim never exactly came out and said it, she hinted that he'd forced them into all sorts of acts – including multi-generational orgies.

At the time it came to an end, Slim was thirteen and calling herself Zock.

She seemed strangely cheerful one morning. Walking to school with her, I asked, 'What's going on?'

'What do you mean?' she asked.

'You're so *happy*.'

'Happy? I'm *ecstatic!*'

'How come?'

'Jimmy' – she never called him Dad or Pop or Father – 'went away last night.'

'Hey, great!' I was ecstatic, myself. I knew Slim hated him, but not exactly why. Not until later. 'Where'd he go?' I asked.

'He took a trip down south,' she said.

'Like to Florida or something?'

'Further south,' she said. '*Deep* south. I don't exactly know the name of the place, but he's never coming back.'

'Are you sure?' I asked, hoping she was right.

'Pretty sure. Nobody *ever* comes back from there.'

'From where?'

'Where he went.'

'Where'd he go?'

'The Deep South,' she said, and laughed.

'If you say so,' I told her.

'And I do,' said she.

By then, we were almost within earshot of the crossing guard, so we stopped talking.

Though the subject of Jimmy's trip came up quite a lot

after that, I never learned any more about where he'd gone. 'Deep South,' was about it.

I had my suspicions, but I kept them to myself.

Anyway, the grandmother died last year. She passed away suddenly. Very suddenly, while in a checkout line at the Super M grocery market. As the story goes, she was bending over the push-bar of her shopping cart and reaching down to take out a can of tomato sauce when all of a sudden she sort of twitched and tooted and dived headfirst into her cart – and the cart took off with her draped over it, butt in the air. In front of her were a couple of little tykes waiting while their mother wrote a check. The runaway cart crashed through both kids, took down the mother, knocked their empty shopping cart out of the way, kept going and nailed an old lady who happened to be heading for the exit behind her *own* shopping cart. Finally, Slim's grandma crashed into a display of Kingsford charcoal briquettes and did a somersault into her cart.

Nobody else perished in the incident, though one of the kids got concussion and the old lady broke her hip.

That's the true story of how the grandmother died (with the help of a brain aneurism) and that's how Slim and her mother ended up living by themselves in such a nice house.

Side by side, Rusty and I climbed the porch stairs. I jabbed the doorbell button with my forefinger. From inside the house came the quiet *ding-dong* of the chimes.

But nothing else. No footsteps, no voice.

I rang the doorbell again. We waited a while longer.

'Guess she's not here,' I said.

'Let's find out.' Rusty pulled open the screen door.

'Hey, we can't go in,' I told him.

Stepping in front of me, he tried the handle of the main door. 'What do you know? Isn't locked.'

'Of course not,' I said. In Grandville, back in those days, almost nobody locked their house doors.

Rusty swung it open. Leaning in, he called, 'Hello! Anybody home?'

No answer.

'Come on,' he said, and entered.

'I don't know. If nobody's home . . .'

'How're we gonna know nobody's home if we don't look around? Like you said, maybe Slim passed out or something.'

He was right.

So I followed him inside and gently shut the door. The house was silent. I heard a ticking clock, a couple of creaking sounds, but not much else. No voices, no music, no footsteps, no running water.

But it was a large house. Slim might be somewhere in it, beyond our hearing range, maybe even unable to move or call out.

'You check around down here,' Rusty whispered. 'I'll look upstairs.'

'I'll come with you,' I whispered.

We were whispering like a couple of thieves. Supposedly, we'd entered the house to find Slim and make sure she was okay. So why the whispers? Maybe it's only natural when you're inside someone else's house without permission.

But it wasn't only that. I think we both had more on our minds than checking up on Slim.

I was a nervous wreck, breathing hard, my heart pounding, dribbles of sweat running down my bare sides, my hands trembling, my legs weak and shaky as I climbed the stairs behind Rusty.

Over the years, we had spent lots of time in Slim's house but we'd never been allowed inside it when her mother wasn't home.

And we'd never been upstairs at all. Upstairs was off limits; that's where the bedrooms were.

Not that Slim's mother was unusually strict or weird. In those days, at least in Grandville, hardly any decent parents allowed their kids to have friends inside the house unless an adult was home. Also, whether or not a parent was in the house, friends of the opposite sex were *never* allowed into a bedroom. These were standard rules in almost every household.

Rusty and I, sneaking upstairs, were venturing into taboo territory.

Not only that, but this was the stairway where Slim's grandfather had met his death. And at the top would be the bedrooms where Jimmy had done many horrible things to Slim, her mother and her grandmother.

There was also a slight chance that we might find Slim taking a bath.

And neither of us was wearing a shirt. That's fine if you're roaming around outside, but it makes you feel funny when you're sneaking through someone else's house.

No wonder I was a wreck.

At the top of the stairs, I said, 'Maybe we oughta call out again.'

Rusty shook his head. He was flushed and sweaty like me, and had a frantic look in his eyes as if he couldn't make up his mind whether to cry out with glee or run like hell.

In silence, we walked to the nearest doorway. The door was open and we found ourselves in a very spacious bathroom.

Nobody there.

The tub was empty.

Good thing, I thought. But I felt disappointed.

What was nice about the bathroom, it had a fresh, flowery aroma that reminded me of Slim. I saw a pink oval of soap on the sink. Was that the source of the wonderful scent? I wanted to give it a sniff, but not with Rusty watching.

We went on down the hall, walking silently, Rusty in the lead. A couple of times, he opened doors and found closets. Near the end of the hall, we came to the doorway of a very large, corner bedroom.

Slim's bedroom. It had to be, because of the bookshelves. There were *lots* of bookshelves, and nearly all of them were loaded: rows of hardbounds, some neatly lined up while others were tipped at angles as if bravely trying to hold up neighboring volumes; books of various sizes resting on top of the upright books; neat rows of paperbacks; crooked stacks of paperbacks and hardbounds; neat stacks of magazines; and scattered non-book items such stuffed animals, Barbie dolls, fifteen or twenty stuffed animals, an archery trophy she'd won at the YWCA tournament, a couple of little snow globes, a piggy bank wearing Slim's brand new Chicago Cubs baseball cap and her special major league baseball – autographed by Ernie Banks.

In one corner of the room stood a nice wooden desk with a Royal portable typewriter ready for action. Papers were piled all around the typewriter. On the wall, at Slim's eye level if she were sitting at the desk, was a framed photo of Ayn Rand that looked is if it had been torn from a *LIFE* or *LOOK* magazine.

Slim's bed was neatly made. Its wooden headboard had a shelf for holding a radio, books, and so on. She had a radio on it, along with about a dozen paperbacks. I stepped over for a closer look at the books. There were beat-up copies of *The Temple of Gold, The Catcher in the Rye, Dracula, To Kill a Mockingbird, Gone With the Wind, The Complete Tales and Poems of Edgar Allan Poe, Jane Eyre, The Sign of the Four, The October Country, Atlas Shrugged* and *The Fountainhead.* I hadn't actually read any of these books myself (except *The Catcher in the Rye*, which was so funny I split a gut laughing and so sad that I cried a few times), but Slim had told me about most of them. Of all the books in her room, these were probably her favorites, which is why she kept them in her headboard.

When I finished looking at them, I turned around. Rusty was gone.

I felt a surge of alarm.

Instead of calling out for him, I went looking.

I found him in the bedroom across the hall. The mother's bedroom. He was standing over an open drawer of the dresser, his back toward me, his head down. He must've heard me come in, because he turned around and grinned. In his hands, he held a flimsy black bra by its shoulder straps. 'Check out the merchandise,' he whispered.

'Put that away. Are you nuts?'

'It's her mom's.'

'My God, Rusty.'

'Look.' He raised it in front of his face. 'You can see through it.'

'Put it away.'

'Dig it, man. It's had her tits in it.' He put one of the cups against his face like a surgical mask, and breathed in. The soft pouch collapsed against his nose and mouth. As he sighed, it puffed outward. 'I can smell her.'

'Yeah, sure.'

'I swear to God. She hasn't washed this thing since the last time she wore it.'

'Gimme a break.'

'C'mon and smell it.'

'No way.'

'Chicken.'

'Put it back, Rusty. We've gotta get out of here before somebody catches us.'

100

'Nobody's gonna catch us.'

He breathed in slowly and deeply, once again sucking the fabric against his nose and mouth.

'For God's sake.'

'Okay, okay.' He lowered it, folded it in half and stuffed it into the drawer.

'Is that the way you found it?' I asked.

'What do you think, I'm a moron?' He slid the drawer shut.

'Let's go.'

'Hang on.' He pulled open another drawer. 'Undies!'

He started to reach in, so I rushed over and shoved the drawer shut. He jerked his hands clear in the nick of time.

But I'd shut the drawer too hard.

The dresser shook.

On top of the dresser was a tall, slim vase of clear green glass with three or four yellow roses in it.

The vase toppled forward.

Gasping, I tried to catch it.

I wasn't quick enough.

It crashed down onto a perfume bottle and they both shattered. Glass, water and perfume exploded, filling the air. Roses flew off the front of the dresser. As they bumped their bright heads against the front of Rusty's jeans, a cascade of scented water spilled over the edge of the dresser, ran down and poured onto the carpet.

Chapter Fifteen

We gazed at the mess, stunned and silent.

The air of the bedroom carried an odor of perfume so sweet and heavy that it almost made me gag.

After a while, Rusty muttered, 'Shit. You really did it this time.'

'*Me?*'

'Huh? You think *I* slammed the drawer?'

'Oh, *you* had nothing to do with it. All you did was open it in the first place so you could paw through her stuff. If you weren't such a degenerate . . .'

'If *you* weren't such a prude . . .'

Then we both fell silent and resumed gazing at our catastrophe: the puddle on the dresser top bristling with chunks and slivers and specks of glass; the wet patch on the carpet that looked as if a dog had taken a leak there; the bits of colored glass sprinkled on and around the wet patch; the yellow roses at Rusty's feet, some of their petals fallen off.

'What're we gonna do?' Rusty asked.

I shook my head. I couldn't believe we'd found ourselves in such a predicament.

'Clean it up?' Rusty asked.

'I don't think we *can*. That perfume . . . we'll never get the smell out of the carpet. The minute someone comes upstairs, they're gonna know something's wrong.'

'Not to mention,' said Rusty, 'we can't exactly *un*break the glass.'

'Whatever we do, we'd better do it fast and get out of here.'

'Wanta just leave?' Rusty asked.

'I want to make it all go away!'

'Rotsa ruck.'

'Okay,' I muttered, sort of thinking out loud. 'We can't make it go away. And it'd probably take us fifteen minutes just to clean up all the glass. Then the place would *still* smell like a perfume factory. And in the meantime, we might get caught up here.'

Rusty nodded, then said, 'If we just go away – leave everything exactly the way it is right now – they might not even realize anyone was here. I mean, if shutting a drawer too hard'll knock that vase over, *anything* will. They'll think it was just an accident.'

'I don't know,' I said.

'C'mon, man. A *lot* of stuff could've knocked the thing over. Like even the front door slamming.'

'Maybe so.'

'So let's haul ass.'

We walked backward away from our mess, watching it as if to make sure it wouldn't pursue us. On the other side of the doorway, we whirled around and ran for the stairs.

When we were a block away from Slim's house, we looked at each other, shook our heads and sighed.

'I feel like such a rat,' I said.

'Accidents happen,' Rusty said. 'Thing is, we got away with it. Long as nobody blabs . . .'

'I don't know.'

'You don't *know*?'

'Lying to Slim . . .'

'You'd rather have her find out we went sneaking through her house? That'd go over big.'

'If we explain why . . .'

'And what were we doing in her *mother's bedroom*?'

'*I* just went in to look for *you*.'

'Oh, so you wanta tell Slim what *I* was doing in her mom's room?'

I shook my head. I sure couldn't tell Slim the truth about *that*.

'You'd *better* not.'

'Why'd you have to *do* that?'

'Felt like it,' he muttered. 'Anyway, *you* would've done the same thing if you had the guts.'

'Would not.'

'Only *you* would've gone through *Slim's* drawers.' Grinning, he raised his eyebrows. 'What *were* you doing by yourself in Slim's room, huh?'

'Looking at her books.'

'Oh, sure.'

'I didn't even know you were gone.'

'Uh-huh. Sure.'

'Go to hell.'

Laughing, he patted me on the back.

'Hands off,' I said.

He took his hand away. His smile sliding sideways, he said, 'Seriously, you're not gonna tell Slim about any of this, right?'

'I guess not,' I said.

'You *guess* not? C'mon, man! I've never told on *you*.'

'I know,' I said, and went a little sick inside at the reminder of all the things Rusty knew about me. 'I won't tell. I promise.'

'Okay. Good deal. It's just between you and me.'

'Right.'

'Shake on it.'

I looked around. There were houses on both sides of the street and a few people nearby, but nobody seemed to be watching us. So I shook hands with Rusty. His hand was bigger than mine, and very sweaty. He didn't pull any funny stuff, so I guess he was being sincere.

'If anything comes up,' he said, 'we didn't even go in Slim's house today.'

'What if somebody saw us?'

'We'll claim it wasn't us.'

'Sure thing.'

'We just stick to our story, no matter what.'

'But if somebody *saw* us . . . somebody who *knows* us . . .'

'Simple. We just say he's confused about which day it was. You know? We'll say we *did* go into Slim's house yesterday, but not today. Get it?'

'I guess so.'

'But don't worry. It'll never come up. It's not like anybody got murdered in there.'

'That's true,' I admitted.

But I got a sick feeling again, because the truth was a lot worse than a broken vase and perfume bottle. Sure, it wasn't murder. If it ever got out what really happened in Slim's house, however, people would be giving me and Rusty (*especially* Rusty) funny looks from now till Doomsday.

'Never happened?' Rusty asked.

'Never happened.'

'Great.' He smiled as if vastly relieved. 'That's that.'

'All we've gotta do now,' I said, 'is find Slim.'

'She'll turn up.'

'I wonder if we should check with her mom.'

'At Steerman's?' Rusty asked. 'Oh, great idea! And tell her what? "Gosh, Mrs Drake, have you happened to see your daughter lately? She seems to be missing. We've already checked at your house, but she isn't there."'

'We don't have to tell her that.'

'We go anywhere near her, she's gonna *know* it was us in her bedroom.'

I supposed he was right about that.

'Anyway,' he said, 'you think they'll let us into that restaurant without our shirts on?'

'We could pick up a couple of shirts at your house,' I suggested.

'We can't go to Steerman's.'

'But we've gotta find Slim! I mean, where the hell *is* she? How can she just disappear? Maybe somebody jumped her or something. You never saw her make it into her house and she isn't *in* her house and she didn't show up at *my* house and we haven't spotted her on the streets – so where *is* she?'

'She might've gone to the hospital.'

At this point, we were only two blocks away from the police station. 'I think I wanta talk to Dad about it.'

'Your *father*? Are you nuts?'

'Maybe he knows something.'

'He's a *cop*!'

'That's the point. If somebody grabbed Slim, the quicker we get the police on it, the better.'

'What'll we tell him about going to Slim's house?'

'Never happened.'

Leading the way, I turned the corner toward the police station.

Rusty reached out, clapped a hand on my shoulder and stopped me. 'Hang on a minute.'

'What for?'

'You'll get us all in trouble.'

I turned around and faced him. 'If that's what it takes to find Slim . . .'

He bared his teeth as if in pain, then said, 'I know where she is.'

'*What?*'

'I know where Slim is.'

'That's what I thought you said. What're you talking about?'

'I didn't exactly tell you everything before.'

'Like what?'

'We didn't exactly walk home together.'

'Right. You split up at her corner.'

'Well, that's not exactly the way it happened.'

'Exactly how *did* it happen?'

'We actually split up . . . back at Janks Field.'

'*What?*'

He shrugged his bare, freckled shoulders and held out his hands, palms upward as if feeling for raindrops. But there was no rain. 'Thing is, Slim wouldn't leave.'

'*What?*'

'Well, we were up on the roof of the snack stand, you know.'

'Where you were supposed to *stay*,' I reminded him.

'Well, that's the thing. Slim *did* stay. But I didn't. When we heard these engine noises, we looked over the top of the sign and pretty soon here comes this hearse outa the woods. I go something like, "Oh, shit, it's *them*." But Slim goes, 'Hey, all right!' like she's excited about it. The dog goes running over to bark at the hearse, so I tell Slim we'd better head for the hills while the gettin's good. Only she won't do it. She says there's no reason to run away, and besides, *you'll* get all bent outa shape if you come back looking for us and we aren't there.'

'So you ran away *without* her?'

'She *refused* to leave. What was I supposed to do?'

'Stay with her!'

'Hey, man, it was her choice to stay.'

'It was *your* choice to run.'

'She *told* me to go on without her. "Don't let me stop you," that's what she said. She also said, "Maybe I can get a look at Valeria and see who wins the bet." So I jumped down and that's the last I saw of her.'

'Jesus,' I muttered.

'She planned to wait for you, man. I figured that's exactly what she *did* do. When you came driving up to your place with Lee, I figured Slim was gonna be with you.'

'She wasn't *on* the roof.'

'Yeah, I know, I know.'

'So why'd you lie?'

'I don't know.' His voice was whiny. 'I figured . . . if you found out I'd left her there, you'd give me all sorts of shit about it . . .'

I almost slugged him in the face, but the sight of my raised fist put such fear in his eyes that I couldn't go through with it. I lowered my arm. I shook my head. I muttered, 'You *left* her there.'

'*You* left both of us.'

'That was to get help, you idiot. Don't you know the difference?'

'Nobody *made* her stay behind.'

'So where the hell *is* she?' I blurted.

'How should I know?'

'Damn it!'

'I thought she'd be at her house by the time we got there.'

'Well, she wasn't,' I snapped. I gave Rusty a scowl, then started walking away. He stuck with me, walking by my side, his head down.

After a while, he said, 'Look, she's gotta be somewhere. She wasn't on the roof of the shack when you and Lee got there, so she must've jumped down sometime after I did. She probably ran into the woods . . .'

'Then why isn't she home yet?'

'Maybe she hung around to keep an eye on things. And to wait for you to show up.'

'But I *did* show up.'

'Maybe she'd quit by then and started for home.'

'Then where *is* she?'

'On her way?' he suggested.

'It's not that far. Lee and I left Janks Field – must've been a couple of hours ago.'

'Hour and a half.'

'Whatever, Slim had *more* than enough time to get home.'

'Maybe we just haven't looked in the right place yet.'

'She'd be looking for *us!* And she would've *found* us a long time ago if she'd made it back to town. Which means she didn't.'

'So what do you think happened?' Rusty asked.

Shaking my head, I told him, 'Somehow, she's out of commission.'

'Huh?'

'Too weak to travel. Passed out. Trapped somehow. Maybe even a prisoner. Or worse.'

'Worse like what?'

'Do I have to spell it out?'

'You mean like raped and murdered?'

Hearing him speak the words, I cringed. 'Yeah. Like that.'

We walked in silence for a while. Then Rusty said, 'I bet it'll turn out that she's fine.'

'She'd *better* be.'

Chapter Sixteen

'We're going to the cops,' I said, and turned a corner toward the police station.

'Do we *have* to?' Rusty asked.

'Yeah.'

'Your dad'll find out we went to Janks Field.'

'I don't care,' I said. I did care, but getting in trouble with my parents didn't seem like much of a big deal just then.

'He'll ground you,' Rusty warned.

'Maybe.'

'What about the show?'

'I'm not gonna be *allowed* to go to that no matter what. And at this point, I don't give a hot crap about that stupid Vampire Show. I just want to find Slim. The best way to do that is to tell Dad everything that happened.'

Rusty looked shocked. 'Not about *Slim's* house.'

'We can say we rang the doorbell, but didn't go in.'

'No! That'll be admitting we were there!'

'We *were* there.'

It went on like that for a couple more minutes, but we both shut up as we approached the front doors of the police station.

I went in first. Right away, I regretted it.

With everything else going on, I hadn't given any thought to Dolly.

The Grandville Police Department comprises six cops, my dad included. Two cops per shift, all of whom could be brought into action in case of an emergency.

Since there were no actual police to spare for desk duty,

civilians had been hired to act as receptionist/clerk/
dispatchers. Dolly worked the day watch.

She was a skinny, bloodless prude. Pushing forty, she
lived with her older sister. She disapproved of men in
general, and me in particular. The only times she ever
seemed happy were when she got to gloat over someone
else's misery.

When I walked through the door, she looked at me from
behind the front desk. The corners of her lips curled upward.
'Dwight,' she said.

'Hello, Dolly.'

One of her thin, black eyebrows climbed her forehead to
show how much she didn't appreciate any hint of a reference
to the Broadway musical.

'Russell,' she said and gave him a curt nod.

'Good afternoon, Miss Desmond.'

She eyed both of us as we approached her. Mostly, she
eyed our bare chests. Even though the office was air-
conditioned, heat was suddenly rushing to my skin. 'Let me
guess,' she said. 'You've come to report the theft of your
shirts.'

Rusty laughed politely. It sounded very fake. On purpose,
I'm sure.

'We've been mowing lawns,' I explained. Not quite a lie. I
had been mowing the lawn, Rusty participating as an
observer. 'Is Dad here?'

'I'm afraid not,' she said, obviously pleased by her
announcement. 'What seems to be the trouble?'

'I just need to talk with Dad about something.'

'Would it be police business?'

'Sort of,' I said.

She tipped her head to one side and fluttered her eyelashes
at me in some sort of mockery of flirtation. 'Perhaps you
would like to share it with me?'

'It's sort of personal,' I said.

'In trouble again, are we?' She glanced from me to Rusty, then back to me. 'What is it this time?'

'Nothing,' I said. 'We didn't do anything. I just need to talk to Dad for a minute.'

'No can do,' she said, oh so chipper.

'Do you know where he is?'

'Out on a call.' Grinning, she batted her eyelashes some more. 'I'm not at liberty to divulge his exact whereabouts. Police business. You understand.'

Rusty nudged my arm and whispered, 'Let's just go.'

'You can radio him, can't you?' I said.

'No can do.'

'Come on, Dolly. Please. This is important.'

Her eyes narrowed. 'This *does* have to do with your shirts, doesn't it.' She spoke it as a fact, not a question.

'No,' I said. Though, in a way, our shirts *were* involved.

She leaned forward, folded her arms on the desktop and slid her tongue across her lips. 'Tell me.'

'No can do,' I said.

Off to my side, Rusty snorted.

Dolly stiffened and her eyes flared. 'Are you smart-mouthing me, young man?'

'No,' I said.

'I don't *like* a smart-mouth.'

'I'm sorry. I didn't mean to –'

'Your father will hear about this.'

I blushed. Again.

She noticed and seemed pleased. 'He'll hear *alllll* about how you and your pal Russell came barging in here half-naked and got *smart* with me.'

'Let's get out of here,' Rusty said.

'Speaking of *pals*,' Dolly said, 'where's Frances? Why isn't *she* here? She's *always* with you two.' Dolly leaned further over the desk top and stretched her long neck forward like a curious turtle. 'Has something happened to her?'

Mouth hanging open, I shook my head.

'She hasn't lost *her* shirt, has she?'

'No.'

'Why isn't she with you?'

While I tried to think of a good lie, Rusty kept silent.

'What've you two *done* to her?' Dolly demanded.

'Nothing! She's fine. Are you out of your mind?'

'*Out of my mind?*' she screeched.

Oh shit, I thought. Now I've done it.

'Frances is fine!' I blurted.

'*OUT OF MY MIND???*'

'I didn't mean it!'

'He didn't mean it!' Rusty echoed.

'*WHERE'S MY GUN???*'

I yelled, '*FUCK!!!*'

Dolly cried out, '*WHAT DID YOU SAY?*'

By then, we were racing for the door, Rusty in the lead.

'*WHAT DID YOU SAY, DWIGHT THOMPSON? WAS THAT THE F-WORD YOU SAID? YOUR FATHER IS GOING TO—*'

The door shut behind me, cutting off the rest of her words.

We ran around the corner before we slowed down. Rusty was out of breath and laughing at the same time.

'It's not funny,' I said.

'The hell . . .'

'If she tells Dad what I said . . .'

'You're fucked.'

'It's not funny,' I repeated, and looked around to make sure nobody was within earshot. We were walking along Central, the main street through Grandville's business district. Though a few cars were going by and I could see a couple of people in the distance, the area was pretty much

113

dead. Just by the deadness, I knew without looking at a clock that the time must be about two o'clock. That's how the town *is* between two and three o'clock on just about every weekday afternoon.

It was a strange time of day. You could go into the hardware store, the restaurants, Woolworths, the barber shop, the pharmacy, or just about any other business establishment in the downtown area and you'd be lucky to find another living soul – expect for those who worked there.

Since nobody was around, we didn't need to worry about being overheard.

I didn't care much for the quiet, though. It gave me an uneasy feeling. If you're in a forest and nobody's around, all the better. A forest is supposed to be quiet and peaceful. Not a town, though. A town is meant to be bustling with people. When it's almost deserted, it feels wrong. At least to me.

It made matters worse, the day being so gray and hot.

It especially made matters worse that Slim was missing.

Just in case I might happen to forget for one minute to worry about her, I couldn't turn my eyes anywhere without seeing posters for the Travelling Vampire Show. They were tacked to utility poles, taped to store windows and doors, and several littered the sidewalk and street. I even saw one in a curbside trash basket.

'Somebody was sure busy putting up posters,' I muttered.

'You should've been here this morning. They were everywhere.'

'They're almost everywhere now.'

Rusty shook his head. 'Half of 'em aren't even here anymore.' He patted his seat pocket. 'I got mine. And we've got *tickets!* I can't believe it.'

I gave him a look.

'Cheer up, buddy.'

114

'I'll cheer up when we find Slim. If my dad hasn't killed me by then for saying fuck to Dolly.'

'You know what?' Rusty said. 'I bet Dolly won't even tell on you. She *can't*. She threatened us with a gun.'

'She didn't really...'

'She went, "Where's my gun?" After that's when you yelled fuck.'

We were walking past the recessed entryway of a toy store just then. The doors stood wide open, but I glanced in and didn't see anyone.

'Stop saying that, okay?'

'What, fuck?'

'Come on, Rusty, quit it. We're in enough trouble already.'

'Dolly won't tell.'

'*Every*body tells in this town.'

Not everybody, I reminded myself. There's Lee. She was probably the only adult I knew who didn't take delight in snitching on people.

'Know why I keep saying fuck?' Rusty asked.

'Cut it out.'

'Because I'm so fucking hungry.'

I was awfully hungry, myself. Here it was, somewhere past two o'clock in the afternoon, and I'd eaten nothing all day except for a bowl of Raisin Bran at about nine.

'Okay,' I said. 'You stop talking dirty and we'll get something to eat.'

'Deal.'

'Central Cafe?'

'Great,' Rusty said. 'How much money you got?'

'Seven or eight bucks.'

'Can I borrow some off you? Just enough for a cheese-burger and fries. And a chocolate milk shake.'

'Sure.'

'I'll pay you back.'

115

He almost never paid me back for anything, but I said, 'Fine.'

As we walked along, Rusty moaned softly. He said, 'I *love* Flora's cheeseburgers.'

'They're pretty decent,' I admitted.

'Decent? They're fabulous. How about the way she butters up those buns and *grills* 'em so they crunch?'

I was on the verge of drooling when we arrived at the Central Cafe. Looking through the windows, I saw nobody at any of the booths or tables, though one guy was sitting at the counter. Behind the counter stood Flora.

Taped to one of the windows was a poster for the Travelling Vampire Show.

'Oh, shit,' Rusty said.

He pointed to a sign on the restaurant's door.

NO SHIRT. NO SHOES. NO SERVICE.

'Oh, well,' I said.

He said, 'Fuck!'

I said, 'Shhh.'

'When did they put *this* up?'

'It's probably always been here.'

'I don't think so. Why don't we give it a try, anyway?'

'Not me. Let's just go someplace else.'

'Chicken.'

Not in the mood to argue, I walked away from the door and Rusty. He hurried after me. 'I *really* wanted one of those cheeseburgers,' he said.

'Me, too. But we lost our shirts in a good cause.'

'If I'd known we were gonna end up starving . . .'

'You'll live,' I said.

He groaned. 'We should've had those sandwiches back at your house when we had the chance.'

'Well, we didn't.'

'We can go back.'

'Your place is closer,' I said.

He contorted his face to let me know what a lousy idea it was.

I decided not to let him off the hook. 'Why don't we go there and get something to eat? You can ask your mom about having supper at my place tonight, and maybe I can borrow one of your shirts.'

He sighed. Then he said, 'Yeah, okay.'

'A clean one, preferably.'

A smile broke out. 'Up yours,' he said.

Chapter Seventeen

When Rusty's house came into sight, so did a crowd of parked cars.

'Oh,' Rusty said.

'What?'

He looked at me and bared his teeth. 'Mom's day to host her bridge club.'

'Oh.'

'Forgot all about it.' Looking pained, he said, 'There'll be like a dozen ladies in the living room.'

I nodded.

My mother also belonged to a bridge club, though not the same one as Rusty's mom. I'd been in our house when she hosted her group. The air was so thick with cigarette smoke you wondered how they could see their cards . . . or breathe. And the noise! I had no problem with the clinking of glasses and coffee cups that sounded as if you were in a crowded restaurant. The constant chatter wasn't so bad, either. What I couldn't stand were the outcries of surprise and delight that kept blasting through the house: ear-splitting whoops and squeals and cackles and shrieks.

'We can't go in,' Rusty said.

'What about the back door? We could sneak into the kitchen.'

Rusty scowled. 'I don't know,' he muttered. 'Mom'll be running in and out . . . and no telling who else.' He shook his head. 'We'd get caught. Then Mom would have to *introduce* us to everyone.'

I grimaced.

Our mothers *always* introduced us to company. It's a horrible, embarrassing experience even when you're fully dressed. I sure didn't want to be paraded shirtless in front of all Mrs Baxter's lady friends.

It would be even more humiliating for Rusty, since his physique was nothing to brag about.

'But I've *gotta* get some food in me,' he said. He frowned down at the sidewalk as if pondering his options. Then he said, 'We might as well try and sneak into the kitchen. We can grab something to eat and then haul ass.'

'What about shirts?'

'Forget it. How'm I supposed to get to my room?'

I gave him a look.

'It's not *my* fault,' he said.

'I know.'

'But at least we can grab some food.'

In case we were being watched from the living room, we kept our eyes away from Rusty's house until we were past it. On the other side of the driveway, we ducked behind the parked station wagon and made our way to the garage. Then we went around the garage to the back yard and crept up the stairs to the kitchen door.

Rusty bent forward. Hands cupped to the screen, he peered in. Then he eased open the door.

I followed him into the kitchen. Nobody was there except for us. Both doors to the rest of the house were shut – probably to keep the bridge club ladies from noticing the kitchen's clutter.

The doors kept out most of the smoke, but not the noise. Mrs Baxter's group sounded exactly like my mother's – like a gang of merry female lunatics.

The kitchen counters were littered with dirty glasses, cups, plates and silverware. By the look of things, Mrs Baxter had served cherry pie à la mode to her friends. On the table in front of us were two pie tins, empty except for crumbs of crust and spilled red filling.

Rusty ran a fingertip across the bottom of a tin, came up with a gob of filling and stuck it in his mouth.

I didn't bother.

Hunched over, head swiveling as he glanced from door to door, Rusty tiptoed around the table and made his way to the refrigerator. He pulled it open. I stepped up beside him. The chilly air from inside drifted against my skin. It felt great.

With both of us standing close to the open refrigerator, Rusty found a pack of Oscar Meyer wieners. He pulled out a hot dog, stuck it into his mouth like a somewhat droopy orange cigar, then offered the package to me. I slipped out a wiener and poked it into my mouth.

Rusty, Slim and I often ate cold hot dogs – but only when no adults were around. Put a mother into the picture, and a wiener *has* to be heated and slipped onto a bun. Like it's the law. Only problem is, the bun is usually dry. To make the bunned hot dog edible, you need to slather it with mustard or ketchup (and Rusty always needed *pickle relish*, a disgusting concoction), which killed the taste of the wiener.

I chowed down my cold dog and accepted Rusty's offer to have another.

While we held them in our mouths, Rusty put the package away and pulled out a big brick of Velveeta cheese.

'Mmm?' he asked.

Nodding, I affirmed, 'Mmm.'

We turned away from the refrigerator, I eased its door shut, and we headed across the kitchen. Rusty took a cheese slicer out of a drawer. At a clear place on the counter, he set down the Velveeta and peeled back its shiny silver wrapper. With the taut wire of the slicer, he cut off an inch-thick slab.

He handed it to me. As I sank my teeth into it, he started to cut off another slab.

One of the doors behind us *swooshed* open.

We both jumped.

Through the swinging door stepped Bitsy.

The actual name of Rusty's fourteen-year-old sister was Elizabeth. Her nickname used to be Betsy. Like everyone else in Rusty's family, however, she was on the husky side. So Rusty started calling her Bitsy. She *liked* it, but her parents didn't. They seemed to think it drew attention to her size, and not in a flattering way.

When the door swung open, I figured we'd had it.

Rusty gasped and whirled around like a burglar caught in the act.

Seeing that the intruder was only Bitsy, though, he rolled his eyes upward. I smiled at her, my tight lips hiding my mouthful of yellow cheese good and my right hand holding a wiener.

'Hi, guys,' she said. She looked glad to see us.

Especially glad to see me. She was always glad to see me. She was smitten with me, and had been for years. Maybe because I was such a handsome fellow. Or maybe because I always treated her like a regular person, never teased her and often stuck up for her when Rusty started giving her crap.

As the door swung shut behind her, Bitsy blushed and smiled into my eyes, then checked out my bare torso, then met my eyes again and said, 'Hi, Dwight.'

I nodded, swallowed some Velveeta and said, 'Hi, Bitsy. How you doing?'

'Oh, fine, thank you.' As if suddenly worried about her own appearance, she patted her hair and glanced down at herself. Her hair, as usual, resembled a shaggy brown football helmet but without the face guard or chin strap. She was wearing an old T-shirt and cut-off blue jeans – the same sort of outfit Slim normally wore, except Bitsy was barefoot. Plus, her T-shirt was more ragged than Slim's and she wasn't wearing a bikini top underneath it. She could've used one. Or a bra. Especially since her T-shirt was so thin you could pretty much see through it.

'Hey, Bits,' Rusty said. 'Wanta do us a favor?'

'Like what?'

'Get us some shirts.'

She frowned slightly at him. 'What for?'

'To *wear*, stupid.'

I gave him a look. One thing that always puzzles me: people smarting off when they're asking for someone's help. It seems not only rude but incredibly dumb.

Trying to sound extra nice to make up for Rusty, I said, 'Our shirts got ruined over at Janks Field.'

Bitsy's eyes widened. 'You were at *Janks Field*?' She glanced at Rusty. 'You're not supposed to go there.'

'Thanks, Dwight. Now she's gonna tell on me.'

To Bitsy, I said, 'You won't tell on him, will you?'

'If you don't want me to.'

'Thanks.'

'You're welcome.'

'Anyway, our shirts got ruined when we were there.' Seeing the concern in her eyes, I explained, 'A dog attacked us.'

'Oh, no!'

'We're all right, but our shirts got wrecked. We've been running around without them all day and we're getting pretty sunburned.'

'You've got a good tan,' she told me, blushing.

'Thanks. But anyway, we just want to borrow a couple of shirts so we don't get burnt any more than we already are when we go back out.'

'What *sort* of shirts do you want?' she asked.

'Anything,' I said.

'Just go in my closet and grab us a couple, okay?'

'In your *closet?*'

'Want me to draw you a map?'

With a sort of pleased, now-the-tables-are-turned look on her face, she said to Rusty, 'But I'm not supposed to *go* in your closet.'

Rusty's eyes narrowed. 'You have my permission. This once.'

'Well well well,' she said.

'Just do it, okay?'

'Why can't you do it yourself? They're *your* shirts. It's *your* closet.'

Before Rusty could answer and probably make matters worse, I told her, 'We don't really want to meet the bridge club, you know?' Shrugging, I glanced down at myself. 'No shirts? It'd be kind of embarrassing.'

Nodding and blushing, she stared at my bare torso.

'C'mon, Bits. We haven't got all day.'

I scowled at Rusty. 'Leave her alone. She doesn't have to get the shirts if she doesn't want to.'

'I'll get them,' she said, speaking to me.

'Thanks.'

'You're welcome. How many do you need?'

'*Twenty-eight, you moron*,' Rusty said.

'Just two will be fine,' I told her.

'What about Slim?' she asked.

The sudden reminder made me go sick inside. Trying not to let it show, I said, 'What about her?'

'Does she need one, too?'

'Let's *ask*,' Rusty said, and looked over his shoulder.

'Slim isn't with us,' I explained.

'Why not?'

Rusty and I spent a little too long thinking about that one. Bitsy suddenly looked worried. 'Is she all right?'

'She's fine,' Rusty said.

'No she's not,' Bitsy said. Her eyes turned to me. 'Something happened to her, didn't it?'

Considering Bitsy's crush on me, you might've expected her to be jealous of Slim. But it didn't work that way. Instead of hating Slim, she idolized her. I'm pretty sure she wished she could *be* Slim: cute and slender and athletic and smart and funny, and hanging out with me almost every day.

'Where *is* she?' Bitsy asked.

I shrugged.

'She had to stay home and do the laundry,' Rusty said.

Bitsy's eyes stayed on me. Clearly, she didn't believe Rusty's explanation. She wanted to hear it from me.

'Why don't you go ahead and get us the shirts?' I said, a gentleness in my voice that surprised me. 'Just two shirts. We'll wait in the back yard, okay? And I'll tell you about Slim.'

'Okay.'

When Bitsy shoved open the door, the noise of the bridge

ladies swelled. The door swung shut, coming half-open again on our side and fanning in a few gray rags of smoke.

Rusty muttered, 'Shit.'

Then he cut off another thick slab of Velveeta cheese, folded the end of the wrapper, and returned the cheese to the refrigerator. While he still held the door open, he asked, 'Another dog?'

I shook my head.

He shut the door and, holding what was left of our wieners and cheese, we hurried outside and down the stairs to the back yard. Over near a corner of the house, we stopped to wait for Bitsy and finish eating.

'Jush wha' we nee',' Rusty muttered, his words mushy from a mouthful of partly chewed lunch.

'Don't worry about it,' I said.

He swallowed and said, 'Why'd you have to go and tell her about *Janks Field*?'

I shrugged. 'I have a hard time lying sometimes.'

'Tell me about it.'

'Sorry. But look, she'll be all right.'

'Easy for you to say, she isn't *your* sister.'

The screen door swung open. Bitsy rushed out and bounded down the stairs. Her hands were empty. I figured something must've gone wrong. As she hurried toward us, though, I saw that the front of her T-shirt bulged more than usual.

'Got 'em,' she said. Stopping in front of us, Bitsy patted her bulge. Her T-shirt was so thin I could see the wrinkled bunch of fabric underneath it.

Rusty put out his hand and snapped his fingers. 'Give,' he said.

Fixing her eyes on me, Bitsy asked, 'Where's Slim really? Something's wrong, isn't it?'

'You have to promise not to tell,' I said.

Rusty groaned.

'I promise.'

'She'll tell.'

'No, I won't.' She raised her right hand. 'I swear.'

'First time something doesn't go her way . . .'

She threw a glare at him. 'I will not.'

I said, 'We're going to look for Slim right now. She was still at Janks Field last time we saw her. So that's where we're going.'

'How come you went off without her?'

I gave Rusty a look, then faced Bitsy and said, 'She wanted to stay behind.'

'How come?'

'To look at some stuff,' I said. 'Anyway, we have to get back and find her.'

Bobbing her head slightly as if she now understood, Bitsy reached with both hands under the bottom of her T-shirt and dragged out a couple of shirts. They were both wrinkled, but looked clean.

'This one's for you,' she said, and handed me a checkered, short-sleeved shirt.

'Thanks,' I said.

'You're welcome.'

'And this one's for you.'

The shirt she held out toward Rusty had nothing wrong with it that I could see, but he snatched it from her grip and muttered, 'Thanks a lot.'

Turning again to me, she said, 'Are you sure Slim doesn't need a shirt, too?'

'Nah,' I said. 'She has ours.'

'What happened to *hers?*'

'The dog got it,' I said.

'I thought you said it wrecked *your* shirts.'

'Indirectly,' I said.

'Huh?' Bitsy asked.

'Shit on a stick,' Rusty said, 'why not just blab *everything*?'

Holding the stub of my wiener in my mouth, I put on the shirt.

'I'm coming with you,' said Bitsy.

Chapter Eighteen

'The hell you are!' Rusty blurted.

'She's my friend, too.'

'You're not coming.'

Glaring at her brother, Bitsy said, If you don't let me come, I'm gonna tell.'

Rusty's eyes flashed at me. '*See?*' Then he shoved the rest of his wiener into his mouth.

Bitsy turned to me. 'You don't mind me coming, do you?'

Here was my big chance to redeem myself with Rusty and ruin Bitsy's day . . . or week, or month. I didn't want to do it. But I wasn't crazy about having her tag along with us, either. 'It's fine with me,' I said.

She gave Rusty a glance of triumph.

'The only thing is,' I said, 'it might be dangerous.'

'That's okay.'

'I wouldn't want you to get hurt.'

'I don't mind.'

'Do you mind if you get *us* hurt?' Rusty asked her.

'I'm not gonna do that.'

'Oh, yeah? What if we get chased and you're too slow and we have to run back to *rescue* your fat ass and Dwight gets *killed* all because of *you*?'

'Quit it, Rusty,' I said.

A stubborn look in her eyes, Bitsy told him, 'You just don't want me to come. But it's okay with Dwight. He said so.'

She looked at me for confirmation.

'Sure,' I said. 'If you really want to, you can. But we *are* going to Janks Field. No telling what might happen. There's the dog, and—'

'I'm not scared.'

'You oughta be, you little twat.'

'Rusty!'

She turned on him. 'I'm gonna *tell*!'

'Go ahead. See if I care.' To me, he said, 'Damn it, Dwight, we can't take her to Janks Field. She's my *sister*. What if something *does* happen to her?'

'We'll make sure she's all right,' I told him. To Bitsy, I said, 'Are you really *sure* you want to come? It's not just dangerous, it's a long walk. Five or six miles,' I added, exaggerating slightly.

'Is not,' she said.

'Round trip.'

'I can walk that far.'

'Sure you can,' Rusty muttered.

'I'm coming,' Bitsy said. 'Right, Dwight?'

'If you really want to,' I told her.

'I do.'

'One thing, though. You can't come with us barefoot. It's a long walk and Janks Field has all sorts of broken glass and stuff . . .'

'Spiders and snakes,' Rusty added.

'You have to put some shoes on,' I told her.

An eager look in her eyes, she said, 'Wait right here.' Then she swung around and trotted to the back stairs. She hustled up them, pulled open the screen door and entered the kitchen. The door banged shut.

Rusty and I looked at each other.

I nodded.

We split.

Ran like hell around the corner of the garage, cut across the neighbor's yard, made it to the sidewalk and didn't stop running till we reached Route 3. Panting and drenched with sweat, we stopped by the side of the pavement. I walked in slow circles while Rusty bent over and held his knees.

When he had his breath back, he straightened up and grinned at me and shook his head. 'Good man,' he said.

'Yeah, well.'

He patted me on the back, and we walked up Route 3. On both sides of us, the woods were tall and thick. Though the sunless afternoon made the road ahead of us look gloomy, in there among the trees there was hardly any light at all.

After a while, Rusty said, 'Bet she never thought *you'd* ditch her.'

'I know.'

'That's why it worked.'

'Yeah.'

He patted me on the back some more. 'I can't believe you did that to her.'

I glowered at him.

'Just kidding, man. It was brilliant.'

'I didn't want to hurt her feelings.'

'Blew that one.'

'If she's just listened to reason . . .'

'Ha!'

'I *tried* to talk her out of coming.'

128

'You did your best. Anyway, she had no business butting in like that. Not to mention threatening to *tell* on us. Serves her right.' Rusty chuckled softly.

'What?' I asked.

'Just thinking about the look she must've had on her face when she came back out and we were gone.'

'It's not funny.'

The humor left his face. 'Just hope she doesn't decide to come after us. I wouldn't put it past her.' Scowling, he looked over his shoulder.

I looked back, too. The road behind us was deserted, at least to where it curved out of sight about thirty feet away. 'Maybe we'd better hurry,' I said.

We picked up our pace.

Every so often, we glanced back.

I felt lousy about ditching Bitsy.

I told myself that she had no business going with us in the first place. She wasn't really one of us and we *might* be running into trouble. If things went bad, she could hardly be counted on to take care of herself. Saving her would be *our* job and we didn't need that sort of responsibility.

Still, I'd tricked her. I'd betrayed her. I'd probably broken her heart.

I almost wished she would show up just so I could stop feeling so guilty.

Because of the twists in Route 3, we couldn't see very far behind us. Bitsy might've been back there, closing in. At any moment, she might come hustling around a bend, jiggling and waving.

I half expected it to happen.

Every so often, cars went by. We stayed along the edge of the road, walking single file, and ignored them. Though most of the people in the cars probably recognized us, nobody called out or stopped. With any luck, we might not even get talked about; it wasn't as if we were doing anything interesting, just walking.

By the time we were about halfway to the Janks Field turn-off, Bitsy still hadn't appeared. Maybe because we were walking too fast. So I slowed down.

Rusty gave me a grateful look. Our fast pace had been rough on him.

We kept glancing back every so often. Rusty, I'm sure, hoped he wouldn't spot Bitsy on the road behind us. I didn't want her with us, either, but I might's been relieved to find her coming along.

When we finally reached the dirt road leading to Janks Field, I stopped and looked back toward town. There was a fairly long stretch before the first bend. Staring at the empty lanes, I realized this was where the sheeted man had come gliding toward us last Halloween night. The memory gave me a little shiver up my back.

What was he doing out here that night? I wondered.

Who was he?

Where is he now?

I almost expected to see the sheeted figure in its silly bowler hat and not-so-silly hangman's noose come drifting up the road toward us.

Would it be as scary on a summer afternoon?

Maybe even scarier.

What if he's just on the other side of the bend?

To stop myself from thinking about it, I said to Rusty, 'Maybe we'd better wait here for a few minutes and see if Bitsy turns up.'

'Are you nuts?'

'What if she *is* coming after us?'

'All the more reason to get going.'

I shook my head. 'And leave her alone out here? We're two miles from town.'

He gave me a disgusted look. 'She knows the way home.'

'But she might keep on looking for us. If she thinks we're somewhere just ahead of her, no telling *where* she might go.'

Rusty sighed. 'She probably never came after us at all. She probably went straight to her bedroom, crying.'

'Maybe,' I admitted. 'But let's at least give her five minutes or something to catch up. In case she—'

'Hi, guys.'

Rusty flinched and gasped, 'Shit!'

Even though I recognized the voice, I jumped. A moment later, warmth and relief spread through me. I turned and searched the deep shadows of the woods alongside the dirt road.

'What's up?' Slim asked, stepping out from behind a tree.

'Hey *hey!*' Rusty blurted. 'I *knew* you were okay.'

'I'd known no such thing, myself. As she came toward us, my throat tightened and tears filled my eyes.

She looked fine.

She looked *great.* Her short blond hair was wet and clinging to her scalp. Her skin was shiny and dripping, scratched here and there from her encounter with the dog. On top, she wore nothing except her white bikini. Her cut-off jeans hung low around her hips. Her feet were wrapped in shirts, mine on her right foot, Rusty's on her left.

Seeing the look on my face, she said, 'Hey, Dwight, it's okay.'

I hurried to her and spread out my arms, aching to hug her. But then I remembered all the cuts on her back, so I didn't do it. She looked into my eyes. She had tears in hers, too. Her lips and chin quivered a little. Suddenly, she threw herself against me and wrapped her arms around me and hugged me hard.

Not wanting to hurt her, I put my hands on her shoulders.

Her hot, wet face nuzzled the side of my neck. She was breathing hard, her chest and breasts pushing against me. I could feel the pounding of her heart. Each time she took a breath, her flat belly touched mine.

'You guys gonna get it on?' Rusty asked.

'Shut up,' Slim said.

'Do I get some of that?'

Neither of us bothered to answer him.

After a while, Slim loosened her hold on me and tipped her head back. 'I sure am glad to see you,' she whispered.

'Same here,' I said.

She looked at Rusty. 'You too, I guess.'

'How's the back?' I asked.

'Not bad.'

I turned her around by the shoulders. The cuts looked raw and gooey. None seemed to be bleeding at the moment, but her skin was ruddy with a mixture of sweat and old blood. The bikini ties in the middle of her back were still white in a few places. Mostly, though, they were red.

'Has it been bleeding?' I asked.

'Not much.' She turned around to face me. 'Just for a little while right after I jumped down off the shack,' she said, and glanced at Rusty.

'What'd *I* do?' he complained.

Instead of answering, she looked over her shoulder. 'Let's get off the road before someone comes along.' As we followed her into the trees, she said,

'I've been staying out of sight.'

'Good idea,' I told her.

'Waiting for you. I knew you'd be coming back for me sooner or later.'

'We've been looking all over for you,' I said.

'I've been right here.' She stopped and turned toward us. 'A long time,' she added.

'How long?' I asked.

She shrugged. 'More than an hour, I bet.'

'Why?' Rusty asked.

She gave him a peeved look. 'We were *supposed* to wait for Dwight.'

'I know, I know.'

'Some of us do what we *say* we'll do.'

'You didn't exactly stay put either,' he told her.

'No, I didn't. But I came here so I could *meet* him.' To me, she said, 'I figured if you came back with a car, you'd have to slow down for the turn and I'd have a chance to run out and stop you.'

'I *did* come back in a car,' I said.

Her head jumped forward, eyes going wide, mouth dropping open – a look of total, dumb surprise. 'Huh?'

'In Lee's pickup.'

'When?'

'I don't know. Around noon, I guess. Twelve, twelve-thirty, something like that.'

With a few minor changes in her face and posture, she looked intelligent again, but perplexed. 'That must've been right after I took off,' she said.

'Should've stayed,' Rusty told her.

'You've got to be kidding. I couldn't get out of there fast enough after what I saw.'

'What?' I asked.

'The way they killed the dog.'

'They killed the dog?'

Chapter Nineteen

'Good for them,' Rusty said.

Slim frowned at him. 'Why don't *you* shut up?'

'What crawled up *your* ass and—'

'Rusty!' I snapped.

'What'd *I* do?'

Eyes on Rusty, Slim said, 'I didn't really appreciate getting *left* up there.'

'You should've come with me.'

'We were supposed to wait for Dwight.'

'Yeah, but . . .'

'Yeah, but,' she mimicked him. 'Yeah-but, yeah-but you turned yellow and ran away and *left* me up there.' To me, she said, 'You should've seen him freak out. Nothing was even *there* yet. We just heard cars coming through the woods, and he goes ape like it's the end of the goddamn world. And then this *hearse* drives onto the field. That did it, the hearse. He goes, "*Oh, shit! It's a hearse! We gotta get outa here!*" I told him to calm down. I mean, big deal. A hearse. It's just part of the vampire show. It's part of what we went there to *see*, you know? It was probably *Valeria's* hearse. I thought he *wanted* to see Valeria. But huh-uh, all he wants is to *vamoos*.'

'You were scared, too,' Rusty said.

'Yeah, a little. But I didn't run away.'

'Duh. Yes you did.'

'*Later*.'

'You should've left when I did. Don't go calling *me* a chicken. I just had the foresight to haul my ass out of there sooner than you.'

'I planned to stick it out.' To me again, she said, 'I told Rusty we should just relax and lie down flat so they wouldn't see us.'

'They *would've* seen us. The minute someone climbed the bleachers. By then, we might not've been *able* to get away.'

'So he said, "You wanta stay, stay. I'm gonna get while the gettin's good."'

I could *hear* Rusty say it.

'Of course, my shoes and shirt were down on the ground. My shirt was no big deal, but I didn't want to leave my shoes behind.'

'But you did,' Rusty pointed out.

'Yeah, that's for sure. After they did that to the dog, I stopped worrying about my feet. I grabbed both your shirts and jumped off the back of the shack and ran like hell for the woods.'

'What *did* they do to the dog?' I asked.

'Right off, it went running toward the hearse, barking like a maniac.'

'I saw that,' Rusty said.

'Yeah, and then you took off.' Turning her eyes to me, she said, 'I got down flat on my stomach and looked around the end of the sign. The hearse was coming straight toward me. It had a bus coming along behind it. Like a school bus, only black.'

'I've seen it,' I said.

'When you drove out with Lee?' Slim asked.

'Yeah.'

'So what did you see?' she asked.

'The hearse, the bus, that big truck that looked like a moving van, a bunch of people unloading stuff.'

'Wait'll you hear,' Rusty said.

'Hear what?'

'He's got . . .'

'Hey!' I blasted him. 'I'll tell her. But I'd like to hear about the dog first, okay?'

'Okay, okay.' To Slim, he said, 'What'd they do, run it over?'

'Let *her* tell it.'

'So sorry.' He smirked at Slim. 'Proceed.'

'Okay, so the dog ran straight for the hearse, barking its butt off. I thought it'd jump out of the way at the last second, but it didn't. What it did, it stopped in front of the hearse and planted its feet in the dirt and sort of hunched down and *barked* like a madman. So then the hearse stops. I'm thinking these are decent people who don't want to run over a dog. Boy, was *I* wrong. What happens next, the bus drives up behind the hearse and stops and its door opens. And these *people* come pouring out. Like maybe fifteen of them, and they're all dressed in black and carrying spears.'

'*Spears?*' I blurted.

'Spears. Big long ones. Like maybe six feet long, with steel tips.'

'You're shitting us,' Rusty muttered.

'Yeah, I wish.'

'What did these people look like?' I asked.

'Jungle bunnies?' Rusty asked.

I winced. Ever since Slim had read *To Kill a Mockingbird*, she'd gone on the warpath if anyone used that sort of language.

She glared at Rusty.

'You know.' He smiled. 'The spears.'

'Don't be an asshole,' she told him.

'Just asking.'

'Well, don't. You want to be a bigoted shit-for-brains, don't do it in front of me.'

I looked at Rusty and shook my head. 'Nice going.'

'Big deal.'

Still looking angry, Slim said, 'Matter of fact, all of them were white.'

'Glad to hear it,' Rusty said.

Ignoring him, I asked, 'What did they look like?'

'Just normal, I guess.' She glanced at Rusty, but he made no comment so she turned her attention to me and continued. 'Mostly men, I think. And a few women. They all wore these shiny black shirts that looked like satin or silk or something. Anyway, they split into two groups. One bunch went around one side of the hearse, one around the other. Before the dog noticed anything was wrong, they closed in on it. They surrounded it, then started poking at it with their spears. They could've killed it with one good thrust, but nobody did that. They just kept poking at it, giving it little jabs.'

Slim went silent. She had a hurt look in her eyes as if she could feel the dog's agonies. After taking a few deep breaths, she said, 'I couldn't see the dog at all . . . just those people around it, going at it with their spears. I could sure hear it, though. It was yelping and squealing and whimpering. You could tell . . . It was like they just wanted to *torture* it.'

'Good God,' I muttered.

'Sick,' Rusty said.

'Finally, they stepped back to let someone through. The dog was down on its side. Its tongue was hanging out and it was panting for air, and it was just *covered* with blood. It was sort of trying to get up.' Slim's voice broke. She shook her head and looked away from us.

Rusty looked as if he might throw up.

With both hands, Slim wiped sweat away from her eyes. Some tears, too, I think. Then she took another deep breath and said, 'The guy they let through, he got down on one knee and shoved his spear . . .' Breathing hard, she shook her head. Then as if in a race to get her story done, she blurted, *'He picked it up off the ground with his spear and ran with it to the back of the hearse and somebody'd already opened the door back there and he shoved the dog in like food on the end of a stick and . . .'* She paused to take a few quick breaths, then went on. *'He pulled the spear back a second later, and the dog wasn't on it anymore. It was like somebody in the hearse . . . I don't know.'*

Rusty and I both stared at her.

Head down, she kept wiping her face with both hands. It took her a long time to calm down. Then she said, 'After that, that's when I figured it was time to go.'

We were silent for a while longer. Then I said, 'God Almighty.'

After more silence, Rusty said, 'So you think somebody in the hearse *ate* the dog?'

She shrugged her shiny, tanned shoulders. 'I don't know,' she muttered.

'Or drank its blood,' I suggested.

'Valeria *is* supposed to be a vampire,' Rusty reminded us.

'I don't know who was in the hearse,' Slim said.

'Maybe nobody,' I said. 'Maybe they just put the dog in there to get it out of sight.'

'I don't know,' Slim muttered. 'Anyway, that's what happened. And I thought if they got their hands on me . . . I might get it like the dog. So I turned around and belly-crawled to the back of the roof and jumped down and ran like hell.'

'Did they see you?' I asked.

'I don't know. Maybe not. I didn't hear any shouts. No one came after me. I don't think so, anyway. When I got into the woods, I kept changing directions to throw them off. Just in case someone *was* after me. Then I hid for a while.'

'Where'd you hide?' Rusty asked.

She shrugged again. 'Under some old tree. It had fallen over and there was a space between it and the ground. I just barely fit in.'

'How long do you think you stayed in there?' I asked.

'Seemed like ages.' She shrugged again. 'Maybe half an hour, I don't know.'

'I bet that's where you were when Lee and I were at Janks Field.'

'Maybe. I don't know.'

'Did you hear anyone calling your name?'

She shook her head.

'I called out for you and Rusty.'

'When was that?'

I shrugged. 'I don't know. Maybe around twelve-thirty, I guess. Twelve-fifteen, twelve-thirty, something like that.'

Slim frowned as if thinking about it, and shook her head again. 'I must've been *some*where in the woods.'

'You weren't on the roof.'

Surprise on her face, she said, 'You looked?'

'Yeah. I went over and jumped up and—'

'Went over to the *shack*?'

'Yeah.'

'What about all those *people*?'

'They weren't paying much attention to us. Julian had gone into the bus . . .'

'Who's that?'

'Julian Stryker. He's the owner of the show.'

Looking surprised but not at all pleased, Slim said, 'You met the *owner*?'

I nodded.

'What'd he look like?'

'I can see *this* coming,' Rusty said.

139

I glanced at him, then looked back at Slim. 'He wore a black shirt...'

'They *all* wore black shirts, numbnuts,' Rusty reminded me.

Ignoring the remark, I said to Slim, 'He had long, black hair. He was... I guess women would probably think he was really handsome.'

'Gorgeous?' Slim asked.

'I didn't think so, but...'

'Was he carrying a spear?' Rusty asked.

I glared at him.

'Did he wear silver spurs?' Slim asked.

'Yeah.'

'That's him,' she said.

'Knew it,' said Rusty.

Me, too. But I asked, 'The guy who... picked up the dog and took it to the hearse?'

Slim nodded.

'Oh, man,' I muttered.

'What?'

'We asked him about you and Rusty.'

'What'd he say?'

'That he hadn't seen you.'

'Wait'll you hear the *good* part,' Rusty said, a strange smile on his face.

'Lee bought tickets from him,' I explained. 'Four tickets for tonight's performance of the Travelling Vampire Show. One for each of us.'

Chapter Twenty

Slim stared at me. She looked a little stunned. 'You're kidding,' she said.

'They cost her forty bucks,' I said.

'But nobody under eighteen's allowed.'

'Julian made an exception for us.'

'He's got the hots for Lee,' Rusty explained.

Slim's upper lip lifted slightly. Eyes turning toward Rusty, she said, 'Maybe that's why. Or maybe he *did* see us. Me, anyway. If he saw me running away – if *any* of them did – he might figure I watched them kill the dog. Maybe he wants to *get* me.'

A touch of scorn in his voice, Rusty said, 'Why would he want to *get* you?'

'To stop me from telling what I saw.'

I could think of other reasons he might want Slim. They made me feel cold and tight inside. I decided not to mention them.

A grin on his face, Rusty said, 'Maybe he wants to stick a spear up your ass.'

'Real funny,' Slim muttered.

I punched him. My fist smacked his soft upper arm through the sleeve of his shirt.

Face going red, he gasped, '*Ah!*' and grabbed his arm and gazed at me with shocked, accusing eyes. As I watched, his eyes filled with tears. 'Real nice,' he said.

I turned to Slim. She looked as if she wished I hadn't hit him, but she didn't seem *angry* at me. More as if she thought the punch had probably not been the most terrific idea.

Though tears shimmered in Rusty's eyes, he wasn't exactly

141

crying. They weren't streaming down his face or anything. Frowning at me, he rubbed his arm.

'I didn't hit you that hard,' I said.

'Hard enough. It *hurt*, man.'

'You shouldn't have said what you did.'

'I was just being funny.'

'You *weren't* being funny,' Slim assured him. 'And you wouldn't be making cracks like that if you'd watched them with the dog.'

'Sorry,' he muttered, still rubbing his arm.

'And as a matter of fact,' Slim said, 'that guy really *might* want to stick a spear up my ass. Or up yours. Anyone who'll do a thing like that to a dog . . . he wouldn't think twice about doing it to a person.'

'Maybe we'd better forget about going to the show tonight,' I said.

Rusty's mouth fell open. He looked as if I'd punched him again. 'Shit,' he said. 'We can't not *go*!'

'I'm not going,' Slim said. 'No way.'

He turned to me. '*I* wanta see the show, man! Don't you? I mean, *Valeria*! If we don't go tonight, we'll *never* see her. *You* wanta see her, don't you?'

'It might not be such a good idea,' I said.

'It'd be a *lousy* idea,' Slim said. '*I'm* sure not going anywhere near those people again, and I don't think you guys should, either. They're a bunch of sickos.'

'Just because they killed that stupid *dog*? Hey, *Dwight* tried to *jump* on the damn thing. Is he a sicko, too?'

'It's different.'

'Dog would've been just as dead. Except he missed. He sure as hell *planned* to land on it.'

She glanced at me, shook her head, and said to Rusty, 'You know good and well it was different. Stop being a creep, okay?'

'I just don't wanta get rooked outa the show,' he said. 'I don't care *what* they did to that stupid dog. Look how it messed *you* up. It deserved what it got.'

'Didn't deserve *that*.' Slim looked from Rusty to me and said, 'Anyway, let's get out of here. I want to go home and get cleaned up.'

Home.

I remembered what we'd done there.

It all rushed in: sneaking into her bedroom, looking at her things, Rusty fooling with her mother's bra, and the awful accident with the vase and how we'd left the mess behind. A nasty flood of heat flashed through my body.

Rusty cast me a warning glance.

And suddenly an idea popped into my head. Trying to keep my relief from showing, I frowned and said, 'Maybe we'd better go over to Lee's house first and tell her about what happened. See what she thinks.'

Rusty looked pained. 'She hears what they did, man, she isn't gonna *take* us.'

I gaped at him, astonished that he didn't realize a trip to Lee's house would save us from going to Slim's. The mess in her mother's room was sure to be discovered sooner or later, but I preferred later. The longer we could put it off, the better.

'She *shouldn't* take us,' Slim said. 'None of us should go to that show.'

'Anyway,' I said, 'we *have* to tell Lee what happened.'

'No, we don't.'

'Yes, we do. Otherwise, she'll be waiting for us.' To Slim, I explained, 'We're supposed to be at her house at ten-thirty tonight.' To Rusty, I said, 'We can't just not show up when she's expecting us.'

'So we *do* show up. I've got no problem with that.'

'I think we'd better tell her now,' I said.

Slim nodded in agreement.

'Besides,' I said, 'her house is closer than Slim's. We can stop there first and borrow some bandages.'

Rusty opened his mouth as if all set to argue. Before any words came out, however, a light of understanding filled his eyes.

He got it.

He got *something* anyway.

'Good point,' he said. 'Bandages. Lee *must* have bandages. Everyone has bandages. Okay. Let's go there first.'

'Okay by me,' Slim said.

Not saying a word, I raised one foot off the ground and pulled off my sneaker.

'What're you doing?' Slim asked.

'Giving you my shoes.'

'You don't have to do that.'

I smiled at her, shrugged and pulled off my other sneaker. Holding them both toward her, I said, 'I insist.'

'Hey, no. C'mon. I can't wear your shoes.'

'Sure you can.'

'If she doesn't want to wear 'em . . .'

I gave Rusty a look that shut his mouth.

'Put them on,' I told Slim. 'Please.'

'I don't know.'

'If it hadn't been for *your* shoes, I would've gotten chomped by the dog.'

'Glad to help.'

'*I'm* the one who threw 'em,' Rusty reminded us.

'You did a good job,' I told him.

'Saved your butt.'

'I know. You both did.'

'Yeah, well, remember that when you wanta rook me outa Valeria.'

'Sure.' To Slim, I said, 'I *want* you to wear them. Please.'

'But what about *you*?'

'I'll be fine.'

With a look of embarrassed but grateful surrender, she nodded and said, 'All right.' Then she took the sneakers from my hands, turned away and walked over to the remains of an old, fallen-down tree. She sat on its trunk, facing us, and set both sneakers beside her. While Rusty and I stood there and watched, she brought up one foot, crossed it over her knee, and removed the shirt that she'd been using to protect it. The bottom of her bare foot looked filthy. I glimpsed some blood on it before she put my sneaker on.

'Are your feet okay?' I asked.

'A few little nicks. No big deal.' She let the shirt fall to the ground, then brought up her other foot.

When she had both my shoes on, she stood up. 'Feels much better,' she said. Then she crouched and plucked our shirts off the ground. Holding them out in front of her, she shook her head. 'These are really wrecked, guys. I'm sorry.'

They were not only covered with dirt and blood, but torn in a few places.

'Want them?' she asked.

Rusty shook his head.

'We can throw them away when we get to town,' I said, holding out my hand. 'I'll carry 'em.'

She was about to give them to me when Rusty asked her, 'Don't you want to wear one?'

'Thanks anyway. They're filthy. You want me to get infected?'

'You can't walk back to town looking like that. Everybody's gonna wonder how you got all wrecked up.'

I nodded. 'You'd better wear a shirt.'

She frowned at the shirts in her hands. 'I'd rather let people see me—'

'You can borrow mine,' Rusty said. He started to unfasten the buttons of the shirt he was wearing.

Shaking her head, Slim said, 'It'll get blood on it. I've wrecked enough shirts for one day.'

'I insist,' Rusty said.

'No, really . . .'

'You can wear Dwight's shoes . . .'

'Okay.'

He pulled his shirt off.

'Thanks,' Slim said. She handed the two ruined shirts to me, then stepped closer to Rusty. 'You'd better put it on me, though.' She turned her back to him.

He gave me a strange smile – somehow smug and embarrassed at the same time – then slipped the shirt up Slim's arms and eased it onto her shoulders. 'There you go,' he told her.

Turning to face us, she fastened a couple of the middle buttons. 'Thanks, guys,' she said.

The shirt was way too large for her. It drooped over her shoulders. The sleeves reached down to her elbows. The single pocket hung below the rise of her left breast. The tails were so long that they completely hid her cut-off jeans.

She looked so cute it hurt to look at her.

I wished I could put my arms around her and hold her and never let go.

Instead of giving it a try, I just stood there, staring at her and feeling like I almost wanted to cry.

I don't know what it was about Slim.

I'd seen Lee a few hours earlier wearing my brother's big old work shirt. Even though it fit Lee pretty much the same way as Rusty's shirt fit Slim, even though Lee was probably the most beautiful woman I'd ever seen, the sight of her hadn't made me feel like my heart might break.

Maybe because Lee wasn't *cute*.

Slim was cute; Lee was spectacular.

I loved both of them. They both had ways of making me ache for them. But different ways. And different sorts of aches. In different places.

'What's wrong?' Slim asked me.

'Nothing.'

'Ready?'

'Yeah.'

'Let's *go*,' Rusty said. He led the way, Slim walking *behind* him.

I followed, staying a few paces behind Slim, watching her.

With only my socks between my feet and the forest floor, I felt pokes and jabs with every step. I didn't mind, though. I was glad that my own feet, not Slim's, were the ones being hurt.

When we reached the pavement of Route 3, I said, 'Wait up.'

Slim and Rusty stopped walking. I checked the bottoms of my socks. They had picked up some dirt and debris, but they weren't really damaged yet.

'Want your shoes back?' Slim asked.

'Nope. I'm fine.' I pulled off my socks, stuffed them into the pockets of my jeans and then we all resumed our hike back to town.

Chapter Twenty-one

As we entered the outskirts of town, I remembered about Bitsy.

She hadn't followed us, after all, probably so hurt by my betrayal that she'd gone back to her bedroom and cried. I once again felt rotten about ditching her ... on top of everything else I felt rotten about.

God, it's hard not to feel rotten.

I should've felt wonderful because we'd found Slim alive and well.

But I didn't. And I felt cheated because I had to feel lousy about Bitsy and about what we'd done in Slim's house and about slugging Rusty and about the poor damn dog getting speared and about God-only-knows what else.

On top of all that, it looked as if we wouldn't even get to see the Travelling Vampire Show.

Things could've been worse, though: at least we weren't on our way to Slim's house.

When we came to Lee's block, I saw her pickup truck in the driveway.

'She's home,' I said.

'How about if we *don't* tell her about the dog?' Rusty suggested, looking over his shoulder at us with a pained expression on his face. 'Please? She doesn't have to know *everything*, does she?'

'She has to know about that,' Slim said.

'We're not going, anyway,' I pointed out. 'So why *not* tell her?'

Rusty stopped walking, turned around and raised his open hands to halt us. 'Hold it up,' he said.

We stopped.

'What if we change our minds?' he asked. 'It's a long time between now and midnight. Maybe we'll wanta go after all, but we won't be able to if we've already spilled the beans to Lee.'

Looking mildly amused, Slim said, 'Oh, you think sometime between now and midnight it'll turn out that they *didn't* gang-stab the dog.'

Gang-stab? Slim sometimes got creative with her language.

'I just mean, you know, maybe we'll decide to go *anyway*. Do we really wanta miss the vampire show on account of a stupid dog?'

'It isn't because of the dog,' Slim said. 'It's because what they did to it was heinous. These are heinous people.'

Rusty looked annoyed.

'Abominable,' I explained. 'Shockingly evil.'

He glanced at me. 'I know what it means. I'm not stupid, you know.'

'I know.'

'Anyway, it's not like they'll do anything horrible *tonight*. They wouldn't dare.' Eyes on Slim, he said, 'I bet they wouldn't even've done that to the dog if they'd known you were watching. They *sure* aren't gonna pull stuff like that in front of an audience.'

'Wouldn't think so,' I said.

'They'd have the cops all over 'em.'

Slim shook her head. 'I don't plan to find out.' Not waiting for any more arguments from Rusty, she stepped past him. He turned to follow her, and I took up the rear.

'Just because *you* don't want to see the show,' he said to Slim's back, 'have you gotta ruin it for the rest of us?'

'Leave her alone,' I said.

We cut across Lee's front lawn. After two miles of walking mostly on pavement, the soft, dry grass felt good under my bare feet. When we reached the porch, I took over the lead and trotted up the wooden stairs. The screen door was shut, but I could see through it. The main door was open. Instead of ringing the doorbell or knocking, I called out. 'Lee? It's Dwight. Are you here?'

'Come on in.' Her voice sounded as if it came from somewhere deep in the house.

I opened the screen door and we all stepped into the foyer. The stone floor felt cool but hard.

The living room was just to our left. Lee's voice hadn't come from over there, but I looked for her anyway. She didn't seem to be there. At least I couldn't see her.

Though all the curtains were open, the afternoon was so gloomy that not much light made it through the windows. The room looked the way it might look at dusk if nobody's turned on any lamps.

'I'll be right in,' Lee called.

'Okay.' I realized she might assume I was alone. Just to play it safe, I let her know, 'Slim and Rusty are here, too.'

'Good deal.'

'Hi, Mrs Thompson!' Slim called.

'Hi, Slim.'

'Hello again,' Rusty called.

'Hello, Rusty.' After a small pause, Lee added, 'Sit down and make yourselves comfortable. I'll be in in a minute.'

Rusty suddenly announced, 'If this isn't a good time for you, we can leave.'

'No, it's fine. Don't go away. I'm almost done.'

'Nice try,' Slim whispered.

Rusty grinned, then walked into the living room and plopped down on the sofa.

Slim glanced at the bottoms of her shoes – my shoes – then entered the living room.

'Take a load off,' Rusty told her.

She looked around at the furniture, then shook her head. 'Think I'll stand. I'm a mess.'

I checked the bottoms of my feet. They felt sore from the hike. They were dirty and even had a couple of dark smudges that made me suspect I'd stepped in a couple of oil drips. I didn't see any blood or cuts, though, so I took the socks out of my pocket and put them on. Then I walked into the living room. The carpet felt good and soft.

I wanted to sit down, but it didn't seem right to leave Slim standing by herself.

After a couple of minutes, Lee came in. 'Sorry about that,' she said. 'I was mopping the kitchen floor.'

She *looked* as if she'd been mopping a floor: some hair drooped across her forehead, her skin gleamed with sweat, the sleeves of her big blue shirt were rolled halfway up her forearms and her feet were bare. The front of the shirt was tied together just below her breasts. She wore small, white shorts. Like her shirt, the shorts looked like what she'd had on when she drove me to Janks Field.

To Slim, she said, 'I understand you had some dog trouble this morning.'

'Just a bit. Thanks for going out to rescue me.'

'Yeah, thanks,' Rusty added.

'Sorry we missed you,' Lee said. Concern coming into her eyes, she said to Slim, 'I thought you went home afterward.'

Slim looked puzzled.

'You aren't cleaned up and it looks like you're wearing someone else's shirt and sneakers.'

'I haven't been home,' Slim said.

Lee gave Rusty a glance.

He seemed to blush, cringe and shrug all at the same time.

'It turns out Slim stayed behind,' I explained. 'At Janks Field. Rusty left, but she stayed for a while. Rusty told us a little fib when he said they'd left together. We went back and found her.'

'Where *were* you?' Lee asked her.

'I ran off and hid in the woods,' Slim said. 'I guess that's how I missed you.'

'That was a *long* time ago.'

Slim shrugged. 'I just stayed hidden. I didn't want to walk all the way home because I'd lost my shirt and shoes. Besides, Dwight was supposed to show up.' She smiled at me. 'And he did.'

'We *both* did,' Rusty pointed out.

To Lee, I said, 'We figured maybe we could borrow some bandages from you.'

She turned to Slim. 'All right if I take a look?'

'Sure.' Slim unbuttoned her shirt, took it off, then turned around.

At the sight of her back, Lee pursed her lips.

'Most of that's from broken glass,' I explained.

'You'd better come with me, Slim. We'll get you cleaned up and bandaged.'

Looking a little embarrassed, Slim nodded.

'You guys wait here,' Lee told us. 'We won't be long.'

We watched Slim and Lee leave the room. A couple of minutes later, water came on and rushed through the pipes.

Rusty met my eyes. 'Sounds like somebody's taking a bath,' he whispered.

'Or a shower.'

'Who do you think it is?'

'Who do you think?'

A smile spreading across his cherubic face, Rusty said, 'Wanta find out?' He started to rise from the sofa.

'Stay put,' I said.

He stood up. 'I know we can't *look*. As if they'd leave the *door* open. But maybe we can hear something.'

'Forget it.'

'Come on, man.'

'Don't you think we've screwed up enough for one day?'

Looking disappointed in me, he said, 'You're such a chicken.'

'If you say so.'

'Come on. It'll be cool.'

'No.'

'I tell you what. You wait here where it's nice and safe and *I'll* go listen.'

'No you won't.'

He lifted his eyebrows. In a quiet, taunting voice, he said, 'Slim's probably *nude* in there, you know.'

'Knock it off.'

'Maybe Lee, too. Maybe she got in the shower with Slim to help wash her back.'

I saw it in my mind. Rusty was obviously seeing it in his mind, too, and I didn't like that. I stepped up close to him – so close that our stomachs touched – and looked him in the eyes.

'Okay, okay,' he muttered. 'Forget it. Never mind.' He backed away and sank onto the sofa.

After a while, I calmed down. I walked to the other side of the room and sat in an armchair.

We both sat in silence.

Rusty was careful not to look at me.

The water kept rushing through the pipes.

Chapter Twenty-two

When the water shut off, Rusty lifted his head and looked at me.

'What?' I asked.

'Nothing.'

'What?'

'Nothing. You're not so pure, that's all. You're no purer than me, you're just scared of getting caught.'

'Up yours.'

'It's the truth.'

'Shut up, okay? They might be able to hear us.'

He closed his mouth and gave me a smug, knowing smile. He knew he was right, and I knew he wasn't far from wrong.

We didn't say anything else.

After a while, we heard a door unlatch. Then came quiet footsteps and voices.

Lee saying, 'I'll have to give him a try.'

Slim saying, 'I've got an extra copy of *The Temple of Gold* I can let you read.'

'Great.'

'I'll bring it over sometime.'

Then they walked into the living room. Lee, dressed the same as before, was carrying my sneakers, Rusty's shirt, and a brown paper grocery bag with its top crumpled shut.

Slim, with nothing in her hands, had the clean, fresh look of someone who'd just taken a bath or shower. She wore clothes that must've belonged to Lee: a loose white T-shirt, red shorts, white crew socks and white sneakers. The T-shirt completely covered her shorts, but I could see through it enough to tell their color. I could also tell where bandages had been applied, and that she no longer wore her bikini top.

Her bikini and cut-off jeans were probably in the grocery bag Lee was carrying.

Evidently, Lee didn't own a bra in Slim's size.

When I realized I was staring at Slim's chest, I quickly turned my eyes to Lee. 'How'd it go?' I asked.

'I think she'll live. But since she refuses to see a doctor, I guess she'll have to go stitchless.'

'My cuts aren't that bad,' Slim said.

'They aren't that *good*, either.' Lee dropped the sneakers in front of my feet, stepped toward the sofa and tossed the shirt to Rusty.

While I put on my shoes and Rusty put on his shirt, Lee set the grocery sack on the coffee table. Then she sank onto the sofa beside Rusty, settled back against the cushion, swung her legs onto the coffee table and crossed her ankles. She sighed as if relieved to be off her feet.

Still fastening his buttons, Rusty turned his head and stared down at her.

Life was suddenly good again for him.

Lee glanced at him, smiled, then said to all of us, 'The kitchen floor's gotta be dry by now. If anyone wants a Coke or something, feel free. I'm not moving, though. You'll have to help yourselves.'

None of us spoke up.

Slim walked past me. She smelled like a strange, wonderful combination of lemons and marshmallows. Through the back of her T-shirt, I saw eight or ten bandages. She went to a wicker chair near the lamp table and sat down. Perched near the front of the seat, she folded her hands on her lap and kept her back straight.

Glancing from Slim to me, Lee asked, 'So, all set for tonight?'

Slim hadn't told her about the dog?

'Not sure yet,' I said.

'We're still working on it,' said Rusty. He gave Slim a perplexed look.

Slim's shoulders moved slightly.

Rusty returned his gaze to Lee's slumped, lounging body. 'Any ideas?' he asked her.

'Nothing spectacular. Anyway, I think you should work it out for yourselves.'

Looking at me, Rusty said, 'I can get permission to sleep over at your house. Your mom and dad still go to bed at ten?'

'Around then.'

'So we wait till they hit the sack, then we sneak out.'

'I don't know about sneaking out,' I said.

'It'll work. It's always worked before.'

I could've killed him for saying that in front of Lee.

She looked at me and lifted her eyebrows. She seemed amused and curious.

'We didn't do anything much,' I told her.

'Hey, don't worry about it. I won't tell.'

'I know.'

'But I'd like to hear about it sometime.'

'Sure.'

'And I'll tell you about the times *I* used to sneak out at night.'

'*I'd* like to hear that,' Rusty said.

She lifted a hand off her belly, reached over and patted him on the leg.

His face went crimson.

Mine probably did, too.

'We'll see,' she told him.

'If we have to sneak out of someone's house,' I said to Rusty, 'why not *yours*? Why does it always have to be *my* house?'

'I'm already invited for supper,' he pointed out.

'What's that got to do with it?'

'I'll already *be* there.'

'Right. So then I explain how you've asked me to spend the night at *your* place. So then we go over *there* after—'

'Just can't wait to see Bitsy again, huh?'

I grunted as if I'd been slugged in the stomach. 'Oh yeah,' I muttered.

'I'm sure she'd *love* to see you . . .'

'Never mind.'

'Here's how to work it,' Slim suddenly said.

I gaped at her.

Rusty actually went, 'Huh?'

'Dwight, you tell your parents you've been asked to spend the night at Rusty's house. Rusty, you tell yours that you're invited to stay at Dwight's. Then you both come over to *my* house.'

Stunned again, I mumbled, 'Your house?'

'It'll be perfect,' she said.

I pictured the mess in her mother's bedroom.

'I don't get it,' Rusty asked. 'Why do we wanta go to your house?'

'We won't have to worry about sneaking out when it's time to leave.'

'We won't?' I asked.

'We'll have the whole house to ourselves.'

'Really?'

Smiling and nodding as if very pleased with herself, she said, 'That's right.'

'What about your mom?' I asked.

'She'll be gone. She's got a date tonight.'

'What do you mean?' Rusty asked. He had a dumbfounded look on his face as if he'd just woken up from a nap and couldn't figure out what was going on.

'A *date*, you know? With a *guy*.'

'Tonight?' I asked. I was feeling slightly dumbfounded myself.

'Who's the lucky man?' Lee asked.

Slim shrugged, this time using only one shoulder. 'I don't know. She met him at Steerman's last night.'

'You don't know his name?'

'Charlie something. From across the river. He lives over in Falcon Bay. Anyway, he's taking Mom out tonight in his cabin cruiser.'

'He's got a *cabin cruiser*?' I asked.

'A thirty-foot Chris-craft.'

'Holy shit!' Rusty blurted. Then he said, 'Sorry, Mrs Thompson.'

Lee reached over and patted his thigh again. I wished she would stop doing that.

'Mom won't even be coming home at the end of her shift,' Slim explained. 'Charlie's meeting her at the restaurant. Then he's taking her out for a night on the river.'

'How do I meet this guy?' Lee asked.

'Hey,' I said.

She laughed.

Eyes on Slim, Rusty asked, 'So when's your mom getting home?'

'I'm supposed to expect her when I see her.' Slim tried to smile, but it didn't come off very well. 'When she says that, I usually don't see her till the next day.'

I tried not to look upset. 'She leaves you alone all night?'

'Sometimes.'

Why was this the first I'd heard about it?

'It's no big deal,' she said. 'I *am* sixteen.'

'So am I, but . . . *I* wouldn't like it.'

Slim met my eyes. 'It's okay. Really.'

'It's not *that* okay,' Lee said. 'If you ever feel like coming over here . . .'

'Thanks.'

'Let me know the next time your mom's planning to pull an all-nighter, okay? You shouldn't have to stay alone like that.'

'Anyway,' Slim said, 'it'll work out great for tonight. After supper, we can all hang out at my house till it's time to go. There won't be anyone around to stop us.'

'Sounds great,' Rusty said.

'Yeah,' I said.

'Why don't you come over, too?' she asked Lee.

'Thanks, but I'll pass. I'll probably take a nice long nap after supper. Wouldn't want to fall asleep in the middle of the vampire show.'

'If you change your mind . . .'

She shook her head. 'Not me. But let's not have any hanky-panky over there. You really shouldn't be having boys in the house when your mom's not home.'

'Yeah, but we won't do anything.'

Looking at each of us, Lee said, 'I want everyone to be on their best behaviour, okay?'

'We will be,' Slim said. She glanced from Rusty to me. 'Won't we, guys?'

'Sure thing,' said Rusty.

I nodded in agreement.

'Okay,' Lee said. 'So then just come on over here around ten, ten-thirty.'

'We'll be here,' Slim said.

Chapter Twenty-three

When we left Lee's house a couple of minutes later, Slim led the way. We hurried after her, but she managed to keep ahead of us until we reached the corner.

There, she turned around, faced us, and set her grocery bag down on the sidewalk. 'Can one of you give me a shirt?'

We must've looked perplexed.

'Come on, come on.' She snapped her fingers. 'Dwight, let me have yours.'

'It's actually Rusty's.'

'She can have it,' Rusty said.

I took it off and handed it to her.

'Thanks.'

'You're welcome,' Rusty said.

As she slipped into the shirt, she said, 'I don't mind much if you guys see me like that, but . . .' She shook her head. 'Not everyone else in town.' She started fastening the buttons. 'Lee wouldn't let me put my own stuff back on after I showered. I wanted to at least put my swimsuit back on, but she said it's too dirty. Which it is. I'm probably better off not wearing it.' Slim finished with the buttons. 'All set.'

'Almost,' I said. 'What happened to telling Lee about the dog?'

'Oh, that.'

'Yeah.'

She shrugged. 'I don't know. I just didn't want to screw things up for you guys.'

'All *right*!' Rusty blurted.

'I mean, it's pretty clear you've both got the hots to see Valeria in action.'

'You betcha.'

'I'm not so sure I do,' I told her.

'Well, it's up to you. I just didn't want to be the one to ruin it. *I'm* still not going. But let's hang out at my place anyway, okay? Then when it's time to go you can just head over to Lee's without me. If you feel like it.'

'She'll wonder why you didn't come,' I said.

'Tell her I got a headache or something.'

'The trots,' Rusty suggested.

She scowled at him. 'Not the trots, a headache.'

'You got your period!'

Slim and I both blushed furiously.

'No,' she said.

'Why not say it's your period?'

'Forget it.'

'Can't go to vampire shows when you've got your period, you know. All that blood? Drives 'em crazy and they come after you.'

'*Jeez*,' I muttered.

'It's the *truth*, man. It'd be like going into bear country or swimming in shark-infested waters.'

Glaring at him, Slim said, 'Get bent.'

Rusty started to laugh.

Slim reached toward his face. Very quickly, she tucked down her middle finger, hooked it in place with the pad of her thumb, built up some force in her finger and let it go. It flicked upward, nail thumping Rusty's nose.

His eyes bulged. His face went red. His laughter stopped. Staggering backward, he cupped a hand over his nose.

'No more talk like that,' she told him.

'Shit,' he gasped.

'You never know when to quit,' she said.

He blinked at her, his eyes red and watery.

161

I didn't feel sorry for him. And I was glad Slim and hurt him. Now, *both* of us had brought tears to Rusty's eyes.

He sniffled a few times. Then he muttered, 'Now you've done it,' and lowered his hand.

Bright red blood was running out of his nostrils and spilling over his upper lip.

'Oh, great,' Slim muttered.

Rusty sniffed and licked the blood. 'Happy?' He tipped back his head.

'You'd better lie down,' I told him.

He stepped off the sidewalk and stretched out flat on someone's front yard.

'You'll be all right in a minute,' I said.

Slim squatted down beside him. Patting him on the chest, she said, 'Too bad, sport. You can't go to a vampire show with a bloody nose. Drives 'em crazy. They'll come right after you and suck you dry.'

'Screw you,' he said.

Calmly, Slim reached toward his face, tucked down her middle finger and gave his nose another hard flick.

'*OW! DAMNIT!*'

'Be nice, Rusty, and these things won't befall you.'

'Go to hell,' he muttered.

Chuckling, Slim stood up. She said to me, 'Poor Rusty, everybody's beating up on him.'

'He likes it,' I said. 'He must.'

'I do not,' he said from the ground.

'Anyway,' Slim said, 'where're we going now?'

'My place?' I suggested. 'We can hang out there till supper time. You're going to eat with us, aren't you? Dad's grilling burgers.'

'Sure. But why don't I meet you there? I want to run home and change clothes.'

She saw the look on my face.

'What?' she asked.

'Do you *have* to?'

She stared down at herself, holding her arms away from her sides, bending her knees, grimacing as if she'd just gotten up from a face-first fall into a mud puddle.

'You look fine,' I said. She looked *great*, but I didn't want to push it.

'Yeah, well, I like to wear my own stuff. Anyway, it'll only take a few minutes.' She started to turn away.

'No, wait,' I said.

She faced me.

'Why don't you not go?'

She raised her eyebrows, put her head forward and spoke slowly as if talking to a goon. 'I want my *own* clothes?' She lifted her voice at the end so it sounded like a question. 'I want clothes that *fit*? And shorts that aren't *red*? And *something* to wear under them?'

'Okay,' I said.

But I must've looked pained, because her mocking attitude changed to concern. 'What is it?'

I shrugged.

Someone was sure to discover the mess in her mother's bedroom, anyway, sooner or later. This might be a good time for Slim to find it. She would have no reason to suspect Rusty and me, especially if she went by herself so she couldn't see the looks on our faces or hear us say something stupid.

I should've told her, 'Nothing's wrong. Go on ahead.'

But I didn't want her to leave.

Before I could think of what to say, Rusty spoke up. 'He's scared you'll get lost.'

Slim met my eyes.

My eyes must've looked astonished, because I could hardly believe that Rusty had come up with an explanation that was so close to the truth.

163

Especially since I hadn't realized it, myself, until the words came out of him.

'I just think we oughta stick together,' I said. 'It's been a weird day, you know? We didn't know *where* you were, and . . . I don't want you to get lost again.'

'I was never lost.'

'But *we* didn't know where you were. We were afraid maybe *they'd* gotten their hands on you . . .'

'And shoved a spear up your ass.'

Just when I was starting to appreciate Rusty again, he had to say that.

Slim smirked down at him. 'You didn't *know* about the spears then, moron.'

'We assumed them.'

Slim and I laughed. But then we looked at each other and I said, 'Anyway, I've spent most of the day *worrying* about you, and we finally found you and now you want to go off by yourself.'

'Just for a few minutes . . .'

'What if they *are* after you?' I asked. 'Somebody might've seen you run away . . .'

'Even if they did, they don't know where I live.'

'They might.'

'They have *ways*,' Rusty said from the ground.

'Bull.'

'*Magic* ways.'

'Yeah, right.'

Rusty sniffed a couple of times, then took his hand away from his face. All around his mouth, he was smeared with blood. He looked as if he'd been eating someone raw. Smiling, he said, 'Maybe they put the *dog* on your scent.'

'It's dead.'

'They put its *ghost* on you.'

164

Slim looked uneasy for a moment. Then she smiled and said, 'Good one.'

'Maybe *you* should be the writer,' I told him.

'Slim can write 'em. I'll be the idea man.'

'Anyway,' Slim said, 'they can't possibly know where I live.'

'What if they're watching us right now,' I asked, 'and they follow you home?'

She almost smirked, but not quite. Instead, she turned her head and looked over her shoulder.

'Maybe they're already *at* your house,' Rusty added, kidding around.

'Yeah, right.'

'Anything's possible,' he said.

'Anything is *not* possible.'

'What if they're *waiting* for you?'

I looked down at Rusty, impressed and a little annoyed. He'd just given a whole new meaning to the mess Slim would find in her mother's room. Now, instead of wondering about the mystery of it, she might figure the gang from Janks Field had paid a visit to her house.

'I'll take my chances,' she told Rusty. 'See you guys later.' Again, she turned away.

Again, I said, 'No, wait.' Then I looked down at Rusty. 'Get up. If she's going, we're going with her.' To Slim, I said, 'Is that okay?'

'Okay by me.'

'How's the nose?' I asked Rusty.

'Hurts.'

'Is it still bleeding?'

He sniffed a couple of times. 'I dunno. Maybe not.'

'Come on. We're going with Slim.'

Chapter Twenty-four

As we climbed the porch stairs, my stomach started to feel funny. Not indigestion funny, scared funny. I was nervous about Slim finding the spilled perfume and broken glass in her mother's room, but it wasn't just that. Dumb as it may seem, I half believed that Julian or some of his gang *might* be hiding in the house.

Because of Rusty's remarks.

Sometimes people say stuff that doesn't make any sense, but it gets to you anyway. This was one of those times.

I *knew* Slim's house was empty, but the fear wouldn't go away.

It didn't help matters, watching her open the screen door and front door without unlocking either of them.

Anybody might be in her house.

When I started to follow Slim through the doors, Rusty grabbed my arm.

I frowned back at him.

'Maybe we should wait out here,' he said.

'Huh?'

'Her *mother's* not home.'

In the foyer, Slim turned around. 'You're coming over tonight, aren't you? So what's the difference?'

'I thought tonight we'd sneak in the back way,' Rusty explained. 'We don't want your neighbors seeing us, do we?'

She made a face to show us what she thought of nosy neighbors. 'If they don't like it, they can lump it.'

'You're only gonna be a minute, right?' Rusty asked. 'Why don't we just wait out here for you?'

'Don't you want to come in and wash up?' she asked him.

'Nah, I'm fine.'

'You're a bloody mess,' she said.

'That's okay.'

'I think we should go in with her,' I said, still worried for no good reason that she might have intruders.

Slim nodded. 'Yeah, come on.'

Leering at her, Rusty said, 'If we come in, can we go upstairs?' Before she could answer, he added, 'We've never seen your bedroom.'

Her eyebrows lifted.

Rusty nudged me. '*You'd* like to see her bedroom, wouldn't you?'

Scowling, I shook my head.

'How about it?' he asked Slim. 'Do we get to see your bedroom?'

'In your dreams.' She whirled around and hurried toward the stairway. As she trotted up, she looked over her shoulder. 'In or out, I don't care. But stay downstairs.'

When she was gone, Rusty grinned at me.

'You jerk,' I whispered. 'What're you trying to pull?'

'Just playing it safe, you know? We don't wanta be around when she finds the surprise in her mom's room, do we?'

'I guess not.'

'Outa sight, outa mind.'

'Sure.'

'No matter what, we act dumb.'

'Right.'

I hated the whole idea of being dishonest with Slim, but we'd already deceived her. If we tried to tell the truth now, we'd look like jerks.

Expecting Slim to shout at any moment, I gazed at the top of the stairs. So did Rusty. We stood side by side, watching and listening. Quiet sounds came from the second floor:

footsteps, the creaking of a board, soft skids and bumps that might've been drawers opening and shutting.

Rusty leaned toward me. 'She hasn't noticed it yet.'

'Guess not.'

'Maybe she won't.'

Nodding, I whispered, 'The smell might've dissipated.'

He turned his head and frowned at me.

'Spread out and faded away,' I explained.

'I know that. I'm not stupid.'

'Hey, guys,' Slim called. 'You want to come up here a minute?' She sounded a little worried.

We glanced at each other. Rusty looked like a school kid ordered to the principal's office.

'Oh, man,' he murmured.

I ran to the stairs and raced up them two at a time, Rusty pounding along behind me. At the top of the stairs, I *knew* I would see Slim down the hallway, standing in front of her mother's bedroom.

She wasn't there.

The hallway was empty.

'Slim?'

'Over here.' Her voice had come from the left – the direction of both the bedrooms.

Heart thumping hard and fast, I hurried down the hallway, certain to find Slim inside her mother's room.

The two doors were on opposite sides of the hallway.

As I neared them, I smelled the sweetness of the spilled perfume. Maybe the scent had dissipated, but it certainly hadn't vanished.

I turned toward the mother's door.

'Dwight?'

I spun around. Slim was in her own room. I hurried to her door and got there just before Rusty. We both stopped and gazed in.

Slim was standing beside her bed, a nervous look on her face. She was barefoot. She still wore Lee's red shorts, but she'd taken off the shirts and put on her own bikini top. The powder blue one, a favorite of mine. The matching bottoms looked as if they been tossed onto her bed along with the two shirts she'd taken off.

'What's wrong?' I asked.

In a small voice as if she feared being overheard, she said, 'Somebody's been in my room.'

I shriveled inside.

Before I could say anything, Rusty asked, 'What do you mean?'

She turned sideways, raised a long, tanned arm and pointed a finger at her pillow.

On top of it lay a paperback book, wet and chewed and torn. Though the book looked as if it had been mauled by a vicious dog, its cover was intact enough for me to read the title.

Dracula.

My breath knocked out, I looked at Rusty. He looked at me. Then we both shook our heads.

Slim still had her eyes on the wreckage of *Dracula*, so I took a fast look at the paperbacks on her headboard. They were lined up neatly, just the same as when I'd seen them earlier. Then, however, *Dracula* had been among them.

'How the hell did *that* happen?' Rusty asked.

I almost blurted out, '*I* didn't do it,' but I caught myself in time.

I'd looked at the books, but I hadn't touched them and certainly hadn't chewed on any of them.

Neither had Rusty. The books had been fine when I went looking for him and found him in the mother's room. After that, neither of us had been alone in the house.

Slim kept staring at the book.

'Did *you* do it?' Rusty asked.

'No!' I blurted.

'Not you. Slim.'

'Huh? Me?' She looked at him. 'Are you nuts?'

He shrugged. 'I don't know. Did you?'

'No!'

'You had *time* to do it.'

'I was changing my clothes.'

'Didn't you *see* it?'

Slowly, she shook her head. 'Not right away. It must've been like that, but ... I got undressed over there.' She nodded toward her dresser. 'Then I came over here and tossed the stuff on the bed and that's when I noticed.'

'That's when you yelled?' I asked.

She shook her head some more. 'I put my top on first.'

An image filled my mind of Slim standing there in just the red shorts, breathing hard as she stared down at the damaged book, her breasts rising and falling.

'This is crazy,' Rusty muttered. He looked worried. Apparently, he didn't suspect me. Maybe he'd glanced into the room on our way out and seen that nothing was out of place.

To Slim, he said, 'Are you sure you didn't do this, like to freak us out or something?'

One glance gave him all the answer he needed – and more.

'Slim wouldn't do that to a book,' I said. 'For *any* reason.'

'That's right,' she said.

'So if she didn't, who did?' Half grimacing, half smiling, he added, 'Or *what*?'

Slim bent over slightly, reached down and picked up the book. 'It's still wet.' She lifted it close to her face and sniffed. 'Smells like saliva.'

'Human or dog?' I asked.

'Or vampire?' asked Rusty.

Slim scowled at him. 'It's broad daylight.'

'We'd better look around,' I said. 'Whoever did this might still be in the house.'

'Or *whatever*,' Rusty threw in.

Slim looked around as if confused about what to do with the book. Then she carried it across her room and dropped it into a wastebasket next to her desk. It hit the bottom with a ringing thump.

She pulled open a desk drawer and took out two knives. One was a hunting knife in a leather sheath. The other was a Boy Scout pocket knife. Not speaking a word, she brought the knives to us. She handed the hunting knife to me, the pocket knife to Rusty. Then she went to her closet, silently opened its door and stepped inside.

In the closet, most of Slim was out of sight.

She stepped backward with her straight, fiberglass bow in one hand and a quiver of arrows in the other.

Turning toward us, she slung the quiver over her back so the feathered ends of a dozen or more arrows jutted up behind her right shoulder. The strap angled downward from her shoulder to her left hip, passing between her breasts.

With both hands free, she planted a tip of her fiberglass bow against the floor. She pulled down at the top, used her leg for some extra leverage, bent the bow and slipped its string upward until its loop was secure in the nock.

Left hand on the grip, she raised the bow. Then she reached up over her shoulder with her right hand and slipped an arrow out of the quiver. She brought it down silently in front of her and fitted its plastic nock onto the string.

At the end of the long, pale shaft was a steel head that looked as if it were made of razor blades.

'Watch my back,' she whispered.

I drew the hunting knife out of its sheath. Rusty opened the blade of the pocket knife. We followed Slim out of the room.

Much of her back was hidden behind the quiver of arrows. The quiver was brown leather and nicely tooled. She'd won it by taking first place in a YWCA Fourth of July archery contest a couple of summers earlier. Most people hadn't expected a fourteen-year-old girl to win it, but I'd known she would.

Chapter Twenty-five

Just a week before the archery contest, we had hiked out to Janks Field for a secret practice session. It was the end of June, a hot and sunny afternoon. The desolate expanse of Janks Field, scattered with a million bits of broken glass, sparkled and glittered in the sunlight as if someone had sprinkled gems over its bare gray earth. Even with our sunglasses on, we had to squint as we walked onto the field. There wasn't so much as a hint of a breeze. The air felt heavy and dead. It smelled dead, too. Or something did.

'What's that *smell*?' I asked.

'Your butt,' Rusty said.

'Something's dead,' said Slim.

'Dwight's butt,' Rusty explained.

'Huh-uh.' Slim shook her head. She was fifteen that summer and calling herself Phoebe. 'It's bodies.'

'Dwight's . . .'

'I bet they never found 'em all,' she said. 'You know, the stiffs. The corpses. And you know what? It *always* smells like this.'

'Does not,' Rusty said. He would argue with a rock.

'Yeah, it does,' Phoebe said. 'I smell it every time we're here. It's just worse sometimes, like on really hot days.'

'Bunk,' Rusty said.

'I think she's right,' I said.

'Oh, yeah, she's *always* right.'

'Pretty much,' I said.

Grinning, Phoebe said, 'Right as rain.'

'Where do you want to shoot?' I asked her.

'Here's fine.'

I'd carried the target all the way from home. We'd constructed it that morning in my garage: a cardboard box stuffed with tightly wadded newspapers, an old LIFE magazine photo of Adolph Eichmann taped to one side.

I set the box down on a mound of dirt so that Eichmann's face was on the front and tilted upward at a slight angle.

Phoebe paced off fifty feet.

Rusty and I stood slightly behind her.

With her first arrow, she put out one of Eichmann's eyes and knocked the box askew.

That's when I knew she would win next week's archery contest.

She held fire while I straightened the box and came back.

Her second arrow poked through Eichmann's other eye. He looked as if his big, black-rimmed spectacles had come equipped with feathered shafts.

Though the impact had twisted the box, she managed to put her next arrow into Eichmann's nose.

Then someone called out, 'Well, if it ain't Robin Hood and his merry fags.'

Even before turning around, we recognized the voice.

173

Scotty Douglas.

When we did turn around, we saw that he wasn't alone. Scotty had his sidekicks with him: Tim Hancock and Andy 'Smack' Malone.

Smack got the nickname because it was what he enjoyed doing to kids like us. But he was no worse than Scotty and Tim.

Sneering and smirking, the three guys swaggered toward us like desperados on their way to a gunfight.

Nobody had any guns, thank God.

Their empty hands dangled in front of them, thumbs hooked under their belts.

Phoebe had the bow.

Rusty and I appeared to be unarmed, but we both had knives in our pockets. So did Scotty's gang, probably. Except their knives were sure to be bigger than ours, and switchblades.

With big greasy hair, sideburns down to their jaws, black leather jackets, white T-shirts, blue jeans, wide leather belts and black motorcycle boots with buckles on the sides, they were a trio of Marlon Brandos from *The Wild One*, half-baked but scary.

Scotty and Tim were older than us by a couple of years, and Smack was at least a year older than them. Bigger, too. In spite of his hood costume, Smack looked like an eight-year-old balloon boy somebody'd pumped up till he was ready to burst. Hairy, though. His belly, bulging out between the bottom of his T-shirt and the belt of his low hanging jeans, was extremely white and overgrown with curly black hair that got thicker near his belt.

Smack was in the same grade as his buddies because he'd gotten held back once or twice. He wasn't exactly a sharp tool. Neither were Scotty and Tim, for that matter.

Scotty raised his hands. 'Don't shoot,' he told Phoebe.

Though she lowered her bow, she kept an arrow nocked and her hand on it. 'We were here first,' she said.

'So what?' Scotty asked.

'So maybe you can go somewhere else till we're done.'

'Maybe we don't wanta.'

'Maybe we *like* it here,' said Tim.

Grinning like a dope, Smack glanced at his two pals and said, 'Anyways, she didn't use the magic word.'

They laughed. Smack was such a card.

'*Please*,' Phoebe said, even though she knew the magic word would work no magic on these three losers. We all knew that. We knew they wouldn't simply go away. Not until they'd had their 'fun' with us, whatever that might be.

Scotty, Tim and Smack came to a halt about four or five paces away from us. They smiled as if they owned us.

Flanked by his buddies, Scotty asked, 'Please what?'

'Please go away and leave us alone.' Though she must've been shaking inside, she seemed very calm.

'What'll you give us if we do?' Scotty asked.

'What do you want?' Phoebe asked.

Pursing his lips, Scotty stroked his chin with his thumb and forefinger and frowned as if giving deep thought to the matter. '*Wellllll*,' he said, 'let me *seeeee*.'

'You guys better leave us alone,' Rusty said, a whine in his voice. 'Dwight's dad's the police chief.'

As if they didn't already know that.

'As if we give a shit,' said Scotty. Fixing his eyes on me, he asked, 'You gonna tell on us?'

'No,' I said.

'That's what I thought.'

Rusty glanced at his wristwatch. Then he looked surprised. 'Oh, gosh, I have to get home.'

'To your *mommy*?' Smack asked. He gave his pals a hopeful

glance, and looked disappointed when they didn't laugh or even crack smiles over his wit.

'Go home if you want,' Scotty said.

'Really? You mean it?'

'Sure. Go.'

Trying again, Smack said, 'You don't wanta keep your *mommy* waiting.'

Rusty acted as if he hadn't heard that. To Scotty, he said, 'You really gonna let us go?'

'Gonna let *you* go, fatso.'

'Me?'

'You.'

'What about *them*?'

'What about 'em?'

'You gonna let them go, too?'

'What's it to you?'

Lips twisting all crooked, Rusty said, 'I don't know.'

'You going or aren't you?' Scotty asked.

'I don't know.'

'He don't know much,' Smack said, and chuckled.

'I'll give you till three,' Scotty said. 'You're still here, you get what they get. One.'

Rusty's mouth fell open. Appalled, he glanced at me, at Phoebe.

'Two.'

He raised a hand and blurted, 'Wait! Wait! What're you gonna do to *them*?'

'Whatever we want,' said Tim.

'Three.'

'*WAIT!*' Rusty cried out, tears coming to his eyes.

'Missed your chance, lardass.'

'Did not! It was a *time-out*!'

'That's what you think.'

Jim spoke again. 'Missed your chance, porky.'

Scared as I was – and I was straining not to mess my pants – it occurred to me as peculiar that these two skinny snakes were making cracks about Rusty's weight when their own pal, Smack, was about a ton heavier than him. Showed how much they cared about their buddy.

Suddenly in tears, Rusty pleaded, 'Gimme another chance. C'mon. Please? It ain't fair.'

The three creeps thought *that* was funny. They laughed and glanced at each other and shook their heads.

I didn't find it very amusing.

'Let him go,' I said.

Scotty smirked at me. 'Gonna tell your *daddy* on us?'

'Just let him go, that's all.'

To Rusty, he said, 'You wanta leave?'

Sniffling and sobbing, Rusty nodded.

'Okay, you can leave.'

'Th . . . thanks.'

'But first you gotta suck my dick.'

For half a second, I thought he was kidding. But then he unzipped his jeans. Walking toward Rusty, he reached into his fly and my stomach sort of dropped because this was getting worse than I'd ever thought and if they did perverted sex stuff to Rusty they'd do it to me and Phoebe, too, and then maybe they would have to kill us so we wouldn't tell on them.

About two steps away from Rusty, Scotty whipped out his tool and said, 'Get on your knees and open wide,' and Phoebe shot an arrow into his leg.

It punched through Scotty's jeans and thunked deep into the side of his right thigh. He squealed, jerked up his leg and grabbed near where the arrow had entered. On one foot, he twisted away and hopped a couple of times. Then he fell sideways. He landed hard on the ground and squealed some more as the pieces of broken bottles jabbed into him.

Instead of attacking us, Tim and Smack just stood there. They looked at Scotty, then at Phoebe, shock on their faces. They couldn't believe Mr Tough Guy had gotten himself shot down. Especially by a skinny little tomboy with a bow and arrow.

Squirming on the ground and whimpering, Scotty cried out, '*Get her, guys! Get 'em all!*'

By then, Phoebe had another arrow on the string of her bow.

When Tim and Smack turned to her, she drew back the string to her chin and aimed at Tim's face.

Flinging his hands up in front of his face, he yelled, 'No! Don't! I give!'

As she swept her weapon in Smack's direction, he gasped something like, '*Eeek!*' and threw both hands toward the sky.

'Get down,' she told him.

'Huh?'

'Get down on the ground.'

He looked as if he wanted to say something else. Then he shut his mouth and sank to his knees.

'All the way down,' Phoebe said. 'Lie down.'

He eyed the ground in front of him. It glittered with bits and chunks of shattered bottles. Also, there were a couple of snake holes in the dirt. If he followed Phoebe's orders, he would have to lie down on them.

His sweaty face flushed a deeper shade of red than before. 'Hey,' he said. 'C'mon. I didn't do nothing.'

'Down,' Phoebe said.

I don't know whether it was the razor sharp arrowhead a few inches in front of his nose or the look in Phoebe's eyes, but something convinced him to obey orders. Hands on the ground, he eased his trembling body down onto the dirt and broken glass and snake holes.

'Stay put,' Phoebe told him. Then she turned toward Tim.

He cringed away from her.

'I want my arrow back,' she said.

Tim looked down at Scotty curled on his side, the arrow jutting up from his leg. Scotty was quietly weeping, and not moving at all except to gasp for breath. Probably he didn't want to get cut up any worse by the glass he was lying on.

Wrinkling his nose, Tim faced Phoebe. 'Your arrow?'

'That one right there.'

'How'm I supposed to . . .'

'Jerk it out.'

'But . . .'

Scotty spoke up. In a tight voice that seemed to vibrate with pain or rage, he said, 'Touch the fuckin' arrow and I'll eat your heart.'

'But—'

'I'll kill your mom and fuck your sister. I'll—'

Giving him a dirty look, Tim bent down and jerked out the arrow. Scotty screamed, clutched his wound and lay there twitching.

Phoebe uncocked her bow and slipped the arrow into her old, raggedy quiver.

Tim handed the other arrow to her. 'Thanks,' she said. She waved it toward me and Rusty. The steel head looked as if it had been dipped in red paint. A couple of drops fell to the ground. 'My lucky arrow,' she said.

Not bothering to clean Scotty's blood of its tip, she swept the arrow over her shoulder and dropped it into her quiver.

'You lie down, too,' she told Tim.

Without protest or hesitation, he stretched out on the ground.

To Rusty and me, Phoebe said, 'I guess that's enough target practice for one day. Let's go home.'

We went to the target first. I plucked the arrows out of

Eichmann's eyes and nose and gave them to Phoebe. Then I picked up the cardboard box.

Scotty, Smack and Tim stayed on the ground.

We started walking away, Phoebe in the middle.

They stayed down.

When we were pretty far away but still within earshot, Phoebe stopped and turned around. She shouted, *'We won't tell if you don't!'*

They never did.

We never did.

In the woods after we got away from them, we laughed nervously, shook our heads, slapped each other on the back, and told Phoebe 'Good going' and 'Way to go' about a million times.

Then I saw she had tears in her eyes.

When I saw that, my own eyes went hot and wet.

I'm not really sure why either of us got weepy like that, but I suspect there were plenty of reasons. They had to do with fear and loyalty and bravery and cowardice and humiliation and pride. They also had to do, I think, with the joy of survival.

I'm pretty sure we didn't spill any tears over damages inflicted on Scotty or his pals.

After that time in Janks Field, by the way, they were no longer pals. They stayed away from each other, and *really* stayed away from me, Rusty and Phoebe.

They were so scared of Phoebe that they never even dared to give us dirty looks. Many times, in the first few months after the incident, I saw each of them cross streets or start walking in the opposite direction just to avoid us – Scotty with a pretty good limp.

One week after her target practice in Janks Field, Phoebe won the Fourth of July archery contest (junior division) with a final, amazing shot that would've done Robin Hood proud.

She made the shot, of course, with her lucky arrow.

And won the hand-tooled leather quiver.

Chapter Twenty-six

On both sides of the quiver, I could see the powder blue strings of Slim's bikini top, her bandages and bare, tanned skin down to the waistband of Lee's red shorts.

I was half lost in how Slim looked from behind, half dwelling on the summer she won the quiver and pretty much paying no attention at all to anything else as I followed her to the door of her bedroom.

One step into the hallway, she stopped.

'What?' Rusty asked.

As if he didn't know.

Slim went, 'Shhhh.' Then she walked straight across the hallway and into her mother's bedroom. We went in after her, spread out, and stared at the mess we'd left behind. A puddle, prickly with broken glass, remained on top of the dresser. The carpet below the dresser now looked dry, but dangerous with shards from the demolished vase and perfume bottle. A few bright yellow rose petals lay among the remains as if they'd been blown there from somewhere else.

The flowers were gone.

For a moment, I thought that Rusty or I must've thrown them away.

Then I remembered that we hadn't touched them.

A chill crawled up the back of my neck.

Rusty and I glanced at each other.

He, too, had noticed the roses were gone.

'We better get outa here,' he whispered.

Ignoring him, Slim stepped around the mess on the carpet and walked slowly through the room. We stayed with her. Since both her hands were busy with the bow and arrow, she stood by, ready to shoot, while I looked under the bed and Rusty opened the closet door. When she entered the master bathroom, I crept in behind her.

The bathroom held flowery scents.

No trace of the yellow roses, though.

And no trace of any intruders.

Turning around, Slim pointed her arrow away from me. Her eyes met mine. She gave me a quick, nervous smile. Then she came toward me and I backed out of the bathroom.

Rusty looked glad to see us.

For the next ten or fifteen minutes – or hour – we searched the house.

It was hard on the nerves.

In some ways, I felt major relief. Because of the *real* intruder, Slim would never have to know about our invasion of her home.

But the relief came with a large price.

Someone *else* had come into her house, roamed its silent rooms, stood beside Slim's bed while neatly slipping the paperback copy of *Dracula* out of her headboard and *chewing* the book. Someone had stolen into her mother's bedroom and made the yellow roses disappear.

Chewing the book seemed like the act of a madman.

Taking the roses seemed like something a woman might do. *Or the Frankenstein monster*, I suddenly thought, remembering Karloff's smile when the little girl gave him a flower.

As we crept through the house, upstairs and down, entering every room, opening every door, glancing under and behind furniture, checking everywhere large enough to conceal a person, I prayed that we would find no one.

I was a nervous wreck.

Not a moment went by that I didn't expect someone to jump out at us.

Julian Stryker, maybe. Or Valeria (though I'd never seen her). Or some of their black-shirted crew.

Maybe armed with spears.

I tried to convince myself that this was impossible, that they had no way of knowing where Slim lived, but it certainly *wasn't* impossible. There were many ways to learn such things.

By following us, for instance.

I gripped the knife tightly. My mouth was dry. My heart thudded. Sweat dripped down my face, fell off my ears and nose and chin, and glued the clothes to my skin. I felt as if a cry of terror was ready to explode from my chest.

But we found no one.

'I want to finish changing,' Slim said when our search was done.

'We'll go with you,' I told her.

If Rusty had said that, she would've answered with a crack. 'In your dreams,' maybe. But I'd said it, so she knew I wasn't being a wiseguy. 'Okay.'

We followed her upstairs. In her bedroom, she dropped her bow and arrow onto her bed. Facing us, she said, 'You guys can wait in the hall.' Then she took off her quiver. Not paying much attention to what she was doing, she dragged the leather strap up against her left breast. It snagged the underside of her bikini and lifted the fabric. As the rising strap pushed at her breast, she realized what was happening, saw us watching, and quickly turned her back.

'In the hall,' she reminded us. 'Okay?'

'We're going, we're going,' Rusty said.

I said, 'I'll leave the door open a crack.'

'Fine.'

We hurried out of her room and I pulled the door almost shut.

Rusty quietly mouthed, 'Did you see that?'

I gave him a dirty look.

He mouthed, 'Oh, like you didn't look.'

Speaking in a normal voice, I said, 'Why don't you go to the bathroom and wash your blood off? I'll start cleaning up the glass.'

He shook his head. 'I'll help.'

'You'll get blood on stuff.'

He inspected his hands. They looked as if they'd been smeared with rust-colored paint. Palms up, he closed and opened his fingers. The stickiness made crackling sounds. 'Maybe I better,' he admitted. 'But you've gotta come, too.'

'You're not scared, are you?'

'Up yours,' he said. He gave me the finger, then turned his back on me, marched to the bathroom at the end of the hall, and vanished through its doorway. A moment later, the door bumped shut. I heard a soft, ringing thump as Rusty locked it. Soon, water began running through the pipes.

I stood alone in the hallway.

And didn't like it.

Even though we had searched the house, we weren't necessarily safe. Separated like this, we could be picked off one at a time.

'Slim?' I asked.

'Yeah?' she said from inside her room.

'You okay?'

'Fine.'

'You almost . . .?'

She swung the door open so quickly it startled me. She grinned. She now wore a clean white T-shirt, cut-off jeans and a pair of old tennis shoes that must've been white on a distant summer when she'd been Dagny or Phoebe or Zock. Through the thin cotton T-shirt, I could see her bikini top.

Stepping out of her room, she looked down the hall. 'Rusty in the john?' she asked.

The water still ran.

'Yeah. He's washing up.'

She nodded. 'Thought so.' Then she looked me in the eyes and said, 'I'm sure glad you guys are here. This stuff would've scared me silly if I'd been by myself.'

'Are you kidding? Nothing scares you.'

'*Everything* scares me.'

'Yeah, sure. You're the bravest person I know.'

A smile broke across her face. 'That's what *you* think.' She glanced toward the bathroom.

The door remained shut. The water still ran.

Tilting her head back slightly, she stared into my eyes.

Slim's eyes, pale blue in sunlight, were dark blue in the dimness of the hallway – the color of the summer sky at dusk. Intense, hopeful and nervous, they seemed to be searching for something in my eyes.

She had never stared at me quite that way before. I wondered what it meant.

What if she wants me to kiss her?

Could that be it? I wondered.

Do it and find out.

But maybe that *wasn't* what she wanted.

We kept gazing into each other's eyes. Soon, I was sure that she *did* want me to kiss her. She didn't just want it, she was *waiting* for it. Waiting for me to catch on and take her into my arms and put my lips on hers.

I wanted to do it, too. I *ached* to do it. I'd been longing to kiss her for so long, and now she was almost *begging* for my lips.

I couldn't force myself to move.

Do it! Come on! She wants me to!

I stood there like a lump – except that lumps don't sweat and tremble.

I felt more frightened than when we'd been searching the house, but this fear was mixed with desire for Slim and disgust with myself for being such a coward.

Just do it!

Making an excuse for myself, I thought, *If I try to kiss her now, Rusty might catch us.*

The water still ran.

What's taking him so long, anyway?

Then I thought, *Who cares if he sees us kiss? Just go ahead do it. Do it now before she changes her mind . . .*

A toilet flushed.

The sound of it came like a signal for Slim to shut down the power of her gaze. Whatever'd been going on, it was over. A mild smile lifted the corners of her mouth. With her eyes and smile, she seemed to be saying, 'Oh, well. Missed our chance. Maybe next time.'

At least that's what I think they were telling me. They might've been saying, 'You dumb jerk, you missed your chance.' But I don't think so.

Then she reached up and flicked my nose the same as she'd done to Rusty, but not as hard. Not nearly as hard.

Gently.

Then she said, 'Want to help me pick up the glass?'

'Sure.'

We turned and entered her mother's room.

Chapter Twenty-seven

We no sooner started picking up the pieces of broken glass than Slim said, 'I'll get my wastebasket.' She hurried off and came back quickly.

When she set it down, I dumped in a handful of glass and saw her ruined copy of *Dracula* at the bottom.

'Mom won't be too happy about this,' Slim said.

'She doesn't get home till tomorrow?'

'Probably not.' Frowning slightly, Slim started to gather shards from the dresser top.

'What if we clean all this up,' I said, 'and get rid of the smell and replace the broken stuff? She'll never have to find out anything happened.'

'Is that what *you'd* do?' Slim asked.

I looked up at her.

'If it was *your* mom's stuff?'

'Maybe.'

'You wouldn't, either.' A grin spread across her face. 'You're *way* too much of a Boy Scout for that.'

'Think so, do you?'

'I know so.'

I suddenly felt ashamed of myself for not living up to her ideas about me.

And I felt very glad she didn't know everything.

'Anyway,' she said, 'I don't think we'd get away with it. We'd have to find a matching vase and perfume bottle . . .' She shook her head. 'Even if we could lay our hands on exact matches, Mom would figure it out somehow. Then I'd be in trouble for trying to trick her.' She dumped a handful of glass into the wastebasket. 'Only thing is, it'll really scare her if she finds out somebody came in the house and did this stuff. It'd be nice if she *didn't* have to find out.'

I dropped more glass into the wastebasket.

Slim continued to clean off the dresser top for a while. Then she blurted, 'I've got it!' She grinned down at me. 'How about this? First, forget about *Dracula*. She hasn't got a clue about what I read. All we have to do is get rid of the evidence. As for this mess . . . I was just being helpful. I came in to water her roses, seeing as how she was having an overnighter with her boyfriend, and had a little accident. Knocked the vase over. It hit the perfume bottle, broke the perfume bottle and *presto*!'

Somebody applauded.

I looked over my shoulder and found Rusty standing in the doorway, clapping his hands. 'Bravo!' he said. 'Good plan.'

Slim obviously thought so, too. Beaming, she said, 'Not bad, huh?'

'It's perfect,' I said.

'You oughta be a writer,' Rusty told her.

'Thank you, thank you, thank you.' She might've performed a full bow if her hands hadn't been full of broken glass. All she did was duck her head.

I dumped more glass into the wastebasket, then said to Rusty, 'Wanta give us a hand here?'

He started clapping again.

'Ha ha.'

'Did I miss anything?' he asked.

I remembered the way Slim had stared into my eyes. Feeling myself blush, I said, 'Not much.'

'You almost missed your chance to help us clean this up,' Slim told him.

'I tried.'

'What'd you do in there,' I asked, 'take a bath?'

His face flushed scarlet. 'I had to *go*, okay? Thanks for bringing it up.'

Slim chuckled.

'Very funny,' Rusty muttered.

'You like it so much in there,' she said, 'how about going back and getting us some paper towels? There should be a roll under the sink where the TP is. Maybe you can bring the whole thing.'

'Sure.' He hurried away.

Slim waited until his footsteps faded, then whispered, 'Do you think Rusty had anything to do with this?'

I felt a blush coming on. Quickly, I asked, 'What do you mean?'

'He's acting sort of funny.'

'He is?' I hoped I wasn't.

'Like he feels guilty about something.'

I shook my head. 'I don't know. He seems okay to me.'

'Do you think he might've done this stuff?'

'Why would he chew up your *book*?'

She shrugged. 'It's *Dracula* and he's all excited about the Travelling Vampire Show? Maybe he thought it'd be a cool trick to play . . . freak us out.'

'I don't know,' I muttered. 'I don't think so. Anyway, he was with me.'

'Maybe he came in and did this on his way back from Janks Field. Before he went over to your place.'

As I shrugged, I heard footsteps coming down the hallway.

We went silent, but we both looked at Rusty when he walked in.

'What?' he asked, handing the roll of paper towels to Slim.

'Thanks,' she said.

'What's going on?'

'We were just trying to figure out how all this happened,'

Slim explained. She turned away, tore off some paper towels, wadded them up and started to mop the top of the dresser.

Rusty gave me an alarmed look.

I almost shook my head, but realized that Slim was facing the mirror and might see me.

'If none of us did this stuff,' she said, 'who did?'

'How about ghosts?' Rusty suggested. The playful tone of his voice sounded a little forced. 'I mean, you've *gotta* have ghosts in this place, everything that's happened here.'

She stopped cleaning and turned around. Frowning, she asked, 'Like what?'

'You know.'

'No I don't. What do you mean, "everything that's happened here"?'

Rusty seemed shocked by her tone. It shocked me, too.

'Like with your dad and grandfather.'

'You've gotta be dead to be a ghost,' Slim said, her voice sharp.

'I know, but—'

'And Jimmy Drake isn't.'

'I didn't say he is.'

'You said his ghost . . .'

'He *might* be dead, right? I mean, he left town and you've never heard from him again. So he *could* be dead, couldn't he?'

Seeming calmer, Slim looked at Rusty with narrow eyes and said, 'I guess so.'

'Anyway,' Rusty said, 'it was just a thought.'

'A lame thought,' I told him, wishing he hadn't brought up the subject of Slim's father. 'You don't even believe in ghosts.'

'This just seems like the sort of thing a guy like Jimmy Drake might do,' Rusty explained. Then his eyes widened.

In a hushed voice, he said, 'Maybe he *was* here. Maybe he came back . . . you know, from wherever he went . . . and did this stuff.'

Slim stared at him.

'In the flesh,' Rusty said. 'Not a ghost or anything, but *him*. What if he's *back*?'

'He's not,' Slim said.

'How do you know?'

'If he came back, he wouldn't piddle around chomping on books and breaking a couple of things. It's not his style. They're just *things*. They're not people. They don't . . .' She turned away and resumed wiping the dresser top.

'I think it has something to do with the vampire show,' I said – partly because that's what I really thought, partly to get the subject off Slim's father because I knew she didn't like being reminded of what he'd done to her and the others. 'Maybe it's a warning.'

Nodding, Rusty added, 'To keep our mouths shut.'

'I don't know,' Slim muttered.

'What I think we should do,' I said, 'is finish cleaning this stuff up and then go over to my house. We can have supper there like we planned, but maybe we shouldn't come back here afterwards.'

'*They* might be waiting for us,' Rusty pointed out, smiling as if he thought it were a joke.

'Where *will* we go?' Slim asked.

'I don't know yet. We oughta think of a place where nobody'll be able to find us. But the main thing is, we should stay together from now on.'

Slim turned around. Finally smiling, she raised her eyebrows. 'From now on?'

'Cool,' Rusty said.

'At least till the vampire show leaves town,' I explained.

'What about tonight?' she asked. 'I'm *not* going to the

show. I'm not stepping foot in Janks Field till those creeps are long gone.'

'Well *I'm* going,' Rusty said. Eyes on Slim, he shook his head. 'I'm not gonna miss it just because *you're* a chicken.'

'Hey,' I said.

'Well, I'm not. We don't even know it was *them*. It might've been anyone.'

'It isn't about this,' Slim said. 'It's about torturing and killing that poor dog.'

'That poor dog went after you like a hunk of raw meat.'

'Let's not start this again,' I said. 'Let's just finish and get outa here before something else happens.'

It took about half an hour longer to complete the clean-up: vacuuming the carpet, wiping it with a damp sponge to take away some of the perfume, dumping the wastebasket in Slim's garbage can in the alley behind her house and throwing in some old newspapers to hide the book and bits of glass, then finally putting everything away.

Back upstairs after returning the wastebasket to her bedroom, Slim brushed her hands against the front of her cut-off jeans. 'I guess that does it.'

'Guess so,' I agreed. 'Anything you want to take with you?'

'Depends on what we'll be doing.'

'Going to the vampire show,' Rusty said.

'Maybe *you* are.' To me, she said, 'Anyway, I guess I'll just leave everything here for now. We can always come back and get stuff, depending on what we decide to do.'

'Go to the vampire show,' Rusty repeated. This time, he grinned.

'Yeah, sure,' Slim said.

Downstairs, we hid all the weapons on the floor behind the living-room sofa where we could get to them quickly if we needed them.

'I'll be right back,' she said. Leaving us there, she hurried toward the back of her house. She returned a couple of minutes later with an inch-long strip of Scotch tape sticking to her fingertip.

'What're you gonna do with that?' Rusty asked.

'Old Indian trick,' she said, and ushered us out of the house.

Standing in the entryway, she pulled the front door shut. Then she squatted down and I realized what she was doing. Not exactly an 'old Indian trick.' More like a James Bond trick. She was sticking one end of the tape to the door's edge, the other end to the frame.

When she stepped away, I glanced down but couldn't quite see the transparent tape.

Neither would an intruder, more than likely.

Opening the door would either break the tape or pull it loose at one end or the other. Then we'd know that someone had entered Slim's house.

'Did the same to the kitchen door,' she announced.

'Good idea,' I said.

Smirking, Rusty said, 'Why not balance buckets of water on top of the doors and *really* nail 'em.'

She looked at him and raised her eyebrows.

I said, 'Make it *holy* water.'

'*There's* an idea,' Slim said.

Rusty frowned. He didn't get it. So we both tried to explain to him about vampires and holy water while we crossed to the sidewalk and turned toward my house.

When we finished, he said, 'I knew that.'

Chapter Twenty-eight

Mom's car was gone from the driveway. The house seemed empty when we entered it, but I called out anyway and got no answer.

'She must've gone somewhere,' I muttered. It seemed odd that Mom would leave the house this late in the afternoon.

'Maybe she went to the store,' Slim suggested.

'Maybe.' That didn't seem likely, since she'd done her grocery shopping that very morning. But maybe she'd forgotten to pick up buns or something, and decided to make a last-minute run.

On the kitchen table, I found a note in Mom's handwriting.

> Honey,
> Your father just called from the hospital. He got hurt, but he tells me it is nothing to worry about. I am going to be with him. Don't know when I'll be back. Go ahead and eat without us. Burgers are in the fridge. I'll call when I can.
> Try not to worry, your dad's fine.
> Love,
> Mom

Slim and Rusty watched in silence while I read the message a couple of times. It gave me a cold lump in my dad's in the stomach. When I finished with it, I said, 'My dad's in the hospital.'

Slim winced. 'What's wrong with him?'

Shaking my head, I handed the note to her. Rusty stepped up close beside her and they read it together.

'He can't be very bad,' Slim said. 'He was in good enough shape to phone your mom.'

'But he can't be that good,' Rusty said, 'or he wouldn't be at the hospital.'

Scowling, I shook my head.

Slim put down the note. 'What do you want to do?'

'I don't know,' I muttered.

'Want us to go away?' Rusty asked.

'No. Huh-uh.' I pulled out a chair and sank onto it. 'Why couldn't Mom tell me what's wrong with him?'

'She said he's fine,' Slim pointed out.

'He can't be *fine*.'

She picked up the note and stared at it for a while. 'Your dad got hurt,' she said, 'but he's fine. That's what it says.'

'Doesn't make any sense,' I muttered.

' "Got hurt," ' Slim said. 'Your mom wouldn't have worded it that way if he'd had something like a heart attack. Sounds like maybe he had an accident.'

'Or got shot,' Rusty suggested.

Slim gave him a dirty look. 'Whatever happened,' she said, 'it's nothing really serious but he does need some sort of treatment.'

'Why couldn't she just *tell* me?' I blurted. 'He must've told *her*.'

'I don't know,' Slim muttered.

'Maybe she thought it'd scare you,' Rusty said.

'But it's not supposed to scare me *not* being told?'

Slim put her hand on my back. It made me feel better, but not a whole lot. 'We don't have to wait for your mom to call. Why don't we phone police headquarters? I bet somebody there can tell us what happened.'

I checked the kitchen clock.

'Dolly'll still be on duty,' I said.

'So?' Slim asked.

I shook my head. Much as I hated the idea of talking to Dolly, I stood up and headed for the wall phone.

Rusty met my eyes. He looked as if he were in pain, himself. 'Or you could call the hospital,' he said.

'How do we know which one?' Slim asked.

While the town of Grandville had a hospital of its own, the county hospital over in Clarksburg was better equipped for major emergencies. In nearby Bixton was a Catholic hospital staffed mostly by nuns. People from our area could end up in any one of them, depending on one thing or another.

'Start with the nearest,' Rusty suggested.

'Easier to ask Dolly,' Slim said.

We hadn't gotten around to telling her about our run-in with the vicious little dispatcher. Under the circumstances, however, I figured Dolly would be sympathetic. Even if she couldn't stand me, she liked my dad. For good reason: anyone else would've fired her a long time ago.

'Guess I'll call her,' I said.

Just as I reached for the phone, it rang. I jumped and jerked my hand back, my heart pounding like mad.

Before the second ring, I snatched the phone off its hook. Hardly able to breathe, I said, 'Hello?'

'Dwight?'

It was a mother, but not mine. And she didn't sound happy.

'Is Russell there?'

'Yeah. Yes. He's right here.'

'Please send him home right away.'

'Would you like to talk to him?'

Teeth bared, Rusty put up his hands and shook his head.

'I'll talk to him when he gets here. As for you, young man, I must say I'm terribly disappointed in you.'

THE TRAVELLING VAMPIRE SHOW

I felt my own lips peel back. My stomach suddenly felt even worse than before.

'I'm sorry,' I said.

'You ought to be. Elizabeth has always been very fond of you.'

'I'm fond of her, too.'

'You have a strange way of showing it.'

'I'm sorry,' I muttered.

'Send Russell home immediately, please.' With that, she hung up.

Rusty and I stared at each other.

'You're supposed to go home right away,' I said.

'Shit.'

'Bitsy must've told on us.'

'Told you she would, man. Shit. The little bitch.'

'Hey,' Slim said.

'Well, she is. I knew she'd spill her guts.'

'What'd you guys do to her?'

'We sort of ditched her,' I said. 'She wanted to go with us to look for you. We tried to talk her out of it, but she wouldn't take no for an answer.'

'Always has to have her own way, or she goes crying to mommy, the little twat.'

Slim scowled at him. 'Quit it.'

'Anyway,' I said, 'I finally said she could come with us but she had to put shoes on. So when she went into the house for her shoes, we took off.'

'That wasn't very nice,' Slim said.

'I know. But she was being a pest. And anyway, it was for her own good. I mean, we were heading for Janks Field. Do *you* think we should've taken Bitsy to Janks Field?'

'You've got a point.'

'So now we're neck-deep in shit,' Rusty said.

'You'd better get going,' I told him.

197

'What about you guys?' he asked.

I shook my head.

'We'll stay here,' Slim said, 'and try to find out what's going on with the chief.'

'What about tonight?'

'You worried about the goddamn vampire show?' Slim blasted him. 'Dwight's *dad's* in the hospital, you cretin! Get outa here!'

She hurried ahead of him and opened the kitchen door.

Watching me over his shoulder as he walked toward the door, Rusty said, 'We'll still try 'n' make it, though, right? I mean, if your dad's okay and everything?'

I just shrugged and shook my head.

'I'll call you,' he said.

Then Slim shut the door behind him and we were alone. Our eyes met.

We'd both had it drilled into our minds that, unless an adult was present, we should never be in a house with a member of the opposite sex.

It had been different when Rusty was with us. Now he was gone. We were suddenly free to do *anything*, and I'm sure we both knew it.

Knew it, and felt embarrassed by the knowledge.

Slim shrugged and said, 'Do you want to call Dolly?'

'I guess I could.' I stepped over to the phone. And stared at it. And kept staring.

I didn't want to make the call.

Not because of Dolly, but because of what she might say about my father.

In a soft voice, Slim asked from behind me, 'Are you okay?'

'Yeah, but I don't know. Maybe I'd better wait for Mom's call.'

'She might not call for an hour or two.'

'I know, but . . . maybe I'd better wait.'

'Want *me* to call Dolly and see what's going on?'

'No, that's okay.'

'Are you sure? I'll do it if—'

The phone rang. Its sudden jangle made me flinch. My insides cringed.

I grabbed the handset. 'Hello?'

'Honey, it's me.'

Mom.

I shriveled.

'Did you see my note?'

'Yeah.'

Tell me!

'I would've called sooner, but people were using the phones. And then I *did* call, but our line was busy.'

'How's Dad?'

'Oh, he's fine. He said to say hello.'

'Well, what happened?'

'He had a little accident in his patrol car, honey. A dog ran out in front of him. You know how your father is about animals. He swerved to miss it, and everything would've been fine except his front tire picked that moment to blow out. So then he lost control of the car and smacked into a tree.'

'Hard?' I asked.

'Hard enough,' Mom said. 'You know how your father feels about seat belts.'

According to Dad, only sissies wore them. It seemed like a strange attitude for a chief of police, but he'd grown up in the Great Depression, fought in World War Two . . .

'How *is* he?' I asked.

'Well, he broke his left arm and cracked a few ribs. He also hit his head on the windshield hard enough to break it. The windshield, not his head.' She laughed, but it sounded a little tense. 'You know how hard your father's head is. Anyway, apparently he *was* knocked unconscious for a while. But then he came to and drove himself over to County General.'

'Why County General?' I asked.

'Well, he feels it's better equipped, and he was almost as close to it as—'

'Where was he?'

'Out on Route 3.'

On Route 3 and a dog ran out in front of his car?

A chill scurried up my back and the skin on the nape of my neck stiffened with goosebumps.

'Anyway,' Mom said, 'he's fine, but they're going to keep him overnight.'

'What for?'

'Just as a precaution. Because of the head injury, mostly. They want to keep an eye on him till morning.'

'Oh. Okay.'

'Anyhow, I thought I'd like to stay here at the hospital with him.'

'All night?' I asked.

'I don't *have* to stay . . .'

'No, it's fine.'

'If you'd rather not stay by yourself, I could come home.'

'No, you don't have to do that.'

'Or I'm sure you could spend the night with Rusty or one of your brothers.'

'Danny's out of town.'

'Well, Lee's home. Or go over to Stu's.'

'I'll be okay here,' I said.

'That's fine. You're certainly old enough to stay by yourself. There's ground beef in the fridge. You can make yourself a hamburger if you want. We were going to grill them on the barbecue tonight . . .' Her voice trembled and stopped and I knew she was weeping. After a while, she sniffed and said, 'If you'd rather get take-out, there's money in the drawer . . .'

'I'll be fine,' I said. 'Don't worry about me. Tell Dad hi for me, okay?'

'I will, darling. Oh, he said I should let you know that he missed the dog.'

'He should've hit the dog and missed the tree,' I said.

I heard Mom laugh softly. 'I'll tell him that. And I'll give him your love.'

'Thanks.'

'Anything else before we hang up?'

'Not that I can think of.'

'Okay then, honey. You can call us here if anything comes up.' She gave me the hospital's phone number and Dad's room number. Then she said, 'I guess that's about it for now.'

'Guess so.'

'Okay, we'll see you in the morning.'

'See you then,' I said.

'Be good.'

'I will.'

'Bye.'

'Bye,' I said, and hung up.

Chapter Twenty-nine

'So he's pretty much all right?' Slim asked when I turned around.

Nodding, I realized she'd heard only my side of the conversation. I wasn't sure what she knew and what she didn't. So I explained, 'They're keeping him overnight because he hit his head, but . . . other than that, he broke his arm and cracked some ribs.'

'But his head'll be all right?'

'They think so.'

'He missed a dog and hit a tree?'

I smiled. It must've looked strange, because it brought a frown to Slim's face. 'He was out on Route 3,' I explained, 'and a dog ran out in front of his car.'

Slim made a face as if she were smelling something horrible but amusing. 'A *one-eyed* dog?' she asked.

'I didn't ask.'

'Woo.'

'Yeah.'

'When did this happen?'

'I don't think it was *that* long ago.'

'*Our* dog's been dead since about noon.'

'Yeah.' I shook my head. 'Had to be a different dog.'

'Maybe the one that chewed up my *Dracula*.'

'The very same,' I said.

She grimaced.

I grimaced.

'Maybe we've got *ghost* dogs,' she said.

'Or someone wants us to *think* so,' I said, which got her laughing. 'Anyway,' I continued, 'it wasn't a ghost *or* a dog that chewed up your *Dracula*.'

'Are you *sure*?'

'Pretty sure. For one thing, there's no such thing as ghosts.'

'Are you *sure*?'

She was seeming very playful.

'Pretty sure.'

'Don't be.'

'Anyway, if there *are* ghosts, they can't *bite* stuff. They don't have any...'

'Teeth?' she asked.

Grinning, I shook my head. 'That's not what ... I mean, they're just ... like *spirits*. They don't have *substance*.'

'A matter of opinion.'

'Anyway, ghost or not, a dog would've had to paw the *Dracula* off your bookshelf. Or bite it out. Either way, it would've messed up your other books. But they were all in a neat row. That could only be done by a human.'

'Or a vampire,' she added, 'speaking on behalf of our absent Russell.'

I laughed. 'Daylight,' I reminded her.

Her smile evaporated. 'Which leaves us with humans. I'm glad we're out of my house.'

'My mom isn't coming home till tomorrow morning, so I guess there's no reason you can't stay here.'

'No reason you can't go to the vampire show tonight, either.'

'I don't know.'

'You don't want to miss that.'

'I might.'

'Oh? You'd rather stay home and watch television?'

'Maybe. If you'll be here.'

'I'll be here unless you throw me out, I guess.'

'I wouldn't throw you out.'

'What about Rusty?' she asked.

'What about him?'

'He *really* wants to see that show.'

'He's probably grounded.'

'He'll find a way to get out.'

'Maybe.'

'He will. And then he'll show up here, all rarin' to go.'

'I almost hope he doesn't,' I said.

We suddenly ran out of words, so we stared at each other. Again, we both seemed awfully aware of being together in an empty house. Nobody to see us. Nobody to tell on us. Nobody to stop us.

We were only a few feet apart. A couple of steps forward

and I'd be close enough to put my arms around her, pull her up against me, kiss her . . .

I couldn't move.

She wasn't moving either, just gazing into my eyes. She looked solemn and hopeful.

I ached to take those steps and hug her, feel her body against mine, feel her lips . . .

A smile broke across her face and she said, 'Maybe we'd better eat.'

Saved! But disappointed.

'Good idea,' I said. 'Cheeseburgers sound okay?'

'Cheeseburgers sound great.'

'We can do 'em outside on the grill.'

'Why don't you get the fire started and I'll make the patties?'

'Great.'

I hurried to the refrigerator, found the package of ground chuck, and gave it to Slim.

'How many you want?' she asked.

'I don't know, how many do *you* want?'

'I haven't thought about it.'

'Do you make 'em thick or thin?' I asked.

'Thin's better. I don't like them raw in the middle.'

'Me either. So if you're making them thin, I'll have two.'

'Okie-doke. Maybe I'll have two, too.'

We both smiled like idiots.

Slim set the package of meat down on the counter, then stepped over to the sink and started to wash her hands. I watched her standing there, bent over slightly, the bottom of her T-shirt hanging crooked across the rear of her cut-off jeans. Her rump filled the seat of her jeans. A fringe of threads brushed against the backs of her thighs. Her legs were smooth and tanned all the way down to her ankles.

She looked over her shoulder. 'What?' she asked.

'Nothing.'

She smiled. 'Nothing, huh?'

'Just looking,' I said, and blushed.

We had another of those staring contests where I wanted to go to Slim, but was afraid to, and she looked as if maybe she hoped I would come over and kiss her.

This time, it didn't go on very long before she said, 'Maybe you'd better go out and start the fire.'

'Yeah, guess so. Back in a while.' I hurried outside.

Nowadays, most people have grills that run on propane. It's easy to use and doesn't pollute the environment (God perserve us from the fumes of backyard barbecues!). When I was growing up, however, we never had a propane grill. We never had charcoal lighting fluid, either. Dad claimed the fuel odor gave food a bad taste, but I'm pretty sure he was just trying to protect my brothers and me from the scourge of doing something 'the easy way'. So while every other family in Grandville started their barbecue fires by squirting fuel on the briquettes, we had to build ours the 'natural way', like Boy Scouts on a camp-out, by crumpling paper, piling on the kindling, then adding the briquettes on top.

At least he allowed us to use matches. Could've been worse.

Usually, I resented that we weren't allowed to use fuel. Tonight, though, I welcomed the distraction of building a fire the hard way.

For one thing, it kept my mind occupied so it wouldn't dwell too much on Dad's accident . . . or on the murdered dog . . . or on the chewed book or the missing yellow roses . . . or on my betrayal of Bitsy . . . or on the Travelling Vampire Show . . .

Also, it kept me out of the kitchen.

I was glad to be outside in the murky afternoon, watching flames lick at my sticks and briquettes, with Slim safely out of sight.

Alone with my fire, I missed her and longed to be with her – but I felt a wonderful sense of relief. At least for a while, there was no need to worry about how to act with Slim in a house without adults.

It remained in my mind, along with all my other concerns, but didn't overwhelm me because my main thoughts were focused on adding sticks and briquettes to the fire.

I jumped a little when the screen door banged shut.

Slim came trotting down the back steps with a bottle in each hand.

They weren't bottles of soda pop.

'You think your parents'll mind if we drink up some of their beer?'

If she'd been Rusty, I would've blown my stack.

But she was Slim, and she looked so good, and she had that smile.

'They'll just kill us is all,' I said, smiling.

'Never fear. My mom drinks the same brand. We can replace these with some of hers.'

'Then *she'll* have missing bottles.'

'She keeps a zillion of them around. She'll never know the difference.'

'We will,' I said. I must've said it funny.

Slim laughed and said, 'Gad-zooks, I hope so.'

Chapter Thirty

We sat on the stairs outside the back door and sipped our beers. We were side by side, so we didn't have to worry about staring at each other. We could look straight forward at the lawn or grill, or down at the beer bottles we were holding, or somewhere else.

When we first sat down, there were a couple of inches between us. As we talked and sipped, they disappeared somehow, through no fault of mine. I didn't move, so Slim must've. Before you knew it, her upper right arm was touching my upper left arm.

I tried not to think too much about it, but I couldn't quit thinking about it.

Even though Slim and I had been best friends for all those years and done so much together, it was almost as if we were on a first date. Everything about her seemed new and wonderful and scary.

When our bottles were about half empty, Slim said, 'Think the charcoal's ready?'

I considered jumping up to check, but that would've broken the contact between our arms. We might not be able to get our positions just the same when I came back.

'I'd give it another ten minutes or so,' I said.

She nodded, sighed, took another sip of beer, then said, 'I'm not in any hurry.'

'Me neither.'

'It's kind of nice, just sitting here.'

'Yeah.'

'Just the two of us,' she added.

207

My heart started pounding like mad. Afraid to look at her, I stared toward the barbecue grill and nodded.

'Not that I've got anything against Rusty,' she said.

I managed to laugh. 'You don't?'

'He's okay.'

'For a pain in the butt.'

This time, she laughed. Then she said, 'What really bugs me is that he's always around. I know he's your best friend and all, but . . .'

I was tempted to turn my head toward her, but I stopped myself. 'But what?' I asked.

'Sometimes I just wish he'd take a long walk off a short pier, that's all.'

'Same here.'

In a low voice, she said, 'Thing is, it'd be nice if just the *two* of us could do stuff sometimes.'

Now I *had* to turn my head. Looking her in the eyes, I asked, 'Really?'

'Yeah. Not that I want to hurt his feelings or anything.'

Our faces were so close together that her eyes made tiny jerking movements from left to right as if she couldn't make up her mind about which of my eyes to look at. I could smell a sweet warm scent of beer on her breath.

'Just that I sort of like being alone with you,' she said. 'Like now.'

'Same here,' I whispered.

Then Slim reached down between her legs and set the beer bottle on the next lower step. Turning herself sideways, she put her arm around my back. I set down my bottle. When I turned, my knee pushed against her knee. We both leaned toward each other and put our arms around each other and kissed.

Her lips were cool from the beer, and soft, and *hers*. I'd kissed girls before. A few times, anyway. In fact, I'd kissed

Slim before, at least on the cheek a couple of times when she was going away on trips with her mom. But there'd never been another kiss like this one.

The way Slim kissed me, I figured she must be in love with me just the same as I was in love with her. She hugged me so hard it hurt. I took it easy on her, though, because I could feel the bandages under her shirt.

The kiss went on and on. I felt as if I were sinking into Slim. I was in her and she was in me. I had her breath in my mouth and in my throat and in my lungs. I had the tips of her breasts touching me softly through our clothes. I wanted it to go on forever.

Way too soon, she loosened her hold on me. Her lips moved away from mine. Her breasts stopped touching me. But she remained so close that our noses almost touched, and she stared into my eyes.

I stared back into hers.

This time, the staring didn't make me nervous. This time, it just felt good.

After a while, she tilted her head sideways and kissed me again. This time, her lips barely touched mine before she took them away. 'You're all spitty,' she whispered. She eased away from me, but not very far. She was wet around the mouth herself, and a little bit red. Smiling softly, she leaned toward me again. She stretched out the neck of her T-shirt and rubbed it across my mouth. Then she moved back and wiped her own mouth in the same place. 'Kissing can be messy, huh?' she asked.

I opened my mouth. For a moment, I thought I might've forgotten how to talk. But I managed to say, 'Guess so.'

'Think the fire's ready yet?'

'Maybe. I'll be right back.'

Leaving my beer on the step, I stood up and started toward the grill. As I walked, I could feel a slippery wetness in the lining of the swimming trunks that I wore under my jeans. It dismayed me. I mean, we'd just been kissing. It had been the most wonderful kiss of my life. It had been overwhelming, but sweet and pure, not sexual. At least that's what I'd thought while it was happening. I hadn't had a hard-on – at least I didn't think so – and I certainly hadn't ejaculated.

I'd sure leaked, though.

A hot, sick feeling flooded through me.

While I still had my back to Slim, I glanced down. The front of my jeans was safely hidden by the hanging front of my shirt. Rusty's shirt, actually.

Vastly relieved, I looked down at the fire. The paper and kindling had burnt away, but the charcoal briquettes were just about right: the gray had almost reached their back centers.

'Looks ready,' I called to Slim.

'I'll get the burgers.' She took another swig of beer, then reached down again and set her bottle on the step. Standing up, she plucked at the legs of her cut-offs, then turned around and rushed the stairs. At the top, she swung open the screen door and vanished into the kitchen.

I waited for the door to bang shut. My back to the house, I looked down and pulled aside the front of my shirt-tail.

No wet spot on my jeans.

One less thing to worry about.

Pretty soon, the kitchen door swung open and Slim came out with a platter of burgers in her hands. Though her hair wasn't much longer than mine, a wispy flap of it draping her forehead and the fringe around her ears bounced as she trotted down the back stairs. So did her bikini top. I could see it jouncing up and down ever so slightly through the front of her T-shirt. The crew neck of her T-shirt drooped a little to the right from when she'd pulled at it to wipe off our mouths.

'I put salt and pepper on them,' Slim said as she came toward me. 'Also, I found the buns.'

'Good deal,' I said.

While she held the platter, I removed the patties one at a time. They felt cold and greasy in my fingers, and sizzled when they hit the grill.

I looked at my hands. 'Guess I'd better wash.'

'You could've used this.' Slim reached behind her back. Her hand returned holding a spatula which must've come from a back pocket.

'*Now* you tell me.'

She grinned. 'Go ahead and wash up. I'll watch the burgers.'

'Right back,' I said. Taking the platter with me, I ran to the house. I set it on the counter next to the buns. The buns were already on another plate, open and slathered on both sides with mayonnaise.

Slim knew what we liked.

I hurried over to the sink. When I tried to wash my hands, I found that cold water wouldn't take off the grease. I had to use hot water and soap.

Through the window in front of my face, I could see Slim standing by the barbecue. Pale smoke was rising in front of her and drifting away on the breeze. She was frowning slightly. I couldn't tell whether she was worried about something or just thinking hard. Maybe she was concentrating on the burger patties, trying to judge when to turn them over. She had the spatula ready in her right hand, but wasn't using it yet. Her left arm hung by her side. She stood with her left leg stiff, all her weight on it, that side of her rump sort of pushing out against the seat of her cut-offs.

I might've kept staring at her forever, but the water burnt

211

my hands. I gasped and jerked them out from under the faucet. They were stinging, so I let cold water run on them for a while. Then I dried them on the dish towel.

Slim was a big fan of cheeseburgers. So was I, for that matter. So I hurried to the fridge and took out our Velveeta. Carrying it to the counter and unwrapping it, I found myself remembering the Velveeta at Rusty's house. And his mother's bridge club. And Bitsy catching us. And how we'd run away from her.

Life had seemed wonderful for the past few minutes, but now I started feeling a little rotten again.

In my mind, I saw the eagerness on Bitsy's face when she thought we'd be taking her with us.

Then I heard Rusty's mother. *Elizabeth has always been very fond of you.*

I found our cheese slicer in a drawer.

I must say I'm terribly disappointed in you.

I pushed the tight wire of the slicer down through the block of Velveeta. When I had four slabs, each about half an inch thick, I put them on the plate with the buns. Then I picked up the plate and hurried outside.

Slim watched me trot down the stairs. She still had that frown on her face. As I neared her, she smiled. 'Velveeta,' she said.

'Yep.'

'Just a sec.'

Fire was leaping around the patties, fueled by their dripping grease. Slim had already flipped them over. Their upturned sides were brown and glistening, striped with black indentations from the grill. They sizzled and crackled and smelled delicious. As I watched, Slim pressed down on each of them with the spatula, squeezing them flatter, making juices spill out their sides. Each time she mashed one, the fire underneath it went crazy.

After pressing all four of them, she switched the spatula to her left hand. With her right, she picked up the slabs of Velveeta. She laid them out, one on top of each patty.

Until she came to the fourth slab of Velveeta.

She gave me a quick grin. 'This'll be mine,' she said, and took a bite. A blissful look on her face, she started to put the remaining three-quarters of the slice on the fourth patty. Instead of letting it go, however, she brought it quickly back to her mouth and snapped off another quarter of it. 'Gotta even up the sides,' she said through her mouthful. Then, reaching through the smoke and flames, she neatly set the remaining strip in the center of the patty.

By then, the cheese on the other burgers was starting to melt. 'These are going to be great,' Slim said.

'Yeah.'

'But you know what?'

'What?' I asked.

'I've been thinking about Rusty.'

'Uh.'

'He really wants to see the vampire show.'

'Yeah, I know.'

'I've been thinking, it might not be so easy for him to get out of his house tonight. They probably won't *let* him out, and he won't be able to *sneak* out in time if they're keeping an eye on him.'

'Maybe it's just as well,' I said. 'It might be better if we *all* miss it.'

'He really has his heart set on it, though.'

'Yeah, I know.'

'He'd be so disappointed,' Slim said, and looked at the grill. Melted Velveeta was starting to spill down the sides of the patties and drip into the flames. 'Uh-oh.' Quickly, she stabbed the spatula underneath one of the burgers, lifted it off the grill and slid it onto a bun.

'Should we go to Rusty's rescue?' I asked.

'I think we'd better.' Slim scooped off another burger.

'I thought you liked it better without him around,' I said.

'I do,' she said. She flashed me a sly smile, then transferred another burger from the grill to a bun. 'But he's still our friend.'

'Yeah.'

'More appreciated in his absence than in his presence . . .'

I laughed.

She took off the last burger, the one with half as much Velveeta. 'This one's yours,' she said.

'Okay.'

'I'm kidding,' she said. 'It's . . .'

'No, really, I'll take it. I'd *rather* have that one.'

She laughed softly and shook her head. 'If you want it that much, you can have it.' She set the top of the bun in place and pressed it down with her open hand. 'She's all yours.'

Chapter Thirty-one

The sun normally would've been blazing in our eyes at this time of the evening, but it couldn't get through the heavy clouds. Though the air felt muggy, a breeze came along every so often. A warm breeze. It felt pretty good, anyway.

We sat at the picnic table near the back of the lawn. It was painted green and had benches along both the long sides. Slim and I sat across from each other.

The cheeseburgers tasted great but they were very

messy to eat. Juices and Velveeta dripped off their sides, ran down our chins, dribbled down our hands and fell onto the table. After just a few bites, I ran into the house to get napkins.

We'd finished our beers and needed something to drink with our burgers. So I went to the fridge. I half intended to grab a couple more beer bottles, but couldn't bring myself to do it. I took out a couple of Pepsis instead.

Then I hurried outside.

Watching me, Slim said, 'Ah, Pepsi.'

'If you'd rather have more beer . . .'

She shook her head. 'This is just what I wanted.'

I put the cans on the table, gave Slim a couple of napkins, then sat down.

'Anyway,' she said, 'we don't want Rusty's parents to smell beer on our breath.'

'Why are they *gonna* smell beer on our breath?'

She gave me a whimsical, tilted smile. 'We drank beer.'

'I know that, but . . .'

'And we're going over to Rusty's house when we get done eating.'

'We are?'

'We want to rescue him, don't we?'

'I guess so.'

'Well, we can't exactly go in and kick butts, you know? I mean, this is Rusty's family.'

'Right.'

Her smile spread. 'What we've got to do is *kiss* butts.'

When she said that, I suddenly remembered the wager about Valeria. Rusty had suggested that the loser would have to kiss Slim's butt. And I'd imagined myself doing it. I imagined it now, too, and my face went red.

'That's a figure of speech,' Slim pointed out.

'I know.'

'Anyway,' she said, 'if we were *literally* going to kiss their butts, we wouldn't need to worry about beer on our breath.'

'We'd have *bigger* worries.'

We both had a pretty good laugh, and then we went on eating. When we were done, we carried everything into the house and cleaned up. Slim washed the spatula, knife and platter. I dried them and put them away. Soon, every trace of our supper was gone except for the two empty beer bottles.

'What'll we do with those?' I asked.

'Find a sack. We'll take them over to my place. We'll put them with my mom's empties, then grab a couple of fresh ones and bring them back here.'

I grinned. 'Good plan.'

'Elementary, my dear Thompson.'

My dear.

She only said it to make a play on Sherlock Holmes, but the words gave me a warm feeling, anyway.

'We'd better take care of that, first,' she said. 'Get it out of the way before we try to liberate Rusty.'

I found a grocery sack. The brown paper kind. (This was before anyone came up with the notion of 'saving the trees' by providing plastic grocery bags – which now *decorate* the trees and fences and streets and rivers and never go away.) Mom used the grocery bags to line our wastebaskets and sometimes to wrap packages for mailing. So she had a good collection of them.

I got one and held it open for Slim. With the empty bottles in her hands, she bent down in front of me, the top of her head almost touching my belly. The bottles clinked together as she set them on the bottom of the sack.

Then she straightened up. We looked each other in the eyes. Smiling softly, she said, 'Let me smell your breath.'

I set the sack down beside me. Slim moved in close, very close. She put her nose in front of my mouth and sniffed I expected a smart remark, but didn't get one. Instead of commenting on my breath, she put her mouth against mine and kissed me. Her arms went around me. She pressed her body against mine.

I thought about hugging her, but was afraid of her cuts. She didn't have any cuts on her rear end, though. I could put my hands down there. I *wanted* to. But I didn't dare. After all, that was below the belt.

While I was still struggling to work up the nerve, Slim took her mouth away and stepped back. 'Your breath's fine,' she whispered.

'Yours, too.'

'Smells like beer and cheeseburgers.'

'I thought you said it's fine.'

'It *is*,' she said. 'Only thing is, Mr and Mrs Simmons are going to know you've been drinking.'

'You, too.'

She smiled. 'Maybe if we don't let them kiss us . . .'

'They'd better not try.'

'Why don't you go and brush your teeth?'

'I don't think that'll take care of it.'

'Can't hurt. I'll brush mine when we get to my place.'

'Well . . .'

'Go ahead, I'll wait here.'

I ran up the stairs two at a time and hurried into the bathroom. After brushing my teeth, I used the toilet. This was the tough part about wearing swim trunks instead of underwear; they had no fly. Usually, I tried to maneuver myself out through the leghole of the trunks and the zipper of my jeans. But I didn't feel like struggling, so I just dragged everything down around my ankles. My skin was hot and damp from being trapped inside all those clothes. In front, I was slippery as if I'd been dipped in liquid soap. I could hardly hold on to take aim.

But the air felt great on all those hot, wet places.

Before flushing, I used a lot of toilet paper to dry myself. Then I pulled up my trunks and groaned at the way their hot, clammy lining clung to me. Quickly, I tugged them down again. I took off my shoes, jeans and trunks, then put my jeans back on.

The dirty clothes hamper was next to the toilet. I dropped my trunks in, put my shoes on, then washed my hands and left the bathroom. Without anything on under my jeans, I felt dry and loose and free.

I could *stay* like this, I thought. Nobody'll ever know.

But I knew I didn't dare.

In my bedroom, I shut the door and turned on the light. I unbuttoned Rusty's shirt, took it off, turned toward my bed and gave his shirt a toss.

On the pillow of my bed was a yellow rose.

My stomach dropped.

I leaped to my open closet, pulled a clean shirt off a hanger, then snatched Rusty's shirt off the bed and ran to the door. I jerked it open.

'*Slim!*' I shouted.

'Yeah?' Her voice sounded far away. 'What is it?'

I slapped the light switch. As darkness collapsed all around me, I raced down the hallway to the top of the stairs and then I ran down the stairs.

Slim was standing in the gloom of the kitchen, the grocery sack in her hand. 'What's wrong?' she asked.

'Somebody's been here.' Holding the two shirts in my left hand, I grabbed Slim's arm with my right. I hurried to the back door, pulling her.

I felt a little better the moment we were outside, but I didn't actually feel safe until we'd reached the sidewalk out front. When we came to the end of the block, we stopped. I tried to put on my shirt, but it wasn't easy with Rusty's shirt in one hand.

'I'll hold it,' Slim said.

I gave Rusty's shirt to her, and put on my own.

'So what happened?' she asked.

'I went to my bedroom to change shirts,' I explained. 'When I looked at my bed, there was a rose on the pillow. A *yellow* rose.'

The left side of Slim's upper lip lifted, baring some teeth. 'Like one of my *mom's* yellow roses?'

'Yeah.'

'Ooo.'

'It was just lying there on my pillow.'

'Everything else was okay?'

'Far as I could tell. But I didn't exactly hang around to find out.'

Or put on underwear, I thought. But Slim didn't need to know that.

'I was afraid they might still be in the house. And I thought about you being alone in the kitchen.' I finished buttoning my shirt. Then I took Rusty's shirt from Slim. 'Figured I'd take this back to him.'

She nodded.

We stepped off the curb and crossed the street.

'Are we still going to your place?' I asked.

'We have to,' she said. 'Then we've got to go to *your* house again. If we don't take care of the beer, you'll get the shaft from your parents.'

'Guess we never should've drunk it in the first place.'

She smiled at me. 'Can't say I regret it.'

'This is a lot of trouble to go through.'

'The cover-up's the price you pay for doing the crime.'

I laughed. 'Did you just think that up?'

'I think so.'

'Good one.'

She slipped her hand into mine. We walked side by side through the quiet evening.

Chapter Thirty-two

When we came to Slim's house, she set the grocery sack down on the stoop and crouched in front of the door. 'The tape looks okay,' she said. 'Stay here. I'll check the back door before we go in.'

I waited. A couple of minutes later, Slim opened the front door from inside.

'*Entre*,' she said.

The sack in one hand, Rusty's shirt in the other, I stepped over the threshold.

Slim shut the door and locked it. 'If anyone came in while we were gone,' she said, 'they didn't use the doors.'

'I guess that's good news,' I said.

She seemed amused. 'Vampires, of course, can turn into bats or wolves . . . or even a mist. You go turning into *mist*, you can get in just about anywhere.'

'It's not dark yet,' I pointed out.

She smiled. 'Not *technically*. Of course, if we want to get picky about it, vampires can't enter *anyplace* without an invitation.'

'That *is* good news.'

'But *people* can.'

'Not so good.'

'I want to brush my teeth. Why don't you put that stuff down and come upstairs with me? You can stand guard. Just in case.'

'Okay.'

We went upstairs together. She turned on the bathroom light, then said, 'I'll be out in a minute,' and shut the door.

She didn't lock it, or I would've heard the ping.

It was good to know that she trusted me.

Standing outside the door, I heard water start to run.

Night hadn't yet fallen, but the hallway was almost dark. I thought about taking a walk to the other end for a quick look into the bedrooms. But I wanted to stay close to Slim. And I really didn't *want* to see the bedrooms: what if they weren't the same as when we'd left?

What if someone was *hiding* in one of them? Hiding in silence, waiting for us . . .

It didn't seem likely. If I'd had to put money on it, I would've wagered that nobody was in either of the rooms, nobody was in the entire house except me and Slim.

Still, I felt chills crawling up my back as I stared into the gloom at the end of the hallway.

I wished Slim would hurry up.

Finally, she shut the water off. I expected the door to open, but it didn't.

Then I heard a steady splashing sound.

Oh.

Not wanting Slim to come out and wonder if I'd been listening to her, I walked away from the door. The sound diminished. Though I could still hear her, I stopped a few strides down the hall.

And stared toward the two bedrooms.

Nobody's here, I told myself. They were here before, but then they left and went to my house.

And to Rusty's? I wondered. He'd been at Janks Field the same as us.

I heard the toilet flush.

Soon after that, the bathroom door opened, light spilling into the hallway.

'Dwight?'

'I'm here.' I hurried to the door.

Slim looked a little worried. 'Where'd you go?'

'Nowhere. Just over there.' I nodded to the side.

Stepping out of the bathroom, she looked down the hallway. 'Did you hear something?'

I shook my head. 'Not really. I was just . . . waiting for you.'

'Let's go to my room,' she said.

'Okay.'

My heart suddenly pounding, I stayed by Slim's side and we left the lighted doorway behind.

Hurrying at the last moment, she entered her bedroom ahead of me and flicked the light switch. We stood motionless. Only our heads turned.

'Looks fine,' Slim whispered.

'Yeah.'

She turned toward me.

Nobody's home and we're in her bedroom . . .

'I've made a decision,' she said.

Oh, God.

I was almost too nervous to ask, but I managed to say, 'What?'

'I'm going after all,' she said.

'Huh?'

'To the Travelling Vampire Show. If you guys are going to it, so am I.'

'But I thought . . .'

'Yeah, well . . . things have changed. If I *don't* go with you, where am I supposed to stay that's safe? They've been *here* – somebody has been, anyway.'

I almost confessed, but stopped myself. Rusty and I had been in her house, all right, and we'd broken the vase and perfume bottle in her mother's room. But we hadn't chewed her book or taken the yellow roses.

'And they've been to *your* place,' Slim continued. '*Your* parents are at the hospital. *My* mom's away for the night. I'm sure as heck not going to stay here by myself. Or at your place. I *wouldn't* stay at Rusty's, since I happen to not be able to stand his parents.' She shrugged. 'Maybe at Lee's, but . . .'

'Not there,' I said. 'Julian has her address on the check she gave him.'

'As if he needs addresses,' Slim said.

'But why are they doing this?' I asked. 'If it *is* them? I just don't get it.'

'To scare us, I guess. So we won't talk.'

'About the dog?'

'I don't know. They might be afraid the cops'll come if I tell. Maybe they've got a *lot* to hide. I mean, you know?'

'If they're so afraid we'll tell on them, why don't they . . .' Not wanting to say it, I shrugged.

'Take us prisoners?' Slim suggested. 'Or kill us?'

'Something like that,' I admitted.

'I don't know,' Slim said. 'But that'd be awfully drastic. If they're trying not to draw attention to themselves, killing some kids doesn't seem like a brilliant way to go about it.'

I almost smiled. 'You're right about that.'

'On the other hand,' she said, 'if they're trying to scare us, why did they give us tickets for tonight's show?'

'They didn't *give* them to us. They *sold* them.'

'And got their hands on Lee's address,' Slim said. 'But why do they need her address? They didn't need *ours*. They just followed us, or something.'

I shrugged. 'Maybe in case they *hadn't* been able to follow us? That sort of thing doesn't always work. They might've lost us. But if they *did*, they'd still know where to find Lee.' When I said that, I got a slightly sick feeling inside.

'I wonder if *she's* had any visitors,' Slim said.

'Maybe we'd better call her.'

'Yeah. In a minute. I want to change first.'

'Huh?'

'Like you.'

I blushed and raised my eyebrows as if I didn't know what she was talking about. Which was pretty much true.

'The dark shirt,' she said.

'Oh.'

'It's a good idea.'

'Thanks.' I hadn't worn a dark shirt on purpose. After seeing the rose on my pillow, I'd just grabbed it. But I saw no harm in allowing Slim to think I'd chosen a dark shirt for purposes of camouflage.

She walked to her closet, turned on its light and began to search through the clothes hangers.

'I'd better wait in the hall,' I said.

'You don't have to.' The words were hardly out of her mouth before she pulled off her T-shirt. Her back was toward me and she had her bikini top on, along with about a dozen bandages. Then she reached behind her. 'Don't get worried,' she said, and untied the back string. As she untied the neck string, she said, 'It's just too hot.'

She let her bikini top fall to the closet floor.

I stood there gaping at her naked back, stunned and thrilled and scared, hardly able to believe that she had actually taken off her top in front of me.

This had never happened before.

Maybe because we'd never been alone together.

She spread some hangers apart. As she reached out for a

blouse with her right arm, she turned her body slightly. Just in front of her armpit, and a little lower, was a pale, smooth slope – the side of her right breast.

She probably didn't know I could see it. And I only did see it for a moment before she pulled the blouse off the hanger and turned away again.

Turned away so that both her breasts were facing the closet. I couldn't see them, but I sure knew they were there.

They'd be in plain sight if only I were standing in the closet.

Or if she turns around.

Please turn around, I thought. Please.

I suddenly hoped something would happen to *make* her turn around. Maybe a sudden noise. Like the telephone ringing? Or a shout?

I could shout.

But I didn't. As much as I ached for Slim to turn around, I didn't want to do anything that might make her think less of me.

She turned around.

Her blouse was already on, however, and most of the buttons were fastened.

I hoped I wasn't blushing too badly when she looked up at me. 'How's this?' she asked.

Her long-sleeved blouse was black and made of a shiny fabric. Somewhat too large for her, it hung down so low it almost hid the front of her cut-off jeans.

'That oughta keep you from being seen,' I said.

'Does it look weird?' she asked.

'Looks great.'

'I mean, with my shorts. A long-sleeved blouse . . .'

'Do you have a black skirt?'

She made a face at me. 'I have one, but I'm not about to wear it.'

225

'Long jeans?' I suggested.

'It *does* look weird.'

'It's fine.'

'How about if I do this?' She rolled the sleeves halfway up her forearms. Then she turned her back to me, unfastened her cut-offs and tucked in the tails of her blouse. Zipped and buttoned, she faced me again. 'Better?'

Pulled tight and smooth, the blouse showed every contour. The smooth mounds of her breasts were tipped with stiff nipples.

'You look fine,' I said.

She frowned. 'What?'

Before I could say anything, she turned around and looked at herself in the mirror. Her frown deepened. Her hands came up and she touched her nipples. 'Can't go around like this,' she said.

In the mirror's reflection, our eyes met.

I shrugged.

Her hands slid down below her breasts, clutched her blouse and pulled it upward, dragging its tails out of her cut-offs. When she stopped, it was still tucked in but now had plenty of slack in it. No longer taut against her breasts, it draped them but didn't reveal every detail.

Her eyes again met mine in the mirror. 'Better?' she asked.

I nodded.

She turned around and came to me, a smile spreading over her face. 'Are you all right?' she asked.

'Fine.'

'Are you sure?'

'Sure.'

'You seem awfully nervous.'

'I do?'

'Yeah.'

'I'm okay.'

'Do *I* make you nervous?'

'Maybe a little.'

Reaching down, she took hold of my wrists. 'These?' she asked, and lifted my hands and placed them on her breasts. Through the thin fabric of her blouse, I felt their heat and smoothness. I felt how springy they were. I felt the push of her nipples.

Chapter Thirty-three

In Slim's bathroom, I tried to clean myself up.

'Are you okay?' she asked through the door.

'Fine,' I said. I tried to make my voice sound calm even though I was so embarrassed I wanted to cry.

'Can I do something to help?' she asked.

'No. Thanks. Everything's okay.'

'Oh, sure.' She didn't sound very chipper, herself.

'Just . . . I'll be out in a minute.'

'I'm sorry, Dwight.'

'Isn't your fault.'

'Of course not.'

I blushed furiously.

What did she think had happened to me?

She hadn't asked.

Does she know?

My hands leaping away from her breasts, I'd blurted, 'Gotta go,' then run from her bedroom and down the hall to the bathroom.

Maybe she thinks I got hit by the trots.

From the other side of the door, Slim said, 'It's fine if you want to take a shower or something.'

A shower might be the best solution, but I said, 'No, that's okay.'

'Come on, Dwight. You take a shower, and I'll throw your stuff in the wash. It won't take that long. We'll get everything nice and clean.'

'I don't know,' I muttered. The wads of toilet paper had taken care of the worst of it, but I was still very sticky and my jeans . . .

'Why don't you just hand your pants out through the door?' Slim said.

'Nah.'

'Come on, Dwight.' Slim opened the door, but only a few inches. Her arm reached in. 'Just hand them to me.'

'They're a mess.'

'It's all right. Come on.' Her fingers waved back and forth, gesturing for me to approach.

'Can't you just leave me alone for a while?'

'Give me your pants, Dwight.' This time, she sounded serious.

'They're gross.'

'They *are* not.'

'That's what you think.'

'I know what happened,' she said, her voice suddenly going soft. 'And I know why it happened. I know all about that sort of stuff. Thanks to Jimmy.'

'Oh, God,' I muttered, and hoped she hadn't heard me.

'*He* was gross,' Slim said. 'Everything *about* him was gross. But nothing about you is gross, Dwight. Nothing. There's nothing for you to be ashamed of or embarrassed about. Okay? So just let me have your pants and I'll wash them for you. Please.'

'Okay.'

Blushing like crazy, I climbed out of my jeans. On the back of the bathroom door was a full-length mirror. I saw myself walking toward it, my hair mussed, my face scarlet, my shirt not quite long enough to cover my equipment, my jeans swaying by my side, my legs bare all the way down to the tops of my white socks.

'Here,' I said, and put my jeans into Slim's hand.

'Thanks,' she said. Her arm retreated. A moment later, she said, 'What about your trunks?'

Expecting the question didn't save me from the embarrassment of it.

'I got rid of them back at my house,' I confessed. 'They were too hot.'

'Ah,' she said. 'Okay. No problem. I'll go downstairs and throw these in the washer. Why don't you go ahead and take a shower?'

'Be careful, okay?'

'I will be. You, too.' The bathroom door eased shut.

I thought about things for a minute or two, then took off my shirt and socks and stepped over to the bathtub. I started the water running. When it felt about right, I climbed into the tub, slid the frosted door shut, and started the shower. The spray came out cold. A few seconds later, however, it was good and hot.

I tried to get myself clean with just my hands and the water. After some rubbing, though, my skin still felt slick and tacky in the places where I'd made the mess.

Bending over, I removed a bar of soap from the tray.

The fresh scent of the soap reminded me of Slim.

Of course, I thought. It's her soap.

Suddenly, the realization struck me that I was taking a shower in the very same tub where Slim took her showers or baths. She had been naked in this very place. She had slid this very bar of soap over her bare skin. It had touched her face, glided over her breasts, slicked the skin of her buttocks, even rubbed her *down there*.

Never mind, I told myself.

But as I stood in the spray, I couldn't stop myself from thinking about it. I got pretty excited all over again. I imagined Slim coming back upstairs after throwing my jeans in the washer ... easing open the bathroom door and sneaking inside ... taking off all her clothes, then sliding open the shower door.

Mind if I join you in there?

Don't mind at all.

It'll never happen, I thought. Not in a million years.

It might.

What had already happened was too fantastic to believe.

She put my hands on her breasts!

If she'll do that, I thought, what *else* will she do?

She knows all about sex, thanks to that bastard Jimmy Drake. She's *experienced*. We're alone in the house. We've got all night – if we skip the vampire show. Taking a shower together could be just the beginning!

I was done washing myself, but I decided to keep on showering.

No hurry, I thought.

She'd already had plenty of time to take my jeans out to the garage behind her house, throw them into the washing machine, start the machine, and return to the house. By now, she might be just outside the bathroom door.

On the rim of the tub was a plastic bottle of shampoo. I picked it up, opened it, and poured some of the yellow goo into the palm of my hand.

I'll be sudsing my hair when she comes in.

I'll act very surprised.

I won't have to *act*, I realized. I really *will* be surprised. I'll be shocked.

It would take a miracle to have Slim get in the shower with me.

But she put my hands on her breasts.

Right. And I had an *accident* like some kind of sex-starved kid.

I *am* a sex-starved kid.

I rubbed the foamy shampoo into my hair and scalp. The shampoo didn't smell the same as the soap. Like the soap, however, its aroma reminded me of Slim.

I lathered my hair for a long time, giving Slim plenty of time to show up.

She isn't *going* to show up, I finally had to admit.

She's probably waiting outside the bathroom door – and wondering what's taking me so long. Maybe she even decided to wait by the washing machine and not come back until my jeans are finished.

I put my head under the hot spray. I spent a fairly long time rinsing away the suds, still hoping for Slim to come in. Finally, I bent down and turned off the water. I rolled the door open. Hanging on to its edge, I leaned out slightly and looked around. The bathroom was aswirl with white steam.

No Slim.

I climbed out of the tub. Dripping, I took a few steps and pulled a pale blue towel off its bar. Slim's towel. It had to be hers: her mother's tub was in the master bathroom. The towel was the same powder blue color as Slim's bikini. The one she was wearing tonight. The one with the top she'd removed in her closet.

Drying myself, I wondered if the towel had been in the wash since the last time she'd used it. I didn't think so. It seemed clean and fresh, but didn't smell or feel the way towels do before they've been used.

This one had been against Slim, all over.

When I was done drying myself, I wrapped it around my

waist and tucked a corner down to hold it in place. It jutted out quite a lot in front, so I didn't go to the door or call out for Slim.

To pass a little time, I stepped over to the counter. The mirror above it was all fogged up. Even though I couldn't see myself in the mirror, I combed my hair with a pink comb I found on the counter. Then I sprayed my armpits with Slim's deodorant. It was Right Guard, and its odor reminded me of Slim.

It seemed that Slim's special scent was made of many different aromas – her soap, her shampoo, her deodorant. Now those scents were on me. I liked having the same smell as Slim – or almost the same.

She had others aromas, too, at different times. Perfumes. Suntan oil. Foods she'd eaten. Sometimes, she carried outdoor scents: she smelled like wind or rain or grass or sunlight.

The towel was no longer sticking out, so I went to the door.

I expected Slim to be on the other side of it.

She wasn't.

I stepped out and looked down the hall. Light from her open bedroom door spilled onto the carpet like a yellow fluid.

'Slim?' I called.

No answer came.

Not from her bedroom. Not from downstairs. Not from anywhere.

What if *they* got her?

The thought made me feel squirmy.

Maybe they were hanging around the house all along, hiding, waiting to get Slim alone . . .

She's probably still in the garage, I told myself. Safe and sound. Waiting to take my jeans out of the washer.

I might as well wait in her bedroom, I thought.

As I walked toward the glow from her room, the towel started to come loose. I grabbed it, held it up, and kept on walking – suddenly very aware of being naked except for the towel.

Stepping into the light, turning toward her doorway, I suddenly imagined Slim was waiting for me in her bed. Maybe with a sheet pulled up almost to her shoulders.

Her shoulders bare.

Her face smiling.

That's why she hadn't answered when I called out; she didn't want to ruin the surprise.

Chapter Thirty-four

Wrong.

Slim's bed was empty. She didn't seem to be in her room at all.

'Slim?' I asked, just to make sure.

A fluttery feeling in my stomach, I left her room and walked to the head of the stairway.

'*Slim!*' I called out.

She didn't answer.

So I trotted down the stairs. Straight ahead of me was the front door. I suddenly imagined it swinging open, Slim's mother coming into the house and gaping up at me in shock, blurting out, *What're YOU doing here, young man? Where are your clothes?*

233

Something had gone wrong with her overnight plans, and here she was.

It could happen.

Of course, it didn't.

It's been my experience that worst-case scenarios are very rare indeed. Rare to the extent that you can almost count on their not happening.

But sometimes they do.

The moment I turned away from the front door, my terror of being caught by Slim's mother vanished and my fears for Slim returned.

The kitchen light was on. The back door stood open and the screen door was shut.

Earlier, Slim had entered the house this way to open the front door for me. She had also, probably, gone out this way to take my jeans to the garage.

I walked across the linoleum floor. It felt clean and slick under my bare feet.

At the screen door, I stopped and looked out.

The two-car garage stood at the far right corner of the lawn. Though its doors were shut, the windows of the laundry room were bright.

Slim has to be in there, I told myself.

But what if she's not?

She *is*! She knows I've got no pants until she comes back with my jeans. She's just staying with them till they're done.

Probably.

I couldn't stand the idea of waiting for her – not knowing for sure if she was there – so I opened the screen door and hurried down the back-porch stairs.

Night had come. It was warm. Soft breezes blew against me, and they smelled of rain – rain that had been holding off all day but was sure to fall sooner or later.

Almost naked, I was glad to have the darkness. The trees

and fences gave me some protection, but not enough, from the eyes of neighbors who might be looking out their windows. If I should be seen in Slim's back yard wearing nothing but a towel . . .

I suddenly realized that *Slim* would be seeing me in nothing but a towel. I couldn't turn back, though. I had to make sure she was safe.

It'll be embarrassing, I thought, but it can't be any worse than what's already happened.

After retucking the towel to secure it around my waist, I opened the laundry room door.

I stepped in.

Slim wasn't there. Neither machine was running, but the air held a moist warmth and smelled faintly of detergent. I stepped up to the washer and opened its top. Bending down and peering into the shadows, I felt heat rise against my face. The machine had been used recently, but it was empty now.

I stepped over to the drier. It was a front-loader. When I bent over to open it, my towel started to come loose. I grabbed the towel at its tuck by my hip. Holding it in place, I bent lower and peered into the drum.

At the bottom was a tangle of damp fabrics.

Feeling a little confused, I squatted down directly in front of the drier, reached in with my right arm, and plucked at the clothes. I separated them enough to find my own jeans, Slim's cut-off jeans and the pants of her powder blue bikini. Nothing else.

'You got me.'

Though I recognized Slim's voice, it came from behind and startled me. My arm hopped up and banged against the top of the drier's door hole. '*OW!*' I yelped. I jerked my arm clear. Grabbing where it hurt, I shot to my feet and twisted around.

The laundry room had its own door into the rest of the garage. Though it housed the big old Pontiac that used to belong to Slim's grandmother (who'd checked out in the Super M checkout line the previous year), it was mostly used for storage. They kept a freezer chest there. And an extra refrigrator.

The door had been shut when I came into the laundry room.

Now it was open and Slim stood in the doorway, a look of concern on her face, a beer bottle in each hand. Her shiny black blouse was large enough so that it reached below her groin. Cut higher at the sides, it let me see bare skin to her hips. Her legs were bare all the way down to the sneakers on her feet.

I noticed all that in about half a second.

During the same half second, while my arm rang with pain, I realized that I'd lost my towel.

The hand of my wrecked arm was almost where I needed it to be. Fast as I could, I cupped myself.

Slim smiled as she watched me squat and snatch up the towel.

When I had it around me again, her smile vanished. 'Sorry I startled you,' she said.

'It's okay.'

'You really whacked your arm.'

'It'll be okay.'

'I keep messing you up.' She looked serious when she said it. But then she must've found some humor in her wording, because a smile crept across her face. 'Rusty would've liked that one,' she said.

'Yeah.'

'Anyway, I'm sorry.' She stepped out of the doorway and came toward me, the bottles swinging by her bare hips, her breasts moving softly under her blouse. She set the bottles on top of the washer. 'Let me see your arm,' she said.

Holding the towel together with my left hand, I raised my right arm. The front of my forearm was crossed by a red mark. Slim frowned at it. Then she gently took hold of my wrist and elbow, lifted my arm toward her face, and kissed the red place. I still felt as if someone had whacked my arm with a crowbar, but now I could feel Slim's lips. They felt cool and soft.

Looking up into my eyes, she asked, 'Does that make it better?'

'Makes it fine,' I told her.

She lowered my arm and let go of it. 'I didn't mean to surprise you,' she said. 'I thought you were in the house.'

'I got worried about you.'

'I was just out here.'

I shrugged. 'Guess so. It's just . . . you were gone so long.'

'I couldn't come in till the wash was done.' She lowered her head to look at herself. Her open hands, down by her sides, gestured toward her bare thighs. As if to point out that she was naked below her hanging shirt-tails.

As if I hadn't noticed.

'Since I was doing a wash anyway,' she said, 'I figured I might as well throw in some of my own stuff.' She blushed slightly, looked as if she might add something, then turned away. 'Only trouble is, I can't get the drier to work.'

I found myself smiling.

'Looking forward to wet jeans?' Slim asked.

I shook my head. 'It's just . . . I thought you'd vanished again.'

Her eyebrows soared. 'What do you mean, vanished *again*? I've never vanished.'

'I *thought* you had.'

'Ah, but I *hadn't*. I always knew where I was.'

'I guess so.'

'I know so.' She laughed a couple of times. Then she said, 'So what'll we do about the drier?'

After shrugging, I asked, 'What's wrong with it?'

'It doesn't go. Watch.' She went to the drier. As she bent over to shut its door, the tail of her blouse slid upward a couple of inches. I tried to look away. Before I could succeed, however, she straightened up.

Before I could feel either relief or disappointment about that, she leaned over the top of the drier and reached for the control knobs and her blouse tail *really* slid up.

'See?' she asked.

I saw, all right.

'It *should* be going. But it's not.'

I said, 'Hmm.'

She straightened up and turned around. I must've been as red as ketchup, but she acted as if she didn't notice. She also pretended not to notice the front of my towel sticking out. 'Why doesn't it want to work?' she asked.

'I'm sure it *wants* to.'

She smirked, but I could see she was a little amused, too. 'You know what I mean,' she said.

'You sure you're turning it on right?' I asked.

'I *know* how to turn on a drier.'

'I'm sure you do.'

'And what's *that* supposed to mean?' she asked.

I tried not to grin. 'Oh, nothing.'

She reached up with her right hand, flicked her middle finger and thumped the tip of my nose. Not very hard, but hard enough to make me blink and take a step backward. Also, my eyes watered.

'Oh, no,' Slim said, suddenly looking appalled. 'I'm sorry. God, why do I keep *doing* this stuff?' She put her hands on both sides of my face, drew my head toward her and kissed me on the nose. Then she kissed me on the mouth.

I almost reached for her breasts. I remembered last time, and how they'd felt. But I also remembered the result.

Taking her by the wrists, instead, I moved her hands away from my face. Her mouth went away, too.

'I'd better take a look at the drier,' I said.

Looking me in the eyes, she nodded slightly. 'Good idea,' she said, her voice low and shaky.

She stepped aside. I went to the drier. 'Nothing at all happens when you turn it on, right?'

'The drier?'

'Right, the drier.'

'Right. Nothing at all happens.'

'Sounds like it might be a problem with the power.'

'Sure,' Slim said.

'Was it working before?'

'Yeah. Mom did the wash a couple of days ago. It was working fine.'

Holding on to my towel, I stepped around the side of the machine and looked behind it with high hopes of finding the power cord unplugged. But it looked secure in its socket.

'It *is* plugged in,' Slim told me. 'I already checked that.'

'You did?'

'I'm not an idiot.'

I looked at her and grinned. 'I know.'

'So what do you think it is?'

'It might be a dead outlet. Have you got an extension cord?'

'Sure. Right back.' She whirled around. Her blouse fluttered and rippled behind her as she ran toward the doorway. The air flapped its tail.

She leaped through the doorway and vanished into the other side of the garage.

While she was gone, I squatted beside the machine,

scooted it away from the wall, reached behind it and pulled the plug out of the wall socket.

Slim came back with the coil of an extension cord dangling from one hand. 'Here you go,' she said.

'Thanks.'

I took it from her and pushed the drier's plug into the extension. Holding my towel with one hand, I stood up and followed Slim to an outlet near the door.

'Try this one,' she said.

I pushed the prongs of the extension cord into the holes of the outlet.

Slim said, 'Ahhh' as the drier came to life.

Chapter Thirty-five

Leaving our clothes in the drier, we went back to Slim's house. I led the way, using my left hand to hold my towel secure. Slim carried the beer bottles.

In the kitchen, she set the bottles on the table. 'Maybe you'd better give Lee a call.'

'Oh, yeah,' I said.

Slim swept her hand toward the wall phone.

'Now?' I asked.

'Don't you think you should?'

'I guess so,' I admitted. I frowned at the phone, reluctant to make the call.

'What's wrong?'

I shrugged. 'I don't know.'

'We'd better make sure she's all right.'

'Yeah.'

'And find out if *she's* had any weird stuff happen.'

'How about if we wait and call later?'

'What's wrong with now?'

'I don't know.' I happened, just then, to glance at Slim's legs.

She grinned. 'It's a *phone* call, Dwight. She won't be able to *see* us.'

'I know, but . . .' I shrugged.

'Want me to leave the room?'

'No!' The word burst from my mouth.

Slim flinched.

'Don't leave,' I said, trying to make my voice calm. 'You'll probably vanish again.'

'I told you, I *haven't* vanished.'

'That's your opinion.'

A glint of mischief in her eyes, she said, 'I oughta know.'

'Don't go anywhere,' I told her.

I stepped over to the phone, made sure my towel was secure, then lifted the receiver off its hook. I knew Lee's number by heart. While I dialed it, Slim pulled a chair away from the kitchen table and sat down.

Lee's phone started to ring.

With the table in the way, I didn't need to worry about seeing anything lower than Slim's belly.

I listened to the quiet ringing and we gazed into each other's eyes.

It started out as that intense, curious, hopeful stare that we'd been giving each other so much lately. Our *love* stare, I guess. But then Slim's gaze faltered, and so did mine. Soon, we were frowning at each other.

'How many times has it rung?' she asked.

'I don't know, seven or eight.'

'Give it a few more.'

'She usually gets it in two or three if she's home.'

'Maybe she's in the bathroom or something.'

Maybe she's busy, I thought, and doesn't want to be bothered by a phone call right now and she's wondering what sort of jerk is keeping at it this long.

As I let it continue to ring, I began to hope Lee *wouldn't* answer. She was one of my favorite people, not only beautiful but one of my best friends, so I hated to make a nuisance of myself.

Finally, I hung up.

'Well,' Slim said.

'Yeah.'

'I wonder what *that* means.'

'Maybe she went somewhere,' I said.

'Or she's taking a bath,' Slim said. 'If she's running the water, she might not even hear the phone. Or maybe she heard it, but didn't want to get out of the tub.'

I pictured Lee lounging in her bathtub, wet and shiny.

'I sure don't get out to answer the phone,' Slim said, and I pictured *her* in her bathtub.

Starting to get excited, I sat down at the kitchen table across from Slim.

'Or she might've been on the toilet,' Slim added. 'There's no telling. Why don't you call her back?'

I didn't relish the idea of standing up just then. 'Why don't we give her a while?'

'Yeah. How about five or ten minutes? Maybe she'll get done with whatever she's doing.'

'Good,' I said.

'I'm sure she's fine.'

'I hope so.'

'I mean, *we* had some weird stuff happen, but nobody *did* anything to us. We might've gotten a little scared, but we didn't get hurt.'

I nodded in agreement.

'While we're waiting . . .' She went silent and let a smile spread over her face.

It was a type of smile I'd seen on Slim before, but not very often. It had a slyness to it. It always meant trouble.

'Uh-oh,' I said.

Slim scooted back her chair. I tried to keep my gaze high as she stood up and turned around. Mostly, I succeeded.

'Where're you going?' I asked.

Striding away, she looked over her shoulder. 'Back in a minute. Don't worry, I won't vanish.'

'Please don't,' I muttered.

I watched the black tail of her blouse drift against her rear end as she left the kitchen. When she was beyond the reach of the kitchen light, all I could see was a pair of walking legs. Soon, they were eaten by the darkness.

I was tempted to stand up and go after her, but I still had a towel problem.

'You okay?' I called.

'Fine.'

'What're you doing?'

'You'll see.'

On her way back, I saw her legs first. Then I noticed the pale shapes of her face and forearms. By her side, she was carrying something more pale than her skin.

It turned out to be a newspaper.

I looked away and tried to seem interested in the clock while Slim sat down and scooted her chair closer to the table.

Then I faced her and asked, 'What's the paper for?'

'Time to put my big plan into action.'

'What big plan is that?'

'Operation Rescue Rusty.'

I groaned.

Slim chuckled.

By the time she finished explaining, I no longer needed to worry about embarrassing protrusions of my towel. I sighed, pushed myself away from the table, and went to the phone. I was trembling slightly and my heart was pounding.

I dialed, then turned toward Slim.

She looked very pleased with herself.

I showed her my teeth and she laughed.

Over at Rusty's house, someone picked up a phone.

'Hello?'

I cringed. 'Hello, Mrs Simmons.'

'Hello, young man.'

'Is Rusty there?'

'I'm afraid he's incommunicado at the moment.'

'Oh. Yeah. I sort of thought so. I feel awful about what we did. You know, ditching Elizabeth.'

'You have no idea how much you hurt her feelings, Dwight. Frankly, I didn't expect such behavior from you.'

'I'm awfully sorry. Really. I just wasn't thinking straight. I was so worried about Slim . . .'

'Well, yes. I can understand your concern, but it was no excuse. Elizabeth fully expected you to wait for her.'

'I know. I feel rotten about it. Anyway, I was thinking about doing something to cheer her up.'

Mrs Simmons was silent.

'I thought maybe Slim and I might come over and take her with us to the movies.'

Mrs Simmons remained silent.

'There's a double-feature at the drive-in. *Whatever Happened to Baby Jane*'s playing with *House on Haunted Hill*.'

'Haven't you *seen* those movies?' she asked.

'*House on Haunted Hill*.'

'I thought so.'

'But that was a couple of years ago, and we missed our chance to see *Whatever Happened to Baby Jane* when it played at the Crown. Anyway, I'm pretty sure Elizabeth hasn't seen either one of them, and Slim and I don't mind seeing *House on Haunted Hill* again. It was really good.'

'I'm not sure I want Elizabeth to see that sort of movie. They're both supposed to be dreadful. I don't want her coming home with nightmares.'

'Bette Davis and Joan Crawford are in *Baby Jane*,' I pointed out.

'I'm well aware of that.'

'They were really big stars in your generation.'

That got a laugh out of Mrs Simmons. '*My* generation, huh?'

I wasn't quite sure what to make of that, so I changed the subject slightly. 'Anyway, I bet Elizabeth would get a kick out of going to the drive-in with us. We'll pay for her ticket and buy her snacks and stuff.'

'And who, exactly, will be driving?'

'Slim. We'll be going in her car.'

'I see.'

She trusted Slim. I figured we had it made.

Then she said, 'I don't know, Dwight.'

'I think Elizabeth might especially like spending some time with me after ... you know, feeling so *abandoned* this afternoon.'

'I suppose you'll want *Rusty* to accompany you likewise?'

'Doesn't matter to us. It's fine either way.'

'He's grounded, you know.'

'He doesn't have to come. The thing is, this is really for Elizabeth.'

'I'll have to ask her.'

I heard some clatter that meant she was setting down the

phone. Pressing the mouthpiece of Slim's phone against my belly, I said quietly, 'I think we're in business.'

Slim looked tickled. She also looked as if she'd known all along that her plan would succeed. Largely because her plans *always* succeeded.

Almost always.

After a while, Mrs Simmons returned to the phone. 'Dwight?' she asked.

'I'm here.'

'My husband and I have talked it over. We've also discussed the matter with Elizabeth, and she's willing to forgive and forget.'

'Oh. Good.'

'So we'll allow her to go with you.'

'Great.'

'Rusty, too. He's still grounded, mind you. This will be the exception to the rule.'

'Fine.' I grinned at Slim.

'But I want you to promise you won't do anything to make us regret our decision.'

'I promise, Mrs Simmons.'

'When will you be picking them up?'

'Maybe in about half an hour?'

Slim nodded her approval.

'Very good. We'll see you then.'

'Great.'

'And Dwight?'

'Yes?'

'This is a very thoughtful thing you're doing. It goes a long way toward putting you back in our good graces.'

'Thank you, Mrs Simmons.'

'See you soon,' she said.

'Real good. Bye.'

'Bye.'

I hung up.

Grinning, Slim began to applaud. 'Bravo,' she said. 'A *fine* performance.'

'Thank you, thank you . . .'

'While you're on a roll, how about giving Lee another try?'

I dialed Lee's number. It rang and rang and rang.

Chapter Thirty-six

Slim picked up the two fresh bottles of beer and we went into the living room. On the foyer floor was Rusty's shirt and the bag containing my dad's two empty beer bottles – just where I'd left them before hurrying upstairs to stand guard on Slim while she brushed her teeth.

At the time, I'd figured we would be out of the house in about five minutes.

Funny how one thing leads to another.

Or not so funny.

Watching Slim squat by the bag to take out the empty bottles and put in the full ones, I could hardly believe what had happened after I'd followed her upstairs. There was a dreamlike quality to it. As if several of my fantasies – and dreads – had come to life. But I knew I hadn't dreamed any of it; there squatted Slim in nothing but her blouse and here stood I in nothing but a towel. Our clothes were in the drier. All of it had actually happened.

And we were still dealing with the consequences.

Not to mention the consequences of drinking my dad's beer.

Drinking those two bottles of beer (and trying to conceal the deed) had led us back to Slim's house ... where she'd gone upstairs to brush her teeth and change into a dark blouse ... and all the rest had happened.

Consequences within consequences.

But *good* consequences. Mostly.

Standing up, Slim said, 'You be in charge of the beer.' Then she walked over to the sofa. Her back was toward me, so I watched the tail of her blouse slide up as she bent over and pulled the sofa away from the wall.

She crouched and took out the weapons: her bow, her quiver of arrows, and the two knives Rusty and I had carried while helping her search the house for prowlers.

'What'll we do with those?' I asked.

'Take 'em with us.' She raised her arm to lift the strap of the quiver over her head. When she did that, her blouse glided up a couple of inches. I kept my eyes on her face until the quiver was on her back and her blouse was down where it belonged.

'Let's go see if the clothes are dry,' she said.

I picked up the bag, the two empty bottles, and the shirt I'd borrowed from Rusty.

'Aren't you forgetting something?' Slim asked.

I must've looked puzzled.

A smile spread across Slim's face. 'I only washed your *jeans*.'

'Oh!'

She laughed.

I set everything down again, said, 'Right back,' and headed for the stairway feeling a little stupid.

I was about halfway up when Slim said, 'Dwight?'

I stopped and looked around. 'You'd better leave my towel up there,' she said. 'Put it back where you got it, okay?'

Leave her *towel*?

'Okay,' I said.

'And check around the bathroom. We don't want to leave any *evidence* behind.'

'Okay.'

'And could you check my bedroom, too? I think I left the light on.'

'I'll check,' I said and continued up the stairs. At the top, I looked back down at her and said, 'Stay put, okay?'

'I will.'

'And yell if anything happens.'

'I will.'

On my way down the hall to her bedroom, the towel started to slip. I held it by the tuck . . . and wondered why I bothered. After all, she wanted me to leave the towel in the bathroom. What would I do then?

Stepping into her bedroom, I was about to flick the wall switch when I saw that the closet light was also on. I walked toward it, striding over the place where Slim and I had been standing when she'd put my hands on her breasts. Then I was in the closet, standing where she'd stood when she took off her T-shirt. I looked down. The powder blue top of her bikini lay on the floor, just where she'd dropped it.

Maybe she didn't want it left on the floor.

As I thought about picking it up, however, I remembered Rusty fooling with Slim's mother's bra. What if I picked up the bikini top and got an urge to bury my face in it . . . and Slim suddenly showed up and caught me?

So I let it stay on the floor.

I yanked the string to shut the light off, then rushed back across Slim's room, hit the switch on my way out, and hurried through the hallway toward the glow from the bathroom.

At the top of the stairs, I paused and saw Slim looking up at me.

'Everything okay?' she asked.

'No problem. Your closet light was on.'

'You get it?'

'Yeah.'

'Thanks.'

'I'll be right down,' I said, and entered the bathroom. I started to shut the door, then changed my mind and left it open a few inches so I would be able to hear her . . . in case.

The first thing I did was take off the towel. Naked, I went to the bar where I'd found it. I folded it neatly and hung it up.

Then I crouched over the bathtub. I turned on the water and rinsed the tub, then used toilet paper to wipe some hairs that had collected over the drain. I tossed the paper into the toilet and flushed.

The counter and sink looked fine.

So I put on my shirt, then my socks and shoes.

And stood there, staring down at myself. The tails of my shirt hung down pretty much the same distance on me as Slim's blouse did on her. But there was a difference. Slim had nothing down there capable of sticking out.

I did, and it was.

Slim had already caught a look at it in the laundry room when I lost my towel. Still, I wasn't about to go downstairs this way.

She *said* to leave the towel up here, I reminded myself.

If she can go around in just her blouse, I can go around in this.

What if her mom comes home?

Never mind her mom coming home; in my condition I wouldn't be able to stand in front of Slim for ten seconds without having another accident.

To solve the problem, I took off my shirt. Obviously, I couldn't tie it around my waist by its short sleeves. When I turned my shirt upside-down, however, the corners of the front tails were able to reach around my waist. I tied them together with a half-knot over my left hip. The arrangement looked ridiculous and didn't cover any of my left leg, but it concealed what needed to be hidden. I looked at myself in the mirror and shook my head.

Then I swung open the bathroom door, flicked its light off, and stepped into the hallway.

From the foot of the stairs, Slim grinned up at me. 'Good grief,' she said.

'I had to put your towel back.'

As I trotted down the stairs, she stared at me and kept grinning. 'You could've just *worn* the shirt, you know.'

'I *am*.'

'Up where it belongs.'

'No, I couldn't.'

'I am,' she said.

'I know, but . . .' I shrugged. 'It's different.'

'Chicken.' Though the grin remained on her face, I caught a hint of disappointment in her eyes.

My God, I thought.

Turning away, Slim said, 'We'd better get a move on. I put the knives in the bag with the beers, by the way.'

'Good idea.' I picked up the bag, the two empty beer bottles and Rusty's shirt. Then I followed Slim into the kitchen. She grabbed her purse off the counter and swung its strap over her other shoulder. Then we went outside.

The wind was stronger than before, but warm. It felt good blowing against me. I watched how it flapped and lifted Slim's blouse.

Was she angry with me?

Did she feel cheated because I'd worn the shirt around my waist? Had she hoped to catch glimpses of *me* underneath its tails?

Even as I wondered about it, the rear of her blouse was flipped up by the wind and I saw her pale buttocks.

Then she opened a door and entered the laundry room. I stepped in behind her, pulled the door shut, and followed her through the other door to the main area of the garage.

She stopped at the rear of the Pontiac. With one hand, she reached into her purse. Her hand come out holding a key case. She fumbled with it, found the key she wanted, then bent over and slid it into the keyhole of the trunk.

When the trunk was open, she set her bow inside. She took the quiver off her back and put it into the trunk, too. Then she took the bag from me, set it down near her quiver and bow, and shut the lid.

Next, she opened the driver's door and tossed her purse onto the seat. After closing the door, she said, 'Over here.'

I followed her to a corner of the garage. We stopped at a collection of cardboard cartons containing empty beer and soda bottles. Slim took our two empties from me, knelt down, studied the situation for a while, then found a carton with four vacant openings. She slipped Dad's bottles into two of them.

Grinning up at me, she said, 'That's half the trick.'

I felt half relieved.

We went into the laundry room. The drier was still going, but it stopped when Slim opened its door. Squatting, she reached inside the machine and pulled out my jeans. She felt them here and there. 'I think they're dry. It's hard to tell when they're hot like this. They might still be a little damp.'

'It's okay.'

She handed the jeans up to me. While she reached into the machine to take out her cut-offs and bikini bottoms, I draped my jeans over the top of the washer.

I tugged the half-knot at my hip.

My shirt pulled free.

Slim turned her head and stared up at me.

Even as I felt myself growing and rising, I swung the shirt behind my back, put my arms into its sleeves, pulled it up, drew it together in front and began to fasten its buttons.

A gentle smile spread over Slim's face.

My heart pounded like crazy.

I've lost my mind, I thought.

'Oh, dear,' Slim said. 'Look at you.'

'Sorry.' I snatched my jeans off the washer.

'No. Don't put them on yet.'

'But . . .'

'Just wait.'

While I waited, Slim stood up. She put her bikini pants and cut-off jeans on top of the drier. Then she leaned over the machine and twisted a knob – to shut it off, I guess.

Coming toward me, she said, 'I know a way to get rid of that.'

'Get rid of what?'

'That.' Her eyes went to it.

'You do?'

There was mischief in her smile. 'I know many things.'

'Jeez.'

She squatted in front of me.

Oh, my God! She's gonna blow me!

My heart hammered. 'I don't know, Slim.'

She tilted back her head and smiled up at me. 'It'll be all right. We don't want you messing up your clean jeans, do we?'

'No, but . . .'

She raised her hand toward me.

Okay. Not the same as her mouth, but still . . .

Her middle finger curled down. She caught it under her thumb and let fly, thumping the tip of my erection.

'*Ow!!!*' I cried out.

Chapter Thirty-seven

Sitting in the passenger seat of the Pontiac on the way to my house, I gave Slim a dirty look. She grinned at me. In the darkness, she couldn't have seen much of the look I'd given her, or known what I was thinking. But she said, 'It worked, didn't it?'

She *did* know what I was thinking. 'Yeah, but jeez!'

'You're fine.'

'Easy for you to say, you're not the one who got thumped.'

'I've had a few thumps.'

Remembering Jimmy Drake, I decided not to pursue the subject.

'The car's working good,' I said.

'She's a peach,' Slim said, and patted the steering wheel.

That's what her grandmother used to say about the car, *She's a peach.*

Up to the moment of her grandma's demise, it had been the old woman's car and nobody else had been allowed to drive it. Slim's mother used the hot little MG that had belonged to Jimmy. (Apparently, he'd gone on his mysterious trip without it.)

Slim, however, hated everything about Jimmy, including his car. *Especially* his car. Before going away, he often forced her to take rides with him. He drove her to secluded places and did terrible things to her.

After Jimmy's departure, Slim refused to go anywhere in the MG Her grandmother drove her in the Pontiac when she *had* to have a ride. Otherwise, she did her travelling by foot. This was fine with Slim. I think, if she'd gotten herself stranded in the middle of Death Valley and her mother came to the rescue in Jimmy's old MG, Slim would've shaken her head and told her, 'Thanks anyway, I'd rather walk.'

When her grandmother died, Slim lost her transportation. Her mother continued to use Jimmy's car, while the Pontiac sat unused in the garage. It seems that Slim's mother wanted nothing to do with *that* car. Who knows why? Maybe she simply enjoyed the nice little MG, even if it *had* belonged to a bastard like Jimmy. Or maybe awful things had happened to her in the Pontiac – or *nice* things that were too painful for her, now that her mother was dead.

Like I say, who knows?

Whatever the reason, the Pontiac got itself abandoned in the garage. It sat there for almost a year.

A few months before the Travelling Vampire Show came to town, Rusty and I went over to Slim's house on a hot, sunny morning, figuring the three of us might head over to the river. The MG wasn't in the driveway, so Slim's mom was probably away. Slim might've been gone, too, but we knew she hadn't taken off with her mother. Not in the MG.

We knocked on the front door, but nobody answered. So then we went around back. The garage door was open. We found Slim in the driver's seat of her grandmother's big green Pontiac, gazing through the windshield. When she heard us coming, she turned her head and smiled. 'Hey, guys,' she said out the open window.

'Hi,' I said.

'What's up?' Rusty asked.

'Not much. Hop in.'

While Rusty nodded and eyed the back door, I hurried around to the other side and climbed into the front seat. Leaving the door open for Rusty, I scooted to the middle.

Slim was in her a T-shirt and cut-off jeans. Her legs looked tan and smooth. Her feet were bare. The way she looked made me feel great. So did the smell of her. I sighed and smiled. 'What're you doing?' I asked.

She shrugged. 'Just thinking,' she said.

Rusty scooted in beside me. 'Gonna take her for a spin?'

When he said that, I noticed the key in the ignition.

'Not today.'

'Come on, Dagny, let's see what she'll do.'

Leaning toward the wheel, she looked at Rusty. 'It's Slim,' she said. 'Slim, not Dagny.'

This was the first we'd heard of it.

'*Slim?*' Rusty asked. 'All of a sudden you're Slim? What happened to Dagny?'

She shrugged, smiled, and said, 'Now I'm Slim, that's all.'

'If you say so,' Rusty said.

I said, 'Fine with me. Any name you want's fine with me.'

Rusty went, '*Oooooo.*'

Ignoring him, I said, 'Anyway, Slim, want to come with us to the river? Maybe we can take a canoe out, or—'

'Forget it, man,' Rusty interrupted. 'Let's go for a spin!'

'Can't,' Slim said.

'Sure we can.'

'A,' she said, 'I don't know how to drive. B, I don't have a driver's license. C, two of the tires are flat. D . . .' she twisted the ignition key. It triggered a few dismal clicking sounds, then nothing.

Rusty muttered, 'Crap.'

'Dead battery?' I said.

Slim nodded. 'That's what I think, too.' Frowning, she stared out the windshield. One of her hands idly stroked the steering wheel, which was sheathed in leopard skin.

You don't see leopard-skin steering-wheel covers too much anymore. In fact, the last one I remember seeing was on

Slim's grandmother's Pontiac. Back in those days, steering-wheel covers weren't at all uncommon. Old people seemed especially fond of them. When you saw a leopard-skin cover on a steering wheel, you could pretty much bet that the car was owned by an old woman.

Anyway, Slim lightly stroked the leopard skin along the top curve of the wheel while she concentrated on her thoughts. After a while, she said, 'I don't know much about cars.'

Rusty let out a laugh.

She leaned forward, looked past me and frowned at him.

'Thought you knew *everything*,' he said.

'I know more than you, numbnuts.'

'Hah!'

'But not about this.'

'Whatcha mean, J.D. Salinger don't teach you how to fix a car?'

Ignoring Rusty's crack, she gave the key another twist. Silence.

'How about Ayn Rand!' Rusty called out. 'Why don't you look up "dead batteries" in *Alice Shrugged*.'

I gave him a shot with my elbow.

'Ow!' He grabbed his arm. 'Damn it!'

'It's *Atlas*,' Slim said. 'Not Alice. Anyway, are you guys interested in helping me fix the car? My mom wants nothing to do with it. She'll just let it sit here forever. But if we can get it running, it's as good as mine. I can get my driver's license and then we can drive *all over* the place.'

'I'll teach you how to drive,' I said, really eager.

'Great.'

I pictured the two of us roaming the back roads together, just as Lee and I had done the previous summer when I was learning to drive in her pickup truck.

'What about me?' Rusty asked.

'You don't have a license,' I pointed out.

'Who cares? I'm a great driver. We can *both* teach her.'

I'd seen samples of Rusty's driving prowess a few times after he had 'borrowed' his family car in the middle of the night. We'd been lucky to live. For various reasons, we'd never told Slim about the excursions, so she had no idea what a lousy, dangerous driver Rusty was.

Shaking my head, I muttered, 'I don't know.'

Slim patted my thigh and said, 'If we get this baby going, you can *both* be my teachers. We'll drive all over the place! It'll be great!'

So we didn't go to the river that day. We worked on the Pontiac, instead.

Apparently, Slim's grandmother had kept it in fine shape while she was alive. Its troubles were mostly the result of the car not being used for almost a year.

Rusty really came through. He figured out all the problems as we went along. Slim and I provided money to buy whatever he suggested: some new belts and hoses, mostly, but also a new battery. He installed them. He also patched the flat tires.

Within a week, we had the Pontiac running.

On back roads outside the town limits, Slim drove. Rusty and I took turns sitting beside her, giving instructions, once in a while grabbing the wheel to keep us on course. We had a few close shaves, but no accidents.

After about two weeks, Slim was driving as well as anyone I'd ever known . . . and a zillion times better than Rusty. Her mom took her over to the DMV in Clarksburg. A couple of hours later, she came back with her temporary driver's license.

There was no stopping us, then. Slim behind the wheel (and sometimes me or Rusty), hardly a day went by when we didn't go for a drive someplace. We had already explored most of the nearby back roads, so we hit every town within fifty miles of Grandville. We followed the roads that ran alongside the river, stopping whenever we felt like wandering around on foot or taking a swim. At night, sometimes we cruised downtown Grandville. Once a week, we took the Pontiac to the drive-in movie show. We were having ourselves a fine time until about the middle of July.

That's when the Moonlight Drive-in had its very first 'ALL-NIGHT SHOCKFEST'. From sunset till dawn, the drive-in out on Mason Road would be showing one horror movie after another.

We wanted to go and stay for the entire event.

Not a chance.

Even though Slim would be driving and everyone trusted her, we were ordered to be home by midnight. By 'we' I mean me and Slim. Both my parents were pretty strict about that sort of thing, and so was Slim's mother, Rusty's parents thought of themselves as strict, too, but they were easy to fool. Rusty could've tricked them and stayed out all night, no problem. He had no reason to do it, though, since Slim and I both had to be back by twelve.

Our parents thought they were being generous, giving us till midnight.

We didn't see it that way. They *always* let us stay out till midnight when we went to the drive-in. But this wasn't just the usual double-feature – this was the first ALL-NIGHT SHOCKFEST. *Six* different horror movies would be shown and we wanted to see them all.

Thanks to our midnight deadline, we would only have time to watch two of them.

Didn't seem fair.

We pushed for one o'clock, figuring we might get in three of the movies. That would at least be *half* of them. Getting to see half sounded pretty good.

But my parents wouldn't go along with it. Therefore, neither would Slim's mother.

Midnight. Take it or leave it.

Midnight, it seems, is the magic hour for parents. Somewhere along the line, maybe someone was too impressed by *Cinderella*. Or maybe midnight was when the gates of the city got locked, back in the old days when cities *had* gates. More than likely, the fixation on being home by midnight had primitive, superstitious origins. Midnight, the witching hour, 'when churchyards yawn' and all that. Who knows?

I do know this. The need to be home by midnight was what got us into trouble . . . the fact that we left the drive-in exactly when we did.

Chapter Thirty-eight

We arrived at the Moonlight Drive-in early enough to find a parking place fairly close to the screen. Though the sun had already gone down, it wasn't quite dark enough yet for the movies to start. 'Big Girls Don't Cry' was coming from the speaker box on the post beside our car. Kids were still playing on the swings and slide and teeter-totters below the giant screen.

We had plenty of time for a trip to the snack bar, where we bought Cokes and hot dogs and buttered popcorn. Back at the car, I took the driver's seat. Slim sat beside me, and Rusty sat by her other side. 'Walk Like A Man' was playing on the speaker. I leaned out the window, grabbed the metal box off its post and brought it inside. I cranked the window up a few inches and hung the speaker over its edge. And we were all set.

About ten minutes later, the Shockfest began.

The first movie turned out to be *A Bucket of Blood*. It's about this goony beatnik who wants to be an artist, but he's no good at it. Then he accidentally kills a cat, which was pretty funny in an awful way. To conceal the cat's body, he covers it with clay. Presto! He has himself a perfectly good sculpture. Everybody's amazed by how detailed and lifelike it is. Knowing a good thing when he sees it, he starts murdering gals and covering *their* bodies with clay.

We loved it. We kept laughing and going, '*Oh, no!*' But it scared us, too. A couple of times, Slim grabbed my leg and squeezed it.

After *A Bucket of Blood* was over, we went to the restrooms. We also paid another visit to the snack bar, where we picked up boxes of Juicy Fruits, Good 'n' Plenty and Milk Duds.

The second show was *The Killer Shrews* and even scarier than *A Bucket of Blood*. Shrews are supposedly the fiercest creatures in the world, but they're so small they don't go after people. *These* shrews, though, were the size of dogs. (Looking back on it, I'm pretty sure they *were* dogs.) They kept trying to get at a group of people stranded on this island. Wanted to rip them up and eat them. The people took refuge inside a house and boarded up the place to keep the shrews out. But the damn things kept getting in, anyway. It was pretty horrible. Several of the people got themselves eaten.

When I saw *Night of the Living Dead* a few years later, it reminded me of *The Killer Shrews* . . . and of what happened after we left the drive-in. I found myself reminded of that night about a zillion times because the main actor in *The*

Killer Shrews turned out to be Festus in *Gunsmoke*. After
Chester got replaced by Festus, I could hardly ever watch
Gunsmoke without thinking about *The Killer Shrews* and what
happened on the way home.

At about eleven-thirty, the movie ended. An intermission started, and the area around the snack stand lit up.
Here and there, headlights came on and engines started.
Apparently, we weren't the only people who needed to get
home.

Since I was already behind the wheel, I asked Slim, 'Want
me to take us back?'

She was *supposed* to do all the driving that night. In fact,
she always drove us to and from the drive-in movies. But I
figured it would be easier if we just stayed in our seats and I
took the wheel.

Slim didn't answer for a few seconds. Then she said, 'We
told everyone *I'd* be driving.'

'Yeah, true. Maybe you'd better.'

'I suppose so.'

Leaning out the window, I reached over and hooked the
speaker box onto its pole. Then I brought myself back into
the car and opened the door.

And realized my mistake. If I went around to the other
side of the car so Slim could scoot over behind the wheel, I
would end up sitting next to Rusty on the way home.

I wanted to sit next to Slim, not Rusty.

'What's wrong?' she asked.

I couldn't tell her. We were pals, buddies, best friends. If
she found out I *needed* to sit next to her, she might realize
how I really felt. It might scare her.

'Nothing,' I said. 'I'm fine.'

'Are you sure? If you really *want* to drive . . .'

'Nah, that's okay.' I climbed out and shut the door. Starting
to feel lousy, I walked around to the other side. By the time

I reached the passenger door, Slim and Rusty had both scooted over.

I sat beside Rusty and swung the door shut.

Leaving the headlights off, Slim drove slowly forward down the slope of the hump from which we'd viewed the movies. At the bottom, she made a sharp turn onto the cross-lane.

She put on the parking lights. A couple of times, she stopped to let people walk by. At the end of the lane, she waited for a car to pass us before she pulled out.

She didn't cut anyone off. She didn't do anything wrong or even rude. Neither did Rusty or I.

In fact, we're pretty sure that what happened a few minutes later had nothing to do with any of the cars from the drive-in. Those exiting ahead of us had all turned the other way at Mason Road. And none came out after us. None that we noticed, anyway.

For a while, Slim's Pontiac seemed to be the only car on the road. We were about ten miles north of town, midway between Grandville and Clarksburg.

We had forest on the right.

On the left was the old graveyard. If it had a name, we didn't know it. Nobody'd been buried there since about 1920. We'd explored it a few times, though never at night. It had a lot of very cool tombstones and statues and stuff.

Driving by, the three of us snuck glances at it the way we usually did. I think we wanted to make sure nobody was digging up bodies . . . or crawling out of any graves.

No one was.

But a car sat between the old stone posts of its entry gate.

A car without any lights on.

'Uh-oh,' Slim said. I felt our speed decrease slightly. 'Was that a cop car?'

'Didn't look like one,' Rusty said.

'It wasn't,' I confirmed. Being the son of Grandville's police chief, I knew what every cop car looked like: not just ours, but those of all the nearby towns, plus the county cars and state cars.

'Thought it might be a speed trap,' Slim said.

'Nope,' I told her.

'Cool place to make out,' Rusty said.

Slim and I both laughed.

'Don't you think?'

'No,' Slim said. 'For one thing, it's right by the road where everyone can see you. Not to mention the *bone* orchard. You wouldn't catch *me* making out there.'

'Wouldn't catch *you* making any . . .' Rusty tipped his head back and stared at the rearview mirror.

'What?' Slim asked.

'I think it's coming,' he said.

'Huh?' Slim glanced at the rearview mirror. 'I don't . . . oh.'

I was already looking over my shoulder and knew why she'd said, 'Oh.' A car was coming, all right, but without headlights on. It looked like a clump of shadow hurling toward us from the rear.

'That the car from the graveyard?' Slim asked.

'Think so,' Rusty said.

Slim groaned.

Rusty and I both looked over our shoulders.

Rusty muttered, 'Shit.'

By the velocity of the car's approach, I expected it to swerve and zip around us. But it didn't. It stayed behind us. Just when I expected it to slam into our tail, Slim hit the gas. We shot forward, the sudden acceleration pushing me into the seat.

The other car shrank into the distance, then started to grow. It looked like a big old black Cadillac.

'Here it comes,' I said.

'What's the *matter* with that bastard?' Slim blurted.

'You'd better get moving,' Rusty told her.

'I *am* moving.'

'Faster.'

We picked up more speed. The Cadillac quit growing. It didn't shrink away, either. It matched our speed and stayed about twenty feet behind us.

Moonlight glinted on its hood and windshield. I couldn't see inside it.

Slim said, 'I don't like this.'

She rounded a bend in the road too fast. The tires sighed. As the forces pulled at me, I grabbed the door handle to keep myself from leaning into Rusty. He let himself tilt against Slim. She muttered, 'Get off me,' and shoved at him with her elbow.

I looked back. The Cadillac was still on our tail.

'I'm slowing down,' Slim said and took her foot off the gas.

'Here it comes,' I warned.

I braced for the impact. There wasn't one. When I looked back again, the car was no more than two feet from our rear. But the space seemed to be growing.

'Looks like they don't want to hit us,' I said.

'What *do* they want?' Slim asked.

I shook my head.

Rusty said, 'Maybe they're just trying to scare us.'

'If that's all,' Slim said, 'they've succeeded. They can go home now.'

'Could be anything,' I said.

'*Is* it the car from the graveyard?' Slim asked.

'You got me,' I said.

'I think so,' said Rusty.

'*It* looked like it might've just been sitting there *waiting* for us.'

'Or for *some*one,' I said. 'Maybe just waiting for *any*one to go by.'

Her voice low and steady, Slim said, 'Either way, we're it.'

'Long as all they do is follow us . . .' Rusty muttered.

'We'll get to town pretty soon,' I said.

'We're not *that* close,' Slim pointed out.

'Five minutes?'

'More like ten,' Rusty said.

'Who do you think they are?' Slim asked.

'God knows,' I muttered.

'How about Scotty or one of those guys?' Rusty suggested.

'They wouldn't dare,' Slim said.

'They'd *love* to nail us,' I said.

'Yeah, but they know what'll happen if they try.'

'You wouldn't happen to have your bow handy, would you?' Rusty asked.

'No. But they don't know that.'

'I almost hope it *is* Scotty,' I said.

'As opposed to whom?' Slim asked.

'I don't know. Some creep like Starkweather or . . .'

'Hey,' Rusty said. 'Maybe it's an *artist* and he wants to make us into statues. Slap some clay on us . . .'

'*Crap!*' Slim cried out.

Startled, I leaned past Rusty and looked at Slim. Her head was turned away, her short hair blowing. Just as I noticed the engine noises growing louder, the dark shape of the Cadillac filled her side window. It was no more than three feet away, in the lane for oncoming traffic.

So far, there *was* no oncoming traffic.

The big car stayed beside us. Its windows were rolled up. I tried to see through them, but couldn't.

Slowly, the front passenger window began to lower.

'*Watch out!*' I yelled.

Slim hit the brakes. We were thrown forward in our seats

and the Cadillac burst ahead. It zoomed up the road for a few seconds, then cut back into our lane.

Its brake lights came on, bright red in the darkness.

'Oh, shit,' Rusty muttered.

'Shit is right,' Slim said.

We stopped dead in our lane.

The Cadillac, about fifty yards ahead of us, also seemed to be stopped.

Its red brake lights went out.

Slim shut off our headlights and darkness slammed down on us.

At the rear of the Cadillac, white lights came on.

'Back-up lights,' I muttered.

They began moving slowly toward us.

'Here it comes,' Slim whispered.

'I don't feel so good,' Rusty said.

'What'll we do?' I asked.

Nobody said anything.

The car continued to back up. About ten feet in front of us, it stopped. All its lights went dark. It sat there.

And sat there.

'If anyone else comes along . . .' I said.

'We'll see their headlights,' Slim said. 'I'll get us out of the way.'

'Speaking of which,' said Rusty, 'where *is* everyone?'

'Still at the movies,' Slim explained.

'That's where *we* oughta be,' I said. 'We wouldn't be in this fix if we'd stayed for the whole thing.'

'Parents,' Rusty muttered as if it were a curse word.

Slim chuckled softly, then added, 'I guess we'll have the last laugh if we end up getting killed.'

'We'll be all right,' I said. 'They obviously aren't gonna ram us, or they would've done it by now. The thing is . . .' I wasn't sure how to say it.

'What?' Slim asked.

'If someone gets out of the car . . .'

She leaned forward and looked at me. 'Someone gets out and tries to come for us on foot, he'll have to deal with Chief Pontiac.'

'Gonna run him over?' Rusty asked.

'If he needs it.'

We waited.

The Cadillac sat in front of us, dark, its doors shut.

Slim looked at her wristwatch. 'I know his game,' she said. 'He's trying to make us late.'

'What time is it?' I asked.

'Quarter till twelve.'

'We can still make it.'

'Not if we keep sitting here.'

'If we're late,' I said, 'my dad's gonna kill me.'

That got a pretty good laugh from Slim and Rusty.

Then Slim said softly as if speaking to herself, 'Let's just see what happens,' and stepped on the gas. As we bolted from a standstill, she cut into the other lane.

The Cadillac sprang forward and swung to the left, blocking us.

Slim hit her brakes and swerved to the right.

The Cadillac swerved and blocked us again.

We stopped. It stopped.

We sat there in the dark, ten feet apart.

'Screw this,' Slim said. She threw her door open.

'What're you *doing*?' I yelled.

'Stay here.' She started to climb out.

'Grab her!'

Rusty didn't even try. Either he knew better than to interfere with Slim or he was eager for her to handle the situation.

Slim dodged her open door and headed for the Cadillac, taking long, quick strides. I jumped out. 'Wait!' I called.

She stopped and waved me away. 'Get back in the car,' she said.

'Slim!'

She whirled away and walked straight to the driver's door of the Cadillac.

I felt my stomach drop as she bent over and knocked on the window.

'Get away from there!' I called.

She knocked again. 'Hey!' she yelled.

I hurried between the two cars. Glancing toward ours, I saw that Rusty had scooted over. He now sat in the driver's seat.

Slim was still leaning toward the window of the Cadillac. As I stepped around its rear, she said, 'What's going on, mister?' From her tone of voice, I figured the window must be open. 'Why're you—'

She suddenly tried to leap backward, but a hand shot out and grabbed the front of her T-shirt. It jerked hard. With a gasp, she stumbled forward and her head plunged into the open window.

'*NO!*' she squealed.

I ran toward her.

Watching.

Not wanting to believe my eyes.

Slim was inside the window to her shoulders, squirming and kicking, shoving at the window frame with her left hand to keep herself from being dragged in.

Her right arm was already inside the car.

I hit her hard in the midsection.

Tore her out of the window.

Tackled her.

Landed on top of her, smashing her against the pavement, where we almost got run over by the Pontiac. 'Get in!' Rusty yelled. The passenger door flew open. 'Get in! Quick!'

I scurried up, pulling at Slim. I hurled her into the front seat. Already in motion, the car started to take off without me. I chased it, running in the V of its open door. 'Hey!' I yelled.

Rusty slowed down and I dived in.

Next thing I knew, we were speeding toward town.

I leaned out and pulled the door shut. Panting for air, I sat up straight.

Rusty was stoked. 'Holy jumpin' Jesus!' he said. 'Wow! Jeez! Did you see that? They *grabbed* her. Holy shit! Couldn't believe it! Shit!' He slapped Slim on the thigh. 'They almost got you.'

Slim quit gasping for breath long enough to say, 'Tell me about it.'

'You all right?' I asked her.

'I'm here. That's what counts. Thanks, guys.'

'No sweat,' said Rusty.

Twisting my head, I looked out the rear window. The road behind us looked empty. 'I don't see 'em,' I said.

'Me, neither,' said Rusty.

'When they come, don't stop. Don't stop for anything.'

'You betcha!'

'They won't,' Slim said. 'They won't be coming.' She lifted her right hand and jangled a bunch of keys.

'Holy shit!' Rusty said.

'You got their *car* keys.'

'It was easy.'

As Rusty raced into town that night, Slim told us that there'd been two men in the car: one behind the wheel and another in the passenger seat. They were strangers to her.

She described them to us – and ten minutes later to my father – as being about thirty years old, white, slender, with crew cuts. They were dressed in blue jeans and white T-shirts. Though she'd only seen them in the darkness for a few seconds, she was fairly certain that the two men were identical twins.

Dad drove off to look for them.

By the time he got out to Mason Road, however, the Cadillac was gone, along with the twins who'd tried to take Slim.

They weren't found during the weeks that followed, either.

Maybe they'd just been 'passing through' and were long gone.

But we were afraid they might be out there, somewhere.

We didn't talk about it much. Hardly ever. Probably because all three of us had a pretty good idea about what they would've done to Slim if they'd taken her away in their Cadillac. We didn't want to think about it.

Especially since they might make another try for her.

We knew their car.

And they knew ours.

After that night, I kept a sharp eye out for dark Cadillacs. I'm pretty sure we all did, though we didn't talk about it.

And our car – Slim's – remained in the garage for almost a month after our close call on the way home from the Shockfest. It didn't come out again until the night of the Travelling Vampire Show.

Chapter Thirty-nine

Slim waited in the driveway while I ran into my house and placed the two full bottles of beer in the refrigerator. I was almost weak with relief as I hurried back to her car.

I climbed into the passenger seat. 'That's it,' I said.

'Beautiful,' she said. 'Pulled that off without a hitch.'

We looked at each other and grinned.

Then she backed out of the driveway and steered for Rusty's house. 'When we get there,' she said, 'maybe you'd better go in without me.'

'You sure?' I was hoping to have her there for moral support.

'I can do without Rusty's mom and dad. Besides, they'll start asking me a lot of questions if I go in. I'm sure they must've heard about my "disappearance".'

'Probably.' The real reason she wouldn't go into the house with me, I figured, was because she didn't want Rusty's parents to see how she was dressed. They were used to seeing her in T-shirts, not fancy blouses. Plus, her shiny, long-sleeved blouse didn't exactly go with her ragged cut-off jeans. Rusty's mom and dad were sure to wonder why she'd dressed so strangely.

'Just say we're in a hurry and I'm waiting in the car.'

I nodded. With Slim waiting in the car, *I* might be able to get out of the house faster.

Too soon, we reached Rusty's house. Slim pulled up to the curb and stopped. 'I'll even leave the engine running,' she said.

'*Sure* you don't want to come in?' I asked.

'You'll be fine.'

'Okay. See ya.'

I climbed out of the car. Somebody must've been watching for us, though, because the front door opened before I could get there. Bitsy came out. Rusty, still in the doorway, called 'We're going now!' to his parents.

An answer came from somewhere inside the house, but I couldn't make it out.

Rusty shut the door.

All *right*! I wouldn't have to face the parents, after all.

As Rusty followed his sister down the porch stairs, I said, 'Hi, Bitsy.'

Smiling and looking shy, she said, 'Hi, Dwight. Thank you for inviting me to the movies.'

'Oh, you're welcome. Glad to have you.'

She had dressed up for the occasion. Instead of her usual T-shirt and cut-off jeans, she was wearing a sleeveless sundress. Instead of being barefoot, she wore sandals. Hanging from one shoulder was a white, patent leather purse.

'You look very nice tonight,' I said. What was I *supposed* to say?

'Thank you, Dwight.'

'You're a life-saver,' Rusty told me.

'No sweat.'

He hurried ahead. I'd left the passenger door open. He climbed in. Smiling at me, he said, 'Maybe you two lovebirds should sit together in the back.'

'That was the plan,' I said.

Sure it was.

I opened the back door and held it for Bitsy. Then I got in and shut the door.

'Hey, Slim,' Rusty said.

'Hey, Rusty.' Looking over her shoulder, she said, 'How you doing, Bitsy?'

273

'Oh, just fine, thank you. Thank you for asking me to come with.'

'Our pleasure,' Slim told her. Facing forward again, she took off.

Bitsy smiled at me from her side of the back seat, but didn't try to come any closer. 'I'm sorry to hear about your father's accident,' she said.

Thanks for reminding me, I thought.

'Thanks,' I said.

'Is he going to be all right?'

'I guess so. They're just keeping him overnight in the hospital to be on the safe side.'

'I'm sure that's a good idea.'

'Hey, Bitsy?' Slim said.

'Yes?'

'We're stopping by Lee Thompson's house before we head over to the drive-in.'

'Really? What for?'

'Don't be such a nosy pain in the ass,' Rusty said.

I said, 'Leave her alone' at about the same moment Slim said, 'Cut it out, Rusty.'

Even though there wasn't much light in the back, enough came in through the windows for me see Bitsy turn her head toward Rusty and cast a self-satisfied smile in his direction. I saw the smile, but he didn't. He was looking straight ahead.

To Bitsy, I explained, 'My brother's out of town for the weekend. We just want to drop in on Lee and make sure she's okay.'

'Is something wrong?'

'A lot of weird stuff's been going on today,' Slim said.

'Like what?'

'Come *on*, guys,' Rusty said, a pleading whine in his voice. 'She *tells*. I don't want my mom and dad knowing *all* my business.'

'I won't tell,' Bitsy said.

'Bullshit,' Rusty said.

Slim stopped the car. Looking out the window, I saw that we were at the curb in front of Lee's house. Her pickup truck was parked in the driveway.

The windows of her house were dark.

'Doesn't look like she's home,' Rusty said.

'I'll go see.' I opened my door.

'I'm coming with you,' Rusty said, opening his.

'Me too,' said Bitsy.

Slim shrugged, shut off the engine and killed the headlights. Moments later, all four of us were walking toward the front door of Lee's house.

'Did Lee *go* somewhere?' Rusty asked in a hushed voice.

'We don't know,' Slim said.

'It's funny the lights are off,' I muttered.

'Maybe she's taking a nap,' Rusty said.

'We tried to call a couple of times,' I told him. 'I don't think she could have slept through the ringing.'

'Might've,' Slim said. 'But not likely.'

On the front stoop, I reached for the doorbell but Rusty grabbed my wrist. 'Don't,' he whispered. 'What if somebody's *in* there?'

'Like who?'

'You know. Like *them*.'

'You mean Julian?' I asked.

'Yeah. Or some of his gang.'

'Who's Julian?' Bitsy asked.

Slim went, 'Shhhh.'

When I lowered my arm, Rusty released my wrist. I stepped up to the screen door, put my nose against it, then cupped my hands on both sides of my eyes to block out the faint glow of light from the street.

I could just barely see in.

The main door was wide open. Beyond it, I saw only blackness and shades of gray.

'*LEE!*' I shouted, startling everyone.

Rusty gasped. Bitsy sucked in a quick breath, making a high-pitched '*Uh!*' Slim grabbed my arm but didn't make any noise.

Only silence came from inside the house.

Though I hated to raise my voice again, I yelled, '*LEE! YOU HOME? IT'S DWIGHT!*'

After my shout, a long silence.

Rusty broke it, whispering, 'Maybe she went over to a neighbor's.'

'Maybe.'

'Who's Julian?' Bitsy asked again.

'From the vampire show,' Slim said.

Bitsy did that '*Uh!*' again.

'Tell her *everything*, why don't you!' Rusty burst out in an angry whisper.

'I'm going in,' I said.

Slim, still gripping my arm, gave it a squeeze. 'Wait here. I'll be right back.' Then she let go, whirled around and ran back to her Pontiac. Bending over behind it, she opened its trunk.

'What's she doing?' Bitsy asked.

Slim reached into the trunk, then took a step away from it and swung her quiver of arrows behind her back.

Rusty groaned.

'What?' Bitsy demanded.

'Nothing.'

Slim bent over the trunk again. This time, she came up with her bow in one hand. I couldn't exactly see what she had in her other hand, but knew it must be the two knives.

She came running toward us, leaped up the stairs and lurched to a halt. 'Here, you guys.' She held out the knives. Rusty took the sheath knife and I took the pocket knife.

'What's going on?' Bitsy asked.

'Why don't you go and wait in the car?' Rusty said.

'Fat chance.'

'Go on. It might be dangerous.'

'So?' Turning to me, she said, 'I don't have to wait in the car, do I?'

'Might be a good idea,' I said.

Slim gave a quick shake of her head. 'We don't really want her in the car by herself.'

'No,' said Bitsy. 'We don't.'

'If you stay,' Rusty told her, 'you've got to do everything we tell you to.'

'I'm not taking orders from *you*.'

'Just stick with us,' Slim told her, then whipped an arrow out of her quiver, fit it onto her bowstring and drew the string back a few inches.

'Who's *in* there?' Bitsy asked.

'We don't know,' I said. 'Maybe nobody.'

Rusty put his face close to Bitsy's. 'Maybe a *vampire*!'

She straightened her back. 'No such thing.'

'Keep telling yourself that, squirt.'

'There *isn't*.'

'Let's go,' Slim said. 'Me first. Dwight, you wanta get the door?'

First, I opened the pocket knife. Holding it in my right hand, I used my left to pull open the screen door.

Slim walked in. Rusty followed, staying close to her back. Bitsy went into the house behind him. I took up the rear and eased the screen door silently shut.

In the foyer, we stopped moving. We listened.

There were a few quiet sounds of the sort that houses

always make: creaks, clicks, hums and buzzes from some sort of appliances. I heard breathing sounds and hoped they came only from us.

Slim's black shirt moved like a shadow in the darkness. She seemed to be swiveling slowly, scanning the living room, ready to shoot.

All of a sudden, my left arm got grabbed. I flinched and gasped, then realized it was only Bitsy.

Only.

She clung to my arm with both hands and pressed her body against it as if she'd mistaken my arm for a pole she hoped to climb. My upper arm was clasped against one of her breasts so tightly that the small, soft mound seemed to be mashed flat. My forearm was pressed to her belly. I could feel her heartbeat and breathing. She wore a flowery perfume so sweet I almost gagged.

It wasn't the same as having Slim pressed again me.

I resisted the urge to push her away.

'Somebody get a light,' Slim whispered.

'Let go,' I told Bitsy.

She held on. I made my way toward a wall switch, anyway, with Bitsy still clinging to me. When I got within reach of where a switch should be, I said, 'Let go. Come on, I need my arm.'

At last, she released me.

Without her body mashed against it, my arm felt strangely cool. I raised it and flicked a light switch. Two lamps came on in the living room, one at each end of the sofa.

No Lee.

No strangers.

No one at all.

Everything looked just the same as usual.

'Okay,' Slim whispered, 'let's check the rest of the house.'

Again, she led the way, walking slowly, her bow partly drawn back, ready to let an arrow fly if we should come under attack.

Chapter Forty

We made our way through the entire house, turning on lights in every room, looking in closets, glancing behind furniture and drapes. In the bedroom, I dropped and peered into the space between the bed and the floor while Rusty checked the adjoining bathroom.

Lee was nowhere to be found.

Nobody seemed to be in the house except the four of us.

Done with our search, we returned to the living room. Slim swung her arrow over her shoulder and dropped it into her quiver. Rusty sank onto the sofa. I folded my knife shut and stuffed it into a front pocket of my jeans.

'Can we go to the movies now?' Bitsy asked.

We all looked at her.

She frowned. 'What?'

'We're worried about Lee,' Slim exlained.

'Don't you think she just *went* someplace? I mean, people *go* places. We don't want to miss the movies, do we?'

'Screw the movies,' Rusty said. 'We were never gonna go to the movies anyway.'

'Were, too.' She gave me a betrayed look. 'We were, weren't we? You *said* so.'

I nodded to Bitsy, but spoke to Rusty. 'We figured to head on out to the Moonlight and take in the first one, anyway.'

'Why not both?' Bitsy asked.

'We're supposed to be back here by ten-thirty...'

'*Dwight!*' Rusty blurted.

'We might as well tell her the truth.'

'She'll *tell* on us.'

'Will not,' she protested.

'Like hell.'

Slim said to Bitsy, 'This has to be a secret, okay? We've let you come along tonight, but if you ever want to do anything with us again...'

'Ever in your whole life,' Rusty added.

'...you'll have to keep quiet about what goes on. We can't have you going home and telling your parents about everything we do.'

'About *any*thing we do,' Rusty said.

Bitsy raised her right hand as if taking an oath. 'I promise.'

Looking disgusted, Rusty shook his head and muttered, 'She'll tell.'

'Will not.'

I gave Slim the nod.

She nodded in return, then said to Bitsy, 'We think somebody's after us. Maybe someone from the Travelling Vampire Show.'

'What for?'

'To shut us up,' Rusty said.

'We don't really know what they're up to,' Slim explained. 'I saw them... do something horrible to a dog today. Maybe they want to scare us into keeping quiet about it. The thing is, weird stuff has been happening ever since. Someone was in my house this afternoon. They chewed up a book in my bedroom...'

'Like a dog,' Rusty added.

'The book was *Dracula*,' Slim pointed out. 'Which is about vampires.'

'Not that we think a vampire did it,' I said.

'But maybe someone from the show. Also, there was this flower vase in my mother's room. It had yellow roses in it. Somebody broke the vase and took the roses. Then one of the roses turned up in Dwight's room.'

'At *your* house?' Bitsy asked me, looking shocked.

I nodded. 'They put it on my pillow.'

'Now Lee's missing,' Slim continued. 'She and Dwight drove over to Janks Field this morning looking for me and Rusty, and they talked to the main guy of the vampire show.'

'Julian Stryker,' I said.

'Lee bought tickets for tonight's performance, but she paid with a check. The check had her name and address on it. So Julian and his bunch had an easy way to find out where she lives.'

'You think they *took* her?' Bitsy asked.

The question made me go cold inside.

'We don't know,' Slim said.

'She ain't *here*,' Rusty added.

'But there're no signs of foul play.' I wanted to talk myself and the others out of believing that Lee had been taken away.

'Not unless you count the open door,' Slim said.

'She might've left it like that for the breeze,' I said. 'Anyway, she isn't expecting us for a couple more hours, so maybe she *did* go somewhere.'

'Without her truck?' Slim asked.

'She might've walked over to—'

'Without her purse?'

'Purse?' I asked.

'It's on a counter in the kitchen.'

'I saw it,' Bitsy threw in.

Slim said, 'I think Lee would've taken it with her if she'd gone off on her own.'

'*You* hardly ever take a purse with you,' I pointed out.

'Yeah, well . . . I'm a little different. Most women take their purses *every*where.'

'Maybe she took a different one,' I said. 'She has more than one.'

'Let's have a look,' Slim said.

All of us followed her into the kitchen. Nodding at Lee's brown leather purse, she said to me, 'Why don't you do the honors? You're family.'

'Sure.' I moved Lee's purse from the counter to the kitchen table, where the light was better. Then I frowned at Slim. 'Do you really think we oughta do this? It's sort of invading her privacy.'

'*I'll* look,' Rusty volunteered.

'No you won't,' I said. 'We don't need *you* going through her stuff.'

'Oh, yeah? What's . . .?' He shut up, no doubt suddenly afraid I might tell what he'd done that afternoon in Slim's mother's bedroom.

Slim said, 'We just need to see how full it is . . . if maybe she went off with some other purse.'

'It feels pretty heavy,' I said.

'Would you rather have me look?' Slim asked.

'Yeah, maybe so.'

I stepped aside. Slim handed the bow to me, then opened Lee's purse. As we all watched, she lifted out the billfold. Holding it out of the way, she bent over the purse and peered in. 'Checkbook, lipstick, keys . . .' Then her lips moved, but she said nothing. She reached down into the purse.

Her hand came up holding four stiff red papers the size of postcards cut in half lengthwise.

The first time I'd seen them, they had been in the hand of Julian Stryker when he came out of the bus at Janks Field.

Then I'd seen Lee tuck them into her purse.

Slim studied one of them. Meeting my eyes, she said, 'Tickets for tonight's performance of the Travelling Vampire Show.'

'All *right*!' Rusty blurted.

Slim and I looked at him. He seemed delighted.

'The *tickets*, guys. We can still *go*.'

'Not without Lee,' I said.

'Go where?' Bitsy asked.

Rusty scowled at her. 'To the Travelling Vampire Show.'

'What about the *drive-in*?'

'Screw the drive-in.'

Bitsy glanced hopefully from me to Slim and back to me again. This time, neither of us came to her defense. Her face turned sullen, lower lip bulging out.

Slim set the tickets on the kitchen table. 'Guess Lee didn't switch purses. This one has all the main stuff in it.' She put the billfold back inside. Leaving the tickets on the table, she closed the purse. Then she turned toward me. She looked worried.

'You really think they took her?' I asked.

'It's a possibility. But maybe Lee just went off without her purse, no big deal. She might've gone for a walk, gone on a ride with a friend, whatever, and she'll turn up before long. I mean, you guys had *me* kidnapped or God-knows-what this afternoon just because you couldn't find me for a couple of hours. Lee could be *anywhere*, perfectly safe, planning to get back here in plenty of time to take us to the show.'

'We're gonna *miss* the show if we don't get going,' Bitsy complained.

'Not *that* show, you wad. The *vampire* show.'

Slim pretty much ignored them. 'If she'd just gone off, though, she probably would've taken her purse and shut the front door. So maybe something happened that made her leave in a big hurry.'

283

'An emergency,' I said.

Slim nodded. 'Maybe she ran out of the house to help someone. Or to get *away* from someone.'

'Maybe she *did* get away,' I said.

In my mind, I saw Lee fleeing out the back door of her house, Stryker and his gang in hot pursuit . . . chasing her with spears as she ran through her yard and down the long embankment toward the river.

What if she didn't make it?

'Another possibility,' Slim said, 'is that someone came into the house and took her away.'

'Stryker?' Rusty asked.

'He's a likely suspect,' Slim said. 'But maybe he isn't involved at all. Look at what's happened to *us*. Like how that car came after us on the way home from the drive-in a few weeks ago. And that weird guy in the sheet on Halloween last year. And all the troubles we've had over at Janks Field *before* today. They had nothing to do with the vampire show.'

'Maybe,' Rusty said. 'Maybe not.'

'Get real,' I told him.

'Who really knows?' he said, wiggling his eyebrows and trying to sound like Karloff. 'Maybe it's the ghost of Tommy Janks. He's doing it all . . . pulling all the strings.'

'Get bent,' Slim said.

'I want to take a look out back,' I said and handed the bow back to Slim. 'If someone *did* come after Lee, maybe she ran off.'

'Out the *back* door?' Rusty asked, using his normal voice.

'Yeah.' I walked toward it.

'The front door's the open one,' he reminded me.

'If someone comes in the front door,' I explained, 'what you do is run out the back and shut it behind you to slow 'em down . . .'

'Or maybe so they don't realize you went out,' Slim added.

'Right,' I said. I stepped up to the back door and opened it. A warm wind blew in against me. I pushed on the screen door.

It stayed shut.

Because its inside hook was fastened.

'Guess she *didn't* run out the back,' I admitted.

'So much for that theory,' said Slim.

'She still could've gotten away.'

'Maybe she didn't *need* to,' Rusty said.

'That's right,' I said.

'So what do you want to do?' Slim asked me.

I shrugged. I had to do something, but didn't know what. I felt miserable: confused, helpless, scared.

Even as we stood in the kitchen chatting about theories, Lee might be running for her life with Stryker or someone hot on her tail. Or maybe she'd already been captured. Someone might be taking her farther and farther away. Or torturing her. Or raping her. Or killing her. Or she might be perfectly fine. Maybe she'd walked over to a friend's house for supper or gone for a stroll to enjoy the wild, windy night.

'I don't know,' I muttered.

Bitsy raised her hand as if she were in a classroom.

'We know, we know,' Rusty said. 'In your brilliant opinion, we should forget about Lee and go to the drive-in.'

'Shows how much you know,' Bitsy said.

'What is it?' Slim asked.

Bitsy frowned and opened her mouth, but no words came out.

'Spit it out,' Rusty said.

'Shut up,' I told him. Then I looked at Bitsy. 'Is there something you want to say?'

She glanced around at all of us, then said, 'Just that you

shouldn't be so worried about Lee. She just *went* somewhere, that's all.'

Rusty smirked. 'Thanks for the newsflash.'

Bitsy scowled at him, then looked at me and said, 'Nobody's *after* anybody. I mean, you've got it all wrong.'

'About what?'

'Everything. That guy you keep talking about . . . Stryker? From the vampire show? He didn't do any of that stuff. You know, sneak into your houses and chew on the book and do things with the roses.' Blushing fiercely and looking ready to burst into tears, Bitsy said, '*I* did it.'

Chapter Forty-one

I think my mouth fell open. I know Slim's did.

Rusty blasted, '*You!*'

'I'm *sorrrrry*,' she brayed, and then started to bawl. Face red and twisted, tears rolling down her cheeks, she sobbed out, 'I didn't *mean* to! I'm *sorrrrry!!!*'

'You little shit!'

'Knock it off,' I told Rusty.

Standing there, Bitsy lowered her face into her open hands. Her shoulders jumped up and down. She gasped and snorted.

Slim started making faces at me and nodding toward Bitsy.

I got the message. Stepping up to Bitsy, I murmured, 'It's all right,' and put my arms around her.

Her arms whipped around me like a springing trap.

I stroked her head with one hand and patted her back with the other while she shuddered and twitched. Her face was shoved against my chest. I felt her hot breath through my shirt. Soon, I felt wetness, too. From her tears. And, I'm afraid, from her slobber.

I kept saying, 'It's all right' and 'Everything's fine' and 'It doesn't matter' and so on for quite a while until Bitsy finally calmed down.

Then Slim said softly, 'Let's go sit down.' She led the way. Bitsy and I followed her, Bitsy sniffing and clinging to my arm.

In the living room, Slim pointed to the sofa. So I sat down on it, Bitsy still holding on to me.

Slim sank onto the front edge of a chair. She propped the bow on the floor between her feet and held it upright in front of her. She couldn't lean back because of her quiver.

Rusty sat in another chair, looking disgusted and shaking his head.

'We're not mad at you, Bitsy,' Slim said.

'You're not?'

'No. Are we, Dwight?'

'No,' I said. 'It's no big deal, Bitsy.'

'No big deal,' Rusty echoed, glaring at her. 'Fuckin' psycho.'

Bitsy gasped. From the look on her face, she was about to blurt, *I'm gonna tell!* But no words came out. Our warnings must've gotten through to her.

Slim frowned at Rusty. 'You're not helping matters.'

He rolled his eyes upward.

To Bitsy, Slim said in a gentle voice, 'What happened, anyway? What made you do it?'

She gave Slim a pouty look, then whined, 'I don't *knowwwww*. They ditched me.'

'Rusty and Dwight.'

287

'Yeah. I got sent in for my shoes, only when I came back out they were already gone. It was all just a trick to get rid of me.'

'A pretty mean trick,' Slim muttered.

Which made me feel crummy again.

'Yeah,' Bitsy said. 'It was really mean. I went after 'em. I could've caught up, too, 'cause I knew they were going to Janks Field to look for you. Only they didn't *want* me with 'em, or they would've waited.' Bitsy looked into Slim's eyes. 'See, the thing is, you've always gotta have it just the three of you. Nobody wants me butting in. They've gotta have you all to themselves, and I guess you *wanta* be the only girl.' She pushed out her lower lip again. 'Maybe you're not the *only* girl around that wants to have fun sometimes.'

I saw Slim's eyes go shiny. She swallowed, licked her lips, then asked in a soft voice, 'You blamed *me* for the guys ditching you?'

'Sorta,' Bitsy muttered.

'And that's why you went over to my house?'

'I guess.' She lowered her head and continued. 'It wasn't locked or anything.'

'It hardly ever is.'

'I knew nobody was gonna be there, 'cause of how your mom works over at the restaurant and you don't have a dad or anything . . . and the guys said you were over at Janks Field. So I just went in.'

'Freak,' Rusty muttered.

'Stop it,' I told him.

'Well, she is.'

'Leave her alone,' Slim said. Then she said to Bitsy, 'Did you go in on purpose to wreck things?'

'No,' she said. It was almost a whimper.

'Why *did* you go in?'

She shrugged with one shoulder. 'I don't know.'

'But you went up to my bedroom and chewed on my *Dracula*?'

'I guess so.'

Rusty sneered. 'You don't *know*?'

'I guess I chewed on some book.'

'Why that one?' Slim asked.

'Just . . . I don't know . . . I knew you liked it a lot.'

'That's why you chewed on it? To hurt me?'

'I guess so.'

'Why none of the others?'

Another shrug. 'I don't know. I guess maybe I didn't feel like it.' She raised her head to meet Slim's eyes. 'It made me feel *awful*, wrecking your book.' Her lower lip bulged, her chin shook and she started crying all over again. 'I'm *sorrrrry!*' she blubbered.

I started patting her back.

Slim said, 'It's all right, Bitsy. Don't worry about it.'

'I'll . . . buy you . . . a new one.'

'Doesn't matter,' Slim said. 'But I don't get it. If you suddenly felt so bad about wrecking *Dracula*, how come you went into my mom's room and started breaking things?'

Here we go.

'I *didn't*,' she blurted.

Meeting my eyes, Rusty shook his head slightly.

'You didn't break the vase?' Slim asked. 'Or the perfume bottle?'

'They was . . . already busted. I just . . . I took the *flowers*, that's all . . . They looked so . . . they was on the floor like . . . like nobody wanted 'em and they got thrown down . . . and they looked so *sad*.'

Looking perplexed, Slim said, 'But you didn't break any glass?'

Bitsy shook her head.

Then Slim laid off the questions for a while and I patted

Bitsy until she calmed down. When she was done crying, Slim asked, 'So what happened after you picked up the roses?'

'Nothing.'

'Nothing else at my house?'

'Huh-uh.'

'So you left my house, and then what?'

Lowering her head, she muttered, 'I guess I went and gave a rose to Dwight.'

'You went over to his house and sneaked in?'

She nodded slightly.

'What time was that?' I asked.

She shrugged. 'I don't know.'

'Wasn't my *mom* home?'

Again, the small nodding motion. Then the soft voice murmured, 'I guess so.'

'You snuck around in my house while my *mother* was there?'

'I'm sorry.'

'Jeez.'

Rusty looked pleased with himself. '*Told* you she's a psycho.'

'I didn't hurt nothing,' Bitsy said.

'What *did* you do in Dwight's house?' Slim asked.

'Nothing. Just gave him the flower, that's all.'

'You put it on my *bed*,' I said.

'I'm sorry.'

'Good God,' I muttered.

'What else did you do?' Slim asked.

The way Bitsy's face suddenly flushed crimson, I wished Slim had kept the question to herself.

'Nothing,' Bitsy said.

'Oooo, boy,' Rusty muttered.

'What did you do?' Slim asked again.

Once too many times.

Bitsy's head jerked up and she snapped at Slim, 'Nothing! I didn't do *nothing*! You can go to hell! You can *all* go to hell!' Then she leaped up and ran for the foyer.

For a moment, the three of us were too stunned to move or speak. Then Rusty yelped, 'Shit!'

Slim called, 'Bitsy, wait.'

From where I was sitting on the sofa, I could see the girl hustle toward the front door. 'Bitsy!' I yelled.

Then Rusty pounded by.

'Good God,' Slim said. She sprang up, dropping her bow to the carpet and struggling to pull off her quiver.

I leaped up and went after Rusty.

'Stop or I'm gonna cream you!' he shouted.

His sister flung open the screen door and ran outside.

The door, starting to swing shut, bounced off Rusty as he charged through.

'Rusty!' I yelled. Hot on his heels, I swept the closing door out of my way, rushed across the stoop and leaped down the stairs.

Bitsy was chugging across Lee's front yard, short hair bouncing, skirt flapping behind her, Rusty closing in. Though he was large and clumsy and slow, his little sister was slower.

'Rusty!' I shouted. 'Let her go!'

He reached out and grabbed a shoulder of her sleeveless sundress. 'Gotcha!'

They matched strides, linked by his arm.

'Let go!' I yelled at him.

'Stop!' he yelled at her.

He didn't let go. She didn't stop.

I reached out and grabbed the back of Rusty's shirt collar. I was about to give it a sharp tug when Bitsy suddenly let out a squeal.

Rusty's body blocked my view of her. When I saw her again, she was careening sideways out of control. Rusty must've jerked her shoulder.

I heard Slim yell, '*Jesus!*'

Letting go of Rusty and trying to slow down, I twisted my head around and caught a glimpse of Bitsy spinning like a frenzied figure skater. Her arms were flung out. Her skirt was twirling high.

I lost track of her for a moment as Rusty and I nearly collided.

By the time I saw her again, she must've just crashed to the ground. She tumbled wildly, flipping over a couple of times, and came to rest on her back.

We hurried toward her.

She was gasping for air. Her arms and legs were spread out as if she hoped to make snow angels in August. The top of her sundress, buttons ripped open down to her belly, was hanging off one shoulder and showing her bare right breast. Her skirt had gotten shoved up so it covered nothing below her waist. I thought at first that she was wearing some sort of tight, skin-colored underwear. Just as I realized my mistake, Slim crouched beside her, blocking my view. She shut Bitsy's dress top and lowered the skirt just before Rusty and I got there.

Rusty scowled down at her. 'Y'okay?' he asked.

She just kept gasping.

'It's your own stupid fault,' he said. 'I *told* you to stop.'

In a gentle voice, Slim said to Bitsy, 'There was no reason to run away.'

'Yeah,' Rusty said. 'We weren't gonna hurt you.'

I glared at him. 'Why'd you have to throw her down?'

'All I wanted to do was make her stop running away. She wasn't supposed to get hurt.'

'Fucker.'

It wasn't a very nice thing for Bitsy to call her brother, but I was glad to hear it. For one thing, I felt the same way. For another, I didn't think she'd be making cracks like that if she had sustained any really serious damage.

Rusty scowled down at her for a while, then said, 'Look, you weren't supposed to get hurt. Okay? I'm sorry. It was an accident.'

'Like fuck,' Bitsy muttered.

'Why don't we get you off the ground?' Slim said to her. 'We can go back inside and see if you need to be patched up. I happen to know Lee's medicine cabinet is full of first-aid supplies.'

'No,' Bitsy said. 'I don't wanta.'

'I know,' said Rusty. 'You wanta go to the movies.'

She shook her head. 'I wanta go home.'

Chapter Forty-two

'Go home?' Rusty said. 'No way.'

'Wanta bet?' Using one hand to hold the top of her dress shut, Bitsy shoved at the ground with her other hand and managed to sit up.

'I'll drive you home,' Slim said. 'But you don't want your mom and dad to see you looking like this. Let's go in the house first, and—'

'Huh-uh. I wanta go home. Right now.'

Rusty looked pitiful. 'Man, it's gonna be my ass.'

'Should've thought of that,' I said, 'before you threw her down.'

'It was an *accident*. Anyway, if you hadn't grabbed my shirt...'

'Oh, so now it's *my* fault.'

With Slim holding her steady, Bitsy rose to her feet. 'Let's go in the house,' Slim said.

'I don't wanta.' She tried to pull away, but Slim held on.

'You're *not* going home looking like this,' Slim said, her voice firm. 'We'll clean you up first and see if you've got any injuries. Then we'll do something about your dress. *Then* I'll take you home. Maybe.'

I almost applauded.

Hobbling toward the front door in Slim's custody, Bitsy started to cry again.

Rusty and I stayed back. By the time we entered the front door, they were out of sight. Soon, we heard water running.

Rusty shook his head. 'I'm really gonna get it,' he muttered. 'They'll ground me so long I'll be gray before they let me outa the house.'

'You should've kept your hands off her,' I said.

'She was trying to get away. She was gonna run home. It would've wrecked everything.'

Slim came striding into the foyer.

'How is she?' I asked.

'*Really* upset. I mean, God.' Slim shook her head. 'At least she's not hurt.'

'She's not?' Rusty asked. He seemed surprised and pleased.

'Not much. Mostly, she's grass-stained. She has a few little scrapes and scratches, but that's about it. I told her to wash up.'

'How about her dress?' Rusty asked.

'Wrecked.'

'Can't you fix it?'

'I could wash it,' she told Rusty, and glanced at me in a

way that brought back memories of her laundry room. 'I might be able to mend it, too . . . sew some new buttons on. But the first time your mother takes a good look at it, she'll know it got wrecked. I mean, there's *fabric* missing where the buttons got torn off.'

'In other words, I'm fucked.'

Almost pleased, I said, 'Yep.'

'Not necessarily,' said Slim. 'There's one way out.'

'Suicide?' Rusty asked.

'A little less drastic than that,' Slim explained. 'As a matter of fact, it's simple. All we've gotta do is win Bitsy over. You're off the hook if she doesn't tell on you.'

'But what about the dress?'

'She can say she was fooling around . . . got into a game of touch football or something and had a little accident.'

'Better make it *tackle* football,' I said.

Slim grinned at me. 'Yeah.'

Rusty shook his head. 'She'll never go along with it.'

'It's your only chance,' Slim said.

'What you've gotta do,' I said, 'is *really* kiss up to her.'

'Barf.'

Giving me a meaningful look, Slim said, 'We've *all* got to be really nice to her.'

'Never should've let her come with us in the first place,' Rusty muttered.

Slim smirked at him.

'Hey, moron,' I said, 'it was the only way to get you out of the house.'

'I could've snuck out.'

'Sure. Maybe by around midnight. Which would've been a little late for catching the vampire show.'

'Not gonna catch it anyway if we let Bitsy go home and rat on me.'

'I shouldn't have pushed her,' Slim muttered.

'That was Rusty.'

'You know what I mean. We wouldn't be in this fix if I hadn't given her the third degree.'

Forgetting his worries for a moment, Rusty flashed a smile at me. 'What the hell *did* she do in your room?'

'Let's drop it,' I said. 'I don't know and I don't *wanta* know.'

'Must've been pretty embarrassing.'

Slim shook her head. In a low voice, she whispered to Rusty, 'The kid's *in love* with him – *everything's* embarrassing.'

I believe I snarled.

'Well, she is,' Slim told me.

'I know.'

'That's right,' Rusty said.

At the sound of a door opening, we went silent and watched Bitsy step into the hallway. She was no longer crying. She seemed calm. Back straight, she limped toward us. She'd used a couple of safety pins to fasten the top of her dress together, but she hadn't done a very good job with them. Her front was open to one extent or another all the way down to her waist.

'How are you doing?' I asked her.

'Not so good.'

'We're really sorry you got hurt.'

'Yeah,' Rusty said. 'I'm sorry.'

'You know what?' Slim asked her. 'We're *glad* you're the one who did that stuff in our houses. I mean, we figured we had those weirdos from the vampire show creeping around, so it's a fantastic relief to find out it was only you.'

'That's for sure,' I said.

It wasn't a total lie. I was very glad we weren't being stalked by Stryker and his gang. But the notion of Bitsy skulking through my house – *while my mom was home* – gave me a bad case of the creeps. I knew that Rusty and I had sneaked into Slim's house that same day, but this seemed different. In fact, this seemed a trifle demented.

What if she sneaks into the house when I'm there?

I imagined her creeping through the hallways and rooms late at night, lurking in shadows, spying on me.

'I'm sorry I upset you,' Slim told her.

'And I'm sorry you fell,' Rusty said.

I just smiled at her and shrugged.

She smiled back at me. A rather sad smile that used only one side of her mouth. 'Anyway,' she said, 'I don't wanta go home, after all.'

'Okay,' Slim said.

Rusty looked as if he wanted to whoop for joy. He held it in, though, and simply sighed as if his death sentence had been commuted.

'All I ever wanted,' Bitsy said, 'was just to hang out with you guys. I didn't wanta wreck anything.'

'That's real good,' I said, trying to sound sincere.

'So can we all be friends?' she asked. 'If I promise not to tell?'

'Sure!' Rusty blurted.

'And nobody tells on me, okay?'

'A deal,' Slim said.

I nodded.

'What's to tell?' said Rusty.

Blushing, she looked away and muttered, 'Nothing.'

'Well,' said Slim, 'I'm glad that's all settled. Now we just have to decide what to do about Lee.' She asked me, 'What do you think?'

'I guess . . . since it was Bitsy who did the other stuff, maybe there really *isn't* anything to worry about.'

Rusty gave his sister a look of exaggerated suspicion. '*You* didn't do something with Lee, did you?'

Bitsy narrowed her eyes. 'No.'

'Anyway,' I said, 'I guess we can either go on to the drive-in or wait here.'

'There's no point in the drive-in anymore,' Bitsy said.

We all looked at her.

'By the time we can get there ...' She shrugged. 'We'd just have to turn around and come back. Wouldn't even get to see a whole movie. Not if we have to be *here* by ten-thirty.'

'We could at least watch part of one,' I told her.

'Nah.' A smile lifted her heavy lips. 'Who wants to see a couple of stupid movies, anyway? I wanta go see the Travelling Vampire Show.'

Silence crashed down on us.

Slim, Rusty and I stared at each other.

Bitsy watched us, a funny smile on her face that made me suspect she knew exactly what she was doing.

Nobody else spoke up, so I did.

'We'd like to have you come with us,' I said, 'but we've only got four tickets.'

She pointed at us, counting aloud. 'One, two, three, four.'

'The problem is, one of the tickets is for Lee.'

'But she's not here.'

'Thanks for the newsflash,' Rusty said.

Slim gave him a dirty look, then said, 'They're Lee's tickets. She bought them, and she's intending to go.'

'In fact,' I added, 'they might not let us in without her. We're all under age. Stryker only sold her the tickets on the condition that she'd come with us.'

'How can she come with us if she isn't even here?' Bitsy asked.

'Well,' I said, 'we're hoping she'll be back in time.'

'So *I* won't be able to go?'

'I didn't mean it that way. We'd *like* for you to come with us.'

'Of course,' Slim said. 'But with only four tickets, I'm not sure we'll be able to manage it.'

Lower lip bulging again, Bitsy said, 'I guess I wanta go home now. If I can't go to the vampire show . . .'

'You can go!' Rusty blurted. 'Jesus! Okay? No problem. We'll get another ticket, that's all.'

'How are we supposed to do that?' I asked.

'For all we know,' Slim said, 'they might be sold out.'

'Even if they aren't,' I added, 'they won't sell us one for a thirteen year old.'

'I'm going home,' Bitsy said.

'No!' Looking frantic, Rusty raised his open hands and flapped them at us. 'Just hang on a minute. Nobody's going anywhere. I've got it all figured out. Okay?'

'Let's hear it,' Slim said.

Calming down slightly, he patted the air in front of his shoulders and said, 'We go now.'

'Go where?' I asked.

'To Janks Field. We take three of the tickets. Slim drives. We leave Lee's ticket here so she can follow along later in her pickup. We leave her a note, too, so she'll know what's going on.'

'That still leaves us a ticket short,' Slim pointed out.

Rusty patted the air some more. 'That's why we go now. We get there good and early, find us an adult and pay him to buy us one more ticket.'

'What'll we use for money?' I asked.

'How much we need?' Bitsy asked.

'The tickets are normally ten bucks,' Rusty said, 'but we might have to pay more. Fifteen or twenty, maybe.'

'I got more'n thirty,' Bitsy said.

I remembered her white patent-leather purse. She didn't have it now. When we first came into Lee's house, she must've left it in Slim's car.

Rusty frowned as if he couldn't figure out how his little sister had gotten her hands on that much money. But he played it smart this time and kept his mouth shut.

'Great!' he said. 'We're in business.' He glanced at Slim, then at me. 'Okay?'

'Might work,' Slim said.

'Worth a try,' I said.

Narrowing her eyes, Bitsy looked at her brother. 'What if we can't *get* another ticket?'

Rusty stared at her for a long time, then said, 'That happens, you can have mine.'

Chapter Forty-three

In the kitchen, I handed three of the tickets to Slim and left the fourth ticket on the table beside Lee's purse. Slim slipped them down a seat pocket of her cut-off jeans.

I found a pen and a pad of scratch paper by the phone. Back at the table, I wrote:

Dear Lee,
Sorry we missed you. We took three of the tickets and went on ahead. We figured we had better get there early and beat the crowd, as the parking has been known to get wierd.
We took Slim's Pontiac. Please come as early as you can. We well be looking for you and save you a seat.
Love,
Dwight

I showed the note to Slim. She read it to herself, then asked, 'Who ever taught you how to spell?'

'What's wrong with my spelling?'

'Aside from it stinks?'

Rusty chuckled.

'Like *you're* some kinda whizzkid,' I said to him.

'Let me see,' Bitsy said, and plucked the note from Slim's hand. Her head bobbed up and down as she silently mouthed the words. About the time she came to the end, her brow furrowed.

'She's my sister-in-law,' I explained.

Bitsy said, 'I know that,' but she looked relieved.

After she gave the note to me, I folded it and placed it beside the red ticket. 'All set,' I said.

'You don't want to correct the spelling?' Slim asked, a glint in her eyes.

'Not really.'

'Lee's a teacher.'

'I know that,' I said, suddenly sounding like Rusty or Bitsy.

Rusty let out a laugh. To Slim, he said, 'Dwighty's hoping to get some private spelling lessons from her.'

'Very funny,' I said. 'Are we going?'

'Let's go,' Slim said.

In the living room, she picked up her bow and her quiver of arrows. Then we left the house. Hanging back, I shut the main door behind us.

We crossed the lawn to Slim's car. When we got there, she put her bow and quiver of arrows into the trunk. Then we all climbed into the car. I sat in the back seat with Bitsy. Slim drove. Within about a minute, we were out on Route 3 with woods on both sides and no other cars in sight.

'What I think we'll do,' she said, 'is walk in.'

'Huh?' Rusty said.

'Walk?' asked Bitsy.

'I'm not driving onto Janks Field,' Slim said. 'For one thing, I don't want the tires getting ruined. For another, we might be the only car there this early. We're too young to be going at *all*, so we sure don't want the whole crew watching us arrive.'

'Good point,' I said.

'Also, the place'll probably end up jammed with cars later on. We don't want to get stuck in the traffic.'

'Hey,' Rusty said, 'maybe they'll have a riot like that other time.' He sounded as if he hoped so and wouldn't mind participating.

'If there *is* a riot,' Slim said, 'we can just take off into the woods free and clear.'

'Are we gonna have to walk through the woods?' Bitsy asked.

'Just if there's a riot,' I explained.

'Or if we get chased by vampires,' Rusty added.

'Quit it,' Bitsy said.

'What we'll do,' Slim said, 'is park along the highway and walk in on the dirt road.'

Bitsy moaned.

'You wanted to come,' Rusty reminded her.

'I know that.'

'You don't *have* to,' I told her. 'We've still got plenty of time. We could drop you off . . .'

'I wanta come with.'

'That's fine,' Slim said. 'The thing is, Bitsy, we might see some really bad stuff happen. *I* sure did. What they did to that dog . . . These are bad people.'

'You're just trying to talk me out of it.'

'No, I'm trying to warn you. You might end up wishing you'd stayed home.'

'So how come *you're* going?' Asking that, she sounded a little snotty.

'Slim's the judge,' Rusty said.

'Huh?'

'Dwight and I, we've got a bet going.'

'What bet?' Bitsy asked.

'I say Valeria's a babe.'

'Who's she?'

'The star of the show,' I explained.

'Dwight says she'll be a loser, but I happen to know she'll be gorgeous. If I'm right, Dwight has to shave his head.'

'*Slim* shaves my head,' I reminded him.

'Oh, yeah, right. Anyways, Slim's the judge.'

'That isn't why I'm going,' Slim said. Turning her head to the left, she said, 'There's the way in.' She started to slow down. 'We'll turn around . . .' she muttered.

'Then why?' Bitsy asked.

'Huh?'

'How come *you* wanta go if it's gonna be so horrible?'

'Gotta watch out for my guys,' she said. Slowing almost to a stop, she made a U-turn. 'Anyway, my mom's away for the night and I didn't much want to stay by myself.'

'Especially since she had a *prowler* today,' Rusty added, and glanced back at his sister.

'I said I was sorry,' Bitsy muttered.

'Here's the turn-off,' Slim announced.

As she drove slowly past it, I glimpsed a couple of Travelling Vampire Show handbills and the makeshift cardboard sign on trees near the narrow dirt road. They were dim shapes in the darkness. If I hadn't already seen them a couple of times in daylight, I wouldn't have known what they were.

I thought, Nobody'll be able to find the place.

Then I realized I was being stupid. Everyone for miles around knew the location of Janks Field. Almost everyone *avoided* it whenever possible, but hardly anyone would have trouble getting there, even in the dark.

Slim eased her Pontiac off the road. We dipped down into a shallow ditch, then climbed out of it and rolled through some deep grass.

'What're you *doing*?' Rusty asked.

'Parking,' Slim said.

The car shook as she steered it over the rough ground. Bushes squeaked against the sides. Fallen twigs crackled under the tires. But not for long.

Slim stopped the car behind some trees, killed its headlights and shut off the engine.

'Jeez,' Rusty said.

'We don't want everybody seeing our car.'

By 'everybody,' I'm sure Slim meant more than just people wishing to do us harm. She also meant any residents of Grandville who might drive by – either on their way to the show or going elsewhere. Because if anyone should see the huge old Pontiac, word would get around. Soon, everyone in town – including our parents – would know that Slim's car had been spotted out near the Janks Field turn-off the night of the Travelling Vampire Show.

The night of my dad's car accident.

The night Slim's mom had her overnight date on the river.

The night the parents of Rusty and Bitsy *thought* we'd taken their kids to a double-feature at the Moonlight Drive-in.

I suddenly had a bad thought.

'Rusty,' I said.

He looked around at me.

'What time are you and Bitsy supposed to get home?'

'What time do *you* think?'

'Midnight?'

'Good guess.'

'We can't be back by then,' I said. 'That's when the show *begins*.'

'No sweat,' Rusty said. 'My folks're *never* awake by midnight. We'll just sneak in real quiet when we get home. They'll never be the wiser.'

Maybe he was right. He had certainly gotten away, many times, with sneaking in and out of his house late at night.

'If we *do* get caught,' he said, 'I'll just say we had car trouble. And anyway, by then it'll be too late. We'll already've seen the show, right?' He chuckled. '*Let* 'em ground me. See who cares.'

Chapter Forty-four

With the rest of us standing nearby, Slim opened the trunk of her car. Then she just stood there as if staring in.

'What're you waiting for?' Rusty asked.

Slim shook her head. 'I'd better leave this stuff here,' she said. 'We might need to blend in with the crowd. Can't exactly do that if I'm armed like Robin Hood.' Leaving her archery equipment inside the trunk, she shut the lid.

We started back toward the dirt road, staying in among the bushes and trees in case of traffic on Route 3.

'Nobody said we'd have to *walk*,' Bitsy complained.

'You're the one that wanted to come,' Rusty reminded her.

'But I got *sandals* on.'

'So wait in the car.'

'Nobody's going to wait in the car,' Slim said.

'My feet are getting all scratched.'

'Tough toenails,' Rusty said, and chuckled.

'Ha ha. That's so funny I forgot to—'

'Let's hold up here a second,' I said. We halted, and I pulled off one of my shoes. As I peeled the sock off, I said, 'You can wear my socks, Bitsy.'

'Really?' She sounded surprised and pleased.

'Sure.' I handed her the sock I'd already removed. Still balancing on one leg, I put my sneaker back on. Then I shifted legs and took off the other shoe and sock. I gave the second sock to her.

'Thank you very much,' she said.

As I put my shoe on again, Bitsy sat on the ground. She brought her knees up and spread them wide apart like a little kid. But she wasn't a little kid and she was wearing a dress. There must've been a break in the clouds. Some moonlight made its way into the forest and she'd found a patch of it.

Almost as if she wanted me to watch.

I looked away and glimpsed Rusty staring down at her. He didn't say anything, just watched.

Being her brother, maybe he was used to seeing that sort of thing. I didn't have a sister, so I wouldn't know. But it seemed funny that he would stare like that.

It made me wonder about Rusty.

About Bitsy, too, for that matter. She had to know her brother was watching, but it didn't seem to faze her.

Bitsy was turning out to be more strange than I had ever imagined.

Slim, keeping watch as if afraid someone might sneak up on us, didn't seem to notice Bitsy's secret show – or audience.

After putting my socks on, Bitsy struggled into her sandals and stood up. She brushed off the seat of her dress. 'Thanks,' she said again.

'You're welcome.'

'Ready?' Slim asked.

'Yeah,' Bitsy said.

So we started off again, Slim in the lead, Rusty next. Instead of moving out behind her brother, Bitsy came over to my side and took my hand. 'I wanta stay by you,' she said.

'Sure.'

She kept hold of my hand. Side by side, we made our way through the dark woods.

'The socks sure help,' she said.

'Good.'

'They're kinda sweaty, but I don't mind. I kinda like it.'

'Ah,' I said.

'Car!' Slim warned.

Off to the right and ahead of us through the trees, pale beams lit the night. A car was coming our way on Route 3. Slim stepped behind a tree trunk. Rusty crouched behind a bush. Pulling Bitsy by the hand, I gasped, 'Come on,' and rushed over to a waist-high boulder. We ducked behind it, Bitsy clutching my hand and gasping for breath.

Huddled together, we heard the car come closer. It sounded like a strong wind rushing through the trees. I felt one of Bitsy's breasts pushing against the side of my arm. It moved slightly, rubbing me, as if she wanted to make sure I noticed. I noticed, all right. And it made me wish I was somewhere else: hiding behind the tree with Slim, for instance.

Soon, but not nearly soon enough, the sound of the car faded like a sigh. We stood up. Slim waved when she saw us. Rusty shook his head. I tried to break contact with Bitsy. Though I got free of her breast, she kept her grip on my hand.

Slim and Rusty waited for us. When we were all together, Slim took the lead again. Rusty trudged after her. Bitsy squeezed my hand and looked up at me. We weren't in moonlight, so I couldn't see the look on her face. Just as well.

A couple of minutes later, we came to the dirt road.

Slim waited until we were all there. Then she said in a quiet voice, 'Let's just stay on this and stick together. A lot easier than traipsing through the woods.'

'What if a car comes?' Bitsy asked.

'We'll duck out of sight same as last time,' Slim said.

Clustered together, we began walking up the dirt road toward Janks Field.

Soon, a car came along from behind us. We heard it and saw the glow of its headlights in plenty of time to hide. No sooner had it passed us than another was on the way. When both had gone, we returned to the dirt road.

'Early birds,' Slim said.

'After the best seats,' Rusty suggested.

'Or the best parking places,' I said.

'*We've* got the best parking place,' Slim said. 'A good safe distance from the action.'

'You still got the tickets?' Rusty asked her.

'Yep.' She patted the seat of her cut-offs.

To Bitsy, he said, 'You sure you got plenty of money?'

Nodding, she patted her purse. She had let go of me while we'd been waiting for the cars to pass. Now she was over to the side and slightly ahead of me. The white purse, hanging from her shoulder, seemed to be floating by her hip.

'You better have enough for a ticket,' Rusty warned, 'or the deal's off.'

'I've got plenty.'

We heard another car coming, so we ran for cover.

Our way was blocked by a fallen tree. All four of us scurried over its trunk and ducked behind it.

As we waited for the car to pass, I suddenly wondered why we were hiding and why we'd bothered to conceal

Slim's Pontiac. If we hoped to buy a ticket for Bitsy, use our tickets to enter the grandstands, then sit among the other paying customers, we were sure to be seen and recognized. We would probably be *surrounded* by people from Grandville.

We started to rise, but then another car came along. It went by. As we began to climb over the trunk, another glow of headlights appeared so we dropped out of sight again.

'I'm not sure why we're hiding,' I said.

Slim, crouched close to my left side, nudged me with her elbow and muttered, 'So they don't see us, Mr Brain.'

'A few minutes, we'll be in the middle of them.'

Was I the only one who'd thought of that?

Slim turned her face toward me. I couldn't see her expression, and she didn't speak.

'What'll we do?' asked Bitsy. She was crouched on my right.

'Should've brought disguises,' Rusty whispered.

'It'll be all right,' Slim said.

'I don't . . .' My voice stopped and I listened to the approaching engine. It had a powerful sound.

Hands on the rough, moist bark, I eased myself upward and peered toward the dirt road. A pickup truck was speeding along the dirt road, shaking and bouncing.

Its headlights ruined my night vision.

There seemed to be only one occupant, the driver. But I couldn't make out who it was – not even whether it was a man or woman.

As the pickup sped away, however, I was able to see its color in the glow of its tail-lights.

Red.

A red pickup truck, the same as Lee's.

'Was that her?' Rusty asked.

We were all gazing over the top of the fallen trunk.

'I don't know,' I said.

'Sure looked like her truck,' Slim said.

'I bet it was her,' Bitsy said.

'Did you see her?' I asked.

'No, but I bet it *was*.'

'I hope so,' I muttered. 'Thing is, it's not like she's got the only red pickup in town.'

'Did *any*one see the driver?' Slim asked.

'Nope.'

'Huh-uh.'

'I wish.'

'Might've been her,' Rusty said.

'She's *supposed* to come,' I added.

'Well,' said Slim, 'we'll find out soon enough, I guess.'

Chapter Forty-five

We walked for a couple of minutes on the dirt road, but then another car came so we hid again. This time, we crouched behind a clump of bushes about twenty feet from the roadside.

'We're *never* gonna get there,' Rusty said.

'Maybe we'd better cut through the woods,' Slim suggested.

'Have we *gotta*?' Bitsy asked.

'We'd better,' Slim said. 'If we keep hiding every time a car comes by . . .'

'We might as well walk up the road,' I said. 'Everybody's gonna see us when we get to the show, anyway.'

Slim looked at me. She was silent for a few seconds, then said, 'I don't know. Maybe you're right. But—'

Rusty gasped out, '*Holy shit!*'

The rest of us looked.

The car bouncing up the road and just about to pass our hiding place was a huge old Cadillac. Slammed by fear, I ducked. Bitsy was still staring at it, so I clamped a hand on her shoulder and jerked her down.

'What's—?'

'Shhh.'

Hunkered low, we waited for the Cadillac to pass.

It's probably not even the same one, I told myself. But I knew better. Around these parts, Cadillacs weren't nearly as common as pickup trucks. This *had* to be the one that had terrorized us after the drive-in.

For the past month, all the cops in the county had been looking for it.

Now, here it was.

The sounds of the Cadillac faded, but not with distance. Its engine noise decreased because someone had taken his foot off the gas pedal. Its tires no longer crunched along the dirt road because they had quit moving.

Cars stop for many reasons, but I *knew* why this one had stopped.

We'd been seen.

'Did they *see* us?' Rusty asked in a hoarse whisper.

Slim went 'Shhh.'

Rusty murmured, 'Jesus.'

'Who are—?' Bitsy started to ask. I cupped an open hand across her mouth, catching the final word, dissolving it into warm breath. Though she didn't try to say more, I kept my hand on her mouth. She breathed into it.

I listened for the sound of a door opening.

What if they're already open?

Through the thick foliage in front of me, I could see nothing of the Cadillac except the glow of its headlights.

I wanted to rise and peer over the top, but I didn't dare.

Then a man's thin voice sang out, '*Weee seee youuuu.*'

I felt as if I had icy snakes in my bowels.

The same voice, but without the sing-song, asked, 'Want a lift?'

I was afraid Slim might answer with a wisecrack, but she remained silent.

'What's the matter, kids? Cat got your tongues?'

A moment later, I felt *Bitsy's* tongue push gently against the palm of my hand.

She's licking me!

I jerked my hand away from her mouth.

'How about a ride to the Travelling Vampire Show?' the man asked.

I rubbed my wet hand on the leg of my jeans.

'Don't worry,' the man said, 'we won't hurt you.' After a pause, he added, 'Much.'

His passenger giggled. That's when I remembered that they were supposed to be twins.

A matching pair of perverts.

The blast of a car horn made me jump.

'Be *seeeeing* you,' the guy called out. The engine revved. The tires hissed and crunched on the dirt road.

Rising slightly, I saw that a pale station wagon now stood just behind where the Cadillac had been. It must've been the car that honked. As the Cadillac disappeared among the trees, the station wagon started forward. After it came a little sports car.

'This way,' Slim said.

On hands and knees, she scurried away from the bush. We followed her into the trees. When the dirt road was a safe distance behind us, we got to our feet.

'It was *them*,' Rusty said.

'Guess so,' Slim said.

'Who?' Bitsy asked.

'Never mind,' Rusty told her.

Bitsy turned to me for an answer.

The Cadillac twins were a well-kept secret. My dad and all the law enforcement agencies in the area knew about them, but hardly anyone else did. We'd been told to keep quiet. If the twins were long gone, there was no reason to panic everyone. If they *were* still around, the cops didn't want them to know they were being sought. 'They find out we're after 'em,' Dad had said, 'they'll jackrabbit or go to ground.'

So I said to Bitsy, 'We can't tell you who they are.'

'But they're very bad guys,' Slim added.

'And they're going to the show,' Rusty said.

'Still wanta go?' I asked him.

'You kidding? You think I'm gonna let a couple of pervs scare me off, you got another thing comin'.'

'You're not the one they're after,' I said.

'Who is?' Bitsy asked.

'Slim.'

Rusty groaned. 'Tell her *everything*, why don't you?'

As if taking up the suggestion, Slim told Bitsy, 'They tried to pull me into their car a few weeks ago.'

'What for?'

Rusty said, 'What do *you* think, dipshit?'

'Cut it out,' Slim told him.

To Bitsy, he said, 'You better not breathe a word of this to Mom or Dad.'

'I won't.'

'Sure you won't.'

Turning toward me, Slim said, 'I'm not so sure anymore.'

'About going?'

'Yeah. It's bad enough, Stryker and his gang. But now *these* guys. It's getting a little *too* creepy.'

Rusty went into his chicken impression, tucking his hands under his armpits, flapping his elbows up and down and going, '*Bwok-bwok-bwok-bwok!*'

'Up yours,' Slim told him.

'*Meow!*'

'Shut up,' I warned.

'I think maybe we'd better call it off,' Slim said.

'No!'

'Yeah,' I said. 'I wanta see the vampire show as much as anyone, but it isn't worth getting killed over.'

'Well, *I'm* going. You guys wanta chicken out, that's your problem. Fuck ya. And the horse y'rode in on.' He jammed an open hand toward Slim. 'Gimme one a those tickets.'

'You don't want to go by yourself,' Slim said.

'Oh, no? Y'wanta bet?'

'Hey, man,' I said.

'Go to hell.'

'Let's just all go back to the car and get out of here,' Slim said. 'We can go to the drive-in.'

Rusty shook his head. 'Not me. I'm going to the Travelling Vampire Show . . . with or without the rest of you chicken-shit pussies.'

'You want to go, go.' Slim jammed a ticket into his hand. 'No skin off my butt.'

'Thanks,' Rusty muttered.

'It isn't worth it,' I told him.

'I'm not scared.'

'The hell you aren't.'

Slim said to him, 'You don't have to prove anything.'

'I don't know what you're talking about.'

'Yeah, you do,' I said.

''Fraid not.'

'Yeah, right.'

He gave me the finger, then headed for the dirt road.

I muttered, 'Damn it.'

'You'd better go with him,' Slim said.

'Huh?'

She called out, 'Rusty, wait! Dwight's going with you.'

'I am?'

Rusty stopped and turned around. 'You coming?' he asked.

'Just a minute,' Slim called. To me, she said, 'We can't let him go by himself.'

'Sure we can.'

She shook her head. 'Besides, what about Lee?'

Lee had temporarily slipped my mind.

'Whether that was Lee in the pickup or not,' Slim said, 'she'll probably turn up at the show sooner or later and she's expecting us to be there.'

'She can hook up with Rusty,' I said. It sounded feeble even to me.

'Suppose the Cadillac twins decide to go after *her*?'

Grimacing, I nodded. 'Yeah,' I muttered. 'Maybe I'd *better* go. I don't want to, but . . .'

'Duty calls,' Slim said. In the dim grayness of the forest, she seemed to smile at me. 'Anyway,' she added, 'I *know* you want to see the vampire show.'

'Don't you wanta see it?'

She shook her head. 'Not hardly. Look, you go to the show and take care of Rusty. I don't think the Cadillac twins are likely to bother you guys if I'm not with you. They might not even recognize you. So just go on ahead. Find Lee. Enjoy the show. Bitsy and I'll wait for you in the car.'

'I don't know,' I muttered.

'Yes, you do.'

'What if something happens to you and Bitsy?'

'We'll be fine. The car's well hidden. It'll be a hell of a lot safer for us than going to the vampire show, I know that much.'

'Maybe you should drive on home.'

She shook her head. 'We'll wait.'

'We'll wait,' echoed Bitsy.

'Here's your ticket,' Slim said. She held it out for me.

As I took it, she stepped in against me. She put an arm around my back, pressed her slender body against mine and kissed me. I felt the warmth of her belly, the soft push of her breasts, the gentle pressure of her lips. But only for a moment. Easing away from me, she whispered, 'Be careful.'

'You, too,' I said.

'What about me?' Bitsy asked.

Slim stepped aside for her. Bitsy put both arms around me and tilted back her head for a kiss.

Slim gave a little nod.

So I hugged Bitsy.

She writhed against me, moaning. Her heavy, open lips mooshed against mine and squirmed like a pair of slugs.

When I eased her away, she whimpered.

'See you later,' I said.

As I lifted a hand in farewell to Slim, Bitsy grabbed my other arm. 'I'm coming with you,' she said.

'You'll be safer with Slim,' I told her.

'But I wanta come with *you*. You *promised!* Everybody *promised*. If you're goin' to see the vampires, I getta go, too!'

'It's too dangerous now,' Slim explained. 'I'm not going, either.'

'But *they* are! If they get t'go, *I* get t'go.'

'You coming or not?' Rusty called to me.

'Hold your horses,' I answered.

Slim patted Bitsy on the back and said, 'Come along with me, Bits. We'll head back to the car.'

'But I don't *wanta*!'

I jerked my arm out of her grip. She reached for me again, but I leaped out of range. So then she lurched toward me, reaching with both hands.

I caught hold of her wrists. In a voice that wasn't exactly gentle, I said, 'Cut it out and go with Slim.'

'But I wanta—'

'*Shut the hell up and go with Slim!*'

She gasped. Then she started to cry. When I let go of her wrists, she sort of sagged and stood there, sobbing.

'Sorry,' I muttered.

As I ran to catch up with Rusty, Slim called out, 'Nice going, Dwight.'

I felt like bursting into tears, myself. But I called, 'I'm sorry,' and kept going.

Chapter Forty-six

Rusty and I trudged through the woods, staying away from the dirt road. With no path and very little light, it was slow going. And painful. We kept bumping into things, falling, getting scratched.

After a while, I muttered, 'We should've gone with the girls.'

'It's gonna be worth it, man.'

'That's what you think.'

'Just wait'll you lay your eyes on Valeria.'

'Sure,' I muttered. No matter how beautiful Valeria might be, she couldn't compare to Slim. I wanted *nothing* more than to be with Slim, but there I was – tromping through the woods with Rusty.

We were both out of breath, panting for air. The night was hot, the air heavy and moist. No wind at all seemed to penetrate the forest. Sweat poured down my body. My sodden shirt and jeans clung to me. Without the socks I'd given to Bitsy, my feet slid around inside my sneakers and made squelching sounds.

Why am I *doing* this? I kept thinking.

Not so I could lay my eyes on Valeria, that was for sure. Not really so I could keep Rusty company, either – though that must've been part of it. The real reason was Lee.

No telling where she was or what had happened to her.

Maybe she was okay. If so, she would find the note we'd left in her kitchen and come to the vampire show. I needed to be there to meet her.

Maybe she had already arrived – if that had been Lee in the red pickup truck.

Or maybe she'd been taken there earlier. She'd given Stryker the check with her address on it. Would've been so easy for him to pay her a visit.

Then again, maybe her disappearance had nothing to do with the Travelling Vampire Show.

Maybe she wasn't even missing.

If nothing happened to her, I thought, she'll see the note and drive over. One way or another, Janks Field was where I stood my best chance of finding Lee.

At last, we saw a pale glow of lights through the trees ahead of us.

'That's gotta be it,' Rusty said.

'Guess so.'

The grandstands of Fargus's Folly were always brightly lit at night to prevent the sort of mischief that often happened in the dark. But the grandstands weren't straight ahead of us. Also, their lights didn't move. Our way seemed to be illuminated, instead, by the headbeams of cars cruising Janks Field in search of places to park.

I thought about how smart it had been to park Slim's Pontiac off Route 3.

I wished I were there.

Slim and Bitsy had probably reached it already. If only I were with them . . . and if Bitsy weren't, so it could be just Slim and me sitting together in the front seat, waiting for Rusty . . .

But Bitsy *is* there, I reminded myself. If I so much as *kissed* Slim, Bitsy would want me to kiss her, too.

Maybe I'm better off here.

Soon, Janks Field came into sight through the spaces between the trees. Cars and pickup trucks were moving about, headlights pushing through the darkness.

We crept closer and closer. With nothing more than a bramble between us and the field, we stretched out flat on the ground, side by side, our shoulders almost touching.

Off to our right, a stream of vehicles poured into Janks Field from the dirt road. They were met by black-shirted members of Stryker's crew who directed them toward the area of field in front of us. The place seemed to be filling up fast, but in an orderly way. Stryker's gang knew how to do their job.

I suddenly pictured them surrounding the one-eyed dog, poking it with spears.

They had no spears now – only flashlights. Watching them, though, I felt chills crawl up my spine.

Slim was smart not to come here, I thought.

Cars and trucks kept lining up, stopping, shutting off their headlights and engines. Doors opened. People climbed out. Doors banged shut. In couples and small groups, people walked away from their vehicles and headed for the brightly lit bleachers. I could hear their voices, their laughter.

People I know, I thought.

I *had* to know plenty of them . . . any who'd come from Grandville, at least.

And they'll know us.

But I couldn't actually recognize anyone because of the darkness and the distance.

I nudged Rusty with my shoulder. His head turned. 'See anyone we know?' I asked.

'Do you?'

'Huh-uh.'

'Me nei—' I gasped and flinched as someone flopped onto the ground beside me. The heat of her body seemed to wash over me. She was panting for breath.

'I'm back,' she huffed.

I jerked my head toward her.

Bitsy's hair was glued down with sweat. Her face was shiny and dripping . . . and smiling. She nudged me with her shoulder.

'Shit, no,' Rusty said. 'What the hell is *she* doing here?'

Ignoring him, I twisted around and gazed behind me. No sign of Slim. 'Where's Slim?' I asked.

'Goin' to the car.'

'Why aren't you *with* her?'

'She said it's okay.'

'*Slim* said you could come with us?' I asked.

'Yeah.'

'She did not,' Rusty said.

'Did so.'

Fat chance, I thought. Keeping it to myself, I asked, 'How'd you get away from her?'

Bitsy smiled. It gave me a creepy feeling. 'I just said how I had to take a leak. That got her to let go of my hand, so then I ran away.'

'Slim could've caught you easy,' Rusty said.

'She did. And she ripped my dress and we fell down and I got hurt. So then she climbed offa me and said she was sorry.'

That sounded like Slim, all right.

'And I was crying and saying how all I wanted was to go see the vampire show like everyone promised, but she said I shouldn't on account of I might get hurt and I said how I didn't care. So then she was gonna make me come with her anyhow. She pulled me off the ground and I tried to get away again but she wouldn't let go, so then I called her a name and she let go.'

'Called her what?' I asked.

'Nothing,' she muttered.

'*What?*'

Bitsy muttered, 'A dirty whore.'

'You called Slim *a whore?*'

Her voice a quiet whimper, she said, 'Yeah.'

Back in those days, you never heard the 'c' word. I didn't, anyway. 'Whore' was the worst thing anyone ever called a girl, and you rarely heard that. It's a commonplace word now, used in everyday speech, in comedy routines, all over the place. But not then. Back then, it was a dark, vile word. Calling a girl a 'whore' was as lowdown as you could get.

I had a tight feeling in my throat – and an urge to punch Bitsy in the face.

'What'd you wanta call her *that* for?' I asked.

'Just to make her let go.'

'She's always been your friend.'

In a stronger voice, Bitsy said, 'I wanted her to let *go* of me.'

'That was really lousy,' I told her.

Softly, she murmured, 'I know. I'm sorry.'

'Real neat play, fatso,' Rusty said.

'So what happened after you called Slim that name?' I asked.

'She let go. She says, "You wanta go with Dwight so bad, go. And go to hell while you're at it." So then she let me have my ticket. I told her thanks and she said, "Fuck you."'

'Sure she did,' Rusty muttered.

'She *did*.'

I'd never heard the word come from Slim's mouth. I doubted she'd said it to Bitsy, but the worthless bitch had just called her a dirty whore so maybe Slim *had* used that language back at her.

'What happened then?' I asked. 'After she called you that.'

'Nothin'. I came looking for you.'

'Where'd Slim go?'

'I don't know. Back to the car?'

I just stared at Bitsy. It was a good thing there wasn't enough light for her to see the look in my eyes. Turning to Rusty, I said, 'I've gotta go and find Slim.'

'Hey, no. Come on, man.'

'You *can't*,' Bitsy whined.

I looked at her. 'Wanta bet?'

'You'll miss the show,' Rusty said.

'Screw the show.'

Bitsy went, '*Dwiiiight.*'

I pushed myself up to my hands and knees. As I started to back away, Bitsy clutched my right arm with both hands.

'Let go,' I said, keeping my voice low.

'Stay. Y'gotta stay.'

'Bitsy, let go!'

'*No!*'

I wrenched my arm out of her grip, then whirled around on my hands and knees. Just as I was about to scurry off, a hand tugged at a seat pocket of my jeans and Bitsy said, 'What about Lee?'

I stopped.

'You gotta find Lee, don't you?'

'Yeah,' Rusty said. 'You left her a note and everything. You can't just not show up.'

Bitsy gave my pocket a couple of pulls. 'Slim's just going back to the car, anyways. She doesn't need you.'

Chapter Forty-seven

I looked around at Bitsy. She was on her knees, leaning toward me, left arm bracing her up while her right arm was extended toward my rear end. Behind her, a few cars were moving slowly toward their parking places. People were walking toward the bleachers. I saw a couple of the black-shirt gang waving flashlights.

Nobody seemed to be aware of us.

'Take your hand out of my pocket,' I said.

She took it out. 'Don't go,' she whispered. 'Please.'

'Rusty, you're the one who's so hot to see the show. Why don't you and Bitsy go ahead? Keep an eye out for Lee. If you find her, stick with her. I've gotta make sure Slim's okay.'

'Slim's fine,' Bitsy insisted.

'I'll know that when I see her.'

Rusty suddenly said, 'I'm not gonna go to the vampire show with my *sister*. Screw that. I'm coming with you.'

'*No*,' Bitsy whined. 'Never mind Slim. We gotta see the show.'

'Forget it,' Rusty said.

Next thing I knew, all three of us were crawling through the forest *away* from Janks Field and the Travelling Vampire Show.

Fine, I thought. Now nobody gets to see it.

We never should've tried in the first place. The whole thing had been a rotten idea from the very start and we'd been in trouble of one kind or another all day long because of the stupid show.

I was *glad* we wouldn't be seeing it.

When we were a safe distance from Janks Field, we stood up. I led the way, moving carefully though the dark woods. Bitsy walked close behind me and Rusty followed her.

'Hold up a minute,' Rusty said.

I stopped and turned around.

So did Bitsy.

Rusty said, 'Here's good.'

'Good for what?' I asked.

'This.' He leaped forward, grabbed Bitsy by the front of her dress with one hand and smashed her in the stomach with the other. The sound was like punching a raw steak. Her breath whooshed out and she started to fold over. 'Nuffa you!' he blurted, and slugged her again.

'Rusty!'

'Stay outa this.'

Before I could make a move to help her, Rusty drove his fist into her belly again and again, very fast. Then he let go and staggered backward. Bitsy sank to her knees. Doubled over, she whined and sucked air. Her head was almost touching the ground.

'Jesus, Rusty,' I muttered.

'She had it coming.'

'God!'

'She asked for it. She's been askin' for it all day. Got no business messin' with us.'

'You didn't have to do *that*!'

'Yeah, yeah.' He stepped behind Bitsy, grabbed her hair and pulled. With a squeal, she struggled to her feet. She and Rusty looked vague in the darkness, but I could see that Bitsy's dress was open, hanging off one shoulder. Her skin was a pale shade of gray, her nipple a black smudge. 'Wanta take a swing at her?' Rusty asked me.

'Hell, no. Are you nuts?'

'Come on, man. She called Slim a dirty whore. You gonna let her get away with that?'

'I'm not gonna *hit* her.'

'Chicken,' he said.

'Leave her alone.'

'Sure. Soon as she leaves *us* alone.' He jerked her hair. She squeaked and went up on tiptoes. Mouth close to her ear, Rusty said, 'You gonna leave?'

'Huh-uh.'

'Wanta bet?'

'Rusty,' I said.

'It's okay, pal. She's gonna go back to the car. *Aren't* you, Bitsy?'

'No.'

'Yes you are.'

'No I'm not.'

'You're not coming with us.'

'Am, too.'

'You're gettin' one chance,' Rusty said. Turning her so she faced the general direction of Route 3, he let go of her hair and shoved her. She stumbled a few steps, then fell to her hands and knees. 'Now *go*!'

She stayed there for a while, her head drooping toward the ground. Then she pushed herself up and turned around.

'I don't see you *leaving*,' Rusty said.

'*Dwiiiiight*.' Though she spoke my name, it sounded as if she were saying, *Why are you letting this happen to me?*

'You'd better go back and wait in the car,' I said.

'But I wanta . . . come *with*.'

'It isn't safe. That's why Slim changed her mind.'

'*You're* going.'

'We're guys. It's different.'

'Now get your fat ass outa here,' Rusty said, 'or you're *really* gonna get it.'

She slowly shook her head.

'That's it,' Rusty muttered. He started toward her.

'*Dwight!*'

'Just go,' I told her.

'No.' She raised an arm and pointed straight at Rusty. 'Better not,' she said. 'I'm gonna tell.'

'Famous last words,' Rusty said.

'*Dwight!*'

I just stood there and let it happen. It was her own fault. We'd told her to leave. And told her and told her. So I just stood there. It made me feel a little sick, just standing there and watching, but she had it coming. On top of everything else, she'd called Slim a dirty whore.

When Rusty was done, Bitsy lay sprawled on her back, wheezing and sobbing.

He stood over her. Gasping for air, he said, 'Want more?'

She didn't answer. Probably couldn't.

He turned around and staggered toward me. 'Let's go, man.'

Side by side, we headed for Janks Field. I looked back a couple of times. The first time, Bitsy was still flat on the ground. The next time, she was propped up on her elbows, watching us.

'Don't go'n leave *meeeeee*,' she whined.

Stopping, I called, 'Go back to the car.'

'I wanta come *with*!'

'No.'

'But *Dwiiiiight*!'

I kept going again, and hurried to catch up with Rusty.

'*Dwiiiiight*, don't leave me! Pleeeeese.'

I called over my shoulder, 'Shut up!' and sounded a lot like Rusty.

'Bitch,' Rusty muttered.

I slugged him in the arm.

'*OW!*' He cringed away, clutching where I'd punched him. 'What'd ya do *that* for?'

'Just felt like it,' I said.

'Jeez.'

'Bastard.'

'Got rid of her, didn't I?'

'You didn't have to beat her up.'

'Got the job done.'

'You're gonna be in *so* much trouble. You and me both.'

'Yeah, well, screw it. She asked for it and I gave it to her.'

'There's no way she's gonna keep her mouth shut after *that*.'

'Let her tell. It's what she's good at. But you know what? Nobody's gonna nail us for it tonight. By the time she blabs, we'll already've seen the vampire show . . . without her.'

As we came to Janks Field, I noticed that it didn't seem as bright as before. I ducked behind a tree and peered around the trunk. In the few minutes we'd been away, so many cars and pickups had shown up that the field was almost packed. Soon, there would be no more space. The dirt road would end up jammed, maybe all the way out to Route 3. Just like the night of Fargus Durge's boxing spectacular.

'Come on,' Rusty said and stepped out of the woods.

'Wait.'

327

He didn't wait.

Nobody seemed to be nearby, so I went out after him and we rushed in among the parked vehicles. They were crowded close together. Staying low to avoid being spotted, we couldn't see where we were going. I simply followed Rusty. He led us through a dark, narrow labyrinth, gravel and bits of broken glass crunching under our shoes.

When we came upon a pickup truck, I wondered if it might be Lee's. It seemed to be a dark color, maybe red. But as I crept past the open passenger window of its cab, out came a reek of stale cigarettes.

Lee didn't smoke. The cab of her pickup always smelled as good as she did.

At the rear of the truck, a VW van blocked our way. We cut to the left and climbed over some bumpers before coming to another straightaway.

Crouched low between a couple of cars, Rusty looked back at me. 'We're home free now,' he said.

'Huh?'

'Bitsy'll *never* find us now. If she even tries.'

'You think she'd *try*?'

'Wouldn't put nothin' past her, the dumb twat.' He chuckled quietly, then moved on.

Every so often, we came upon pickup trucks. None of them seemed to be Lee's, though. Which didn't mean her truck wasn't there. So far, we hadn't even stumbled upon the red pickup that we *knew* had arrived. We saw nothing much except what was beside us and straight in front of us.

About halfway through the labyrinth, we came upon a big old black Cadillac.

Chapter Forty-eight

Parked close behind some sort of boxy delivery truck, the Cadillac took us by surprise. There it suddenly was, its front bumper close enough to touch.

Rusty must've noticed it an instant before I did. He gasped and dropped to his knees. At first, I didn't know what was wrong. I thought maybe someone had spotted us. Then I saw the hood ornament and felt as if my wind had been knocked out.

I hit the ground behind Rusty.

Twisting his head around, he whispered, 'Is it *it*?'

'Uh-huh.'

'You sure?'

'Pretty sure.'

'Anyone in it?'

'I don't know.'

Rusty moaned. 'What if they're *in* it?'

'Got your knife?' Even as I asked, I shoved a hand down the front pocket of my jeans and wrapped it around Slim's folding knife.

Rusty reached back under the hanging tail of his shirt and pulled out Slim's sheath knife.

I opened my blade. My hands were shaking. 'They're probably in the stands,' I whispered.

'They better be.'

I raised my head. The windshield had no glare. A pale glow from the grandstands lit up the rear window so I could see straight through the car.

If I'd found the twins staring back at me from the front seat, I probably would've dropped dead. Or at the very least filled my jeans. Instead, I let my breath out.

'It's okay,' I whispered. 'They're gone.'

Rusty took a look for himself. Then he muttered, 'Thank God.'

We started forward again, moving through the narrow space between the side of the Cadillac and the station wagon beside it.

I suddenly got an idea. It sent a jolt of fear through me. Fear and excitement.

'Rusty, wait.'

He stopped and looked around at me. 'Huh?'

'Think it's really their car?' I whispered.

'Must be.'

'Yeah. Look. I'm gonna check it out. Maybe we can find out who they are.'

'But the show.'

'Screw the show. Anyway, it's not gonna start for a while. Wait here.' I switched the knife to my left hand. With my right, I reached up for the handle of the passenger door.

'Are you nuts?'

'Shhh. Keep an eye out. Yell if anyone comes.'

The door wasn't locked. I opened it. No lights came on. Cigarette stink filled my nostrils. When I climbed into the car, stuff slid and crunched under my feet. There seemed to be a lot of junk on the floor in front of the seat. Magazines or maps, bags, food wrappers, maybe some small boxes. I couldn't see much in the darkness, but that was the impression I got.

I sat down and opened the glove compartment. It was full. I took out some cigarette packs, matches, maps, napkins, rubber gloves like my mom usually wore when she washed the dishes.

Rubber gloves.

I kept on searching, pausing to look at papers, hoping to

find the car registration. There didn't seem to be anything of the sort, but I found an ice pick with a wooden handle.

'Jeez,' I muttered.

'What?' Rusty asked through the door.

'An ice pick.'

'Let's get outa here,' Rusty said.

I put Slim's knife back into my pocket. Keeping the ice pick, I crawled out of the car. I eased its door shut and showed the pick to Rusty.

'Nasty,' he said.

'Yeah.'

'Gonna keep it?'

'I don't know.'

'These've gotta be our guys.'

'Oh, yeah.'

'Find out who they are?'

I shook my head. 'There's probably *something* with their names on it, but . . . too much crap in there. And it's too dark to see anything. Maybe if we took everything with us . . .'

'Forget it.'

'Anyway, that'd take a gunny sack.'

'Let's just get going,' Rusty said.

'Wait.'

'Now what?'

'We can make sure it stays here. The car, everything in it.' I grinned. 'Maybe *them*, too. The twins.'

'Huh?'

Instead of trying to explain, I scurried over to the right front tire and rammed the ice pick into its side. The point punched easily through the rubber. I shoved the shaft in deep, then jerked it free. Air chased it out, hissing.

'Terrific,' Rusty muttered.

At the front of the Cadillac, I checked for a license plate. There wasn't one. I opened the hood and propped it up.

Leaning inside, I poked holes in all the hoses I could find. And I removed the radiator cap and gave it a toss into the darkness. Silently, I shut the hood.

I crouched by the left front tire, jabbed it with the ice pick, then hurried to the rear tire and gave it the same treatment.

No back plate, either.

I stabbed the right rear tire.

Looking up, I saw Rusty shake his head. '*Now* can we go see the show?' he asked.

'Yeah, I guess so.' I rubbed the pick with my shirt tail to get my fingerprints off its handle, then tossed it under the Cadillac.

We moved on.

Rusty led the way, and I kept an eye out for Lee's pickup. We made good progress. Everything went okay for a while. But as we were sneaking alongside a Volkswagen, I glimpsed pale movement in its driver's seat. Couldn't see what it was, but I blurted, '*Watch out!*'

Not knowing what the problem was, Rusty stopped and twisted around to look back at me. The twisting swept his face past the open window.

'*No! Get . . .!*'

But he kept turning, luckily. His right upper arm, not his face, caught the dog's teeth. They clamped him through his shirt. He cried out in pain and lurched away.

The dog, hanging on, flew out of the car window. Might've been a white poodle. What they call a 'toy.' It looked like a toy, all right. Like a kid's stuffed doggie doll. But it growled like a real dog.

It swung by its jaws as Rusty twirled. 'Get it off! Get it off!'

I tried to grab it, but it swung by too fast. And then it lost its hold, sailed off, and slammed against the shut window of the Chevy that was parked beside the VW. The dog yipped, bounced off the window and fell to the ground at Rusty's feet. He tried to kick it, but missed.

To get away from us, it scurried underneath the Chevy. About half a second later, it screamed.

If dogs can scream, that's what this one did – as if it had run into a nameless horror on the ground beneath the car.

One quick shriek, then silence.

Rusty and I stared at each other. His mouth was drooping open. He held Slim's knife in his right hand while his left arm was across his chest, hand clutching his wound.

We didn't say anything, just stared at each other.

No sounds at all came from under the Chevy.

Rusty suddenly whirled around and took off. I went after him. We cut to the right, climbed over bumpers and hurried through a narrow gap.

Rusty leaped over the side of an old gray pickup truck. I didn't, but I hung onto the side and gasped for air. Sprawled on his back in the bed of the truck, Rusty held his chomped arm while he panted.

We were both too breathless to talk.

From where I stood, I could see that we'd made our way across most of Janks Field. There was only one more row of parked vehicles before the BEER-SNACKS-SOUVENIRS stand.

The shack was open, its door-sized flap raised and propped up at each end. It was brightly lighted inside. Julian Stryker, in his shiny black shirt, stood behind the counter, apparently selling tickets for the show. There must've been twenty people waiting in line. I recognized about half of them.

I saw no twins.

Lee wasn't in the line, either. But why should she be? She already had her ticket. Maybe she was already in the bleachers.

Or dead in the back of the hearse.

333

Where *is* the hearse? I suddenly wondered.

The Travelling Vampire Show's hearse, the black moving van and the bus were nowhere in sight. Maybe they'd been moved to the area on the far side of the bleachers.

Normally, I could look all the way through the stands and see whatever was over there. Normally, though, the stands were empty. Not tonight.

Now, the nearest bank of bleachers, about twenty-five or thirty feet high, was jammed with people. Through the spaces above and below the bench seats, I could see the backs of their legs. But I couldn't see much of the arena or the stands on the other side.

Down on the ground, the ticket line looked no shorter but had a few different people in it. Several customers were entering the stands. Others were heading for the ticket line from the direction of the dirt road where they'd probably left their cars.

'Hey,' Rusty said.

I looked at him. He was still on his back, still clutching his arm, but now he had his knees up.

'What the hell's goin' on?' he asked.

'Stryker's selling tickets . . .'

'The dog, man, the dog.'

'It's a bad day for dogs,' I said.

'What *happened* to it?'

'How should I know? How's your arm?'

'How the hell y'think it is?' He took his hand away. The sleeve of his shirt, dark with blood, was clinging to his upper arm.

'You're gonna need rabies shots,' I said.

'Awww, man. Don't say that.'

'And we'd better forget about trying to get into the vampire show.'

'Huh?'

'You can't go in there. Not all bloody like that. The blood'll bring vampires like chum brings sharks. You said so yourself.'

'Me?'

'This morning. To Slim.'

'Yeah, well . . . Screw that. I'm not gonna miss the show.' He lowered his knees, sat up and took off his shirt. Then he looked at his arm. 'Can't believe it,' he muttered. 'Fuckin' dogs.'

I nodded, but he didn't see me. He was too busy studying the holes in his arm.

'What is it,' he grumbled, 'a fuckin' conspiracy?'

I shrugged. 'Just coincidences, I guess.'

'A fuckin' dog made your *dad* crash.'

'Guess so.'

'Not to mention the fuckin' one-eyed wonder.'

When he said that, I pictured that dog getting speared to death by Stryker and his gang.

Where *is* his gang? I wondered.

Looking around, I spotted a couple of them near the entrance to the grandstands, taking tickets. I didn't see any others. Just those two, and Stryker in the shack.

Rusty used his wadded shirt to pat the bite wounds.

Just that morning, we'd tended to *Slim's* wounds on the roof of the shack after escaping from a different dog.

Strange.

And if some other dog hadn't caused Dad to crash his car, everything tonight would've happened differently. Much of it wouldn't have happened at all.

Including what went on with Slim and me.

Very strange, I thought.

'Y'wanta give me a hand?' Rusty asked.

I clapped softly.

'Har har.'

So then I climbed over the side of the pickup truck and sat beside him. He thrust the bloody shirt at me. 'Make me a bandage, okay?'

'With your shirt?'

'Why not? It's wrecked anyways.'

'It's a day for wrecking shirts.'

He frowned at me. 'This has been a very weird fuckin' day.'

'You're telling me.'

I looked at his wounds. The poodle had left two small, curved rows of punctures near the back of his arm a few inches below his shoulder. Most of the bleeding was over, but they seemed to be leaking slightly. I tore a long strip off the back of Rusty's shirt, then wrapped it around his upper arm. With another strip, I tied it in place. 'There you go,' I said.

'Grassy-ass.'

I looked toward the shack. Stryker still stood behind the counter, but the ticket line had dwindled down to three people. A few others were straggling in from the area of the dirt road.

'You sure you wanta go through with this?' I asked.

As if there were any doubt.

'You kidding me?' he said.

'How'll we get in?'

'We got our tickets, man. Why not walk in like anybody else?'

'We're under age.'

'BFD,' he said. I don't think anyone says BFD anymore. In those days, it stood for 'big fucking deal'.

Chapter Forty-nine

Rusty leaned over the tailgate of the pickup truck and stared at the ground. I knew why. He was thinking about the poodle, wondering what had gotten it and wondering if the same thing might make a try for him.

So was I.

'Whatever it is,' I said, 'I guess it's full.'

'I don't know, man. That was an awful small dog.'

'Wanta stay here and *listen* to the vampire show?'

He groaned, then leaped down. I jumped to the ground after him. Staying low, we rushed through the gap between a couple of cars. At the end of it, there were no more cars to conceal us. We stood up straight and walked toward the grandstands.

Over to the right, people were still in line to buy tickets. More were on the way. Stryker seemed busy behind the counter. I wanted to watch him the whole time to make sure he never looked at us, but I had to keep glancing at the ground.

In the glow of the stadium lights, the dirt looked pale gray. Broken glass glittered. Bumps and rocks cast dark shadows. Holes were blotches of blackness. I was looking for creatures. What I saw instead were cigarette butts, a mashed pack of Lucky Strikes, a flattened beer can, a dirty white sneaker . . .

Slim's sneaker?

It might've been one of those Rusty had thrown at the one-eyed dog. I was tempted to pick it up. But it looked as if it had been run over. No telling what else had happened to it – maybe a spider had crawled in. Maybe if I reached down for it something would spring at my hand. Besides, what good would *one* sneaker do Slim?

If Rusty saw the sneaker, he either didn't recognize it or didn't care. He kept on walking.

I caught up to him.

Just in front of us, a man and woman were about to encounter the ticket-takers. The man turned slightly and extended two tickets to a black-shirted member of Stryker's crew.

Rusty nudged me with his elbow, leaned toward me and whispered, 'It's Hearn.'

Sure enough, the man in front of us was Mr Hearn, a history teacher from our high school. I didn't recognized the woman beside him, but figured she was probably his wife. Though we hadn't taken any classes from Mr Hearn, we'd seen him around school and knew who he was. He probably knew who we were, too.

Everybody knew everybody.

He hadn't seen us yet, but . . .

Recognizing someone from our town came as no surprise to me. I'd expected it. It was inevitable. Before, however, it had been inevitable in some sort of distant, abstract way. Now, it was real.

Too real.

Even if plenty of spectators had come to the show from places like Clarksburg and Bixton – from all over the county – we were bound to be surrounded by people from Grandville who would recognize us and spread the news.

We're gonna get in so much trouble!

I stopped dead. Even as I reached for Rusty, he handed his ticket to one of Stryker's gang.

She was a slender, pale woman with straight black hair down to her shoulders. She wore a shiny black shirt and black leather pants. Her eyes narrowed slightly as she took

Rusty's ticket. Her lips were bright red. She smirked and said to Rusty, 'You're a big fella.'

He nodded.

She slid a fingertip down his bare chest. He squirmed and grinned. 'Not eighteen, though, I bet.'

'Sure I am.'

She turned to me. 'And you.' Still smirking, she shook her head. 'I'm sorry, boys, but this event is for adults only.'

Thank God, I thought.

Nodding, I was about to turn away.

'We have special permission from Mr Stryker,' Rusty said.

Away went her smirk. To the other ticket-taker, she said, 'I'll be right back.' Then she stepped past us. 'Come with me, boys.'

Rusty started to follow her. I put my hand on his shoulder. His bare skin was hot and moist. He scowled back at me and kept walking.

I tried to speak, but was too choked at first. Then I forced it out. 'We don't have to see the show, ma'am. If it's a problem . . .'

Rusty gave me a murderous glance.

'If you've got Mr Stryker's okay,' the woman said, 'it's fine with me. They're his rules.'

Rusty's turn to smirk.

I gave *him* a murderous look. Didn't he know we were being taken to see Stryker? Had he forgotten what Slim had told us? Or didn't he care that this was the same guy who had rammed his spear up the butt of the one-eyed dog, picked it up with the same spear and delivered it to the hearse?

I glanced toward the parking area.

If I made a run for it, would they come after me?

Probably not. Not with all these people around. The trouble was, Rusty might not come after me, either.

He *really* wanted to see the show.

So I stuck with him. The woman led us to the side door of the shack and rapped on it with her knuckles. A moment later, it was opened by Stryker. Light spilled out around him. He frowned as if annoyed by the interruption.

'Vivian?' he asked.

'I'm sorry to bother you, Mr Stryker, but these boys claim they've got your permission to see the show.' She stepped out of the way.

Stryker's eyes swept up and down Rusty. Looking somewhat disgusted, he shook his head. But when he saw me, his heavy black eyebrows slid upward and he smiled. 'Ah, it's you.'

I nodded. My heart was thudding. I wanted to whip around and run like hell, but I just stood there.

'Where are the others?' Stryker asked.

I just gaped at him and struggled to breathe.

'The lovely Lee Thompson and the spunky tomboy?'

I collapsed inside.

'They're on their way, sir,' Rusty said. 'We had to park pretty far off, so they sent us on ahead to save seats for 'em.'

'I see,' Stryker said. And the way he smiled . . .

He knows *everything*, I thought. Knows it's a lie, knows Lee isn't coming because he's already been to her house and knows exactly where she is.

Glaring into his eyes, I thought, *What have you done to Lee?*

Smiling into *my* eyes, he seemed to be thinking, *Wouldn't you like to know?*

He turned his smile on Vivian. 'We'll make an exception to the age rule for my two friends here. See that they have excellent seats, will you?'

'Yes, sir,' Vivian said.

'And stay with them until their friends arrive.'

She nodded.

'Enjoy the show, boys.' Stryker closed the door, shutting out the light.

'Come with me,' Vivian said.

As we walked behind her, Rusty cast a smile at me. A very smug one, as if he had single-handedly made it possible for us to see the show.

In a way, he was right.

I wanted to slug him.

'You've really done it now,' I muttered.

'Hey, man, we're gonna see it.'

'Yeah, right.'

'Valeria, here we come.'

Didn't he realize we were now prisoners? Didn't he realize Stryker knew about Slim witnessing the death of the dog? She *must've* been seen, or why had Stryker thought to call her a spunky tomboy? And most of all, didn't Rusty catch on that Stryker had been to Lee's house? The bastard *knew* she wouldn't be showing up tonight.

What if he'd killed her?

An image filled my mind of Lee down on her elbows and knees, naked, Stryker driving a spear . . .

No, I thought. She's fine. She *has* to be fine. Maybe she's his prisoner and we'll be able to rescue her. Maybe she's tied up on the bus, or . . .

'Oh, man,' Rusty muttered.

We followed Vivian past the other ticket-taker and into the bright lights. With the noise, it was like entering a football stadium. A very small one. I walked beside Rusty, keeping my head down, hoping nobody would notice us.

I guess you'd call it the ostrich principle; if I can't see them, they can't see me.

Of course, I knew it was foolish. Even as we walked past the front of the bleachers, dozens of Grandville locals were certain to be watching us. Probably pointing us out to each other. *Hey, look, there's the Thompson boy. And Rusty Simmons, too. What're they doing here? Didn't anyone tell 'em this is 'adults only' entertainment? You can bet your bottom dollar their FOLKS don't know about this.*

Within a day or two, Mom and Dad would be hearing about it from everyone in town.

I'd be grounded. Worse, I'd be humiliated. My parents had always trusted me to follow their rules. I often *didn't* follow their rules, but I rarely got caught at it.

This time, I'd be caught big time. Everything would come out. Well, maybe not everything, but enough.

I heard my dad saying, *This is a real disappointment, Dwight.*

My mom saying, *Of all things, to take advantage of your father's accident that way.*

Lee yelling, '*DWIGHT! RUSTY! UP HERE!*'

Lee's voice was real.

My head jerked up and turned. I searched the faces of the audience. Saw so many familiar ones. Neighbors, store clerks, teachers, friends of my parents . . .

'*DWIGHT! HEY, DWIGHT! UP HERE!*'

This time, I found the source of the voice.

There stood Lee, about halfway to the top of the bleachers, waving her arms overhead.

Chapter Fifty

'Holy shit,' Rusty said.

I couldn't believe it, myself. But the woman in the stands was Lee, all right. When she saw that we'd spotted her, she lowered one arm and waved with the other, beaming a smile down at us.

My eyes filled with tears, I was so glad to see her alive and free.

Rusty tapped Vivian on the shoulder. She looked back at us. 'Our friends are already here,' he announced.

Vivian frowned.

'Up there.' Rusty pointed.

Vivian looked.

'The blonde in the blue shirt,' Rusty said.

Nodding, Lee smiled and patted herself on the chest as if to say, *Yeah, it's me. I'm their adult.*

'That's your friend?' Vivian asked.

'Yeah,' Rusty said.

'That's her,' I threw in.

'I thought there was supposed to be a girl with her?'

'She's probably wandering,' Rusty said. 'She's my sister. A real pain in the butt.'

The missing girl *wasn't* his sister, she was Slim. The switch was just part of his lie, but it annoyed me. Maybe because I didn't like to be reminded of Bitsy. Maybe because I wished Slim were with us.

It was her choice to stay behind, I reminded myself. She never really wanted to see the vampire show, anyway.

But *I* wanted her to see it . . . wanted her sitting beside me.

343

Slim on one side, Lee on the other.

'Okay, guys,' Vivian said. 'Go on ahead.'

We both thanked Vivian. She stepped around us and headed away.

Apparently, I'd been wrong about our being prisoners.

I'd been wrong about a lot.

Rusty and I trotted up the nearest section of bleacher stairs. When we were level with Lee, I stepped into the row and waded toward her, audience knees on one side, heads and backs on the other. A few people nearby said, 'Hi, Dwight,' and 'Hey, young man,' and so on. I smiled, nodded, and greeted some of them by name.

Sitting two rows up was Dolly Desmond, the dispatcher. She didn't say hi, though. Just glared at me and Rusty.

We've had it for sure, I thought.

But it suddenly didn't bother me. Not very much, anyway. Trouble with Mom and Dad about coming to the vampire show didn't seem very significant anymore. Kid stuff. Not worth worrying about, now that I'd found out Lee was safe.

She had spread a folded blanket over about six feet of the bench to save space for us. She was sitting in the middle, her purse by her left hip. It was the brown leather purse we'd last seen in her kitchen.

The one Slim had searched.

I stepped past Lee, brushing against her knees, and sat on the blanket near her right side.

Rusty sat on her left.

She looked great. Her long, blond hair hung behind her in a ponytail. She had no makeup on, and looked about nineteen years old. She was wearing a blue chambray shirt, white shorts and white sneakers. The shirt didn't have any sleeves. Its top couple of buttons were open, and it was so short that it didn't quite reach the waist of her shorts. The shorts were white, small, and tight. Her white sneakers looked brand new, and she didn't have any socks on.

She watched the way I looked her over. 'I'm glad to see you, too,' she said, smiling. Then she turned her head. 'And you, Rusty.'

'Thanks, Mrs Thompson.'

'I've been looking for you guys. Thought you would've been here *before* me.'

'We walked in from the highway,' I explained.

'To avoid the parking tie-up?'

I nodded.

'No wonder I got here first,' she said. Turning again to Rusty, she asked, 'What happened to your arm?'

'Aaah, nothing. Some crappy little poodle took a bite outa me.'

'A *dog* bit you?'

'Yeah. When we were coming through the parked cars.'

'The same dog as this morning?'

'Nah. Different one.'

'It's been a bad day for dogs,' I remarked.

'I'll say,' Lee said. 'You'd better see a doctor about it, Rusty. You might need shots or something.'

'*Rabies* shots,' I added.

A disgusted look on his face, he said, 'Yeah, I know.'

'Are *you* all right?' I asked Lee.

'I'm fine.' She spoke as if everything were perfectly ordinary. 'Where's Slim?'

'Waiting in her car.'

'What for?'

'Just . . . she didn't want to . . . where *were* you? We were over at your house and . . .'

Nodding, she said, 'I got your note.'

'We thought something had *happened* to you.' I almost got

345

through the sentence before my voice broke and tears again filled my eyes.

'Oh, God,' Lee murmured. She leaned against me and put a hand on my back. 'I was fine, honey. I just went out, that's all. I never expected you to show up so early.'

Sounding amused, Rusty said, 'Dwighty here, he had you kidnapped and murdered.'

Not trusting myself to speak, I nodded.

'Your truck was still there,' Rusty explained. 'Same with your purse.'

'I . . . thought Stryker got you,' I said.

'Jeez.' She rubbed my back. 'I'm so sorry. I just went down to the river, that's all. It's such a wonderful, windy night. I sat out on the end of the dock to enjoy the weather and have myself a little cocktail.'

'My God,' I said. I'd almost looked for her there. 'But the screen door was locked.'

'The back screen? Was it?' She frowned and shrugged. 'I must've gone out the front.' She was silent for a few seconds, then nodded. 'Yeah, I *did* go out the front. Sat on the stoop for a few minutes before I got the idea to see what the river was doing.'

'Man,' Rusty said, and chuckled.

Lee rubbed my back some more. 'I'm so sorry, honey. I had no idea . . .'

'That's okay,' I said. 'We shouldn't have shown up so early.' Why *had* we gone to her house so early? It took me a moment to remember. Then I explained, 'We were worried about you. That's why we didn't wait till ten-thirty. I was afraid Stryker was gonna try something . . .'

'Because I gave him that check?'

A few other reasons, too – but Bitsy, not Stryker, had turned out to be the culprit behind most of them. I didn't want to get into all that with Lee.

'I guess it was mostly because of the check,' I told her.

'I pay with checks all the time,' she said.

'But Stryker's so creepy.'

She smiled gently. 'Oh, I don't know.'

'He *is*.'

'He's a pretty bad guy,' Rusty affirmed.

'And he . . . he *likes* you.'

'That's not so terrible. He probably wouldn't have sold us the tickets if he hadn't liked me.'

'You know what I mean.'

'Dwight thinks he's got the hots for you.'

'He *does*,' I said.

Looking mildly amused, Lee said, 'Well, that may be so, but he never tried anything. I haven't even spoken to him since you and I were out here.'

I stared at her.

'And he hasn't spoken to me. I did see him selling tickets on my way in, but he looked really busy so I didn't bother him. And he didn't bother me. I don't think he even *noticed* me. I figured he must've already let you guys in . . . So *why* isn't Slim here?'

'It's her time of the month,' Rusty proclaimed.

I couldn't believe my ears. I wanted to kill him.

'She got it all of a sudden on our way over.'

'Rusty!' I gasped.

He leaned forward and smiled at me. 'It's all right, pal. I'm sure Lee knows all about this sorta thing.'

'Does Slim need . . . anything?' Lee asked. She seemed a little flustered, herself.

'You mean like a tampon?'

Lee nodded.

'Nah. She had some in her glove compartment. She walked off into the trees to put one on. Dwight and me, we waited in the car so as not to embarrass her.'

world

If Slim ever heard about this, I wouldn't have to kill Rusty – she would beat me to it.

'So *where* is she now?'

'Back in the car, waiting for us.'

Lee looked at me, frowning. Apparently, she wasn't completely buying Rusty's tale.

I shrugged.

She gave Rusty a perplexed look.

'You *can't* go to a vampire show when you've got your period,' Rusty said, sounding exasperated by the need to explain something so obvious.

Lee looked at him as if he were nuts. She said, 'Huh?'

'A *vampire* show? Your period? *Blood!* Get it?'

'You've gotta be kidding me,' Lee said.

Rusty raised his right hand. 'I kid you not.'

'Jesus H. Christ,' Lee muttered.

Rusty's eyes bulged. 'It's not *your* time of the month, is it?'

She choked out a laugh. 'As if I'm going to discuss that with *you*.'

'Well, if it is . . .'

'LADIES AND GENTLEMEN, MAY I HAVE YOUR ATTENTION, PLEASE?'

Chapter Fifty-one

Though the loud speakers hissed and crackled, I knew the voice. It belonged to Julian Stryker.

For the first time since entering the stadium, I turned my eyes to the arena. There stood Stryker on top of a canvas object that looked like some sort of large, rectangular tent. About ten feet high, maybe twenty feet long and wide, it took up most of the arena. The wind shook the canvas walls with a sound that reminded me of sailboats on the river.

It blew Stryker's long black hair and fluttered his loose black shirt, which, half unbuttoned, gleamed in the stadium lights. His black leather pants looked as if they'd been oiled. He held a microphone in one hand, and turned slowly like the ringmaster of a circus. As he turned, the microphone in his right hand picked up the jangle of his spurs.

'WELCOME TO THE TRAVELLING VAMPIRE SHOW!'

Some polite applause came from the audience.

'MY NAME IS JULIAN STRYKER. I AM THE OWNER OF THE SHOW AND YOUR MASTER OF CEREMONIES FOR TONIGHT'S EXTRAVAGANZA.'

Lee nudged me, grinned, and said, '*Extravaganza!*'

'TONIGHT, YOU'LL FEAST YOUR EYES ON THE WORLD'S ONE AND ONLY KNOWN VAMPIRE IN CAPTIVITY ... A DIRECT DESCENDANT OF THE GREAT COUNT DRACULA HIMSELF ... THE GORGEOUS AND DEADLY *VALERIA!*'

More applause, along with some whispers and titters.

Stryker raised his arms for silence. When the audience quieted down, he continued, 'NOT LONG AGO, VALERIA ROAMED THE WILD REACHES OF THE TRANSYLVANIAN ALPS, FALLING UPON PEASANTS AT NIGHT, SINKING HER TEETH INTO THEIR THROATS AND DRAINING THE BLOOD FROM THEIR BODIES. AT MY RANCH IN ARIZONA, I KNEW NOTHING OF THESE STRANGE, UNGODLY MURDERS. NOT UNTIL THE NEWS ARRIVED THAT MY OWN UNCLE AND HIS FAMILY HAD BEEN VICIOUSLY SLAIN IN THEIR HOME

NEAR BUDAPEST. LEARNING OF THIS, I UNDER-
TOOK AN EXPEDITION TO BRING THEIR SLAYER
TO JUSTICE.

'FOR THREE LONG YEARS, MY TEAM AND I
SEARCHED FOR THE VAMPIRE KNOWN AS
VALERIA. GUIDED BY REPORTS OF EACH NEW
ATROCITY, WE SLOWLY CLOSED IN ON HER. AT
LAST, WE TRACKED VALERIA TO HER MOUNTAIN
LAIR. WE ENTERED AFTER DAYLIGHT AND
FOUND HER SLEEPING – AS IF DEAD – INSIDE HER
COFFIN.

'THOUGH I HAD EVERY INTENTION OF PUT-
TING VALERIA TO DEATH, I FOUND MYSELF
OVERWHELMED BY HER BEAUTY AND WAS
UNABLE TO PERFORM THE DREADFUL TASK.
STILL, SHE HAD TO BE STOPPED. I COULD NOT
ALLOW HER TO CONTINUE HER RUTHLESS
CAMPAIGN OF MURDER. AT LAST, WITH THE
AID OF A WISE MAN WELL VERSED IN THE ARTS
OF MESMERISM, I GAINED CONTROL OVER
VALERIA'S MIND AND THUS ENSLAVED HER TO
MY WILL.

'AND SO I REMOVED HER FROM HER NATIVE
TRANSYLVANIA AND BROUGHT HER TO MY OWN
COUNTRY ... *OUR* COUNTRY, YOURS AND MINE,
AMERICA.'

Good patriots, most of the people in the bleachers cheered
and applauded.

When the noise subsided, Stryker continued his speech.
'UNFORTUNATELY, DUE TO HER BLOOD-
THIRSTY NATURE, VALERIA IS NOT A WELCOME
GUEST IN OUR LAND. LIKE THE WANDERING
JEW, SHE MUST FOREVER CONTINUE HER
TRAVELS, NEVER STOPPING LONG ENOUGH TO

REST, NEVER FINDING A HOME. AND SO WE ARE HERE TONIGHT, PAUSING BRIEFLY ON OUR JOURNEY TO PROVIDE YOU GOOD FOLKS WITH A CHANCE TO VIEW AN ACTUAL VAMPIRE ... VIEW HER *AND MORE!*'

While he paused, I heard whispers hissing through the audience.

Then he said, 'LADIES AND GENTLEMEN, I'LL MAKE YOU WAIT NO LONGER. HERE SHE IS! THE WORLD'S ONLY LIVING VAMPIRE IN CAPTIVITY! THE LOVELY! THE LETHAL! THE MOUTH-WATERING TEMPTRESS OF TRANSYLVANIA! *VALERIA!*'

He flung his arms high and the audience erupted. As we clapped and cheered, several members of his black-shirted crew hurried into the arena. For the first time, I noticed that ropes were hanging down the canvas walls ... three on my side of the enclosure and three (I assumed) on the opposite side.

Each of the ropes was picked up by a member of Stryker's crew. I spotted Vivian in the arena with the center rope from our side. She and the others walked backward, pulling. The ropes came off the ground and were lifted away from the canvas, stretched taut to the place where they were secured on top of the enclosure.

Stryker swung his arms down. It was a signal.

Vivian and the others tugged their ropes.

'*VALERIA!*' Stryker cried out.

All around him, crackling and whapping, the sheets of canvas fell to the ground.

Stryker was standing atop a steel cage. Its roof and every side were made of thick bars like a jail. It was raised a couple of feet off the ground on cinder blocks. It seemed to have a floor of some kind – maybe wood over more bars. Whatever the floor was, it seemed to be covered by a foot-thick layer of dirt.

Near the center of the floor lay a simple, wooden casket. Its lid was shut.

I took my eyes away from the coffin for a moment and looked around. Every spectator seemed to be staring at it.

For a while, the only sound came from the wind blowing through the trees around Janks Field.

Hands on hips, Stryker gazed down through the bars.

'*VALERIA!*' he shouted. '*ARISE!*'

The coffin lid flew off as if kicked. I flinched. So did people all around me. Most of the audience seemed to gasp. A few people let out startled squeals. The coffin lid flipped over a couple of times and hit the dirt floor. Dust drifted up and blew away.

Valeria sat up as if in a trance.

At first, I could only see her in profile. Then, very slowly, she turned her head away. She seemed to be studying the audience in the bleachers across from ours. While she did that, I studied the thick, black hair flowing down her back.

Slowly, her head turned to the front, then to *our* side.

All around me, people moaned and whispered.

Rusty was one of those who moaned.

To say that Valeria was gorgeous would be like calling Mount Rushmore a nice piece of sculpture. Rusty won our wager by a landslide. I would get my head shaved by Slim.

Valeria's head turned toward the front again.

She sat motionless. The audience was dead silent.

'*Valeria, arise,*' Stryker commanded in a low, firm voice from the top of the cage.

She glided upward, rising to her feet with the elegance of a ballerina. Standing upright inside her casket, she must've been well over six feet tall. She spread her cape wide open like the wings of a bat and slowly began to turn.

When she turned toward us, I saw the outfit she was wearing beneath her cape: a top that looked like a bright red leather bra, a very short skirt of matching red leather, and red leather boots. The coffin blocked my view of the boots except for their very tops, which came up nearly to her knees.

All around me, people were murmuring. I heard Rusty say, 'Holy shit.'

I might've said it, myself. I don't know what I said, if anything. I only know that I gazed at Valeria, stunned.

Gazed at her amazing, beautiful face.

Gazed at her deep cleavage.

Gazed at the magnificent globes of her leather-encased breasts.

Gazed at her flat belly and the swell of her hips and her smooth, solid-looking thighs.

Then I saw her in profile. Then I saw only her back: the wide-spread cape and her thick, raven hair.

Completing her full turn, she lowered the cape and wrapped it around herself. As she walked toward the foot of her casket, I heard the jangle of spurs and glanced up at Stryker. He stood motionless on top of the cage, staring down at her.

She stepped out of the casket. The spurs were on her scarlet boots. She halted and stood motionless, staring straight ahead.

Stryker raised the microphone to his mouth. 'LADIES AND GENTLEMEN, VALERIA HAS BEEN ENCLOSED IN HER COFFIN SINCE OUR LAST PERFORMANCE SEVERAL NIGHTS AGO.' He paused for a few moments, then said, 'AND SHE IS HUNGRY.'

Murmurs swept through the audience.

353

Lee glanced at me and grinned.

'SHE IS HUNGRY FOR BLOOD.'

Laughter, cheers and applause.

Stryker raised his arms, signaling for silence.

When the audience settled down, he announced, 'THE TRAVELLING VAMPIRE SHOW IS *MORE* THAN A PERFORMANCE BROUGHT HERE FOR YOUR EDIFICATION AND ENTERTAINMENT, LADIES AND GENTLEMEN. IT IS ALSO OUR METHOD OF SUSTAINING VALERIA'S EXISTENCE.

'BEFORE BEING TAKEN INTO CAPTIVITY, SHE ROAMED THE NIGHT AND SUPPED AT RANDOM, DRAINING HER PREY OF THEIR BLOOD – TAKING THEIR LIVES. SHE NO LONGER KILLS. NOW, IN THE COURSE OF EACH PERFORMANCE, SHE GAINS HER NOURISHMENT NOT FROM ONE SOURCE BUT FROM SEVERAL . . . *MEMBERS OF THE AUDIENCE!*'

The people in the stands went wild with cheers, applause, whoops and whistles.

When the noise subsided, Stryker continued. 'WE MAKE A CONTEST OUT OF IT, LADIES AND GENTLE-MEN. A CONTEST OF STRENGTH, COURAGE AND ENDURANCE. AUDIENCE MEMBERS MAY VOLUN-TEER TO ENTER THE CAGE OF VALERIA. ONE AT A TIME, OF COURSE. AND ONE AT A TIME, SHE WILL DRINK THEIR BLOOD . . . OR PERHAPS NOT. THOUGH SHE POSSESSES UNCOMMON STRENGTH AND AGILITY, HER CHALLENGERS FROM THE AUDIENCE ARE SOMETIMES ABLE TO RESIST HER.

'RESIST HER FOR A PERIOD OF FIVE MINUTES . . . PREVENT HER FROM DRINKING SO MUCH AS A SINGLE DROP OF YOUR BLOOD DURING A

BOUT OF FIVE BRIEF MINUTES ... AND YOU WILL
WIN THE SUM OF FIVE HUNDRED DOLLARS.
THAT'S FIVE HUNDRED DOLLARS CASH MONEY,
LADIES AND GENTLEMEN – HALF A THOUSAND
DOLLARS.'
Someone in the grandstands on the other side of the arena
called out, 'You mean we gotta *fight* her?'
'ONLY IF YOU VOLUNTEER, SIR. BUT THAT'S
EXACTLY WHAT I MEAN. VALERIA IS VERY
HUNGRY. SHE'LL WANT THE BLOOD OF ANY-
ONE WHO STEPS INTO THE CAGE WITH HER –
SHE'LL WANT IT *BADLY*. WHOEVER TAKES
HER ON WILL HAVE A DESPERATE FIGHT
ON HIS HANDS. OR ON *HER* HANDS. WOMEN
ARE WELCOME ... EVEN ENCOURAGED ... TO
CHALLENGE VALERIA.' He chuckled in a way that
sounded very phony, then said into his microphone,
'FIVE HUNDRED BUCKS WILL BUY A LOT OF
GROCERIES, WON'T IT, LADIES?'
Another audience member, a woman this time, yelled,
'Ain't enough groceries to *die* for!'
'VALERIA'S CHALLENGERS RARELY DIE, MA'AM.
SHE KNOWS WHEN TO STOP. HAVING YOUR
BLOOD SUCKED BY VALERIA IS NO MORE
DANGEROUS THAN DONATING A PINT TO THE
RED CROSS ... BUT MUCH MORE PLEASURABLE.'
Laughter and murmurs came from the crowd. A man
shouted, 'All *right*!' Another man yelled, 'Sounds good to
me!' Someone else, 'I'm in!'
'BEFORE I ASK FOR VOLUNTEERS,' Julian contin-
ued, 'I MUST WARN YOU THAT THOSE WHO
CHALLENGE VALERIA DO RUN A RISK OF INJURY.
OVER THE YEARS, A FEW HAVE EVEN SUC-
CUMBED TO THEIR INJURIES.'

Lee leaned toward me and I felt her upper arm against mine as she said in a quiet voice, 'They died.'

I nodded.

'SHE IS VERY POWERFUL. THOUGH I'VE TAMED HER TO SOME EXTENT, SHE *IS* A VAMPIRE AND EXTREMELY DANGEROUS. I MUST ASK EVERY CHALLENGER TO SIGN A WAIVER BEFORE STEPPING INTO THE CAGE . . . RELEASING US OF LIABILITY FOR WHATEVER MISFORTUNES MAY OCCUR IN THE COURSE OF THE STRUGGLE.'

He looked down through the bars at Valeria. She still stood motionless just past the end of her coffin, staring straight ahead.

'VALERIA, ARE YOU HUNGRY?'

She flung off her cape, threw her arms wide open as if to embrace the night, and *roared*.

'AUDIENCE, DO WE HAVE A VOLUNTEER?'

Chapter Fifty-two

We did.

Scattered throughout both grandstands, maybe twelve or fifteen people stood up. Those of them who were timid or polite raised one hand like a school kid, while others waved both arms overhead. A couple of them even shouted and whistled. Though I didn't get a good look at everyone who volunteered – including some who had their backs to me – they all seemed to be men.

They had friends in the audience who cheered and yelled.

Stryker, from his perch atop the cage, pointed toward someone on our side of the stands and said, 'YOU, SIR!'

The man punched both fists at the sky as if he'd already won. He was nobody I recognized. As the audience cheered, he sidestepped through a crowded row, reached the cleared area of stairs, and hurried down to the arena.

He wore a plaid shirt, blue jeans and work boots. The shirt and jeans fit him snugly. He looked handsome and rugged. His haircut was a flat-top, brushed straight up so it looked like a bristly triangle. I figured he was probably some sort of construction worker.

When he got to the ground, however, he shoved both fists at the air again and shouted, '*Semper Fi!*'

A United States Marine!

Back in those days, with fathers who had fought in World War Two and Korea, we all knew about places like Guadalcanal, Tarawa, Iwo Jima and the Chosin Reservoir. To most of us, every Marine was a hero. We held them in awe. Some of us still do.

Realizing that the volunteer was a leatherneck, I think I muttered, 'Wow.'

The audience went crazy, cheering and whistling.

He took off his shirt. He had a dark tan and the sort of muscles that made guys like me want to keep our shirts on forever.

I looked over at Lee. She was leaning forward slightly, staring down at the volunteer. She must've caught the motion of my head, because she turned to me and smiled. 'This should be good,' she said.

'A Marine,' I said.

Leaning way forward, Rusty said, 'Anybody know this guy?'

'Not me,' I said.

Lee shook her head.

'Good thing I'm not a homo,' Rusty said. 'I'd fall in love.'

Lee swatted his leg, but not very hard.

Down in the arena, Vivian walked up to the Marine with a clipboard. She took his shirt, spoke to him, and handed him the clipboard. He signed, then gave it back to her.

As she led him toward the cage, Stryker leaped to the ground. The microphone cord came down after him like long black rope. When he landed on the ground, his spurs jangled. They jangled some more as he stepped up to the volunteer.

Stryker said into the mike, 'AND YOUR NAME IS?'

'WALLACE, SIR.'

Vivian skidded the fingernails of one hand down his spine. He squirmed a little and smiled.

People in the audience laughed.

'CHANCE WALLACE,' the man said.

'CHANCE, IS IT? WELL, DO YOU THINK YOU STAND A *CHANCE* AGAINST VALERIA?'

'YES, SIR!'

Vivian patted his rear end through the tight seat of his jeans.

'GOOD LUCK TO YOU.'

'THANK YOU, SIR.'

Stryker stepped away from him and swung open the door of the cage.

Valeria continued to stand motionless just past the foot of her coffin, her back to the door, the cape wrapped around her body.

'LADIES AND GENTLEMEN . . . WE WILL LEAVE THIS DOOR WIDE OPEN SO THAT THE VIC . . . THE *VOLUNTEER* . . . WILL BE ABLE TO MAKE A QUICK ESCAPE IF THE NEED SHOULD ARISE.' He nodded at Chance. 'ARE YOU READY?' he asked.

'MAY I ASK A QUESTION, SIR?' Chance asked into the mike.

'FIRE AWAY.'

'WHAT ARE THE RULES, SIR?'

'YOU DON'T HAVE A WEAPON, DO YOU?'

'NO, SIR.'

'THEN FEEL FREE TO DO WHATEVER YOU DEEM NECESSARY IN ORDER TO PREVENT VALERIA FROM SUCKING YOUR BLOOD. LAST FIVE MINUTES IN THE CAGE WITH HER AND YOU WIN FIVE HUNDRED DOLLARS. ARE YOU READY?'

'Yes, *SIR!*'

Stryker gestured for the Marine to enter the cage.

Chance climbed a couple of wooden stairs and stepped through the doorway.

Stryker removed a timepiece from a pocket of his leather pants. From where I sat, it looked similar to the stopwatch that always dangled around the neck of my high school track coach. Also like my track coach, he wore a silver whistle around his neck. He glanced at the stopwatch, then spoke into his microphone. 'LADIES AND GENTLEMEN, LET THE CONTEST BEGIN!'

Chance moved forward, eyes on Valeria. He walked slowly, hunkered low but keeping his head up, his arms open and his knees bent like a wrestler approaching his opponent.

Valeria remained motionless, her back to him.

With one foot, Chance shoved the coffin out of his way. Another couple of strides took him within reach of Valeria. He halted.

The audience watched in utter silence. All I could really hear were the sounds of the wind.

I don't know why, but it struck me just then that somewhere in the audience were the two degenerates who had tried to take Slim – the Cadillac twins. They might be sitting directly behind me . . . or in the stands on the other side of the arena . . . or anywhere.

Peering around, I started to look for them.

And missed Valeria's first move. As gasps exploded from the audience, I jerked my eyes back to the cage.

Already, Chance was draped from head to waist by the black shroud of Valeria's cape. While he struggled get rid of it, she twirled away and raised both her arms in triumph, her spurs ringing out with each stride. She looked glorious, her raven hair blowing, her skin golden under the stadium lights, her red leather outfit gleaming.

Chance flung the cape aside. The wind caught it, carried it across the cage and pinned it to the bars.

Facing Valeria, he smiled. Then he shook his head and said something, but I couldn't hear what.

They started circling each other.

Chance might've been happy just to circle her for whatever was left of the five minutes. Plenty of us in the audience might've gone along with it, too. If Lee's reaction meant anything, the handsome and shirtless Marine was a real treat for the gals to watch. And every guy in the audience could've sat there all night watching Valeria. She would've been fine to watch if she were simply standing still. In motion, though, she was spectacular. The way the muscles moved under the smooth skin of her thighs and calves, the way we kept getting different views of her leather-harnessed breasts, and how they wobbled and shook.

She was a wonder to behold.

But Chance would be winning five hundred dollars in the next couple of minutes unless she did more than circle and prance and look gorgeous.

She had to know it, too.

We all knew it.

What's she waiting for? I wondered.

Maybe she's afraid of him. Who wouldn't be? A Marine, for godsake.

She attacked.

Went straight at him, roaring, leaping, reaching out with both hands.

People in the audience gasped. Others yelped with fright. Must've been Judo.

Suddenly, Chance twirled and bent, took Valeria down across his hip and threw her. I glimpsed her red boots high in the air. An instant later, her back slammed the dirt. Dust rose around her.

She lay sprawled on her back, apparently stunned.

Chance stared down at her for a few seconds as if not quite sure what to do next. If she'd been an enemy soldier, he probably would've finished her off. But she was a beautiful woman. And he didn't *need* to finish her off: all he had to do was remain unbitten for a while longer.

The audience, sensing Valeria's defeat (and maybe fearing that her loss might put an end to the entire performance), started cheering her on.

'Get him, Val!'

'Come on, honey, you can do it!'

'Time's a-wastin', darlin'! Nail this gyrene's hide!'

She rolled onto her side. Instead of rising, however, she curled up as if she had a stomach ache.

We clapped and stomped our feet and chanted, *'UP! UP! UP!'*

Chance, assuming the victory was his, began to stride around Valeria, waving at the audience, smiling and nodding.

And got too close to her.

With a sweep of one leg, she kicked his right foot forward. Chance's leg flew high. He yelped with surprise and waved his arms. It looked as if he would slam down on his back. In

361

the moment before he hit the ground, however, he turned his body. He shouted – 'YAH!' – and slapped the ground, landing on his side.

Unhurt, he rolled to get away from Valeria. But not fast enough. She hurled herself onto his back, hooked an arm across his throat, and darted her face down against the side of his neck.

He let out a yelp of surprise and pain.

Then he just lay underneath her, not resisting. Valeria no longer seemed to be struggling, either. She was sprawled on top of him, hands on his shoulders, her body squirming as if Chance were her lover, not her victim.

I couldn't see what was happening with her mouth, but I was pretty sure what must be going on.

Stryker entered the cage, trailing the microphone cord. 'AND THE WINNER IS . . . *VALERIA!*'

The audience erupted with clapping, cheers, shouts and whistles.

Valeria stayed on top of Chance's back, face still down against his neck.

Stryker frowned at her. 'VALERIA! QUIT!'

She didn't quit.

She went on with Chance as if they were all alone in the world.

'*VALERIA!*'

She ignored him.

Stryker stepped over to her, raised his right leg and raked the rowel of his big silver spur across her bare back just above the waist of her skirt.

Her head darted up and swung around. Glaring over her shoulder at Stryker, she roared. Blood flew from her mouth.

As I gaped at her, shocked, she turned her head the other way to let those in the other bleachers get a good look.

Silence.

Nobody spoke or laughed or clapped . . . or moved. The wind blew, hissing through the forest and lifting the long black hair from Valeria's shoulders.

Into the microphone, Stryker said, 'IT'S OVER, MY DARLING. YOU'VE WON.'

Chapter Fifty-three

After Valeria climbed off the Marine, several members of Stryker's black-shirted crew came into the arena wheeling a gurney. While they hurried toward the cage, Chance rolled onto his back and managed to stand up.

Applause rippled through the crowd even before Stryker's voice boomed out, 'LET'S HEAR IT FOR A REAL CONTENDER!'

The applause grew to a roar.

Chance raised his hand in a game but embarrassed wave, sort of like a cowboy who has just gotten tossed off the back of a Brahma bull. Staggering out of the cage, he waved off the gurney in spite of the fact that he appeared to be bitten on the right side of his neck. He had blood all over his shoulder and running down his back and chest. He must've not considered it very serious, though. Not serious enough to merit a visit to an emergency room – or wherever the gurney crew had planned to take him.

As he hobbled back toward the bleachers, Vivian came along with his shirt. She didn't give it to him, though. Instead, she took hold of one arm and spoke to him. He nodded, then walked off with her.

Maybe to get himself bandaged.

Stryker proclaimed, 'CHANCE WALLACE, LADIES AND GENTLEMEN!'

More wild applause. Chance waved again, then walked out of sight with Vivian.

'CHANCE'S TIME IN THE CAGE WITH VALERIA . . .' Stryker glanced at his stopwatch. 'THREE MINUTES, FORTY-EIGHT SECONDS! A FINE DISPLAY OF COURAGE!'

Valeria, standing near Stryker in the cage, was using a wet towel to wipe the blood off her face and neck and chest.

'THAT WAS ONLY THE BEGINNING, LADIES AND GENTLEMEN! CHANCE'S BLOOD DID LITTLE MORE THAN WHET THE APPETITE OF THE GLORIOUS . . . AND VERY THIRSTY . . . VALERIA!'

She dropped the towel to the ground. One of the helpers hurried in to retrieve it.

'WHO WOULD LIKE TO GO NEXT?'

Leaning forward, Rusty looked past Lee and said to me, 'Was that bitchin', or what?'

'Pretty cool,' I said, and suddenly wished Slim could've been here to watch it with us. She would've gotten a kick out of seeing this woman wipe out a Marine. Also, I would've liked to have her sitting beside me. Lee on one side, Slim on the other.

I supposed she was probably sitting in her Pontiac, listening to the radio.

Or maybe listening to Bitsy. I could just see the poor thing sitting in the front seat with Slim, crying her eyes out, sobbing her tale of getting pounded by her brother . . .

Why didn't I stop him?

Slim would be shocked and outraged by what we'd done. And sympathetic toward Bitsy in spite of the names the girl had called her.

'YOU! YOU THERE. YES, YOU.'

Stryker's tinny, amplified voice startled me, tore me out of my daydreams and planted me in the present.

I saw a man climbing down the bleachers across the arena from us. He was a skinny guy, bald on top, and wearing glasses. He couldn't be more than forty years old, but he was dressed like a codger in a white polo shirt, plaid Bermuda shorts, knee socks and loafers. He sort of laughed and waved at the crowd as he made his way down to the arena.

'Here's a sure winner,' Lee said.

Rusty and I laughed.

Down in the arena, he kept his shirt on and signed Vivian's clipboard. Then she led him up the stairs and through the doorway of the cage.

Stryker asked his name. The gawky man leaned close to the microphone in Stryker's hand and said, 'I'M CHESTER.'

'*Go, Chester!*' yelled someone in the audience.

Grinning, he nodded and waved.

'READY TO TAKE ON VALERIA?' Stryker asked.

'OH, WELL, SURE.' He shrugged. 'CAN'T SEE WHY NOT.'

'THAT FIVE HUNDRED DOLLAR PRIZE MUST LOOK AWFULLY GOOD TO YOU.'

'IT AIN'T HAY,' said Chester.

Rusty leaned forward. 'This guy's a goner.'

'WOULD YOU LIKE TO LEAVE YOUR GLASSES WITH OUR BEAUTIFUL ASSISTANT?'

Chester shook his head. Into the mike, he said, 'I'LL KEEP 'EM ON, THANKS.' Stryker started to pull the mike away, but Chester grabbed it and pulled it close to his mouth. 'YOUR GAL HERE, THIS VALERIA, SHE'S A

FINE-LOOKING WOMAN. A GUY'D HAVE TO BE NUTS TO GO IN THAT CAGE WITH HIS GLASSES OFF.'

With that comment, he won the audience. The grandstands erupted with laughter and cheers.

I looked at Valeria. She had her eyes on Chester, and didn't crack a smile.

Stryker was chuckling, though. He patted Chester on the back and said, 'BEST OF LUCK, MY FRIEND.'

Chester bobbed his head, grinning.

'ANY QUESTIONS?'

'NOPE. JUST LET ME AT HER.'

Stryker walked out of the cage and trotted down the stairs, his spurs jangling. At the bottom, he hauled out his stopwatch. 'LADIES AND GENTLEMEN,' he announced, 'LET THE CONTEST BEGIN!'

Valeria planted her hands on her hips and stared at Chester.

He stood there, arms hanging by his sides, and studied her. He didn't even try to be sneaky about it, just ogled her, his head moving slowly up and down. After doing that for a while, he wiped the back of a hand across his mouth.

Nervous-sounding laughter ruffled through the crowd.

Chester looked around, grinning at his audience. Then he leered at Valeria, raised both hands to chest level, and flexed his fingers as if honking her breasts.

That bought him wild laughter and cheers . . . along with a chorus of *boos*.

Smirking, Valeria walked toward him. She moved slowly, her back arched, arms by her sides, as if offering to let him squeeze more than just air.

He pointed a finger at himself and mouthed, 'Me?'

She nodded.

He reached out, actually clutched the red leather cups and

squeezed them. He squeezed them a couple of more times, turning his head and mugging for the audience.

'I bet he's a ringer,' Lee said.

'Huh?' I asked.

'Someone they planted in the audience. He can't be for real.'

Rusty leaned forward. 'I bet you're right. She isn't gonna let some *stranger* grab her . . . her you-know-whats.'

Lee chuckled and shook her head.

Down in the cage, Chester had stopped making faces. He'd stopped pretending to honk Valeria's breasts. Now he was stroking their bare tops while she stood there motionless, letting him.

Lucky Chester.

Then one of her hands glided forward and she rubbed the front of his Bermuda shorts.

His mouth fell open and his back arched.

Everyone in the grandstands probably couldn't see where Valeria had put her hand – the angle was only right for some of us – but half the crowd went '*EWWWWWWWWW*' and so many shrill whistles ripped through the air that my ears cringed.

Chester stood as if frozen.

I heard Rusty murmur, 'Man, oh man.'

Lee grinned at him and patted his knee.

My mouth was dry, but I managed to say, 'This guy *has* to be a ringer.'

'Oh, yeah,' Lee said.

I wondered how much time he had left. At least a couple of minutes must've gone by so far. If he really was a ringer, maybe the plan was to let him win.

Valeria pulled down the zipper of his shorts.

'Oh, great,' Lee grumbled. 'You guys shouldn't be . . .'

Valeria reached into Chester's open fly.

'. . . seeing this.'

The reaction of the audience was a wild mixture of joy, consternation and excitement. Through all the hoots and whistles and applause, I heard shouts of, '*No!*' and, '*Go for it!*' and, '*All right!*' and '*Someone put a stop to this!*' and several suggestions that were extremely foul and vulgar.

Instead of doing what most of us probably expected, however, Valeria turned her hand upward and clutched Chester's pants: not only the upper areas of the zipper, but apparently the waistband of his Bermudas and also his belt buckle. Then she hoisted him off his feet.

He squealed, flapped his arms and kicked.

With just her one arm, Valeria rammed him all the way up. Luckily (or due to plenty of rehearsals), his head missed the bars. It passed through a space between two of them and poked out the top of the cage. The bars stopped him at the shoulders.

Letting go of him, Valeria twirled out of the way.

Chester yelped and started to fall. Then suddenly he grabbed the bars. He pulled himself up until his head was again jutting out the top of the cage.

'*Help!*' he yelled.

Far as I could tell, nobody in the audience seemed very upset by his plight. A good many of us must've already suspected he was a ringer. And some of the audience, especially women, probably figured he was getting his just deserts.

There was nervous laughter – and cheering – when Valeria reached out with both hands and jerked his Bermudas down. For underwear, he wore baggy white boxer shorts decorated with red polka dots.

This guy was *definitely* a ringer. His antics had been nothing but a stage performance.

I felt a strange mixture of relief and disappointment.

Is it ALL fake?

Most likely, I thought.

Then Valeria jerked the boxers down to Chester's ankles. From the waist down, he was naked.

She pulled the Bermudas and boxers down over his shoes and tossed them across the cage. Now Chester was dangling there in nothing but his Polo shirt, knee socks and loafers. He had a skinny, pale butt. He also, much to the shock and delight and amusement and dismay of the spectators, had a boner.

It didn't matter where you were sitting; the way he kicked and twisted, everyone in the bleachers got to see both sides of Chester.

I was suddenly very aware of why they tried to keep kids away from the show.

And I was suddenly embarrassed to be watching this with Lee sitting beside me. And glad that Slim had decided against coming.

Chester's groin area was just about level with Valeria's face.

She stepped up to him and opened her mouth.

Some people screamed. Including Chester. Others cried out '*No!*' and, '*Oh, my God!*' and a few suggestions such as, '*Bite it off!*'

I figured the five minutes must be running out. Valeria had better do something fast or Chester would win the five hundred bucks.

She slowly leaned closer, her mouth wide open as if ready to take him in . . .

He squealed, '*No!*' and kicked out, driving his right shoe into Valeria's midsection. She grunted and stumbled backward, bending over, hugging her belly. As she fell to the dirt, Chester let go of the bars and dropped.

Huffing for breath, he stared down at her. He was standing

at her feet. Her legs were parted, her knees up. Chester seemed to be staring up her short leather skirt.

He swung around and looked toward the open door of the cage.

Thinking about it.

Wondering how much time he had left.

Or maybe no longer caring about the time or about the five hundred dollars or about anything other than what was sprawled on the ground behind him.

Pulling the Polo shirt over his head, he whirled around. He flung the shirt away. Naked down to his knee socks, he dived for Valeria, arms extended, hands all set to grab her breasts. He would've landed between her knees in perfect position for thrusting into her body, but one of her feet shot up.

In an instant of silence, I heard the jingle of a spur.

Then Chester squealed. Braced up by Valeria's right leg, he was thrown over her body. He flipped over in midair and landed on his back across her open casket.

He'd been split open from navel to sternum.

'Holy shit,' Rusty muttered.

Lee blinked, shook her head and said, 'Maybe he's *not* a ringer,' as Valeria, down in the cage, buried her face in Chester's bloody abdomen.

Chapter Fifty-four

The black-shirted crew hustled into the cage and lifted Chester onto the gurney. As they rolled him away, Valeria took a wet towel from one of the helpers and started to wipe the blood off her body. Stryker spoke into the microphone: 'LET'S HEAR IT FOR CHESTER, LADIES AND GENTLEMEN! A REAL SCRAPPER!

Down beside him in the cage, Valeria raised her right leg and propped her boot on an edge of the coffin. Bending down, she used the towel to wipe the blood off her spur. As she did that, I stared at the red mark across her back . . . the wound inflicted by Stryker's spur.

Hers was just a scratch.

She'd really opened Chester up.

'AND HOW ABOUT THAT PHYSIQUE!' Stryker went on. 'IF ANY OF YOU LADIES ARE INTERESTED, I'M SURE YOU'LL HAVE NO TROUBLE FINDING CHESTER LATER AT THE LOCAL EMERGENCY ROOM.'

Here and there, people were making their way down the bleachers. Mostly women. Several towed men along behind them.

Apparently, they'd had enough.

Ignoring the exodus, Stryker studied his stopwatch. 'CHESTER LASTED A GRAND TOTAL OF FOUR MINUTES AND FORTY-THREE SECONDS. CAME UP ONLY SEVENTEEN SECONDS SHORT, LADIES AND GENTLEMEN.'

Vivian hurried over to Stryker and leaned in close to his side. As she started speaking into his ear, he lowered the

371

microphone. Whatever she was telling him, we couldn't hear it.

'Maybe we should be going, too,' Lee said.

Rusty blurted, 'No! We can't!'

'This is worse than I thought it'd be. You boys shouldn't be seeing this sort of thing. *I* shouldn't either.'

'*Please*, Mrs Thompson.'

She shook her head. 'I don't know what I was thinking, bringing you boys to a show like—'

'It's not so bad,' Rusty said.

'That man was naked.'

'So? It was just a *guy*. I mean, maybe *you* didn't like to see that, but it wasn't any big deal for me and Dwight. It ain't pretty, but we see that sorta stuff in gym class all the time. Right, Dwight?'

I just shrugged.

'You don't see guys get ripped open,' Lee said.

'It's just a show, Mrs Thompson. You said so yourself. I'll bet Chester didn't even get a scratch on him. It was probably all a big fake-out. They can do that sorta stuff, magicians and people like that. It's easy.'

Lee frowned and shook her head, but I noticed she was still sitting down. In my opinion, she felt that she *ought* to take us away from the evil show, but she didn't much want to miss the rest of it, herself.

I finally opened my mouth. 'Why don't we just stick around for one more bout and see what happens?'

Lee frowned and sighed. 'I suppose we can stay for *one* more.' Glancing from Rusty to me, she said, 'But you guys have to promise you'll never breathe a word about any of this to your parents.' To me, she added, 'Or your brothers. If they find out I dragged you guys to something like . . .'

'I'll never tell,' Rusty said.

'I sure won't,' I said. 'I promise.'

'Okay. Well, I guess we can stay a little while longer.'

Rusty grinned and clapped. 'You're the best, Mrs Thompson.'

'Yeah, sure.'

Just about then, Vivian got finished whispering to Stryker. As she hurried out of the cage, he raised the microphone to his mouth. 'I'VE JUST BEEN ASSURED THAT CHESTER WILL NEED A FEW STITCHES, BUT HE'LL BE FINE. LET'S HEAR IT AGAIN FOR HIM!'

Some applause came from the crowd, but not much.

'PERHAPS HE DESERVED WORSE THAN HE GOT.'

With that comment, Stryker won over a good portion of the remaining spectators. They laughed and cheered.

'BUT THE SCRAWNY LITTLE BASTARD CAME WITHIN A MERE SEVENTEEN SECONDS OF WALKING HOME WITH FIVE HUNDRED DOLLARS CASH MONEY IN HIS POCKET! HE LASTED *THAT* LONG, FOLKS. IF HE CAN STICK IT OUT – NO PUN INTENDED . . .'

Laughter, groans, applause.

'IF CHESTER CAN *LAST* THAT LONG, WHY NOT YOU? OUTLAST HIM BY A MEAGER SEVENTEEN SECONDS AND YOU'LL WIN THE BIG PRIZE. NOW, HOW ABOUT IT, FOLKS? DO WE HAVE A VOLUNTEER?'

'*I'll take her!*' shouted someone behind me.

I recognized the voice.

As shouts and cheers erupted from the crowd, I twisted around and saw Scotty Douglas near the top of the bleachers. Though standing up, he wasn't going anywhere yet. He stood there smirking, flanked by five or six of his hoodlum friends including a couple of tough-looking gals. Not letting the hot night get in the way of fashion, they *all* wore black leather jackets. I didn't know any of the others, but I had no trouble recognizing Scotty.

Even though I hadn't seen him in a long time (he'd dropped out of high school after his junior year and moved to Clement), the sight of him gave me a sickish feeling in my stomach. It was pretty much the same feeling I'd gotten a couple of years earlier when he and his two buddies, Tim and Smack, went after Slim and Rusty and me when we were at Janks Field for archery practice.

He looked about the same as always: greasy hair piled high on his head, long sideburns, black leather jacket, white T-shirt and blue jeans. He wore a familiar sneer on his face. A cigarette dangled from a corner from his lips.

'YOU!' Stryker announced. 'YOU UP THERE IN THE LEATHER JACKET!'

Scotty nodded, winked toward Stryker, then turned to his friends. He spoke to them for a few seconds – probably cracking wise about how he would decimate Valeria. After that, he stripped off his leather jacket and handed it to one of the gals. Then he started to work his way across the row.

He'd gained a scar on his left cheek since the last time I'd seen him. Also, he looked as if he'd gained about twenty pounds of muscle.

Rusty said, 'Jesus H. Christ, is that who I think it is?'

'It's him, all right,' I said.

'The Douglas kid?' Lee asked.

'Yeah.'

'I knew his big brother. A real . . . jerk.'

'Must run in the family,' I said.

I watched Scotty make his way down the bleachers and enter the arena. He didn't seem to have a limp anymore, but I bet he still had a scar from Slim's arrow.

He was wearing motorcycle boots, the same as always.

Cigarette hanging off his lower lip, he took the clipboard from Valeria and signed it. Then he tossed his butt into the dirt, climbed the stairs and entered the cage.

'NAME'S SCOT DOUGLAS,' he said into Stryker's microphone. 'I'M HERE TO COLLECT MY FIVE HUNDRED BUCKS.'

The grandstands went wild with shouts and hoots and whistles. The worst of the noise came from behind us. Looking over my shoulder, I saw what I expected: Scotty's friends were on their feet, a couple of them waving and shrieking while three were busy giving out ear-splitting whistles with the help of fingers buried in their mouths.

'THINK YOU CAN BEAT CHESTER'S RECORD?' Stryker asked.

'DAMN RIGHT, SPORT.'

'WELL, GOOD LUCK TO YOU.' Spurs jingling, Stryker walked out of the cage and trotted down the stairs to the ground. He raised his stopwatch. 'LADIES AND GENTLEMEN, LET THE CONTEST BEGIN!'

For a while, Scotty and Valeria stood a few feet apart, looking each other over . . . Scotty smirking, Valeria glaring back at him with narrow eyes. Then they started circling like a couple of wrestlers.

The crowd went silent.

Scotty peeled off his T-shirt. Holding it in one hand, he swung it like a towel, sweeping it past Valeria's face, snapping it at her bare midriff.

Way off beyond the other bleachers, the sky flashed as if a monstrous light bulb had burst to life inside a thunderhead, shuddered and quickly died.

Scotty whipped his T-shirt at Valeria's face. She tore it from his hands and the wind tossed it across the cage.

Thunder grumbled through the night.

Here it comes, I thought. All day long, the sky had been grim with clouds, the air heavy and moist and hot. *Now* the storm would come . . . in time to spoil the show.

It isn't here yet, I told myself.

Besides, Lee's going to drag us out of here as soon as Valeria finishes with Scotty.

Maybe.

While I'd been busy worrying about the storm, Scotty had been busy pulling his thick leather belt out of the loops in his jeans. Now he was swinging it instead of the T-shirt, snapping it at Valeria as she circled him.

She didn't seem to be in any hurry to rush him. Nor did she seem very concerned by the belt. Though she dodged and feinted fairly often, she didn't make any great efforts to avoid its lash. Every so often, the leather smacked against her skin with a sound like a face being slapped. Each time that happened, she flinched but just kept circling Scotty.

Why didn't she close in and put a stop to it?

I started to wince myself each time the belt struck her.

Turning to Lee, I said, 'Why doesn't she . . .?' But even as the words started to come out, I noticed that Lee seemed entranced by the spectacle. Her eyes had a glazed look and her mouth hung open.

Though I hadn't finished my question, she blinked and turned her head. 'Huh? What was that?'

'I was just . . . why is she letting him *do* that? He's hurting her.'

Lee shook her head, muttered, 'Don't know,' and returned her attention to the cage.

Rusty leaned forward and said to me, 'Bet she *likes* it. Some gals *like* to get knocked around, you know? Turns 'em on.'

I nodded. 'Yeah, that's probably it.'

We both stopped talking.

Eyes on the show again, I flinched as the tip of Scotty's belt cracked against Valeria's belly. That one must've *really* hurt, because she cried out and twisted away.

As Scotty rushed after her, swinging his belt, she backed away from him. A couple more strides, and a wall of the cage would stop her retreat.

Suddenly, she reached behind her back, undid whatever fasteners were there, and swept off the bright red leather top of her costume. The sight of her naked breasts tore my breath away. All through the audience, people gasped. I could feel myself growing hard. A moan came from Rusty's direction, but I didn't look over at him. Couldn't look anywhere except at Valeria.

Clad only in her short red skirt and boots, she whipped the bra-like garment through the air in front of her. The quick motion swung her breasts.

In midair, the red leather of Valeria's top met the black leather of Scotty's belt.

They tangled.

Valeria's arm leaped back and the belt flew from Scotty's hand.

The crowd roared with delight.

Most of the crowd, that is. The bunch behind us – Scotty's friends – hissed and booed. Someone from back there shouted, 'Get her, Scot!' Another shouted, 'Ream her!'

Down in the cage, Valeria flung away the tangled leather of Scotty's belt and the top of her costume. They landed inside her open casket. Scotty watched them drop out of sight with a look on his face as if his favorite hat had just been blown over the edge of a cliff.

Beyond the other bleachers, a jagged dagger of lightning ripped through the night.

Scotty made a dash for the casket.

He wanted that belt.

Valeria raced to intercept him, her large breasts leaping and swinging.

Thunder grumbled.

She dived, wrapped her arms around Scotty's waist as he ran, and tore him to the ground. They rolled through the dirt. Then Scotty was on his back. Valeria, straddling him, grabbed his shoulder with one hand and his head with the other. She shoved his head sideways, then plunged her face against the side of his neck.

He thrashed and writhed underneath her.

Stryker's voice boomed from the speakers, 'AND THE WINNER IS . . . VALERIA!'

She stayed on Scotty, not done with him yet.

Stryker ran into the cage. 'THAT'S ENOUGH, VALERIA! STOP IT.'

She didn't stop.

'NEED ANOTHER TASTE OF THE SPUR?'

She clung to Scotty for a few seconds more, then raised her head and rolled off him. She flopped on her back, gasping for air. Her lips and cheeks and chin – even the tip of her nose – were crimson with Scotty's blood. The rest of her body gleamed with sweat.

As the crew rushed into the cage, Stryker announced, 'SCOT'S TIME WITH VALERIA, THREE MINUTES AND TWENTY SECONDS.'

He hadn't lasted nearly as long as the frail Chester, but the audience showed lots of appreciation. Maybe because he'd gotten Valeria to remove her top.

The crew lifted Scotty onto a gurney and hurried away with him.

There was a lot of blood on the dirt floor where he'd been sprawled.

The audience cheered Valeria as she rose to her feet. Her

body gleaming with blood and sweat, she thrust both arms toward the sky in triumph and pranced around in a circle as if doing some sort of victory dance. The way she looked – beautiful and shiny, hair blowing in the hot wind, breasts bouncing and swinging – drove the audience to a frenzy. All around us, people stood up.

My view was blocked, so I stood up, too. As did Lee and Rusty.

Apparently enjoying her ovation, Valeria danced around even more wildly.

As she leaped and twirled, lightning in the shape of an upside-down tree turned the sky brilliant. Every detail of Valeria trembled in stark relief – the wild look on her face, the curves of her muscles and ribcage, the jutting tips of her breasts . . .

I felt hard and achy. Without underwear on, I was pushing tight against the inside of my jeans. I started to worry about having another accident so I sat down. This not only relieved the pressure, but it took Valeria out of sight.

Thunder roared, shaking the night.

Lee sat down beside me. 'You okay?' she asked.

I nodded.

'We'd probably better get going,' she said.

'I guess so.'

'Before something *else* happens.'

'Guess so,' I said.

She patted my leg, then turned her head the other way. Toward Rusty.

But he wasn't there.

Chapter Fifty-five

All I could figure was that Rusty must've had an accident, himself, and hurried away to prevent Lee or anyone else from noticing it.

'Come on,' Lee said. She started to stand up.

'No, wait.'

'What?'

'Why don't we wait here for him? He probably just went . . .'

Lee shook her head. 'He knows we're about to leave. Maybe he just went on ahead.'

We were both wrong.

In front of us, the spectators sat down and we saw Rusty halfway down the bleacher stairs, waving both hands overhead. Shirtless and bandaged, he almost looked as if he'd *already* been in the cage with Valeria. Racing toward the bottom, he shouted, *'Me! Me! I'm next! I call it! My turn!'*

The audience cheered him.

Lightning ripped through the sky.

'Oh, my God,' Lee muttered.

I couldn't believe my eyes – oh, yes I could. Though stunned, I wasn't very surprised. Of *course* Rusty wanted to get into the cage with Valeria. He probably saw this as the opportunity of a lifetime.

And maybe he was right.

The thunder came . . . a long, rumbling noise. I could feel its vibrations in my chest like the drums of a parade band.

The storm was coming closer.

But wasn't here yet.

Valeria stood in the cage, breathing hard, slowly rubbing her body with the towel. She hadn't put her top back on. It was probably still inside the casket.

'*Rusty!*' I shouted. The crowd was clapping and yelling, so maybe he couldn't hear me. '*Don't!*' I called out.

'Come on,' Lee said. She stood up, sidestepped past the empty space left by Rusty, and started to make her way through the seated spectators.

I stayed close to her.

'Excuse me,' Lee said to the people we had to disturb.

We were facing forward. The knees of those behind us jammed the backs of our legs. Our thighs rubbed the backs of people the next row down. I'd lost my boner by then, or it would've poked some heads.

'Excuse me,' Lee said. 'Excuse me. Excuse me.'

A few people stood up to let us by. Others didn't budge and we had to shove past their legs.

'Excuse me. Excuse me.'

'*Sit down!*'

'*Down in front!*'

'*Y'make a better door than window!*'

As we struggled across the row, I watched Rusty scribble on Vivian's clipboard. She took his arm and led him up the steps. As they entered the cage, another tree of lightning cracked across the night.

Lee and I broke through the end of the row.

Thunder crashed.

But still no rain.

If the rain starts, I thought, will they stop the fight?

Probably not.

I followed Lee as she raced down the stairs toward the arena.

'I SEE WE HAVE AN EAGER YOUNG VOLUN- TEER,' Stryker said, his amplified voice loud and crackling.

'I'M RUSTY,' Rusty said into the microphone.

The audience cheered.

Rusty turned all the way around, grinning like a dope and waving at the crowd.

Someone called out, '*Go get her, Rusty!*'

Another, '*Nail her!*'

'*Give them titties a squeeze for me!*'

And worse.

Suddenly, near the bottom of the bleachers, our way was blocked by half a dozen black-shirted members of Stryker's crew.

'READY TO TAKE ON VALERIA?' Stryker asked.

'Excuse me,' Lee said, and tried to keep going.

'YOU BET,' Rusty said.

The man directly in front of Lee shook his head and spread out his arms.

'Let us through,' Lee said.

'You'll just have to wait your turn, miss.'

'*Down in front!*'

'*Hey, sit down!*'

'That kid can't fight Valeria,' Lee said.

'Sure, he can.'

'He's under age.'

The man smirked. 'Big deal.'

'*Outa the way, for cry-sake!*'

'I'm his mother and I forbid . . .'

'BEST OF LUCK, RUSTY!'

'His mother, my ass.'

'THANK YOU, MR STRYKER.'

A thin, tough-looking woman beside the guy said, 'We don't want any trouble here.'

'Then don't let Rusty fight!'

'*Move yer asses!*'

'*Down in front!*'

The woman shook her head. 'Why don't you both return to your seats and enjoy the show?'

'LADIES AND GENTLEMEN, LET THE CONTEST BEGIN!'

Another harsh flash of lightning.

'You can't *do* this!' Lee shouted.

'Hell we can't. Sit down or we'll have you removed from the premises.'

The crowd roared.

So did the thunder.

The fight had started. We didn't stand much chance of stopping it, now. I wanted to watch. And so did a dozen or so people whose views we were blocking.

Apparently, so did Lee. 'Okay, okay,' she said.

Though there were empty spaces down low, Lee raced halfway up the stairs before moving toward the center, squeezing past half a dozen spectators and taking a seat. If she couldn't stop the fight, at least she wanted a good vantage point for watching it. Breathless, I sat beside her.

The black-shirted crew watched us for a few more seconds, then spread out and seemed to vanish.

From the look of things in the cage, we hadn't missed much. Rusty and Valeria were both hunched over, arms out, circling each other slowly.

Which seemed to be the standard way to begin such contests.

I felt scared for Rusty. But I also envied him. There he was, face to face with Valeria, probably one of the most beautiful women to ever walk the earth – three or four feet away from that amazing face and those incredible, naked breasts.

It seemed like madness.

Glorious madness.

This must've been like a dream come true for Rusty.

He was sure to pay dearly for it, but it might be worth the payment.

Valeria seemed in no hurry to attack. Neither did Rusty – not with the kind of view he had. But I knew him. What he really wanted, now, was to reach out and feel those breasts.

He *had* to get his hands on them.

Even in front of an audience brimming with people who knew him and his parents?

You bet, I thought. He won't let a little thing like that stop him.

I could just see him grin and hear him say, *Hey, man, by the time someone tells on me, it'll be over. What're my folks gonna do, ground me? They can't make it not've happened, know what I mean?* And he would be showing me his hands as if they were trophies.

He went for her.

Rushed forward, ducking and reaching out with both hands. I thought he was going for her breasts, but then he dived and grabbed the sides of her leather skirt. His weight tore the skirt from her hips.

As Rusty fell, Valeria stumbled backward until the skirt tripped her. She landed on her back. The impact jolted her entire body, bounced her head off the dirt floor and jarred her breasts.

The audience exploded with delight.

The night exploded with lightning.

On his knees, Rusty snatched Valeria's skirt off her boots. The spurs seemed to give him trouble for a moment. Then the skirt pulled free and he flung it out of reach.

Thunder pounded through the air.

Valeria was now naked except for the crimson boots that reached almost to her knees.

She just lay there, sprawled out and limp, staring at the

sky . . . either knocked into a stupor by the blow to her head or faking it.

I figured she *had* to be faking. Vampire or not, she'd outmatched much tougher men than Rusty tonight.

'*Get away from her!*' I shouted.

He probably couldn't hear me through the tumult of the crowd.

Lee joined my shouts. In unison, we yelled, '*Get away from her, Rusty!*'

If Valeria really *was* stunned or unconscious, Rusty actually stood a chance of winning the contest. Five hundred bucks was a ton of money for a guy who forever spent his allowance the day he got it. But he needed to keep his distance . . .

Instead of getting away from her, he scooted forward on his knees, sliding his hands up her bare legs.

The audience cheered him on.

'*Rusty!*' I yelled. '*No!*'

But the lure must've been irresistible. I knew him well. He claimed he'd never seen a naked woman in real life, much less touched one. And he'd never *seen* a woman as beautiful as Valeria.

These were probably the most fabulous moments of his entire life.

'Is he nuts?' Lee asked.

As his hands travelled up Valeria's thighs, the crowd roared with delight and advice.

Lee yelled, '*Rusty, watch out! She's playing 'possum! Get away from her!*'

Rusty spread Valeria's legs apart. Either that, or she moved them herself. I missed who did it. I just suddenly realized her thighs were wider apart than a moment earlier.

'*It's a trick!*' Lee shouted. '*Get away from her! Run!*'

On his knees between her legs, Rusty leaned forward and put a hand on each of her breasts. He rubbed them slowly as

if she'd asked him to spread suntan oil on them. They
wobbled around under the motions of his hands. When he
squeezed them, they seemed springy.

Valeria just lay there, not reacting.

Maybe she *isn't* faking, I thought.

If she's hurt, shouldn't Stryker put a stop to this? Was he
planning to just let Rusty spend the rest of the five minutes
feeling her up?

Rusty hunkered down and put his mouth on Valeria's
right breast. He seemed to be kissing or sucking its nipple.
Then his head was moving all around. I didn't know
what he was doing at first, then realized he was *licking* her
breast.

A dagger of lightning stabbed down from the sky, roaring,
and struck the top of one of the light poles. It was just
behind the other bleachers. The bank of stadium lights
exploded . . . along with the top of the pole.

All the lights surrounding the grandstands suddenly died.

Chapter Fifty-six

We were plunged into darkness . . . except for a fluttering
yellow-orange glow of firelight. It came from the blazing
top of the pole that the lightning had struck.

Suddenly, warm rain was pouring down.

The blazing pole loomed over the bleachers like a giant
torch, dimmed by the rain but still on fire.

All around us, people began leaping to their feet.

They wanted *out*.

As they shoved and bumped us in their rush to escape, Lee and I stood up. We climbed onto our seats and looked down. On both sides of the arena, people were fleeing through the downpour. Some were falling. Others were fighting. But I didn't care what was happening to them.

I turned my eyes toward the cage in the center of the arena.

By then, the fiery light post had nearly been extinguished. Through the heavy rain, I could barely make out the shapes of Rusty and Valeria.

Then came another blast of lightning.

It turned the rain into slanting silver streaks and filled the cage with a shuddering white glare. I glimpsed Rusty on top of Valeria, jeans down around his ankles, his white rump shoving, flexing.

Darkness.

Someone bumped me from behind. I don't know whether it was deliberate or one of those careless collisions of the kind that happens when people are in a hurry. Either way, the result was the same. I yelped and teetered.

Lee grabbed me. She couldn't stop me, though. We both fell forward, grappling with each other, colliding with a few people below us, knocking them off their feet before we crashed down on the slick, wet bleachers. We rolled and fell between two rows.

I struck a board. Then Lee crushed me against it.

She seemed very heavy for such a slender woman. I couldn't budge. She lay on top of me, gasping for breath. Her cheek was warm and wet against the left side of my face while the right side got pelted by rain. Under my back, I felt the vibrations of all the shoes and boots and sandals and bare feet pounding their way down the bleachers.

Nobody stopped to help us.

For that matter, with the darkness and downpour and the way we were down in a low place between the rows, maybe no one even *saw* us.

The bleachers trembled and shook.

Out behind the stands, car doors thumped. Engines began to sputter and cough and race. Headlights came on, casting a pale glow into the rain-filled air above Janks Field. Horns honked. People shouted. More doors slammed. More engines revved.

I suddenly remembered the Cadillac twins and what I'd done to their car.

I'd intended to strand them, but I hadn't planned on *our* being trapped in the grandstands when it happened.

Brilliant move, Thompson.

Directly above us, lightning fluttered across the sky and thunder crashed. Lee flinched.

Which surprised me. She seemed too strong for that. But all her weight was on top of me, so there was no mistake about it: she jerked like a startled little girl. Suddenly feeling protective of her, I raised my arms and wrapped them around her back.

'You okay?' I asked.

She nodded, her cheek sliding against my face. 'How about you?' she asked.

'Guess I'm okay.'

'Am I crushing you?'

'Nah.'

'Maybe we'd better stay here for a few minutes. Give the crowd a chance to clear out.'

I almost told her that I wanted to get up and check on Rusty . . . but then I remembered my last glimpse of him in the lightning flash. It made me feel a little sick.

Valeria obviously wasn't a vampire, after all. Just a beautiful woman with a very strange and dangerous job. And she hadn't been playing 'possum, after all. She'd been stunned or out cold.

You don't *do* things to someone in that condition.

You just don't.

Not even if she's gorgeous and naked and pretends to be a vampire.

I knew Rusty was always horny, always making crude remarks, always talking (when Slim wasn't around) about how much he'd like to 'do it' to this or that girl. Or 'jump her bones' or 'give her a taste of the one-eyed monster' or so on. Maybe it shouldn't have been a shock to catch him doing that to Valeria.

But it was.

How did he even know *how*?

The way he'd been going at her, I couldn't help thinking that maybe he'd had some previous experience.

No. He would've bragged about it.

Unless the girl was . . .

From somewhere behind the bleachers came a scream.

Looking back toward Janks Field, all I could see was a pale glow given off by headlights. I was too high in the stands for a view of the ground or even the vehicles.

'Glad we're not mixed up in that,' Lee said.

'Yeah.'

'How you doing?'

'Fine.'

'You're not squished yet?'

'Nah. I'm okay.'

'You make a pretty good mattress.'

'Thanks.'

'Maybe a little lumpy here and there.' She squirmed as if looking for a more comfortable position.

All of a sudden, I was acutely aware of being flat on my back with *Lee* on top of me.

389

Through her soaked, clinging shirt, my hands felt her back – and no bra straps. Her breasts were mashed against my chest. The way her belly touched mine, I could feel each breath she took. Her groin was tight against my crotch. Though we were thigh to thigh, her legs were slightly apart and squeezing mine together as if to hold herself in place.

I started to get a boner.

Squirming, I pushed at Lee. 'We'd better get up.'

'I'll try.'

She reached up to the bench on her right side, pulled at it, shoved at my shoulder with her other hand, unclenched her thighs and managed to sit up on me, straddling my hips, her legs dangling off the sides.

If anything, this position was worse for me. Didn't she realize what she was sitting on?

Didn't she care?

Maybe she *liked* it.

Lightning flashed.

Lee flinched again.

For just a moment, through the slanting streaks of silver rain, I saw her sitting upright on top of me with her head turned toward the arena. Her soaked hair was flat against her head. Her face, shiny as oil, streamed with water. So did her bare arms. Her drenched shirt was half unbuttoned. It adhered to her body and took on the shapes of her breasts. Her stiff nipples pushed out the clinging fabric.

I saw all this in the starkness of the lightning, a glare that probably lasted no more than a second but seemed to go on much longer. And just before the darkness returned, I saw Lee's jaw drop open.

'Oh, my God!' she gasped.

'What?'

'He's down! She's on him!'

My insides cringed. I tried to sit up but I couldn't – not the way Lee was sitting on me.

She began to climb off. Trapped between the bleacher seats, her legs dangling, it was a struggle. Finally, she freed herself.

The moment she was off me, I lurched upright and looked for Rusty. Whatever cars remained on Janks Field, their headlights weren't pointing in our direction. All we had in the arena was darkness and pouring rain. I could hardly see the cage, but there seemed to be pale shapes inside it. They might've been naked bodies squirming in a tangle, but I couldn't be sure.

Lee dropped onto the bench in front of me, twisted around, reached out and squeezed my arm. '*Let's get down!*'

She helped me climb out from between the bleacher planks. Then, side by side, we hopped carefully but as fast as we dared down the slick boards like a couple of hikers leaping from rock to rock in an effort to cross a stream.

No one was in our way.

The stands on both sides of the arena looked empty. It seemed that everyone except us had already fled. By the sounds of engines and car horns and shouts, many of them were still in Janks Field, fighting the traffic jam.

What're the Cadillac twins up to?

I hardly got a chance to start worrying about them, however, before several dark shapes hurried into the cage with a gurney.

Then several more came running toward Lee and me.

We almost reached the bottom of the bleachers before they stopped us.

The man blocking our way said, 'Show's over, folks. Time to go home.'

'We're not going anywhere,' Lee said. 'Not without my son.'

'Your son, right.' Though I couldn't make out the details of his face, it was obviously the same man who had stopped us the last time. 'Go on, get outa here.'

'You can't make us,' I blurted. I was angry and scared. I needed to get past these people and stop the others from taking Rusty away. 'This is public property. And anyway, my dad's the chief of police. So you'd better just get out of our way.'

'Sure, kid.'

'Please,' Lee said to him. 'We only want to . . .'

I broke to the side, my feet somehow not flying out from under me, and leaped. One of the gang tried for me. I shouldered him or her out of the way, but the impact knocked me crooked. I managed to plant one foot on the bottom row of the bleachers and spring off. In mid-air, I saw several dark figures moving inside the cage . . . rolling the gurney. A pale body was sprawled on top of it. Someone else stood nearby, hands on hips.

Balance gone, I landed on the ground with a splash, stumbled and started to fall.

I was caught by strong hands. They clamped me just below my armpits and hoisted me upright. When I was standing, they still didn't let go.

'What seems to be the problem here?'

It was the voice of Julian Stryker.

'My friend,' I blurted. 'They're taking away my friend.' In case he didn't know who I meant, I said, 'Rusty. The one who . . .'

'I know who he is,' Stryker said. 'He's been hurt. They're taking him to an ambulance.'

The sky suddenly trembled with lightning.

Stryker's mane of black hair was plastered to his head, his stark white face dripping and shiny, his lips crimson. So much like a beautiful woman, but rugged and craggy like a man. His silk shirt was clinging like ebony skin to his powerful shoulders and chest.

In the last moment of brilliant light, I saw past Stryker's side – the gurney gliding by, weighted down by Rusty.

Rusty, naked except for his white socks. Chubby, pale, shiny.

His arm was no longer bandaged.

Where he had been nipped by the poodle, there was now a mouth-sized patch of gory pulp.

The blood'll bring vampires like chum brings sharks.

Thunder rumbled.

Darkness clamped down and Rusty was gone.

Chapter Fifty-seven

'Let go of me!' I shouted into Stryker's face.

'Just settle down.'

'They're taking him away!'

'Nothing to worry about.'

'Where're they *going*?'

Stryker ignored my question. He called out, 'Bring the woman here.'

Over my shoulder, I looked for Rusty. No sign of him or the gurney or those who'd been bearing him away.

But I saw Lee being led toward us, members of Stryker's gang clutching both her arms. Though she struggled to pull free, they hung on. I realized that the rain was no longer falling so hard. It still poured down, but with less force than before. I could see better . . .

Lee's chambray shirt, sleeveless and hardly long enough to reach her waist, was no longer buttoned. Down its middle was a strip of skin the same dusky shade as her bare legs. Her white shorts looked like snow on a cloudy midnight.

Stryker released my sides. Before I could make a move, however, he grabbed my upper right arm. 'Just take it easy,' he said. 'Everything's fine.'

'Like hell,' I said.

'Let her go,' Stryker told his people.

They released Lee's arms. Facing Stryker, she said, 'Now *you* let go of Dwight.'

Stryker's teeth showed. They were as white as Lee's shorts. 'Giving me orders?' he asked. But his hand dropped away from my arm.

I almost took off to go after Rusty, but changed my mind. With half a dozen of Stryker's gang spread out close behind us, I wouldn't have gotten far.

'We want Rusty back,' Lee said.

'I'm afraid he was seriously injured in the competition, but we'll see that he gets proper attention.'

'We'll take care of him,' Lee said.

'He's already being looked after.'

'*We'll* look after him.'

'Where *is* he?' I demanded.

Stryker's head turned toward me. By the way the white showed, he was obviously smiling. 'Wouldn't you like to know?' he said.

'Yes!'

He chuckled.

Lee took hold of my hand. 'Come on, Dwight.'

'We can't leave without Rusty!'

'Come on.' Her voice was firm.

I had an urge to jerk my hand from her grip and refuse to

leave, but then I realized she probably had a plan. Lee wasn't a quitter.

Maybe she figured we should leave peacefully, then double back and spy on the gang.

Or maybe the plan was to hurry into town and come back with the police. My dad was in the hospital, but Grandville still had a police department of sorts. If necessary, they could bring reinforcements from the county sheriff and even the state troopers. We could come back in force and rescue Rusty.

'Let them go,' Stryker ordered.

His gang spread out.

As we walked away from them, I looked over at the parking area. The structure of the bleachers blocked some of my view. So did the BEER-SNACKS-SOUVENIRS shack. But I could see plenty of Janks Field, anyway.

Just about the only people still wandering around over there appeared to be members of Stryker's crew. Equipped with flashlights, they were busy directing traffic. From the look of things, they'd been doing a good job. Though a few cars and pickups sat motionless as if abandoned, the field was mostly empty. A line of vehicles inched toward the mouth of the dirt road.

Not an ambulance among them.

No sign of Rusty, either.

'What're we gonna do?' I asked.

'I'm not sure,' Lee said.

'We can't just leave Rusty.'

'I know.'

'I don't think they're sending him to a hospital. Or the others, either. I haven't even seen an ambulance.'

'Ambulances couldn't get out of here, anyway,' Lee pointed out.

When we rounded the end of the bleachers, I had a clear view of Janks Field. I spotted Lee's pickup truck, the disabled

Cadillac and a couple of other cars. And then I heard the jangle of spurs behind us.

Something seemed to crumple inside me. 'Uh-oh,' I muttered.

'Lee! Dwight!'

We stopped and turned around.

'What is it that you want?' Stryker asked, sounding almost as if he'd forgotten. But you could tell by his voice that he was playing with us.

'Rusty,' Lee said. 'We just want Rusty.'

'How badly?'

In a solemn voice, Lee asked, 'What've you got in mind?'

'You give me what I want, I give you what *you* want.'

'And what is it that *you* want?' Lee asked.

'You and Valeria. Five minutes.'

'What?'

'In the cage.'

'You want me to *fight* her?'

'That's the idea.'

'Why? The show's over. Everybody's gone.'

'Not everybody.' Stryker placed a hand on his own chest. 'I love a good contest of strength and will. Frankly, I feel cheated. The show usually goes on for a couple of hours, at least.' He shrugged elaborately. 'It was especially disappointing that our only challengers were men. I *love* to see an attractive woman take on Valeria. Warms the cockles of my heart.'

Lightning flashed again. All I noticed was Stryker's dripping, grinning face.

When the darkness returned, he said, 'Take her on. I *know* you'll give us a great show.'

I pulled at Lee's hand. 'Let's get out of here.'

She stayed put. 'What if I don't win?' she asked.

'If you don't win, my dear, Valeria will suck your blood.'

Scared that Lee seemed to be considering it, I pulled harder at her hand. 'Come on!' She didn't budge.

Thunder grumbled through the night. It came from a distance. Rain continued to fall, but I realized the worst of the storm had moved on.

'What about Rusty?' she asked.

'What about him?'

'Do we get him even if I lose?'

'Certainly.'

'*No!*' I blurted. I wanted Rusty back, but not if it meant Lee getting ripped up by Valeria. '*Are you crazy?*'

Lee turned her head toward me. 'I'm the reason Rusty came here tonight. I bought the tickets, remember?'

'I know, but—'

'And I'm not leaving without him. Not if I can help it.'

'Then we have a deal?' Stryker asked.

'We have a deal,' said Lee.

'*You can't fight her!*'

She gave my shoulder a gentle squeeze and said, 'It'll be all right.'

'*Leeeee!*'

'Don't worry, honey. Please.'

Stryker stepped away and spoke to some of his crew. Three of them went hurrying off through the rain. Two others came over to me.

While Stryker stayed in the arena with Lee, I was led up the empty bleachers. My two guards were Vivian and a muscular man with a crew cut. They chose seats in the middle, about halfway up, and positioned themselves on both sides of me.

From there, we would have the best view possible of the activities inside the cage.

Vivian patted my leg. 'This is gonna be good,' she said.

I didn't respond.

397

'So who's the lucky gal? Not your mom, is she?'

I shook my head.

'Didn't think so. She looks way too young. What is she, your big sister?'

I had no reason to tell this woman the truth, so I said, 'Yeah, my sister.'

'Good-lookin' gal,' said the guy on my right.

Go to hell, I thought. But I didn't say it. I'm not that stupid.

'Your mom know you're here?' Vivian asked.

I shook my head again.

'Bet your folks think you're home in bed, don't they?'

'Maybe.'

'Glad you came?'

I frowned at her. 'Not very.'

'Bet your friend Rusty had himself a good time. For a while there, anyway . . . till Valeria put the bite on him.'

Her attempt at humor angered me. I opened my mouth. Mostly, I intended to tell her to shut up. But different words came out. 'Is she real?' I heard myself ask.

'Real? Sure she's real.'

'I mean, a vampire.'

Vivian let out a harsh laugh. 'What do *you* think, kid?'

'Is she?'

'Nah. She's the tooth fairy.'

The guy laughed. 'Good one,' he said.

Off ahead of me, behind the other stand of bleachers, three sets of headlights lit the night. I couldn't see the vehicles behind them, but figured they must be the Travelling Vampire Show's hearse, bus and truck.

The beams of the headlights reached through the stands. In their pale glow, I saw Stryker and Lee standing together on the ground, and Valeria alone in her cage.

She no longer wore her boots. Totally naked, she was

leaning back against the bars, arms and legs spread out, stretching and writhing as if she relished the flexing of her muscles and the feel of the rain on her bare skin.

When the light beams shifted, I looked away from Valeria.

One pair of headlights continued to aim at the arena, but the other two sets slid away through the rainy night.

In the jittery glare of a lightning flash, I caught a glimpse of the vehicles. The hearse remained in place behind the opposite bleachers. Moving slowly to the right was the large black truck. Moving to the left was the black bus.

Where're they going? I wondered.

Is Rusty in one of them?

We had no guarantee that Stryker would keep his part of the bargain.

What if they're taking Rusty away?

Through the sounds of their engines and the hiss and patter of the falling rain came a soft rumble of thunder.

The truck and bus rounded the ends of the bleachers, then turned. They weren't leaving, after all.

They drove straight toward each other until the bright beams of their headlights filled the cage. Then they stopped. I heard brakes squeak.

Now, headlights reached through the night from three directions. All of them met in the cage.

Stryker climbed the steps and entered.

Lee walked in after him.

Valeria let go of the bars. Still stretching and writhing in a languid way that seemed almost catlike, she glided toward the middle of the cage. Her sleek black hair was flat against her scalp and clinging to the sides of her face and neck. In the glare of the six headlights, her skin looked like alabaster gleaming and dripping with baby oil.

Stryker raised a hand and signaled her to stop.

She halted.

Like a boxing referee, Stryker spoke to both contestants. I couldn't hear a word he said.

For our benefit, he held up an open hand – the upstretched fingers apparently representing five minutes. Then he hurried backward from between the two women and brought his arm down fast.

As Lee and Valeria started to circle each other, Stryker left the cage. Outside it, he shut the door and did something to its latch.

I gasped, 'Hey! He shut the *door*!'

'No sweat, kid,' said the man on my right.

'Don't worry about it,' Vivian told me. She patted my thigh. 'Door or no door, your gal won't be getting out of there alive.'

Chapter Fifty-eight

Down in the cage, Lee and Valeria kept circling each other, staying apart but bent over, their arms wide open, their heads up.

Though both women were about the same size and I couldn't make out their faces very well, they were easy to tell apart. Lee's blond hair swung and flipped behind her head in a soaked, stringy ponytail; Valeria's straight black hair was plastered down against the back of her skull. Lee wore her sleeveless chambray shirt, white shorts and blue sneakers; Valeria was stark-naked. Every so often, I glimpsed the smooth, inner slopes of Lee's breasts through the gap of her open shirt; except when her back was to me, Valeria's breasts were in full view, bouncing and swaying with the motions of her body.

Suddenly, Valeria growled and swept an open hand at Lee's face as if to claw her cheek open.

Lurching back, Lee grabbed the hand. She seemed to fall away, stretching Valeria's arm. Valeria staggered toward her, then stumbled sideways, breasts leaping. Lee let go. Valeria twirled away and her back slammed against a wall of the cage. The impact shook her. She stayed against the bars as if she needed them to hold her up.

Instead of rushing in to take advantage of the situation, Lee retreated to the other side of the cage.

'*Get her!*' I shouted. '*Knock her out!*'

Hearing me, she looked over her shoulder. She probably couldn't see me, though, because of all the headlights and how I was sitting up in the darkness.

It only took a few seconds for Valeria to recover. Then she came for Lee.

Darting sideways with her back to the bars, Lee put the casket between herself and Valeria.

Valeria chased her around the casket. It was like some sort of lame comedy skit . . . goofballs circling a dining-room table. Except both the goofballs were beautiful women and one was completely naked and I hated to think of what would happen if she caught Lee.

I got the impression that Valeria was enjoying the chase. But she couldn't let it go on forever. In whatever remained of the five minutes, she needed to catch Lee and sink her teeth in.

Suddenly, she bowed at the waist, grabbed the casket with both hands and swung it off the ground. On its way up, it overturned. Out fell a red leather skirt and top, red boots with spurs attached, and a black leather belt. Holding it high, she marched straight toward Lee.

Oh, God, she was something to behold!

Though I knew that she planned to smash Lee with the casket, I suddenly noticed a stiffness in my jeans. No telling how long I'd had it. I felt guilty and ashamed, but it didn't go away.

'*Look out!*' I yelled at Lee.

She needed no warning, though; she could see what was coming. She backed away until she was stopped by a wall of the cage.

Then she ducked and charged. Apparently, she meant to go in under the casket and crash her head into Valeria's belly. But she wasn't quite fast enough.

Valeria slammed the casket down on Lee's back. I heard the whomp of its impact, heard a grunt from Lee. An instant later, she was face down on the mud floor of the cage, sprawled flat.

Valeria tossed the casket out of the way. Then she leaned over Lee, grabbed her by the ponytail and the seat of her shorts, picked her up and hoisted her overhead.

Lee's arms and legs drooped. Her shirt hung open. I could see her breasts.

I didn't want to look at them, but I couldn't help myself. My eyes were latched to them. I grew harder. I felt as if I were betraying her. Betraying Slim, too. But I couldn't look away. I'd been wanting to see them for so long, and here they were, pale and shiny, glorious . . . and suddenly lurching on her chest as Valeria ran with her across the cage.

Oh, my God!

Valeria planned to ram her into the wall of bars.

'*NO!*' I cried out. '*LEE! WATCH OUT!*'

I don't know if she heard me, but both her arms suddenly darted up and she grabbed a bar above her face and came to an abrupt stop.

Unprepared for it, Valeria almost tore Lee loose, but not quite. Though Lee cried out in pain, she clung to the ceiling bar. Valeria lost her hold on Lee's ponytail and shorts and stumbled on, waving her arms, trying not to fall.

Suspended by her arms, Lee twisted and swung.

As Valeria came back for her, she chinned herself up and kicked a foot toward the ceiling of the cage. If only she could hook a foot through the bars, she might be able to pull herself all the way up . . . maybe out of Valeria's reach.

But one leg was still hanging down. Valeria grabbed it with both hands.

I yelled, '*NO!*'

On both sides of me, my guards clapped and cheered.

Valeria tugged at Lee's leg until the other one came down beside it. At that point, it would've been simple to pluck Lee down from the ceiling bar. She didn't do it, though. Instead, she pulled off both of Lee's sneakers and tossed them aside. Then she smiled over her shoulder – at me?

After the smile, she stepped behind Lee and peeled her white shorts down and off. First her shorts, then her panties.

Lee dangled from the bar, facing me, her open shirt barely reaching past her ribcage, her body naked from there down. She looked as if she were being stretched by her own weight. Her arms almost seemed longer than usual. Her belly looked taut. I saw a golden tuft of hair between her legs.

Her legs began to spread apart. Then a hand appeared between them. Valeria's hand. Stroking her.

Lee's jaw was clenched. She had a strange, tight look on her face. A tightness that trembled. She was wet and shiny all over, so there was no way of knowing if she had tears running down her face.

But I knew she was crying.

When I see a girl cry, something happens to me.

Especially if it's a girl I love. Like Slim or Lee.

Shouting, '*Leave her alone!*' I leaped up and drove the point of my elbow into the face of the big man on my right. He grunted and grabbed his nose. Vivian grabbed my other hand, but I didn't let her stop me. Pulled by my weight, she rose off the bench. I tried to fling her and we both tumbled down the bleachers.

When we came to a stop on top of a wet board near the bottom, Vivian was sprawled under me. She raised her head. I slugged her in the nose. Her nose crunched. The back of her head struck the wood with a sound like knuckles on a door.

I scurried off her.

The big guy was coming for me, leaping down the slippery face of the bleachers.

I jumped off the bottom row and ran for the cage.

I still had to get through Stryker.

But he wasn't even looking at me. He stood with both hands on the cage door.

Racing toward him, I looked into the cage. Lee no longer hung from the ceiling bar. She had Valeria backed up against the rear of the cage. Head down, she was slamming punches into Valeria's belly.

Yes!

Maybe she didn't need my help, after all, but it was too late to back out.

'*Open the door!*' I shouted as I ran toward Stryker.

I hardly thought he would do it.

But he stepped backward, swinging it open, grinning at me through a space between its bars. 'The more the merrier,' he said.

I rushed into the cage.

He swung its door shut. *Clang!*

Valeria was still on the bars. Lee kept landing punches to her belly. They were strong punches. Her fists sounded like mallets smacking wet meat. Each blow shook Valeria and made her breasts lurch. With each blow, she grunted.

'Good going, Lee!' I called out.

'Very good going,' Valeria said, smiling at me. She spoke with a fluid, languid drawl. 'For a girl,' she added. Though Lee was still pounding her, she wasn't reacting. Just calmly talking to me. 'Do you suppose you can do better, Mister Thompson?'

Okay, so she knew my last name. I wasn't going to let that bother me. Much. It bothered me a lot more that Valeria didn't seem the least bit fazed by the punches.

'Lee's doing just fine,' I said.

'Is she?' Valeria grabbed the front edges of Lee's shirt, swung her around and slammed her against the bars. Lee's whole body jerked with the impact. She started to sag.

A hand to Lee's throat, Valeria pinned her to the bars. With her other hand, she dragged the shirt off Lee's right shoulder, baring her upper arm and breast.

Then she stepped back, keeping Lee pinned to the bars. 'Lee *is* doing just fine, isn't she?'

'Let go of her!'

'Oh, I don't suppose so.' Reaching out, she slipped a hand beneath Lee's right breast. 'Lovely, isn't it?' She squeezed, but Lee didn't react.

Out cold?

Maybe that's good, I thought.

'How do you suppose it tastes, Mister Thompson?'

'Leave her alone.'

Valeria licked her lips, then spread her mouth open wide.

'*NO!*' I yelled.

As I plowed into her, she stumbled away and let go of Lee. Out of the corner of my eye, I glimpsed Lee sliding to the floor.

Arms clamped around Valeria, forehead pressed between

her breasts, I chugged with my feet and drove her across the cage. I had a vague notion of slamming her against the far wall and going at her with my fists the same as Lee had done.

But Lee's punches hadn't hurt Valeria, so why should mine?

Anyway, we didn't make it to the far wall. Valeria fell flat on her back and I landed on top of her.

Aren't the five minutes up yet? I wondered.

Maybe they've stopped counting.

'TIME?' I shouted.

Valeria, beneath me, said, 'This is not a game anymore.'

She was under me, breathing hard. I felt the quick rise and fall of her chest against the side of my face. It was wet and hot and I heard her quick heartbeat.

She's no vampire!

Of course not, I thought. No such thing.

Just a woman.

Just.

I pushed myself up. Sitting on her pelvis, I pinned her wrists to the muddy ground by her sides.

She smiled up at me. 'Now what?' she asked.

I had no idea.

I looked to Lee for an answer, but she was sprawled on the ground, apparently unconscious.

'Give up?' I asked.

'I don't believe so.' Smiling, she writhed. I watched the rain bounce off her shiny breasts. Her nipples were dark and rigid. 'I know what you would *like* to do.'

I shook my head.

'Go ahead. I'll let you. I let your friend Rusty do it, and he's not *nearly* as cute as you.'

'You *let* him?'

'Did you honestly believe he'd over*powered* me?' She chuckled softly. 'I hardly think so. Nothing happens to me unless I *allow* it. And I hereby allow *you*, Dwight Thompson.'

I shook my head.

A smile spread over her face. 'I know you *want* to. I know you *lust* for me.'

'If you say so.'

'Now's your chance,' she said. 'You have me at your mercy, Mr Thompson.'

'Yeah, well . . .'

'I'm all yours.'

'Forget it. All I wanta do is get outa here. Come on, okay? It's been five minutes.' I looked over my shoulder and saw Stryker outside the cage door, staring in. My two guards were standing beside him. 'Come on!' I yelled. 'The five minutes are up! Let us have Rusty back and we'll . . .'

Smiling, Stryker shook his head.

'You don't want to die a virgin, do you?' Valeria asked. I suddenly didn't feel too good.

'Dié?'

'This may be your one and only chance to avoid such a miserable fate.'

I just sort of stared at her.

'Kiss me,' she said.

I shook my head. 'We just wanta get out of here. With Rusty.'

'Kiss my breasts.'

I shook my head.

'Fuck me.'

'No thanks.'

'Last call. You're about to die, either way. You might as well die happy.'

'You're really beautiful and everything,' I said, 'but I don't even like you. I wouldn't *do it* to you if you were the last woman on—'

She roared in my face and flung me off her body. As I rolled across the floor of the cage, she sprang to her feet. She swept down, grabbed my shirt and ripped it open. Then she picked me up by it.

She raced across the cage, holding me out in front of her, and rammed me into the bars. My ears rang. Barely conscious, I felt her rip the shirt off my shoulders and down my arms.

She rubbed her wet, slippery breasts against my chest. Writhing against me, she kissed me on the mouth. 'See what you'll be missing?' she asked. Then she clutched my right shoulder and my head. She shoved my head sideways, stretched her mouth open wide and went for my neck.

Shrieking, I pushed at her.

I knew it wouldn't do any good, but I shoved at her breasts with both hands and a weird little part of my mind thought how nice they felt.

I knew that the next thing I felt would be her teeth sinking into my neck.

Instead, I felt Valeria yielding to my push.

She's just letting me think . . .

Then I saw the thin wooden shaft protruding from her right eye. Sort of like a pencil . . .

Someone stabbed her with . . .

As she stumbled backward, I saw how long the shaft was. I saw the feathers near its end. Then came a heavy *thunk*, a second arrow hitting her. This one popped through the nipple of her right breast and blood squirted. The arrow went in deep, skewering her breast, holding it rigid while she staggered backward.

Still on her feet, backing away from me, she got it with a third arrow. This one caught her high on the left side of the chest, just over the heart. Her left breast jumped. Unsteady now, she raised her arms for balance. Only a couple of inches of the last arrow showed. She looked as if she had a strange, feathered brooch pinned to the skin of her chest.

Waving her arms, she fell. She landed with a splash and lay spread-eagled on her back in the mud.

Chapter Fifty-nine

I stared at Valeria. She twitched and shuddered. Blood poured out of her wounds, but was quickly washed away by the rain. When she stopped moving, I looked toward the cage door.

Nobody there.

Stryker and the others must've run when the arrows flew. Probably to their bus. It was parked about twenty-five feet away, its engine running, its headbeams bright in my eyes.

The cage door was shut.

Lee, conscious now, was braced up on her elbows. Except for her shirt, she was naked. Her shirt was mostly off, though. It covered her left shoulder, and that was about all. Face scrunched, she scowled through the rain at Valeria's body.

'You okay?' I called to her.

She looked at me, frowning. 'What happened?'

'I guess Slim happened.'

'Jeez.'

I hurried over to the sodden rag of Lee's shorts and snatched them out of the mud. They were white in front, filthy in back. I turned them over and the rain sluiced off some of the dirt.

When I got back to Lee with them, she was on her feet

and leaning back against the bars. I handed the shorts to her. 'Thanks,' she said. She shook them open. As she raised a leg to put them on, I turned away and tried to spot Slim.

I figured she must've shot her arrows from somewhere under the bleachers where I'd been sitting earlier. Because of the headlights on me, though, I couldn't see very well into the darkness. If Slim was crouched beneath the bleachers, I sure couldn't see her.

I could see through them, though. To the back of the BEER-SNACKS-SOUVENIRS shack, to the area that had earlier been crowded with parked cars and trucks. There, all the headlights and tail-lights were gone. The field was dark except for the thin, moving beams of six or eight flashlights.

Stryker's crew.

Apparently unaware of what had just happened in the cage, they seemed to be checking on the abandoned vehicles and other things they found interesting in Janks Field.

'Damn,' Lee said.

I looked at her. She was bending over, shoving the shorts down her legs.

'What's wrong?'

'Can't get 'em on.'

'Huh?'

'Too tight.' With a kick of her right foot, she sent the shorts flying. Then she ran toward the other side of the cage. She slid to a stop, bent down and plucked Valeria's red leather skirt out of the mud. Stepping into it, she said to me, 'Try the door.'

I hurried over to it. There was no handle. I grabbed the bars and shoved. The door rattled in its steel frame and stayed shut.

On the other side was a hasp and a padlock.

Groaning, I turned my head. 'We're locked in!'

Lee came running over. The red leather skirt was so short

it hardly covered her groin. She'd straightened her shirt, but only fastened one button, down near her belly.

'Let's see,' she said.

I stepped out of her way. Lee studied the situation, then reached through the bars, grabbed the lock and jerked at it.

'Oh, boy,' she muttered.

'What'll we do?'

'I don't—'

'Hey!' Slim's voice. It seemed to come from the area of the bleachers.

Lee and I both started to turn.

'Don't look.' She sounded a little strange, her voice tight like someone talking through pain. 'They're in the bus. Probably watching you. Fiddle with the door or something.'

We turned again to the cage door.

'Locked in?' Slim asked.

'Looks that way,' I said.

'It's a combination padlock,' Lee explained.

Slim didn't say anything.

'You still there?' I asked.

'Yeah.'

'Maybe you'd better go get help,' Lee called.

'Nice outfit, Lee.'

'Thanks.'

'Red becomes you.'

'You'd better get going,' Lee said. 'Try to get the police out here . . .'

'Not a good idea. I need to keep you covered.'

'Are you okay?' I asked.

'Okay enough. Took care of Valeria, anyway.'

'You sure did. That was great shooting. But what's wrong?'

'I'm a little beat up, that's all.'

At first, I thought she meant her earlier injuries . . . those from the dog and falling down.

411

'I got worked over a little,' she said.

'What?'

'Bitsy. She jumped me from behind.'

'*Bitsy?*'

'Yeah. Clobbered me with something. Then she beat the crap out of me. Turned out my lights.'

Through my rage, I felt confusion. 'When did she do it?'

'A few minutes after we left you guys. Guess she wanted to "go with".'

'That creepy little . . .!'

'She adores you, pal.'

'Yeah,' I muttered, suddenly glad that Bitsy had gotten herself pounded by Rusty. If I'd known what she'd done to Slim, things would've gone a lot worse for her.

'Seen her around?' Slim asked.

'Yeah. She said you got mad and told her to F off.'

'Real nice.'

'Anyway, we sorta ditched her in the woods. Haven't seen her since.'

'So where's Rusty?' Slim asked.

'We don't know. They took him away after Valeria bit him.'

'She *bit* him?'

'After he *made* it with her.'

'Huh? Rusty *made it* with Valeria?'

'Yeah.'

'You mean sex?'

'Yeah. Right in the cage here. In front of everyone.'

'Holy jeez.'

'Then she tore into him. Next thing you know, they were taking him away on a gurney. We don't know where he is now.'

'Maybe in their bus or something,' Lee said.

'They were gonna give him back to us,' I explained, 'if

Lee went five minutes with Valeria. That's how we ended up like this.'

'Looked like she was about to take a piece out of your neck.'

'Thanks for saving it,' I said.

'Hey, it's my favorite neck.'

I blushed.

'You still have the knife?' Slim asked.

The knife?

I slapped the front right pocket of my blue jeans and felt a solid bulge. Slim's folding knife?

I couldn't believe it.

I'd forgotten I had it.

'Take it out,' Slim said.

I shoved my hand into the tight, wet pocket of my jeans. No wonder Lee hadn't been able to get her shorts back on. Something about wet cloth . . . But I managed to shove my hand in deeply enough to grab the knife.

I pulled it out.

'Now come over to my side of the cage. Make it fast.'

I wanted to ask why, but didn't bother. Whatever her reasons, they were probably good. As I've mentioned before, Slim had more brains than me and Rusty put together.

So I whirled away from the door and rushed across the muddy floor. Through the bars on the other side, I saw a vague shape squirming on the ground in front of the bleachers. It had to be Slim belly-crawling toward the cage.

Suddenly, an engine revved.

Slim scrambled up. Rushing the final few feet to the cage, she entered the headbeams. Her short blonde hair was matted and curly with rain. Her black silk shirt, torn in several places, was clinging to her body. She had her bow in one hand and her quiver of arrows in the other.

It felt great to see her.

But she had a gash above one eyebrow and her face was swollen.

I felt like killing Bitsy.

A moment before slamming against the cage, Slim shoved her bow and quiver of arrows through the bars. 'Trade,' she gasped.

'Huh?'

The bus was on its way. Though I didn't look at it, I heard it going through its gears, picking up speed like a school bus after dropping off a load of kids.

'Take my stuff! Gimme the knife! Quick!' I did as she asked.

'Protect yourselves,' she said. Then she put her face between two of the bars. 'Kiss me.'

Valeria's words exactly. This time they came from Slim and the sound of them hurt my heart.

I dropped to my knees and kissed her on the mouth, forgetting about her puffy, split lips. She winced. I started to pull away, but her hand caught the back of my head. We continued to kiss. I felt the warmth of her lips, the heat of her breath. I tasted her blood.

The brakes of the bus groaned.

Though I didn't look, the sound told me that the bus was stopping somewhere near the front of the cage.

Slim pulled back. 'I love you, Dwight. Don't let yourself get hurt, or I'll have to kill you.'

'Oh God, Slim.' I had a catch in my throat.

'See you.'

'What're you gonna do?'

She tugged open the blade of the knife. 'Tell you after I've done it.'

I heard the familiar hiss of a bus door opening.

'*Run!*' Lee yelled.

In a low crouch, Slim rushed for the bleachers.

414

A big man sprinted in from the side at an angle to intercept her. He was my guard, the guy I'd elbowed in the nose.

As he chased Slim, I heard the bus engine roar. I glanced toward the sound and glimpsed the bus racing backward, as if to put a safe distance between itself and the pursuit.

Just in front of the bleachers, Slim flopped to her belly and squirmed forward.

'Leave her alone!' I yelled.

The man didn't even so much as glance at me.

He was about to leave his feet for a dive at Slim when I let an arrow fly. I was no expert archer like Slim, just a normal American kid of my times ... a kid who'd done plenty fooling around with all things lethal: knives, firearms, blowguns, home-made spears, explosives, swords, bows and arrows.

My arrow went in just under the man's armpit and sank into his ribcage. He hit the mud skidding.

Slim scurried under the bleachers and vanished.

Bleachers I'd thought were empty.

From somewhere near the top, however, came applause. It sounded like one or two people clapping their hands.

Chapter sixty

My skin went all crawly with goosebumps. I couldn't see who was up there, but I knew anyway.

As I peered toward the top of the bleachers, the beam of a flashlight reached up through the darkness, swept this way and that, and found two men at the very top of the stands –

found them for an instant, then lost them as they lowered themselves behind the structure.

'Look out, Slim!' I yelled, getting to my feet. 'The Cadillac twins! They're coming after you!'

She didn't answer.

The beam of the flashlight lowered and whipped back and forth through the lower rows of the bleachers. Shadows jerked and leaped. I looked for Slim, didn't see her, then turned my head to find out who was holding the flashlight.

Its beam came from a cluster of three or four people standing just outside the door of the bus. The bus had stopped about twenty feet back from the cage. Not very far, but the people were in darkness and I had headlights shining in my eyes so I couldn't tell who they were. Stryker was probably one of them, though. And Vivian.

I turned in their direction, readied an arrow and drew the bowstring back to my chin.

'Shut off the flashlight or I'll shoot!' I yelled.

The light went dead.

'Thanks,' I said. A dumb thing to say, but it came out before I had a chance to think. 'Now come over here and let us out.'

'Why would I do that?'

Before I had a chance to think about it – much, anyway – I released the arrow. It vanished into the darkness. Then came a quiet *thump*.

'*Ah!*' a woman cried out. A dark figure broke away from the group, hunching over and twisting away, then dropping to its knees. '*You fucking bastard!*' yelled the same voice. It didn't sound like Vivian, but I'd noticed earlier that Stryker had several women in his crew.

I reached down to the quiver clamped between my knees and pulled out another arrow. Before I could shoot it, though, my targets had disappeared inside the bus. They'd left the wounded one on the ground, writhing and whimpering.

'That's two down,' Lee said. 'Three, counting Valeria. Not bad.'

'Except they've got us trapped and surrounded.'

She shrugged one shoulder. 'Big deal.'

I laughed and so did she. As she came toward me, I slipped the arrow back into the quiver.

When she hugged me, the quiver fell over. But I didn't care.

My shirt had been ripped off by Valeria, so Lee's chambray shirt was the only thing between me and her skin.

'You're doing really well,' she said into my ear.

'Thanks.'

'I always knew you were a good guy, but you're even better than I thought.'

'Well . . . I'm trying.'

Her arms tightened around me. The way she was standing, I figured she could see the bus over my shoulder. And I could see the headlights of the truck over hers. If anything started to happen in either direction, we would know it.

'The thing is to stay brave,' she said.

'I'll try.'

'Me, too.'

I let out a sad little laugh. 'And we don't have to worry about Slim.'

'Huh?'

'Staying brave. That's the least of her problems.'

'I just hope she's careful,' Lee said.

'Yeah, me too.' Then I started to cry.

Lee stroked the back of my head. 'It'll be all right,' she whispered. 'She'll be fine.'

'I don't know,' I blubbered. 'If anything happens to her . . .'

'It's okay, honey. It's okay.'

I kept crying, Lee holding me and stroking my head.

'You know what?' she asked. 'It's like you said when Valeria got shot. "Slim'll happen to *them*."'

I sort of laughed and sobbed at the same time. Then I mumbled, 'God, I hope so.'

Lee stepped back slightly, moved her face in front of mine and looked me in the eyes. To me, she looked blurry. As I blinked, she wiped the tears and raindrops off my face with her fingers. All that touched me were her fingertips and breasts. It would've been very sweet and exciting if I hadn't felt so scared.

After a while, she asked, 'Feeling any better?'

I nodded. 'A little.'

She eased forward and kissed me gently on the mouth. Then she stepped back and put her hands on my shoulders. 'We'd better get ready for the attack.'

'What attack?'

A smile flashed across her face. 'The one that's sure to come.'

'Oh, that. What'll we do?'

'First . . .' She stepped away from me, bent down and picked up the quiver. After counting the arrows, she muttered, 'Eight. Plus three is eleven.'

'Three?'

'Put it on.' She gave me the quiver.

While she held the bow, I swung the quiver onto my back so its strap rested on my left shoulder and ran diagonally down my chest like a bandolier. Then she handed the bow back to me. 'Keep us covered, okay?'

Nodding, I slipped an arrow out of the quiver and nocked it on the bowstring. Then I followed Lee toward Valeria's body.

She crouched beside it.

I said, 'Oh, my God,' as she reached for the feathered

shaft that protruded from Valeria's eye socket. 'Hey, no. Come on.'

'Sorry,' Lee said. 'But we might need these.'

She started to pull at the arrow. I turned away fast.

And took the opportunity to check our situation. The truck was still in position, engine rumbling quietly, headbeams reaching into the cage. The hearse remained motionless behind the other bleachers, shining its headlights at us. And the bus was where they'd stopped it after dropping off the guy who chased Slim.

The wounded gal was gone. She'd either gotten away on her own or someone had helped her.

On the other side of the bleachers into which Slim had vanished, the parking area was dark. No headlights, no tail-lights, no brake lights. Except for the abandoned vehicles such as Lee's pickup truck and the twins' Cadillac, all the vehicles were gone.

Stryker's gang no longer directed traffic or roamed the field. They were over here, now, sneaking through the darkness. I couldn't see them very well – not with so many headlights aimed into the cage, not with the darkness and falling rain.

They wore black clothes and they'd switched off their flashlights. They looked like human shadows. I almost couldn't see them at all. They were easier to see when I didn't look straight at them.

They were all around us, crouching and skulking under the bleachers on both sides, kneeling in the darkness near the bus and truck.

'Here,' Lee said.

I turned. She held an arrow. The first few inches of it were dripping blood. I glanced at Valeria's eye socket and almost gagged.

'Catch.' Lee tossed the arrow to me.

I snagged it out of the air.

'They're all around us,' I said.

'I noticed.'

She reached for the arrow that had gone through Valeria's nipple, so I turned away again.

I held out the bloody arrow that she'd just handed me, hoping the rain would wash it clean. Its shaft was so thin that not many raindrops landed on it. Each time one hit, I saw a tiny explosion of pink.

'This one's really stuck,' Lee said.

'Maybe just leave it?'

'Huh-uh.' Lee stood up, planted a bare foot on Valeria's ribcage – directly between the breasts – bent down and grabbed the arrow with her right hand. She started to tug at it. I turned away again.

Off in the distance, someone raced past the front of the truck, sprinting through its headbeams. I couldn't tell whether it was a man or woman, but it held a long, thin shaft in one hand.

A spear?

My skin prickled.

'Oh, jeez,' I murmured.

'You'd better give me a hand here,' Lee said.

I didn't want to. More than that, though, I didn't want to disappoint her. I guess I would've done *anything* she asked. So I handed the bow and arrow to her, then put a foot on Valeria's chest, just as she had done. Only three or four inches of the arrow protruded – enough room for just one hand.

I wiped my right hand on my jeans (which were also wet), then grabbed the arrow around its feathers, being careful to stay away from what remained of Valeria's nipple. Squeezing the shaft, I gave it a hard pull. A quick slip and my hand flew off it.

'Damn,' Lee said. 'Give it another try, okay? If we end up one arrow short . . .'

'I'll get it,' I said.

And I meant it. I wasn't going to let Lee think I was weak or chicken. 'Get me a rag,' I said. Not waiting for it, I cupped Valeria's breast with my left hand, my thumb hooked around the arrow. Her breast felt slippery and cool. I pushed, mashing it, sliding it down the shaft until there was room on the arrow for both my hands to fit.

Lee muttered, 'Oh jeez.' Then she gave me my shirt.

Released, Valeria's breast swelled upward, climbing the arrow.

Though my shirt was wet, it took some of the slipperiness off my hands. I used it to dry the protruding shaft. Keeping the shirt around my hands, I once again compressed Valeria's breast to make space for two hands on the arrow. Then I clutched the shaft with both hands, put most of my weight on her chest, and pulled with every ounce of my strength. The shirt, I think, gave me the extra friction that was needed.

I felt a force under my shoe as if Valeria were trying to sit up, but my weight kept her down.

The arrowhead, embedded in God-knows-what, suddenly let go. I glimpsed her breast stretching upward, pulled into the shape of a tall cone. Then the arrow leaped out like Excalibur, flinging blood. I held it high in both hands as I stumbled backward.

I slammed into Lee. She grunted, but stayed up. So did I.

'You okay?' she asked.

'Guess so.'

'Good work.'

'You too,' I said, knowing that she must've thrown herself in my way on purpose to stop me from falling.

We stood there, back to back. The quiver was in the way, but I could feel Lee's rear end against mine.

Under the bleachers in front of me, a shape flitted across the headlights of the hearse. It was hunched low and carrying a spear.

'What's going on?' I asked.

'They've got us pretty much surrounded,' Lee said. 'But they're staying back. So far.'

'What're they waiting for?'

'No idea. Maybe they're just afraid of catching an arrow.'

'I'll get the last one,' I said, feeling very powerful and brave now that I had retrieved the breast arrow.

'Better leave it,' Lee said.

'Huh?'

'Just in case.'

I thought about that for a moment. 'Because it's the one in her heart?'

'She's probably *not* a vampire, but . . . I don't know, everything's so crazy. I don't know what to make out of all this, but . . . I'd hate to be locked in this cage if she suddenly comes to life.'

'You and me both,' I said.

'I know she won't, but . . . I don't want to stake my life on it.'

'That arrow's probably broken anyway,' I said. 'It went all the way through her and she fell on it.'

'Might've just buried itself in the dirt. But let's leave it. For now, anyway.'

'Okay.'

'If we start to run out . . .'

. . . *if we last that long*, I thought.

'. . . I'll try to get it out of her later.'

Chapter Sixty-one

'*I'll make you a deal!*' Stryker shouted.

Lee whirled, drawing back the bowstring.

I saw a dark shape hunkered by the front door of the bus.

'That him?' Lee asked.

'Not sure.'

Lee called out, '*What sort of deal?*'

'We'll let you and the kids live if—'

Her arrow flew, hissing through the rain.

'*Fuck!*' Stryker yelled.

The arrow must've come close, but it missed him.

Lee shook her head, then turned and handed the bow to me. 'You'd better do the shooting.'

As I got ready with the arrow I'd plucked from Valeria, Stryker shouted, '*Don't do that again or I'll have you writhing on lances, screaming your lungs out.*'

Lee yelled, '*Chuck you, Farley!*'

'*Just listen to my offer! Do you want to die in that cage? Do you want the kids to die?*'

Kids? He meant me, of course, but who else? Rusty and Slim? Bitsy?

Though I took aim at the shape that was probably Stryker, I didn't release the arrow. At this distance, I'd be lucky to hit him. So I lowered the bow.

'*You said you'd let Rusty go if I went up against Valeria,*' Lee shouted. '*So where is he?*'

'*You weren't supposed to KILL her.*'

'*Fortunes of war, buddy.*'

'*Here's the new offer.*'

'*You didn't keep the OLD offer. Screw you.*'

'*Would you like a demonstration?*'

I didn't like the sound of that.

Suddenly, Stryker blew his whistle. It shrilled through the night like the sound of an angry track coach.

For a few seconds, nothing happened.

Then spears were flying out of the darkness toward our cage. Lee threw me to the ground and shielded me with her body. I heard a clamor as if something had struck a bar and bounced off. Then came the wet thunking sounds of spears punching into the mud.

Lee climbed off me. Raising my head, I saw six or seven spears sticking out of the ground. They formed a rough circle around us.

We got to our feet. I still held the bow, but it didn't seem like much of a weapon after the storm of spears. And I'd lost the arrow.

'*Next time I blow the whistle*,' Stryker yelled, '*they won't miss. Interested in hearing my offer?*'

'*What is it?*' Lee asked.

'*You killed our sole attraction.*'

'*Not me*,' Lee said.

'*You, your friends, it's all the same. Valeria's dead. We're out of business unless we replace her. I want YOU to be her replacement. Agree to surrender and come with us as our vampire, and I'll let the kids go home.*'

'*Why me?*' Lee asked.

'*You're perfect. You're brave and strong . . . and luscious.*'

'*I'm not a vampire.*'

'*No problem. All you need to do is travel with our show and take on all comers in the cage.*'

'*For how long?*' Lee asked.

'You can't!' I blurted at her.

'*For as long as I say.*'

'*And you'll let everyone else go?*'

'Certainly. I would HAVE to, wouldn't I? If I don't release them, you won't keep your side of the bargain.'

'You're right about that.'

'How about it?'

'Give me a few minutes to think it over.'

'Of course.'

We turned away from Stryker and faced each other. 'You can't do it,' I said.

'What other choices do we have?'

'Fight.'

'They'll kill us easily.'

'Maybe, maybe not. At least maybe we can take some of them with us.'

'I don't want you to get killed, Dwight. Or *me*, for that matter. Not to mention Slim and Rusty. For all we know, maybe they've even got Bitsy. We might *all* die if I don't take his offer.'

'You *can't*!'

'I've got to.'

'What about Danny?' I asked.

At the mention of my brother's name, her chin started shaking. In a voice that trembled, she said, 'Tell him that I love him. This . . . this is something I had to do. Tell him I'll always love him. And I'll come back to him if I can.'

I started bawling again. This time, I didn't feel embarrassed about it. I was in too much anguish for embarrassment.

'I have to do this, honey. It's the right thing to do. You know it and I know it.'

'*No!*'

'Let me have the bow,' she said, her voice gentle and sad.

Though I blurted, '*NO!*', I didn't resist when she pulled it from my hand. Nor when she removed the quiver from my back. 'I thought we were gonna *fight*,' I protested.

'I'm sorry,' she said.

She carried the bow and the quiver of arrows to the side of the cage, reached through a space in the bars, and let them fall to the ground.

Turning toward Stryker, she raised her arms in surrender and called, *'It's a deal!'*

'Very good. You won't be sorry.'

He stood up, stepped in front of the bus and made some gestures with his hands. All around us, black-garbed men and women came out of the darkness. Some appeared from behind the bus and truck. Others climbed out from under bleachers. I didn't count, but got the impression there must've been fourteen of fifteen of them. About half of them carried spears.

They all walked toward our cage.

A few paces from the bars, they stopped. One of them bent down and picked up the bow and quiver. All of them gazed at the body of Valeria. Some were scowling. Many shook their heads and looked dismayed. Others appeared to be weeping.

Stryker stepped up to the cage door.

Looking around at his crew, he said in a loud voice, 'This has been a terrible night.' Heads nodded in agreement. 'I know how much Valeria meant to all of you . . . and to me. She was a very special lady. Very special. We'll all miss her terribly.' He took a deep breath and sighed. 'However, the show must go on. To that end, let me introduce the woman who will take over Valeria's role . . . our *new* vampire, Lee Thompson.'

Murmurs and quiet applause came from the crew.

Stryker stepped forward, bent over slightly in front of the door and turned the dial of the combination lock. A few seconds later, he removed the lock and swung the door open.

Lee moved toward it, but Stryker entered. Taking her by

the shoulders, he guided her backward toward the middle of the cage. 'You're already in part of the outfit,' he said. 'Let's see how you look in the rest of it.'

The crew applauded again, this time with some eagerness.

Standing rigid in the middle of the cage like a proud soldier, Lee removed her sleeveless chambray shirt. She stood there in the rain, naked except for the very short skirt of red leather.

Stryker picked up Valeria's red, bra-like top.

Lee stood motionless while he slipped the straps up her arms, cupped her breasts inside its stiff leather, and stepped behind her to fasten its back.

Vivian entered the cage, carrying the black cape.

Stryker took the cape and swept it over Lee's shoulders.

As he backed away from her, she spread the cape wide open, swept it high like bat wings and called out, '*I AM LENORA THE VAMPIRE!*'

Stryker's black-shirted gang of thugs went crazy, cheering and clapping and shouting.

I thought to myself, *Holy shit. What's this?*

With all eyes fixed on Lee and with so much noisy appreciation coming from the crew of the Travelling Vampire Show, nobody seemed to notice the hearse.

Including me.

Not until it came roaring through the rainy night, headlights off. At the last moment, half a dozen of Stryker's people turned and yelled and tried to jump out of the way.

They didn't make it.

The hearse, probably doing sixty, roared between the side of the cage and the bleachers under which Slim had disappeared, ramming through everyone there. They bounced off the grill and hood and roof. They did cartwheels through the rain. A few spears, along with Slim's bow and quiver of arrows, leaped from hands and flew off into the night.

Stryker gaped at the mayhem.

I whirled around, crouched and snatched an arrow out of the mud – the arrow I'd struggled so hard to pluck from Valeria's breast.

I'd dropped it when Lee threw me to the ground during the storm of spears.

Leaping up, I spun around and drove its razor-sharp point into the side of Stryker's neck so hard it popped out the other side.

His eyes bugged out.

I grabbed Lee's arm. '*Let's go!*' I yelled. I jerked her arm.

She looked at me, a frenzy in her eyes, then flung off the vampire cape and let out something that sounded the way I always imagined one of those 'rebel yells' from the Civil War must've been . . . an ear-splitting cry full of rage and wild joy.

On our way toward the cage door, we each jerked a spear out of the mud.

We were just outside the cage when the hearse skidded to a stop near the rear of the bus.

We ran for it.

It started backing toward us.

I had a pretty good idea who must be behind the wheel.

A few spears flew past us, but missed.

Somebody leaped out of the bus door and confronted us with a machete. Before he could swing it, Lee shoved her spear into his mouth and I plunged mine into his stomach.

Leaving the spears in him, we sprinted for the hearse.

It slid to a halt. I was first to reach its passenger door. I grabbed the handle and jerked it open.

'*In!*' I yelled at Lee. '*Jump in!*'

She dived in and I scurried in after her.

Slim turned her head. 'I'm back,' she said.

She stepped on the gas. The hearse lurched forward, its passenger door slamming shut without any help from me.

I figured we should finish the escape, but Slim had different plans. She made a high-speed pass along the other side of the cage. This time, she didn't have quite the same element of surprise working for her. She only managed to mow down one of Stryker's people.

'Can we go now?' I asked.

'Sure.'

With that, Slim steered around the end of the bleachers, put on the headlights and sped across Janks Field. The hearse juddered and shook over the rough muddy ground. We bounced and swayed.

I saw the crippled Cadillac sitting abandoned. And Lee's pickup truck. And two or three other cars that had been left behind.

'Want me to drop you off at your pickup?' Slim asked.

'No thanks,' Lee said. 'Just get us out of here.'

'You sure? I'd be glad to.'

'I lost my keys.'

'We'll go back to my car,' Slim said, and sped toward the dirt road that would return us to Route 3.

Chapter Sixty-two

On the narrow and curvy dirt road, Slim slowed down a lot. She kept glancing at the side mirrors.

'I don't think they'll come after us,' Lee said.

'I don't know,' Slim said.

'Can't hurt to keep an eye out,' I added. I didn't mean it as any sort of pun, but the words forced a picture of Valeria's eye socket into my mind. And then I pictured the arrow embedded in her nipple.

'They've got so many dead,' Lee said.

'We decimated their sorry butts,' Slim said.

'You did a great job,' Lee told her.

'Saved our lives,' I added.

I half expected a quip, but Slim only nodded. In the glow of the dashboard lights, her face looked grim.

'What happened, anyway?' I asked her.

'Huh?'

'After you went off under the bleachers.'

'Just sort of snuck around.'

'Did you see the Cadillac twins?' I asked. 'They were up at the top. Looked like they were on their way down to get you. I yelled to warn you.'

'Yeah, thanks. I took care of them.'

'Huh?'

'You know, the knife. I was sort of waiting for them when they climbed down the back of the stands. Did away with them.'

'You *did away* with them?'

'Yeah. Sent them south. Deep south.'

'Jeez,' Lee said.

I said, 'Holy shit.'

'As Mike Hammer says, "It was easy." '

'So you *killed* them?' I asked, hardly believing it.

'Yeah. Some others, too. I sort of snuck up on anybody I found and cut their throats. A couple of them saw me coming, but I think they figured I was with the show because of the black shirt.'

'The morons,' I said.

'I was trying to find Rusty,' she said.

'Any luck?' Lee asked.

I think we both knew what the answer would be.

'No. I don't know where they took him. I searched the truck. It's where they keep the cage and stuff when they're on the road, I guess. Nobody was in it, though. Just the driver. He was in the cab. I took care of him before I searched the back. Then I didn't get a chance to search the bus or the back of the hearse. Just about the time I got to the hearse, I looked over at the cage and saw they were moving in on you guys. So all I did was kill the driver and come to the rescue.'

'Mighty good job of it,' Lee said.

'Thanks. I just wish . . .' She shook her head. 'I wanted to find *Rusty*.' As she said that about Rusty, her voice cracked. 'I don't want to leave him *behind*.'

I put my hand on Slim's thigh. The leg of her cut-off jeans was warm and damp. 'Wanta go back?' I asked her.

'I don't know. I think maybe.' She must've taken her foot off the gas pedal; the engine quieted and we slowed down. 'What about you?' she asked.

I *hated* the idea of going back to Janks Field. We'd been lucky to get out of there alive, and the chances of finding Rusty alive were slim.

'Yeah,' I said. 'Let's go back and find him.'

'What the hell,' Lee said. 'In for a penny . . .'

'"And gentlemen in England now a-bed,"' quoted Slim, '"shall think themselves accursed they were not here, and hold their manhoods cheap . . ."'

'You bet,' Lee said.

Slim stopped the hearse. She shifted to reverse, started speeding backward, then twisted toward me in her seat to look back over her shoulder. 'Damn!' She slammed on the brakes.

I looked over my shoulder. The window behind the front seat was shrouded with a curtain.

Slim glanced at the side mirrors. 'I can't drive backward without a rearview mirror.'

'Guess you'll have to turn around,' I said.

'Too narrow.'

'Maybe go on to the highway,' Lee suggested. 'Easy enough to turn . . .'

From behind us came a *thud* as if someone riding in back – in the coffin area – had stomped on the floor or dropped something.

Slim looked over her shoulder at the glass just behind our heads. '*Rusty!*' she called.

Lee was already throwing her door open.

As Lee leaped out, Slim shut off the engine and plucked the key from the ignition. Then she flung her door open.

I scurried out Lee's side.

Lee was first to reach the rear of the hearse. She was trying to open its door, but not having any luck. 'I think it's locked,' she said.

'I've got the keys,' Slim said. She picked one and tried to put it into the lock hole. Her hand was shaking so badly that she couldn't get it in for a while. When she finally poked its tip into the slot, it wouldn't go in any farther.

Wrong key. So she pulled it out and tried another. Again, she had trouble because she was trembling so badly. Then it went in.

She turned the key and worked the door handle. The door unlatched. She stepped back, pulling it toward herself, swinging it wide open.

The night, until then fresh and sweet with the aromas of a rain-soaked forest, suddenly went foul. The stench made me hold my breath. Lee clapped a hand across her mouth. Slim stepped around the open door, her lips pressed shut and her chest out. It was the way she sometimes looked out on the river just before she plunged below the surface.

I *wished* we were out on the river. Or anywhere else, just so we were miles away from here.

Inside the hearse a light had come on. It must've been triggered by the opening door.

We all gazed in.

The volunteers who'd gone up against Valeria in the cage were there: Chance Wallace, the handsome Marine; geeky Chester; our old enemy Scotty Douglas, the hoodlum; and our chubby, sweet, stupid best friend, Rusty.

They were all naked.

They were all in pieces, piled up next to the casket within easy reach of . . . its occupant.

Inside the casket, propped up with his head against the curtains of the window we'd been trying to look through, sat an obese, legless, hairless man. I *guess* it was a man. He looked like a bloated sack of slippery white skin. Except the skin was mostly scarlet with blood.

His bulgy eyes looked like a pair of bloodshot golfballs.

Clutched in both hands, upside-down just under his chin, was Rusty's head. Snuffling and grunting, he shoved his maw into the raw gore of the neck stump. He ripped out a large gob, then raised his head, bumping it against the window, and seemed to smile at us . . . with a dripping load of Rusty slopping out of his mouth.

Chapter Sixty-three

All things considered, I think we handled ourselves very well up to the point at which we looked into the back of the hearse.

What we saw in there . . . it knocked out whatever remained of our brains and guts.

I have vague memories of noises coming from us. Things like, '*Whoa!*' and, '*Yahhh!*' and, '*Eeee!*' as we backed away from the rear of the hearse. And someone – Slim, I think – slammed the door shut. And then we were running down the middle of the dirt road as if we had the bogeyman after us.

We ran and ran and ran. Finally we came to Route 3 and Slim led the way to her Pontiac. We all piled into the front seat. The three of us sat side by side, me in the middle, all of us huffing and whimpering while Slim tried to get her key into the ignition.

At last, the engine roared and we were off.

We sped down Route 3 toward town.

At Lee's house, we turned on all the lights. Then we took turns taking showers. After our showers, we got into clean dry clothes that Lee had gathered for us. I wore my brother's stuff. Lee and Slim wore Lee's.

We got together in the living room. Lee let us drink beer. She even made popcorn. We were so freaked out that we hardly talked . . . not for a while, anyway. By the time we'd each polished off a couple of beers, though, we had calmed down.

The talking began. And decisions were made.

In the early morning hours before dawn, we went out to Lee's garage to start getting ready. We made a couple of stakes by sawing off a broom handle and whittling a point on one end of each shaft. We gathered a hammer and a hatchet. We also equipped ourselves with the tin of gasoline that Danny kept around for his power mower. And a box of wooden matches and a cigarette lighter.

We loaded all this into Slim's Pontiac.

After sunrise, we climbed in and Slim started the car. But Lee said, 'Wait a minute. I just thought of something.' She climbed out of the car and hurried back into her house. A couple of minutes later, she came back with my brother's Winchester .30-caliber lever-action repeater. As she climbed in with it, she said, 'In case we have human trouble, too.'

'Always thinking,' Slim said.

Then she drove us up Route 3 until we came to the turn-off. She made the turn and drove slowly up the dirt road toward the place where we'd left the hearse and its awful cargo.

It was a lovely summer morning. Sometime before dawn, the rain had stopped. You could still smell it, though. There is nothing like the scent of a forest after a heavy rainfall.

The sky was cloudless. Birds were twittering all around us, bugs buzzed and sunlight slanted down through the treetops like transparent rods of gold.

It was one of those mornings that make you feel great.

At least if you're not on an errand like ours.

After a while, Lee said, 'Where is it?'

'I don't know,' Slim said, and kept on driving.

435

I think we all expected to find the hearse around every bend, but the dirt road ahead of us remained empty.

'Somebody must've moved it,' Lee said.

Then we came out the other end of the dirt road. Ahead of us was Janks Field, all rutted and muddy, puddles and bits of broken glass flashing sunlight.

Lee's red pickup was still there. So was the Cadillac I had disabled. So was a VW bug. I supposed it had probably belonged to one of the other volunteers – Chester, most likely. Scotty had been with a bunch of his hoodlum friends; they must've gone off without him after the lightning struck. As for Chance the Marine, who knows?

On our way over to the bleachers, I noticed several fresh holes in the dirt. They weren't filled in. Just holes. I didn't know who or what had made them, or why, but I suddenly remembered the poodle that had nipped Rusty's arm and how it had squealed underneath one of the cars.

Slim drove us all around the bleachers and between them. There was no sign of the black bus or the black truck or the black hearse or the black-shirted crew of the Travelling Vampire Show.

The cage was gone, too.

'"Folded their tents like the Arabs,"' said Slim, '"and silently slipped away."'

It seemed they had left nothing behind except Slim's bow, her arrows, and the special quiver she'd won at the Fourth of July archery contest.

When she spotted them, she cried out, 'Ah-*ha!*' and stopped the car. Lee jumped out and retrieved them.

A few minutes later, Lee jumped out again. This time, she ran through the mud with spare keys in her hand and climbed into her red pickup truck.

We followed close behind her all the way back to town.

Chapter Sixty-four

There was a big investigation, of course, but the Travelling Vampire Show was never seen or heard of again. Neither were the bodies of the volunteers or Stryker or Valeria or any of the workers we'd killed.

Or Bitsy.

Yeah, Bitsy vanished that night, too. I don't know, she simply never turned up again. Searchers, including me and Slim and Lee, scoured the woods for her. Parts of Janks Field were even dug up. Four bodies were found, but not Bitsy (no one else from that night, either, strangely enough). To this day, Bitsy is a big mystery. I keep hoping she's alive and happy somewhere, that she chose that night to run away from home, that she didn't end up getting grabbed by remnants of the vampire show or by some other form of degenerate . . . or whatever it was that got the poodle. If anything bad happened to her, it would've been partly my fault.

I won't get into the whole mess about Mr and Mrs Simmons, the parents of Rusty and Bitsy. Let's just say it was grim.

Rusty had won the wager about Valeria's beauty, no doubt about that. We didn't have to go through with the payoff, but we did. As sort of a tribute to Rusty, Slim shaved my head. We never told anyone why. Only Lee. We pretty much told her everything.

My father recovered nicely from the injuries he'd sustained in the car accident.

The next year, Lee and my brother Danny had a baby girl.

Slim started calling herself Fran, short for Frances, and

we began going steady and everything was just about as great as it could possibly be ... except for Rusty being dead and Bitsy being gone and Lee and Fran and me never being able to completely get away from memories of what we saw that night in the back of the hearse.

I guess maybe it was the 'real' vampire, and maybe Valeria had been some sort of bait ...

I don't want to think about it.

Anyway, that's my story.

I just want to say, if you ever get word that a Travelling Vampire Show is coming to your town, stay away from it. For God's sake.

Dreadful Tales

Table of Contents

Bibliographic Information

'Invitation to Murder' – c.1991. First appeared in *Invitation to Murder* edited by Ed Gorman and Martin H. Greenberg, published by Dark Harvest, 1991, published by Diamond, 1993.

'The Grab' – c.1982. First appeared in *Gallery* magazine, January, 1982. Reprinted in the anthology, *The Year's Best Horror Stories: Series XI*, edited by Karl Edward Wagner, published by DAW Books, 1983. Reprinted in *100 Hair-Raising Little Horror Stories*, edited by Al Sarrantonio and Martin H. Greenberg, published by Marboro Books, 1993. Reprinted in my collection, *A Good, Secret Place*, published by Deadline Press, 1993. Performed by the New Hampshire Radio Theater group on Halloween, 1997. To be reprinted in 8th grade Australian textbook, *English Magic 2*, published by Addison Wesley Longman.

'Saving Grace' – c.1991. First appeared in *Cold Blood*, edited by Richard Chizmar, published by Mark Zeising, 1991.

'Barney's Bigfoot Museum' – c.1981. First appeared in *Creature*, edited by Bill Pronzini, published by Arbor House, 1981. Reprinted in *A Good, Secret Place*, 1993.

'Herman' – c.1996. First appeared in *Cemetery Dance* magazine, edited by Richard Chizmar, Fall, 1996.

'The Champion' – c.1978. First appeared in *Cavalier* magazine, October, 1978. Reprinted in the anthology, *Modern*

Masters of Horror, edited by Frank Coffey, published by Coward, McCann & Geoghegan, 1981. Paperback reprints by Ace, 1982 and Berkeley, 1988. Reprinted in *A Good, Secret Place*, 1993. Reprinted in *100 Fiendish Little Frightmares*, edited by Stefan Dziemianowicz, Robert Weinberg and Martin H. Greenberg, published by Barnes & Noble, 1997.

'The Maiden' – c.1994. First appeared in *Dark Love*, edited by Nancy Collins & Edward Kramer, published by New American Library, ROC, 1995.

'A Good Cigar is a Smoke' – c.1976. First appeared in *Ellery Queen's Mystery Magazine*, February, 1976. Reprinted in *A Good, Secret Place*, 1993.

'I'm Not a Criminal' – c.1993. First appeared in *After the Darkness*, edited by Stanley Wiater, published by Maclay, 1993. Belgium (French language) translation published in PHENIX, 1997.

'Oscar's Audition' – c.1975. First appeared in *The Executioner Mystery Magazine*, June, 1975 under the pseudonym, Dick Kelly. Reprinted in *A Good, Secret Place*, 1993.

'Into the Pit' – is original to this collection.

'Spooked' – c.1981. First appeared in *Mike Shayne's Mystery Magazine*, October, 1981. Reprinted in *A Good, Secret Place*, 1993.

'The Good Deed' – c.1993. First appeared in *A Good, Secret Place*, 1993.

'The Direct Approach' – c.1977. First appeared in *Alfred Hitchcock's Mystery Magazine*, January, 1977. Reprinted in *A Good, Secret Place*, 1993.

'Good Vibrations' – c.1996. First appeared in *Night Screams*, edited by Ed Gorman and Martin H. Greenberg, published by ROC, 1996.

'Phil the Vampire' – c.1995. First appeared in *Vampire Detectives*, edited by Ed Gorman and Martin H. Greenberg, published by DAW Books, 1995.

'Paying Joe Back' – c.1975. First appeared in *Ellery Queen's Mystery Magazine*, September, 1975. Reprinted in *Masters of Suspense*, edited by Ellery Queen and Eleanor Sullivan, 1992. Reprinted in *A Good, Secret Place*, 1993.

'The Fur Coat' – c.1994. First appeared in *The Earth Strikes Back*, edited by Richard Chizmar, published by Mark Zeising, 1994.

'Blarney' – c.1981. First appeared in *Mike Shayne's Mystery Magazine*, September, 1981. Reprinted in *A Good, Secret Place*, 1993.

'Dracuson's Driver' – c.1992. First appeared in *Dracula, Prince of Darkness*, edited by Ed Gorman and Martin H. Greenberg, published by DAW Books, 1992.

'Roadside Pickup' – c.1974. First appeared in *Ellery Queen's Mystery Magazine*, December, 1974. Reprinted in *A Good, Secret Place*, 1993. Reprinted in *100 Tiny Little Terror Tales*, edited by Robert Weinberg, Stefan Dziemianowicz and Martin H. Greenberg, 1996.

'Wishbone' – c.1989. First appeared in *Night Visions 7*, edited by Stanley Wiater, published by Dark Harvest, 1989.

'First Date' – c.1997. First appeared in *Love in Vein II*, edited by Poppy Z. Brite, published by HarperCollins, 1997.

'Stickman' – c.1993. First appeared in *A Good, Secret Place*, 1993.

'Mop Up' – c.1989. First appeared in *Night Visions* 7, edited by Stanley Wiater, 1989.

Preface

Me, I don't read prefaces, forewords or introductions. Not until *after* I've read the book. I'm always afraid that the writers of such pre-story material might give away details about what awaits me in the body of the book.

In many cases, they do.

I hate to know anything in advance about a story I'm about to read – or watch on the television or at the movies. As audiences, we're not *meant* to know what happens until we encounter it in the course of the story. For that reason, I avoid reading book covers or dustjackets. When movie previews start to roll, I often shut my eyes and plug my ears.

You may, therefore, feel free to read this Preface without fear that I'll spoil the stories for you. Not me. No way.

You may prefer to avoid it, anyway, and get straight to the stories. (If so, of course, you probably haven't read this far.) I find it perfectly understandable to leap-frog such introductory material and 'skip to the chase'. After all, you're here for the stories, not for authorial observations and assorted blather.

You may wish to return and peruse this material *after* you've read the stories. That's what I do. When finished with a novel or a collection of stories, I usually sit back and check out the details: the cover design, the blurbs, the plot description, the introductory material (if any), the interesting assortment of information to be found on the back of the title page, and so on. By then, none of it can hurt me. I may even find it to be edifying or entertaining.

So why am I writing a 'Preface'? Wouldn't it be more sensible, considering my own habits, to write an 'Afterward' or nothing at all?

Providing an 'Afterward' is like introducing a guest at the end of a party.

And I couldn't simply write *nothing*. Readers of story collections *expect* some sort of additional material. (As do agents and publishers.) The piece needs to be written by the author himself or by a *guest* author – someone with clout. Well, Dean Koontz wrote the introduction for my other collection, *Fiends*. I can't do better than Dean, so I'm stuck writing my own introductory material.

And you're stuck reading it.

(You've gone this far, so you might as well see it through to the end.)

Don't worry. It'll soon be over and you'll be able to move along to the actual stories.

They're *Dreadful Tales*.

I looked up 'dreadful' in my *Webster's Seventh New Collegiate Dictionary*. According to the definitions I found there, you might expect my tales to 'inspire awe or reverance' (reverance?), to be 'extremely distasteful, unpleasant or shocking' (more like it), or perhaps to be 'cheap and sensational' (humph).

Pretty much the sort of thing you might expect from a guy like me.

The twenty-five stories collected in this book – some more dreadful than others – were written over a period of more than twenty years. The earliest, 'Roadside Pickup', was published in *Ellery Queen's Mystery Magazine* in 1974. The most recent, 'First Date', was published in *Love in Vein II* in 1997.

When combined with the Headline editions of *Out are the Lights* (the title novel and five pieces of my short fiction) and

Fiends (the title novella and twelve short stories), *Dreadful Tales* offers *all* of the adult short stories and novellas that I've had professionally published from the start of my career until 1997.

These stories have seen print in a variety of American magazines and anthologies and in my own limited edition collection, *A Good, Secret Place*, which was short-listed for a Bram Stoker award in 1993. To my knowledge, nothing in this volume has ever been published in the United Kingdom. Every dreadful tale will be new to anyone who has not had access to the US publications. Many will be new to American readers as well, because they've appeared in magazines and books that are difficult to find.

Hope you like them.

You'll be able to start in on the first tale very shortly, because my Preface is almost over.

It's 'Invitation to Murder', about an author trying to write a short story about . . .

Never mind. I'll let you find out for yourself.

Ready to read it?

My Preface is almost over.

It *is* over.

Now.

Richard Laymon
April, 1999

Invitation to Murder

A story. Gotta have a story. Time's running out.

The week in Hawaii wouldn't be any vacation at all with a deadline looming.

You've got tonight and tomorrow, pal. Otherwise, you'll be scowling into your Mai Tais, worrying your damn head off.

Shane booted up the word processor, typed the date, and got started.

'Ed wants a story for his *Invitation to Murder* anthology. Every story in the book must have something to do with a twenty-two-year-old female being found dead in her apartment. That's the anthology's unifying premise.'

Oughta be a cinch. A million ways you can go with that.

Has to be tricky, though. I need a nifty reversal for it.

Can't be a whodunit. Not from me. He'll probably get plenty of those from the mystery writers. From me, he'll expect horror or a thriller. It has to be a grabber. There'll be names a lot bigger than mine in that book. I don't want to look like a slouch.

Gotta come up with something hot.

Hot. Christ, it's hot in here.

West LA usually cooled off at night. But this was one of those periods that seemed to come around a couple of weeks each summer when the daytime temperatures hit the upper nineties, the cooling sea breeze took a hike, and the heat lingered on through the night. Even with the windows open, the still air in the apartment felt stifling. Shane's T-shirt and shorts were already damp and clinging with sweat.

A long, cool shower would feel great.

Come up with a plot first. A shower can be your reward.

All right. Shouldn't be all that difficult.

Shane stared out the window and tried to concentrate. A gimmick. A reversal. Okay.

'Idea. A guy picks out this gal. She's twenty-two, of course. And a knockout. He's got the hots to mess around with her. One fine night, intending to rape her, he breaks into the gal's apartment. Only to find her stretched out on the floor, dead. Murdered. Neat. But then what? Is the killer still in the apartment?'

Shane stared at the computer screen, read the amber lines again and again.

How does it end? What's the twist?

Nothing came.

Forget it.

'I like the idea of a guy obsessed with a woman. Maybe he's alone in his hot apartment. Goes out on the fire escape for some fresh air.'

I wish *I* had a fire escape. Or a balcony, for god-sake.

'Just across from his building is an old, abandoned apartment house. Condemned, maybe. But while he's out there trying to get cool, a beautiful young woman appears in a window of that creepy old place. The most beautiful woman he has ever seen.'

All right! Now we're cooking!

A sudden blare of raucous music shattered Shane's thoughts.

Shit!

Was it coming from outside? Yeah, but it also seemed to be driving straight through the wall.

Standing, Shane leaned over the computer screen and touched the wall. It *vibrated* like the head of a drum.

Goddam modern cheap apartment houses!

Calm down, calm down. Just ignore it.

What if it goes on all night?

It won't.

Forget about it.

Guy on fire escape trying to get cool. Gal appears in window across the alley. 'The lighting is bad,' Shane typed. 'No electricity, of course, since the building is condemned. He sees her by firelight. Candles. Can't make her out very well. In fact, all he can really see is her gorgeous face, her shimmering blonde hair. They talk. She has sultry voice. Invites him over. He's reluctant to go. Worried. Who is she? What's she doing there? He REALLY wants her, but he's hesitant about venturing over there. It's a lousy neighborhood. Weirdos around. Only that evening, he'd run into a bag lady at the mouth of the alley between the two buildings. A real hag.

'Reluctantly, he declines to go over. He's about to go back inside his apartment to avoid further temptation when the woman lifts a couple of candles onto the windowsill. She is visible from the waist up. She is naked. She fondles her breasts and again asks him to come over.

'He goes. Spooky stuff while he searches the alley, finds a broken door, and enters. Makes his way through the dark corridor, up a creepy staircase. (Give him a flashlight.) Goes along the second story corridor to the door of the apartment across from his. The door is ajar. A glow of candles from inside. He enters.

'And finds a body sprawled in a corner of the room. He shines his flashlight on it. The body is that of a female (twenty-two, of course). Her clothes are strewn around the floor. She has no face, no hair. From shoulders to waist, she is a mass of gore.

'Out of the shadows steps another woman. Naked. Wearing a mask of the dead gal's face. Withered old arms and legs. But with a fresh, young torso tied in place with a harness of twine. She hobbles toward the guy, caressing the full, perfect breasts she's taken from the corpse.

'She cackles, tells him he's such a hunk. Tells him that she knew, from the way he'd reacted in the alley earlier, that she couldn't hope to have him – he's too picky to be interested in someone like her. So she borrowed good looks from a gal she caught walking past the alley.

'He stands there stunned as she comes closer. "Ain't I pretty now? Ain't I a knockout?" '

Shane grinned at the screen.

Terrific! That story'll be prime Shane Malone: creepy, perverse, sexy, with a touch of black humor. And nice thematic touches about loneliness, desperation, the dubious merits of physical beauty. It'll blow Ed's socks off.

But what if it's too much? Ed had explained that he didn't want stories that were too extreme.

This is pretty damn extreme. That old babe's wearing a dead gal's tits.

A vest of tits.

Shit! Harris used that in *Silence of the Lambs*. A goddam best-seller! Everyone'll think I stole it from him. He got the idea from Gein, no doubt. Gein really did it. But still, they'd figure I copied Harris's gimmick.

Shane sank back in the chair and gazed at the computer screen.

And gazed at it.

That idea's dead in the water. Gotta come up with something else.

The music was still blaring.

It hadn't really gotten in the way, though. Shane had hardly been aware of it once the story idea began to flow. But now . . .

What kind of cretin plays music that loud?

Who the hell *is* playing it? The noise was obviously coming from 210. That apartment had been empty for the past month.

Somebody must've moved in while I was at work.

Some fucking lunatic.

Just block it out. Ignore it.

A twenty-two-year-old gal is found dead in her apartment. Need a twist.

How about something from the point of view of a young woman?

Damn that racket!

'Open with gal walking alone through city streets. Nervous about being out so late. Maybe she thinks someone is following her. She's spooked, quickens her pace. At last, she gets to her apartment building. Unlocks the foyer door, enters. She's safe at last. Relieved, she climbs the stairs to the second floor. The door of her apartment is ajar. She looks in. Her room-mate, a twenty-two-year-old gal (of course), is dead on the floor. And the killer, crouching over the body, grins over his shoulder at the main gal, lurches up and rushes her.'

Rushes her. Then what?

'She whirls away and runs . . .'

Shane glared at the wall. That music!

Am I the only person in the whole damn place it's driving nuts?

This *is* Saturday night. Maybe everyone's out – gone to the movies, gone to visit friends, gone to parties.

Was the creep in the next apartment having a party? Didn't sound that way. No voices, no laughter, no sounds of anyone moving around. Just that blasting music.

Shane stood up, leaned over the computer screen, and pounded the wall. 'Hey! Could you please hold it down in there? I'm trying to work.'

The volume of the music lowered.

'Thank you.'

'Get fucked!' shouted a female voice from the other side of the wall. Then the music blared, even louder than before.

Shane's heart thudded.

Calm down, calm down.

I oughta go over and clean that bitch's clock for her!

What I oughta do is calm down.

What about complaining to the landlord? Right. That moron. Dudley. A dud, all right. I'd get nothing but grief from him. If he's even home. Saturday night. Probably out somewhere, pursuing his hobby – 'bagging babes' as he liked to put it.

What about calling the cops?

Oh, that'd be a neat move. If they do come over and give that bitch a warning, I'll have a real enemy on my hands. No telling what kind of shit she might start pulling.

What about taking the shower?

Come up with a story first. That was the deal.

Shane blinked away some sweat and read the last few sentences on the computer screen.

Okay. The gal finds her room-mate dead. The killer leaps at her and she whirls away and runs 'through the doorway. Runs down the corridor, shouting for help. Nobody comes out to help. The killer races after her with his knife.'

What next?

That bitch! Told me to get fucked!

Pound on the wall again? Lot of good that would do. She'd probably turn the music up even louder – if that's possible.

'The guy hot on her tail, she pounds on an apartment

door. It swings open. She rushes in. Trips over a body. Sees another body slumped against a wall.

'Neat idea. Suppose the . . .'

Sweat stung Shane's eyes. Nothing within reach to wipe them dry.

My shirt.

The T-shirt came off. Though damp, it did a fine job mopping the sweat away. There *was* a breeze from the window. Very slight. But it felt good. Shane tossed the shirt to the floor, sighed, and studied the computer screen.

'. . . killer has murdered everyone in the whole building? But why would he do something like that? Just because he's nuts? Suppose he's the owner and there's rent control and he wants to get rid of all his tenants so he can convert the place into a condo?'

Stupid.

'Forget him killing any other people in the building. His targets are the two gals, nobody else. He lived in the apartment next to theirs. He decided to knock them off because he just couldn't stand them always playing their fucking stereo too damn loud!'

Oh, man, I'm getting nowhere fast.

Too noisy! Too hot!

The breeze was better than nothing, but hardly cool enough to stop sweat from running down Shane's face and sides and chest.

This might easily qualify as the most miserable night of my life. Thanks a lot, Ed. And *you,* you bitch!

Shane kicked the wall, then hunched down sideways and picked up the T-shirt and attacked some tickling runnels of sweat.

I'll *never* come up with a decent idea. Not with all this racket. Not with all this heat making the sweat pop out as fast as I can wipe it off.

So take the shower.

Yeah!

Feeling better already, Shane hurried to the bathroom. Its shut door muffled the maddening beat of the music. And the sounds of water splashing into the tub obliterated the noise completely.

Maybe I'll just stay in here. Never come out again.

You left the computer on, stupid. Good move. Hope it doesn't explode or something. That'd be a fitting finale for this misbegotten night.

Hey, I'd have a good excuse for Ed. Sorry, afraid I can't do that story for you. My computer blew up.

Peeling the shorts down, Shane scowled at a haggard twin in the full-length mirror: short hair clinging in wet points; specks of sweat under the eyes, above the upper lip; tanned skin gleaming as if it had been slicked with oil; untanned skin, hidden from the sun by swimsuits, that looked white and felt clammy.

Oughta get some air conditioning in this dump. Maybe buy one of those window units.

Sure. With what?

With the $5,000 advance I got for *The Black Room*?

That was reserved for Hawaii.

In two days, I'll be soaring out over the Pacific. Away from all this. Hawaii. Beaches. Soft breezes. Mai Tais. Maybe meet someone nice . . .

The bod's not half bad. Trim and firm. The tan looks pretty good, and nobody'll see the white. Not unless I get lucky.

Shane smirked at the face in the mirror, then stepped to the tub, climbed in, swept the curtain shut and turned on the water. It gushed from the spout. Nice and cool. A tug at the little knob on top of the spout sent it raining down.

Wonderful!

Maybe I can pick up some kind of air-conditioning unit with the money I get from Ed.

Have to write the story, first.

Have to think of *an idea*, first.

How about a twenty-two-year-old babe gets offed in the shower? Some kind of a twist on the *Psycho* thing. Maybe the gal in the shower turns out to be a guy. Right. Only then we've got a *male* dead. Has to be a female.

Besides, it's stupid. Everybody would say I was ripping off Bloch. I could say it's not a rip-off, it's a *homage*. That's what everyone else calls it when they swipe somebody's stuff.

Shane sat down on the tub's cool, slick enamel.

Think think think.

Eyes shut, legs crossed, the deliciously cool water pattering, sliding, caressing.

I could almost fall asleep.

You can't.

Think! Twenty-two-year-old gal found dead in her apartment.

What if she's a bitch who deserved to die? A nag. Always at her husband. And her husband's a cripple in a wheelchair. Totally at her mercy. One fine night, she steps out of the bathroom after taking a shower and he zaps her.

How does he zap her?

With darts. That's his only fun in life, throwing darts. And she's always giving him shit because he misses the target sometimes and puts little holes in the wall.

Maybe the bitch hid his dart board. And that was the last straw. She steps out of the bathroom, maybe onto a sheet of plastic he's spread on the carpet to catch the blood, and whammo! Nails her with some darts in the face.

Not half bad.

Smiling, Shane stretched out along the bottom of the tub.

Now we're getting someplace!

Could you kill someone with a dart? Probably. A good hard shot right to the forehead. Penetrates the skull. Pokes the brain. And maybe he puts one in her eye.

Bull's-eye!

Make her a lesbian, you'd have a nifty play on words: bull's-eye, bull dyke.

No. The pun's going too far. Pushing the ludicrous.

But nice and sickening, a dart jabbing into her eyeball.

Anyway, she winds up dead. Twenty-two-year-old gal dead in her apartment.

And the perp is a cripple in a wheelchair. So he needs help disposing of her body. So he phones his best friend, and invites the guy to come over for a game of darts. The friend is reluctant to come. Doesn't want to face the guy's shrew of a wife. Guy says, 'That's okay, she's out.'

Out, all right.

This is great.

So the friend shows up, finds the bitch dead on the floor. He's shocked, but not especially upset. He needs some convincing, but finally agrees to help get rid of the body. He's afraid he might be seen if he tries to carry it out through the apartment building, but there's a balcony over the alley. So he and the crippled guy lower the body with a rope.

How about giving it a toss, instead? More fun that way.

Either way, it ends up in the alley. And the friend goes down, planning to drive it away. But the body isn't there. He can't find it anywhere. He goes back up to the apartment.

The two guys are discussing what to do, when suddenly they hear voices. Shouts. They go to the balcony and look down. Half a dozen creepy, ragged derelicts are gathered in the alley, all of them gazing up at these fellows. 'Give us another one! We want another!'

What did they do with her? Eat her? And they're still

hungry, and if the boys don't throw down seconds for them, they might just come up and help themselves.

So then what?

Shane sat up, shivering.

Too much time under the cold shower? Or am I shivering with excitement because of the story?

Hell, it's not that good. But it's not that bad.

Is it good enough?

Shane turned off the water, groaned at the muffled sound of the music, but climbed out of the tub and pulled a towel off its bar.

Just don't think about the damn noise or that slimy scum-sucking bitch next door. Think about the story.

Is it really the end of the story when we figure the bums want more? Maybe the guy in the wheelchair could push his friend off the balcony. But then what? It would sure be the end if I tell the story from the friend's point of view. But that way, how would I work in the neat business of the cripple darting his wife to death?

Dry, Shane draped the towel over its bar and opened the bathroom door. The music pounded in.

'Shit!'

At least the apartment no longer felt like an oven. Probably as hot as before, *I'm* just cool. Won't be for long, though, especially if I let that music get to me.

Shane put on a fresh pair of running shorts and a short-sleeved shirt, left the shirt unbuttoned so air could get in, and sat down in front of the computer.

Stick with the idea of the wheelchair guy? Cannibalism. Derelicts. I've used both those things a lot lately. And the ending isn't all that terrific.

The story seems okay until the bums show up in the alley. But if I get rid of them, where did the body go?

Walked away? She's dead, for Christsake. Make it a

zombie story, and she comes stumbling back up, seeking vengence.

Crapola.

Damn it! The story hadn't seemed half bad while I was under the shower – and couldn't hear that bitch's music. With that noise messing up my head, maybe *nothing* will seem any good.

I oughta go over there and break her face. Or break her stereo, even better.

No, just be polite. Explain the situation. Ask her nicely to turn the volume down.

The thought of it made Shane's heart pound.

Chicken.

You've gotta do it. Otherwise, you'll just sit here getting more and more steamed and you'll never accomplish anything.

Do it!

Heart hammering, mouth dry, Shane got up from the chair and walked to the door. Paused to button up.

Shit. I don't want to do this.

Opened the door.

She might be nice. Who knows? Nice, sure. She told me to get fucked.

Stepped into the corridor, left the door open, and walked on shaky legs to the neighbor's door. Knocked.

Bitch probably can't hear me through all that noise.

Knocked again.

The volume of the music dropped. 'Yeah? Who's there?'

'It's me from next door.'

'What do you want?'

'I'd just like to talk to you for a second.'

'Yeah?'

Shane heard a metallic click.

'If you came over here to give me shit about . . .' The door swung open. The woman's glower softened. So did the tone of her voice as she said, 'Well, now. So you're my new neighbor, huh?' She made a little toasting gesture with her cocktail glass, and said, 'Pleased to meet you, neighbor.'

Shane managed a nervous smile.

Jeez, the gal was practically naked. All she wore was a black negligée. It had spaghetti straps. Its low front exposed the tops of her breasts. Its skirt was hardly long enough to reach her thighs. And Shane could see right through the gauzy fabric.

Any gal who would open the door in an outfit like that must be weird or half polluted. Maybe both. Her eyes looked a little red. From the booze, or had she been crying?

'I'm Francine,' she said, holding out her hand.

Reluctantly, Shane shook it. 'I'm Shane.'

'Nice to meet you. Come on in, why don't you?'

'Oh, I don't want to intrude.'

'Please?' A smile twitched on her heavy lips. 'Come on in and have a drink, okay? Hey, it's my birthday. Nobody oughta have to be alone on her birthday, huh?'

Shane suddenly felt a little sorry for the woman. 'I guess I can come in for a minute. But no booze. I'm trying to work.'

'Sure, sure. How about a Pepsi?'

'That'd be fine, thank you.'

Francine shut the door, gestured with her glass toward a sofa, and headed for the kitchen area.

Shane sat at one end of the sofa.

This is not bright. Francine's obviously a bit mental. But not really a bitch. After this, she might be willing to cooperate and keep the music down.

The stereo and its twin speakers were on the floor, right up against the same wall that Shane faced when sitting at the word processor.

If the wall weren't there, I could've knocked them over with my feet.

No wonder the noise had been so bad.

The turntable was empty. In front of the stereo were stacks of cassette cases.

'How do you like this heat?' Francine called.

'I don't.'

'My last place was air conditioned.'

'This close to the ocean, you usually don't need one. Just for a couple of weeks each summer . . .'

'Makes me wanta scream.'

She came back, a full glass in each hand. A strap had slipped off her shoulder. When she bent down to hand the soda to Shane, that side of her negligée drooped, exposing her entire breast.

On purpose?

What've I gotten myself into here?

She stepped by, and lowered herself next to Shane. Turning sideways, she rested an arm across the back of the sofa, brought up one leg and hooked its foot behind her other knee.

Shane glanced down. The negligée was hardly long enough to conceal Francine's groin.

Man oh man.

'Here's how,' Francine said, and gulped some of her drink.

'Happy birthday.'

'Happy. It's been the shits till now.'

'Birthday's can be that way.'

'See how *you* feel when you hit the big two-two.'

'Already did,' Shane said.

This gal is twenty-two! Talk about your coincidences and ironies of life!

'You don't look any older than nineteen,' Francine said.

'Neither do you,' Shane lied. The gal looked closer to thirty.

'You're just saying that.'

'No, it's true.'

A corner of Francine's mouth curled up. 'Do you think I'm attractive?'

Her dark hair was mussed, her face a little puffy and red. Though she looked older than her age, she was beautiful. No denying that. And she certainly had a body.

'Sure,' Shane said. 'Of course you're attractive.'

The other corner of her mouth trembled upward. 'You're not bad, yourself. I'm so glad you came over. I was feeling so down in the dumps you just wouldn't believe it.'

'It hasn't been a banner night for me, either.'

'I guess I'm partly to blame, huh?'

'Well, it's all right.'

She took another drink, then set her glass on the table. 'I'm sorry I yelled at you.' She leaned a little closer. Her fingers began to caress the back of Shane's neck. 'Can you forgive me?'

'Sure. No problem. But I'd better . . .'

Her other hand, wet and chilly from the glass, squeezed Shane's thigh. 'Doesn't that feel good? Nice and cold?'

'Look, Francine . . .'

'You have such lovely blue eyes.'

'I'm really busy tonight. I have to get back to my work.'

'Do you? Do you really?' The hand crept higher, fingertips slipping under the leg hole of Shane's shorts.

'Hey!'

The hand retreated. Staring into Shane's eyes, Francine said, 'You want me. I know you want me.'

'I don't. Really. Thanks all the same.'

There was pain in the woman's eyes. Loneliness. Despair.

'I'm sorry, Francine, but . . .'

With a noise that seemed partly growl, partly whimper, she hurled herself onto Shane. The Pepsi glass went flying.

'No! Get off!'

Lips. Wet, sloppy lips. A sour reak of gin. Hands plucking feverishly at buttons, yanking open Shane's shirt. Grabbing, caressing, squeezing.

I don't believe this. God, I don't believe this!

The mouth and hands suddenly went away. Shane, slumped on the sofa, hips pinned down by Francine's weight, gasped for breath as the frenzied woman arched her back and peeled off her negligée.

'Don't. Please.'

'You love it.' Hunching down, she pushed a breast against Shane's mouth.

And tumbled off as Shane bucked and twisted.

Her back struck the edge of the coffee table. Her head pounded it. The table skidded, capsizing her glass. Then she flopped off and dropped to the floor.

She lay there face-down, sprawled between the table and the front of the sofa.

Shane scurried over the end of the sofa. Stood. Stared down at Francine. Felt a hot surge of shame and revulsion. Whirled away, doubled over and vomited.

Shouldn't have shoved her. Oh, God, shouldn't have shoved her.

Why didn't I just let her do what she wanted?

Shane backed away from the mess on the carpet, and gazed at Francine.

What if she's dead and I killed her?

Who says she's dead? Probably just unconscious. That's cheap movie stuff, people getting shoved during a struggle, falling, dying from a little bump on the head. She'll probably wake up in a few seconds.

When she does, I don't want to be here.

Watching the body, Shane knelt beside the coffee table and picked up the Pepsi glass.

Anything else with my fingerprints?

Probably just this glass.

Don't take it! Jesus! That's like admitting she's dead, admitting your guilt.

But Shane kept the glass. Rushed to the door. Wrapped a hand in a shirt-tail before turning the knob. Checked the corridor.

Empty. Silent.

Stepped out, swung the door shut, and walked fast.

She can't be dead. But if she is, there's no way they can pin it on me. No physical evidence. The vomit! They'll know somebody else was there. But they won't know who. They'll end up deciding it was an accident. She was drunk, she fell and hit her head. They'll check her blood alcohol level during the autopsy, realize she was polluted, and . . .

There won't be an autopsy! She's okay.

What if I'm locked out?

But the door was still open. Shane lunged in, locked the door and leaned against it, gasping.

Safe.

God, *why* did I have to go over there!

She's all right. Just a little knock on the head.

Shane pushed away from the door, staggered over to the desk, and dropped onto the chair. The music came softly through the wall.

Turn it up, Francine. Come on, make it blast.

On the computer screen was Shane's last sentence. 'He decided to knock them off because he couldn't stand them always playing their fucking stereo too damn loud!'

No no no no no!

'Shane?'

Little more than a whisper through the wall.

'Francine?' Rising from the seat. Heart thumping. Relief like a flowing warmth. 'Francine, are you okay?'

'Fuck you.'

'I'm sorry you got hurt, but –'

A blast pounded Shane's ears. White dust and flecks exploded from the wall a foot to the right. Something zipped by.

In the wall was a hole the size of a dime.

She shot at me!

'Francine!'

The next shot punched Shane in the chest.

Twenty-two-year-old female found dead in her apartment.

Oh, shit.

Shane dropped onto the chair, saw blood hit the computer screen, the keyboard – then stared down at the spurting hole between her breasts.

The Grab

My old college roomie, Clark Addison, pulled into town at sundown with a pickup truck, a brand-new stetson, and a bad case of cowboy fever.

'What kind of nightlife you got in this one-hearse town?' he asked, after polishing off a hamburger at my place.

'I see by your outfit you don't want another go at the Glass Palace.'

'Disco's out, pardner. Where you been?'

With that, we piled into his pickup and started scouting for an appropriate watering hole. We passed the four blocks of downtown Barnesdale without spotting a single bar that boasted of country music or a mechanical bull. 'Guess we're out of luck,' I said, trying to sound disappointed.

'Never say die,' Clark said.

At that moment, we bumped over the railroad tracks and Clark punched a forefinger against the windshield. Ahead, on the far side of the grain elevator, stood a shabby little clapboard joint with a blue neon sign: THE BAR NONE SALOON.

Short of a bucking machine, the Bar None had all the trappings needed to warm the heart of any yearning cowpoke: sawdust heaped on the floor, Merle Haggard on the jukebox, Coors on tap, and skintight jeans on the lower half of every gal. We mosied up to the bar.

'Two Coors,' Clark said.

The bartender tipped back his hat and turned away. When the mugs were full, he pushed them toward us. 'That's one-eighty.'

'I'll get this round,' Clark told me. Taking out his wallet, he leaned against the bar. 'What kind of action you got here?' he asked.

'We got drinking, dancing, carousing, and The Grab.'

'The Grab?' Clark asked. 'What's that?'

The bartender stroked his handlebar mustache as if giving the matter lots of thought. Then he pointed down the bar at a rectangular metal box. The side I could see, painted with yellow letters, read, TEST YER GUTS.

'What's it do?' Clark asked.

'Stick around,' the bartender said. With that advice, he moved on.

Clark and I wandered over to the metal box. It stood more than two feet high, its sides about half as wide as its height. THE GRAB was painted on its front in sloppy red letters intended, no doubt, to suggest dripping blood. Its far side was printed with green: PAY $10 AND WIN.

'Wonder what you win,' Clark said.

I shrugged. Leaning over the bar, I took a peek at the rear of the box. It was outfitted with a pound of hardware and padlocked to the counter.

While I checked out the lock, Clark was busy hopping and splashing beer. 'No opening on top,' he concluded.

'The only way in is from the bottom,' I said.

'Twas ever thus,' he said, forgetting to be a cowboy. He quickly recovered. 'Reckon we oughta grab a couple of fillies and raise some dust.'

As we started across the room toward a pair of unescorted females, the jukebox stopped. There were a few hushed voices as everyone looked toward the bartender.

'Yep!' he cried, raising his arms. 'It's time! Step on over the face The Grab. But let me warn you, this ain't for the faint of heart, it ain't for the weak of stomach. It ain't a roller coaster or a tilt-a-whirl you get off, laughing, and forget. This is a genu-wine test of grit, and any that ain't up to it are welcome to vamoose. Any that stay to watch or participate are honor bound to hold their peace about the doings here tonight. Alf's curse goes on the head of any who spill the beans.'

I heard Clark laugh softly. A pale girl, beside him, looked up at Clark as if he were a curiosity.

'Any that ain't up to it, hit the trail,' the bartender said.

He lowered his arms and remained silent while two couples headed for the door. When they were gone, he removed a thin chain from around his neck. He held it up for all to see. A diamond ring and a small key hung from it. He slid them free, and raised the ring.

'This here's the prize. Give it to your best gal, or trade it in for a thousand bucks if you're man enough to take it. So far, we've gone three weeks with The Grab, and not a soul's shown the gumption to make the ring his own. Pretty thing, ain't it? Okay, now gather 'round. Move on in here and haul out your cash, folks. Ten dollars is all it takes.'

We stepped closer to the metal box at the end of the bar, and several men reached for their wallets – Clark included.

'You going to do it?' I whispered to him.

'Sure.'

'You don't even know what it is.'

'Can't be that bad. *They're* all gonna try.'

Looking around at the others as they took out their money, I saw a few eager faces, some wild grinning ones, and several that appeared pale and scared.

The bartender used his key to open the padlock at the rear of the metal box. He held up the lock, and somebody moaned in the silence.

'Dal,' a woman whispered. She was off to my left, tugging on the elbow of a burly, bearded fellow. He jerked his arm free and sneered at her. 'Then go ahead, fool,' she said, and ran. The muffled thud of her cowboy boots was the only sound in the room. Near the door, she slipped on the sawdust and fell, landing on her rump. A few people laughed.

'Perverts!' she yelled as she scurried to her feet. She yanked open the door and slammed it behind her.

'Gal's got a nervous stomach,' Dal said, grinning around at the rest of us. To the bartender, he said, 'Let's get to it, Jerry!'

Jerry set aside the padlock. He climbed onto the bar and stood over the metal container. Then he raised it. The cover slid slowly upward, revealing a glass tank like a tall, narrow aquarium. All around me, people gasped and moaned as they saw what lay at the bottom, barely visible through the gray, murky liquid. A stench of formaldehyde filled my nostrils, and I gagged.

Face up at the bottom of the tank was a severed head, its

black hair and mustache moving as if stirred by a breeze, its skin wrinkled and yellow, its eyes wide, its mouth agape, its neck full of ragged pulp.

'Well, well,' Clark muttered.

Jerry, kneeling beside the glass tank, picked up a straight-bent coat hanger with one end turned up slightly to form a hook. He slipped the diamond ring over it. Standing, he lowered the wire into the tank. The ring descended slowly, the brilliance of its diamond a dim glow in the cloudy solution. Then it vanished inside the open mouth. Jerry flicked the hanger a bit, and raised it. The ring no longer hung from its hook.

I let out a long-held breath, and looked at Clark. He was grinning.

'All you gotta do for that pretty diamond ring is to reach down with your hand and take it out of the feller's mouth. Who'll go first?'

'That's me!' said Dal, the bearded one whose girl had just run off. He handed a ten-dollar bill to Jerry, then swung himself onto the bar. Standing over the tank, he unbuttoned his plaid shirt.'

'Let me just say,' Jerry continued, 'nobody's a loser at the Bar None Saloon. Every man with grit enough to try The Grab gets a free beer afterwards, compliments of the house.'

Throwing down his shirt, Dal knelt beside the tank. Jerry tied a black blindfold over his eyes.

'All set?'

Dal nodded. He lowered his head and took a few deep breaths, psyching himself up like a basketball player on the free-throw line. Nobody cheered or urged him on. There was dead silence. Swelling out his chest, he held his breath and dipped his right hand into the liquid. It eased lower and lower. A few inches above the face, it stopped. The thick fingers wiggled, but touched nothing. The arm reached deeper. The tip of the middle finger stroked the dead man's nose.

With a strangled yelp, Dal jerked his arm from the tank, splashing those of us nearby with the smelly fluid. Then he sighed, and shook his head as if disgusted with himself.

'Good try, good try!' Jerry cried, removing the blindfold. 'Let's give this brave fellow a hand!'

A few people clapped. Most just watched, hands at their sides or in pockets, as Jerry filled a beer mug and gave it to Dal. 'Try again later, pardner. Everyone's welcome to try as often as he likes. It only costs ten dollars. Ten little dollars for a chance at a thousand-buck ring. Who's next?'

'Me!' called the pale girl beside Clark.

'Folks, we have us a first! What's your name, young lady?'

'Biff,' she said.

'Biff will be the very first lady ever to try her hand at The Grab.'

'Don't do it,' whispered a chubby girl nearby. 'Please.'

'Lay off, huh?'

'It's not worth it.'

'Is to me,' she muttered, and pulled out a ten-dollar bill. She handed her purse to the other girl, then stepped toward the bar.

'Thank you, Biff,' Jerry said, taking her money.

She removed her hat and tossed it onto the counter. She was wearing a T-shirt. She didn't take it off. Leaning forward, she stared down into the tank. She looked sick.

Jerry tied the blindfold in place. 'All set?' he asked.

Biff nodded. Her open hand trembled over the surface of the fluid. Then it slipped in, small and pale in the murkiness. Slowly, it eased downward. It sank closer and closer to the face, never stopping until her fingertips lit on the forehead. They stayed there, motionless. I glanced up.

She was tight and shaking as if naked in an icy wind.

Her fingers moved down the face. One touched an open eye. Flinching away, her hand clutched into a fist.

Slowly, her fingers fluttered open. They stretched out, trembled along the sides of the nose, and settled in the mustache. For seconds, they didn't move. The upper lip wasn't visible, as though it had shrunken under the mustache.

Biff's thumb slid along the edges of the teeth. Her fingertips moved off the mustache. They pressed against the lower teeth.

Biff started to moan.

Her fingers trembled off the teeth. They spread open over the gaping mouth, and started down.

With a shriek, she jerked her hand from the tank. She tugged the blindfold off. Face twisted with horror, she shook her hand in the air and gazed at it. She rubbed it on her T-shirt and looked at it again, gasping for air.

'Good try!' Jerry said. 'The little lady made a gutsy try, didn't she, folks?'

A few of the group clapped. She stared out at us, blinking and shaking her head. Then she grabbed her hat, took the complimentary beer, and scurried off the bar.

Clark patted her shoulder. 'Good going,' he said.

'Not good enough,' she muttered. 'Got spooked.'

'Who'll be next?' Jerry asked.

'Yours truly,' Clark said, holding up a pair of fives. He winked at me. 'It's a cinch,' he said, and boosted himself onto the bar. Grinning, he tipped his hat to the small silent crowd. 'I have a little surprise for y'all,' he said in his thickest cowboy drawl. 'You see, folks . . .' he paused and beamed, '. . . not even my best friend, Steve, knows about this, but I work full-time as a mortician's assistant.'

That brought a shocked murmur from the audience, including me.

'Why, folks, I've handled more dead meat than your corner butcher. This is gonna be a pure cinch.'

With that, he skinned off his shirt and knelt behind the tank. Jerry, looking a bit amused, tied the blindfold over his eyes.

'All set?'

'Ready to lose your diamond ring?'

'Give it a try.'

Clark didn't hesitate. He plunged his arm into the solution and drove his open hand downward. His fingers found the dead man's hair. They patted him on the head. 'Howdy, pardner,' he said.

Then his fingers slid over the ghastly face. They tweaked the nose, they plucked the mustache. 'Say ahhhh.'

He slipped his forefinger deep between the parted teeth, and his scream ripped through the silence as the mouth snapped shut. His hand shot up, a cloud of red behind it. It popped from the surface, spraying us with formaldehyde and blood.

Clark jerked the blindfold down and stared at his hand. The forefinger was gone.

'My *finger*!' he shrieked. 'My God, my *finger*! It bit . . . it . . .'

Cheers and applause interrupted him, but they weren't for Clark.

'Look at him go!' Dal yelled, pointing at the head.

'Go, Alf, go!' cried another.

'Alf?' I asked Biff.

'Alf Packer,' she said without looking away from the head. 'The famous Rocky Mountain cannibal.'

The head seemed to grin as it chewed.

I turned to Biff. 'You knew?'

'Sure. Any wimp'll make The Grab if he doesn't know. When you know, it takes real guts.'

'Who's next?' Jerry asked.

'Here's a volunteer,' Biff called out, clutching my arm. I jerked away from her, but was restrained by half a dozen mutilated hands. 'Maybe you'll get lucky,' she said. 'Alf's a lot more tame after a good meal.'

Saving Grace

At the top of the hill, Jim stopped his bike, planted a foot on the pavement and twisted around. Mike was far back, red-faced and huffing, fat bouncing as he pumped his way up the slope.

While he waited for his friend, Jim took off his shirt. He wiped his sweaty face with it, then stuffed it into the basket on the rack behind his seat.

'It's all downhill from here,' he said.

Mike rolled to a halt beside him. He draped himself over the handlebars, gasping. 'Shit on a stick,' he muttered. Sweat dripped off his nose and chin. 'Gonna have a heart attack.'

'Beans. Nobody fifteen has a heart attack.'

'Oh yeah?'

'Just think how neat it'll be at the lake.'

'If we ever get there. You and your great ideas. I bet there won't even *be* any babes there.'

'You'll see.' Yesterday, when trying to talk Mike into a bike trip to Indian Lake, he'd told all about the girls who'd been there last Saturday when he picnicked on the shore with his family. 'There were some real yucks,' he'd said, 'but some were fantastic. This one, she had on a white suit you could see right through. You could see *everything*. Everything! And some had on these bikinis you wouldn't believe. It was just incredible. We'll take our binoculars, you know?' Mike had listened, nodding, his lips pursed, and readily agreed to make the twelve-mile trip.

'Man,' Mike said, 'if you're wrong . . .'

'Trust me. Your eyes are gonna fall out.'

'They better.'

'Let's get going.' A shove at the pavement started Jim's bike rolling. He pedaled a few times, picking up speed. Then the road slanted downward through the dense forest. He coasted faster and faster, sighing as the summer air rushed against him. It was better than standing in front of a big fan, the way it blew his hair and buffeted his face and rubbed his arms and chest and belly and sides. It felt really wonderful against the heat of his armpits. It felt best where it slid up inside a leghole of his swimming trunks, cool on his hot groin.

With a glance back at Mike, he saw a car come over the crest of the hill. 'Watch out behind you!' he called.

Mike looked around, then steered toward the edge of the road. The car swung out and crossed the center line a bit, giving him a wide berth. As it sped down, Jim eased his bike over. The car stayed far to the side. It shot past him, and quickly returned to its own lane before disappearing around a curve to the right.

'Did you see that babe?' Mike called.

Jim looked over his shoulder. 'Huh?'

'The gal driving. Hope *she's* on her way to the lake.'

'Hot stuff?'

'Didn't you . . . look out!'

Jim snapped his head forward. Just in time to see a black van straight in front of him. Parked. Its rear jutting into the road. He braked and swerved to the left. Missed it. But his bike was skidding sideways, tires sliding out, dropping him toward the pavement. He shot his foot down, swung his other leg clear and hopped a couple of times as the bike flew out from under him. From the feel of things, he knew that dismounting hadn't solved his problem. A twister suddenly seemed to grab him. It whirled him, whipped him down, tumbled him.

He lay there.

Mike came to a stop and grimaced down at him. 'Are you okay?'

'Shit fuck damn hell.'

'Should've watched where you were going.'

Groaning, Jim sat up. The side of his left knee was filthy, scuffed and bloody. So was a patch of his left forearm, just below the elbow. He tried to brush some of the grit out of the wounds, and winced. I'll wash up when we get to the lake, he thought. He struggled to his feet and limped to his bike.

His shirt and towel were still in the basket. His lunch bag and binoculars had fallen out.

'Oh, man,' he muttered, picking up the binoculars. He pulled them out of the case, glanced at the lenses.

'They okay?'

'Yeah, I guess so.' He stuffed them back into the case. 'Asshole. Why didn't he pull *all* the way off the road?'

'Well, there's a ditch.'

'The bastard.' He hobbled close to the van and kicked its side.

'Jeez! Don't! What if someone's in there?'

That hadn't occurred to Jim. With a grimace, he hurried over to his bike. Mike was already starting off. 'Hey, wait up.' He jammed his binoculars and lunch back into the basket and lifted his bike by the handlebars. Giving the van a nervous glance, he planted a foot on the lower pedal, gave himself a push and swung up his other leg.

And heard a high-pitched shriek.

It seemed to come from somewhere nearby in the woods.

Mike stopped and looked back at him. 'Jeez!'

Jim rolled past him, then steered to the roadside in front of the van and braced a foot against the pavement. He stared into the thick, shadowy woods.

Mike glided over and stopped. 'It was a scream, wasn't it?'

'Sure was.'

'A gal.'

'Yeah. But I don't know.'

'Don't know what?' Mike asked.

'You know girls. They scream all the time just for the fun of it. I mean, it doesn't mean she's in trouble, or anything. She might've just been messing around.'

'Yeah, or she saw a spider.'

They stopped talking and listened. Jim heard a soft breeze stirring the treetops, birds squawking and twittering, insects buzzing.

Then, *'Please!'*

'God,' he muttered, 'maybe she *is* in trouble.'

Mike's eyes widened. 'Maybe she's *screwing*.'

Jim felt his heartbeat quicken. 'Yeah,' he said. 'I bet that's it.' He dismounted and lowered the kick stand. 'Let's check it out.'

'Are you kidding?'

'No, I'm not kidding. Besides, what if she *is* in trouble?' He plucked his binoculars out of the basket, removed them from the case, and slipped the strap over his head.

'Oh man, oh man,' Mike muttered, propping up his bike. He took out his own binoculars.

Jim led the way, Mike close behind him as he hurried to the bottom of the shallow ditch and climbed its other side. He entered the shadows of the forest. He walked slowly, weaving around bushes and trees, setting his feet down as softly as possible, cringing at the quiet sounds of leaves and twigs crunching under his shoes.

Flies buzzed around the scrapes on his knee and arm. Mosquitos settled on him. He wished he were wearing more clothes. But this was neat, in a way. Exciting. Creeping through the woods like an Indian, nearly naked.

What if there really *is* a gal getting screwed?

It'd be like a dream coming true, getting to watch something like that.

As long as we don't get spotted.

What if the guy sees us and comes after us?

God, he'd kill us.

Jim stopped and looked around at Mike.

'What?' Mike whispered.

'Maybe we'd better not.'

'Oh, man.'

'I mean, what if we get caught?'

As if stabbed with pain, Mike bared his upper teeth. The expression pushed his cheeks so high they seemed to squeeze his eyes shut. 'We've gotta at least take a peek,' he whispered. 'This is our big chance.'

Jim nodded. He knew Mike was right. They'd seen naked women in movies and skin magazines, but never in the flesh. If he should turn back now, he would want to kick himself later.

Probably won't see much, anyway, he thought as he turned away from Mike and began walking deeper into the forest.

Probably won't even be able to find her.

Less than a minute later, he glimpsed movement beyond some trees far to the right. His heart gave a lurch. Halting, he pointed.

'Yeah,' Mike whispered.

They made their way slowly in that direction. Jim couldn't

see much. The trees were too close together, offering only glimpses of someone through the tiny spaces between their trunks. Soon, however, he began to hear a rustle of dead leaves and twigs. There were also a few muffled moans and squeals.

Crouching low, he crept up to a tree that he hoped might be near enough so he could get a good view. He squatted, one hand on its trunk. Mike came up behind him. He felt Mike's knees push against his back.

Hearing a soft intake of air, he realized that Mike was already looking.

Jim eased his face past the side of the trunk.

And gasped.

And felt his bowels shrivel.

The girl in the clearing ahead was naked, just as he'd hoped. She was slim and beautiful, probably no older than eighteen. Sunlight slanting down through the trees made her hair shine golden, her damp skin gleam. She was sweaty, dripping. She had a dusky tan except for where a skimpy bikini must've hidden her skin from the sun. Her breasts were creamy mounds. The darker flesh of her nipples jutted. Lowering his eyes, Jim gazed at sunlit hair so fine and meager that he could see right through it, see the soft edges of the split between her legs.

This was so much better than he'd ever hoped.

But so much worse.

Worse because the girl was suspended from a tree branch by a rope looped around her neck, because she was writhing and weeping, because her mouth was stuffed with cloth to stifle her noises and the man behind her was doing something that must be hurting her terribly.

As Jim watched, stunned and breathless, the man stepped around to the front. He was not very old, maybe twenty. He was very handsome. He was grinning. He was naked except for his socks and sneakers. He had a huge boner. He had a hunting knife in one hand, pliers in the other.

He turned toward the girl. Crouching slightly, he put his face against one of her breasts. She jerked her head from side to side, a wild look in her eyes. She made whimpery noises through the gag. She tried to kick him, but lost her balance. The rope yanked at her neck. Her eyes bulged. She made choking sounds. Then she found her footing and shut her eyes.

The guy moved his face to her other breast. The one he'd left behind was no longer creamy. It had a reddish hue. Above the nipple was a curving row of dents – teeth marks.

When he sank to his knees, both her breasts looked that way.

His face pushed against her groin.

Though the girl twisted and squirmed and shook her head, she didn't try to kick him away. Nor did she reach for him. Obviously, her hands were bound behind her back.

He tilted his head back. Then he reached up with the pliers.

He shut their jaws on her right nipple.

As the girl let out a muffled shriek, Jim leaped up and ran, raced at the man, swinging his binoculars by their strap.

The guy looked over his shoulder.

Started to turn around.

But he was on his knees. Not quick enough.

The binoculars smashed against the side of his face. His head jumped as if he wanted another quick look at the girl's crotch. Her knee pumped up. Jim heard teeth crash together. He leaped out of the way. The man flopped backward and slammed the ground. His head struck with a quiet thump. He had landed with both knees up. Now, one slowly sank sideways. The other leg straightened out, his sneaker sliding in between the girl's bare feet. She stomped on his ankle and he let out a groggy groan.

He groaned again when Mike stomped on the wrist of his right hand. Bending over, Mike took the knife away. The pliers, Jim noticed, had already fallen from the other hand.

The man raised his head off the ground.

'Get him again,' Mike gasped.

Jim twirled the binoculars by their strap. Faster and faster. Then he whipped his arm down and crashed the binoculars against the man's temple. The head jerked sideways, sweat and spit spraying.

He lay motionless.

'Out like a light,' Mike said.

Jim and Mike both faced the girl. She had tears in her eyes. Her chest was heaving as she sucked air through her nose. Jim glanced at her rising, falling breasts. Saw their redness, the marks left by the bastard's teeth. Her right nipple was bright red and looked as if it were swelling up because of what the pliers had done.

He felt no desire. He felt only weak and shaky and nauseous.

'You'll be all right,' he told the girl. Stepping over the man's legs, he pulled the cloth from her mouth. Red, lace panties, moist with her saliva. As he tossed aside the wadded garment, the girl gasped air through her mouth. 'We'll get you down,' he said.

Mike, using the assailant's knife, cut through the rope above her head.

She slumped forward. Jim caught her. He wrapped his arms around her and held her up. Her face rested against the side of his neck. He felt her slick, hot skin against his bare chest. The soft push of her breasts. And something warm running down the backs of his hands.

Mike stepped behind the girl. He winced. 'God, the guy cut her.'

Moments later, her arms went around Jim. She clung to him, gasping and sobbing. Mike raised the severed ropes for Jim to see, then tossed them down.

'You'll be all right,' Jim whispered.

And realized that, in spite of his shock and revulsion, he was starting to get hard. The feel of the naked girl was just too much. Embarrassed, afraid she might notice his arousal, he eased her away.

'Maybe you'd better sit down.'

She sniffed, nodded, wiped her eyes.

Holding onto her upper arms, Jim guided her sideways. He watched her head turn as she tried to look past him at the man.

'It's all right. He's out cold.'

'He . . . he might wake up.'

'Don't worry,' Mike told her. 'We'll take care of him.'

She started to sag. Jim lowered her gently. When her knees met the ground, he released her. She hunched over and braced herself up with straight arms.

He saw her back.

It was slick with blood.

Mike stepped up beside her. He'd found a T-shirt. He wadded it and patted the bloody mess. When he lifted the rag, Jim saw a design carved into the girl's skin.

'My God,' he murmured.

'A face,' Mike whispered.

'It's a *skull*. It's a goddam *skull*.'

As he stared at the skull, its lines of blood thickened and began to trickle down the slopes of her back.

'We oughta kill the bastard,' Mike said.

'I'll kill him,' said the girl.

'Just take it easy. Mike, why don't you pull down that rope and tie him up? I'll take care of the girl.'

Mike lowered the bloody cloth to her back, then hurried away. Jim gently mopped the cuts. Sidestepping, he rubbed the crimson mounds of her buttocks, then the backs of her legs. He returned to the skull, blotted it, and left the rag there. 'I'll get your clothes.'

She stayed on her hands and knees, her head drooping.

The man was still sprawled flat, motionless.

Mike, face to the tree, was busy working at the knot that bound the rope to its trunk.

The girl's clothes were scattered on the ground. Jim picked up the damp ball of her panties. Pulling them open, he found that their sides had been severed. The man must've cut them off her. He dropped them and saw a red bra nearby. Sliced apart the way it was, it would be of no more use than her panties.

Her skirt and blouse were not far from the bra. Jim went to them. The short, denim skirt appeared to be all right. The plaid blouse was pretty much intact, though one sleeve hung loose from its shoulder and all its buttons were gone.

He glanced around, but couldn't find her shoes and socks.

The T-shirt used to clean her back, Jim realized, must belong to the man. A pair of jeans were neatly folded on top of a boulder near the edge of the clearing. No shirt. Just jeans.

'Want to help me tie him up?' Mike asked, dragging the rope down from the limb.

'Okay. Just a second.' He returned to the girl. She raised her head and watched him approach. Crouching, he set down the skirt and blouse in front of her. 'Here, you can put these on.'

'Thanks.'

'Your other stuff's wrecked.'

She reached out a shaky hand and lifted the blouse. Then

she pushed herself back and settled onto her haunches. She seemed much calmer now. She rubbed her face with the blouse.

'How are you feeling?'

'I guess I'll live. Thanks to you and your friend.'

'Jim,' he said. 'I'm Jim. That's Mike over there.' He nodded toward Mike, who had already managed to roll the man over. Knife clamped between his teeth, he was straddling the guy's rump and tying one of the hands.

'I'm Grace,' the girl said. 'I owe you two my life, I really do.' She gave him a sweet, trembling smile. 'Could you help me with this?' She held the blouse toward him.

He took it, and tried not to look at her breasts as he slid a sleeve up her outstretched arm. He remembered how they'd felt, pushing against his chest. He wondered how they would feel in his hands.

Don't even think about it, he warned himself. After what she's been through . . .

Embarrassed, he leaned forward and pulled the blouse across her back. He held it while she struggled to get her other arm in.

'Thanks.'

'That's all right. I'd better go and help Mike.'

She nodded.

Jim stood up and hurried over to his friend.

Now, both wrists were bound together behind the man's back. Knife in hand, Mike was climbing off.

'Looks like you've got him taken care of.'

'Yeah. But what about his feet? We don't want him running off.'

'I don't know.'

'What are we gonna do with him?'

'I wonder if that was his van.'

'Probably.'

Jim turned around. Grace was on her feet, bent over and stepping into her skirt. She straightened, pulling it up her legs. Jim caught a last glimpse of her downy public hair before the denim ruined his view.

'That van by the road, is it his?'

'Yeah.' Grace raised the zipper and fastened the button at her waist. Then she came toward them, walking a little stiffly, making no attempt to close her blouse. She halted in front of Mike. 'I'm Grace,' she said, and held out her hand.

'Nice to meet you. I'm Mike.' He blushed fiercely as he shook her hand.

'You two saved my life.'

Mike shrugged. 'Glad we did.'

'We're trying to figure out what to do with him,' Jim said. 'If that's his van, I guess we should try to get him into it. We could drive him into town and turn him over to the cops.'

She stared down at the man, and said nothing.

'Or we could stay here with him,' Mike suggested, 'and she could go for the cops.'

'I'll stay,' Grace said. 'You guys go for help.'

'Are you kidding?' Mike blurted.

'Yeah, you don't want to do that. He's bound to wake up.'

'I'll be okay. He's tied. Just leave me the knife.'

'But we're on bikes,' Mike pointed out. 'It'd take us a long time to reach town.'

'We could take the guy's van,' Jim said, though he thought it was crazy to let Grace stay behind. 'Maybe just one of us should go.'

'Meaning me,' Mike said, looking a little sour. 'You're the one with the learner's permit.'

'This is an emergency. The cops aren't gonna worry about whether you've got a driver's license.'

'Why don't you just take your bikes?' Grace suggested. 'I

don't think anybody oughta use the van. When the cops come, they'll want to search it for evidence. It shouldn't be . . . you know, tampered with. I think he's had other girls in there besides just me.'

'Really?' Mike sounded surprised.

'Yeah. There were some clothes in the back. And I saw stains. I think he's one of those guys who goes around . . . getting a lot of people.'

'A serial killer?' Jim asked.

'Yeah, something like that.'

'Geez,' Mike said.

'How'd he get you?' Jim asked.

She pressed her lips together hard. She looked as if she were struggling not to cry. After a few moments, she said, 'He just grabbed me.' Her voice sounded way too high. 'I was going to my car.' She sniffed. 'He came up behind me and . . . gave me a jab. With his knife. And he said, 'Come with me. I wanta show you something.' And he made me go to his van. And he pushed me in. He didn't even know me. I never did anything to him.'

Jim's throat had gone tight while he listened and watched her painful struggle to communicate. Now, he reached out and put a hand on her shoulder. She sniffed. She wiped her nose.

'I've never been so . . . scared. And then . . .' Her breath hitched. 'The things he did to me.'

The way she looked at Jim, the way she leaned toward him, he knew she needed to be held. He took her into his arms. The back of her blouse felt sodden and sticky. She squeezed herself against him. He wished her blouse were open wider so her breasts would be bare against him like last time.

Mike was watching. Frowning. 'Come on. We'd better do something about this guy.'

'Why don't you go for the cops?' Jim told him. 'I'll stay with Grace.'

'Thanks but no thanks.'

'You should both go,' Grace said. 'I'll be okay here.'

'We can't leave you alone with him.'

'Yes, you can.' Easing out of his arms, she wiped her eyes. 'Go. I mean it.'

He suddenly realized why she wanted them both to leave. A thick weight seemed to sink inside his stomach. 'You're gonna *do* something to him.'

'No, I'm not. Just go. Please.'

'So you can kill him.' It made Jim hurt, talking to her this way. He wanted to hold her, to kiss her, not to stand here accusing her. 'You'll kill him. Then you'll probably take his van and leave.'

'Oh, man,' Mike said. 'You're right.'

'You saw what he did to me. *Some* of what he did.' Her face was red, twisted with agony, tears spilling down her cheeks. 'He would've ... My God, don't you think he deserves whatever he gets?'

'Yeah, but ... you can't just murder him in cold blood.'

'That's *just* what he was gonna do to me. Once he got done torturing me. And raping me. And I bet I'm not the first. I bet he's done it to a lot of girls.'

'I don't know about killing him,' Mike said.

'You guys don't have to watch. Just go. I'll wait till you're gone.'

'We'd still *know*,' Jim said.

'So would you,' Mike told her. 'Right now, you want to make him pay for what he did. But what about later? If you kill him, you'll have to live with it for the rest of your life.'

'I'll always have to live with what he did to me,' she said. She took a deep, shaky breath. 'As long as he isn't dead, I'll be ... afraid he might come after me again.'

486

'He won't be able to,' Jim said. 'They'll never let a guy like him out of prison.'

'Yeah, sure.'

'What if they can't prove any murders on him?' Mike said. 'He might get . . . I don't know, ten or twenty years for what he did with Grace. And they give time off for good behavior.'

'That's right,' Grace said. 'He could get out in five or ten years, and then what'd happen? Even if he doesn't come after me, he might get someone else.'

'She has a point.'

'And it'd be *our* fault.' She was no longer crying. She seemed completely focused on changing Jim's mind. 'If they let him out or he escapes or something and kills somebody, we'll be to blame. We've got a chance, right now, to get rid of him. Nobody will ever know but us. And he'll never, never be able to hurt anyone again.'

'It'd be murder,' Jim said.

'*I don't care!*' She suddenly lurched sideways, grabbed the knife from Mike, and threw herself at the tied, motionless man. His body shook as she dropped onto his rump. She raised the knife high.

'No!'

Even as the knife slashed down, Jim slammed her to the ground with a flying tackle. She rolled and squirmed under him. 'Get off me!' she gasped. 'Leave me alone!' He caught her wrists and pinned them down.

'Let go of the knife!'

'God, Jim,' Mike blurted from behind.

'We can't *let* her!'

She stopped struggling. She stared up into Jim's eyes. 'Let me do what I want,' she said, 'and you can have me. You both can.'

'What?' Jim gasped.

'You want to. I know you do.'

'Oh, my God,' Mike said.

Breathless, Jim gazed down at her. He was sitting across her hips. Her blouse hung open, showing her breasts. He could feel her heat through his trunks and her denim skirt. He thought about how she was wearing no panties. He started to get hard.

'I mean it. I like you both. We can make love right here. Right now. If you'll let me keep the knife and . . . take care of him.'

'Oh, man,' Mike murmured.

'Kiss me, Jim. Kiss my breasts.'

'Geez. Go for it.'

He released her left hand – the one without the knife. Gently, he caressed her breast. He thought he had never touched anything so smooth, so wonderful. Grace moaned softly. 'Am I hurting you?'

'No. No.'

He fingered the crescent of dents made by the man's teeth.

And flinched with surprise as Grace's hand rubbed his penis through the trunks. No girl had ever touched him there before.

She's only doing this so I'll let her kill the guy.

So what? Let her.

It'll be the same as if I killed him with my own hands.

He's the price.

He's a monster, anyway.

Grace's hand slipped inside his trunks. Her fingers curled around him, glided slowly up and down. He shuddered. He felt as if he might explode.

'No!' he shouted. He grabbed her wrist, forced her hand away and pinned it to the ground. 'We can't. We can't do this. It'd be wrong.'

'Please,' Grace said.

'No.'

'Don't be an idiot,' Mike said. 'When'll we ever get another chance like this?'

'It doesn't matter! We can't just murder the guy. I don't care what he's done, we can't just murder him. We'll take him to the cops. This is something for the law, not for us. If we kill him, we wouldn't be any better than he is.'

'Shit,' Mike muttered.

Releasing Grace's left hand, Jim reached across her body and tried to take the knife from her right hand.

She held on tightly. 'You don't know what you're doing,' she said. 'Please.'

'I'm sorry.' He pried Grace's fingers away from the handle. He picked up the knife, then scrambled off her and got to his feet.

Mike, frowning, shook his head. 'Man, we could've . . .'

'It wouldn't have been any good.'

'Oh, yeah, right. *Look* at her.'

Grace lay on her back, braced up with her elbows, looking from Jim to Mike. Her blouse was wide open. Her skirt was rumpled high around her hips. Her knees were up, and spread apart. 'Please,' she said. 'If we don't kill him . . . I don't know what I'll do. I'll always be afraid. I don't want to always be afraid. Why can't you understand that?'

'I do understand. I'm sorry. I really am. God, how I'd love to . . . but I'm not a murderer. I don't want you or Mike to be murderers, either.'

'It'd be kind of like self-defense,' Mike said. 'You know?'

'He's *tied up*, for godsake. And out cold.'

'We could untie him.'

'Oh, that's a neat idea. Come on, let's get going. It'd be nice if we can get him to the cops before he wakes up.'

'What're we gonna do, carry him?'

'Drag him, I don't know.' Jim walked over to the man's folded jeans. He picked them up. As he searched the pockets, he watched Grace struggle to her feet. She straightened her skirt. She closed the front of her blouse and held it shut. She stared at him. She looked betrayed.

Jim found the car keys and a wallet.

Curious, he flipped open the wallet. The driver's license identified the man as Owen Philbert Shimley. 'Shimley,' Jim said.

The man on the ground moaned as if awakened by the sound of his name.

'Oh shit,' Mike said.

'Maybe it's better this way,' Jim said. 'He can walk under his own steam.'

Mike, looking alarmed, snatched up the length of rope he'd cut away after binding Shimley's hands. He quickly made a slip knot in one end, dropped to his knees, and pulled the loop down over the man's head. A tug sent the knot skidding until it stopped against the back of his neck.

Jim let the jeans fall. He had no pockets, so he tucked the key case and wallet under the elastic waistband of his trunks. They seemed secure there. Knife clenched in his right hand, he hurried over to Mike.

Mike, standing behind the man's feet, held the rope taut.

'Get up, Shimley,' Jim ordered.

Face pushing against the ground, he struggled to his knees. A tug at the rope yanked him backward, choking. Upright on his knees, he glared at Jim. Then at Grace. She hunched over and seemed to shrink as he looked at her.

Jim ducked, picked up his binoculars, and dropped their strap over his head. 'On your feet,' he said.

Shimley stood up.

'We're taking you in,' Jim said. 'Don't try any funny stuff, or you'll be sorry.' Boy, did that sound trite and dumb.

But the man didn't make any remark about it. He nodded his head.

'Let's go.'

'I want my pants.'

'Fuck you,' Mike said.

Shimley glanced around at him.

'Come on!'

Shimley started walking.

Grace stayed behind him, stayed with Mike.

She hates me, Jim thought.

But this is for the best. We're doing the right thing.

He walked backward, watching Shimley. The man really looked pitiful, stumbling along with his head down, his shoulders slumped, his limp penis wagging.

Big, tough monster.

But not so tough now.

With a roar, Shimley charged. The rope clamped his neck like a choke collar. His head jerked. His face went scarlet. But he didn't stop coming.

'Shit!' Mike yelled. Either he'd lost hold of the rope or . . .

Jim thrust his knife straight forward at Shimley's chest.

The man lurched to a halt inches from its tip. He hunched over. He bared his teeth. He growled.

'Don't move!' Jim shouted in his face.

'Abracadabra, motherfucker.' Shimley's arms came around from behind him. He dangled a knotted tangle of ropes in front of Jim's eyes.

Mike and Grace hit him at the same instant.

Mike slamming against Shimley's back.

Grace tackling him low.

They hit him hard, smashing him forward.

Jim's knife plunged into his chest.

Shimley crashed into him. As he went down backward, he knew he'd killed the man, after all.

Then his head struck something.

* * *

Jim awoke with a horrible, raging headache.

He sat up, and saw that his feet were bound together with rope.

Then he saw Mike's head. It was near enough to touch. It was upside-down. A big red ball with teeth and open eyes. Some spinal column, jutting from a ragged stump of neck, pointed at the sky.

Then he saw Grace. She had a rope around her neck. She was hanging from the limb of the tree. Her feet didn't quite touch the ground. Her tongue was sticking out. From just below her neck all the way down to her knees, she was raw and pulpy and strange. Skinless.

Shimley stepped out from behind the tree.

He was red all over. And grinning.

His left hand was pressed tight against his ribcage. His right hand held the bloody knife.

He walked toward Jim.

'Too bad you slept through the fun, asshole.'

Jim lurched forward and started to vomit on his thighs.

He was still vomiting when Shimley kicked him in the forehead.

Dazed, he dropped backward and hit the ground.

'But you didn't miss *all* of it. Get a load of this.'

Jim bucked as the knife punched deep into his belly.

Barney's Bigfoot Museum

All day long, people stopped by. Not just for a beer or a meal, or to stock up on minnows or bug spray, or to have a look at my Bigfoot Museum. That's not why. I'll tell you why.

It was the gray, lonely weather out there, the kind that makes you ache for a brightly lighted diner, a cup of chili, a familiar tune on the jukebox. You can get all that at my place. Mine's the first spot after almost fifty miles of forest so heavy and bleak you think you'll never see another human face. I call it Barney's Bigfoot Museum 'n' Diner.

My wife was working the lunch counter, late that afternoon, when this fellow came in. He climbed out of a Dodge pickup with a Pathfinder camper on the back, and came up the porch steps. At the door, he stopped and glanced around like he thought someone might be sneaking up on his back. Then he came in.

He looked lean and hard, and banged up. The sleeve of his flannel shirt was torn. His face and neck were threaded with scratches.

Turning away from the counter, he limped toward the museum entrance. He had my curiosity up, so I followed him through the door. He must've heard me. With a small sound, he spun around and grabbed under his shirt. I glimpsed black steel – the butt plate of an automatic – before he dropped his hand and the shirt-tails fell shut.

'Damn,' he said.

'Are you all right?'

He didn't answer. He just turned away and gazed up at the Winchester. It hung on the wall above a display case, its barrel bent toward the ceiling.

'Bigfoot did that?' he asked.

'So I'm told.'

'Where'd you get it?'

'Bought it off a fellow.'

He lowered his eyes to the display case and looked for a while at the plaster casts of giant footprints.

'Buy these, too?'

'Some. I made two of them, myself, from prints I found near Clamouth.'

'Authentic?'

'Far as I know.'

He limped to the next display case and peered through the glass at half a dozen photos.

'Ever seen one?' he asked.

'A Bigfoot?'

'Yeah.'

'No. Not yet. I keep hoping, though. There've been several sightings in the area. And I've seen the footprints, like I said. I go out searching when I get the chance.'

He stepped over to the corner and peered at the plaster bust.

'That's lifesize,' I told him. 'A sculptor over in Kalama claims he saw one, back in seventy-eight.'

'Pay much for this?'

'It wasn't cheap.'

'You got taken. It's all wrong.'

'Oh?' I'd been suspicious, at the time, but finally agreed to pay the artist's exorbitant price. Whether or not he'd actually seen the beast, the simian features conformed with other eyewitness accounts and blurred photos. 'What makes you think it's wrong?'

The man turned to me. He rubbed a scabbed-over scratch above his eye, as if it might be itchy.

'My God,' I gasped. 'You've seen one, haven't you?'

A grim smile creased his face. 'More than that.'

'Tell me – tell me *all* about it! I mean, what I'm doing, I'm writing a book. It'll be *the* book on Sasquatch. I've been working on it for five years, collecting artifacts and stories . . . My museum, it draws everyone who –'

He held up a hand for me to stop. He smiled as if amused by my eager babbling. 'I'll tell you about it.'

'Great! Just great! Wait and I'll get my recorder. That okay, if I record you?'

'Help yourself.' He glanced out the window at the gloomy sky. 'Make it quick.'

'Right.'

I hurried to my office and lugged my heavy reel-to-reel tape recorder back to the museum room. The man was still alone. I shut the door to keep intruders out, plugged in the machine. I put on a fresh spool of tape and ran it through.

'One thing before I start,' he said.

I glanced up, ready for bad news.

'I want something in return. Do you have a car?'

I nodded.

'What kind?'

'A seventy-nine Bushmaster, four-wheel drive.'

'Do you have the pink slip?'

'In my office.'

'I'll leave you my Dodge and Pathfinder. You sign your Bushmaster over to me.'

'I don't—'

'It'll be worth it, believe me. So far, you've paid out a lot of money for junk. Nothing but junk.' He gazed at me with weary, red eyes. 'I'll let you in on something that'll put your museum on the map.'

I hesitated.

'Wait till I'm done, then decide.'

I couldn't see any objection to that. 'I guess . . .'

'Start the machine.'

I turned on the recorder, and the man began to speak. He talked swiftly, staring at the floor, often turning for a quick glance out the window.

'My name is Thomas Hodgson. I'm thirty-two. I come from Enumclaw. For the past two weeks, I've been hunting Bigfoot in the woods about thirty miles north of here.

'I had three friends with me – Charles Raider, Bob Chambers, and Armondo Ruiz – all from Enumclaw. It was Chambers's idea. He'd run into some tracks back in early June. He figured we'd all be millionaires if we could capture Bigfoot. Or kill it. Either way. I don't suppose we really figured we'd find the thing, though. Just an excuse to spend our vacation running wild. We'd all been together in the Marines – that's where we met – in Nam. We all came to Enumclaw in seventy-two and started a sporting goods . . . forget all that. The thing is, we went out looking for Bigfoot and we sure as hell found it.

'Ruiz saw tracks on the twelfth day out. He was picking up firewood and sucking on a brew. *Cerveza*, he called it. You never saw Ruiz, he didn't have a *cerveza* in his fist.

'We spent the next day and a half following the tracks. We finally lost them at a stream about twenty miles from our base camp. They just ended at the stream. Couldn't pick them up again, so we decided to stick around and see what developed.

'We camped near the stream that night. Ruiz had first watch, then Chambers. At about two in the morning, a gunshot woke me up. Chambers started yelling his head off. "Hey, I bagged one! I bagged one!"

'I grabbed my rifle and got outside just as he came running into camp. Raider and Ruiz popped out the other tent. They hit Chambers with their flashlight beams. Christ, what a . . . He stood there with his feet planted and lifted this . . . *thing* by its arms. It hung there like it was dead. Blood kept pumping out, though. You could hear it pattering on the ground.

'Chambers put the thing down.

'Ruiz shined his light on it, and we all saw it wasn't human. It was covered with bristly fur, and the shape wasn't right: the arms too long, the rump more like a bear than a man. But its face was bare and pale, and it somehow made you think of a little kid.

'"It came along for a drink at the stream," Chambers told us. He sounded pretty upset. "I figured, you know, it's Bigfoot."

'"Kind of small, don't you think?" Raider said.

'"I think it is a Sasquatch," I said. "A young one. What else could it be? Have you ever seen anything like it?" None of us had. "We've got a hell of an opportunity here," I said. "We came in after Bigfoot and by God, we got one! You're looking at the one and only specimen, guys. We'll be famous. And rich! We can sell this thing, or tour with it, or parlay it into a whopping book contract. The possibilities are staggering!"

'After that, Chambers went on about how we should dig a grave and bury the thing. Nobody bought it, though. While Ruiz and Raider were still dazed with the idea of riches, I tried another pitch on them.

'"We'd be better off, though, with a full-grown version. If this is a baby Bigfoot, its parents are probably nearby." They all looked at me as if they'd been thinking the same thing, and not liking the idea much. But I went on. "We'll put out the kid as bait. When papa or mama come along, *wham!*"

'"No way," Chambers said. "Count me out."

'"What've you got against money?" I asked him.

'"There's ways and there's ways, Hodgson. I just killed this thing. That's enough for me. More than enough."

'"How about you?" I asked the others.

'Ruiz shook his head. "I don't know, man."

'"I say we get while the gettin's good," Raider said. "A bird in the hand, you know."

'Ruiz nodded. "We killed the kid, man. If its folks come looking . . ." He shook his head, fear in his eyes.

'I argued for staying, but the others wouldn't give in. Finally, we tied up the carcass, slipped it under a tent pole, and started out. Raider led the way, with Chambers and me on the pole, and Ruiz bringing up the rear. None of us talked. I guess we were listening, expecting to hear footsteps or a roar or something. None of that happened. The woods were silent except for the usual night sounds: owls and frogs, that sort of thing.

'Then Raider shrieked and left his feet. He went straight up, flapping his arms and kicking. I couldn't see anything but him. He just hung there, squirming and yelling, for a second. Then he fell. He landed right at my feet, and he didn't have a head any more.

'Yeah, his head was still up there about twelve feet above the ground. In the hands of this *thing*. This huge, dark *thing*! Bigfoot. It had to be. It threw Raider's head to the ground and stomped on it – crushed it.

'We'd dropped the pole by this time. While the creature was busy mashing Raider's head into the ground, I shouldered my rifle and fired. The thing flinched and staggered back. Then it left. It just ran off.

'The three of us stood around for a while, looking at what was left of Raider and staring off into the woods. Ruiz kept shaking his head and muttering, "Holy Jesus."

'"It's gonna get us all!" Chambers was yelling.

"'It's had its chance," I told him. "Probably going off someplace to die in peace."

"'It'll be back," Chambers said. "It'll keep coming back."

"'Since when are you psychic?" I asked him. But Chambers ignored me.

"'It wants the kid," Ruiz said. "I say we leave the kid."

"'I'm not leaving it," I told them.

"'That's your problem," Chambers said. He gestured to Ruiz, and they started away together.

'That's how I found them, an hour later. Together – their arms and legs all broken and intertwined like a terrible bloody knot.

'I kept moving. I hardly expected to survive the night, but I kept trudging along, the creature on my back, its tied hands pulling at my neck like a kid riding piggyback.

'Dawn came and I kept moving. The sun beat through the trees and the body stank and flies swarmed all around us, but I kept moving. Finally, I reached base camp. I threw the carcass in the back of my Pathfinder, then drove like hell.

'That was this afternoon,' he said.

'You mean . . .?'

He nodded, anticipating my question. 'Yeah. The thing's in my camper.'

'My God! Can I . . . can I *see* it?'

'Just sign over your Bushmaster. I'll give you the papers on my Pathfinder and truck. Fair trade.'

I hesitated. 'Something wrong with them?'

A smile twisted his face. 'Not a thing. Just want to trade, that's all.'

'You don't think Sasquatch could follow a truck!'

'Of course not. I'd just feel better.'

'I'll be right back.'

With a nod, he turned toward the window and stared out at the dark forest.

I left him. I ran for my office, ignoring the curious looks from my wife and half a dozen customers at the lunch counter.

In the office, I searched madly through my desk. My hands trembled as I flipped through the papers, searching for the pink title slip. Finally, I found it. As I shoved the drawer shut, I heard a burst of glass out front. Then a gunshot.

I ran for the museum room ahead of the customers and shoved open the door.

Hodgson was gone.

The room reeked of a foul, musty stench that made me think of mold and dead things.

Gagging, I raced to the broken window. I looked out, but saw only the dark road and the timber on the other side of it.

I climbed out. I ran through the windy night. To the side of the diner. To the parking lot. To Hodgson's battered Pathfinder.

Its rear door lay on the gravel.

Stepping over the door, I peered into the camper and saw a dark shape on the floor. I scurried inside. On hands and knees, I picked up the thing by its hair.

Voices. Rushing footsteps.

Before the curious arrived, I had it safely concealed in a cupboard.

It's the pride of my Bigfoot Museum, but I show it to no one, not even my wife. I stuffed and mounted it myself. I keep it inside a locked case, in the corner below the twisted metal door of the Pathfinder.

Perhaps, when my Bigfoot epic is complete, I'll reveal it to the world.

Perhaps not.

It's mine, and I want to keep it that way.

Often, late at night, I lock myself in the darkness of my

museum and open the case. I hold Hodgson's head on my lap as I listen to the tape of his voice. Sometimes, I half expect to feel his lips move with the words.

But they never do.

Herman

Charlotte, who went by Charlie, was thirteen and a very brave girl who thought of herself as a tomboy. She also thought of herself as an explorer of territories unknown, as a teen detective, and as a crusader against injustice. She thought of her bicycle as a stallion named Speedy, and she thought that she had an invisible friend named Herman who went everywhere with her and who would, against any and all odds, keep her from harm.

She was a very imaginative girl.

But not completely out of touch with reality.

She knew trouble when she saw it.

When the car sped toward her from the rear, she pulled way over to the edge of the road. She flinched when it raced by, engine roaring, radio blasting, guy yelling out the passenger window at her, 'Eat me!'

The car, an old blue Mustang, zoomed past her so quickly that she didn't get a chance to see who was inside.

A couple of jerks, that's all Charlie knew for sure.

Her left hand let go of Speedy's handlebar.

She jabbed at the noon sky with her upraised, stiff middle finger.

Ahead of her, the car braked.

That's when she knew she was in trouble.

She muttered, 'Uh-oh,' skidded to a stop and caught the pavement with her feet.

Holding Speedy between her legs, she looked over her shoulder. The road was a sunlit strip of pavement bordered by bright green forest. All the way back to the bend, its lanes were empty.

She looked forward. The only car in that direction was the Mustang.

It began backing slowly toward her.

'Oh, man,' she muttered. 'Now I've done it.'

She glanced from side to side as if checking the woods for an escape route. Then she faced the Mustang.

About twenty feet in front of her, it stopped. The doors opened and two young men stepped out. What with school, church, the band and choir and softball team and her general roamings about the town of Maplewood and the county in general, Charlie knew just about everyone who lived in the vicinity. These guys were strangers to her.

They looked the right age to be high-school drop-outs. Both of them wore T-shirts, blue jeans and cowboy boots. The driver looked scrawny and mean. He had a cigarette pinched between his lips, but it wasn't lighted. The passenger looked fat and mean. He was chewing on something.

At the rear of the Mustang, they stopped. They both stared at Charlie. Then they gave each other a smirk.

Look what we got here.

The scrawny one flicked his Bic and lit up.

'Hi, guys,' Charlie said. 'What's up?'

'Your number,' the fat one said. His voice sounded mushy through the mouthful of whatever he was chewing.

'I guess that was supposed to be cute,' she said.

'What're you doing on our road?' the scrawny one asked.

'This isn't your road. This is a *public* road, State Highway Sixty-three as a matter of fact, and I have every right to use it.'

'Wrong.'

'Dead wrong,' added the fat guy.

Charlie looked over her shoulder again.

'Who you looking for back there?' the scrawny one asked. 'John Wayne?'

'Dead,' said the fat one.

'The Seventh Cavalry?'

'Dead.'

'Batman?'

'Dead.'

'Is not,' Charlie said.

'Might as well be,' the scrawny one said, 'for all the good he's gonna do you.'

'You're up Shit Creek,' said the fat one, 'and *we're* the shit.'

'Shut up, Tom,' the skinny one said.

Tom scowled like a kid scolded by his father. Then he started to swallow whatever he'd been chewing. The swallowing seemed to take a lot of effort.

While he worked on it, Charlie said, 'Look, I'm sorry I flipped you guys off. I mean, not that you didn't sort of have it coming. Him, anyhow. Tom. It's not exactly nice manners to shout at me like he did. I mean, *eat me*? That's a really crude thing to say to someone, especially a total stranger. So I like lost my temper. But I'm sorry. Okay?'

'Okay,' the scrawny one said.

But they didn't turn around and head for their car. They just stayed put, and kept staring at her.

'Can I go now?' Charlie asked.

'What's your name?' the skinny one asked.

'Why do you want to know?'

He darted the cigarette at her. She flinched. Before she had a chance to dodge it, the lighted tip poked softly against the front of her pink T-shirt, just below her shoulder. It made a circle of ash the size of a pencil eraser. As the cigarette fell, she brushed at the gray dot and said, 'Nice going. Jeez. Real nice.'

'What's your name?'

'Charlie.'

'That's a boy name,' Tom said.

'You a boy?' asked the other.

'She ain't a boy,' Tom said.

'May I go now?' she asked the scrawny one. He seemed to be in charge. 'Please?'

'Say "pretty please with sugar."'

'Pretty please with sugar.'

Tom suddenly got an urgent, happy look on his face. He leaned in close to his friend's side, cupped a hand by his mouth as if he was afraid Charlie might be a lip-reader, and whispered something. At the end of his message, he faced her, folded his arms across his huge chest, and grinned.

The other one spoke. 'Tom wants you to pull up your shirt.'

For a few seconds, Charlie just stood there, staring at them and holding her bike up. Then she said, 'Tom can blow it out his kazoo.'

Tom lost his grin. 'Make her do it, Bill.'

'If you do it,' Bill said, 'maybe we'll let you go.'

She shook her head. 'I'd better warn you guys, you'd *better* let me go or you'll be really really sorry.'

'Just do like we—'

'No!' she suddenly snapped. 'Now go away and leave me alone!'

'All we wanta do is get a little look at your tits. What's the big deal?'

'Maybe she's 'shamed of 'em,' Tom said. 'Seeing as how they're so teeny.'

'You'd better just get out of here.' She glanced over her shoulder again.

'Nobody's coming,' Bill pointed out. 'Not yet. And if a car just *should* happen to come along, it won't do you any good. Nobody's gonna help you.'

'I'm warning you. Get back in your car and go away! You might think we're all by ourselves out here, but you'd be wrong. You see what kind of bike this is?'

'What about it?' Bill asked.

'It's a bicycle-built-for-two.'

'So what?'

'What does that tell you?' she asked.

'That you're some kind of a fuckin' dweeb,' fat Tom said, and grinned. 'Nobody but a dweeb goes around by herself on a bike like that.'

'That's 'cause I'm not by myself.'

'Yeah, right,' Tom said.

'Herman's with me.'

'Yeah, right.'

'Herman?' Bill asked.

'He's my best friend. And he's so big and strong you wouldn't believe it. He makes Arnold Schwarzenegger look like a weenie.'

Bill and Tom grinned at each other.

'I'm scared,' Bill said. 'Are you scared?'

'I'm petrified,' Tom said. He raised his open hands and fluttered his fingers and said, 'Ooooooo, I'm so scared! Look at me! I'm shaking!'

Bill, the skinny one, didn't seem so amused. He said, 'What's your friend's name? Helen?'

'*Her*man.'

'And he's, like, your riding companion on this two-seater?'

'That's right.'

'Well, shit. *I* don't see him.'

Tom broke out laughing. His huge belly shook and wobbled. He slapped Bill on the back a couple of times.

'Knock it off,' Bill told him. To Charlie, he said, '*How* big is this Herman of yours?'

'Real big. He's almost seven feet tall.'

'That *is* big. So how come I can't see him?'

'Because.'

'Oh, be*cause*.' He glanced at Tom. 'That explains it.'

Tom laughed some more, but he kept his hand off Bill's back.

'Nobody can see him,' Charlie explained.

'Oh, I get it. You mean he's invisible.'

'That's right.'

'Now I'm *really* scared.'

'I'm so scared I'm gonna shit!' Tom blurted, and did a little dance as if he were trying to hold it in.

'You won't think it's so funny if you try anything with me. He'll rip you guys from limb to limb.'

'Oh, yeah?' Bill looked at Tom. 'You stay here, I'll take care of him.' Then he came forward, strutted past Charlie, and halted beside the second set of handlebars. She twisted around to watch him. 'All right, Herman, give me your best shot.' He stuck out his chin.

Charlie said, 'Herman isn't there.'

Looking at her, Bill lifted his eyebrows. 'Really? You wouldn't be kidding me, would you?' He reached out and patted the leather seat. 'You're right. Darn! I was *so* looking forward to meeting him.'

'Me, too,' Tom said.

'So, where *is* this Herman of yours?'

'He got off when we stopped.'

'You mean, he *was* here but now he's not?'

'That's right.'

'Where *is* he?'

'Close enough to take care of you guys if you don't leave me alone.'

'How do you know that?' Tom asked. 'You can't see him.' He sounded pleased, as if he'd outsmarted her.

'I just know,' Charlie said. 'He's right here, and he's waiting for you guys to try something funny, and then he's gonna lambast you like you wouldn't believe.'

Bill shook his head slowly from side to side. 'Aren't you kind of like too *old* to have a make-believe friend?'

'He isn't make-believe.'

Behind her, Tom said, 'Betcha it's that Snuffleupagus.'

She faced Tom and said, 'His name is Herman.'

'Yeah, right.'

'And he's gonna rip us limb from limb if we try to mess with you?'

She twisted around to face Bill again. 'That's right. He's not just my best friend, he's my bodyguard. And you'd better let me go right now. All I've gotta do is give him the signal, and . . .'

'So give it,' Bill said.

'Don't make me. You'll regret it. I'm warning you. You'd better just go –'

Bill rammed his hand against the front of her left shoulder. The blow twisted her toward him and knocked her backward. She gasped, 'Yah!' and tried to hop clear of her bicycle. The saddle caught the back of her left thigh. Crying out and flapping her arms, she fell. She slammed the pavement. The bike crashed down on her right leg.

She yelled, 'Ow!'

'Ooo, nasty fall,' Bill said.

He hurried around to the other side of the bike, grabbed

one of Charlie's arms, and dragged her clear. Then he hoisted her to her feet. 'Get rid of the bike,' he said to Tom.

'Don't you *dare!*' Charlie snapped. 'Leave it alone, you big ox!'

'Fuck you, babe.'

'You won't be needing it,' Bill told her.

'What'm I s'posed to do with it?' Tom asked.

'Take it off into the trees. Throw it someplace. Just so nobody can see it from the road here.'

'Right.' Tom hitched up his drooping jeans, then bent down and lifted the bicycle-built-for-two onto its tires. Holding the front set of handlebars, he rolled Speedy to the edge of the road and into the woods.

Charlie watched it go.

When it was out of sight, she tried to break free from Bill's grip.

'Knock it off,' he warned.

She kicked him in the shin.

He decked her.

She was still sprawled on her back, moaning, when Tom returned from concealing her bike.

'What'd you do to her?' Tom asked.

'Gave her a taste of my famous knuckle sandwich.'

Tom scowled. 'You gotta not do that sort of stuff when I can't watch.'

'Don't worry, you didn't miss much. Tell you what, I'll pull the car off the road, and you can stay with her. Maybe take her into the trees over there.'

'Hey, great.' He clapped his hands a couple of times, then headed for Charlie while Bill returned to their Mustang.

Stopping by Charlie's hip, Tom gazed down at her. 'You got a boyfriend?' he asked.

'Maybe.'

'Huh? Do you or don't you?' He tapped her with the toe of his cowboy boot.

'Maybe Herman. But –'

He kicked her. 'Don't give me this Herman shit. I mean a *real* boyfriend.'

'Herman's real,' she muttered.

'Yeah, right.'

'He is. And you guys are gonna be sorry you were ever born by the time he gets done with you.'

'Sure.'

'He's right behind you!' Charlie blurted.

Tom glanced around.

Charlie flipped from her side to her belly. As she scrambled to get up, Tom stomped her on the back. His boot slammed her against the blacktop. Her breath whooshed out. 'Think I'm an idiot?' Tom asked.

Bending over her, he grabbed the neck of her T-shirt and the waistband at the back of her shorts. He lifted her off the road. The T-shirt stretched and ripped, but its shoulders held. The waist button popped off her shorts. The zipper skidded down a little bit at a time as she was carried into the woods.

When Tom got her where he wanted her, he let go of the T-shirt and used both hands to shake Charlie out of her shorts. She fell headfirst toward the ground, but caught herself with her arms.

On hands and knees, she scurried over the forest floor.

And halted when Tom pulled the elastic waistband of her panties.

'You ain't going nowhere.'

'Leave me alone!' she gasped.

He tugged the elastic and let it go. It snapped her across the buttocks. He laughed.

At the sound of footsteps hurrying through the dry pine

needles, Charlie raised her head and saw Bill striding into the clearing.

As he approached, he pulled his T-shirt off. His jeans hung very low. The brass buckle of his belt looked like a skull. At the right side of his belt hung a knife in a brown leather sheath. Charlie hadn't noticed the knife before.

He was very skinny and bony and white. He looked as if he had never before been out in the sun without a shirt on. In the middle of his chest, directly between his nipples, was a cluster of bright red pimples.

'Let's see what we got,' he said to Tom.

Tom's broad, oily face grinned. He stepped behind Charlie and slipped his fingers under the drooping shoulders of her T-shirt.

'Don't,' she said, her voice shaking. 'I'm warning you.'

He jerked the T-shirt, stretching and tearing it. As he dragged it down to her ankles, she clutched her breasts and called out, 'Herman!'

Bill, an odd smile on his lips, helped. 'Herrrmannn?' he called in a lilting voice. 'Yooo-hooo, Herrrr-mannnn! Where arrrrre you? Charlie neeeeeeds you.'

Tom, still behind her, tugged her panties down. He tongued her rump, and she flinched.

'Herman!' she cried out. 'Help!'

'Can I have firsties?' Tom asked.

'No way.'

'Hey, come on. You *always* get firsties.'

'That's 'cause they're too messed up by the time you get done with 'em. Just hold her for me.'

'Yeah yeah yeah. Hang on.'

Charlie stood stiff and trembling, legs tight together, hands cupping her breasts, while Bill took the knife from its sheath and clamped it between his teeth. The handle of the

510

knife was wrapped with black tape. The blade, at least five inches long, looked sharp on both edges.

With his hands free, Bill unfastened his skull buckle and pulled down the zipper of his jeans.

He didn't have any underwear on.

Charlie looked away fast.

Then Tom's hands came around from behind her. They clutched her wrists and forced her arms high. He raised them until her shoulders hurt and she had to stand on tiptoes.

She could feel his bulging belly against her back.

Bare skin, hot and slippery.

In front of her, Bill finished taking off his boots and jeans. Then he stepped toward her, grinning behind the handle of the knife in his teeth.

'Get away from me,' she blurted.

He took the knife out of his mouth.

Charlie shook her head.

He touched the tip of the knife to the underside of her chin, then scraped it lightly down her throat and sideways.

'Please,' she murmured.

'Please? Who you talking to?' he asked. 'Me or your buddy Herman?'

'Don't hurt me.'

'Guess ol' Hermy must've deserted her,' Tom said, and writhed so his belly slid against her back.

'What's the world coming to,' Bill said, 'when you can't count on your invisible friends in a pinch? A sorry state of affairs, that's what I think.'

'Don't,' she said. 'Please.'

Gritting her teeth, she watched the tip of the knife scratch a line down the top of her left breast. She jerked when it nicked the tip of her nipple. A speck of blood, very bright red, bloomed, then disappeared.

Vanished between Bill's lips.

He licked. He sucked. He moaned and sucked harder, drawing her small breast deep into his mouth as his right hand came up and shoved the entire five-inch blade of the knife into his own right eye.

The impact shoved his head back.

Charlie's breast popped out of his mouth.

Behind her, fat Tom let out an odd, high-pitched laugh as if he figured his buddy was pulling some sort of a weird stunt with the knife.

'Hey,' he said.

Bill said nothing. Mouth wide open, he stumbled backward two steps, three, with the black-taped handle of the knife sticking out of his face.

'What're you doing?' Tom asked.

Bill fell flat on his back. As he lay twitching on the ground, Tom let go of Charlie's wrists and hooked an arm across her throat. He squeezed her tightly against him, his belly forcing her back to bend, his chin above her left ear.

'Fucking shit!' he gasped. 'Bill? What the fuck? Bill? Why'd you go and do that?'

Bill, no longer twitching, answered with a loud, moist farting noise.

'Shit!'

The knife began to rise. Its blade slid upward, pulling slowly out of the bloody mess in Bill's eye socket.

'Oh, hey,' Tom said.

The knife came the rest of the way out. It lingered motionless above Bill's face. Blood dripping from the blade made soft splashes in the socket puddle.

'Oh, hey,' shit.'

'Herman,' Charlie groaned out.

'No way. Huh-uh. Bull*shit*.'

'Let . . . me . . . go.'

The knife drifted higher. Higher and higher as if it were

being offered, pommel first, to someone on a tree branch above Bill's body.

Arm still tight across Charlie's throat, Tom started backing away. His belly shoved at her back, forcing her feet off the ground. She started to choke.

Eight or nine feet above Bill's face, the knife's rise halted.

Charlie, being hustled backward by her throat, kicked her legs and flapped her arms and choked.

The knife flew at her.

Or at Tom.

Tumbling blade over hilt, flinging off a wispy spray of blood.

It struck with a thunk above and just to the side of Charlie's left ear.

Tom went, '*Uh!*'

His arm jerked against her throat. He dropped backward. Charlie followed him down, riding the soft hill of his belly. It sank in when she landed. Air blew out of him.

Legs still kicking at the sky, Charlie shoved his arm away from her throat. Then she flung herself off his body. She crawled clear and scurried to her feet before turning around for a look.

Where the knife should have been sticking out of Tom's forehead, he had a red mark the side of a quarter.

The size of the knife's pommel.

Gasping for breath, Charlie rubbed her throat and grimaced. She stepped closer to Tom.

His big white belly moved up and down with his breathing.

His eyes were shut.

He still had his boots on, but his jeans were down around his shins. He was very white and lumpy. He looked like an effigy made from loaves of uncooked bread dough that had been basted with oil.

She glanced at his *thing*. Wrinkling her nose, she turned away fast.

'Herman?' she asked.

'Yo.'

The voice came from straight in front of Charlie, but somewhat higher than her head.

'Thanks,' she said.

'My pleasure.'

'But jeez, you sure took your time about it.'

'Well . . . Better late than never. Right?'

She shook her head. 'You let them hurt me.'

'I know. I'm awfully sorry. I truly am.'

'Why didn't you stop them? I mean, jeez!'

Herman didn't answer.

'Didn't you see that guy slug me?'

'Yes.'

'Why didn't you *destroy* him right then?'

'I . . . I was curious, I suppose.'

'Curious? What do you mean, curious?'

'I wanted to see what they had in mind.'

'Jeez, wasn't that pretty obvious? I mean, by the time fatso *stripped* me, it should've been pretty—'

'I'm afraid I was . . . rather caught up in the situation.'

'You *what*?'

He hesitated for a few seconds, then said, 'I . . . wanted to watch.'

'*Watch?*'

'I'm afraid so.'

'Oh, isn't *that* wonderful. I thought you were supposed to be a gentleman.'

'I know. I'm sorry. Oh, Charlie. I've always . . . I've *never* spied on you. I've always left the room whenever you . . . needed privacy. But . . . I don't know. I'm so sorry. The thing is, you're not quite the child you used to be, and I'm afraid that I . . . I should've intervened much sooner. I know that. I just couldn't quite force myself . . . You're so beautiful, Charlie.'

'Oh, man.'

'Do you hate me?'

She scowled. 'No. Don't be dumb. I could never hate you. But . . . you let that guy actually . . . cut me.' She touched the small slit on her nipple and showed Herman the blood on her fingertip. 'See?'

'Yes. I see. Can you . . . will you forgive me?'

She licked the blood off her finger. 'Maybe.'

'Please, Charlie.'

'You've got to kiss it and make it well,' she said.

Herman hesitated. Then he murmured, 'All right.'

At the touch of his lips, Charlie gasped and stiffened. The blood smeared and swirled. Her nipple began to stretch. Trembling, she moaned. She found Herman's shoulders and held on to them and shuddered.

His mouth went away from her breast.

'How's that?' he asked.

And she saw his lips move when he asked. Phantom lips, stained by her blood.

'The other,' she said.

'But it's not cut.'

'I don't care.'

By the time he finished, she was gasping for breath and she could hardly stay on her feet. She clung to his shoulders.

'I want to see you,' she gasped. 'I want to see what *you* look like.'

'We've been through all that, Charlie.'

'I know, I know. You're naked . . . wouldn't be decent. That's . . . not hardly a problem any more, is it? I mean, you let those guys strip me. Now it's only fair . . . And anyhow, I love you.'

'You do?'

'Yes. Of course. But I've gotta *see* you. I've never seen you.'

'I suppose we could go home and get some make-up.'

'No, now. I've gotta see you right now.'

'Ah. But I don't see how . . .'

'The knife,' she gasped.

'Huh?'

'Where'd it end up?' She let go of his shoulders and turned around. She glanced at Tom, still sprawled on his back. The mark on his head had become a livid lump. His eyes were still shut. She scanned the floor of the forest beyond his head, then blurted, 'There it is.' She ran, crouched, and picked up the knife.

Then she hurried back to Tom.

He opened his eyes as she knelt on the ground above his head.

He opened them very wide.

'Over here, Herman,' she said. 'Quick.'

'Hey,' Tom said, his voice groggy.

'Hey yourself,' she told him.

His belly sank and widened when Herman sat on it.

He raised his head off the ground as if he hoped to see who was there. His fat red face dripped sweat . . . and maybe a few tears. He began to make a high-pitched whimpery sound.

'That's good,' Charlie said. 'You just sit there, honey. I'll do all the work.'

Tom squealed when she tore open his throat with the knife.

Blood shot high.

Charlie tossed away the knife. She started to splash Herman with the blood. Then she leaned into the gushers herself, grabbed Herman by his red-splattered shoulders and pulled him toward her. She wrapped her arms around him.

Blood hosed his face.

Coated it.

Dripped.

She kissed his slippery lips.

He was slippery all over – massive and gentle and very slippery – as they tumbled off Tom's body and rolled on the grass and wrestled and kissed and made love in the sunlit clearing.

Soon, the blood began to make them itchy. They licked each other clean.

Then they lay side by side on the grass.

After a while, Charlie said, 'I hate it that I can't see you. I used to think it was great, but now . . . God, how come you have to be invisible? It isn't fair. I can't look at you.'

'It has its advantages,' Herman pointed out.

'I guess so, but . . . I know we can try make-up on you, and stuff. *Paint* you.' She wrinkled her nose. 'It's not the same, though. I want to really *see* you. How will I ever get to see what you'd look like if you were . . . like *real*?'

'I am real, Charlie.'

'I know, but . . . I mean, actual flesh and blood. With skin. What would you look like if you had skin just like . . . Hey! I've got it!'

She gave him a pat, then pushed herself up and crawled toward the knife.

'Wait, now, Charlie.'

'No, this'll be cool.'

'It'll be *hot*. Not to mention *messy*.'

'Oh, don't be a spoilsport. It'll be great.'

Herman groaned. 'Besides, I'm bigger than Tom. It'll never fit.'

'Hey, there's two of them, only one of you. There'll be plenty, maybe even some left over for a hat.'

The Champion

'You're not going anywhere,' said the man blocking the door.

He was smaller than Harry Barlow, with neither the bulk nor the muscle to make his words good. But he had a friend on each side. Though Harry figured he could take the three of them, he didn't want to try. Like most big men, he'd been pestered all his life by people wanting to prove their toughness. He was tired of it. He wanted never to fight again.

'Please move,' he said to the man.

'Not on your life, bud. You're staying right here. This is your big night.'

The entire restaurant erupted with cheers. Harry turned slowly, studying the faces around him. Most belonged to men. Funny, he hadn't noticed that during the meal. He hadn't noticed much of anything, really, except his dinner of top sirloin.

When he first saw Roy's Bar and Steak House, he'd been surprised by the crowd of cars in its parking lot. The town, hidden in a valley deep in northern California's timber country, seemed too small to have so many cars. Once he'd tasted the rich charbroiled steak, however, he'd realized that folks had probably driven miles for supper at Roy's. He'd been glad he'd stopped in.

Until now.

Now, he only wanted to leave. He took a step toward the three men barring his way.

'Hold up,' someone called from behind.

Harry turned around. He'd seen this man before. During supper, the fellow had wandered from table to table chatting and laughing with the customers. He'd even exchanged a few words with Harry. 'I'm Roy,' he'd said. 'This your first time here? Whereabouts are you from? How's your beef?' He'd seemed like a pleasant, amiable man.

Now he had a shotgun aimed at Harry's midsection.

'What's that for?' Harry asked.

'Can't have you leave,' Roy told him.

'Why's that?'

Except for a few scattered clinks of silverware, silence hushed the restaurant.

'You're the challenger,' Roy said.

'What am I challenging?' Harry asked. He waited, feeling a tremor of fear.

'It's not a what, it's a who.'

Harry heard some quiet laughter. Looking around, he saw that every face was turned toward him. He rubbed his hands along the soft corduroy of his pants legs. 'Okay,' he said. '*Who* am I challenging?'

'The champion.'

'Am I?'

More laughter.

'You sure are. You ever hear of the Saturday Night Fights? Well, here at Roy's Bar and Steak House, we have our own version.'

Cheers and applause roared through the restaurant. Roy held up his hands for silence. 'The first man through the door after nine on Saturday night, he's the challenger. You walked in at nine-o-three.'

Harry remembered the group of seven or eight men who had been standing just outside the door, talking in quiet, eager voices. A few had looked at him oddly as he stepped by. Now he understood why they were there. They'd arrived at nine. Knowing the score, they'd been smart enough to wait for a chump to come along and enter first.

'Look,' Harry said, 'I don't want to fight anyone.'

'They hardly ever do.'

'Well, I'm not *going to*.'

'We had a guy about two years back,' Roy said. 'Some kind of chicken pacifist. He wouldn't fight the champion. Just wouldn't do it. Made a run for the door.' Roy grinned and waved the barrel of his shotgun. 'I cut him down. I'll cut you down if you make a run.'

'This is crazy,' Harry muttered.

'Just our way of having a good time.' Roy turned his attention to the crowd. 'All right, folks. For any newcomers to the Saturday Night Fight, I'll tell you how she works.'

A waitress stepped up to his side, holding a fish bowl stuffed with red tickets.

'We got a hundred tickets here in the bowl. Each ticket has a three-second time period on it, going up to five minutes. Never had a fight go more than that. You pay five bucks for each chance. Winner takes the pot. Any tickets aren't sold by fight time, they belong to the house.' He patted the arm of the woman holding the bowl. 'Julie, here, she's time-keeper. I'm referee. The fight's over when one or the other contestant's dead. Any questions?'

No questions.

'Buy your tickets at the counter. Fight starts in ten minutes.'

During the next ten minutes, as customers filed past the cash register and drew their tickets from the bowl, Roy stood guard. Harry considered running for the door. He decided, however, that he would rather face the champion than Roy's shotgun. To pass the time, he counted the number of tickets sold.

Seventy-two.

At five dollars each, that came to $360.00.

'Fight starts in one minute,' Roy announced. 'Last call for tickets.'

The ticket buying was done.

'Elmer?'

A thin, bald old man nodded and went out the rear door.

'The champion will be right in, folks. If a couple of you could help move these tables outa the way . . .?'

Six tables from the center of the room were moved toward the sides, leaving a clear area that seemed awfully small to Harry.

The crowd suddenly cheered and whistled. Looking toward the rear door, Harry saw Elmer enter. A tall, lean man walked behind him.

'Ladies and gentlemen!' Roy called. 'The champion!'

The champion scowled at the crowd as he hobbled toward the clear space. From his looks, he'd fought many times before. His broad forehead was creased with a scar. He wore a patch over his left eye. The tip of one ear was missing. So was the forefinger of his left hand.

Looking down, Harry saw the cause of the champion's strange, awkward gait. A three-foot length of chain dragged between his shackled feet.

'I'm not fighting this man,' Harry said.

'Sure you are,' Roy told him. 'Elmer?'

The skinny old guy knelt down. Opening a padlock, he removed the shackle from the right ankle of the champion.

Harry took a step backward.

'Stand still,' Roy ordered.

'There's no way you can make me fight this man.'

'The folks with low numbers'll be glad to hear that.'

'Right!' someone yelled from the crowd.

'Just stand there,' called another.

Others joined the shouting, some urging him to wait passively for death, some demanding that he fight.

Elmer locked the iron onto Harry's left ankle. The yard-long chain now connected him to the champion.

'Time?' Roy called.

The yelling stopped.

'Ten seconds to starting,' Julie said.

'Elmer?'

The old man scurried away. From behind the counter, he took a matching pair of knives.

'Five seconds,' Julie said.

The knives had wooden handles, brass cross guards, and eight-inch blades of polished steel.

'We won't do it,' Harry said to the champion. 'They can't make us.'

The champion sneered.

Elmer handed one knife to the champion, one to Harry. He rushed out of the way as Julie said, 'Go!'

Harry flung down his knife. Its point thunked the hardwood floor, biting deep. Its handle was still vibrating as the champion jabbed at Harry's stomach. Harry jumped away. The chain stopped his foot, and he fell backward. The champion stomped on his knee. Harry cried out as his leg exploded with pain.

With a demented shriek, the champion flung himself down on Harry. Using both hands, Harry held back the knife that the champion was driving toward his face. The blade pressed closer. He blinked, and felt his right eyelashes brush the steel tip. Turning his head, he shoved sideways. The blade ripped his ear and stabbed the floor beside his head.

He smashed a fist upward into the champion's nose. Rolling, he got out from under the stunned man. He crawled away from the grasping hands and stood.

'Enough!' he shouted. 'That's enough! It has to stop!'

The crowd booed and hissed.

The champion, tearing his knife from the floor, leaped to his feet and swung at Harry. The blade sliced the front of Harry's plaid shirt.

'Stop it!'

The champion lunged, growling. He punched the knife toward Harry's belly. Chopping down, Harry knocked the hand away. The champion stabbed again. This time, the blade slashed Harry's blocking hand. It struck at his stomach. Spinning aside, he dodged the steel.

He gripped the champion's right arm at the wrist and elbow and pumped his knee up. The forearm broke with a popping sound like snapped kindling. Screaming, the champion dropped his knife.

But he caught it with his left hand and thrust it wildly at Harry, who dodged out of the way.

Dropping to one knee, Harry grabbed the chain and tugged. The champion's leg flew high and he tumbled backward. Harry sprang onto him. With both hands, he clutched the champion's left hand and pinned it to the floor.

'Give up!' he shouted into the man's blood-smeared face.

The champion nodded. The knife dropped from his hand.

'That's it!' Harry raised his eyes to the crowd. 'He gave up! He quit!'

Abruptly, the man sat up and clamped his teeth on Harry's throat. Blind with pain and enraged by the deception, Harry slapped the floor. He found the knife. He plunged it four times into the champion's side before the jaws loosened their grip on his neck. The champion flopped. His head hit the floor with a solid thunk.

Harry crawled aside, fingering his wounded neck. He wasn't bleeding as badly as he'd feared.

Sitting on the floor, he watched Roy kneel at the champion's side.

'Is he dead?' someone shouted from the crowd.

Roy checked the pulse in the champion's neck. 'Not yet,' he announced.

'Come on!' someone yelled.

'Hang on, champ!' shouted another.

'Give it up!' called a woman's voice.

The crowd roared for a few seconds. Then silence fell. Complete silence. All eyes were fixed on Roy kneeling beside the fallen champion.

'Gone!' Roy announced.

Julie clicked her stopwatch. 'Two minutes, twenty-eight seconds.'

'That's me!' a man cried out, waving his red ticket. 'That's me! I got it!'

'Come on up here,' Roy said. 'We'll just verify that and hand over your loot.' He turned to his skinny old assistant. 'Elmer?'

Elmer knelt between Harry and the body. He unlatched the dead man's shackle. Before Harry could move to prevent it, the iron cuff was clamped around his own right ankle. Elmer shut the padlock.

'Hey!' Harry protested. 'Take 'em off! I won! You've got to let me go!'

'Can't do that,' Roy said, smiling down at him. 'You're the champion.'

The Maiden

'I don't know about this,' I said.

'What's not to know?' Cody asked. He was driving. His car was a Jeep Cherokee and he had it in four-wheel drive. We'd been bouncing along a dirt road through a forest for about half an hour, it was dark as hell out there except for the headlights, and I didn't know how much farther it might be to our destination, a place supposedly called Lost Lake.

'What if we break down?' I asked.

'We aren't gonna break down,' Cody said.

'It sounds like the car's shaking to pieces.'

'Don't be such a weenie,' said Rudy, who sat in the passenger seat.

Rudy was Cody's best pal. They were both a couple of pretty cool guys. In a way, I felt very honored that they'd invited me to come with them. But I felt nervous, too. Maybe they'd asked me to come along because I'm the new kid in school and they just wanted to be nice and get to know me better. On the other hand, maybe they planned to screw me.

I don't mean 'screw' in the literal sense. There was nothing the least bit funny about Cody or Rudy, and they both had girlfriends.

Rudy's girl wasn't much. Her name was Alice. She looked like someone had taken hold of her by the head and feet, then stretched her out till she was way too long and skinny.

Cody's girl was Lois Garnett. Everything about Lois was perfect. Except for one thing; she *knew* that she was perfect. In other words, she was a snot.

I had a bad case of the hots for Lois, anyway. How could I *not*? All you've got to do is look at her, and she'll drive you crazy. But I made the mistake of getting caught, last week. She dropped her pencil on the floor in Chemistry. When she bent down to pick it up, I had a view straight down the front of her blouse. Even though she had a bra on, the view was pretty terrific. The problem is, she looked up and saw where my eyes were aimed. She muttered, 'What're you looking at, asshole?'

'Tit,' I answered. I can be a wiseguy, sometimes.

It's a good thing looks can't kill.

Boyfriends can, though. Which was one reason I was a little bit worried about going off into the woods in the middle of the night with Cody and Rudy.

Nobody had mentioned the incident, though.

Not so far.

Maybe Lois hadn't told Cody about it, and I had nothing to worry about.

On the other hand . . .

I figured it was worth the risk. I mean, what was the worst that could happen? It's not like they would actually try and kill me just for looking down Lois's blouse.

What they *said* they wanted to do was set me up with some gal.

I was eating my lunch in the quad, just that afternoon, when Cody and Rudy came over and started talking to me.

'You doing anything tonight?' Cody asked.

'What do you mean?'

'He means,' Rudy said, 'we know this babe that thinks you're hot stuff. She wants to *see* you, know what I mean? Tonight.'

'Tonight? Me?'

'Midnight,' Cody said.

'You sure you've got the right guy?'

'We're sure.'

'Elmo Baine?'

'You think we're morons?' Rudy asked, sounding steamed. 'We *know* your name. *Everybody* knows your name.'

'You're the one she wants,' Cody said. 'How about it?'

'Gosh, I don't know.'

'What's not to know?' Rudy asked.

'Well . . . Who is she?'

'What do you care?' Rudy asked. 'She *wants* you, man. How many babes *want* you?'

'Well . . . I'd sort of like to know who she is before I make up my mind.'

'She told us not to tell you,' Cody explained.

'Wants it to be a surprise,' Rudy added.

'Yeah, but I mean . . . How do I know she isn't some sort of a . . . you know . . .'

'A dog?' Rudy suggested.

'Well . . . yeah.'

Cody and Rudy looked at each other and shook their heads. Then Cody said, 'She's hot stuff, take my word on it. This might be the best offer you ever get, Elmo. You don't wanta blow it.'

'Well . . . Can't you tell me who she is?'

'Nope.'

'Is she someone I know?'

'She knows you,' Rudy pointed out. 'And she *wants* to know you a lot better.'

'Don't blow it,' Cody told me again.

'Well,' I said. 'I guess . . . okay.'

After that, we made plans about where and when I would meet their car.

I didn't ask if 'anyone else' would be going with us, but I figured there was a chance they might show up with Alice and Lois. The possibility had me really excited. As the day went on, I got myself so sure Lois would come along that I pretty much forgot all about the mystery girl.

I fixed myself up and snuck out of the house in plenty of time to meet the car. When it showed up, though, it didn't have anyone in it except Cody and Rudy. I guess my disappointment must've showed.

'Something wrong?' Cody asked.

'No. Nothing. I'm just a little nervous.'

Rudy grinned at me over his shoulder. 'You sure smell good.'

'Just some Old Spice.'

'You'll have her licking you.'

'Cut it out,' Cody told him.

'So,' I said, 'where are we going? I mean, I know you're not supposed to tell me *who* she is, but I'm sort of curious about exactly *where* you're taking me.'

'Can we tell him?' Rudy asked.

'I guess so. Have you ever been out to Lost Lake, Elmo?'

'Lost Lake? Never heard of it.'

'You have, now,' Rudy told me.

'Is that where she lives?' I asked.

'It's where she wants to meet you,' Cody said.

'She's sort of a "nature girl",' Rudy explained.

'Besides,' Cody said, 'it's a great place for fooling around. Way out in the woods, a nice little lake, and you've got all the privacy in the world.'

That crummy dirt road seemed to go on forever. The Jeep shook and rattled. Branches or something squeaked against the sides. And talk about dark.

There's nothing like a forest when it comes to darkness. Maybe that's because the trees block out the moonlight. It was like driving through a tunnel. The headlights lit up the stuff just in front of us, and the tail lights made a red glow out the back window. Everything else was black.

I was okay for a while, but I started to get more and more nervous. The deeper into the forest we went, the worse I felt. They'd told me that the car wouldn't break down, and Rudy had called me a weenie for even asking. A while later, though, I went ahead and said, 'Are you sure we aren't lost?'

'I don't get lost,' Cody said.

'How are we doing on gas?'

'We're fine.'

'What a pussy,' Rudy said.

What a shithead, I thought. But I didn't say it. I didn't say anything. I mean, we were out in the boonies and nobody knew I was with these guys. If I made them mad, things might get pretty drastic.

Of course, I realized that things might take a turn for the ugly, anyway. This whole deal could be a set-up. I hoped not, but you just never know.

The trouble is, you can't make any friends at all if you don't take a chance. Whether or not a friendship with Cody and Rudy was worth this much of a risk – and I was having some real doubts about that – an 'in' with them would mean an 'in' with Lois.

I could just see it. There might be triple dates: Cody and Lois, Rudy and Alice, Elmo and Mystery Girl. We would travel crowded in the Jeep. We'd sit together at the movies. We'd go on picnics, have swimming parties, maybe take camping trips – and fool around. My actual partner would be Mystery Girl, but Lois would be right there where I could watch her, listen to her, and maybe more. Maybe we would trade partners sometimes. Maybe we would even have orgies.

No telling what might happen if they accepted me.

I guess I would do just about anything to find out – even take a ride into the middle of nowhere with these guys, where they might be planning to leave me stranded, or beat me up, or worse.

I was pretty scared. The deeper we got into the woods, the more I suspected a bad time from these two. But I kept my mouth shut after Rudy called me a pussy. I just sat there in the back seat and worried and kept telling myself that they didn't have a good enough reason to really *demolish* me. All I'd done was take a look down Lois's front.

'Here we are,' Cody said.

We had come to the end of the road.

Ahead, lit by the white beams of the headlights, was a cleared place big enough for half a dozen cars to park. There were logs on the ground to show you where to stop. Off beyond the parking area, I saw a trash barrel, a couple of picnic tables, and a brick fireplace for barbecues.

Ours was the only car.

We were the only people.

'I guess she isn't here yet,' I said.

'You never know,' Cody told me.

'There aren't any other cars.'

'Who says she drove?' Rudy said.

Cody steered toward one of the logs, stopped and shut off the engine.

I couldn't see any lake. I almost made a crack about it being lost, but didn't feel much like joking around at that moment.

Cody shut off the headlights. Blackness dropped on us, but only for a second. Then both the front doors swung open, making the overhead light come on.

'Let's go,' Cody said.

They both climbed out. I did, too.

When they shut their doors, the light inside the Jeep died.

But we were standing in the open. The sky was spread above us. The moon was almost full and the stars were out.

Shadows were black, but everything else was lit up, almost like a dirty white powder had been sprinkled around.

That was one extremely bright moon.

'This way,' Cody said.

We walked through the picnic area. I've got to tell you, my legs were shaking.

Just past the tables, the ground slanted down to a pale area that reminded me of how snow looks at night – only this seemed dimmer than snow. A sand beach? It had to be.

Beyond the curve of the beach, the lake was black. It looked beautiful, the way the moon made a silvery path on the water. The silver came straight at us from the far end of the lake. It stretched past the side of a small, wooded island and came all the way to the beach.

Cody had said that this place had 'all the privacy in the world', and he was right. Except for the moon and stars, there were no lights in sight: none from boats on the water, or from docks along the shores, or from cabins in the dark woods around the lake. The way things looked, we might've been the only three people for miles around.

I wished I wasn't feeling so nervous. This could be a great place if you weren't here with a couple of guys possibly planning to mess you over. A great place to be alone with a really terrific babe, for instance.

'I don't think she's here,' I said.

'Don't be so sure,' Rudy told me.

'Maybe she changed her mind about coming. I mean, it's a school night, and everything.'

'It's gotta be a school night,' Cody explained. 'Too many people here, weekends. Look at this, we've got the whole place to ourselves.'

'But where's the girl?'

'Jeez,' Rudy said, 'will you knock off the whining?'

'Yeah,' Cody said. 'Relax and enjoy yourself.'

Just then, we walked out onto the sand. After a few steps, both the guys stopped. They took off their shoes and socks. I took off mine, too. Even though it was a warm night, the sand felt cool with my feet bare.

Next, they took their shirts off. There was nothing wrong with doing that; they're guys and the night was warm and a soft breeze was blowing. But it made me so nervous, I got a cold wad in the pit of my stomach. Cody and Rudy had really fine physiques. And even in the *moonlight*, you could see they had good tans.

I untucked my shirt and unfastened the buttons.

They left their shirts on the beach with the shoes and socks. I kept mine on. Nobody said anything about it. As we walked down the sand toward the water, I almost decided to go ahead and take my shirt off. I wanted to be like them. And I sure liked the way the breeze felt. I just couldn't do it, though.

We stopped at the water's edge.

'This is great,' Cody said. He raised his arms and stretched. 'Feel that breeze.'

Rudy stretched, flexed his muscles, and groaned. 'Man,' he said, 'I sure wish the babes were here.'

'Maybe we'll come back Friday, bring 'em. You can come, too, Elmo. Bring your new honey and we'll have ourselves a big ol' party.'

'Really?'

'Sure.'

'Wow! That'd be . . . really neat.'

It was *exactly* what I wanted to hear! My worries had been stupid. These two were the greatest pals a guy could have.

A few more nights, and I'd be right here at the beach with Lois.

I suddenly felt terrific!

'Maybe we oughta just, you know, put off everything till then,' I said. 'My ... uh, date ... she isn't here anyway. Maybe we should just leave, and we can *all* come Friday night. I wouldn't mind waiting till then to meet her.'

'That'd be okay with me,' Cody said.

'Same here,' said Rudy.

'Great!'

Smiling, Cody tilted his head sideways. 'Wouldn't be okay with *her*, though. She wants you tonight.'

'Lucky bastard,' Rudy said, and slugged my arm.

Rubbing my arm, I explained, 'But she isn't here.'

Cody nodded. 'You're right. She's not here. She's *there*.' He pointed at the lake.

'What?' I asked.

'On the island.'

'On the *island*?' I'm no expert on judging distances, but the island looked pretty far out. A couple of hundred yards, at least. 'What's she doing *there*?'

'Waiting for you, lover boy.' Rudy punched my arm again.

'Quit it.'

'Sorry.' He gave me another slug.

'Cut it out,' Cody told him. To me, he said, 'That's where she wants to meet you.'

'*There?*'

'It's perfect. You won't have to worry about anyone barging in on you.'

'She's on the *island*?' I was having a fairly difficult time believing it.

'That's right.'

'How'd she get there?'

'She swam.'

'She's sort of a "nature girl",' Rudy said. He'd pointed that out once before.

'How am *I* supposed to get there?'

'Same way she did,' Cody said.

'Swim?'

'You know how to swim, don't you?'

'Yeah. Sort of.'

'Sort of?'

'I mean, I'm not exactly the world's greatest swimmer.'

'Can you make it that far?'

'I don't know.'

'Shit,' Rudy said. 'I *knew* he was a pussy.'

Screw you, I thought. I felt like slamming him in the face, but all I did was stand there.

'We don't want him drowning on us,' Cody said.

'He won't drown. Shit, his *fat*'ll keep him up.'

Part of me wanted to pound Rudy for saying that, and part of me wanted to cry.

'I can swim to that island if I want to,' I blurted out. 'Maybe I don't want to, that's all. I bet there isn't even any girl there.'

'What do you mean?' Cody asked.

'It's just a trick,' I said. 'There isn't any girl, and you know it. It's just a trick to make me try and swim to the island. Then you'll probably drive off and leave me, or something.'

Cody stared at me. 'It's no wonder you don't have any friends.'

Rudy nudged him with an elbow. 'Elmo here thinks we're a couple of *assholes.*'

'I didn't say that.'

'Yeah, right,' Cody said. 'We try to do you a favor, and you think we're out to screw you. Fuck it. Let's go.'

'What?' I asked.

'Let's go.'

They both turned their backs to the lake and started

walking up the beach toward the place where they'd left their stuff.

'We're leaving?' I asked.

Cody glanced back at me. 'That's what you want, isn't it? Come on, we'll take you home.'

'To your mommy,' Rudy added.

I stood my ground. 'Wait!' I called. 'Hold on, okay? Just a second. Let's talk this over, okay?'

'Forget it,' Cody said. 'You're a loser.'

'I am not!'

They crouched and picked up their shirts.

'Hey look, I'm sorry. I'll do it. Okay? I believe you. I'll swim to the island.' Cody and Rudy looked at each other. Cody shook his head.

'Please!' I yelled. 'Give me another chance!'

'You think we're a couple of liars.'

'No, I don't. Honest. I was just confused, that's all. It's just strange. I've never had a girl . . . like *send* for me. Okay? I'll go. I'll do it.'

'Yeah, all right,' Cody said. He sounded reluctant, though.

They tossed their shirts down. As they walked back to where I was standing, they kept shaking their heads and looking at each other.

'We don't wanta be here all night,' Cody said to me. He checked his wristwatch. 'What we'll do, we'll give you an hour.'

'And then leave without me?'

'Did I say that? We're not gonna leave without you.'

'He *does* think we're assholes,' Rudy said.

'I do not.'

'If you're not back,' Cody said, 'we'll yell or toot the horn or something. Just figure you'll have about an hour with her.'

'Don't keep us waiting,' Rudy warned. 'You wanta

screw her till dawn, do it some time when we ain't your chauffeurs.'

Screw her till dawn?

'Okay,' I said. I faced the water, and took a deep breath. 'Here goes. Anything else I need to know?'

'Are you planning to keep your jeans on?' Cody asked.

'Yeah.'

'I wouldn't.'

'They'll drag you down,' Rudy pointed out.

'You'd better leave them here.'

I didn't like the sound of that, at all.

'I don't know,' I said.

Cody shook his head. 'We aren't gonna take them.'

'Who'd wanta *touch* 'em?'

'The thing is,' Cody went on, 'those jeans'll soak up a lot of water. They'll get damned heavy.'

'You'll never make it to the island in 'em,' Rudy said.

'They'll sink you.'

'Or *she* will.'

'*What?*'

'Don't listen to Rudy. He's full of crap.'

'The Maiden,' Rudy said. 'She'll get you if you don't swim fast enough. You gotta lose the jeans.'

'He's just trying to scare you.'

'The *Maiden*? There's a *maiden* who's gonna *get* me or drown me or something?'

'No no no,' Cody said. He scowled at Rudy. 'Did you have to go and mention her? You idiot!'

'Hey, man. He wants to keep his jeans on. He keeps 'em on, he'll *never* stand a chance of out-swimming her. She'll nail him, for sure.'

'There's no such *thing* as the Maiden.'

'Is, too.'

'What are you two *talking* about?' I blurted.

Cody faced me, shaking his head. 'The Maiden of Lost Lake. It's some bullshit legend.'

'She got Willy Glitten last summer,' Rudy said.

'Willy got a cramp, that's all.'

'That's what you think.'

'That's what I know. He ate that damn pepperoni pizza just before he went in. That's what killed him, not some stupid ghost.'

'The Maiden ain't a *ghost*. That shows how much you know. Ghosts can't grab you and . . .'

'Neither can gals who've been dead for forty years.'

'*She* can.'

'Bull.'

'*What are you two talking about?*' I snapped.

They both looked at me.

'You wanta tell him?' Cody asked Rudy.

'You go ahead.'

'You're the one that brought it up,' Cody said.

'And you're telling me I'm full of shit. So you tell it *your* way. I'm not saying another word about her.'

'Would *some*body please tell me?'

'All right, all right,' Cody said. 'Here's the deal. There's this story about the Maiden of Lost Lake. Part of it's true, and part of it's bull.'

Rudy made a snorty noise.

'The true part is that a gal drowned out there one night about forty years ago.'

'The night of her senior prom,' Rudy added. He'd broken his word about keeping his mouth shut, but Cody didn't call him on it.

'Yeah,' Cody said. 'It was Prom Night, and after the dance was over, her date drove her out here. The whole idea was to fool around, you know? So they park in the lot back there, and start in. Things get going pretty good. Too good for the gal.'

'She was a virgin,' Rudy pointed out. 'That's how come they call her "the Maiden".'

'Yeah. Anyway, it's all getting out of hand, as far as she's concerned. So to slow things down, she says they oughta go and take a swim in the lake. The guy figures she means a skinny-dip, so he's all for it.'

'Nobody else was around,' Rudy said.

'That's what she thinks, anyway,' Cody said. 'So they climb out of the car and start stripping. The guy takes off everything. Not her, though. She insists on keeping her underwear on.'

'Her panties and bra,' Rudy explained.

'So they throw their clothes in the car and run down here to the beach and go in the lake. They swim around for a while. Play games. Splash each other. That sort of thing. Then they get hold of each other and, you know . . . things start getting hot again.'

'They were still in the water?' I asked.

'Yeah. Out where it isn't very deep.'

I wondered how he knew all this.

'Pretty soon, she lets him unhook her bra. It was the first time he'd ever gotten that far.'

'Finally got to feel her titties,' Rudy said.

'He figures he's died and gone to heaven. And he figures he's finally gonna score. So then he tries to pull her panties down.'

'He was gonna put it to her, right there in the lake,' Rudy explained.

'Yeah. But then she tells him to stop. He doesn't listen, though. He just goes ahead and tries to pull her panties down. So she starts fighting him. I mean, this guy is bare-ass naked and probably has a boner to beat the band, so she *knows* what's gonna happen if he gets her panties down. And she isn't about to let it. She pounds on him and scratches him and kicks him until she finally manages to get loose and head for shore. Then, just when she's wading out of the lake, her boyfriend starts shouting. He yells, "Guys! Quick! She's getting away!" And all of a sudden, these five other guys come running down the beach at her.'

'They're his buddies,' Rudy explained.

'A bunch of losers who hadn't even *gone* to the prom. The guy, the Maiden's date? He'd collected five bucks from each of them, and set up the whole deal. They'd driven out earlier that night, hidden their car in the woods, then waited around, drinking beer. By the time the guy showed up with the Maiden, they were plastered out of their minds . . .'

'And horny enough,' Rudy added, 'to fuck the crack of dawn.'

'The Maiden never had a chance,' Cody said. 'They caught her while she was running up the beach, and they held her down while her prom date banged her. That was part of the deal, that he'd get to go first.'

'Didn't want no sloppy seconds,' Rudy explained.

'After him, all the rest of them took turns.'

'Two or *three* turns each,' Rudy said. 'Some of 'em nailed her in the butt, too.'

'That's . . . awful,' I muttered. It *was* cruel and terrible – which made me feel guilty about how the story made me sort of hard.

'She was messed up pretty good by the time they were finished with her,' Cody explained. 'They hadn't *beaten* on her, though. There were four or five of them holding her down, the whole time, so they never had to punch her out or anything like that. They figured she'd look all right, once she'd washed up and gotten dressed. The plan was for the boyfriend to drive her back home, just as if nothing had happened. They figured she wouldn't dare tell on them. Back in those days, you looked like the town slut if you got yourself gang-raped. She'd be ruined if she tried to get them in trouble.

'So they tell her to go in the lake and clean herself up, and while they're thinking everything's gonna turn out great, she goes stumbling into the water and wades out farther and farther. Next thing they know, she's swimming hell-bent for the island. They don't know if she's trying to escape or wants to drown herself. Either way, they can't let it happen. So they go and swim out after her.'

'All but one,' Rudy said.

'One of the guys didn't know how to swim,' Cody explained. 'So he stayed on shore and watched. What happened is, the Maiden never reached the island.'

'She *almost* made it,' Rudy said.

'Had about fifty yards to go, and then she went under.'

'God,' I muttered.

'Then the *guys* went under,' Cody said. 'Some were faster swimmers than others, and they were spread out pretty good. The guy on shore, he could see them in the moonlight. One by one, they each sort of let out a quick little cry and splashed around for a few seconds, and vanished under the water. The gal's prom date was the last to go. When he saw his buddies were going down all around him, he turned tail and tried for shore. He made it about halfway. Then he yelled out, "No! No! Let *go* of me! Please! I'm sorry! Please!" Then, down he went.'

'Wow,' I muttered.

'The guy who'd seen it all, he jumped in one of the cars and went speeding for town. He was so drunk and shook up, he crashed after he got out to the main road. He thought he was dying, so he confessed while they were taking him to the hospital. Told everything.

'It was a couple of hours before a search party made it back here to the lake. And you know what they found?'

I shook my head.

'The guys. The boyfriend and his four buddies. They were stretched out side by side, right here on the beach. They were all naked. They were lying on their backs with their eyes wide open, gazing up at the sky.'

'Dead?' I asked.

'Dead as carp,' Rudy said.

'Drowned,' Cody said.

'Jeez,' I said. 'And it's supposed to be the Maiden who did it? She actually drowned *all* those guys?'

'You couldn't exactly call them guys anymore,' Cody said.

Rudy grinned, then chomped his teeth together a couple of times.

'She *bit* off their . . .?' I couldn't bring myself to say it.

'Nobody knows for sure *who* did it,' Cody said. 'Someone or some*thing* did. I'd say she was the most likely candidate, wouldn't you?'

'I guess.'

'Anyway, they never found the Maiden.'

'Or the missing weenies,' Rudy added.

'People say she drowned out there on her way to the island, and it was her ghost that took vengeance on those guys.'

'It's not her *ghost*,' Rudy said. 'Ghosts can't do shit. It's *her*. She's, you know, like "the living dead". A zombie.'

'Bull,' Cody said.

'She just sort of hangs around out there under the water and waits till a guy tries to swim by. Then she goes for him. Like she did Willy Glitten and all those others. She gets 'em by the dingus with her teeth . . .'

Cody elbowed him. 'She does not.'

'Does, too! And pulls 'em down by it.'

I suddenly laughed. I couldn't help it. I'd been pretty wrapped up in the story, and actually *believing* most of it, up till Rudy said that about the Maiden turning into some sort of a dick-hungry zombie. Maybe I can be a little gullible sometimes, but I'm not a complete dope.

'You think it's funny?' Rudy asked.

I quit laughing.

'You wouldn't think it's so funny if you knew how many guys have *drowned* trying to swim out to the island.'

'If they drowned,' I said, 'I'll bet it wasn't because the Maiden got them.'

'That's what *I* say,' Cody said. 'Like I told you, only part of the story's true. I mean, I'm willing to believe the business about the girl getting raped, and then drowning. But the rest of it, I think somebody made it up. I don't think it's true about the guys getting *picked off* when they went after her. Much less that she bit off their cocks. I mean, that's complete bull. It's just somebody's idea of poetic justice, you know?'

'You can believe whatever you want,' Rudy said. 'My gramps was there with the bunch that found the guys that night. And he told my dad about it, and my dad told me.'

'I know, I know,' Cody said.

'And he *didn't* just tell me it to scare me.'

'Sure, he did. 'Cause he knows you're just the kind of guy that might pull a stunt like those jerks.'

'I never raped nobody in my life.'

'That's 'cause you're scared you'll get your whang bit off.'

'I sure won't go swimming in *there*,' Rudy said. He stuck an arm out and pointed at the lake. 'No way. You believe what you want, the Maiden's in there and she's just waiting.'

Cody, looking at me, shook his head. 'She *is* out there, I guess. I mean, I think she *did* drown that night. But that was forty years ago. There's probably nothing much left of her by now. And she doesn't have anything to do with the drownings we've had. People just drown sometimes. It happens. They get muscle cramps . . .' He shrugged. 'But I sure won't hold it against you if you've changed your mind about swimming out to the island.'

'I don't know.' I stared out at it. There was a lot of black water between me and that patch of wooded land. 'If so many people have drowned . . .'

'It's not *that* many. Only one guy last year. And he'd just finished wolfing down a pepperoni pizza.'

'The Maiden got him,' Rudy muttered.

'Did they find his body?' I asked.

'No,' Cody said.

'So you don't know if he'd been . . . eaten.'

'I'd bet on it,' Rudy said.

I looked Cody in the eyes. They were in shadows, actually, so I couldn't see them. 'But *you* don't believe any of the stuff about the Maiden . . . you know, waiting around in the lake to . . . uh, do that to guys who swim by?'

'You've gotta be kidding me. Only dorks like Rudy believe in crap like that.'

'Thanks, pal,' Rudy said to him.

I took a deep breath, and sighed. I looked once more toward the island, and saw all that blackness along the way. 'I guess maybe I'd better skip it,' I said.

Cody gave Rudy an elbow in the side. 'See what you did? Why didn't you keep your big mouth shut?'

'*You* told him the story!'

'*You* brought it up in the first place!'

'He had a right to know! You can't just send a guy out like that without warning him! And he was gonna wear his *jeans*! Your only chance is if you can outswim her, and you can't do that with *jeans* on.'

'Okay, okay,' Cody said. 'Anyway, it doesn't matter. He's not going.'

'We shouldn't have tried to make him in the first place,'

Rudy said. 'The whole idea was dumb. I mean, you-know-who's as hot as they come, but she ain't worth *dying* for.'

'Well,' Cody said, 'that's what she wanted to find out, isn't it?' He turned to me. 'That's the main reason she picked the island. It was supposed to be a test. What she told me, if you aren't man enough to make the swim, you aren't man enough to deserve her. The thing is, she didn't figure on Bozo here shooting off his mouth about the Maiden.'

'It's not that,' I said. 'You don't think I believe that stuff, do you? But, you know, I'm really not such a great swimmer.'

'It's all right,' Cody said. 'You don't have to explain.'

Rudy said, 'We just gonna leave now?'

'Guess so.' Cody turned toward the lake, cupped his hands to the sides of his mouth, and yelled, 'Ashley!'

'Shit!' Rudy blurted. 'You said her name!'

'Ooops.'

Ashley?

I knew of only one Ashley.

'Ashley Brooks?' I asked.

Cody nodded and shrugged. 'It was supposed to be a surprise. And you weren't supposed to find out, at all, if you didn't make the swim.'

My heart was slamming.

Not that I believed a word of it. Ashley Brooks could not possibly have the hots for me and be waiting for me on that island. She was probably the one girl in school who was just as stupendous as Lois. Beautiful golden hair, eyes like a summer morning sky, a face to dream about, and a body . . . a body that didn't quit. Talk about *built*!

But her personality wasn't at all like Lois. She had a kind of innocence and sweetness that made her seem like she was from another world – almost too good to be true.

I couldn't come close to believing that Ashley even knew I existed.

She was too much to hope for.

'It can't be Ashley Brooks,' I said.

'She knew you'd be shocked,' Cody told me. 'That's one reason she wanted us to keep it secret. She wanted to see the surprise on your face.'

'Oh, sure.'

Facing the island again, Cody called out, 'ASHLEY! Might as well show yourself! Elmo's not interested!'

'I didn't say that!' I gasped.

'ASHLEY!' Cody called again.

We waited.

Maybe half a minute later, a white glow appeared through the trees and bushes near the tip of the island. The glow seemed to be moving. It was very bright. It probably came from one of those propane lanterns people use on camping trips.

'She's gonna be awfully disappointed,' Cody muttered.

A few more seconds passed. Then she stepped out onto the rocky shore, the lantern held off away from her side – probably to avoid burning herself.

'And you thought we was liars,' Rudy said.

'My God,' I muttered, staring at her. She was awfully far away. I could only make out vague things. Like the goldness of her hair. And her shape. Her shape *really* caught my eye. At first, I thought she was wearing some sort of skintight garment – tights or a leotard, maybe. If that's what she had on, though, it must've been the same color as her face. And it must've had a couple of dark spots where her nipples belonged, and a golden arrowhead pointing down at . . .

'Holy shit,' Rudy said. 'She's butt naked.'

'Nah,' Cody said. 'I don't think—'

'Sure is!'

She raised the lantern high. Then her voice drifted over the lake. 'Elll-mo? Aren't you coming?'

'Yes!' I shouted.

'I'm waiting,' she called. Then she turned around and walked toward the woods.

'She *is* naked,' Cody said. 'Man, I don't believe it.'

'*I* do,' I said. She was out of sight by the time I got my jeans off. I kept my boxers on. They were a little limp in the elastic, so I hitched them up as I headed for the water. I glanced back at the guys. 'See you later.'

'Yeah,' Cody muttered. He seemed distracted. Maybe *he* wanted to be the one going to the island.

'Swim fast,' Rudy said. 'Don't let the Maiden get you.'

'Sure,' I said.

As I waded into the lake, I could still see the pale light from Ashley's lantern and knew she was in the woods, just out of sight, naked and waiting for me.

The night was pale with moonlight and stars. A warm breeze drifted against my skin. The water around my ankles felt even warmer than the breeze. It made soft lapping sounds, and climbed my legs. In my loose boxer shorts, I felt almost naked.

I trembled as if I were freezing, but I wasn't cold at all.

It was just from too much excitement.

This can't be happening, I thought. This sort of thing just doesn't happen to guys like me. It's too fabulous.

But it is happening!

I'd seen her with my own eyes.

As the warm water wrapped my thighs and I imagined how she would look *close up*, I could feel myself rise hard and slide out through the fly of my boxers.

Nobody can see, I told myself. It's too dark, and my back's to the guys.

A couple more steps, and the lake water took me in. It was all soft, sliding warmth. I shivered with the pleasure of it.

'Better get *moving*!' Rudy yelled. 'The Maiden's homing in on you.'

I scowled over my shoulder at him, angry because he'd shouted and ruined the mood. He and Cody were still standing beside each other on the beach.

'You can quit trying to scare me,' I called. 'You just want to make me chicken out.'

'She's too good for you, barf-bag.'

'Ha! Guess *she* doesn't think so.'

The water was up to my shoulders by then, so I shoved at the bottom and started to swim. Like I said before, I'm not the greatest swimmer in the world. My 'crawl' pretty much stinks. I've got an okay breaststroke, though. It's not fast like the crawl, but it gets you where you're going. And it doesn't wear you out. Also, you can see where you're going if you keep your head up.

I like the name, breaststroke. But most of all, I like how it feels to be gliding softly through the water that way. The warm fluid just slides and rubs against you, all over.

Or would, if you didn't have anything on.

Like boxer shorts. They were down low on my hips, clinging, trapping me. They wouldn't even let me spread my legs enough for good kicks.

I thought about taking them off, but didn't dare.

Anyway, they didn't have me *completely* trapped. I was still sticking out the fly, and I loved having it out and feeling the caress of the water.

This was all the more exciting because of the Maiden.

The risk.

Offering her bait.

Taunting her with it.

Not that I believed for one minute in all that garbage about the Maiden drowning guys and devouring their whangs. It was like Cody said: bull. But the *idea* of it turned me on.

You know?

I didn't believe in her, but I could picture her. In my mind, she was sort of suspended in the darkness maybe ten feet below me, her head about even with my waist. She was naked and beautiful. In fact, she looked sort of like Ashley or Lois. She was down there, drifting on her back, not swimming but keeping pace with me, anyhow.

The darkness didn't matter; we could see each other through it. Her skin was so pale that it seemed to glow. She was grinning up at me.

Slowly, she began to rise.

Rising to the bait.

I could see her gliding closer. And I knew she wasn't going to bite. The guys had it all wrong. She was going to suck.

I kept breaststroking along, imagining the Maiden coming up and latching on. The guys had meant the story to scare me. It *had* scared me. But the mind is a great thing. You can turn things around. With a bit of mental legerdemain, I'd changed their dong-chomping zombie into a seductive water nymph.

But I told myself to stop thinking about her. What with everything else – the sexy Prom Night story, seeing Ashley naked, the feel of the warm water – I was so excited that the last thing I needed was to imagine the Maiden underneath me, naked and ready to start sucking.

I had to think about something else.

What'll I say to Ashley?

That gave me a quick scare, until I realized there wouldn't be much need to say anything. Not at first, anyway. You swim to an island for a rendezvous with a naked girl, the last thing you do is chit-chat.

I raised my head a little higher and saw the glow of the lantern. It was still among the trees, just in from shore.

I'd been making good progress. I was past the halfway mark.

Getting into Maiden territory.

Yeah, right.

Come and get it, honey.

'You better quit dawdling and get your ass in gear!' Rudy shouted.

Yeah, right.

'She's gonna get you! I'm not kidding!'

'You'd better swim faster!' Cody yelled.

Cody?

But he doesn't believe in the Maiden. Why's he telling me to swim faster?

'Move it!' Cody shouted. 'Go!'

They're just trying to scare me, I told myself.

It worked.

Suddenly, the water no longer felt like a warm caress; it gave me chills. I was all alone on the surface of a black lake where people had drowned, where rotting bodies lurked, where the Maiden might not really be dead after forty years and where she might be a sharp-toothed, decayed huntress with nothing in her head except revenge and a taste for penis.

Mine shrank like it wanted to hide.

Even though I *knew* there was no Maiden coming after me.

I started swimming hard. No more breaststroke. I churned up a storm, kicking like a madman, windmilling my arms, slapping the water. There were shouts from behind me, but I couldn't make out the words through the noise of my wild splashing.

Head up, I blinked water out of my eyes.

Not much farther to go.

I'll make it! I'm gonna make it!

Then she touched me.

I think I screamed.

As I tried to twist away from her hands, they scurried down from my shoulders, fingernails scraping my chest and belly. They didn't hurt me. But they made me tingle and squirm. I quit swimming and reached down to get them away from me. But I wasn't fast enough. Gouging some skin, they clawed at the band of my shorts. I felt a rough tug. My head went under. Choking, I quit trying to grab the Maiden. I reached up as if trying to find the rungs of a ladder that would lead me to the surface, and air. My lungs burned.

The Maiden dragged me lower and lower.

Dragged me down by my boxer shorts.

They were around my knees, then around my ankles, then gone.

For a moment, I was free.

I kicked for the surface. And got there. Gasping, I sucked at the night air. It took both hands to tread water. I swiveled around. Spotted Cody and Rudy standing on the beach in the moonlight. 'Help!' I yelled. 'Help! It's the Maiden!'

'Told you so!' Rudy called.

'Tough luck,' called Cody.

'Please! *Do* something!'

What they did, it looked like they each raised a hand into the moonlight and flipped me off.

Then a pair of hands underneath the water grabbed my ankles. I wanted to scream. But I took a deep breath, instead. An instant later, they yanked me down.

This is it! She's got me! Oh, God!

I clutched my genitals.

Any second, her teeth . . .

Bubbles came up.

I heard the gurgling sound they made, and felt sort of a tickle as some of them brushed against my skin.

For a second, I thought the bubbles might be gas escaping from the Maiden's rotting carcass. She'd been dead forty years, though. The rotting should've been over and done with, long ago.

My next thought was *air tanks*.

Scuba gear!

I stopped kicking. I squatted, reached down between my feet, made a sudden lunge with both hands and caught hold of some equipment that I think turned out to be her mouthpiece. I gave it a tug for all I was worth.

She must've taken in a mouthful when I did that, because the rest was fairly easy. She hardly fought back, at all.

From the feel of things, she was naked except for her face mask, scuba tank and weight belt. And she wasn't any corpse, either. Her skin was slick and cool, and she had wonderful tits with big, rubbery nipples.

I hurt her pretty bad, right there in the lake.

Then, I towed her ashore at the side of the island, so the guys wouldn't be able to see us. From there, I dragged her a few yards to the clearing where she'd left her lantern.

In the lantern light, I saw who she was.

Though, of course, I'd already guessed.

After doing her Ashley routine to lure me over, Lois must've gotten into her scuba gear real fast and snuck into the lake for her Maiden routine.

She looked great in the lantern light. All shiny and pale, her breasts sticking out between straps. She'd already lost the face mask. I took off her tank and belt so she was naked.

She was sprawled on her back, coughing and choking and having spasms, which made her body twitch and shake in ways that were very neat to watch.

I enjoyed the show for a while. Then I started in on her. This was *the best*.

Richard Laymon

For a while, she was too out of breath to make much noise. Pretty soon, though, I had her screaming.

I knew her screaming would bring Cody and Rudy to the rescue, so I started swinging her weight belt. It caved her head in nicely, and finished her off.

Then I hurried to the tip of the island. Cody and Rudy were already in the lake and swimming fast.

I planned to take them by surprise and bash their heads in, but guess what? I was spared the trouble. They got about halfway to the island. Then, one at a time, they let out squeals and went down.

I couldn't believe it.

Still can't.

But they never showed up.

I guess the Maiden got them.

Why them, but not me?

Maybe the Maiden felt sorry for me, the way I was being abused by my supposed 'friends'. After all, we'd both gotten betrayed by guys we'd trusted.

Who knows? Hell, maybe Cody and Rudy suddenly got cramps, and the Maiden had nothing to do with it.

Anyway, my little excursion to Lost Lake turned out way better than I ever would've dreamed.

Lois was stupendous.

It's no wonder people like sex so much.

Anyway, I eventually sank Lois and her gear in the lake. I found the canoe she must've come over in, so then I climbed aboard and paddled back to the beach. I took Cody's Cherokee most of the way home.

I wiped it to get rid of fingerprints. Then, for good measure, I set it on fire. I made it home just fine, with a while to spare before dawn.

A Good Cigar is a Smoke

Just before 10:00 p.m., the stench came. Beth shut her eyes and breathed deeply through her mouth, but it wouldn't go away. Bourbon always helped, so she got to her feet, turned off the television, and went into the kitchen.

She took a half-empty bottle from the top of the refrigerator. Her glass, resting upside-down over the bottle's neck, clinked quietly as she returned to the living room. She sat on the couch and put up her feet.

Then, holding the bottle beneath her nose, she twisted off the cap. The bourbon fumes mixed with the terrible odor, masking it.

'Damned cigars,' she muttered into the silence.

Randy had never smoked before their marriage. The smoking started seven months later, on a mild June evening. The Eden Street apartment was windy with blowing fans. Randy came in and tossed his necktie over the back of a chair. His upper lip was moist with sweat when he kissed her.

'How were things at the office?' she asked.

'Hey, we got the Harrison account!'

'Wonderful.'

'Quite a coup.'

'That's just wonderful.'

'And Jim Blake had twins. A boy and a girl.' Smiling and roguishly wiggling his eyebrows, Randy withdrew a pair of cigars from the breast pocket of his shirt. Each cigar was long, as slender as a finger, and brown beneath its cellophane wrapper.

'Twins, huh?' Beth sat on his lap and put an arm around his shoulders. 'We've got a lot of catching up to do.'

'We'd better get started.'

Beth kissed him and whispered, 'Dinner first, before it wilts.'

They ate Crab Louis by candlelight. Afterward, as Beth sipped her coffee, she heard a filmy crinkling sound. She looked up. Randy was peeling the wrapper off a cigar.

'You wouldn't dare,' she said.

'Join me?'

'Are you kidding? I wouldn't *touch* one of those vile . . .' She went silent and her smile withered as Randy's shadowy, distorted face loomed above one of the candles. The flame wavered toward the tip of his cigar. 'Please, Randy, don't. I can't stand the smell of those things.'

The face above the candles, bruised with moving shadows, grinned. Its lips blew smoke toward her. 'Doesn't smell so bad, does it?'

'It smells awful.'

The cuckoo clock began to strike ten, startling Beth from her memories. She watched the plastic bird bow down to 'ku-ku' each of the hours. Then she waited for the tiny Balkan villagers to start their cheerful dance below the clock face. They didn't move. And she remembered. They hadn't danced since the old apartment on Eden Street.

Such a shame. She and Randy had bought the clock in Solvang on their honeymoon – the cuckoo clock and the kerosene lamp they always kept on the bedroom dresser to light when they wanted the room rosy with a romantic glow.

She gripped her glass tightly as the terrible smell seemed to grow stronger. A wave of nausea rolled through her. She gulped down the bourbon, then refilled her glass.

* * *

Somehow, she had withstood the stink of Randy's first cigar. 'Thank God you're done with *that*!'

'Hey, these are really great. Quite a revelation. If I'd known how good they are, I'd have—'

'You can't mean it.'

'*Quite* a revelation. Now I know what Kipling was talking about. "A woman is only a woman, but a good cigar is a smoke." That guy knew his stuff.'

'Thanks a bunch.'

Grinning, he opened the cellophane wrapper of the second cigar.

'Randy, don't.'

'It's all right.' He lighted it.

'Please. Put it out.'

'Why?'

'Please? Because I ask you to. The smell makes me sick.'

'You'll get used to it.'

'Will I? Oh, will I? Think so?' She sprang up. Her chair skidded backward and crashed to the floor.

'Elizabeth!'

She slammed the front door behind her.

On the balcony, she gazed through tears at the swimming pool in the courtyard a story below.

Then Randy was behind her, his hand warm on the back of her neck. 'Hey, honey, it's no big deal.'

'No?' She faced him. The cigar was tilted sideways from his mouth. She snatched it away and threw it from the balcony.

'*Loo*-kout!' yelled a voice from below. 'What's going on?' Cleo, a downstairs tenant, grinned up at them from the pool's apron. She held a bag of groceries in her arms. 'Trying to burn my supper?' Her husky laugh floated up to them.

'Sorry,' Randy called. Then he clutched Beth's collar, jerked her into the apartment, and kicked the door shut.

'That was quite a display,' he snapped. His open hand smacked her cheek. 'Don't you *ever*' – another slap – 'do *that*' – another slap – 'again.'

That night in bed, he held her gently and said, 'I'm sorry, honey. I shouldn't have hit you. But you shouldn't have taken my cigar. You had no right to do that.' When she began to cry, he cradled her head against the side of his neck and whispered, 'It's all right, honey. Everything's all right.'

'Think so?'

'Sure. Hey, what say we give the Blakes a run for their money?'

'Why not?' Beth said.

To her it was a mourning rite for what was lost.

The awful smell grew stronger. Beth lifted her glass. She stared at the comforter covering the high slope of her belly, then put down the glass without drinking.

Poor kid. He would have enough strikes against him. He didn't need bourbon in his veins before he could even see the light of day.

'Where's dinner?' Randy demanded three weeks and three dozen cigars after the first.

'In the fridge, I guess.'

'What?' He set down his briefcase and stared at her.

'I fixed myself a lamb chop.'

'That'll be fine.'

'Nobody's stopping you.'

'Hey, what *is* this?'

'Around here, we eat by seven. It is now nine.'

'So?'

'So I don't know where you've been – and I don't think I want to know – but you weren't here where you belonged.

Here with me. It's part of the bargain. If you can't keep your part, you can damn well fix your own supper.'

'That's quite enough. Now, please get me a couple of lamb chops and –'

The front door slammed off his sentence.

Beth went downstairs to Cleo's apartment. The door stood open. 'Don't be bashful, sweetheart.'

Cleo was reclining on a couch, her carrot-colored hair disarrayed. She wore a bright, glossy kimono. The way the clinging fabric showed her body, Beth had little doubt that she wore nothing beneath it.

'If this isn't a good time . . .' she started.

'Hey, it's always a good time for a friendly visit.' Cleo twisted a cigarette into the tip of a long holder. 'You look like a woman with Randy trouble.'

'That's me.' Beth had to smile.

'Well, sit yourself down, sweetheart. I'm all ears.'

'I just don't know what to do,' Beth began.

Cleo listened, often nodding agreement, sometimes shaking her head in sympathy, twice lighting new cigarettes.

'Maybe I should ask him for a divorce,' Beth finally said.

'Mistake, sweetheart. Don't ask. File first, then tell him. Take it from an old hand who's been there and back, don't ask. That is, if a divorce is really what you're after.'

'It's *not*! I want Randy back the old way, the way he used to be. That's what I want. But I guess we can't ever go back . . .' She trailed off, thinking about how good it used to be.

'Might as well bail out then, sweetie. You know what they say about sinking ships? Rats leave first? Let me tell you, it's not just the rats. It's the survivors, too.'

'But I . . .' Beth began to cry.

'Aw, now don't . . .' The ringing telephone interrupted. Cleo said, 'Damn,' and got to her feet.

Beth needed a tissue.

'Hi back, big fella,' she heard Cleo say.

Heading toward the bathroom, Beth passed the bedroom doorway. She glanced inside. On a lamp table beside the bed was a Kleenex dispenser. She went to it and plucked out a tissue. She wiped her eyes and blew her nose . . .

Then she noticed the odor.

A faint lingering smell, bitter and disgusting.

From the wastebasket. She reached inside, pushed aside a wadded tissue, and found the butt of a dead cigar.

She picked it up. It was soggy and cold where his mouth had been.

'I'm sorry, sweetheart.' Cleo stood in the doorway, shaking her head sadly. 'I could tell you it isn't Randy's, but . . .'

Beth shoved past Cleo, ran outside and dashed upstairs to her own apartment. Randy's quiet, hurried voice came from the bedroom. He hung up the extension when he saw her.

'So you know,' he said, gray smoke pouring from his mouth. He was lying on the bed, the telephone resting on his belly, a freshly lit cigar clenched in his teeth.

She flung the wet cigar butt at him. It thumped against the headboard.

'That's quite enough,' he said. 'Knock it off.'

On the dresser was the lamp, the honeymoon lamp from Solvang, its red chimney dusty from disuse. She grabbed it and threw. The glass shattered above Randy's head, splattering kerosene onto his hair. Into his eyes and his open, startled mouth. Onto his shoulders and chest. Onto his cigar.

It made a quiet *whuh!*

Beth's shaking hand lifted the glass to her lips. She held it there, wanting to drink away the foul, wretched odor. But that wouldn't be fair to little Randy. The poor kid would have enough problems: no father, a murdering mother – manslaughter, they'd called it.

The smell of the bourbon helped, but not enough.

Leaning forward, she took a cigar from the box on the lamp table. She tore off the wrapper and wadded it into a ball. The crinkling cellophane sounded like fire.

She struck a match. Soon the cigar was smoldering. Beth sucked and gratefully breathed in the smoke.

Not such an awful odor, really. So much better than the other, the stench of burning flesh.

I'm Not a Criminal

'Of *course* he's not,' Wade said.

'You've gotta give him points for originality,' said Karen.

'Wanta pick him up?'

'Oh, sure.'

They both turned their heads to watch the hitch hiker as they sped past him. He stood motionless by the side of the road. His hair was slicked down by the rain, his cheeks ruddy. The way his dripping poncho bulged behind him, Wade figured he was lugging a backpack. The letters on the wet cardboard sign held at his chest looked as if they'd been printed with a black crayon.

This wasn't the first hitch hiker they'd spotted since embarking on their journey up the California coast four days ago. Nor was this the first carrying a cardboard sign. But the other signs had announced destinations: Crescent City, Eureka, Portland.

Not on this trip, and never before in his life, had Wade seen a hitch-hiker bearing a placard that read, I'M NOT A CRIMINAL.

Karen twisted around and peered back. In the rearview mirror, Wade saw the young man resume walking.

'Second thoughts?' he asked.

She faced Wade and smirked. 'Oh, let's rush right back and pick him up. After all, he's not a criminal.'

'That's what he says.'

'And it's gotta be the truth, right? Could anybody actually fall for something like that?'

'He's probably *not* a criminal.' Wade rounded a curve and glanced again at the rearview mirror. All he saw through the rain was empty road bordered by Redwoods. 'Probably a student, or something.'

'Something, all right. Like a serial killer.'

'Whatever he is, he's clever.'

'I don't know about that. The sign's sure an attention-grabber, all right, but the first thing you've gotta think is that it might be a lie. I can't imagine *anybody* being stupid enough to give him a lift.'

'You wouldn't necessarily have to be stupid.'

'No, you might just have a death wish.'

'I can imagine some people taking pity on him. Clean-cut young man stuck out in the rain in the middle of nowhere. A good, decent person might stop for him just to be kind. Or someone lonely might do it for companionship. Or a serial killer who prefers guys.'

Karen chuckled a bit at that one.

The rain came down harder. Wade twisted the knob at the end of the turn signal to speed up the wipers. 'You might even pick him up just out of curiosity. Hell, I'm tempted, myself. Find out what his story is.'

'If you do that, you can let me out and *I'll* hitch-hike.'

'Maybe he'd let you have his sign.'

'I wouldn't need it.' With a grin and a wink, Karen hoisted her skirt a few inches up her thighs.

Wade reached over and stroked her smooth, warm skin.

'That'd be really safe,' he said.

A few minutes later, they followed signs up a side road, paid a woman at a ticket booth, and made their way slowly through the forest to the Chandelier Tree. Though they hadn't seen another car since passing the hitch hiker, there were several here. Lined up. Each waiting its turn to drive through the mammoth Redwood that had a tunnel through its trunk. There were even more cars – maybe twenty or thirty – scattered about the unpaved parking area near the gift shop.

In spite of the rain, people wandered about with cameras and bags of souvenirs.

Wade stopped behind a Porsche. Three cars waited ahead of it while a Mazda rolled into the Redwood.

'Will we fit?' Karen asked.

'Hope so.'

'It'd be neat to get a picture.'

'If we'd picked up "I'm not a criminal", we could've had *him* run out and take a snapshot.'

'He might've run off with the camera.'

'But we'd stay dry.'

'I don't mind. Just try not to crash.' Karen unbuckled, reached between the seatbacks for the camera, then swung open the door and hopped out. The door thumped shut. Hunched over, she rushed for the other side of the tree. The wind blew her long brown hair. Her white blouse looked very bright in the gloom. Her skirt whipped against her legs.

She's getting drenched, Wade thought.

In front of the Porsche, a station wagon tried to enter the tree. Its driver changed his mind, backed out and circled around to the other side. Then a man leaped from the passenger seat of the Porsche and reached inside for a video camcorder. He walked backward into the trunk, taping while his friend steered.

Finally, Wade eased his Cherokee forward.

Gonna be a tight squeeze.

When his front bumper entered the gap, he stopped. No more than a couple of inches to spare on each side.

Great.

A good chance I'll knock off the mirrors.

Squinting through the rain-splashed windshield, he saw Karen step into the light at the far end of the tunnel. Her hair was matted flat. She raised the camera to her face, then lowered it and gestured for him to come ahead.

Wade shook his head.

Frowning, she called out something he couldn't hear.

It's not worth the risk, he thought. They'd been driving a heap for years. Even their arrogant mechanic had enjoyed referring to it as 'the junk'. Only two weeks ago, after the advance from his English publisher had finally arrived and cleared the bank, were they finally able to buy their bright new Jeep Cherokee.

I'm not gonna bash it up trying to drive through a goddamn Redwood tree.

He checked the rearview mirror. The car behind him was a safe distance away. He shifted into reverse.

Karen, a look of annoyance on her face, waved him forward.

With a final shake of his head, he slowly backed clear of the tree. He turned out, then steered around the trunk. Karen came rushing up to the passenger door, yanked it open and jumped in.

'Jesus, Wade!'

'I couldn't have made it.'

'You had *plenty* of room.'

'No, I didn't.'

'Yes, you did. Jesus! *I* should've driven. I'm soaked to the bone and you didn't even *do* it!'

He crossed the parking area and stopped. 'Do you want to try? Feel free. I'll take the pictures.'

'Never mind. There's no point in *both* of us getting drenched. God, you're such a wuss sometimes.'

'I just didn't want to wreck the car.'

'You had plenty of room. Why did we buy the Jeep anyway if you're scared of *doing* things with it? The whole idea was to have fun with it. God, where's your sense of adventure?'

'It's no great adventure driving through a hole in a tree. But if it means that much to you, I'll go ahead and do it. Or you can. It's not worth fighting about.'

'It wouldn't be any fun now, anyway.'

Women, he thought.

Deciding it was long past time to change the subject, he said, 'Why don't we check out the gift shop?'

'Oh, that's a terrific idea. We can pick up mementos of the drive-through Redwood you wouldn't drive through.'

'Come on, honey. They've probably got some neat stuff.'

'You hate gift shops.'

'I'll make the sacrifice for you.'

A corner of her mouth turned up ... Almost a smile. 'Let's just get going,' she said. 'There'll be plenty of other gift shops.'

'You're telling me.'

'I can't go inside anyplace looking like this, anyway.'

The pink of her skin and the white of her bra showed through her clinging blouse.

'Maybe you should get out of those wet clothes.'

'In your dreams, buster.'

But moments after their return to the main road, she

asked Wade to pull over. He stopped on the muddy shoulder. Karen climbed out and got into the backseat. Wade twisted around to watch her. Kneeling on the cushion, she reached into the luggage area and unzipped her suitcase. She pulled out a towel and rubbed her hair.

'You can get moving again.'

'Oh, that's all right.'

'Then don't just stare at me. Keep an eye out for cars.' She dug into the suitcase, pulled out a sweatshirt, then took off her blouse and bra. She rubbed herself with the towel.

'Shouldn't you turn around to do that?'

'Ha ha ha.'

Hearing a faint engine noise, Wade faced the front. A logging truck came around a bend. 'Better cover up.' As the truck rumbled closer, he checked on Karen. She was bare-backed, holding the open towel against her breasts.

Their car shook as the truck roared by with its load of three huge Redwood trunks. Its horn blasted out a few quick toots.

'Guess he liked what he saw.'

'He didn't see anything,' Karen said.

She dropped the towel to the seat and shook open her sweatshirt and Wade saw a man through the rear window. Walking toward them, but still thirty or forty feet away. The man carried a cardboard sign.

'Company.'

'Shit!'

Karen ducked. Wade stepped on the gas pedal. The Jeep lurched forward, bouncing over the rough ground for a moment before its wheels got onto the pavement.

In the rearview, he saw Karen peer over the seatback.

'It's him,' she said.

'"I'm not a criminal"?'

'I hope he didn't see me.'

'I'm sure he didn't.'

In seconds, the hitch hiker was out of sight.

Karen struggled into her sweatshirt. She caught Wade watching the mirror. 'Keep your eyes on the road.'

He obeyed. For a while. When he glanced through the gap between the seats, she was facing forward, bent over and pulling a pair of skimpy black panties up her legs.

'*Wade!*'

'What?'

'Don't be a jerk.'

'Just looking.'

'Don't trouble yourself. You might crash your precious Jeep.'

He forced a smile, then turned away. 'This is the thanks I get for saving you from the clutches of "I'm not a criminal"?'

'If you'd been keeping a proper lookout, he never would've gotten that close.'

'Maybe I should've just waited for him. I'm sure he'd appreciate a lift. And he wouldn't be giving me a lot of grief because I committed the horrible sin of not driving my car through a fucking *tree*.'

'No, I'm sure he wouldn't. He'd be too busy cutting our throats.'

'You're so hot for adventure, you might enjoy it.'

She didn't say anything to that. Wade heard only the quiet rhythm of his wipers, the patter of raindrops on the roof, the hiss of his tires on the wet pavement.

Great. Now she's pouting. Giving me the famous silent treatment.

After a while, he looked back. She was wearing blue jeans. One knee was raised as she pulled a fresh sock onto her foot. She gave him a sullen, bitter glance. He turned away.

'Are you planning to stay back there?' he asked.

She didn't answer.

'Geez, what did I do? I didn't drive through a tree. I'm sorry, all right? Are you going to screw up the whole day pouting about it?'

'I'm not pouting.'

'That's a good one.'

'How am I supposed to get into the front seat without getting wet?'

She could squeeze through the space between the backs of the bucket seats. An awkward maneuver, but it could be done. If she wanted to. Obviously, she preferred staying in the back, away from the wuss.

Wade drove on in silence. More than an hour passed before his stomach began to grumble. He looked back. Karen was slumped in the seat, her eyes shut.

He hoped she was asleep. Maybe she would wake up in a better mood.

There was no point in disturbing her right now, anyway. They'd been eating picnic lunches during the trip, but they certainly wouldn't be doing that today. Not with the rain pouring down. And he didn't much like the idea of eating in the car.

We'll just wait, he decided. There's bound to be a restaurant sooner or later.

Half an hour later, he came to an area with pullouts on both sides of the road, cars and vans and RVs parked near various gift shops, a gas station, a general store and the Big Trees Cafe.

As Wade swung onto the gravel in front of the cafe, Karen's groggy voice asked, 'What're we doing?'

'I thought we might stop for lunch. Are you hungry?'

'I guess so.'

'We could eat in the car if you don't want to get out in the rain, but . . .'

'No, this is fine.'

No argument. Not even a hint of annoyance in her voice. Maybe things are all right now.

Wade felt optimistic as he parked the Jeep. They both leaped out and ran through the rain. They met beneath the roof of the cafe's porch, and walked side by side to the entrance.

Though the place wasn't crowded, they chose to sit at the counter so they could watch the cook in action. He wore a floppy chef's cap. He whistled 'Listen to the Mockingbird.' He was a master of the spatula. Karen seemed to get a kick out of the show he put on.

They drank Pepsi, ate cheeseburgers, and shared an order of chili fries.

They didn't talk much. Wade knew she was still annoyed with him, but at least she was making an effort to act friendly.

He let her eat most of the chili fries.

By the time they left the cafe, the rain had stopped. The heavy clouds were off to the east, letting the sun glare down.

They crossed the road. They explored a gift shop. Karen picked out a refrigerator magnet and a Christmas tree ornament, both depicting Redwoods. She kept eyeing a vase made of polished Redwood burl. It cost sixty bucks, but Wade insisted they buy it.

On their way back to the Jeep, Wade said, 'I'll bet Reagan had just finished a trip like this when he made his infamous comment.'

'"You've seen one Redwood tree, you've seen them all"?'

'Yeah. Puts it in a different light, I think.'

Karen laughed and nudged him with her elbow.

We're almost back to normal, Wade thought.

He opened the door for her.

They were on the road less than five minutes when they spotted a hitch-hiker, a young man striding along under the weight of a backpack.

He didn't wear a blue poncho, so Wade assumed he wasn't 'their' hitch-hiker.

Then the man turned to face them, smiled, and raised his 'I'm not a criminal' sign.

'My God,' Karen said. 'I don't believe it. How the hell did he get *ahead* of us?'

'Obviously, he got a lift.'

They sped past him.

Wade eased off the accelerator. 'I guess the guy's not a criminal, after all.'

'What makes you think so?'

'Elementary, my dear Karen. Someone gave him a ride, and now he's on foot again. Which means he didn't slit their throats and steal their car. Should we stop for him?'

'Are you kidding?'

He slowed the Jeep and eased it off the edge of the road.

'Wade. Come on.'

'Chicken?' *Now* who's the wuss? he thought, and smiled.

'We *never* pick up hitch-hikers.'

'This will be the exception. Hey, consider it an adventure.'

In the rearview, he saw the young man jogging toward them.

'It's not a good idea.'

'He's proven he's not a criminal,' Wade explained. 'But he's gotta be an interesting character. And this *is* supposed to be a research trip, you know. I'd bet anything I'll get a story out of him.'

'Jesus,' Karen muttered.

The door behind her swung open. The stranger stuck his head inside. He had a friendly, boyish smile. Wade doubted that he was much older then eighteen.

'Can you use a lift?'

'Thanks. Sure can.' He shoved his pack across the

backseat, climbed in after it with his cardboard sign, and shut the door.

Wade checked for traffic, waited for an RV to pass, then steered onto the road. Karen was sitting up very straight, very stiff, face forward, hands gripping her thighs.

She probably thinks I did this to get back at her, Wade thought.

He smiled at the young man. 'We don't usually pick up hitch-hikers.'

'Well, I sure appreciate it.'

'That's quite a sign you've got.'

'"I'm not a criminal"? Yeah, it works real fine for me. The way I see it, you know, most people are pretty good-hearted and the only reason they don't stop for a fellow is because they're scared. And I don't blame them. Not a bit. I mean, they don't know me. They're scared I might be one of those homicidal maniacs you're always hearing about. So I figure if I put their minds at ease on that score, maybe they'll give me a try.'

'It sure caught our interest,' Wade told him. 'Let's say we were *intrigued*. But we didn't necessarily believe it. In fact, it made us think you actually *might* be a criminal.'

'Then how come you stopped for me?'

'Well, we didn't. Not at first. But you obviously got a ride with someone after that, because you managed to get ahead of us while we were stopped for lunch.'

'Ah.'

'That convinced us that your sign wasn't a . . . fabrication.'

'Those folks were only going up to some diner back there.'

Wade grinned at the cheerful face in the rearview. 'The way we saw it, you would've taken *their* car if you were the type who does away with people who stop for you.'

A soft laugh came from the backseat. 'Glad I didn't, then.

But they were a couple of old farts driving a goddamn piece of junk. Now, if they'd been tooling along in a brand new Cherokee and one of them had been a juicy babe . . . might've turned out different.'

Wade's bowels went ice cold.

'Oh, Jesus,' Karen murmured.

'This is my lucky day, huh?' Leaning forward, he reached through the space between the seats and scraped the blade of a pocket knife against Wade's neck. 'My name's Chip. And you are?'

'Wade.'

The blade went away. With the back of his hand, Chip caressed Karen's cheek. 'And you?'

'Karen,' she murmured. She was staring straight ahead. She was squeezing her legs. Wade could see her shaking.

'You can have the car,' Wade blurted. 'Just let us out, okay?'

'Oh, I don't think so.'

'Come on, man. We picked you up, for godsake.'

'Big mistake, Wade. Not a bright move.' He prodded Wade's shoulder with the knife point, but not hard enough to hurt. 'You should've known better. Just asking for trouble, you pick up a stranger.' He laughed. 'You two apparently don't believe in playing safe. Look at you, not even wearing your seatbelts. Put them on now, why don't you? Come on, buckle up for safety.'

Buckle up so we can't jump out and run for it, Wade thought.

Karen reached over her shoulder. She pulled the harness down across her chest and lap. She tried to latch it. Her hand was shaking too much. Chip took hold of her hand and guided the buckle down onto the steel tongue.

Wade wondered what he'd done with the knife.

Probably just switched it into his left hand.

'Don't you feel a whole lot safer now?' Chip asked. 'How about you, Wadeboy? What are you waiting for?'

Wade drew down his harness and latched it.

'Now all we need is a little privacy. Once the party starts, we wouldn't want any interruptions. Let's find a nice, secluded road.' He let go of Karen's hand. Then he stretched forward, knocked the rearview mirror upward, and dropped back out of sight. 'I'll tell you when to turn,' he said.

Karen looked at Wade. Her eyes were frantic.

I'm sorry, he thought. God, I'm sorry.

This can't be happening. Not to us.

There must be a way out!

Two of us, only one of him. But we're strapped in, and he's behind us and he's got the knife.

As soon as we stop, he'll slit my throat.

Then it'll be just him and Karen.

Wade felt like throwing up.

'Okay. Coming up on the right. Take it.'

Wade saw a narrow road ahead. He checked the rearview mirror. It showed only ceiling. He glanced at the side mirrors and saw a logging truck. It seemed to be about a hundred yards behind them. But he wasn't used to side mirrors, didn't trust them, so he looked over his shoulder.

Chip, in the backseat, had the pocket knife clenched between his teeth. His shirt was gone. With both hands, he was pulling down his jeans. He didn't have underwear on.

He grinned around the knife. Then he plucked it from his teeth. 'Don't miss the turn, pal.'

Wade twisted around, hit the brake and swung onto the one-lane road. Its asphalt surface was rough with ridges and potholes. He drove slowly, hands tight on the wheel.

'We'll find a nice, sunny clearing,' Chip said.

That'll be a good trick, Wade thought. Redwoods pressed

in close on both sides. Only a few specks and strips of sunlight found their way down to the road.

When we do come to a clearing, he knew, *that'll be it.*

The bastard's already naked. So he won't get blood on his clothes. So he'll be all ready for what he plans with Karen.

Why is this happening to us?

Because I wouldn't drive through the goddamn Redwood tree, that's why. Triggered the whole thing. If only . . .

Chip leaned forward. His left arm appeared between the seats. He squeezed Karen's breast. She gasped, grabbed his wrist and shoved his hand away.

'Let go,' he told her, his voice calm.

'Damn it!' Wade blurted. 'Leave her alone!'

'Let's have some cooperation here, folks. You don't want to piss me off, do you?'

'You're gonna kill us anyway,' Karen said.

'Not if I have a really good time.'

'Yeah, sure,' she said, but she released his wrist.

'Very good.' He dragged her sweatshirt up until it was bunched above her breasts, the bulk of fabric mashed flat in the middle by the safety harness. He leaned forward for a view. 'Nice,' he said. 'Very nice.' He curled his hand beneath her left breast.

The breast, bouncing with the motions of the car, slapped softly against his open hand.

Karen began to sob.

'You bastard,' Wade said.

As if to punish Wade for the remark, he pinched Karen's nipple. She yelped and flinched and jerked his hand away.

'Let go!' Chip snapped.

'No!'

'I'll cut off your fuckin' tits and make you eat 'em!'

She let go.

He squeezed her breast. Karen squealed.

The engine roared as Wade punched the gas pedal to the floor.

'Slow down, you . . .!'

He jerked the wheel. The Jeep swerved toward the broad trunk of a Redwood.

'Shit!' Chip yelled.

Then the Jeep slammed the trunk, hurling Wade hard against his safety harness, throwing Chip forward between the seatbacks and crashing his head against the windshield. The glass didn't break. Chip's head rebounded off it. He dropped limp across the control console.

Wade and Karen sat motionless, looking down at him. Karen gasped out quiet whimpery sounds.

After a while, Wade realized the engine was still roaring. He took his foot off the gas pedal. He looked toward the front. The left side of the Jeep was crushed against the tree, but he saw no steam or smoke rising from under the hood. He turned off the engine.

'It wasn't exactly a drive-through Redwood,' he said.

Karen said nothing. She was gently rubbing her left breast as she stared down at the body. Her eyes were red and wet. Her nose was running. She sniffed.

'Are you all right?' Wade asked.

She shook her head a bit from side to side, and muttered, 'He's . . . naked.'

'Yeah.'

'God.' She pulled her sweatshirt down.

Wade unfastened his seatbelt. Twisting sideways, he grabbed Chip's bare shoulders, lifted and shoved.

Chip fell in a slump into the backseat, head drooping. His hair was matted with blood. His face was shiny red. Bloody drool hung in strings from his open mouth. Blood dripped from his face, splashed his chest and trickled down.

Karen, free of her harness, looked around at the body. 'Is he dead?'

'I don't know. But he's gonna get blood all over the upholstery.'

Wade didn't think that was funny, but apparently Karen did. She let out a strange, high laugh.

'I'm getting him out of here.'

Wade climbed out, opened the back door, tossed the pack to the ground, then leaned inside and dragged Chip from the car.

Chip groaned when his head bumped the earth.

'Was that him?' Karen asked from inside.

'Yeah.'

'Good.'

Wade didn't know what was so good about it. The groan meant Chip was still alive, probably meant he was regaining consciousness. What could possibly be good about *that*?

He looked up and saw Karen crawling across the front seats. Hair hung in front of her eyes. Her chin was thrust forward, the edges of her lower teeth against her upper lip. Her sweatshirt drooped away from her body. Through its loose neck hole, he could see her breasts swaying.

She looked . . . wild.

Wade felt a sudden hot surge in his groin.

He half expected her to spring down from the Jeep on all fours like a panther. But she didn't do that. She grabbed the steering wheel and knelt on the driver's seat and came out feet first. Wade gripped her forearm and helped her down.

He wanted to pull her against him. For starters.

That's crazy, he told himself. We've got a maniac here.

They turned to Chip. He was sprawled motionless on his back, head to one side. His eyes were shut. The lids had blood on them. His chest rose and fell slightly, its bright red dribbles shimmering in the sunlight.

Karen stepped close to his side.

'He might be playing possum,' Wade warned.

As if to test that theory, Karen nudged his hip with the toe of her sneaker. He shook a little. His penis, limp against his thigh, wobbled.

'We'd better tie him up, or something,' Wade suggested.

'Or something,' Karen muttered. She lifted her sweatshirt, pulled it up over her head, and started folding it.

'What are you doing?' Wade asked. He felt light-headed, breathless.

'Don't want to ruin my clothes,' she answered. She carried her sweatshirt to the Jeep and tossed it onto the driver's seat. She shut the back door. Rump against it, she started taking off her shoes and socks. She kept her eyes on Chip.

'You're . . . taking off everything?'

'You, too.'

'Jeez.'

'He wanted a party. That's what he's going to get.'

Wade shook his head. He didn't understand. But watching Karen pull down her skirt and panties was like watching a stranger – a very exotic, exciting stranger. He wanted very much to please her. He wanted to have her.

She's my *wife* for godsake. She's Karen.

But she hardly seemed like Karen, at all.

Wade began to take off his clothes.

He glanced at Chip, who still appeared to be unconscious. Then he watched Karen open the back door and crawl onto the rear seat. Her buttocks looked pink and smooth. When she reached down to the floor, he could see the folds between her legs and he wanted to hurry over to her and mount her and thrust himself in.

Chip moaned again.

Wade whirled around.

The guy's eyes were squeezed shut as if trying to pinch out the pain in his head. But he wasn't moving.

Karen came up beside Wade. In her hand was Chip's pocket knife.

'Use your belt,' she said. Her voice was low and husky. 'Bind his feet.'

Wade crouched over his jeans and pulled his belt from the loops.

This is too far out, he thought. This is wild. What the hell is she up to?

Every muscle in his body seemed to be trembling as he knelt at Chip's feet, pulled at them to straighten the legs, and wrapped his belt around the ankles.

He hadn't been shaking like this, he realized, even when Chip had been holding the knife to his throat. His heart hadn't been thundering like this, either. Nor had he been so breathless. He most certainly hadn't felt any sexual arousal, much less this incredible hard-on.

He'd *never* felt this way before.

When he finished strapping Chip's ankles together, Karen said, 'Go to the other end and grab his hands.'

He scurried past the body, knelt at Chip's head and leaned forward, pinning his wrists to the ground.

And watched Karen.

Watched her straddle Chip, watched her squat, watched her sit down on his pelvis.

Her skin was flushed. It was shiny with sweat. Her left breast looked as if it had been scorched by a hot glove.

She leaned forward. The knife was in her right hand. With her left hand, she slapped Chip's face. The sweep of her arm made her breasts lurch. The impact rocked Chip's head and splashed out a spray of blood and spittle. He groaned. One of his eyes opened. Then the other. He blinked up at her.

'It's your party,' she said. 'Are you having fun yet?'

He squirmed a bit. He made a feeble effort to move his hands, but Wade had no trouble keeping them down.

'This is pretty much what you had in mind, isn't it, Chip? A get-naked-and-fool-around kinda party? In a nice, sunny clearing in the woods? Wishes *can* come true.'

She grinned down at Chip.

'Do you still feel up to cutting my tits off? Making me eat them?'

His lips moved, but no words came out.

'Is that a yes or a no, Chipper?' She cupped the underside of her left breast. She slowly scraped the top of it with the blunt edge of the knife. Wade saw goosebumps rise on her skin. The blade slid down over the front. Her nipple bent beneath it, then sprang up. 'Wanta slice it off for me?' she whispered.

'No.' The word came out quiet and whiny.

'How about fucking me? Huh?' Her hips shifted. She was rubbing herself against him.

Wade wondered vaguely if he ought to feel jealous about that. But all he felt was excited. As if she were doing it to him.

Chip's face contorted, and he started to sob as he shook his head from side to side.

'Isn't that what it's all about, really?' Karen asked. 'Fucking me? Torturing me and fucking me and killing me?'

'Don't hurt me!' he blurted. 'Please.'

'Not even to mention killing Wade, huh? Just to get him out of the way.'

Wade felt strangely pleased that she had remembered that aspect of the situation.

'I . . . I wasn't gonna . . . hurt anyone.'

'Oh, we know. We know that. You're not a criminal.'

'*Please.*'

'You just wanted to have a little party, didn't you?'

'Y . . . yeah.'

'I like parties. Do you know what I like to do at parties?'

He shook his head wildly. He didn't know. He didn't want to know.

'I like to have a *drink*,' Karen said, and swept the knife across his throat. Her breasts lurched, just as when she'd slapped him. Then blood shot up and splashed them and splashed her face and she leaned into the geyser with her mouth.

Chip gurgled and thrashed. He jerked one hand from Wade's grip, but didn't go for Karen with it. Instead, he clutched his throat. The hand didn't stop the blood, just made it fly in different directions.

Karen, sheathed in blood, sank down on top of him and scurried backward.

Scurried until her face was between his thighs.

Her eyes looked very white in the red mask of her face. 'I like to drink at parties,' she said. 'And I like to eat chips.'

She chomped.

By the time Wade was done with Karen, he was bloody all over.

They went to the stream and washed off.

Then they got dressed and climbed into the Jeep. Karen tossed the I'M NOT A CRIMINAL sign out the window.

The Jeep, though bashed up a bit in front, seemed to work fine.

They drove back to the main road.

'This is turning out to be quite a vacation,' Wade said.

Karen reached over and squeezed his thigh.

Soon, they came upon a hitch-hiker. He was a young man

with a beard. He walked backward along the roadside, watching their approach. He carried a sign that read, COOS BAY.

Wade and Karen looked at each other.

Oscar's Audition

I came out of the Blue Light Bar just short of midnight with a head that felt like it'd run into the business end of a buzz saw. The fresh air helped. I fired up a cigar, zipped my coat, and was starting to feel like a human being when I rounded a corner and walked into a fight.

Three on one.

Since the single guy was a shrimp and didn't have command of judo, Karate, Kung Fu or sprint, he was getting trounced.

'Knock it off, guys!' I shouted.

They tried, but the shrimp's neck was stronger than it looked.

I walked right up to the scuffling quarter, took a long draw on my cigar, and tapped the ash off. A big, meaty character was holding the shrimp's arms. He let go as soon as he felt the hot end of my cigar inside his ear. He also screamed.

His buddies got indignant. One lunged at me, bellowing like a maniac. I almost lost my glasses as I deflated him with a knee. The other guy pulled out an eight-inch blade, and grinned. I pulled out a .357 magnum, and grinned bigger.

He was smart enough to run like hell. His buddies joined him.

The shrimp, who'd been sitting on the sidewalk in the middle of everything, smiled up at me thankfully. He didn't smile too well, though – only half his face was working right.

I touched my head to make sure my new rug was still in place. The thing took some getting used to. 'Want an ambulance?' I asked.

'Nah, I'm okay.'

He probably was, too. These young people heal up so fast they're good as new before they know they've been hurt.

I holstered my magnum, reached down, and helped the shrimp to his feet. While I still had a grip on his hand, I introduced myself. 'The name's Clare,' I said. Just like I thought, the shrimp gave a lopsided grin. A real funny name, Clare. I gave his hand a bone-crusher. 'Something amusing?'

'Nothing,' he gasped. 'Not a thing.' His voice had the tight, choky sound you get when you talk and groan at the same time.

'What's your name?' I asked, not letting go of his hand.

'Oscar.'

'Aren't you gonna thank me, Oscar, for saving your tail?'

'Sure, sure. Thanks, Clare.'

'Sure.'

He looked plenty thankful when I finally let go of his hand.

I wasn't happy about returning to the Blue Light Bar. Awful booze, too much noise and smoke, and a couple of topless dancers that kept looking up at the ceiling. They hoped it would fall in, I think, to relieve their boredom. But what the hell – I had business to conduct, and the Blue Light was handy.

I wiped the steam off my glasses as Oscar and me walked to a corner table. It was a stubby little table, made so lovers can sit close and play kneesies. I didn't love Oscar the shrimp, so I stretched my legs out sideways. When the barmaid came with our beers, I pulled in. Once she was gone, I stuck them out again.

'How long have you been out?' I asked.

'Huh? What d'ya mean?'

'Outside the joint. You just got your walking papers, it's written all over you.'

His eyes narrowed. One did, anyway. The other was puffed up and shiny, and already as narrow as it could get. 'Are you a cop?' he asked.

'Not hardly.'

'Then why're you carrying?'

'Makes me feel good,' I said, and took a swallow of beer. It had a sour taste. 'You oughta be glad I do, pal. If I'd been clean when I saw those three jerks follow you outa here, I might've let them have you.'

'Why'd you help me, anyway?'

' 'Cause I got a heart of gold. Also, 'cause I got a good eye, and my good eye tells me that you're the kind of guy I'm looking for. Now, how long you been out?'

'Two days. After nine big ones at Q.'

'I called Soledad home for twelve. But that was a long time back – the only time they ever made one stick.'

'Yeah?' His good eye looked plenty interested.

'That's right. What'd they get you on?'

'They said I put it to some chick.'

'What, rape?'

'That's what *they* called it.'

'Is that what *you* call it?'

'Hell, no. What d'ya think, I gotta rape some chick to get what I want? She was willing and eager.'

'Eager, huh? And they shipped you off to Q for nine years?'

'So I had a knife. Big deal.'

'Cut her?'

'No way!' He looked insulted.

'Why not? You ever see the DA put a corpse on the stand?'

'Hey, man, you're talking Murder One. That's not for me. No thanks.'

'So you've never iced anyone?'

'Me? Hey, not a chance.'

I grinned through my cigar and said, 'That's good, Oscar. I don't like working with guys that might change a simple armed robbery into murder.'

'What're you talking about?' His voice sounded suspicious, but real interested.

'Maybe I can use you.'

'What for?' He leaned forward. He back-handed some beer foam off his upper lip and folded his arms on the table. The centerpiece, a candle with a red chimney, made Oscar's swollen face look wet and sticky.

'Ever knock over a liquor store?' I asked.

'Maybe.'

'We'll hit one together,' I said. 'Call it an audition. I want to see how you handle yourself. If you do good, maybe I'll let you in on something bigger.'

'Yeah? Like what, for instance?'

'Something bigger,' I said again, and took a long time sucking on my cigar. Oscar spent the time staring at me. He looked like he might be thinking, or maybe just trying to remember how many green ones he'd seen in his billfold the last time he looked. He finally nodded. 'Meet me here tomorrow night at ten,' I said. 'I'll bring you a clean piece.'

'What about wheels?'

'I'll take care of it. I'll take care of everything, Oscar, my friend.'

* * *

The next night, Oscar showed up at the Blue Light on time. 'That's a point in your favor,' I told him, and lit up a cigar to mask the cigarette stench of the place.

'If I'm one thing, I'm prompt.' He grinned proudly with the working half of his face. Over night, the broken half had turned purple.

'It's good in this business, being prompt. But it's even better being something else.'

'Like what?' he asked.

'Like obedient.'

'Sure, sure. I'll do whatever you say. I mean, you know, as long as . . .'

'Let's get going.'

Oscar wasn't overly impressed by the '68 Buick out front. We got into it anyway, and I pulled onto the street. 'Don't worry,' I said, 'your girlfriend won't see you in it. The thing's hotter than a hundred-watt bulb. We'll dump it two minutes after we hit the store.'

'What girlfriend? I haven't got a girlfriend.'

'Not even what's-her-face? Old Willing and Eager?'

'Her? After what she done to me? You gotta be kidding.'

'Yeah. Which reminds me. If there's a chick in the store, don't touch her. This is business, understand?'

'Sure.'

'See that sack on the floor? Take the stuff out of it.'

He picked up the cloth bag and took out a snub-nosed .38.

'A mean-lookin' sucker, isn't it?' I asked.

'Wicked.'

'That's the point. If you scare them bad enough, you won't have to shoot. And you'd better *not* shoot, Oscar. This is for peanuts, remember that. Anyone gets hurt, it's your tail. Understand?'

'Sure,' he muttered. He was plenty scared. He set the

revolver down on his lap and grabbed a deep breath. Then he pulled a wool ski mask out of the sack, then a pair of rubber gloves.

'We're almost there. When you get inside, stick the muzzle up the owner's nose. Make him empty his cash register into the bag. There won't be much. They empty the register all the time into a floor safe. Don't worry about what's in the safe. We just want the ready cash. We're not greedy. Like I said, it's your audition. The bigger stuff's for later, if everything goes smooth.'

'Sure.'

'I'll wait for you in the car.'

'Hey!' He didn't like that. Not a bit.

'Yeah?' I asked.

'I mean, aren't . . .? What if there's customers or something? You want me to go in there alone? Is that it? Geez! I don't know, man.'

'Okay,' I said. 'It's off. Easy as that.'

'I mean . . .'

'I know what you mean. You don't want to go in there alone. Fine. Fine and dandy. So you're not the kind of guy I need. You're a real hot-shot with a knife and a woman, but when it comes to a .38 and hard cash, you turn into cold spaghetti.' I pulled over to the curb. 'You can get out.'

'Now wait. Just a minute . . .'

'Forget it. I thought I was a good judge of character. I saw you lapping up brew in the Blue Light and I said to myself, "This guy's fresh outa the joint and has enough guts to get into something big." So I followed you out and gave you a hand with those mugs. So I wasted my time. Get outa my car.'

'WAIT JUST A GODDAMN MINUTE!'

'Yeah?'

'I'll do it.'

'Yeah?'

'I will. I'll do it. Take me to the store, you'll see.'

I grinned real big. 'I don't have to take you there, Oscar, my friend.' I aimed my finger at a neon sign halfway up the block. It read, 'Barney's Liquor.'

'That's it?'

'That's it.'

'Okay.' He was breathing real hard while he pulled the gloves on.

'You can walk from here. Don't put on the mask till you're ready to step inside.'

'Sure.'

'Once you're in, I'll pull up in front of the place. I'll have the door open for you when you come out. Just climb in, and we're off like a shot. My own car's parked six blocks from here. We'll pile into it, and we're home free.'

'Sure. Sounds okay.'

'Remember what I said about plugging someone.'

'Yeah.' He nodded with quick, nervous jerks.

'Go.'

'Right.' He nodded some more, like a goddamn woodpecker whacking at concrete.

'Now!'

He threw open the door, bailed out, and went rushing up the sidewalk real fast, like he wanted to get it over with before his guts melted. At the store's entrance, he stopped long enough to pull the ski mask over his head. Then he charged inside.

I didn't pull up to the door. Nope. Instead, I climbed out of my trusty Buick and headed for the door on foot. Real slow. Taking off my glasses so I could see better. Unzipping my coat.

I was thirty feet from the entrance when two things

happened: a gal in a yellow windbreaker stepped out of a doorway in front of me, and Oscar backed out of the store with the money bag in one fist and the pistol in the other.

'Out of the way!' I gasped, grabbing for my cannon. The gal jumped sideways and crouched in the doorway. 'Hold it!' I yelled at Oscar.

He swung around, snapping off a couple of shots. With a snub-nose, most guys can't shoot their way out of a wet popsickle bag. Oscar wasn't an exception. His bullets hit nothing but air.

I fingered my trigger. The piece jumped. Through the tail end of its roar, I heard my slug thump Oscar. Before he went down, I put a second one on top of it. Then I ran toward him.

Barney O'Hara, the liquor-store owner, got to the body at the same time as me. Our eyes met. 'Clare?'

'Hi, Barn.'

'I didn't recognize you. New hair, huh?' He shook his own bald head, grinning. 'Say, I guess I owe you for this one.'

'You owe me nothing, pal. Pay your debt to Lady Luck. I was just dropping by for a six-pack.' I reached down and pulled the ski mask off Oscar. Then I muttered, 'My God, I don't believe it!'

'What'sa trouble?' Barney asked.

'This guy . . . It's Oscar Morton. I'd heard he was in town, but . . . ' I shook my head, trying to look confused and shocked.

'So who's Oscar Morton?'

'The guy that raped Peggy.'

'Peggy? Your kid, Peggy? *Cheese-Louise*, talk about Lady Luck!'

'Luck, nothing,' I said. 'I've got some mighty fancy explaining to do. The shooting board's gonna ride my tail like . . .'

Barney clapped me on the shoulder. 'Hell. That was a righteous shoot if I ever saw one. You—'

'Shouldn't somebody call the police?' asked the gal in the yellow windbreaker.

I flashed her my shield.

Into the Pit

1.

In the year 1926, William Brook's father traveled to Egypt for the purpose of lending his expert assistance to the famed Howard Carter, who had recently unearthed the tomb of the child king, Tutankhamen. William accompanied his father on that journey.

In Luxor, they met Mr Carter. He welcomed William's father heartily, for they had worked together several years earlier with Theodore Davis at the tomb of Mentuhotep I. He was not so enthusiastic, however, about the presence of William. He must have felt that a youth of eighteen years, no matter how mature, would prove a hindrance. William was pleased to note that Mr Carter's attitude in this matter changed remarkably once he saw how the young man aided his father in the intricate details of the work. His copious, exact notes soon earned the archaeologist's respect.

It was his bravery, however, that won the respect of the Egyptian youth, Maged. They met on a December night. Suffering from the oppressive heat, William had wandered beyond the boundaries of the encampment in hopes of chancing upon a stray breeze. He longed for the winters of his Wisconsin childhood: to be sledding down a slope, a chill wind battering his face, snowflakes blowing, the night lit by a full moon. He was near weeping with frustration when suddenly an urgent cry startled him.

Never one to flee in the face of a crisis, he rushed forward and discovered half a dozen youths engaged in beating a young fellow senseless. He attacked. In the brief affray that followed, he struck several telling blows on the bullies and sent them scurrying for safety.

The victim introduced himself as Maged, using passable English. (His father, William later learned, had served with the British during the Great War.) He offered William his gratitude and his friendship.

At first, he explained that the boys had fallen upon him for the purpose of committing robbery. After the friendship had grown, however, he finally confided in William. It seems that Maged, no innocent victim, had made vile suggestions to the sister of one of the boys. When she refused him, the young Maged had shown his hostility by defecating on the family's doorstep. The brother, together with several friends, had reacted with violence.

Over the weeks, Maged proved to be an invaluable companion. The little Egyptian led William about in the night. They fought his enemies. They drank stolen raki. On regular occasions, they whiled away the nights in the arms of tawny, lusting women who showed William delights he had never known.

On a warm January night, after saying goodnight to his father, William met Maged at their usual rendezvous point. From there, they traveled a long distance on foot until they reached a village of mud huts. In one of these, Maged assured him, they would find a pair of twin sisters whose beauty and sexual talents would spoil him for all other women.

William waited outside while Maged entered one of the huts to fetch them. Soon, the Egyptian reappeared. The two girls behind him were beautiful indeed, though no older than sixteen. For long moments, William stared at them in the moonlight, struck with awe. He greeted them in Arabic. They smiled lasciviously, but spoke not a word. Maged quickly informed him that they were deaf-mutes. At first, William was troubled by this revelation. He soothed his conscience, however, by reminding himself that the five piasters (amounting to twenty-five cents) he intended to pay the girls was a handsome amount for such peasants. The fellahin who worked at the tomb, after all, received only three piasters for an entire day's labor.

Taking the hand of one girl, William followed Maged into the desert beyond the village. There, they spread blankets on the earth. The girls disrobed. William was ready to take his at once, but Maged restrained him and indicated that he should be seated.

The girls stepped away from the young men. With olive oil cupped in their hands, they caressed one another until their skin had a glossy sheen in the moonlight. Then they danced.

Never had William seen such a dance. He watched the flow of their bodies moving as if to a wonderfully haunting, erotic melody. But there was no music. The only sound was the distant barking of pariah dogs.

He saw the naked girls caressing themselves, hands rubbing pointed breasts, sliding over bellies and thighs, stroking the darkness between their legs while they turned and writhed as if spitted on great phalluses.

He saw them move closer to one another. Reaching out, their fingers met. Then they were drawn together like lovers long apart, lovers starved for the touch of one another, starved for the taste.

How long they continued, William didn't know.

He wanted them to go on forever; he wanted them to stop instantly so that he might satiate the appetite that strained his entire being.

At last, their bodies slid apart. They stepped toward William and Maged, chests heaving, hair wild. They had, no doubt, expended themselves several times in the course of their strange dance, but their half-shut eyes held a promise of boundless delights.

William stood motionless as one of the twins slowly removed his clothing. She smelled of blowing sand, and olive oil, and woman. A moonlit droplet of sweat or oil slid to the tip of her nipple and shimmered there. William longed to lick it off, and did so once his clothing was removed.

Had he been cheated out of the next minutes, he should have counted his life a waste. But whispers of the girls' departure from the village were tardy in reaching Kemwese, their father. Before his arrival, William found time to gratify himself with both of the girls. He was standing, a twin upside-down in his embrace, his head hugged by her slick thighs, his tongue darting into her hot depths, his phallus throbbing within the tight constriction of her sucking mouth, when a sharp blow to the back of his leg toppled him.

As he rolled in the sand, he glimpsed Maged making a dash for freedom. A sandaled foot kicked his breath away. Hearing a struggle behind him, he managed to look around. The naked girls were at their father, clutching his legs and arms, fighting to save William.

They proved no match for the enraged monster. He battered them aside and rushed at William, roaring.

His foot lashed out. Catching it in both hands, William twisted it, throwing Kemwese down. At this moment, he might have chosen to run and save himself. This, however, was against the young man's nature.

Never one to abandon a fight, he attacked the growling savage. He fell upon the man, fists pommeling the face. He heard a satisfying, gristly crunch as his knuckles smashed the bulbous nose. No sooner did blood begin to gout from the nostrils than an arm swung up and struck William's head with the force of a club.

Dazed, William tumbled away.

He was only vaguely aware of the huge man lifting him. Kemwese raised him high, then tipped his head downward and drove him toward the sand. The blow shocked every inch of William's body.

Kemwese lifted him again. William knew, in what remained of his conscious mind, that he would soon be dead.

Rather than throwing him down again, however, the man began to carry him. Where he was being taken, William had no idea. Nor did he care. He only hoped, in a fogged and dreamy way, that if he were carried far enough, some of his strength might return and he might yet save himself.

At length, Kemwese reached his destination. He flung William to the ground.

Though William hadn't the power to raise his head, he could see that they were near the ruins of the Temple of Mentuhotep. Grunting, Kemwese pushed aside a large block of stone.

The young man immediately recognized his intentions. Horror coursed through him, clearing his mind and giving him new strength. Raising his head, he saw a small, black patch in the sand beneath where the rock had rested.

Just as he'd feared. A hole.

When Kemwese came for him, he threw a handful of sand at the grinning face. Blinded and coughing, Kemwese groped for him. William rolled away. He got to his hands and knees.

Crawling, he tried to gain his feet but his body obeyed the commands of his mind in only the slowest fashion and soon the raging man had him by the foot.

William was dragged backward, dragged toward the awful hole. His fingers clawed at the sand and gravel. All sense of manhood broken by the horrible prospect awaiting him, he cried out for forgiveness. He begged Kemwese. He offered money. At the end, he threatened the man with terrible vengeance.

It was useless.

William's feet were lifted high above him. He saw the black pit, like a tunnel to Hell, below his face. His hands dug into the debris at its edges, but to no avail.

Kemwese released him.

He plunged headfirst into the darkness, screaming.

2.

William fell, petrified by an unreasoning fear that he might plunge forever through the lightless void. He had little time, fortunately, to dwell upon the horror of that thought. Abruptly, he hit the bottom of the shaft and lost consciousness.

When his mind returned to him, the aches in every limb of his body quickly reminded him of his situation. The darkness was so intense that he blinked several times to be certain his eyes were indeed open. The lumpy pressure on his back told him that he was lying face upward.

He raised his arms. He found great relief and comfort in touching himself: his face, his chest and belly, his privates, his thighs. The hands, touching familiar places, gave him a warm feeling that he was not entirely alone in this strange and frightful pit. They also confirmed that he was still whole, at least so as far as he could reach. He stirred his legs. They seemed unbroken.

As he lay there continuing to stroke his body and regain a sense of reality, he began to assess his situation. The devil, Kemwese, had undoubtedly left him here to die. That being the case, he must have covered the opening of the pit with the enormous block of stone that had originally sealed it. Even should William succeed in climbing to the top, he would be powerless to stir the rock. His best chance of survival, however, lay in that direction.

Gazing into the black space above him, he tried to determine whether Kemwese had, indeed, replaced the stone. No light came in from the stars or moon. Nothing was visible. Nothing.

William decided he must attempt to climb out, nonetheless. First, however, it would be necessary to explore the confines of his prison.

As he stirred himself to sit up, the uneven ground beneath him seemed to wobble. Lowering a hand to the lump beneath his hip, he touched a plant surface that he immediately recognized as animal hide.

His fingers explored further. The hide felt dry, wrinkled, shrunken. Pressing it, he detected the solid roundness of a bone below its surface. With a gasp of alarm, he flung his naked body clear of the creature.

He huddled in the darkness and gazed in its direction. He could see nothing, of course. To confirm his fears, he finally ventured forward. His hands again encountered the dead flesh. He explored it briefly before realizing, with an agony of horror and revulsion, that his fall had been cushioned by the desiccated corpse of a man.

He, like William, was naked. William wondered if this man, too, had been caught in debauchery with the daughters of Kemwese. The thought chilled him in spite of the pit's dreadful heat. Perhaps William would meet a similar end.

'No,' he said. The sound of his voice was horribly loud. Silly, of course, but he feared for a moment that he might have startled his companion awake. He listened, half expecting the man to speak.

From that point on, William took pains to remain silent.

Starting at the feet of the dead man, he began to inch his way along the boundary of his cell. He crawled on hands and knees, and let his shoulder brush along the stone wall to keep his orientation. After proceeding in this manner for a short time, he set his hand down on someone's face and screamed.

Petrified, he crouched against the wall, panting the hot air, and struggled to regain his composure.

Finally, he ventured forward. With hesitant hands, he familiarized himself with his new neighbor. The flesh felt more stiff than that of the other man, leading William to the assumption that his residence here had been more prolonged.

He left the body behind and continued his exploration. His reaction to the next body was more easily controlled. He didn't scream. He merely removed his hand rapidly from the foot.

This man was fully clothed. William checked the pockets. In the shirt, he found a pack of cigarettes and a small box of matches.

He slid open the box. It contained eight matches. He struck one.

Its head sparked in the darkness, then burst alight with such brilliance that pain shot through his eyes. In a moment, however, the pain passed. He gazed upon the awful scene and groaned.

Gathered around him in the bottom of the shaft no larger than a dozen feet in diameter were the dried corpses of five men. The one in front of him, the clothed one, still held a revolver in his shrunken hand. William saw a hole in his right temple.

Another corpse, across the floor, had gaping wounds on his thigh. William had little doubt how they had gotten there. The grim thought entered his mind that he, too, might soon be driven by extremes of thirst and hunger to consider partaking of his companions.

One in particular, a bald, lean man clad only in undershorts, looked more fresh than the others. Perhaps his body still retained enough moisture to quench the thirst that would shortly begin its slow torture. No. That would be . . .

The fire scorched William's fingers. He dropped the match. Darkness swallowed him and he stood motionless among the dead, considering his next course of action.

At length, he crouched beside the man who had taken his own life. Groping blindly, he found the pistol. He tried to pry it loose from the stiff fingers, and finally snapped three of them before freeing the gun.

He carefully released the cylinder catch. The cylinder swung sideways. He tipped the barrel upward. Six cartridges dropped into his palm. Among them, he found two empty shells and four live rounds. From their size and weight, he guessed them to be of .38 caliber.

He reloaded, then set the revolver by his side.

For the present, he had no need for the weapon. The fact of its presence, however, was a great comfort. He knew that, should circumstances offer no alternative, he need not be reduced to a groveling, inhuman beast. He would simply take his own life and be done with it.

With that settled, he stripped the man of his trousers. He found a penknife in one of the pockets. Using that, he cut the legs into long, narrow strips. When he had a dozen of them, he struck another match. He applied its flame to the end of a strip and found that he had created a rather satisfactory source of light. Paying out fabric as needed, he made a close inspection of the chamber.

The smooth stone walls, he noticed, sloped gradually inward above him. This ruled out the possibility of scaling the shaft.

Might there be another way out?

Certainly, his predecessors hadn't found one.

Their failure, he told himself, constituted no proof that such an exit did not exist.

Here, his knowledge of Egyptian tombs stood him in good stead. The pit, his prison, had obviously been constructed in ancient times. Its proximity to the Temple of Mentuhotep might indicate that it had been built during his reign, possibly as a secret entrance to his tomb. It was not unusual to find such passages, often designed as elaborate mazes complicated with false entries, dead ends and portals concealed in walls and ceilings for the purpose of foiling tomb robbers.

William exhausted most of his supply of makeshift wicks in a fruitless search of the walls and floor. While his flame still burned, he quickly fashioned more strips from the dead man's trousers. Then he renewed his search, looking for the slightest clue that a secret passage might lie behind the stone blocks of his cell. He found no such clue.

Allowing his light to die, he sank against one of the walls. He was sweaty and exhausted. His hopes of escape had faded to a dim prayer.

As he sat in the blackness, surrounded by his silent companions, an idea began to form. It seemed impractical at first. It seemed less so, however, as he gave it more thought. Though the top of the shaft was higher than his frail light had carried, any project which might take him closer to it seemed worthwhile.

Perhaps, after all, the passage to the tomb had been placed

partway up the shaft wall. Such a manner of concealment was not unknown to the wily priests of those times.

Thus, with the project justified in his mind, he set about constructing a platform of bodies. It was a ghoulish task. In the darkness, he dragged each from its place of rest. Their joints were stiff, their skin tough. He grew to know them apart from one another by touch: by the firmness of their flesh, by their manner of undress, by the various configurations of their limbs. Some had died prone, others sitting. He made use of these differences in constructing his platform, often sacrificing height for sturdiness.

At last, by clever stacking of four cadavers against the wall, he had a platform as high as his chest.

He lifted the last body, the one most recently dead. This one was less brittle than the others. Also, his limbs had stiffened into convenient positions.

William stood him upright on top of the others, leaning him slightly backward against the wall. When the cadaver was securely in place, William lit a strip of cloth, the upper end of which he had earlier inserted into the corpse's mouth. He adjusted the burning tip at the side of his platform so it wouldn't hinder his progress.

Then he began the awful climb.

3.

The bodies trembled precariously under William's feet, but he was careful to place his weight only on the strongest of places: a hip here, a shoulder there.

At last, he reached the top of his platform. He stood motionless, gripping the wall, gathering his strength for the most strenuous part of the climb.

The flame had inched slowly up the strip of cloth,

scorching flesh. As he paused, it ignited the hair of one man. The hair blazed, filling his nostrils with a terrible, acrid stench. When the fire died a few seconds later, he inspected the end of the taper.

Half the strip yet remained. William intended to use its flame, when he reached the summit, to ignite another makeshift taper which was wound around his neck. This would save him the use of a precious match. The match box was tied at his throat, however, so he wouldn't be at a loss for light should the flame of the taper expire during his climb.

Without further hesitation, he inched sideways. He swung the burning strip of cloth away from the knees of his ghastly companion and let it hang at the side, out of his way.

Pressing his body to the man, he began to climb. It was a horrible business, all the more so because of William's nudity.

He was perched upon the man's bent knees, one hand pressed to the wall, the other gripping the left shoulder of the corpse, when the light failed.

The sudden darkness unnerved him, but he knew that he would soon fall if he didn't continue upward. Sliding a foot up the dry leg, he sought the bony protuberance of a hip. Perched more precariously than ever, he leaned forward, his knees gripping the body as if he were a child shinnying up a tree.

Carefully, he straightened up, leaning full against the man. He felt the face against his belly, his privates. Nightmarish images passed through his mind as he made his slow way higher.

He was almost onto the shoulders when the man moved. His hands sought purchase on the stone wall, but found none. The corpse continued to slide out from under him.

Then he was falling.

One foot struck the top body of his platform and punched through as if it were a plank of rotten wood.

From there, he tumbled backward through the darkness.

The ground struck him a terrible blow. As he lay there, stunned, a body fell on him. Then another. He flung them aside and scurried away.

Hunched against a wall, he gazed at the darkness. He listened intently. Beyond the drumming of his own heart, beyond the windy gasping of his lungs, he heard other sounds.

Muted, incoherent babbling.

The papery sounds of dry flesh dragging across the gravel floor.

'*NO!*' he shrieked.

He heard their sandy laughter.

With palsied hands, he unlooped a strip of cloth from his neck. He tore open the box of matches. Poised to strike one, he hesitated.

Better to die in the darkness, certainly, than to look upon the creatures crawling toward him.

But he *had* to see!

He struck a match. In its sudden glare, he saw a cadaver reaching for his foot. Another, sitting upright, grinned at him. The others, still in a heap, writhed as they tried to untangle their twisted limbs.

His trembling hand dropped the match.

Its light died.

'*NO!*' he cried out. '*Stay AWAY!*'

But on they came, the dry sounds of their dragging bodies quiet in the silent blackness, their clicking teeth loud.

4.

Their calls drew no response, so William's father and Mr Carter lowered Maged on a rope.

The boy heard nothing as he descended into the pit. At last, his feet found the gravel floor. Stepping away from the rope, he turned on his electric torch. He swept it around the pit. The sight of the tumbled, awkward bodies chilled him. Tight with dread, he stepped through the bodies and crouched behind the naked form of William.

He put a hand on his friend's sweaty back.

William flinched and whimpered.

'I've come for you,' Maged whispered.

William rolled onto his back. His wild eyes gazed up at Maged. 'They want to eat me,' he explained.

'No. We'll leave now.'

'They want to . . .' His eyes darted to the darkness behind Maged.

Maged looked. The bodies, sprawled in their grotesque attitudes, were motionless. He turned to his friend. 'They can't eat you, my friend. They're dead.'

'Are they?' William sat up. He stared at the bodies. 'They are, aren't they?'

'Most surely.'

With a sudden laugh, William leaped to his feet. He kicked the nearest corpse. It rolled onto its side. He bent over and gazed at it, then reached down and tore off one of its arms.

'*Dead!*' he cried out.

He cast the arm aside, then crouched and twisted off the corpse's head and flung it against a wall.

He grinned at Maged. 'He can't eat me *now*, can he!'

Giggling, he fell upon the next corpse and twisted its head off.

Maged quickly climbed the rope. At the top, the men helped him from the mouth of the pit. He gulped the fresh air.

'Is William quite all right?'

'He will come up soon, Mr Brook. Most surely.'

Spooked

Selene woke up, wondering vaguely what had disturbed her sleep. She glanced at the lighted face of the alarm clock. Nearly 3:00 a.m.

If only Alex were here. How could he leave her alone on a night like this – on Halloween, of all nights! He knew very well how nervous she got . . . Well, he would be home in the morning. Only a few hours from now.

Taking a deep breath that seemed to fill her entire body with peaceful weariness, Selene curled up on her side and snuggled her face against the pillow.

Then she heard someone else taking a deep breath.

Someone under the bed!

She went rigid.

Couldn't have been, she told herself.

She felt faint, and realized that she was holding her breath. She opened her mouth, eased air out silently, and breathed in. But not much. Too much, and her chest might expand enough to make the bedsprings creak. If the springs should creak . . .

You're acting like a fool, she thought. There is nobody under the bed. Can't be.

A drop of sweat stung her eye. She wanted to wipe it away, but that would require moving her arm. She didn't dare.

Nobody down there. Not enough room. Plenty of room for the suitcases, though. Only yesterday, she'd dragged out one of them for Alex. A man isn't much thicker than a suitcase.

Selene imagined a man on his back directly under her, his pale eyes staring upward.

Knock it off. Go to sleep.

Selene closed her eyes and rolled onto her back. From beneath her came a stifled cough.

She flung the sheet aside, flipped over, and got to her hands and knees in the center of the king-sized bed. Her nightgown stuck to her back with sweat. 'Who's down there?' Her voice was a dry rasp. She cleared her throat and said firmly, 'I know you're under there. Who are you?'

A long silence answered her question.

'Who?'

A breeze filled the curtain above her. It chilled her wet face. She heard the whisper of a distant car.

'Please! Who's down there?'

From beneath the bed came a single laugh. A shiver scurried up her back like quick, furry spiders.

'It isn't you, is it, Alex?'

What on earth made her think it could be Alex? Because he'd acted so weird before his trip? Because one minute he was gazing into space, the next acting more loving and considerate than he'd been in years? They say that's a sure sign a husband's having an affair.

Ridiculous.

'That isn't you, is it?' she asked.

Silence.

'Alex?' She began to crawl toward the edge of the mattress, trying to see over its side. In her mind, she saw an arm lash up to grab her. She retreated to the center of the bed.

Then she heard a groan.

Alex never groaned like that. *Nobody* ever groaned like that. Nobody but those demented, shadowy mutes that sometimes hulked down the alleys of her nightmares.

Maybe this is a nightmare.

Don't you *wish*.

A low, whispery voice said, 'Se-leeeene.'

She heard herself whimper.

Her eyes roamed the borders of the mattress. Except for the headboard against the wall, a sea of darkness lay beyond its edges. The bedroom door stood open, but so far away!

If she could reach the door without being overtaken, a long hallway lay beyond it. Then a flight of stairs. And finally the front door, chained against burglars. But maybe, with luck . . .

She slowly stood up, the mattress giving beneath her feet.

'SELENE!'

Gasping with fright, she lost her balance and fell backward. Her shoulders hit the headboard. Her head knocked the windowsill, the curtain fluttering against her cheeks and eyelids.

The window!

A way out! She could jump to safety, avoiding the awful darkness where hands were waiting to snatch her ankles . . .

But it would be a long fall to the ground.

She remembered Alex's recent advice. 'If you're ever trapped up here by a fire or something when I'm out, jump. You might break a leg, but that's a far cry better than the alternative. Besides, the saplings will cushion your fall.'

Spinning around, she ripped the curtain off the window and smashed the screen with her fists. It dropped easily away.

She squirmed headfirst through the window. The wooden framework was rough, and full of splinters. One splinter ripped her arm.

'I'LL TEAR YOU UP!' the voice shrieked.

She was halfway out, gazing fearfully at the rows of pine saplings far below, when her nightgown snagged on the sill. She tugged at it, couldn't jerk it free. She squirmed and writhed, whimpering, kicking, waiting for the rough grip to catch her ankles.

'No!' she cried out. 'Oh God, NO!'

Shortly after dawn, Alex entered the bedroom. He noticed that the screen was missing from the open window, saw the curtains piled on the bed. And he smiled.

His smile died when he saw the suitcase on the mattress.

He rushed to the window. The rows of saplings below stood upright against the wind, braced in place by the tall, iron stakes which he'd pounded into the ground last week while Selene was at the beauty parlor. The stakes were green and barely visible.

Selene was not impaled on any of them.

'Damn,' he muttered.

Something had gone wrong.

At the bed, he opened the suitcase. The timer was there. So was the tape recorder. He flicked its switch.

'I'LL TEAR YOU UP!'

He gazed at the recorder, stunned. His words. Yes, the very words he'd screamed into the microphone only a few days ago. But not *his* voice – *Selene's!*

Trembling, he turned off the recorder.

Hands gripped his right ankle and jerked, smashing his shin against the metal bed frame. Pain surged up his leg.

He fell.

Selene, on her belly, scurried from under the bed with madness in her eyes and a butcher knife clenched in her teeth.

The Good Deed

She was asleep when I spotted her. Asleep, or playing possum. Either way, she was curled on her side at the bottom of the cage, not moving.

The first thing that went through my mind was *Holy shit!*

Here I was, taking a leak in the woods, a gal no more than twenty feet away. What if she rolls over? I wished like hell that I'd noticed her before unleashing, but I couldn't stop now. Too much coffee at that diner down the road. So I turned around quick and strained to finish fast. Fast. Before she heard the splashing. Before she turned over and saw me. Before she *said* something.

What's she doing here? I kept thinking.

In a cage, no less.

Shit!

I've gotta get outa here!

I felt shocked, confused, embarrassed, spooked. And then ashamed of myself because my dick was starting to get hard. Because it was out, I suppose, in the presence of a woman. Even if she couldn't see it.

She'll see it if I turn around, I thought. If she's looking.

I didn't turn around, of course.

At last, I finished and shook off. By then, I had to really work at getting myself tucked back into my jeans.

I zipped up. I glanced over my shoulder.

The gal still lay curled on the floor of her cage, her back to me.

I hurried away. The matted dead leaves underfoot crackled and snapped, no matter how softly I tried to step. I kept expecting the gal to call out. She didn't, though. When I looked back, she and her cage were safely out of sight. I saw only thick forest, gloomy with shadows except for a few streaks of morning sunlight that slanted down through the treetops.

I made my way to the Jeep. It was parked to the side of the dirt road, the passenger door open and waiting for me. I climbed in.

'Took you long enough,' Mike said. 'Have to take a dumper?'

'Just a piss.'

'You hiked a mile just to take a piss? Could've done that right here.'

'I didn't hike any mile.'

He started the engine. 'All the traffic we had, you could've done it in the middle of the road here.'

'I like my privacy,' I said.

'Like I'm sure I'd wanta watch. Gimme a break. Do I *look* like a homo?'

'You look like a dork.'

By the way, we were sixteen years old. In case that isn't obvious from the sophisticated nature of our repartee.

Mike and I were buddies, and we'd just finished our sophomore year at Redwood High. If you're wondering what we were doing out in the boonies without adult supervision, it's because we'd begged and pleaded with our parents till they caved in.

It helped matters that the parents on both sides were intelligent, reasonable people. It also helped that Mike and I were a pair of polite, responsible over-achievers. Aside from having four-point grade averages, we were Eagle Scouts. Upstanding citizens, self-reliant, experienced in the wilds. What parent could *not* trust whizzbangs like us, in spite of our youth, to spend a couple of weeks on our own?

When we proposed our plan to explore the scenic wonders of California via Mike's dad's Jeep, camping out at night and calling in every few days to assure everyone that all was well, they went for it. Eventually. None of the folks was tickled by the idea, but the dads soon came around. They admitted it might be a good experience for us, a chance to see a bit of the world and to gain some maturity. Hell, they probably wished *they* could do it. Once we had the dads on our side, the rest was easy.

Which is how we ended up out here by ourselves.

If you're wondering how come we weren't discussing my leak in the dignified manner befitting a couple of brainy, reverant Eagle Scouts, it's because we're guys and we were out here by ourselves, no adults to impress.

'You oughta know, dickhead,' Mike said. (Before embarking on the aside, I'd said he looks like a dork. Remember? We're back in the car, now.) 'It takes one to know one. Are you gonna shut the door?'

I looked at him.

'Well?' he asked.

'Maybe we'd better . . . not drive off yet.'

He grimaced. 'Oh, man. You got the runs?'

I shook my head. My face felt hot. My heart was suddenly thumping awfully hard. 'There's a girl,' I explained.

'A *what?*'

'A girl. A female. A woman. You know.'

'A *babe?*'

'Yeah.'

'Shit. What're you talking about? Where?'

'In there.' I pointed toward the woods.

'Bullshit. No way.'

'It's true.'

'A *babe?* Over there in the trees?'

'I saw her when I went in to take my piss.'

Mike grinned. 'She hold your dick for you?'

'She's in a cage.'

'A *what?*'

'A cage. You know. Like a zoo cage or something. With bars.'

He chuckled. 'Bullshit.'

'I'm serious.'

Mike knew me. When I said that about being serious, he knew I meant it. He narrowed his eyes. 'A babe in a cage. I'm supposed to believe that?'

'Go and take a look for yourself.'

He kept staring at me, frowning. 'What did she look like?'

'All I saw was her back.'

'You didn't talk? Like maybe ask her what the fuck she's doing in a cage in the middle of Fort Boondocks?'

'I think she was asleep.'

'Jee-zus.'

'Hey, man, I was taking a piss. All I wanted to do was get outa there. But she's in a *cage*, you know. She probably can't get out. I don't think we can just drive off and leave her. She might die, or something.'

Mike scrunched his eyes tight and gazed at me through slits. 'You'd better not be shitting me, man.'

'I swear to God.'

He shut off the engine, pulled out the ignition key and threw open his door. Leaping out, he glanced over his shoulder and said, 'This I gotta see.'

I went with him, of course.

I led the way. I felt nervous for a lot of reasons. Part of me hoped we wouldn't find her at all. Then we wouldn't need to deal with the situation. But she and her cage couldn't have walked off, and I'm not one to hallucinate. Besides, Mike would give me no end of crap if we failed to find the mysterious, caged babe.

My heart nearly bashed through my chest when I spotted the cage. I came to a quick halt. Mike stepped up beside me. We both stared.

'What'd I tell you?' I whispered.

'Oh, man, I don't believe it.'

The girl looked as if she hadn't stirred. She lay curled on her side, her back toward us. She was mostly in shadow, but dappled with sunlight that made her hair gleam like gold. She wore a white blouse. It was untucked, its tail hanging crooked so it showed a strip of bare skin above her cut-off jeans. The jeans, low around her hips, were cut away very high so that they really had no legs at all. They were also pretty ragged. One of the rear pockets drooped, ripped halfway off, leaving a rectangular gap. Her skin showed there, too.

Mike nudged me with his elbow. 'Look,' he whispered. 'You can see her butt.'

'I know, I know. Big deal.'

'Man.'

'Get your mind out of the gutter.'

'Yeah. Right. Come on.' He started toward the cage, but I grabbed his arm. 'What?'

'Just hold it. What're we going to do?'

'Check her out.'

'I don't know. I don't like this. It's too damn weird.'

'I just hope she ain't a dog.'

'Would you cut it out? This is *serious*. What the hell is a cage doing out here? Why's she in it? I mean, maybe this is some kind of a trap.'

'A trap, all right. And she's in it.'

'No. I mean like a trap for us.'

He smirked. 'Get real.'

'Maybe some crazy maniacs put her in there as bait.'

His smirk slipped. 'Bullshit,' he said.

'I've read about hunters doing stuff like that. Say they're after a lion? They'll stake out a lamb or something and hide. Pretty soon, along comes a lion. When it goes for the lamb, they blast it.'

'If anyone wanted to blast us, we'd be blasted by now.'

'Maybe they want us alive. There might be a pit over by the cage. You know, covered over so that when we step on it . . .'

'Knock it off, huh? Good God.'

I knocked it off. We both stood silent for a while, peering into the bushes and trees along the borders of the clearing. We even looked up into the higher limbs.

'There's nobody here,' Mike finally whispered.

'Just because we can't see them . . . I mean, *somebody* put her here.'

Mike frowned the way he does when he's concentrating. 'That's true. Or at least somebody brought the cage. *She* sure didn't lug that thing through the woods.' He nibbled his lower lip. 'Could be some guy used it to bring a wild animal out here.'

'That's possible.' I liked the idea. A nice, reasonable explanation that sapped away some of the menace.

'Maybe an environmentalist,' Mike went on. 'Brought out a bobcat or bear to return it to its natural habitat. Let it go, but left his cage behind. And this gal wandered along. Stepped inside to check it out. Shut the door, just for the hell of it. But the damn thing locked on her. Presto, she's caught.'

'Nice theory, Einstein,' I said.

'What?'

'I guess you were too busy scoping her butt to notice the padlock. She didn't fasten a *padlock* by accident, did she?'

He scowled over at the cage. 'Shit.'

'Right.'

Shrugging at me, he said, 'So somebody did put her in there. Doesn't mean she's bait.'

'So what *does* it mean?'

'I guess we'll have to ask her. Come on.'

This time, I didn't try to stop him. Nervous as I was about the whole deal, we couldn't just walk away and leave her. But I let Mike go first. I stayed a few paces behind him and kept a sharp lookout.

Mike didn't seem to be in any great hurry. He stepped along slowly, hunched over a bit, setting his feet down with great care, actually *creeping* toward the cage. I followed his example. Though we tried to be quiet, we couldn't help but make a lot of crunching sounds. Every footstep sounded like somebody balling up a sheet of paper.

The girl didn't move, though.

We got to the front of the cage without getting nailed by any sort of boobytrap. Mike stopped, and I eased over to his side. We gazed through the bars at the girl.

She still hadn't moved.

From where we stood, we could see one side of her face. Part of it, anyway. It was turned downward because of the way her head was resting on her arm. Also, most of it was hidden under a drape of shiny blonde hair. We couldn't really tell what she looked like.

'Hello!' Mike blurted. It came out so loud that I flinched. The girl didn't. She lay motionless. 'Excuse me? Ma'am? Lady? Hello?'

No response.

I snapped my head this way and that, afraid a lunatic – or a family of lunatics – might suddenly come charging out of the woods. But nothing stirred.

'Jeez,' Mike whispered. 'You don't suppose she's dead?'

I quit looking around and concentrated on the girl. 'She doesn't *look* dead.'

'How many stiffs have you met?'

'I've *read* about plenty. They're supposed to have a funny color.'

We both studied her. The slight bits of face that weren't hidden by hair looked healthy enough. Her legs looked sleek and tawny. The portion of her back that showed above her cut-offs wasn't as tanned as her legs, but it had no sickly pallor. Even the creamy skin we could see through the ripped seat of her pants looked *alive*. Looked *great*.

'I don't know,' Mike whispered.

'She isn't dead.'

'Just because she hasn't started to rot yet . . .'

'They do stuff like evacuate their bowels.'

'They take a dump?' He sounded astonished and appalled.

'That's what I've read.'

'Shit! Man, that's disgusting!'

'Shhhh.'

'What do you mean, "Shhhh"? She's out of it. If she's not dead, there's sure as hell *something* wrong with her. Let's see what she looks like from the front.'

When he said that, my heart started pounding really hard. I got a hot, squirmy feeling inside as we made our way around to the opposite side of the cage.

There, we crouched and gazed in at the girl.

Still, not very much of her face showed because of all the hair hanging down across it. Maybe half of her forehead. The tip of her nose. Her lower eye, which was shut. She looked to be about the same age as us, and not at all bad looking from the little I could see.

Her head rested on her left arm, the elbow sticking out past her face. Her right arm hung across her chest. The upper part of it was pushed against the side of her breast. Her blouse was snug over the breast. Her nipple made it really jut out.

Mike nudged me.

'I know, I know.'

'Wow.'

'Shhh.' Feeling turned on and a bit raunchy, I quit looking at the breast. Her blouse was buttoned. Except for leaving a bare triangle above her hip, it covered her all the way down past the waist of her jeans. Those were cut off so high that the bottom of a pocket lining hung out. It lay flat against the front of her thigh like a pale tongue. Her legs were on top of each other, and pulled up so that they were angled toward us, her knees not very far from the bars.

'Look,' Mike said. 'She's breathing. See her hair?'

Sure enough, after studying her face for a few moments, I saw the hair stir slightly where it draped her mouth.

'I *told* you she isn't dead,' I whispered.

'She doesn't even look like she's hurt. What's the matter with her?' In a loud voice, he said, 'Hey! Hey, you!'

Nothing.

So he reached between the bars, leaning forward until his shoulder met the cage. Before he could touch her, I said, 'Wait. Don't.'

He hesistated, his hand hovering above the top knee. 'What?'

'You'd better not.'

'Just gonna give her a little shake.'

'What if she's . . . I don't know . . . infected?'

'Are you nuts?'

'Maybe she's got something, you know? A disease. Maybe she's contagious, and that's why they put her out here. So she wouldn't spread it around. I mean, *something's* wrong with her. And she was *left* here. Maybe she was left here to die, you know?'

'What kind of asshole would do that?'

'Who knows? Somebody ignorant. Or scared. He didn't have the heart to kill her, maybe, so he just . . .'

'Hey, I bet she's a vampire.'

'I'm serious.'

'Or a werewolf. Yeah, that's the ticket. She's a werewolf. It'll be a full moon tonight. Her folks locked her up so she won't run wild and rip out the throats of innocent children.' He let out a howl.

'Cut it out.'

'Gimme a break, huh?' He lowered his hand, clasped her right knee and gave it a shake. 'Come on, girl. Wake up. What's the matter with you?' She didn't respond, so he shook her more roughly, jostling her whole body. I found myself watching her breast, the way it jiggled inside her blouse.

She moaned.

My heart gave an awful kick. Mike's arm jumped and he jerked it back outside the bars.

The girl moaned again, then slowly brought her right hand up to her face. While she rubbed her face like someone waking from a heavy sleep, she rolled onto her back and stretched her legs out.

Suddenly, she froze. She lay motionless for a few moments, then bolted upright, sweeping her hair out of the way. Eyes all wide with alarm, she glanced this way and that, taking in the cage, the forest, and us. She gaped at us. Her mouth hung open. She was breathing hard.

'It's all right,' I told her.

She sprang to her feet, whirled around, and threw herself at the door. It made a clanky sound and stayed shut. The cage rocked a bit. She tugged and shoved at the bars, putting her whole body into it, struggling like a madwoman to force the door open. When that didn't work, she turned toward us. Her face was red. She was huffing for air.

Mike and I were both standing up by this time. But we hadn't moved away from our side of the cage.

'You ought to calm down,' Mike told her. 'We aren't going to hurt you.'

She thrashed her head from side to side, hair flying.

'We'll try to get you out,' I said.

She quit throwing her head, but kept on gasping. She held onto a couple of bars down low by her hips as if there was a current or something that she was afraid might drag her toward us.

Though she still had some wisps of hair in front of her face, I could see what she looked like now. She wasn't any great beauty, I guess. But better than average. Kind of pretty, but not stunning.

In a way, I was glad she'd turned out not to be gorgeous. The ones who are really great-looking make me awfully nervous. I felt shaky enough without having to deal with something like that.

The way she stared at us, you'd think we were a couple of Frankenstein monsters or something.

To Mike, I said, 'Why don't you go back to the car and find something we can use to bust the lock?'

'Me?'

'Just do it, huh?'

'Hey, buddy, you're the one who said she might be contagious. Maybe we'd better find out what's going on before we start trying to break her out.'

'Come on. She's scared to death. We'll both go. It'll give her a chance to calm down.' I took Mike by the arm and pulled him. When we started to move alongside the cage, the girl sidestepped toward the far corner. 'We're just going back to our car,' I explained. 'We'll be right back. We need some tools for the lock. Okay? All we want to do is let you out.'

'Yeah,' Mike added. 'We're the good guys.'

She didn't look as if she believed us. She kept lurching sideways, her back to the bars, watching us from behind swaying slips of hair with panic in her eyes.

By the time we got to the front, she was pressed against the back of the cage where we'd been crouching when she woke up.

We hurried away.

'Christ,' Mike said, 'she's like a madwoman.'

'She's just scared.'

'How do we know she *isn't* mad? Maybe she's a total nutcase. Maybe that's why they put her here.'

'Well, we can't just leave her. That's for sure.'

'I'm not saying that.'

'What are you saying?' I asked.

'We'd just better watch out.'

'Right. She might be a werewolf.'

'I don't know what she is, but we'd better find out before we bust her out. Remember that *Twilight Zone*?'

Mike didn't even need to describe which episode. Right away, I knew the one he meant. For years, we'd been getting together at my house to watch an annual *Twilight Zone* marathon where they showed reruns of the old show for twenty-four hours straight. It was funny that I hadn't thought of the story, myself, before now.

I wished he hadn't reminded me.

I shook my head and forced myself to laugh. 'You think she was caged by a bunch of monks? You think she's the Devil?'

'Don't be a jerk.'

'You're the one who brought it up.'

'The principle of the thing.'

'She was caged out here to protect the world from her evil ways?'

'Who knows? Do you know? I don't. I'm just saying we'd better find out what gives.'

'Well, I'm all for that.'

About then, we reached the Jeep. Mike dug out the tire tool. One end of the iron rod had a head for wrenching off lug nuts and the other end had a prying wedge. I pulled my old Boy Scout hatchet out of my pack, figuring we could bash the lock to pieces if it resisted the tire iron.

I decided to take along my canteen and a chocolate bar. Even if the gal wasn't thirsty or starving, the offer might help to show our good intentions.

When I stepped away from the Jeep, Mike was busy slipping the sheath of his Buck knife onto his belt.

'What the hell do you want that for?'

'You never know.'

'It might spook her.'

'And just suppose we let her out and she goes ape and attacks us?'

'Gimme a break.'

'She might.'

'I guess it's possible.'

'Fucking-A-right it's possible. I'm all for being a good Samaritan and shit, but it's not worth dying for. Besides, *you've* got a goddamn *ax*.'

'Okay, okay.'

With the knife at his hip, he buckled his belt. Then he pulled the tire tool from between his knees, and we headed into the woods.

'At least she ain't ugly,' Mike said after we'd walked a short distance. 'I'd hate to put my butt on the line for a dog.'

'She's probably harmless.'

'They always put harmless people in cages.'

Not wanting to get into another round of pointless speculation as to why she might be locked up in that thing, I changed the subject. 'I guess we might have to take her with us.'

That idea seemed to cheer Mike up. 'Only two seats. You'd better take over the driving. She can sit on my lap.'

I grinned. 'Hey, it's your car. You drive. Besides, you don't want a werewolf sitting on your lap.'

'A werewolf that looks like her? Wearing cut-offs like that? No panties? No bra? Lycanthropy, where is thy sting?'

'Horny bastard.'

'Oh, yeah, and like she doesn't turn *you* on.'

'I'm above such things.'

'Right.'

The cage came into sight. We quit talking, and stayed quiet as we approached it.

The girl was standing, her back to the bars at the far side, but she didn't seem quite as rigid and jumpy as before. Hair no longer hung in front of her face. She was no longer panting for air.

'That didn't take long, did it?' I asked her.

She didn't answer.

At the door of the cage, I dropped my hatchet and Mike put down the tire iron. 'Here's some water and chocolate.' I reached through the bars with the canteen and candy bar. She stayed put. So I gave them a toss and they fell to the floor near her feet. She didn't even glance down at them. Just stared at me and Mike.

Mike started to say, 'Knows better than to take candy from stra—'

And she spoke. 'Why'd you bring me here? What do you want?'

'Huh?'

'Oh, man,' Mike said. 'She thinks *we* ... hey, we had nothing to do with this. We *found* you here.'

'That's right,' I added. 'All we did was find you. You were already here.'

'Oh, yeah?'

'Yeah!' Mike blasted her. 'Christ on a crutch!'

'Calm down,' I told him. To the girl, I said, 'You don't *know* who did this to you?'

As she shook her head slightly from side to side, her eyes seemed to lose some of their terror. She frowned. She looked wary, confused. 'It really wasn't you guys?' she asked.

'No way,' I told her.

'We left our shining armor back at the car,' Mike said. He sounded a bit snotty.

'If you two didn't . . . what are you doing here?'

'We're just out driving around and camping and stuff,' I explained.

'Ed came over to take a leak.'

'Oh, thanks a heap.' I gave Mike a jab with my elbow. But then I saw the girl crack a smile. The smile only lasted an instant, then vanished. It had looked good on her, though. 'I'm Ed, by the way. The jerk is Mike.'

'I'm Shanna.'

'Nice to meet you, Shanna.'

'Hi,' Mike said.

'He's not really a jerk.'

That brought another fleeting smile from Shanna.

'Look, we'll get you out of there and—'

'Not so fast, buddy. We had an agreement, remember?'

'She doesn't know why she's here. She thought *we* were the ones who . . .'

'So she claims.'

I gave her a smile and kind of rolled my eyes upward. 'Mike's afraid you might be a werewolf or something.'

'Hey,' he said, 'screw you.'

'Tell him you're not a werewolf.'

'Just tell me what the hell you're doing in a *cage* in the middle of the goddamn boondocks.'

Shanna frowned, shook her head some more, and took a deep breath. 'I don't know,' she said. 'I fell asleep on the beach.'

'On the beach? At the ocean?'

'Yeah. Stanley Beach. Or Stanton?'

'Stinson Beach? In Marin?'

'That's the one.'

'That's a couple of hundred *miles* from here.'

'Where are we?' she asked.

'In the mountains. The foothills, actually. A ways north of Yosemite.'

'God,' she muttered.

'Anyway, you were at the beach. Then what happened?'

'I woke up here.'

'If you were at the beach,' Mike said, 'then where's your swimming suit?'

Apparently, she didn't like his tone of voice. She gave him a resentful look. 'I didn't have it on.'

'What was it, a nude beach?'

'Come on, Mike. Jeez.'

'It was night. I was wearing what I've got on.'

'Must've been awfully cold,' Mike said.

'I had my sleeping bag.'

'You were spending the night on the beach?' I asked.

'Sure. I did it all the way down the coast.'

'Alone?'

'Yeah. Something wrong with that?'

'What are you,' Mike asked, 'a runaway?'

'That's my business.'

'It's our business if you want us to let you out of there.'

'Look,' I said, 'it doesn't matter. The thing is, you went to bed in your sleeping bag on the beach, and you don't know what happened after that? You just woke up here?'

She nodded. 'Yeah.'

'That's really weird. You weren't beat up, or . . . have you got a sore head or anything?'

'No, huh-uh.' She slipped the fingers of one hand through her hair and felt about as if examining her scalp. 'I do feel kind of funny, though.'

'Funny how?'

'I don't know. Heavy? Tired? Like maybe . . . maybe they drugged me.'

Mike and I looked at each other. Drugs would account for a lot: how she'd come to be here without any awareness of what led to it; how she'd gone on sleeping soundly when Mike had called out to her.

'Seems mighty convenient,' he said. 'Drugged. So she doesn't know anything.'

'I *don't* know anything!' she snapped. 'I can sure figure a few things out, though. Some creeps found me sleeping on the beach, shot me up with something, and drove me out here while I was unconscious. And locked me up.'

'Maybe, maybe not.'

'Hey, come on, Mike.'

'How do we know she isn't lying about everything?'

'It's the truth!' Shanna blurted, 'Don't be such an asshole.'

'Oh, now I'm an asshole.'

'Would you guys please just get me outa here before they come back?'

'Oh, now it's please.'

'Before *who* comes back?' I asked her.

'Whoever brought me here. What are you, retarded? You don't really think they just put me in a cage and that's it? This is just to hold me. That should be obvious even to a moron.'

'She's now called you retarded and a moron,' Mike pointed out.

621

I'd already noticed. And wasn't too happy about it.

'You sure aren't behaving very well for a gal who needs a favor,' I told her.

'Okay, okay. I'm sorry, okay? I didn't mean it. But they're *going* to come back. Isn't that obvious? They must wanta *do* something to me.'

'I know what *I'd* like to do to you,' Mike said.

'Cut it out,' I told him.

'If some creeps just wanted to molest me, they would've done it right there on the beach. This is . . . I don't know. Maybe there are others. Maybe it's a cult or something and they want to sacrifice me. Maybe they'll be meeting here tonight.'

I turned to Mike. 'That might be it.'

'A cult? Give me a break.'

'It makes sense,' I said. 'An advance man for some weird kind of group, it's his job to provide a gal for the evening's festivities. It doesn't have to be devil worship, necessarily. But they need a gal for it.'

'Yeah. She would come in handy for a gang-bang.'

'And they'd want someone who wouldn't be missed. Like a runaway camping on the beach.'

'Might be something like that,' Mike admitted. He grinned. 'Maybe we oughta stick around and watch.'

'Damn it!' Shanna blurted. 'Get me out of here!'

'We could climb a tree, have us a bird's-eye view.'

'You bastard!'

'He's just kidding,' I told her. 'But you oughta quit calling us names.'

'You think I'm kidding?' Mike asked. 'It might be a real kick. Wouldn't you like to watch and see what they do to her?'

I actually began picturing it. Night. Mike and I in a tree, gazing down as rednecks with flashlights and Coleman lanterns gathered around the cage. Shanna terrified, weeping and pleading.

'Neat?' Mike asked.

Already, I was feeling pretty excited, and the imaginary rednecks hadn't even started to work on her. 'We can't do that,' I said.

'Why not? It's none of our business what they do with her. We'd just be innocent observers.'

'It'd be our fault.'

'Hell, no. If we hadn't come along, it would've happened to her anyway. Right? This would just be like letting nature take its course.'

'I don't know.'

'Maybe nothing will even happen. We don't know what's going on. Shanna might be lying through her teeth. For all we know, she might've locked *herself* in there.'

'You're nuts,' Shanna said. 'And if you guys think you're gonna hide and watch what happens . . . go ahead and try it. Whoever shows up, I'll tell 'em right where you are. Then maybe all three of us can end up getting massacred.'

'Listen to her,' Mike said. 'The bitch is threatening us.'

'Yeah. Why don't we just go on back to the car and leave her? Who needs this?' I didn't actually mean it, but she had me peeved.

'I'd rather stick around and watch the fun,' Mike said.

'You heard her. She'd tell on us. Let's just split. She's acting like a jerk.'

'I'm with you.'

I picked up my hatchet. Mike picked up his tire iron. We both turned away from the cage.

'You want your canteen?' Shanna asked.

I looked back. She'd stepped away from the bars and picked it up.

'Toss it over.'

'Huh-uh. You can have it when you let me out.'

'I'll buy you a new one,' Mike told me.

'Fine. You can have that one, Shanna. You might get thirsty while you're waiting for tonight.'

She hurled it down. It thumped against the floor of the cage. 'Get back here! You can't go!'

'Oh, really?' I asked. 'Just watch us.'

We went on walking away.

'Please!' she cried out. 'You can't just leave me! You can't! Please!'

We kept walking.

'We really gonna do it?' Mike whispered.

'Leave?'

'Yeah.'

'Why not? The hell with her.'

'What a bitch.'

'No!' she called. 'Don't go!'

I looked back at her. 'And why the hell shouldn't we? Give us one good reason.'

Her hands scurried down the front of her blouse, rushing from button to button. In a flash, all were unfastened. She pulled her blouse wide open.

'My God,' I muttered.

Mike and I stared. While we watched, she let her blouse fall to the floor of the cage.

'*Now* will you come back?' she asked.

We didn't need to discuss it. We headed back, our eyes pinned to her. She was watching us, standing rigid, arms hanging down at her sides, fists clenched. She was breathing hard again.

She looked great.

Her hair gleamed golden. Her skin, partly in shadows but splashed here and there with sunlight, had a soft, light brown color. Not her breasts, though. They looked pale, creamy. Their nipples were dark and pointing at us.

She was slender and bare to the waist of her cut-offs. Which wasn't at her waist, but a lot lower. Below the jeans, her legs reached down slim and tawny to her bare feet planted somewhat apart on the cage floor.

I'd never seen anything like this.

Nothing even came close.

I felt like I might faint. Or explode. Or wake up.

'Is this what you wanted?' she asked, her voice trembling.

'You didn't have to . . .' I murmured.

'Yeah, sure. Now get me out of here.'

'We'll think about it,' Mike said.

'Give me that.' I reached for the tire iron, but he swept it aside so I missed. 'Hey. Come on. Hand it over.'

'What's the big rush? Let's just relax and enjoy the scenery for a minute.'

I know. I could've wrestled him for the tire iron. Or I could've started whacking the padlock with my hatchet. But I didn't feel much like doing either of those things.

We both turned our attention to Shanna.

She glared at us. Her lips were pinched shut. Her breath hissed through her nostrils. I didn't spend much time, though, studying her face.

After a while, she said, 'Why don't you just take a picture.'

'Wish we had a Polaroid,' Mike said.

'Yeah.'

'Man.'

'You creeps!'

'Lose the shorts,' Mike told her.

She looked like she might start to cry. 'Guys,' she said. 'Hey.' Her eyes went to me as if searching for an ally.

'You don't want us to leave, do you?' I asked.

'Hey. Please. Come on.'

'What's the big deal?' Mike asked. 'We didn't even *ask* you to shuck the shirt. You thought that up all by yourself.'

'Yeah,' I said. 'You started it.'

She nibbled on her lower lip, eyes flicking from me to Mike. Finally, she said, 'If I do, will you get me out of here? No more . . . messing around?'

'Sure,' Mike said.

'Sure,' I said.

Grimacing as if it hurt, she unbuttoned the front of her cut-offs. She didn't bother to unzip, but hooked her thumbs under the sides of the shorts and tugged them down. She bent over as she lowered them. Her breasts swayed a little. When the jeans were about halfway down, she let go and they dropped around her ankles. She stood up straight. She freed her left foot. With her right, she swept the cut-offs aside. Then she pressed her legs together tight.

'Oh, man,' Mike said.

I didn't say anything.

Shanna must've spent some time under the sun in bikini pants. Very skimpy ones. Her skin had narrow pale strips slanting down from the hips toward the center, where the cords must've run into a bit of fabric not a whole lot larger than an eyepatch. Her skin there was white, stubbled with golden bristles.

'Turn around,' Mike told her.

She let out a shaky sigh, then followed orders.

I was glad she did. I couldn't have taken it, staring much longer at her front. This gave me a chance to calm down some.

Her back was tanned all the way down to the pale strips from her bikini cords. The seat must've been no more than about four inches across at the top and tapered down from there, covering the crease of her rump but not a lot more than that. The smooth, firm mounds of her buttocks were mostly tanned. I like a nice tan. But I found my eyes drawn mostly to the area that hadn't been touched by the sun.

'Okay,' Mike said. 'Face us again.'

She did.

'Now get down on your back and spread your legs.'

'No!'

If she did that, I'd lose it for sure. Besides, making her do that seemed really low. 'Come on, Mike,' I said.

'You wanta see her pussy, don't you?'

I could already see it. So could Mike. 'We shouldn't be doing this,' I said. 'We shouldn't be doing any of this.'

'Don't be such a wuss.'

'She's done enough.'

'You promised,' she said.

'Promised what?'

'If I took off my pants, you'd let me out. You said no more messing around.'

'Did we say that?' Mike asked.

'Yeah, we did.'

'Who's side are *you* on?'

'We gave her our word.'

'So what?'

'So plenty.'

He sneered at me. Facing Shanna, he said, 'Okay. Just come over here.'

She shook her head.

'No?'

'No.'

Mike looked at me and raised his eyebrows. 'Is that too much to ask?'

In spite of our promise, I wanted Shanna to come closer. 'I don't guess so. Come on over here,' I told her.

'No!'

'Shall we leave now?' Mike asked me.

'Sure,' I said. 'Let's go.'

'All right!' She stepped over the canteen. Her foot landed on the chocolate bar, but she didn't seem to notice. She walked slowly toward us, the patches of sunlight sliding along her skin, her breasts hardly jiggling or bouncing at all. Halfway across the cage, she stopped.

'Closer,' Mike said.

'This is close enough. I'm not taking another step until you've busted that lock off.'

'Unless we start to leave, right?' I'm the one who said that.

'You won't leave,' she said.

'We will if we feel like it,' I told her. 'You'd just better do what we tell you.'

'If I come any closer, you can reach me through the bars.'

'Maybe that's the point,' Mike said.

'Yeah.'

'You guys wanta touch me.' It wasn't a question.

'I guess it's crossed *my* mind,' Mike said.

I laughed, but it came out sounding funny.

'Of course, we could always drive away,' Mike said. 'Is that what you want?'

She gave us a twitchy smile. 'There's only one way you'll ever get your hands on me. That's to open the cage.'

Mike and I glanced at each other.

'I think we'd better open it,' he said.

'What're we waiting for?'

Then he grinned at Shanna. 'You wouldn't have the key on you?'

'Oh, yeah. Sure.'

'Guess we'll have to do it the hard way.'

He started by slipping his tire iron between the shackle and the case. He braced the end of the rod against the door's steel frame for leverage, and shoved down with all his weight.

The lock didn't give. But he didn't quit. He rammed the rod down again and again. Then he sat in front of the lock, feet against the bars, and jerked the rod again and again until he was huffing and drenched with sweat.

Shanna stood silent, watching. She nibbled her lower lip. She rubbed her open hands against her thighs. She looked plenty nervous. Maybe she was worried that we wouldn't be able to get the lock off. Maybe she was worried that we would.

I only looked at her once in a while. Because my eyes wouldn't stay on her face. And where they went got me too worked up. So I spent most of the time watching Mike.

Finally, he flopped backward with the tire tool across his belly and lay there, panting.

'Move,' I told him.

He scooted out of my way. I crouched and whacked the door hasp just above the padlock's shackle. I only hit it once, though. The way it rang out and my hatchet hopped off, I decided that I might have better luck dealing with the padlock. So I started bashing the lock with the blunt side of my hatchet. Sometimes I missed, but mostly I hit its case.

With each blow, the lock rebounded with a wild bounce and I had to wait for it to settle down. I must have struck fifty times before taking a breather. I stood back and wiped sweat out of my eyes. The shackle was still inside its hole, but the body of the lock looked really battered and caved in.

'I think we've almost got it,' I gasped. 'Give me the tire iron.'

Mike handed it to me.

I positioned it the same way he'd done, held it steady with my left hand, and struck it near the top with my hatchet. One hit. Another. On the third, the case dropped a bit and swiveled, loose at one side.

'My God!' Mike blurted. 'You got it!'

'Yep.'

I tossed the hatchet and tire iron aside. As I slipped the lock off the door hasp, I looked up at Shanna.

She had moved, was squatting near the other side of the cage, her back to us as she picked up her clothes.

'Me first,' Mike whispered.

He pushed me out of the way, threw open the cage door, and rushed in. Shanna only had time to glance over her shoulder before he was on her. He grabbed her from behind, hoisted her up, and rammed her straight forward. Her head pounded the bars. He swung her around and let go. She hit the floor hard, rolled a couple of times, and came to rest on her back, sprawled out and gasping.

It had happened very fast. I had watched, stunned. Now I shouted, 'Mike! Christ!'

He looked startled. He blinked at me. 'Just watch and enjoy. You're next.' He stepped between her legs, dropped to his knees and lunged forward, shoving his face into her groin.

'Don't,' Shanna muttered. Her voice was really feeble. 'No.' She tried to reach down for him, but her arm didn't make it and fell.

'Stop!' I shouted, rushing into the cage.

He raised his head and turned it toward me. He was all wet and shiny around the mouth.

I stopped right beside him.

'Leave her alone. I'm serious.'

'She wants it, man. Fuck. Don't be a wuss.' He got up to his knees and unbuckled his belt.

'You hurt her. That wasn't part of the deal.'

'What deal?'

'Damn it, Mike!'

'You wanta go first? Is that it? Okay, be my guest.' He stood up and stepped backward. 'Help yourself.'

I shook my head.

'Look at her. Look at her!'

I did. Her eyes were squeezed shut, her face contorted with pain. She was gasping for breath. Her breasts rose and fell. They were shiny with sweat. She was shiny all over, splashed with sunlight. Her legs were wide apart.

'Have at her,' Mike said.

'I can't.'

'Fuck her, man! Do it!'

'Fuck you,' I said.

'You feeling sorry for her? Shit, man, she called you a retard. Remember? A moron and a retard.'

'Yeah, I know. But . . .'

'So ream her! Ream her out!'

'I can't.'

'Forget it. I'll go first.'

He took a step toward her, but I blocked the way.

'Move.'

'No way.'

'I mean it.'

'We aren't gonna do this.'

'Like hell.' He pulled his knife. He shoved it toward my face.

'Go ahead and use it. Kill me. That's the only way you're gonna get at her.'

'You're asking for it.'

'If you're gonna kill me, do it.'

For a long time, we faced each other. I really figured he might go ahead and slash my throat. Hell, I knew how he felt. I wanted her, too. Or I *had* wanted her until Mike drove her head into the bars. It had changed, then, somehow. When I'd looked down at her, sprawled out all exposed and hurting and vulnerable, barely conscious, she'd stopped being a thing I ached to grope and fuck. Stopped being a collection of sweaty breasts, jutting nipples, and pussy. Instead, she was a person, a girl named Shanna who didn't deserve any of this.

Corny, huh?

Sue me.

'This is nuts,' Mike finally said.

'Yeah. I know.'

Grimacing, he shoved his knife back inside its sheath. He said, 'Shit.'

I stuck out my hand.

He scowled at it. Then reached out and shook it. 'You're such a fucking wuss.'

All of a sudden, I felt really good. Buoyant, in fact. Have you ever been in a bad earthquake? This is how you feel after it's over and you realize the house hasn't come down on your head. You're trembling and weak, and so glad it's over that you damn near feel drunk.

'Don't know what you're grinning about,' Mike said. 'We just blew the chance of a lifetime.'

'More than likely,' I said.

He shook his head.

We stepped over beside Shanna. She blinked up at us.

'We aren't going to do anything to you,' I said.

'That's right,' Mike muttered.

'We'll leave the door open and go back to our car. You're free.'

Shanna started to weep.

We left the canteen and chocolate bar in the cage with her, picked up the hatchet and tire iron, and walked through the woods to the car.

About half an hour later, just after Mike said, 'She isn't coming,' Shanna walked out of the trees.

She'd put her clothes on. The canteen swung by her side.

She poked the last of the chocolate bar into her mouth, and was still chewing when she reached the car.

'You guys wanta give me a lift?' she asked.

'Where to?' I asked.

'Wherever you're going.'

'You'll have to ask Mike,' I said. 'It's his car.'

'You drive,' he told me.

We switched places. Shanna, standing by the open passenger door, stared at Mike for a second. Then she whapped the top of his head. Quite hard. 'You're still an asshole.'

'Do you want a ride or don't you?'

Shanna climbed in and sat on his lap. She pulled the door shut. 'Let's get outa here.'

And that's what we did.

We never found out who'd put Shanna in the cage, or why.

Maybe a bunch of guys showed up that night only to find themselves robbed of their fun. Maybe not. Maybe she'd been locked up for some other reason.

By someone who just wanted rid of her.

By someone with good intentions who hoped to save the world from her evil.

Maybe she *was* the Devil, or a vampire, or a werewolf.

If so, she behaved herself around Mike and me. I won't go so far as to say she was an angel. Sometimes, she could be a real pain in the butt.

Which isn't all that unusual for a girl.

But she stayed with us for eight days and nights. Not once did she sprout horns and a tail, suck our blood or grow a hairy snout and rip out our throats. Not even when the moon was full.

We bought her a lot of stuff in the first town we found. Including clothes and a pack and a sleeping bag. She took all of it with her when we finally dropped her off at Half Moon Bay. But she never used the sleeping bag while she was with us.

She slept in ours. She took turns.

Somebody once said that no good deed goes unpunished. Whoever said that was nuts.

The Direct Approach

'I was about to leave.'

'I'll only take a few minutes of your time, Mrs Morton.'

'Miss,' she corrected. 'It's Miss.'

'*Miss* Morton.'

'You got my name from the mailbox, right?'

'That's very astute, Miss Morton, very astute. If I might have a few moments of your time?'

'I really should be leaving.' She started to shut the door, but the man's black case blocked it. 'Will you please remove your sample case?'

'Miss Morton, I'm offering you the opportunity of a lifetime.'

'What are you selling?'

'If I might just step inside for a moment?'

'I really don't think I'd be interested, Mr . . .'

'Snye. Marvin Snye. It'll be worth a great deal to you.'

'Just what *are* you selling?'

He smiled. His mouth was too red, his teeth too white, his hair too slick and black. 'Miss Morton, I'm in the mortality business.'

'Cemetery plots?'

'No, no. Hardly that. The firm I represent deals in discreet homicide.'

Peggy Morton's heart raced.

'Murder?'

'Precisely.'

'You're kidding me.'

'I'm quite serious, Miss Morton.'

Shutting her eyes, she rubbed her temples. 'I . . . I don't know. Murder? Okay, let's hear what you've got to say.' She opened the door wide. 'Come in.'

Marvin Snye stepped into her house. He looked slight in his gray suit. His face looked white except for the slash of his mouth. He sat on the couch. Peggy hoped he wouldn't lean back; his hair, she was certain, would leave a dark smudge on the upholstery.

'You may be wondering, Miss Morton, about the exact nature of the service I'm making available to you.'

'You might say that.' She smiled nervously, and sat on a chair facing him.

'I represent the firm Futures Unlimited. We believe that the future lies in the hands of the strong, Miss Morton, in the hands of those individuals with the courage to make it theirs. If you're that kind of person – and I think you are – then you may find our service perfectly suited to your special needs.'

She cleared her throat. 'What do you do, exactly?'

'I'm glad you asked that question. It shows you're a woman who likes the direct approach, and so do I. You believe in confronting situations head-on, don't you?'

'Usually, yes.'

He smoothed his hair, then glanced at his hand as if to see whether anything had rubbed off. 'Our firm believes,' he explained, 'that situations arise from time to time that cannot be solved by conventional means. For a modest sum, we remove those obstacles, those irritants which stand in the way of a more satisfying life for our customers – often with astounding results. If I may?'

He lifted the black case onto his lap, opened it, and took out a leaflet.

'Allow me to read you comments from a few of our satisfied customers.' From the back of the leaflet, he read, '"When I was recently passed over for a promotion, I was truly despondent. Futures Unlimited changed all that. I am now vice-president of a major manufacturing company, and have a brilliant career ahead of me. My gratitude goes to you."

'And here's another. I'm sure you'll appreciate this one. "The old goat simply wouldn't pass on. I thought he'd live for ever, and I was penniless. You did good. You're worth every red cent." We get all kinds, don't we, Miss Morton?' He grinned, and chuckled softly.

'One more? "My husband was a drunken brute. Futures Unlimited worked wonders for my peace of mind." I think that speaks for itself, doesn't it? I have many others in a similar vein, but these ought to be sufficient to indicate the positive response of our customers.

'Now, Miss Morton, tell me this: is there someone in either your personal or professional life whom you feel to be an obstacle, a nuisance, a threat?'

'Yes,' she said. 'Yes, there sure is.'

'Wonderful. I'm sure you'll be totally satisfied with our handling of the matter.'

'What will it cost?'

'Five thousand dollars. Twenty-five hundred in advance, the rest to be paid in full upon completion of the task.'

'That's an awful lot, isn't it?'

'We *do* offer a five percent discount if you agree to provide a testimonial for advertising purposes. An additional fifteen percent discount is available if you purchase two disposals. That would mean, in effect, that you could purchase each for a mere $4,000.'

'I'd only want one.'

'With the testimonial?'

'I guess that'd be okay.'

'It would come to $4,750.'

'That's still awfully steep.'

'Frankly, I'm disappointed to hear you say that, Miss Morton.' He shook his head with regret.

'I'm sorry,' she said.

'If you shop around, you'll find that our fees are entirely reasonable. Certainly, you *could* have the job done for less, but you would invariably be dealing with amateurish thugs. Highly dangerous. In matters as sensitive as this, you would be unwise to settle for anything less than the very best. And we, at Futures Unlimited, *are* the best. We offer you complete confidentiality and prompt, efficient service of the highest professional quality. Naturally, the best costs a little more.'

'Naturally.'

'Now, shall we get down to basics?' He took a gold-plated pen from his shirt pocket, and a note pad from his suit coat. 'Your name?'

'Margaret Morton.'

'Address including zip code?'

She gave it to him. He scribbled in the notebook, never looking up.

'Occupation?'

'Police officer.'

The pen stopped. His lips formed a sickly smile. 'You are joking, of course.'

'Of course.'

'I'm certain you realize, if you are a police officer, that a charge of conspiracy to commit murder requires an overt act?'

'I'm not a cop.'

'All we have done so far is – fantasize.' He cleared his throat. 'Occupation?'

'Salesperson.'

'Employer?'

'Western Cosmetics.'

'Annual income?'

'Is that necessary?'

'I'm afraid so. We need to—'

'About thirty thousand.'

'Very good, Miss Morton. Now, I'll need the name of the subject.'

'Steve Hayes. H-A-Y-E-S.'

'Address?'

'This address.'

'Oh?'

'He lives here.'

'When can he be found at this location?'

'Every evening. He gets home from work at a quarter-past five, and leaves at ten-after seven in the morning.'

'Weekends off?'

'Yes.'

'Very good. Now, Miss Morton, what would you like me to put down as your motive?'

'What?'

'Your motive. Your reason for wanting Futures Unlimited to remove this man from your life.'

'He's been stepping out on me,' she muttered.

Marvin Snye shook his head. 'If I may say so, Miss Morton, it's difficult to believe that a man could find any woman more beautiful and alluring than you.'

'Thank you.' She squirmed under the man's watery gaze. 'You want a snapshot of him or something?'

'That would be very helpful.'

'Just a moment.' Peggy went to the front door where she'd left her purse. She removed her wallet, opened it, and took out a color photo. 'Here's one,' she said. She brought it to the couch and handed it to him.

'Very good. Excellent. This will be of considerable help. Now, if you'll just sign here?' He held out his pen.

Peggy took it. 'What's this you want me to sign?'

'Your agreement to provide a testimonial at the completion of our task. It will mean a saving to you in the amount of $250.'

'Okay.' She scanned the document. 'I'll bet you get a lot of business.'

'We do quite well.' He smiled with pride. 'I've just been transferred from back east to handle this region, and I certainly find my hands full.'

'I guess there's lot of people around who want somebody dead.'

'Almost everyone. Of course, many can't pay the price we ask and others haven't the moral courage to deal with us. Still, I've managed to sign up half a dozen prospects within the past week.' He fondly patted his notebook. 'Now, if you'll sign right here?'

She signed.

'We'll require cash, of course, for the down payment.'

'Of course. But I don't keep that much in the house. I'll have to make a withdrawal from my savings account.'

'I'll be more than happy to pick it up at your convenience. When would that be?'

She grinned down at him.

'Miss Morton?'

'How about never?'

'Miss Morton, really, I fail to . . .'

'I won't pay you a single cent. How do you like that, sleazoid?'

His face went red. 'I fail to see . . .'

He tried to duck away as Peggy thrust the pen at his throat, but he wasn't quick enough. It punched in deep.

'Amateurish thugs, huh?'

She looked at the blood spilling onto her couch and groaned. Cutthroat competition could get *so* messy.

Good Vibrations

Kim spread her blanket on the sand. She stepped onto the middle of it, set down her beach bag and pulled off her sneakers and socks. She placed her sneakers at two corners of the blanket in case the wind should pick up.

Then she unbuttoned her blouse.

She wondered who might be watching. The beach was hardly deserted. At least a dozen guys – some playing volleyball, a few tossing Frisbees, others sunbathing alone or with friends or families or lovers – had turned their heads to inspect her as she'd made her way along the beach in search of an empty place to put down her blanket. Some would be staring at her now, eager to watch the clothes come off.

The beach was aswarm with beautiful young women in scanty swimsuits, but most of the guys within range would have their eyes on Kim. Because she was the one still wearing a blouse and shorts. And they wanted to watch her strip.

She'd come to the beach often enough to know how they were.

Right now, any number of men were staring at her back, aware that she'd unbuttoned her blouse, waiting for her to slip it off her shoulders. Most, she suspected, hoped that by some miracle of recklessness or mischance she'd left the top of her swimsuit elsewhere.

Sorry to disappoint you, fellas, she thought.

She removed her blouse, dropped it to the blanket, then quickly pulled down her shorts and stepped out of them. That should pretty much end the suspense for her audience. Now, she was just another gal in a string bikini. She hadn't forgotten to wear a suit, after all. And it wasn't transparent. And it hadn't fallen apart to give them a thrill.

The guys could turn their attention to other matters.

Some, of course, were bound to keep on watching. There were always a few of those.

It's just part of coming to the beach, Kim told herself. You know you'll be stared at and admired. You know you'll be getting some guys turned on. Like it or not, that's the way it is.

Relax and enjoy yourself.

Clasping her hands behind her head, she stretched. She shut her eyes, arched her back, rose onto tiptoe, clenched her buttocks, and moaned with the good feel of her straining muscles. She sniffed the fresh, briny air. She heard the surf roaring in and washing out, the squeals of seagulls and children, laughter and shouts, rock 'n' roll and rap and country music and the manic voices of DJs from nearby radios. She felt the heat of the sun. She relished the way the soft, cool breeze stirred her hair and roamed over her bare skin.

This is really the life, she thought. It doesn't get much better than this.

It would be better without the bikini, she thought.

And laughed softly.

The fellas would *really* have something to look at, then.

No way.

Kim opened her eyes. Even through the tinted lenses of her sunglasses, the gleam of the sunlit waves was so bright that she was forced to squint. Some kids were playing in the surf. A couple of lovers strolled by, the foam sliding over their feet. A man in skimpy trunks ran past them, muscles leaping, bronze skin flashing.

He didn't look toward Kim. After he'd run by, she watched his back, the way his buttocks flexed under the tight sheath. She was still watching him when she noticed the young man stretched out on the sand a couple of yards off to her left.

He lay on his belly, arms folded under his face. His head was turned toward her. He wore a strange pair of goggles. They didn't look at all like swimming goggles. They were leather, with small round lenses, the green glass of the lenses so dark that she couldn't see his eyes at all. She felt certain that they were open, though. Open and staring at her.

He'd probably been one of those spying on her from the start.

She frowned at him. 'What're *you* looking at?'

He didn't answer. He didn't move. Playing possum.

No point in getting upset, Kim told herself. He has a right to be here. And there's no law against looking at me.

Not even if you are wearing weird goggles.

Something else seemed wrong about him, though.

Something more than the goggles and the sneaky way he was ogling her.

For one thing, she realized, he was sprawled on the actual sand; he had no towel or blanket under him. He didn't have a shirt or shoes. Instead of a real swimsuit, he wore faded cut-off blue jeans.

He didn't look wet at all, so he hadn't simply come wading out of the water and flopped here to let the sun dry him.

His beltless jeans hung so low that the top of his crease showed. A seat pocket was torn loose at one corner, and Kim could see skin through the hole.

The skin there seemed as tanned as the rest of him.

Look who's staring now, Kim thought.

She knew she ought to turn away from him. In those goggles, he just *had* to be a space cadet. She certainly didn't want him to get the impression that she might be interested in him.

All you need is a guy like this deciding to put moves on you.

He's gotta be a nutcase.

But a good-looking one, from what she could see of him. Muscular, slim, with smooth skin tanned a shade darker than the sand and bare all the way down past his hips where his cut-offs hung carelessly low. Or intentionally low. Maybe he wanted her to notice the sleek curve of his back and how it rose to the mounds of his buttocks. Wanted her to think about him being naked under the faded, torn denim.

Kim swung her gaze to his face. It rested on his crossed arms. Those goggles were so damn queer. He might be quite handsome, but who could tell with his eyes out of sight? His hair was cinched in against his head by the leather strap, but neatly trimmed, gleaming like gold, blowing a little in the breeze.

He looked as if he might be a few years younger than Kim. Still a teenager, for sure.

That might explain why he wore the goggles. Teenaged guys often seemed to take a perverse pride in being strange. They enjoyed calling attention to themselves. Not only that, but they were constantly horny. He might be wearing the goggles just so he could spy on the girls in secret.

Maybe he isn't watching me.

Maybe he really is asleep.

His lips suddenly pursed out. Kissed at her twice.

Kim flinched. She turned away fast, knelt on her blanket and stuffed her blouse and shorts into her beach bag.

Her heart was thumping.

He'd been watching her all along, knew she'd been staring at him, the creep.

Those kissing gestures! Only a jerk would do something like that. They'd been like a crude remark – 'kiss my ass', or 'suck me off'.

Or maybe he'd meant nothing of the kind. Maybe he'd only wanted to suggest he wouldn't mind kissing her.

Whatever, it was damned embarrassing.

Kim wondered if she ought to pick up her things and move to a different section of beach. She didn't want to do that, though. She'd been here first. At least, she *thought* she'd been here first. She certainly hadn't noticed him when she'd picked this spot, or she wouldn't have put her blanket down so close to him.

No, he'd come along afterwards. He must've snuck over and flopped nearby to watch the strip show.

Maybe while I was spreading the blanket.

This is where I stay, she decided. I'm not about to let him scare me off.

Scare me off?

I'm not scared. Why should I be? He might be a weirdo, but so what? It's not like he can *do* anything to me, not with so many people around.

All he can do is look. So what?

Let him look to his heart's content.

Jerk-off.

Scared of him. Right. Sure.

Kim dug into her beach bag and pulled out a plastic

bottle of suntan oil. She moved the bag out of her way. Then she turned around slowly. Though trembling a bit, she felt quite pleased with herself as she taunted him with a good frontal view of her body shifting and twisting inside the bikini.

Turning you on, goggle eyes?

She resisted a sudden temptation to make kisses at him.

That might start something.

So she kept her face toward the water, stretched out her legs, and uncapped the bottle of suntan oil. She squirted a thin stream of warm fluid down the top of each leg to the ankle. The oil gleamed in the sunlight, tickled her as it started to dribble. She set the bottle aside. With open hands, she spread the oil over her shins and knees. Then her thighs. She lingered on her thighs, sliding her hands slowly up and down and between them, slicking her skin all the way to the edges of the blue patch that stretched down from its low cord and hugged her like a narrow, glossy membrane.

Catching all this, Goggles?

Eat your heart out.

Done with her legs, she squirted oil into the palm of her right hand and slicked her belly, fingertips drifting along the cord that slanted down from high on both hips. Her hand drifted over the cord, then came up for more oil. This she spread over her sides and across her ribcage below her bikini top.

She oiled her shoulders and arms next. She grinned to herself as she did it.

Make him wait for the grand finale.

She took off her sunglasses. Eyes shut, she carefully dabbed oil on her face.

Bet I'm driving him nuts.

He's probably *already* nuts, or he wouldn't be wearing those idiotic goggles.

Kim put her sunglasses back on, then filled her hand with oil and began to rub it on her chest. She caressed herself, enjoying the hot slippery feel of her skin and savoring the way she must be tormenting the kid. He had to be watching, had to be wishing this was *his* hand sliding between her breasts and stroking their bare sides.

One hand at a time, she eased her fingers beneath the cords that suspended the garment from her neck. She smoothed oil over the top of each breast. She went in under the clinging fabric and brushed her fingertips over nipples already turgid and jutting.

Bet you never expected a show like this, dipshit.

Right hand still inside her top, oily fingers sliding on her nipple, she turned her head for a glance at her spectator.

He was gone.

Nothing there except the shallow imprint his body had pressed into the sand.

Where the hell'd he go?

Kim slipped her hand out from under the bikini and scanned the beach. She looked from side to side. She swept her gaze across the shoreline and the surf. She even twisted her head around to search the area behind her.

She saw plenty of people, even a few guys wearing cut-offs instead of swimsuits. Nobody was near enough, fortunately, to have enjoyed a ringside seat for her show. But the goggled kid who was supposed to be only a few feet away, who was supposed to be agonizing over her, was nowhere to be seen.

The bastard bailed out on me!

Good, she told herself. I didn't come here to get ogled by some freak.

Damn it! How could he just get up and walk away?

Must be gay. No other explanation. A straight guy would've stayed or come over and put moves on me.

Unless he left just to piss me off.

I'm not pissed off.

I'm glad he's gone. Good riddance. I didn't come here to get pestered by some freaky teenager.

Kim capped the bottle of oil. Her hands were trembling. Calm down, she told herself. He's gone. Now you can just forget about him and enjoy yourself.

Twisting around, she propped the bottle against her beach bag. Then she lay down. She closed her eyes. She shifted about on her blanket, snuggling against the sand to shape it with the curves of her body.

She took a deep breath that pushed her breasts more tightly into the bikini's smooth, hugging pouches. She liked the feel of that. She liked the feel of the sun's heat and the way the mild breeze brushed over her skin like gentle fingertips.

It's wonderful, she thought. It's perfect, now that the creep is gone.

Almost perfect. She didn't like the way a lump in the sand pressed against her rump. She squirmed until it settled into the groove between her buttocks.

Probably a beer bottle left behind by some damn litterbug. She thought about getting rid of it. But that would take so much effort: crawling off the blanket, moving it out of the way, digging into the sand, and then she'd have to *touch* the thing. Somebody else's garbage. Probably filthy. It might not even *be* a bottle. Might be an old bone, or something. Yuck. Forget it.

Besides, it didn't really cause any discomfort now. In fact, it felt rather good. She gave it a squeeze with her buttocks.

I ought to roll over and get the most out of it, she thought.

But she had already oiled her front. And she felt too lazy and contented to move. She yawned. She stretched. She snuggled down against the sand and the bump, and soon she fell asleep.

In her dream, the young man in goggles knelt between her legs and slid his hands up her thighs. 'I knew you'd come back,' she told him. 'I knew you wanted me,' he said. She laughed and said, 'Don't flatter yourself.' He smiled. Then he ducked low and licked her. From the feel of his tongue, she realized her bikini bottom was gone. She looked down at herself. The top was missing, too. Gasping, she flung up her hands and covered her breasts. His mouth went away. 'It's all right,' he said. 'Nobody's watching.' She said, 'I'll just bet.' He opened his button and slid the zipper down. 'Would I do this?' he asked, 'if we had an audience?' He let the cut-offs fall to his knees. 'My God,' Kim muttered. 'All for you,' he said. She let her arms fall to her sides. Bending down, he kissed and licked her breasts. He sucked on them. She moaned and writhed. Then she gasped, 'No, wait.' He lifted his head. He smiled down at her and licked his glistening lips. 'What?' he asked. 'I don't even know you.' He answered, 'That's all right. You want me. That's all that matters.' She shook her head. 'I don't care about your name,' she told him. 'But I need to *see* who you are. It's like you're hiding from me behind those stupid goggles.' He smiled again. 'Help yourself.' Easing forward, he lowered himself onto her. As the length of his hot body pressed against her and his tongue slipped between her lips, she reached up and pushed the goggles to his forehead.

He had no eyes.

Empty sockets. Dark, bloody pits.

Kim yelped and pushed him away and flinched awake as she bolted upright. Sweat spilled down her body. She sat there, gasping for breath. A dream. It had just been a dream. A real doozy.

A great dream, there for a while. But those *eyes*!

Yeah. What eyes?

'Man,' she murmured. 'What's wrong with me, imagining something like that?'

She leaned back, braced herself up with stiff arms, and rolled her head to get the kinks out of her neck.

And saw him.

He'd returned.

He lay stretched out on the sand a few feet away, but on her right. He'd switched sides. Like before, however, his head rested on his folded arms, turned toward her. Like before, he wore the strange round goggles that hid his eyes behind their dark green lenses.

If he's *got* eyes, Kim thought.

She realized she was grimacing.

'Something wrong?' he asked.

'Yeah. You. What're you doing here?'

'Enjoying the beach.'

'It's a big beach. Why don't you go somewhere else?'

'I like it here. A very beautiful view.'

'Yeah? I thought maybe you were blind, or something.'

He smiled, showing straight white teeth. Then he rolled over and sat up and turned to face her. As he crossed his legs, he brushed sand off his shoulders and chest. 'You were asleep a long time,' he said.

'And I suppose you were watching me.'

'You looked like you were having a nightmare.'

'Why do you wear those stupid goggles?'

'They keep the sand out of my eyes.'

'They make you look like a dork.'

'Sorry.' A corner of his mouth turned up. Then he raised his hands to the sides of his goggles.

Kim's heart gave a lurch. Her stomach seemed to fall. She lost her breath.

'No,' she gasped. 'You don't . . .'

Too late.

He lifted the goggles to his forehead.

And Kim found herself staring at a pair of eyes as blue as the sky, with long silken lashes. They seemed amused, knowing, gentle.

He's gorgeous!

'Is that better?' he asked.

'A lot better,' Kim said. Her voice came out husky, barely making its way through the tightness in her throat.

'My name's Sandy,' he said. Smiling, he shook his head. Some sand came out of his fine, glossy hair, sprinkling his shoulders, falling past his face.

'You're sandy, all right,' Kim said.

'Named after Koufax.'

'Ah. I'm Kim.'

'Pleased to meet you, Kim. But you're going to burn that lovely skin if you don't turn over pretty soon.'

She eased herself down and rolled onto her side. Facing him. Very aware of how her breasts shifted within the flimsy, yielding patches of her bikini.

'If I turn over,' she said, 'my back will burn. Unless you'd like to help me.'

'Help you?'

'With the suntan oil.'

'Ah. I suppose I could do that.'

'Thanks.' She rolled off her side and stretched out. She crossed her arms beneath her face. And watched Sandy gaze at her as she squirmed on the blanket to smooth and shape the sand. She remembered the lump that had been pressing up against her, earlier. She didn't feel it now.

She stopped moving.

Sandy just sat there.

'Well?' she asked. 'Coming over?'

He shook his head. Some more sand fell from his hair. 'I've got a better idea,' he said. 'Why don't you come over here?'

Suddenly playing control games?

Maybe he just wants to watch me stand up and walk, wants to enjoy the bod in motion.

'My blanket's here,' she said.

'That's what I mean. You don't need it. It's in the way. You should be on the sand.'

'I'd get it all over me.'

'Shower afterwards.'

She stared into his wonderful eyes. He's seeing me naked in a shower, she thought. Maybe seeing himself *with* me under the spray. Soaping me.

She pushed herself up. She clutched the slippery bottle of suntan oil and crawled off the blanket. Crawled toward him, head up, watching him, the hot sand sinking under her hands and knees. It was a shame he couldn't see how her breasts swayed, but he must have a nice view of her back, bare except for the two tied cords that held her top on and the third that descended from her hips to the narrow sheath clinging to her buttocks.

She stopped in front of his crossed legs. She pushed herself up. Kneeling, she held out the bottle.

He took it from her.

'Here?' she asked.

'Here's fine.'

She turned aside and lay down flat. The sand felt almost hot enough to scorch her. After a few moments, she got used to the heat. She squirmed, enjoying the way the surface molded against her body.

'Doesn't that feel better than the blanket?'

'It's different.'

'It's like floating,' he said. 'Floating on a warm sea that

loves you. Feel how it hugs you? Feel how it holds every curve of you, every hollow?'

'I guess so.' It's nice, she thought, but it's not *that* nice. This guy may be gorgeous, but he's still a little weird. 'Are you going to oil my back for me?'

Smiling, he nodded. As he got to his knees and crawled to her, Kim swept her hair aside to bare the nape of her neck. She untied the cord there. She lowered its ends to the sand, then reached up behind her back and plucked open the bow at her spine.

'I don't want strap marks,' she explained.

'More like strings,' Sandy said.

'Now there aren't any strings in the way.' Kim folded her arms under her face. She stretched and wiggled. It felt very good to be free of the cords, exciting to know that her top was loose, held against her breasts by nothing more than the pressure of the cupping sand. 'I'll have to remember to stay down.'

'If you forget, I doubt that anyone would mind. I know I wouldn't.'

She trembled with delight as Sandy squirted a stream of warm oil across the backs of her shoulders and down her spine. Then his hands were on her, gliding, sliding. They drifted all over her back and sides. They spread the oil. They massaged her. They explored her, even roaming low enough to slick the sides of her breasts. When he did that, she raised herself slightly out of the sand. But he didn't take advantage of it, didn't reach into the space and fill his hand. He simply moved on and Kim, with a sigh, sank down again.

When his hands went away, she lifted her head and looked around. She found Sandy kneeling by her hip. He bent forward and squirted oil down both her legs. His cut-offs hung so low they looked as if they might fall off.

God, he's fantastic, she thought.

Then she was lost in the feel of him kneading her calves. She lowered her face against her arm and shut her eyes.

When he's done, she thought, maybe he'll let me oil him. That would be wonderful. But she would need to tie her top again and get up. She didn't want to do that. She liked being just where she was.

I couldn't get up if I wanted to, she thought.

And moaned as his hands worked their way up her thighs. Slid between them. Slicked her bare skin all the way to her groin, then went up and caressed her hips with oil before swirling over her buttocks. He rubbed them, squeezed them. But stayed away from the little that was covered, as if her bikini were a border he didn't dare cross.

Probably doesn't want to stain it with oil.

Or afraid people might be watching.

I've got to take him home with me, Kim thought. I've got to. Take him home to bed. He can oil me all over, and I'll oil him. It'll stain the sheets, but who cares?

Then he was done.

Kim let out a shaky breath. She opened her eyes, and watched Sandy crawl alongside her. He lay down, crossed his arms, and gazed into her eyes.

'That was great,' she whispered.

'My pleasure,' he said.

'I just wish nobody else was here. And we had the whole beach all to ourselves.'

'I know.'

'Would you like to come over to my apartment?'

He frowned slightly. 'I don't think so.'

You can't mean that, Kim thought. Please. 'There won't be anyone there. Only us.'

'I like it here.'

'We don't have to leave right away. We can stay as long as

you want.' She tried to smile. 'I'm not sure I'd be able to move right now, anyway. You've got me so . . . lazy and excited.'

'This is where I belong,' he said.

'Hey, come on.' That sounded a bit whiny. She struggled for control, then tried again. 'Don't you get it? I *want* you. I want us to make love.'

'So do I.'

'Well, then . . .'

Sandy drew the goggles down over his eyes. He straightened his arms overhead, then turned his face downward and pushed it into the sand.

'What're you . . .?'

He began to shake, his whole body shuddering, vibrating.

Kim raised her face. She gaped at him. 'Sandy? What're you doing?'

He didn't answer. He kept on quaking.

My God! He's having some kind of fit!

'Are you all right? What's wrong?'

Reaching out, she clutched his shoulder. It juddered in her grip. Then sand was pushing up around her fingertips.

My God! He's sinking!

She jerked her hand away.

The sand shivered around his palsied body, seemed to be melting beneath him, sucking him down. His arms were already gone. His face was buried past the ears.

His shoulders vanished competely. Sand spilled in across his lower back, trembled above his legs.

Gotta help him!

Kim almost thrust herself up, then remembered her loose top. She groped for the strings, found them in the sand beside her breasts, strained her arms up behind her back to tie them. Then let them fall again.

Because all that remained of Sandy was the seat of his cut-offs and the back of his head – the leather strap matting down his hair.

The goggles.

He's doing this on purpose.

It's what he does.

It's how he disappeared last time.

He's doing it because of me.

Now he was completely gone, leaving behind an imprint of his outstretched body in the sand.

Holy shit!

Kim looked around. Not far away, people were sunbathing. Others were sitting up, reading, talking. One group was having a picnic. A kid walked by with a bottle of soda.

Nobody was gazing, thunderstruck, at the patch of beach where Sandy had pulled his disappearing stunt.

Nobody had noticed.

Nobody knows but me.

Maybe it didn't happen, at all. A person can't just wiggle down like that and vanish. It's impossible.

But I *saw* it happen. And I'm not dreaming, now.

Reaching up behind her, Kim stroked the small of her back. Her hand came away slick.

I didn't dream him oiling me. I'm not dreaming any of this. He really buried himself. Somehow.

Her throat felt tight and tickly. She kept her mouth shut to hold in the scream or wild laugh that wanted to burst free. From her nose came a high-pitched humm.

It's crazy! Get the hell out of here!

She slapped her hands against the sand, ready to push herself up, then paused, wondering if she should tie her bikini first. No time to lose. Better to risk a little embarrassment than to delay her escape even for a . . . the sand beneath her breasts trembled.

Rubbed her.

My God!

All thoughts of fleeing dissolved as the sand shifted against her breasts and fell away. She felt them hanging free inside hollows. Then hands were cupping them, squeezing them gently. Warm, grainy hands on her bare skin. Kim didn't know what he'd done with her bikini top, but she didn't much care.

It's down there somewhere, she thought.

I can worry about it later.

Trembling, she crossed her arms beneath her face.

This is just too weird, she thought.

He's under me. Touching me. And nobody knows. It's our little secret. Our big secret.

How the hell can he breathe?

It's only been a minute or two, she thought. She'd heard of pearl divers who could stay under water for ever. Ten minutes? Fifteen?

This is incredible. Fabulous.

She writhed and moaned as the hands plied her breasts, stroked and pulled her nipples.

This is why he didn't want me on the blanket, she realized. So he could get to me.

Something hard nudged her groin.

Something like the mouth of a beer bottle buried in the sand.

Oh, Sandy! You devil!

It tore her breath away as it thrust.

Not here. Is he nuts?

I can't untie my bottoms. Somebody'd notice that, for sure. And I don't want sand in me.

Gasping and moaning as Sandy teased her breasts and pushed at the flimsy shield between her legs, she lifted her head. She began to sweep away the sand beneath her face. All she found was more sand.

'Where are you?' she whispered.

And scooped out more. And more. And uncovered his nose. Then his goggles. Then his lips. They were shut tight, a line of sand resting across the crease between them. Kim blew the sand away. She lowered her face into the depression and kissed them. They parted. His tongue pushed into her mouth. She sucked it, moaning.

The sand beneath her body began to shiver and slide.

His hands went away from her breasts, slid down to her hips, fingered the ties, plucked them open.

Don't. Somebody'll see.

But she didn't want to tell him no. Didn't want to pull her mouth away from his. Didn't want to stop what was happening. Because now she could feel all of Sandy. Somehow, he'd done away with the thickness of sand keeping them apart. And with his cut-offs.

Who does he think he is, Houdini?

She chuckled softly into his mouth.

He was long and hot against her oiled skin, smooth except for the rough grains that rubbed her as he shook.

He was shaking like crazy.

Vibrating.

It felt wonderful.

He didn't even stop shaking when he plucked the loose fabric and it slid down between her legs and away.

My ass is bare!

Everyone'll see!

Nobody'll see, she realized. It's all right.

Because sand was rushing in to cover her buttocks. It felt wonderful like warm water flooding down, caressing her bare skin, licking into crevices.

Kissing her shut eyes. Dribbling into her ears.

She realized her face was buried. But she could still breathe. No sand was coming into her nostrils as she sucked air. Couldn't get in between their faces. Not yet. And this shouldn't take long.

As Sandy pushed up at her, she tried to spread her legs wider. The sand held them motionless.

He thrust into her, anyway.

Big and thick and sandy.

Quivering in a frenzy deep inside her while his tongue plunged deeper into her mouth and his lips vibrated against her lips and the tremors of his chest rubbed and shook her breasts and his belly and pelvis and thighs all buffeted her with their mad fluttering.

How does he do this?

Doesn't matter how.

All that mattered was how it felt to be pinned down by the heavy sand, naked against his shuddering body, filled with him, lost in the feel of him.

She gasped into his mouth and quaked.

Sandy jumped in her depths, spurting.

Then he quit the wild shaking. He lay motionless beneath her.

We did it. My God, we actually did it here on the beach right in front of everyone . . . and nobody's the wiser.

His tongue began to slide out of Kim's mouth. She squeezed it between her lips, savoring the thickness of it. When it was gone, she kissed his mouth.

This was the best ever, she thought. I've got to bring him home with me.

She tried to lift her head.

The clutching sand held it firm.

Hey, come on.

'Sandy,' she whispered against his lips. 'Get us out of here.'

His quivering started again.

'Thanks,' she whispered.

Ride him up like an elevator.

Uh-oh, she thought. *Where's my bikini? I'll be popping up bare-ass.*

Then she realized that her beach blanket should be within reach. She could drag it over and cover herself, hide beneath it while she got into her shorts and blouse.

Then she felt sand sliding against her lips. Her next breath sucked dry particles into her nostrils.

Shit!

She blew out air to clear the passages, and held her breath.

Sandy!

Sand, not Sandy, was trembling beneath the length of her body. He was no longer pressed against her. But he was still in her. Hard and vibrating, slowly sliding out.

No!

She willed herself to reach down and grab hold before he was gone entirely. But the sand refused to let her arms move.

She clenched muscles around the retreating shaft. Hugged it, but couldn't stop it.

It went away.

Please! My God!

Don't get crazy, she thought. He'll be back. He's just fooling around, trying to throw a scare into me. Playing some kind of masculine control game. Wants to show me who's boss.

He can't just leave me here!

She tensed her muscles, made them shiver.

Two can play this game. If he can vibrate through the sand, so can I.

But the sand only squeezed her. Didn't slide away at all.

Her lungs began to burn.

She went limp.

He'll be back. He won't let me . . .

The sand began to shimmy beneath her trapped body.

I knew it! Thank God!

A pocket opened beneath her right breast.

A tongue slid against her nipple.

Damn it, Sandy! This is no time to fool around! I'm suffocating here!

She felt his lips, the edges of his teeth, his swirling tongue as he sucked her breast into his mouth.

You bastard! Get me out of here!

When his teeth snapped shut, Kim screamed.

When the scream was done and she gasped for air, sand filled her mouth.

Choking, on fire with agony, she struggled to shove and kick and buck, to get away from his teeth, to get free of the sand.

It clutched her, wouldn't let her move.

Held her for Sandy while he ate.

Phil the Vampire

'It's my husband,' she said.

'I see.'

'I don't think so.'

'Tell me about it, then.'

'He's . . . seeing other women.'

I nodded. It was what I'd figured.

The gal's name was Traci Darnell. She looked too young, too sweet, too terrific to have a husband stepping out on her. But all that doesn't matter if you're hooked with the wrong kind of guy. Some fellows don't care how good they've got it at home.

I'd seen it plenty of times before.

It never made much sense. It always made me a little sad, and more than a little disgusted.

'I'm sorry,' I told Traci.

'Well.' Her shoulders gave a quick, nervous hop. The rest of her didn't move at all, just sat rigid in the chair across from my desk, leaning forward slightly, hands folded on her lap. 'It's not as if . . . I mean, I knew what I was getting into.'

'What do you mean?'

'I knew there would be other women. A lot of them. I knew that going in. But . . .' She pinched her lower lip between her teeth. Her shoulders hopped again. 'I thought I could handle it. I thought it wouldn't matter. But it does.' Her eyes met mine. They were blue, intelligent, the sort of eyes that should gleam with fun. But they were grim. They made me want to hurt the guy responsible. 'I love him,' she said. 'I love him so much. It just . . . rips me apart. I can't stand it any more.' Her eyes brimmed.

'Are you sure he's seeing other women?' I asked.

She sniffed. 'Oh, he's never made any secret of it.'

'He admits it?'

'Admits? He doesn't *admit* anything, he *shares his experiences* with me. He tells me every detail of every conquest. Her name, what she looked like, what she was wearing – or not wearing – exactly where he had her. He tells me everything that was said. What she did, what he did. The feel of her, the smell of her, the taste.'

Leaning forward, I shoved a box of tissues closer to the edge of my desk. Traci plucked one out and blew her nose.

'Why did he tell you those things?' I asked. 'To rub it in? To make you squirm?'

'Oh, no. It wasn't anything like that. It was like I said, his way of sharing. He wanted me to know what was going on in his life, that's all. It was never meant to hurt me. He thought it would bring us closer.'

'Bring you *closer*? Telling you about the women he's . . .' I hesistated, reluctant to use any graphic terms in front of a gal who seemed so innocent and vulnerable.

'Sucked?' she suggested.

For a second there, I wondered if Traci had a lisp. 'Did you say "sucked"?' I asked.

'Sucked.'

'Sucked or fucked?'

Her face blushed scarlet. 'Ssssucked.'

'Oh. Sorry.' I felt my own face get hot. 'He told you about *sucking* these other women?'

'That's right. And he . . . he certainly didn't do that *other* thing.'

I couldn't see one whole hell of a lot of difference, myself. It seemed to me that Traci was splitting hairs.

Indignant, she said, 'He's never been unfaithful. He's not a lech, he's a vampire.'

I didn't miss a beat. 'Ah,' I said. 'I see.'

'Do you?' She looked hopeful.

'Sure. He's a vampire. He isn't having affairs with any of these women, he's just sucking their blood.'

'You really *do* understand?'

'Sure. *Dracula, Salem's Lot*, Lugosi and Christopher Lee, Barnabus Collins – you'd have to be culturally illiterate not to know a thing or two about vampires. And your husband's a vampire. What's his name, by the way?'

'Phillip.'

'Phil the vampire.'

I wished I hadn't said that. Traci looked betrayed.

'You think this is all a great big joke.'

'No. I really don't. Whatever's going on, it's obvious that you're . . .'

'I *told* you what's going on.'

'Well, not exactly.'

'Every night, he leaves me alone and goes off stalking victims. He drinks their blood. Then he comes home and *tells* me all about it. I hate it that he's seeing these other women ... that he *needs* them. It makes me feel so ... inadequate. You know, that *I'm* not enough for him.'

'No woman would be enough for his kind,' I said.

'Is that another wisecrack? Because if it is, I'm going to waltz right out that door and ...'

'I was being entirely serious,' I explained. 'As a vampire, he couldn't possibly subsist on your blood alone. You'd be depleted in no time flat. You'd be dead. Phil *has* to play the field. He would kill you otherwise. His roaming, actually, might be viewed as an act of love. Love for you.'

'I know that.' She looked ready to start weeping again. 'But that doesn't make it any easier ... to live with.'

'You're jealous of these women he sucks?'

'Of course I am.'

'Does he ever suck you?'

'Sometimes.' She dipped her fingers under the collar of her blouse and pulled it aside. Her top button came undone, but she didn't seem to notice. The side of her neck had a pair of wounds just where you'd expect to find them in a Dracula movie. Healed, though. Scar tissue that looked like small, pink craters.

Real or make-up? I wondered.

Only one way to find out. I knocked my chair back on its rollers, stepped around my desk, and crouched in front of Traci. Close up, the scars looked pretty authentic.

'Do they hurt?' I asked.

'No. They never did hurt. Not even when he had his teeth in me.'

'Getting bit like that didn't hurt?'

'Oh, no.' With a dreamy look on her face, she fingered the tiny remains of the punctures. 'It felt . . . incredible.'

I raised my index finger. 'Do you mind?'

Shaking her head, she moved her hand out of the way. I gently probed both the scars. They felt real, all right. 'Phil actually made these with his teeth? He actually sucked blood out of your neck?'

'Yes.'

While Traci straightened her collar, I stood up and sat on the front edge of my desk. She didn't fasten the button that had come undone.

'And you're here because you don't like him doing it to other women?'

'That's right.'

'Has Phil killed any of these women?'

'No. Oh, no, I'm sure he hasn't. He's not at all like – you know, Dracula. He's a kind, gentle man. He respects life.'

'Wouldn't harm a fly, huh?'

'Oh, he sometimes eats them. But he doesn't have a malicious bone in his body. He wouldn't kill a *person*. He's very careful never to harm anyone.'

'Is he taking their blood by force?'

She looked confused. 'Well, he's sucking it out.'

'But with their permission? Are they willing partners?'

'Oh, of course. Who wouldn't be? Phil's . . . a hunk, you know? And smart and witty. I think most women find him irresistible. But he also has his powers.'

'Powers?'

'What I mean is, he can pretty much zap the mind of anyone he meets. He has this hypnotic thing he can do. Puts them under.' Traci snapped her fingers. 'Just like that, they're zombies. Not *literally* zombies. You know what I mean.'

'He can put them into a trance, and they'll comply with whatever he wants.'

'Right. But also, the main thing is they can't remember anything afterwards.'

'And Phil uses this power on his victims?'

'I don't know if I'd call them victims.'

'Whatever. The women he sucks. He zaps them?'

'All the time. Not me, though.'

'Why's that?'

Her look suggested it was a dumb question. 'Because I'm his wife, of course.'

'Ah. All right. But here's the thing. If your husband is putting these women under – by hypnosis or whatever – he's compromising their ability to consent. In other words, he does not legally have their permission. If he was having sex with them . . .'

'He's not.'

'But if he *was* having sex with them, it would be rape. So I'm pretty sure he's violating some sort of law by biting them and taking their blood without permission. That would make it a police matter. I'm just a private investigator, and don't have the authority to—'

'I don't want Phil *arrested*!' Traci blurted, shaking her head. 'That's not why I came here. I don't want anything like that.'

'What exactly *do* you want?'

'I want him to stop. I want him all to myself. I want him to quit using all those others!'

The way she looked made me want to take her into my arms. To comfort her. To make her hurts go away. But I knew better. My self-control isn't always terrific when it comes to gals, especially the pretty, vulnerable ones. So I kept to my perch.

She gazed up at me with shiny, imploring eyes. 'Will you help me?' she asked.

'I'd like very much to help you,' I said. 'But maybe what you need is a shrink or . . .'

'A shrink? Are you saying I'm crazy?'

'Nothing of the sort. You obviously didn't put those bite marks on your own neck.' A moment after I'd said that, I wondered how she *might've* gone about putting them there. Self-inflicted wounds are a fairly common trick. Perps think them a very clever way to deceive cops, lawyers, doctors, insurance companies, and even PIs like me.

Traci might have made the punctures herself. Physical evidence to back up her weird tale. If she'd made them, though, she'd done some major advance planning. From the appearance of the scars, the injuries must've been inflicted at least a month ago.

Either she was a major-league schemer, or she was telling the truth – the truth as she saw it, anyway.

'The thing is,' I explained, 'a therapist might be better equipped to help you confront your problem.'

She studied me with narrowed eyes. 'My problem?'

'I want to help you, Traci. I honestly do. You wouldn't believe the creeps and losers and slimes that I have to deal with all the time – mostly attorneys. My clients. So I tell you, it really brightened my afternoon when you showed up. You seem to be a very nice young lady. Easy on the eyes, to boot,' I added.

She gave me a smirk for that one. And blushed as she smirked. And kind of rolled her eyes toward the ceiling in a way that said, *Boy, what a line.*

'I'll do what I can for you, Traci. But we won't do each other any good unless we're honest about the situation. I intend to be honest with you. It might not be pleasant, but it's how I work. Okay?'

'Okay.'

'Your problem. You come in here and tell me your husband's a vampire. Now, we all know about vampires. The living dead. They sleep in coffins during the day, prowl at night, suck the blood out of people. They've got magical powers. They can control people's minds, turn themselves into bats, wolves, fog, pretty much anything that suits their fancy. They're immortal – or as good as. Live hundreds of years, who knows? They're afraid of the cross, find garlic disagreeable. Their reflections don't show up in mirrors. They can't cross moving water. They can't be killed by ordinary means, you've gotta nail them with a wooden shaft. Or trick them into the sunlight. Probably other ways, but I'm no expert. I just know what every red-blooded American guy knows on the subject. Which includes that such things just don't exist.'

'That's what you think.'

'It's what I know, Traci. It's what everyone knows. I'm not saying there aren't weirdos who *think* they're vampires and maybe even act accordingly. But the actual supernatural-Dracula-immortal-batman-vampire is nothing but fiction. You just aren't gonna meet one, not in this life. That means Phil isn't one. That's for starters.'

'So, you are saying I'm crazy.'

'I told you. I'm not a shrink. I'm just a gumshoe, the poor man's Spade. What I'm doing here with you is trying to apply some tricks of my trade, and the best tricks I've got are my instincts and common sense.'

'So what do they tell you?'

'First, I don't think you're crazy. Second, I'm pretty sure you aren't trying to put one over on me. So I'm forced to conclude that Phil has convinced you he's a vampire.'

'He *is* a vampire.'

'He bit your neck and sucked your blood.'

She nodded. 'Many times.'

'He goes off by himself every night and comes back with stories of his conquests. Of women he entranced and sucked.'

'Yes.'

667

'And you believe him.' I gave one of my bushy eyebrows a meaningful hoist. 'Have you ever followed him during one of his nightly prowls?'

She frowned. 'You're saying it might all be a lie?'

'Do you have any proof that it isn't?'

'He sometimes comes home with blood on his clothes.'

'A *lot* of blood, or . . .'

'No, just a few little spots or smudges.'

I fished my Swiss Army knife out of my pants pocket, opened the main blade, and nicked the back of my hand. A dot of blood bloomed out. I blotted it on the front of my white shirt. 'Now I'm a vampire, too,' I said.

And Traci smiled. It was the first time I'd seen her smile. It looked great. 'You've ruined your shirt.'

'Hire me, and I can afford a new one.'

'Hire you?'

'That's why you came in here, right?'

'Well. Yes. I guess so.'

'We were exploring the nature of your problem, right? Your husband has convinced you he's a vampire. As a vampire, he needs to drink human blood. So he goes out and sucks women, and you're jealous. You want it stopped. You want him to devote all his attention on you, not spread it around among strangers.'

'That's pretty much it, I guess.'

'That's your problem. But here's the question: what's Phil *really* up to? You can bet it's not sucking necks.'

'You're saying . . . it might all be like a cover while he's doing something he doesn't want me to know about?'

'I say you can bet on it. He might just be boozing with his buddies, something as innocent as that. Or maybe he's into some kind of criminal activity. Could be anything. But I've got to warn you, the most likely thing is that he's seeing another woman.'

'That's what I *told* you. He's seeing another woman every night.'

'But not to suck blood. To have sex.'

'No.'

'I realize it's a painful—'

'It's not painful because I know he doesn't mess around with anyone.' Though she spoke calmly, her face was bright red. 'He *tells* me what he does to those women. Everything. Every small, intimate detail. And he . . . we . . . make out while he talks. We, you know, get naked. And then we fool around while he tells me all about the woman he'd been with that night, and when it comes to the part where he sinks his teeth into her, that's when he . . . sinks his, uh . . . that's when he enters me.'

She wasn't so much red, really, as pink. Her face, her ears, her throat, the smooth skin that showed between the edges of her blouse where the button was undone.

I had a bulge in my lap. I folded my hands down there to hide it.

Dry-mouthed, I said, 'So, he uses his stories to excite you. As a form of foreplay?'

'Something like that.'

'And the story always finishes with . . . intercourse?'

'Not always.' She gazed down at her own folded hands. 'Sometimes he . . . we . . . use our mouths. You know.'

'Oh.'

She raised her eyes. 'Anyway, so I guess you can see how come I know he's not having any affairs.'

'It may very well be that he's not. I hope he isn't, but obviously he's up to something. Something he means to keep secret from you, so he fabricated the vampire story.'

'I don't think it's a fabrication.'

'Does Phil have a job?'

'He doesn't need one. He's very rich.'

'What does he do during the day?'

'He sleeps. In his coffin. In the basement.'

That shouldn't have surprised me, but it did. Obviously, Phil was carrying his act to some rather major extremes.

'Have you ever seen him go outside in the sunlight?'

Traci shook her head. 'He never leaves his coffin from dawn till after sunset.'

'As far as you know.'

'Well, I don't stand guard, if that's what you mean.'

'What do *you* do during the day?'

'Sleep, do the shopping.' She shrugged. 'Different chores.'

'Do you look in on him often?'

'At first I did. I couldn't . . . you know, believe he'd stay down there so long. But he always did. It was a waste of time, checking on him. So I don't do it much any more.'

'So you can't say for sure whether he stays in the coffin.'

'Not absolutely for sure,' she admitted. 'But pretty sure. What's the big deal?'

'No big deal. Just curious. Have you ever seen Phil turn into a bat or anything?'

'He knows I can't stand bats.'

'Have you ever seen him change into . . .?'

'He changed into a dog once. A big black lab.'

Right, I thought. But I kept the opinion to myself and asked, 'He changed into it before your eyes?'

'Look, if you don't want to believe any of this . . .'

'I just want to get at the truth, that's all. If you actually watched Phil turn himself into a dog, I guess I'd have to believe he's got supernatural powers.'

'You wouldn't have to believe any such thing. You'd figure I was either lying or hallucinating, or that Phil had fooled me with some kind of magic trick.'

'Is Phil a magician?'

'He's a vampire.'

'Did you watch him turn into the dog?'

'No.'

'Then what makes you think . . .?'

'The dog was Phil.' She'd turned pink again. 'I know it was him.'

'How do you know?'

'Never mind. Can we change the subject?'

'All right. Let's change it to mirrors. Does Phil show up in mirrors?'

'Yes.'

I managed not to blurt, *Ah-ha!* But I couldn't help smiling. 'You've seen his reflection in mirrors.'

'Yes.'

'Well, doesn't that suggest a hole in his vampire story?'

'I asked him about it.'

'And?'

'He told me that mirrors aren't the same as they were in the old days. A lot of them used to be backed with silver, but that's pretty rare now. He said he wouldn't show up in a mirror that has a real silver backing. I don't have one like that, so I don't know.'

'Convenient for Phil.'

She frowned. 'You know, I've never felt any great need to *prove* he's a vampire. I know what he is. So I haven't gone around *testing* him.'

'If he's not a vampire, Traci, he has no excuse to go roaming at night.'

'I know that. I know that better than anyone.'

'If he's not a vampire, then he's not sucking those women you're so jealous of.'

'I know. But he *is* one.'

I let out a sigh. 'Then how do you expect me to stop him from seeing those other gals? He *needs* blood, right? If he doesn't take it from strangers, where's he supposed to get it?

He can't rely only on you. It'd kill you. Is that what you want?'

'No.'

'What *do* you want?'

Traci bent down and reached for her handbag. She had placed it on the floor beside her chair immediately after sitting down. It was a large leather bag with a shoulder strap. As she took hold of the bag, I glanced down the front of her blouse. She wore a pale blue bra that was too skimpy to cover much. What it did cover, it was too transparent to hide. What I could see was her entire right breast.

My view went away when Traci sat up, lifting the handbag onto her lap. She slipped her hand inside the top and came out with a wooden stake.

It looked like a foot-long section of broom handle that had been whittled with a knife until it tapered down to a point.

'You're kidding me,' I said.

She stared into my eyes.

'You want me to kill Phil?'

'It's the only way to stop him.'

'Terrific,' I muttered.

She handed the stake to me. I looked it over, thumbed its point. The point was very sharp.

'You said you wanted to help,' she reminded me.

'You've got the wrong guy.'

'I don't think so.'

'I don't do murder.'

'It wouldn't be murder.'

'No, sure, of course not. He's a vampire. Right.'

'It's the truth.'

'Yeah, and I'm Tinkerbell.'

'You've *got* to do this for me. Please. I'll pay you whatever . . . How much do you want? Five thousand? Ten?'

'I don't get it. Why do you want him dead? I thought you loved him?'

'I do.'

'You're just so jealous of these other gals . . .?'

'Yes!' Her eyes flashed. 'Is that so hard to understand? Every night – every night he leaves me alone and goes to someone else. I can't stand it!'

'But he always comes home to you,' I said. 'Those others are nothing to him except . . . nourishment? It's you he loves. It's you he *makes* love to. And it sounds pretty damn passionate, if you ask me.'

Lowering her head, she murmured, 'It is. But . . . *they're* the ones he sucks.'

'You'd *rather* be sucked?'

'It's so much more . . . more everything. Than sex. There's no comparison. It's a kind of rapture that you . . . you just can't imagine.'

'Does Phil know how you feel about this?'

'Of course he does. But he won't give in. He says that he likes me the way I am, that if he sucks me too often, I'll lose my spark. My spark. That's a laugh.'

'It sounds as if he cares a lot about you.'

'Well, he does. But not enough to stay home and bite *my* neck. That's all I want.'

'And since he won't do it, you want me to kill him? That doesn't make any sense at all.'

Her eyes darkened. 'If I can't have him, nobody else will. You know what I mean? I'm sick to death of it.'

All of a sudden, I believed her.

I didn't believe the part about Phil being a vampire. I knew she believed it, though, and I knew she wasn't kidding that she wanted him dead.

If I can't have him, nobody else will.

The magic words.

Graveyards are full of people who died because someone loved them – loved them too much, would rather see them dead than lose them to another person.

'I'm not a killer,' I explained again.

'It's not as if you'd be killing a man.'

'He *is* a man. You may think he's a vampire, but he's flesh and blood. If I took your money and whammed that stake through his heart, it'd be murder. In this state, it'd be first-degree murder with special circumstances. That'd make it a capital crime. Not me, lady.'

'How much?' she asked.

'Uncle Sam doesn't print enough.'

'What if I can prove to you that Phil's a vampire?'

'Ain't gonna happen.'

'But just suppose. How would you feel about killing a real ... what did you call it? A real, supernatural-Dracula-immortal-Batman-vampire? There's no law against *that*, is there?'

'Of course not. But ...'

'*Would* you be willing to kill an actual vampire? For ten thousand dollars? And for me?'

I didn't miss a beat. What was to think about?

'Sure I'd do it,' I told Traci. 'But it won't happen. There's no way, not a chance in hell, you could ever prove to me that Phil's a vampire.'

For the second time that afternoon, Traci smiled. 'Want to bet?' she asked.

She glanced past me at the office window, then checked her wristwatch. 'Sunset isn't till six-twenty-five. That gives us almost an hour and a half.'

I suddenly got an ucky feeling in my gut. 'You want to do this now? Today?'

She nodded. 'Before Phil wakes up.'

* * *

Traci drove. I rode with her in the passenger seat of her Porsche. Normally, I would've driven my own car. There wasn't much normal about this trip, though. No telling what I might be getting in to. If it got messy, I didn't want some neighbor or passerby giving the cops a description of my vehicle.

Besides, riding with Traci gave me more time to enjoy her. She didn't talk much. She smelled good, and had a fine profile. Her black leather skirt was very short, her legs long and smooth.

I thought a lot about how Phil told his stories every night while they worked on each other. How he timed things. *When it comes to the part where he sinks his teeth into her, that's when he sinks his* . . . That's when he put it to her.

Lucky stiff.

The whole vampire thing seemed to be a huge turn-on for both of them.

Assuming, of course, that Traci'd been telling me the truth.

I didn't like to think that she'd been lying about any of it. Lying would mean I'd signed on for a whole different ballgame. Maybe not even a ballgame, at all.

There wasn't much traffic, so we made good time. We left the city behind. Traci sped us through the woods on narrow roads shrouded with shadows.

It took us nearly an hour to reach the house.

A nicely kept two-story colonial. Normal looking. Nothing creepy about it, if you don't count finding it all by itself at the end of a half-mile of unpaved road.

'Where does Phil find all these gals he sucks?' I asked as Traci stopped the car.

'In the city, mostly.'

'A commuter vampire.'

'We'd better hurry.'

As I followed her toward the front door, I checked my

wristwatch. Five-fifty. If Traci was right about the sunset, Phil would be rousing himself in thirty-five minutes.

Not much time.

Not much, right. I felt like a dope for letting myself worry about it. Who cares when the sun goes down? It would only matter if Phil was a vampire, and I knew better.

I had better things to worry about.

What's really going on? for instance.

Traci entered the house first. I stepped in behind her. Even though the sun hadn't gone down yet, the house was pretty dark and gloomy inside. She didn't turn on any lights. Not till we stood at the top of the basement stairs. The basement was very dark. She flipped a switch. Lights came on. They made it a little better, but not much.

'He's down there?' I whispered.

Traci nodded. She removed the stake from her handbag and offered it to me.

I shook my head. I reached under my jacket and unlimbered my .45. It was a big heavy Colt, army model. Out of fashion, I know. These days, it's all 9 mm Berettas and such. But the Colt auto was good enough for my old man in the Pacific. You remember the Pacific? That's when the Japs were too busy killing us to buy the country out from under our sorry butts.

I jacked a round into the chamber.

'That won't do you any good against Phil,' Traci warned.

'Let's go,' I said.

No reason to waste time explaining that vampires were the least of my worries.

For all I knew, this whole bit might've been a trap they'd laid for *me*. Maybe Phil was a guy I'd pissed off, one time or another. Maybe Traci was his cute little helper.

As Yogi Bera might've said, *You never know till you know.*

Traci kept hold of the stake, and started down. I let her

get a few stairs below me, then followed. The stairway was wood. It creaked and moaned. It had open spaces between the treads, spaces that somebody could reach through and grab your ankle. I tried to brace myself for something like that.

The basement air was cool. It had the normal basement smell of dank concrete.

The walls and floor were concrete.

Phil's coffin was on the floor just beyond the foot of the stairs, just beneath a glaring, bare lightbulb.

He was inside. Stretched out on a lining that looked like red satin. Eyes shut. Hands folded on his belly. Dressed to the hilt in a vampire garb that looked like it might've been filched from the Universal Studios wardrobe department.

He looked a lot younger than Lugosi'd been back in those days. He had sort of a clean-cut, boyish appearance. Long, blond hair. He might've looked like a Santa Monica surfer if he'd had a good tan. But his face was pale, pasty. And his lips were bright red.

I stopped beside Traci. We both stood over the coffin, staring down at Phil.

'Now do you believe me?' she asked. She spoke in a normal tone, and her voice resounded through the basement, damn near echoed.

'Shhh.'

'It's all right,' she said. 'We won't disturb him. He's totally out of it till the sun goes down.' She checked her watch. 'That's almost half an hour from now.'

'Sure,' I said.

Five minutes ago, the guy probably had his face pressed to the living-room window. Saw us coming and hightailed for the basement, his black cloak flapping.

If that's how it had gone, though, he hadn't winded himself.

From where I stood, I couldn't tell whether he was breathing at all.

'Will you do it now?' Traci asked. She held the stake out for me. Again.

'No such thing as vampires,' I said.

I gave the side of the coffin a good, rough kick. It gave the box a jolt. It shook Phil. But it didn't wake him up.

'Just take it.' Traci pressed the stake into my hand. Then she hurried across the basement, heels clacking, rump flexing nicely against the seat of her skirt. She snatched something off a workbench near the wall. When she turned around, I saw it was a claw hammer. She gave it a little shake. 'You'll need this.'

'Not likely.'

She stopped in front of me. She held out the hammer. 'Please. Take it.'

'My hands are full,' I muttered.

'The gun won't do you any good, anyway. Here.'

'No thanks.'

'You *said* you'd do it.'

'Yeah. And I will. If you can prove he's a vampire.'

'Just look at him.'

'That's no proof. That's a guy in a coffin and an outfit.'

'I mean *look* at him. He's not alive.'

He's not alive.

Holy shit!

I suddenly knew the score.

I jammed the muzzle of my .45 into Traci's gut. Her mouth sprang open. 'Lose the hammer, honey,' I said.

She dropped it. The steel head struck the concrete with a clank.

'Put your hands on top of your head and interlace your fingers.'

She blinked at me. 'What's—'

'Do it.'

She did it.

'Stay put.'

'What's *wrong*? she blurted. 'Why are you *doing* this?'

I didn't answer. I dropped the stake, shifted the Colt to my left hand, and crouched beside the coffin. Keeping the pistol aimed at Traci, I reached into the coffin with my right hand and found Phil's neck.

Its skin felt cold.

I fingered around, searching for the pulse. From the temperature of the skin, though, I knew I wouldn't find one. And I didn't.

'He's dead, all right,' I said.

'That's what I *told* you. He's not a man, he's a vampire.'

'He's dead.'

'He's *un*dead.'

'Right. Where'd you get the idea I'm an idiot, lady?'

'What are you *talking* about.'

'This.' I stood up and stepped toward her. 'Keep your hands on your head and turn around.'

She turned around.

I stepped in close behind her. I started patting her down. 'You murdered him. You put together this vampire story, got him into the outfit and coffin, checked your phone book for a likely—'

'You're crazy!'

'Not crazy enough to fall for your game.' She was clean. I holstered my piece, brought her arms down behind her back, and cuffed them.

I go plenty of places without my Colt. I never leave home without my handcuffs.

They come in useful when I need to keep someone in custody. And they're a turn-on for a lot of my lady friends.

Traci fell into the former category.

Too bad. I'd liked her. I'd wanted her. Beautiful, sexy, innocent and vulnerable.

Cancel those last two.

Still beautiful and sexy, but about as innocent and vulnerable as a sidewinder.

A sidewinder. Rattlesnake or missile, take your pick.

After she was cuffed, I let go of her. She turned around and gazed at me with wide, stunned eyes.

'You had me going,' I said. 'Thing is, I'm an open-minded sort of guy. You tell me far-out stuff, I'll listen to reason. You had me about eighty percent convinced Phil might really *be* a vampire. But you fell a little short. Short to the tune of a murder rap.'

Traci shook her head.

'If you'd just been a little more convincing, I might've given Phil the stake treatment and taken you off the hook.'

'It's not too late,' she said. 'There's ten thousand in my handbag. Cash. Just kill him and—'

'And take the fall for you. Right. 'Fraid not.'

'I've seen how you look at me.'

'You're a good-looking woman.'

'I'll be yours.'

'Nope. I'll be in prison. Either that, or dead. More than likely dead. Otherwise, I might explain your little vampire fairy tale, and the cops might buy it. You planned to kill me, didn't you? I guess you'd claim you caught me in the act of staking your hubby ... How were you going to explain his getup?'

'Please!' She started to weep.

'Forget it. I'm no one's patsy.'

Cuffed and all, she made a break for the stairs. I grabbed for her but missed, so she got a short lead. I raced after her. She was partway up the stairs before I got hold of her. Just reached up, caught the hem of her skirt and gave it a tug.

I meant to yank it down around her ankles, hobble her, trip her up.

But the skirt didn't pull down. When I gave it that tug, I plucked Traci backward off the stairs and she came falling at me. I had time to dodge her. But I stayed my ground. It was either catch her, or let her crash to the concrete floor. I couldn't allow her to crash, not with her arms cuffed behind her back. Even a gal who'd tried to frame me for murder deserved better than that. So I braced myself and spread my arms.

I almost stayed on my feet.

But not quite.

Her weight hit me. I grabbed her, stumbled back, and fell. She pounded down on top of me. The cuffs got me in the nuts. The back of her head clopped my chin, and the impact of that bashed my head against the concrete.

I went out.

When I came to, Traci wasn't on top of me any more. But I spotted her easily enough. Opened my eyes, and there she was. Didn't even need to raise my head off the floor.

She was hanging from a ceiling girder. Dangling by her tied ankles. She was naked. Her skin was the color of a gloomy, overcast morning. Except where it was smudged with red handprints and lip marks, and where it trickled blood from punctures.

The punctures were bite marks like those she'd shown me on her neck. But these were fresh. Open, raw. And they were all over her, as if her attacker had been a connoisseur sampling tastes from her different regions – her thighs, her groin, her navel, her breasts, her face and the undersides of her drooping arms.

She still wore my cuffs. They were no longer connected, though. With the links between them broken, they encircled Traci's wrists like quirky silver bracelets.

I had reasons of my own for feeling miserable. But the way Traci looked made me feel a lot worse. She'd been broken. Used and trashed. And I was to blame.

I'd fucked up.

And she'd paid for it.

Without moving, I could feel the weight of the Colt in my shoulder holster. I snatched it out, tossed myself sideways, and rolled fast, ready to blast trouble.

What I saw while I rolled was Phil.

I came up to a squat, facing him, taking aim.

He was sitting on the basement stairs, watching me. Second stair from the bottom, feet on the concrete floor, elbows resting on his knees, hands folded. He didn't have his outfit on. He had nothing on, at all. Except a lot of Traci's blood.

Sighing, he shook his head. 'Women,' he muttered. 'You know what I mean?'

I put two slugs in his chest and one in his forehead.

They went through him like he was jelly. The holes flowed shut, and he was good as new before the bullets had time to quit ricocheting around the basement.

'Oh, shit,' I muttered.

He acted like it hadn't happened. 'You know what I mean?' he asked again.

I just gaped at him.

'You know?' he said. 'I mean, what'd I ever do to Traci? I loved her. I treated her great. And what does she do? She brings you over to put a hit on me. Jesus H. Christ on a rubber crutch.'

'She was jealous,' I said.

'Jealous? Shit. I screwed her head off, man. Every single night . . .'

'She didn't want that,' I explained. 'She wanted you to suck her.'

'Figures. They never listen. I told her over and over again, "Traci," I said, "I'd *love* to suck you every night. You *know* that. But it'd *kill* you." That's what I told her. But does she listen? Shit.'

'Looks like she finally got her wish.'

Phil gave me a weary smirk. 'Well, she died happy.'

'Will she become a vampire now?'

Phil huffed. 'No way. I'm leaving her dead, man. She tried to have me snuffed. Good riddance.' He shook his head again. He backhanded some blood off his lips. 'Broads,' he muttered. 'You can't live with 'em, you can't live without 'em.'

'Know what you mean,' I said.

'What's your name?' he asked.

'Matthews. Cliff Matthews.'

'Go on home, Cliff. I got no beef with you.'

Paying Joe Back

Folks say everything changes, but that's not so. I've lived in Windville all my life, and Joe's Bar & Grill looks just the same to me as always.

It has the same heavy steel grill, the same counter, the same swivel stools. Those long tables sticking out of the walls aren't much different than they were thirty years back, when Joe first opened – just older and more beaten up. The booth cushions got new upholstery seven years ago, but Joe had them fixed up in the same red vinyl stuff as before, so you can't hardly tell the difference.

Only one thing has changed about Joe's place. That's the people. Some of the old-timers keep dropping by, regular as clockwork. But time has changed them considerably. Lester Keyhoe, for instance, fell to pieces after his wife kicked over. And old Gimpy Sedge lost his conductor job, so he just watches the train pull in and leave without him, then comes by here to tie one on with Lester.

Joe's gone, too. Not *gone*, just retired. I've kept the place going for the past three years, since I turned twenty-one. When Joe isn't shooting deer in the mountains, he comes in for coffee and a cinnamon bun every morning. He likes to keep an eye on things.

I sure wish he'd been after deer the morning Elsie Thompson blew in.

The place was empty except for me and Lester Keyhoe, who was sitting down the bar where he always sits, getting a start on the day's drinking.

I was toweling down the counter when the car pulled up. I could see it plain through the window. It was an old Ford that looked like somebody'd driven it a dozen times back and forth through Hell. It sputtered and whinnied for a minute after the ignition key was turned off.

I stopped toweling and just stared. The old gal who jumped out of the Ford was a real sight – short and round, dressed in khakis, with gray hair cut like Buster Brown, and wearing big wire-rimmed glasses. She chewed on some gum like she wanted to kill it. A floppy wicker handbag hung from her arm. I said, 'Get a load of this,' to Lester, but he didn't even look up.

The screen door opened and she thumped toward the counter in her dusty boots. She hopped onto the stool in front of me. Her jaw went up and down a few times. One time when it was open, the word 'coffee' came out.

'Yes, ma'am,' I said, and turned away to get it.

'Does this establishment belong to Joseph James Lowry from Chicago?' she asked.

'Sure does,' I said, looking at her.

Behind the glasses, her round eyes opened and shut in time with her chewing mouth. She gave me a huge grin. 'That's mighty good news, young man. I've been driving through every one-horse town west of Chicago looking for this place, looking for Joe Lowry and his damned tavern. There's a place called Joe's in every single one of them. But I knew I'd find Joe Lowry's place sooner or later. Know why? Because I've got willpower, that's why. When do you expect him in?'

'Well . . . what did you want to see him about?'

'He *is* coming in?'

I nodded.

'Good. I expected as much. I'm only surprised not to find him behind the counter.'

'You know him, huh?'

'Oh, yes. My, yes.' Her eyes turned sad for a second. 'We used to know each other very well, back in Chicago.'

'How about if I give him a ring, tell him you're here?'

'That won't be necessary.' Snapping her gum and grinning, she opened the handbag on her lap and pulled out a revolver. Not a peashooter, either – one of those long-barreled .38s. 'I'll surprise him,' she said. Her stubby little thumb pulled back the hammer and she aimed the thing at me. 'We'll surprise him together.'

I didn't feel much like talking, but managed to nod my head.

'What time will Joe be in?' she asked.

'Pretty soon.' I took a deep breath and asked, 'You aren't planning to shoot him, are you?'

She pretended like she didn't hear me, and asked, 'How soon?'

'Well . . .' Far away, the 10:05 from Parkerville let loose its whistle. 'Well, pretty soon, I guess.'

'I'll wait for him. Who's that slob over there?'

'That's Lester.'

'Lester!' she called.

He turned his head and looked at her. She waved the gun at him, grinning and chewing, but his face didn't change. It looked the same as always, long and droopy like a bloodhound's, but more gloomy.

'Lester,' she said, 'you just stay right on that stool. If you get up for any reason, I'll shoot you dead.'

His head nodded, then turned frontwards again and tipped down at his half-empty glass.

'What's your name?' she asked me.

'Wes.'

'Wes, keep Lester's glass full. And don't do anything to make me shoot you. If some more customers come in, just serve them like everything is normal. This revolver has six loads, and I can take down a man with each. I don't want to. I only want Joe Lowry. But if you drive me to it, I'll make this place wall-to-wall corpses. Understand?'

'Sure, I understand.' I filled Lester's glass, then came back to the woman. 'Can I ask you something?'

'Fire away.'

'Why do you want to kill Joe?'

She stopped chewing and squinted at me. 'He ruined my life. That's enough reason to kill a man, I think. Don't you?'

'Nothing's a good enough reason to kill Joe.'

'Think so?'

'What'd he do to you?'

'He ran off with Martha Dipsworth.'

'Martha? That's his wife – was.'

'Dead?'

I nodded.

'Good.' Her jaw chomped, and she beamed. 'That makes me glad. Joe made a mistake, not marrying me – I'm still alive and kicking. We'd be happily married to this day if he'd had the sense to stick with me. But he never did have much sense. Do you know what his great ambition was? To go out west and open up a tavern. Martha thought that was a *glor*ious idea. I said, "Well, *you* marry him, then. Go out west and waste your lives in the boondocks. If Joe's such a romantic fool as to throw his life away like that, I don't want him. There's plenty of fish in the sea." That's what I said. More than thirty years ago.'

'If you said that . . .' I stopped. You don't catch me arguing with an armed woman.

'What?'

'Nothing.'

She shifted her chewing gum over to one corner of her mouth and drank some coffee. 'What were you going to say?'

'Just . . . well, if you said they could get married, it doesn't seem very fair of you to blame them when they went ahead and did it.'

She put down the cup and glanced over at Lester. He still sat there, but he was staring at the gun. 'When I said that about the sea being full of fish, I figured it'd only be a matter of time before I'd land a good one. Well, it didn't work out that way.'

She chewed a few times, gazing up at me with a funny distance in her eyes as if she was looking back at all the years. 'I kept on waiting. I was just sure the right man was around the next corner – around the next year. It finally dawned on me, Wes, that there wasn't ever going to be another man. Joe was it, and I'd lost him. That's when I decided to gun him down.'

'That's . . .'

'What?'

'Crazy.'

'It's justice.'

'Maybe the two of you could get together. He's unattached since Martha died. Maybe . . .'

'Nope. Too late for that. Too late for babies, too late for—'

All at once, Lester flung himself away from the bar and made a foolish run for the door. The old gal swiveled on her stool, tracked him for a split second, then squeezed off a shot. The bullet took off Lester's earlobe. With a yelp, he swung around and ran back to his stool, cupping a hand over what was left of his ear.

'You'd better pray nobody heard that shot,' she said to both of us.

I figured nobody would. We were at the tail end of town, so the closest building was a gas station half a block away. The cars passing by on the highway kicked up plenty of noise. And around here, with all the hunting that goes on, nobody pays much attention to a single gunshot unless it's right under his nose.

But I was nervous, anyway. For five minutes, we all waited without saying a word. The only sound was her gum snapping.

She finally grinned and squinted as if she'd just won a raffle. 'We're in luck.'

'Joe's not,' I said. 'Neither's Lester.'

Lester said nothing. He was pinching his notched ear with one hand and draining his glass with the other.

'They shouldn't have run,' the woman said. 'That was their mistake – they ran. You aren't going to run, are you?'

'No, ma'am.'

'Because if you do, I'll shoot you for sure. I'll shoot anyone today. Anyone. This is my day, Wes – the day Elsie Thompson pays Joe back.'

'I won't run, ma'am. But I won't let you shoot Joe. I'll stop you one way or another.' I went over to fill Lester's glass.

'You can't stop me. No one can stop me. Nothing can. Do you know why? Because I've got willpower, that's why.'

Grinning mysteriously, she chomped three times on her gum and said, 'Today I'm going to die. That gives me all the power in the world. Understand? As soon as I gun down Joe, I'll drive out of this burg. I'll get that old Ford up to seventy, eighty, then I'll pick out the biggest tree . . .'

I made a sick laugh, and came back to her.

'Think I'm fooling?' she asked.

'No, ma'am. It's just kind of funny, you talking like that about crashing into a tree. Not funny ha-ha, funny weird. You know?'

'No.'

'That's 'cause you don't know about Joe. He crashed into a tree – an aspen, just off Route 5. That was about three years back. Martha was with him. She got killed, of course. Joe was in real bad shape, and Doc Mills didn't give him much chance. But he pulled through. His face got so broken up he didn't look quite right, and he lost the use of an eye. His left eye, not his aiming eye. He wears a patch over it, you know. And sometimes when he gets feeling high, he flaps it up and gives us all a peek underneath.'

'You can stop that.'

'He lost a leg, too.'

'I don't want to hear about it.'

'Yes, ma'am. I'm sorry. It's just that . . . well, everyone that crashes into a tree doesn't die.'

'I will.'

'You can't be sure. Maybe you'll just end up like Joe, hobbling around half blind on a fake leg, with your face so scarred up that your best friends won't recognize you.'

'Shut up, Wes.'

She stuck the pistol into my face, so I slowed down and said quietly, 'I just mean, if you want to make sure you die, there's a concrete bridge abutment about a mile up the road.'

'Warm up my coffee and keep your mouth shut.'

I turned around to pick up the pot. That's when I heard the footsteps outside. Boots against the wood planks out front, coming closer. I faced Elsie. She grinned at me. Her jaw worked faster on the gum. Her eyes squinted behind her glasses as the unsteady clumping got louder.

Through the window I saw his mussy gray hair, his scarred face with the patch on his left eye. He saw me looking, smiled, and waved.

I glanced at Lester, who was holding a paper napkin to his ear and the glass to his mouth.

Elsie pushed the pistol close to my chest. 'Don't move,' she whispered.

The screen door swung open.

Elsie spun her stool.

'Duck, Joe!' I cried out.

He didn't duck. He just stood there looking perplexed as Elsie leaped off the stool, crouched, and fired. The first two bullets smacked him square in the chest. The next hit his throat. Then one tore into his shoulder, turning him around so the last shot took him in the small of the back.

All this happened in a couple of seconds as I dived at Elsie. I was in mid-air when she wheeled on me and smacked me in the face with the barrel. I went down.

While I was trying to get up, she jumped over the body and ran out. I reached the door in time to see her car whip backwards. It hit the road with screeching tires, then laid rubber and was gone.

I went back inside.

Lester was still sitting at the bar. His stool was turned around, and he was staring at the body. I sat down at one of the booths, lit a cigarette, and kept Lester company staring.

We spent a long time like that. After a while, I heard the sheriff's siren. Then an ambulance's. The cars screamed by and faded up the road in the direction of the bridge abutment.

'Guess that's Elsie,' I said.

Lester just kept staring.

Then the screen door swung open.

'My God!' The big man looked at me, then at Lester, and knelt down over the body. He turned it over. 'Gimpy,' he muttered. 'Poor old Gimpy.' He patted the dead conductor on the back, and stood up. His eyes questioned me.

I shook my head. 'Some crazy woman,' I muttered. 'She came in here dead set to kill you, Dad.'

The Fur Coat

Janet wore her white ermine coat to the theater that night. The play was *Cats*. She went alone.

The evening was meant to signal a new beginning for her. She hadn't treated herself to a play since Harold's death. He had adored the stage. They'd seen *Cats* together many times during their eight years of marriage. He'd been dead, now, for more than two years. Janet knew that she had to quit mourning, quit feeling sorry for herself, and get on with her life.

She attended *Cats* as a final tribute to Harold.

She wore the ermine coat as a tribute to him, too.

It was a lovely coat, its fur as white as a drift of fresh snow and soft as down. A gift from Harold. She'd yelped with delight the morning she found it under the Christmas tree. Because they had no children and were celebrating the holiday alone, she had immediately thrown off her robe and nightgown. She'd caressed her naked body with the luscious fur coat, then slipped her arms into its sleeves and twirled around for Harold. In his arms, she thanked him for the coat. She kissed him. She hugged him. She stripped him. She urged him to the floor. There, kneeling over him in nothing but her wonderful new coat, she had stroked him, kissed him all over, licked and sucked him, and finally eased down onto him.

Afterward, he'd said, 'My God. Wish I'd bought you this coat years ago.'

'You couldn't have afforded it.'

'So what? Debt, where is thy sting?'

During the next few months, she'd worn the coat every time Harold took her out to dinner or the theater. A few times, when their evening activities were such that she wouldn't need to remove her coat, she'd worn only a garter belt and stockings underneath it – which drove Harold crazy.

The coat never failed to make Janet feel special. Partly because Harold had blown a small fortune on it, she supposed. Partly because it looked so pure and beautiful, felt so soft and smooth against her skin. But mostly, she thought, because of how it had changed their marriage. The coat not only inspired its share of raw lust, but also tenderness, laughter, a fresh assortment of surprises and adventures.

Her first night alone in the house after Harold's accident, she took the coat to bed with her. She wept into its silken fur and fell asleep hugging it.

Soon, however, the coat ceased to give her comfort, became only a reminder of her loss. She couldn't stand to look at it, much less touch it, wear it.

And so she had put it in storage.

Left it there.

For over two years.

Until the day she was brushing her rich brown hair in front of the medicine cabinet mirror and spotted the silver thread.

Her first gray hair.

But I'm only thirty-six! Thirty-six isn't old!

Old enough to start going gray.

It was then that she decided to get on with her life. She phoned the Barkley Theater and made a single reservation for the Saturday night performance of *Cats*. Then she took her ermine coat out of storage.

At Bullocks, she bought an elegant black evening gown for the occasion.

On the day of the performance, she went to the beauty shop. She'd considered having her hair dyed. But she liked her natural color. Besides, the idea of masking the gray hair seemed cowardly. Better to accept it, to face the knowledge that her life was moving on, and make the most of each day ahead.

She had her hair trimmed very short. It made her look spritely. And quite a bit younger.

That evening, ready to leave, she stood in front of the full-length hall mirror for a while and gazed at herself.

The sleek, low-cut gown was brand new. The ermine coat *looked* brand new. And Janet *felt* brand new.

If only Harold could see me now, she thought.

Her eyes filled with tears.

She had to redo her mascara before leaving the house.

The drive into Hollywood took half an hour. Rather than hunt for street parking, she left her Mercedes in a brightly lighted pay lot four blocks from the theater.

The autumn wind had a chill to it. Janet was snug in her fur coat.

She picked up her ticket at the box office. In the warmth of the Barkley's lobby, she removed her coat and draped it over one arm. In her seat, she folded it and set it on her lap. She stroked it during the play. It was almost like having a cat on her lap. But no cat ever had such lovely, smooth fur.

She went nowhere during intermission. Instead, she stood in front of her seat and looked about. She saw no familiar faces, of course. But she noticed several women in furs. More in stoles than in coats, it seemed. Most of the women who wore furs were considerably older than Janet. Most, in fact, were very old.

Was she the only person under sixty, in the entire theater, who'd worn a fur to the play?

Sure looked that way.

Had it always been like that?

Janet didn't think so.

Could things have changed so much in such a short period of time? In less than three years?

Maybe it's because of those animal-rights fanatics, she thought. Had they turned an entire generation away from wearing furs? Sure looked that way. *Something* had happened.

Unless it's the bad economy, and most people simply can't afford the luxury . . .

The lights dimmed.

Janet sat down.

At the end of the play, she wept and clapped. Then she wiped her eyes, pressed the coat to her belly and sidestepped to the aisle.

On her way to the lobby, she was aware of feeling proud.

She had taken such a large step, coming here tonight. She'd actually dressed up and come to the play all by herself. And she'd enjoyed the performance. In a way. If only Harold had been with her . . .

I'm on my own, she reminded herself. *And I got along just fine*.

Things would be easier from now on.

She would try a new play next week. Maybe, sooner or later, she would actually gather enough courage to dine alone in a fine restaurant.

Eventually, she might even meet a man as wonderful as Harold.

Fall in love.

God, wouldn't that be something!

Sighing, she slipped her arms into the sleeves of her coat. The lobby was hot, so she didn't fasten the buttons. Stuck in the mob waiting to exit, she wished she had left the coat off entirely. People pressed against her. The air seemed hot, heavy, suffocating.

Until finally she made her way through the door.

The chilly autumn night felt great.

She breathed deeply. The air beneath the theater marquee was fragrant with scents of myriad perfumes, with men's musky after-shave colognes, with liquor aromas, with smoke from cigarettes and cigars. Whether exotic or comforting or disgusting, the odors excited Janet. They were old, familiar friends. She filled her lungs and smiled.

This is so wonderful, she thought. *I'm really out in the world again*.

Look at me, Harold. I didn't wither up and die. I wanted to, but I didn't. I survived.

The crowd loosened as people headed off in different directions. Janet paused to recall where she had parked her car.

The parking lot. That way.

She turned to the right.

And took only three strides before a voice shouted, 'Murderer!'

Janet was twisting around when a woman cried out, 'No!'
She spotted her at the curb. Old, frail, silver-haired, wrapped in a mink stole, flinging up her arms as she was rushed by a pair of young women.

The two women looked vicious.

'Murderer!' the skinny one shouted into the old woman's face.

'Evil bitch!' shouted her partner, a tubby woman with stringy brown hair. 'Those minks died for your sins!'

Both women dug into their handbags. Janet's heart thumped. She thought they were going for guns. But they came up with cans of spray paint.

'No, please!' the old woman whined.

Red paint sprayed her hands as she scuttled backward, trying to get away. Some got past her hands, misted her hair and forehead and glasses.

At least twenty people seemed to be frozen beneath the theater marquee, watching the attack.

Why was nobody trying to help?

Because the assailants were women? Or were all the spectators on their side, hating the old lady for wearing fur?

The old lady, sandwiched between the pair, whimpered and hugged her head as they sprayed her. Her hair dripped red paint. The fur of her stole was matted down, scarlet.

'Leave her alone, goddamn you!' Janet shouted.

The heads of both assailants snapped toward her. The chubby one squinted through glasses that were speckled with red paint. Round lenses in wire frames. Granny glasses.

'She didn't do anything to you!' Janet yelled. 'Look what you've done to her! What's the matter with you?'

The one in the granny glasses grinned.

The skinny one raised her spray can high overhead. 'Listen up, all you rich capitalist fucks! We're ADF. Hitters for the Animal Defense Front. What you've seen here is a lesson. It's what we do to assholes we catch wearing dead animals.

'You've been fucking Mother Earth long enough! Butchering her forests, poisoning her air and water, slaughtering her innocent creatures. *Murdering* her creatures! Bashing their heads! Slashing their throats. *Experimenting* on them! Eating their flesh! Clothing yourselves in their skins! No more! No more!'

'No more!' the chubby one joined in.

'ADF forever!'

'ADF forever!'

'Get *her*!' The skinny one hurled the old lady aside and rushed toward Janet.

The other grinned.

Janet whirled away.

The tight skirt of her evening gown bound her legs, but not for long. With her third stride, her knee punched through its front. A kick finished the job. The skirt split open from hem to waist, freeing her to run.

People nearby dodged clear, some yelping with alarm, others watching as if amused, none trying to help.

Janet glanced over her shoulder. Her pursuers were side by side, no more than fifteen feet back.

What sort of range did the spray cans have?

I'll die if they ruin my coat!

But she knew that she couldn't outrun them – not in her heels.

The shoes, like the gown, could be replaced.

Without slowing, she kicked off her right shoe. The left gave her some trouble, but after a few strides she managed to fling it clear. Shoes gone, her feet felt light and quick.

She dashed along the sidewalk, silent except for her huffing breath and the slap of her feet and the whispery sounds that her pantyhose made as she whipped one leg after the other out through the split front of her skirt.

The girls behind her made a lot more noise. One seemed to be wheezing. One wore footwear, probably sandals, that smacked the concrete with harsh claps. One jingled with Christmas bells. From their spray cans came rattling sounds, as if each contained nothing more than a ball-bearing.

The sounds of the pair didn't seem to be getting any closer. But not fading, either.

So far, Janet was keeping her lead.

Just ahead, her way was blocked by a knot of people standing at the corner. Waiting to cross the street.

'Help!'

Some looked around at her.

'What's the trouble?' asked a young man in a sweater. He looked innocent, collegiate.

'They're after me!' Janet cried out.

'What for?'

'Animal Defense Front!' shouted one of the gals. 'Keep out of it!'

'Huh?' He wrinkled his nose.

And it was already too late. Janet had no time to stop and explain. Give the attackers two or three seconds, and her coat would be dripping crimson paint.

Just short of the group, she cut to the right.

'What's going on?' the kid called after her.

She didn't bother to answer. She poured on speed.

The sidewalk in front of her was deserted. Just as well, she thought. Nobody was likely to help her, anyway – not without an explanation. No explanation was possible. They'd be on her too quick.

If only someone would take out the two bitches on general principles!

Isn't it obvious who's the victim here?

Apparently not.

Or people just don't care.

It'd all be different if guys were chasing me.

Men would be climbing all over each other to save me.

But these're gals after me. So I'm fucked.

Wonderful.

Her pursuers sounded farther away than before. Thinking that she was beginning to outdistance them, Janet risked a look back.

And gasped.

The skinny one was closer than ever before. No more than seven or eight feet separated her from Janet.

The heavy one was much farther back. She was the noisy one. The one with a wheeze. The one who wore sandals and sleighbells. The one who now carried both clinking canisters of paint.

Her friend in the lead was sprinting almost silent. Long blonde hair streaming. Lips peeled away from teeth that looked very white in the streetlights. No earrings or necklace or bracelets or rings. No bra. No shoes or socks. Dressed in a white T-shirt, old cut-off jeans and apparently nothing else. Stripped for action, for silent running.

'Leave me alone!' Janet blurted.

'Butcher!'

'I'm *not*!'

'Gimme the coat!'

'No! Go away!'

'Yeah! After I've . . . ripped that fur . . . off your fucking back!'

Janet twisted sideways and hurled her clutch bag. Like the coat, it had been a gift from Harold. But she had nothing else to throw.

Inside the black satin bag were several odds and ends: some cash, tissues, a tampon, her parking-lot ticket, the stub of her theater ticket, the folded playbill, and her driver's license. Also her key case, her compact and opera glasses – which gave the bag some weight.

Her pursuer saw the airborn bag. She flung up an arm to block it, but missed. She tried to jerk her head out of the way. The bag caught her in the right temple. Her face scrunched. She turned and tripped herself, hit the sidewalk shoulder first, and skidded.

Janet rushed back to her. She snatched up her purse.

'I warned you to leave me alone!' she said as the gal, moaning, tried to push herself up.

'Hey!' yelled the chubby one. 'What'd you do to her! Leave her alone!'

'You leave *me* alone!' Janet snapped, backing away. While the big one chugged toward her, the other got to her knees. The fall had torn down the sleeve of her T-shirt. Teeth clenched, she took a quick look at her dark, scuffed shoulder.

'Are you hurt?' her friend asked, staggering to a halt.

'Get her!'

'No!' Janet yelled. 'Quit it! She's already gotten hurt.'

'Damn it, Glory, *spray the fuckin' coat!*'

Glory lurched past her, bells jingling.

'No,' Janet said. 'Come on. Please.'

Glory kept coming, so she flung herself around. As she broke into a run, the cans hissed. She glanced back. Glory, firing with both barrels, was hidden from the chest up behind clouds of red mist. The paint didn't seem to shoot far enough to hit Janet.

But if Glory got much closer . . .

Janet rammed the clutch bag to her mouth. She bit it. The bag flopped, whapping her beneath the chin as she dashed along the sidewalk and struggled out of her coat. She brought the coat in front of her. Mashed it into a thick bundle. Clamped it to her chest with her left arm. Took the bag from her mouth with her right hand. And kept on running, hugging the coat.

They won't get you now, she thought.

The corner ahead looked deserted. Approaching it, she glanced both ways.

The parking lot.

If I can get to the parking lot . . .

Where the hell is it?

She had no idea.

But the traffic light was green for her and the intersection looked clear, so she leaped off the curb and raced into the street.

A horn blast stunned her.

She snapped her head to the left.

A cab running the red light sped straight at her. It swerved. She lurched to a stop, teetered backward. It rushed by, fanning her with a warm breeze.

Stunned by the near miss, Janet hardly noticed the sounds of smacking sandals and tinkling bells. The *sssssssss* took her by surprise.

She sprang forward.

But not fast enough.

Her evening gown was backless, so the cool paint plastered her bare skin from the nape of her neck and downward almost to her waist before she put on enough speed to leave Glory behind.

That would've been it for the coat, she thought.

Thank God! Got it off just in time.

At the other side of the street, she bounded over the curb. Then looked over her shoulder.

Glory, still pursuing her with a canister in each hand, had stopped spraying. Her hair was matted, her face slick with red paint. Janet wondered how she could possibly see through her glasses. The gal had obviously been racing

into her own spray, soaking herself. Her sleeveless
sweatshirt looked sodden. It was mostly red, only a hint of
its original gray still visible low on the belly. Her plaid
Bermuda shorts and heavy legs had caught some spatters.
Janet noticed that the jingling came from a leather collar of
bells around her left ankle.

Leather?

And what about those sandals?

Leather?

Maybe not. Maybe fake.

Or maybe the bitch is a hypocrite.

Fake?

Janet yelled over her shoulder, 'My fur isn't real! It's
simulated! You've got no reason to . . .'

Her voice went dead as the skinny one – the fast one –
raced up behind Glory, overtook her and left her behind,
charging toward Janet with shocking speed.

Janet bolted.

With the coat in her arms, she'd been able to stay ahead of
Glory. But this one was so much quicker. Janet couldn't hope
to outrun her – not without her arms free to pump.

Just a matter of time.

Janet began to weep.

*I don't want them to ruin my coat! Please! Why do they want to
do this?*

She heard the girl's bare feet slapping the sidewalk, heard
the girl's quick, sharp breaths.

'Please!' she yelled.

The word was still on its way out when a tackle took her
down. Her arms, wrapped around the coat, were first to
strike the concrete. Then her knees. The coat cushioned her
like a big pillow, saving her face and chest as she slammed
the sidewalk.

The girl scurried up her body, squirming, sliding on Janet's painted skin, embracing her, reaching for the coat. Janet tried to elbow the hands away.

'All *right!*' Glory called, rushing closer.

Just as Glory halted, sandals and bells going silent, a sudden writhing tug by the other flipped Janet over. She found herself on top, the girl pinned beneath her back, Glory looming above her.

'Nail the bitch!'

Grinning, Glory squatted, stretched her arms toward Janet, and sprayed. Both canisters spat red paint.

Janet felt the spray on her arms.

On her arms, wrapped around the ermine coat.

And she knew that the coat was finished.

'You getting her?' asked the girl underneath Janet.

'You bet.'

'Got the coat good?'

'Yep.'

'Nail her in the face.'

Janet let go of the fur. She squeezed her eyes shut, closed her mouth, and flung up her arms to protect her face. An instant later, the spray hissed at her.

While it showered her, she felt the coat being snatched off her chest.

She felt hands rip open the bodice of her gown. They plucked and tore, savaging her gown and under-garments.

'Nail her!'

The spray slathered her breasts, worked its way down her belly, burnt between her legs.

'Okay,' Glory said.

The spraying stopped.

With a shove from below, Janet was sent rolling off the girl. She tumbled over the curb, dropped, and landed face-down in leaves and debris at the edge of the street. She lay there motionless. She didn't dare to breathe.

She heard quiet sounds of fabric being torn.

She knew they were ripping her coat to shreds.

Soon, the pieces of it fell softly onto her bare back and rump and legs.

'You think this was bad?' asked the nameless one.

Janet didn't answer.

'This wasn't bad. This was nothing. Imagine how the ermines felt.'

'Ermines have feelings, too,' Glory added.

'You had no right to slaughter them for your vanity,' said the other.

She stepped on Janet's back, stepped down to the street beside her, knelt, grabbed Janet's painted hair and lifted her face off the pavement. 'They were poor, innocent creatures. They only wanted to live, just like the rest of us. They didn't want to be made into a coat for a rich bitch like you.'

'You had no right,' said Glory.

The other one jerked Janet's hair down quick and hard. Janet's face crashed against the pavement. Her nose burst. Three teeth crumbled.

'Animals have feelings, too.'

'Do you think they *enjoy* being skinned?' Glory asked.

'How do you think *you'd* like it, bitch?'

Janet began to struggle, but the girl bounced her face off the street again.

She was unconscious when they dragged her into the alley.

She woke up screaming when they started in with the razor blades.

Blarney

'What's that?'

Deke looked to the right, where Val was pointing. Half a mile up the coast, on a rocky point high above the surf, stood the gray stone walls of a castle ruin. 'A castle, I guess,' he said.

'In California?'

'Probably some nut put it up. Some guy didn't know what to do with his money.'

She tugged his arm. 'Can we go over to it?'

'Leave off my arm.'

She let go. 'Can we?'

'We'll see,' Deke said. He slipped a .32 automatic out of his belt.

'Hey, what are you doing?'

'Kissing it goodbye.'

'You're not throwing it away!'

'Oh yes I am.'

'Deke!'

He generally didn't dislike Val. After all, she wasn't bad looking for a gal her age. Her hair was dyed a gaudy reddish-brown. Her face had a few sags, same as her body, but what can you expect? Gals start downhill at eighteen, and Val was pushing fifty. No, he didn't dislike her looks much. Her big trouble was she didn't have much common sense. 'I have to ditch it,' he told her.

'Maybe we'll need it.'

'We can always get a new one. They catch us with this baby, they can tie it into the shooting of that idiot clerk, and it's *adios* for both of us.'

Val's wide eyes looked shocked. '*I* didn't shoot him!'

'Doesn't matter, stupid. You were there. You were in on it. That's the same as if you dropped the hammer.'

'It is?' She looked desolate, and ten years older.

Deke grinned. 'It's okay. Don't let it worry you. I'll just deep-six this baby . . .' With all his strength, he hurled the automatic. It flipped and spun, its blue-steel dark against the overcast sky, dropping like a shot raven. In the tumult of the surf far below, he couldn't see it splash.

'Now we're off the hook. No hard evidence, no witnesses . . .'

'*I'll* never speak a word,' said Val.

'Oh boy,' he muttered. In the two months he'd known her, he never quite trusted her. Now she comes up with a remark like that. If she thought about squealing enough to deny she would ever do it . . .

'What's wrong?' she asked.

'Nothing,' Deke said.

He'd been too quick to throw away the gun.

He looked again at the distant stone fortress. That tower on the ocean side looked like a great place for an accident. 'Still want to visit the castle?' he asked.

Val beamed.

They hurried back to the car.

Walking the barren ledge, Deke took a long look at the castle. It stood on an outcropping of rock, cut off entirely from the bluff. A rickety footbridge, about thirty feet long, reached over to it.

He could heave Val off the bridge easy enough. But what if it gave out under the weight of two people and he took the dive with her?

The castle itself seemed to be nothing more than four stone walls with the big tower on the southwest corner.

Forget the footbridge. The tower was the place to do it.

'Isn't it lovely!' Val blurted. 'It's so . . . I don't know . . . *majestic*! You'd think it would be in the guide books.'

'Maybe it is.'

'Oh, it's not. I've read them all. I know California like my own face, and I've never heard of a castle like this. There's the Hearst Castle, of course, but it's so different. I've been there twice, you know. Once with my second husband, and . . . Where's the ticket booth, do you think?'

'I don't think there is one.'

'Oh, there *has* to be.'

'Maybe inside,' Deke said. He was sure there would be no ticket booth. The place looked deserted and forlorn. He didn't feel like explaining, though. Val would see for herself, soon enough.

They reached the footbridge. Far below it, the surf beat and churned.

'So far down!'

'I'll go first,' Deke said. 'You stay put till I'm across.'

Val nodded.

Deke hurried across the swaying bridge, and sighed with relief when he reached the far end. He was trembling. As he tried to calm down, Val appeared beside him.

'Oh look!' she said, and pointed at a sign above the castle gate. '"Herlihy's Castle",' she read. '"May age ne'r wither thy brow."'

'Cute,' Deke said.

They stepped beneath the arch of the gateway. Except for a dozen seagulls taking shelter from the wind, the courtyard was deserted. 'Guess we don't have to buy tickets, after all.'

Val pushed her hands into her coat pockets. 'I don't like this place, Deke. It makes me jumpy.'

'A minute ago you said it's majestic.'

'Yeah, but . . .'

'Yeah but, yeah but,' Deke mimicked.

'It shouldn't be here, you know what I mean?'

'No, I don't.'

'I mean, a castle in California?'

Ignoring her, he started walking across the court-yard. Seagulls in his way took flight, circled, and landed again.

Val hurried to catch up. She gripped his elbow, but he kept walking. 'I've got this crazy weird feeling, Deke. Like we're in a nightmare. We oughta get out of here. Something bad's gonna happen, I can feel it in my bones.'

'That's arthritis.'

'Very funny. Please, let's go back to the car.'

'You're the one who wanted to see this place. "Can we go see it? Can we, can we?" Well, now we're here. And I don't leave till I've been up that tower. You stay here and wait, if you want, but I'm going up.' Jerking his arm free, he stepped toward the dark entryway.

'Don't leave me here.'

'Stay or come, it's up to you.'

'Deke, please! We shouldn't be here. I can feel it.'

'Sure. See you later. Probably won't take me half an hour.'

He entered the opening and began to climb the spiral stairs. His shoes made loud scuffing sounds on the concrete. He realized, by the third stair, that there was no handrail.

'Wait!' Val cried. 'Don't leave me!'

'Then put a move on.' He waited until she reached the step below him. 'Stay close,' he said, and continued to climb.

The stairs were shaped like wedges, a foot wide near the outer wall and tapering down to nothing at Deke's right. He stayed close to the wall. He kept his left hand against its cool, damp stone.

After one full turn of the stairs, the light from below was lost. The stairway was dark except for a thin band of light from a window slit.

'Deke, let's go back.'

'Forget it.'

'I feel like I'm gonna fall.'

You must be psychic, he thought, and grinned. 'Just keep a hand on the wall,' he advised. As he spoke, his right foot found only enough stair for his toes, and slipped off. His knee slammed the concrete. 'Damn!' he snapped.

'I *told* you—'

'Shut up.'

They kept climbing with only the light from the window slits to show the way. Once, the light vanished so completely that Deke could see nothing. Disoriented and dizzy, he stopped climbing. He flinched as Val touched his back.

'It's getting to you, isn't it?' she asked.

'Nothing's getting to me but the darkness. I'll be okay in a minute.'

'Let's go down, Deke.'

'We're almost to the top.'

'How do you know?'

'Don't worry, I know.'

As he started to climb again, his legs felt shaky.

'How're we gonna get down?' Val asked.

'Walk,' he said.

'It'll be dark outside. We won't be able to see a thing.'

'So we spend the night.'

'I don't want to go any higher. Not now. It's all too creepy.'

'Suit yourself.'

He suddenly saw light above him. 'Ha! We made it!' He hurried up the final stairs and stepped through the doorway. Directly in front of him, back to the tower wall, sat a man.

'Is it come to kiss the stone, you are?' he asked in a lilting accent Deke took for Irish. He wore an old gray jacket, and baggy trousers with leather knee patches. He had a sly look on his face.

'What stone?'

Val stepped up beside Deke. She smiled when she saw the stranger.

'Why, the Herlihy Stone. Have you not heard of it, then?' Deke shook his head.

The man stood up, using a blackthorn walking stick. A young, powerfully built man, he didn't appear to need the stick. 'You know of the Blarney Stone, no doubt?' he asked. 'It's a bit of marble you find on a castle wall near Cork, in Ireland.'

'If you kiss it,' said Val, 'it's good luck.'

'A common bit of misinformation that's on your tongue, ma'am. It's not good luck you'll be getting from the Blarney Stone, but the gift of eloquence. Your tongue'll walk circles 'round all who listen, and they'll not understand a word of it. That's the gift of the Blarney Stone. Now you take the Herlihy Stone, it's a different story altogether. One kiss of it, and you'll stay forever young.'

'I've never heard of the Herlihy Stone,' Val said.

'It's not many as have. We don't let it get around, you see. It's a hundred years the Herlihys have kept this castle keep, and we've all been modest men. We like our quiet and solitude. We like a bit of desolation, for it's calming to the soul. Crowds are the curse of God, after all, and it's surely crowds we'd be getting if the gift of our Stone got around. A few wanderers, now and again, put money enough in our pockets. We are not greedy men.'

'What does it cost to kiss this stone of yours?' Deke asked, trying to keep the anger and frustration out of his voice. All that work, all that climbing, for this! He should've known the castle wouldn't be deserted.

'Would two-fifty a head be too dear?' the man wanted to know.

'Two dollars and fifty cents?' Val asked.

'That's all it would cost, and you'd have a kiss of the Herlihy Stone and never lose your youth.'

Val smiled. 'I wish I'd come here thirty years ago.'

'I shouldn't worry. It's still a lovely woman you are.'

She gave Deke a superior, accusing smile, as if he'd been too ignorant to notice the qualities so obvious to this stranger.

'Go ahead and kiss the damned thing,' Deke said. 'What've you got to lose?'

'Before you decide, have a look at the stone itself.' The man pointed his stick at a gap between the stone walkway and the parapet. 'Step up and have a look.'

Deke and Val moved closer.

'My God!' Val said.

Kneeling beside the gap, the man reached down with his cane and tapped the wall. 'There's your Herlihy Stone, the bit of marble down there.'

Two hundred feet below the bit of marble, waves crashed and exploded against the rocks of the promontory.

'It's not so dangerous as it might appear,' the man said. 'You must sit on the edge of the walk here and lean back, same as if you were giving the Blarney Stone a kiss. I'll be holding your legs, of course.'

'How many have you lost?' Deke asked, and grinned.

The man grinned back. 'Hardly enough to mention.'

'Well,' Val said, 'I don't think I'm up to it. I really don't.'

'A good many folk feel that way, at first. I must tell you with all me heart, however, a kiss of the Herlihy Stone will keep you young, indeed. How would you guess my age?'

'Thirty?' Val tried.

'And you, sir?' he asked Deke.

'Thirty-five?'

'It's eighty-three I'll be come October.'

Deke laughed.

'Fifty years it's been since I kissed the Herlihy Stone.'

'Sure,' Deke said.

'Is it a liar you're after calling me?'

Deke considered the man's size, and the walking stick. 'No. Not me. Go ahead and kiss the stone, Val. Look what it did for him.'

She shook her head.

'I'll be holding your legs good and tight, ma'am. Me hands have not failed me yet.'

'Well . . .'

Deke could see that, in spite of her hesitation, she wanted to go ahead with it. Did she really believe that garbage about eternal youth? She couldn't be that stupid. More likely, she was looking forward to the feel of those big, powerful hands pressing down on her legs.

'Okay,' she said. 'I'm game. Deke?'

Maybe he could figure a way to lose her through the hole. Grinning, he took out his billfold. He handed the man three dollars.

'It'll be five dollars for you and the lady both.'

'Right. You owe me fifty cents.'

'Are you not going to kiss the Stone yourself, then?'

'You kidding?'

'Deke, you've got to.'

'I haven't *got* to. You go ahead and have your fun, you two. I'll watch.'

'Deke, please! Don't you want to stay young?'

'Do you believe that bunk?' Deke pointed toward the small slab of marble. 'He ought to call it the Hooey Stone.'

'Well, I'm doing it anyway.'

'Be my guest. I'm not trying to stop you.'

'Okay then,' Val said.

The man reached into a pocket and took out a pair of quarters. 'Your change, sir.'

Deke put them away. He zipped his coat against the cold wind.

The man tapped his stick on a stone platform beside the gap. 'If you've any valuables in your pockets, ma'am, set them here or they'll be in for a great long fall.'

Val put her purse on the platform. She took gloves from her coat pockets. Last, she removed her glasses. The man held her arm as she sat down on the walkway, her back to the battlements.

Deke grinned. 'Say, do you want *me* to hold your legs?'

'No,' Val said. 'That's okay.'

'Come on. Why not?'

'I couldn't allow it,' the man intervened. 'It's *I* must do the holding.'

'I don't see why.'

'It's the rules, sir.'

'Whose rules?'

'If you wish the lady to kiss the stone, it's I must hold her. I'll not be arguing about it.'

Deke shrugged. 'Do it your way,' he said.

As the man knelt beside Val, Deke glanced at the blackthorn stick. Its knobby handle looked lethal. A good bash at the right instant, he could wipe them both out. Unfortunately, the stick was propped against the parapet within the man's reach.

'Ready?'

Val nodded.

The man gripped her thighs. 'Now gently lie backwards. Aye. Don't be afraid.'

Deke watched Val's head lower into the gap. He glanced at the blackthorn stick.

What if he couldn't nail the guy fast enough? He'd stand little chance against a strong, young man like that.

Val was bent backward like a bow, her shoulders and head completely out of sight.

Now or never!

Never, Deke decided. Not up here. Not with this fellow to deal with. He'd wait for a better chance. Maybe the dark stairs on the way down. Or the footbridge.

'Have you kissed the Herlihy Stone?' the man called down.

'Yes,' came Val's strained voice.

He flipped her legs upward and let go. Deke watched, astonished, as Val's feet vanished through the gap.

She screamed for a long time.

The man picked up his blackthorn stick and got to his feet.

Deke backed away. 'What're you doing?' he demanded. 'You dropped her on purpose!'

'I surely did, and there's no denying it. Now it's your turn, sir, to kiss the Stone.' He raised the stick to his shoulder and stepped toward Deke.

'No! Stay back!'

The stick cut through the air and pounded Deke's shoulder. His arm went numb. The next blow glanced off his head. Dazed, he dropped to his knees.

'It's down you go,' said the man, dragging him to the gap.

His back bent painfully as he was lowered headfirst. He saw the smooth marble inches from his face.

'Have you kissed it yet?'

'No!'

'Doesn't matter, actually.'

'Let me up!'

'I can't do that. It's me job. It's the family line, so to speak, conferring the gift of the Herlihy Stone.' As he let go of Deke's legs, he called, 'You'll not grow old now, my friend, not at all!'

Dracuson's Driver

The graveyard shift at the Wanderer's Rest Motel suited Pete fine. It went from midnight to 8:00 a.m. Between those hours, there wasn't much to do: answer the phone, though it rarely rang; once in a great while register a guest arriving unusually late. The job consisted mostly of simply being there to keep an eye on things.

Pete liked keeping his eye on things.

In particular, the younger and more attractive of the motel's female guests.

Few of them ever visited the motel office during the long, late hours of Pete's shift. But he made up for their absence by visiting them.

All the ground level rooms had rear windows. None of the rear windows had curtains that worked quite properly – Pete had seen to that. The curtain gaps gave him many wonderful sights. As did the bathroom windows. Because the bathrooms had no ventilation fans, and because the rear of the motel was sheltered by a steep rocky slope, the windows were often left open. As a result, Pete had spied many sweet things stripping for showers, stepping into and out of the stalls, afterward rubbing gleamy slick skin with thread-bare towels.

'Yo, Boydy-babes,' Pete said as he entered the motel office to relieve Boyd Marmon. 'How's it swinging?'

Boyd abandoned the rear of the registration counter fast enough to avoid a friendly smack on the shoulder or back.

Alone, Pete inspected the registration cards. All but three of the downstairs rooms were supposedly taken for the night. So he waited until 12:30, then did what he called a 'window

715

run'. And another at 1:00 a.m. Still others at 1:15, 1:30, 1:45 and 2:00.

For all his efforts, Pete viewed two dumpy women, one cute teenaged girl who'd already changed into her Garfield nightshirt and would probably not be removing it in the near future, and a gal who sat in an armchair, her back to the window. Though this one had lush blonde hair and bare shoulders, she would not stir from her chair. She looked wonderful from behind. Was she beautiful? What was she wearing that left her shoulders bare? Something strapless? Maybe a towel? Or nothing at all?

She was the main reason Pete kept making window runs that night. After first spotting her during the one o'clock trip, he pretty much ignored the other windows and spent his few minutes gazing in at her, aching, *willing* her to get out of the chair and turn around. But she never did. Not while he was watching. And when he made his two o'clock run, her window was dark.

He peered in, anyway, but saw nothing.

She must've already gone to bed.

He'd missed her.

He thought, *Shit!*

He thought, *No damn fair!*

On his way back to the office, he nearly tripped over a black cat that had been hanging around the motel lately. He tried to give it a punt. It scooted, however, so his shoe only nicked its rump. He threw a rock at it, but missed.

At the office, he kicked open the glass door. He kicked the front of the registration counter.

If you had any guts, he thought, you'd kick open that babe's door and *take* her.

She might even like it. A sweet, balmy night like this, she's *got* to be horny.

'Course, the card says she's in there with her husband.

So what? Break his head open, and *then* nail her.

It perked up Pete to imagine such things.

He sat behind the counter and dwelled on his fantasies. What she would look like naked. How she would feel. What he would do to her. What he would force her to do to him.

Pete had only been with one naked girl. Beth Wiggins. Last June in his dad's car after the Senior Ball. She was the worst-looking girl in school – therefore the only girl he could work up enough guts to invite.

She'd been as eager as a puppy dying for affection.

In the car after the dance, she'd been all over him.

She had onion breath and boobs like uncooked bread loaves and a jumbo gut and an ass a mile wide. She'd wanted it bad. Pete had always thought *he* wanted it bad. Confronted with a lusting and unattired Beth, however, he found out that all he wanted was to get away. He didn't even get hard when she sucked on him. So then she'd started to cry.

So then he'd smacked her.

When he smacked her, he *did* start getting hard. So he did it again, and got harder. But she squealed and slugged him in the nose, and that put a stop to everything. They both got dressed and she sobbed all the way back to her house.

Never again, he'd vowed that night.

No more pigs.

Unfortunately, he was terrified by the idea of speaking to – much less asking out – any female he found the least bit attractive.

He could *look* at them, though.

Spy on them through windows.

Dream about sneaking into their rooms, subduing them, stripping them, forcing them to comply with his every wish.

Hardly a night went by that he didn't pursue such thoughts about one or another of the motel guests.

He would *love* to make the dreams come true.

If only he were invisible . . .

Or if he could figure out a way to hypnotize or drug one of them without her ever suspecting . . .

A way to have his fun with a gal and get away with it, that's what he wanted. And he savoured the problem, toyed with it, considered possible solutions. He knew there *was* no solution. No way, ever, to act out his fantasies and be totally, absolutely, utterly one hundred per cent certain of not being so much as suspected.

Still, it was fun to think about.

Pete spent a lot of time, during the long silent hours after quitting his window runs for the night, imagining what he might do to the bare-shouldered woman. And then he spent even longer toying with various plans he might employ for getting away with it.

At times, all of it seemed very real.

He could see her, smell her, taste her, hear her rough breathing and gasps and squeals. Shrieks of ecstasy and pain sounded so much alike.

If he drugged her, of course, she would feel neither.

Maybe bash her on the head. Tie her to the bedframe. Wait till she comes to before starting in on her. Yes.

Shiny with sweat. Striped with bright red ribbons of blood. *Writhing, squirming, screaming* . . .

Pete was startled from his reveries, just after 4:00 a.m., when a hearse glided to a stop beneath the motel's portico. It looked like the real thing – long and black and shiny, its rear side windows draped with curtains.

The moment he saw it, icy prickles raced up Pete's spine, stiffened the nape of his neck, made his scalp crawl.

'Oh shit,' he muttered.

A hearse!

Why's a *hearse* stopping here?

For just a second, he considered a quick drop behind the counter. He could pretend not to be here.

But maybe the driver had already spotted him.

Anyway, he told himself, that'd be chicken.

Nothing to be scared of.

Instead of trying to hide, Pete lowered his head and gazed at the stack of registration cards. He heard a car door thump shut.

A hearse had never stopped here before.

Pete had never *heard* of a hearse stopping at a motel.

Weird. Awful fucking weird.

The bells above the office door jingled.

Sweat trickled down Pete's sides. He drilled his eyes into the stack of cards, terrified of looking up.

Footsteps approached.

Make him go away! Please! I don't like this!

'Hi.'

The sound of the voice shocked him. It sounded cheerful. Cheerful and young and female.

He raised his eyes.

The girl on the other side of the counter wore a black uniform: a black, visored cap tilted up in a jaunty way atop a head of very short, pale blonde hair; a black tunic with two rows of brass buttons down its front; black slacks that hugged her legs; gleaming black leather boots as high as her knees.

The uniform might've looked grim and severe on someone else. On this smiling, slender girl, it looked like a lark. She was a pixie playing dress-up.

Gazing at her, Pete felt as if his heart might quit.

He'd never seen anyone so . . . so fine.

He felt stunned nearly senseless by the curve of bangs that hid her entire right eyebrow, by her huge blue eyes, by the smooth warm cream of her skin and the delicate curves of her cheekbones, nose, lips and chin, by the long smooth glide of her neck.

'Are you quite all right?' she asked.

'Me? Sure. Fine.' He bobbed his head. 'You . . . You just reminded me of someone, that's all. Would you like a room?'

'That I would. It's been a mighty long night.' She raised her index finger. 'A single should do nicely. My companion won't be requiring a bed.'

'Your companion?'

She swung a thumb over her shoulder. 'My stiff friend out in the bone-mobile.'

'*What?* You've got a . . . a dead person in there?'

'Don't fret. I won't allow him out of his coffin.'

Pete stared out at the hearse. 'My God,' he muttered. 'There's really a dead guy. . .?'

'Oh, yes, quite. Does that present a problem?'

'I don't know.'

'He needn't be registered, you know.' She gave Pete a quick, gamine grin.

'I guess it'll be all right,' he said.

'Super.'

'How long would you be staying with us?'

'Ah, the rub.' She sighed. 'You see, the thing of it is, I've been at the wheel since sunrise.'

'Sunrise *yesterday*?'

'If I stay up a few more hours, it'll be an even twenty-four. In other words, I'm wasted. So what I should like to do is climb into bed and sleep through the day.'

'Mmmm.'

'Not the way things are usually done, eh?'

'You're right about that. Check-out time is noon.'

She shrugged. 'I'll really need to stay on until evening. Perhaps as late as nine o'clock.'

'That is sort of a problem.'

'I know. I've been around this particular bend a few times before. Next, you'll be explaining that you've no choice but to charge me for two days occupancy.'

I can't lose her.

'No. That wouldn't be fair. I tell you what, I'll fix things so you only need to pay for one night.'

'You can do that?'

'Sure. My parents own the place.' It was a lie, but the girl had no way of knowing any better. 'I'll give you a nice ground-floor room at the end of the wing. If you'll just fill this out?' He peeled a registration card off the stack, slid it across the counter to her, and snapped a pen down on top of it.

Pete was good at reading upside-down.

The girl's name was Tess Hunter.

She was with the Greenfields Mortuary of Clayton, New York.

'You're a long way from home,' Pete said.

'So's he.' She gestured again with her thumb. 'The poor bloke burnt himself up in a yacht fire on the St Lawrence. His family intends to finish what the fire started, and spread his ashes on their beach property in Malibu.'

Pete found his nose wrinkling. 'He *burnt up*?'

'Not quite. Charred on the outside, though I should imagine he's still rather rare on the inside.'

She pushed the card toward Pete.

'And how will you be paying?'

'Cash.'

He charged her for one night in the room. After receiving the payment, he gave her the key to room ten. 'There's an ice machine right next to the office here, and . . .'

She shook her head. 'Won't be needing it. It's just a quick shower for me, if I can stay awake long enough, and then to bed.'

A shower!

'Could I give you a hand with your luggage?' Pete asked. He knew his face was red.

'Does the offer include a hand with the coffin?'

'Huh?'

'Oh, I'm afraid I can't leave poor Mr Dracuson in the hearse. Somebody might make off with him, you know.'

'I'm sure nobody would . . .'

'It's quite a responsibility, chauffeuring the dead.'

'But . . .'

'I'd be sacked for sure if I should lose him.'

'Where do you want to put him?' Pete asked.

'In my room, of course.'

'In your *room?*'

'You haven't a rule against it, I hope.'

'Not that I know of. But . . . do you *do* that? Keep the dead guys with you in your *room?*'

'Oh, sure. Doesn't bother me a whit, actually. 'Cept for those that snore.'

Pete surprised himself by laughing.

'What's your name?' Tess asked.

'Pete.'

'So, Pete, you'll lend me a hand with the box?'

He gave her a nod, then hurried around the end of the registration counter. He opened the office door for Tess. She stepped quickly to the hearse and opened its passenger door for Pete.

She wants me to ride with her!

The thought of sitting beside Tess in a car made Pete's heart pound fast. To be so close to her! In the darkness!

Not in a hearse, though.

No way.

'Thanks anyway,' he told her.

'Pop in. I'll give you a ride to the room.'

'That's okay. I'll walk.'

'The hearse puts you off, does it?'

Already on his way, he looked back at Tess and said, 'No, no. Just that there's no point. The room's just over there.'

'You may not get another chance, you know, to ride in the front of one.'

'That's okay.'

She entered the passenger side, herself, swung the door shut behind her, and slid across the seat. She was no sooner stationed behind the wheel than the engine *voomed* to life. The headlights came on.

Pete was already halfway across the parking lot by the time the hearse began rolling forward. It turned slowly, beams creeping over the blacktop until they found him. Framed in their brightness, he followed his long shadow to the parking space in front of room ten.

He faced the car, squinting until its headlights died. The engine went silent. The door swung open and Tess climbed out. She walked toward him briskly, swinging an overnight case at her side.

'Let me get the door for you,' he said.

'Thanks.' She handed the key to him.

He unlocked the door, reached into the room and flicked a switch. The chandelier came on. Though it was suspended above the front table, its six small bulbs brightened all but the farthest end of the room. Beyond the shadows there, Pete glimpsed the window. *His* window.

The sight of it sucked his breath out.

Oh, to be standing on the other side of it! Staring in at Tess! This'll be the best ever!

The very best!

And she mentioned a shower!

In just a few more minutes . . .

Tess stepped past him, tossed her bag onto a bed and swung around, grinning. 'Spiffy room,' she said.

Pete nodded. 'Is that all the luggage you have?' he asked.

'It's all I need.'

He backed out of the doorway as she approached. Then he followed her. The seat of her trousers looked very tight. It hugged her rump, flexed and shifted with every step she took.

At the rear of the hearse, he kept his eyes on Tess, savoring her looks, thrilling himself with the knowledge that he would soon be spying on her, and also avoiding the sights that he preferred not to see.

He watched Tess, not the hearse, as she swung open its rear door. He watched Tess, not the coffin, as she pulled at it and dragged it toward her.

'Poor Mr Dracuson isn't very heavy,' she said. 'But if you'd like to take hold of the front . . .?'

Pete realized she was standing motionless, waiting for his help, an end of the coffin braced against her chest, the other end resting at the edge of the hearse.

He hurried to the front, found handles on both sides of the dark wood box, and swung it clear.

The coffin wasn't nearly as heavy as Pete had expected. In spite of Tess's comment about the weight, he'd thought it would be a lot tougher to carry. He supposed that large amounts of Dracuson must've been left behind in the boat or river. Ashes.

Tess maneuvered herself close to the rear of the hearse. She shut the door with her rump. 'Okay,' she said.

'You got it?'

'I'm fine. How about you?'

'No sweat,' Pete said.

As he lugged the coffin backward, he imagined dropping it. He pictured it smashing down, the lid dropping away, a charred black husk tumbling out. A withered thing, faceless, hunched like a fetus. Black dust rising off its skin shell. Flakes falling. Pieces – a nose, a finger – silently breaking off.

But it didn't happen.

Together, they carried the coffin into the room.

Just inside the doorway, Tess said, 'Right here's fine.'

They lowered it to the floor.

'Have you ever seen him?' Pete asked.

'Oh, yes. I helped put him in, you know.'

'How does he look?'

'Bloody awful.' She tapped the box with the toe of her boot. 'I'd open it up and show you, but the smell might be rather off-putting.'

He tried to laugh. 'I wouldn't want to see him. Thanks anyway.'

'Well, thank you for the help. He's a bit tough to manage by myself.'

Pete returned the room key to her.

She put it on the table, then pulled the wallet out of her back pocket. Pete held up his hands.

'No. It was my pleasure.'

'A pleasure, was it? Lugging a stiff?'

'Well . . .' He shrugged. 'You know.'

As he stepped past the coffin, Tess returned the wallet to her pocket. She moved out of his way, but extended her hand. 'Thank you again,' she said.

'You're welcome.' He shook her hand.

It sent heat rushing up his arm, heat that spread and filled his entire body.

The heat stayed, even after her hand went away.

Pete swallowed. His voice trembled slightly as he said, 'If you need anything, I'll be right in the office.'

'Have a good night, now,' Tess said.

He stepped outside, and she shut the door.

He headed straight for the office. Walking fast. It would've been much quicker just to hurry around the corner of Tess's room, but he wanted to *appear* to be returning to the office. Just in case.

He entered the office, glanced about. Saw it was deserted. Heard no phone ringing. Then turned around and left. He rushed around to the rear.

No light spilled into the darkness from *any* of the windows. Not even from Tess's at the far end of the building.

This can't be!

If I get cheated out of this . . .!

It's okay, he thought, that the bathroom light isn't on. Only means she hasn't started her shower. Good. I haven't missed anything yet.

But the window at the back of her *room* looked dark.

That light *has* to be on, he told himself. I just can't see it from here.

After all, the gap between the edges of the curtains was only a couple of inches wide. It wouldn't allow more than a narrow strip of light to shine out.

Maybe she pinned the gap shut, or something.

Pete crept toward Tess's windows.

Not even so much as a flicker of television light showed within any room along the way.

He stopped at Tess's bathroom window. Frosted glass, gray in the darkness. One side open all the way.

Fantastic, Pete thought. Incredible.

When she takes that shower . . .

If she takes it.

He rushed in a crouch to the main rear window and peered in.

Peered into a black void.

She just got here! I was only gone a minute! What the hell's going on!

726

Calm down, he told himself. You didn't miss anything. She hasn't had time to change for bed, much less take a shower. She probably just left the room for some reason.

What if she's on her way to the office?

She needs something. No towel in her room? Something like that. Phoned the office. Now she's looking for me.

Shit! What if she finds me?

As fast as he could move without making too much noise, Pete made his way to the end of the building and alongside the windowless far wall. At the front corner, he leaned forward.

The hearse was parked in front of the room, just where Tess had left it.

The lighted walkway leading to the office looked deserted. Except for the cars lined up in front of the ground-level rooms, the parking lot was empty. Even the road beyond the parking lot seemed abandoned and desolate.

Pete studied the windshield of the hearse. When he opened the driver's door, a courtesy light came on.

Tess was not in the hearse.

He went to the motel office. Tess was not there, either.

She's gotta still be in her room, he thought. Maybe she just turned off the light, flopped on one of the beds and zonked out.

Too worn out for that shower she wanted.

So tired she probably fell asleep in her clothes.

Wasted.

What if she's so wasted she can't wake up?

Nobody will ever know, Pete told himself as he slipped his spare key into the lock of room ten.

He wished he had gotten started earlier.

It had taken him a while, though, to work up the nerve. By the time he'd left the office, light had already begun to creep across the sky from the east.

He'd nearly lost his nerve.

But all the windows along the front of the motel were still dark.

Even if somebody does see me, he thought, it won't matter. I'm the night manager. I have every right to go into a room. Besides, none of the guests had signed up for more than one night. All of them would be gone by noon.

It'll work out fine.

If Tess doesn't wake up.

She won't.

As long as I'm very quiet . . . and don't shine the flashlight on her face.

Anyhow, Pete knew that he might not be able to get into her room, at all. Most guests, before retiring, fastened the safety bolt. If Tess had done that, the game was over. Pete sure couldn't risk breaking in. It was silently with the key, or nothing.

If she was dead tired, though, maybe she'd neglected to fasten the latch.

Maybe.

Pete turned the key, twisted the knob, and pushed. The door swung inward.

Oh, my God! Fantastic!

The door hinges squeaked a bit. Pete cringed, but he didn't quit. He inched the door open wider and wider, then slipped inside the room and eased the door shut behind him.

The room was not totally dark. Strips of dim gray showed between the curtains of the big front window, the small rear window. The vague hints of light were useless, however. Pete could see no details of the room's interior. Not the furniture, not the coffin, not Tess.

He heard nothing except his own quick heartbeat.

Then the quiet rub of his hand against cloth as he slipped

the key into the front pocket of his jeans, another rub as he drew his hand out.

He switched the heavy, steel-cased flashlight to his right hand. He curled the fingers of his left hand over its lens. Turning the light toward his face, he thumbed the switch. His fingers went rosy, so nearly transparent that he could see their shadowy bone-shapes.

Though the darkness had prevented him from seeing either bed, he knew exactly where each had to be. He aimed his flashlight, spread his middle fingers slightly, and watched a bright ribbon stretch down to the surface of the nearer bed.

No feet or legs. Not so much as a bulge in the covers.

He swept the light sideways.

The bed was neatly made, empty except for Tess's overnight bag. The top of the bag was spread open a bit. She must've been into it.

Pete lit the other bed, and gasped.

For just an instant, he thought Tess was sprawled out, dismembered, decapitated. Then he realized he was looking at her strewed clothes. Cap, tunic and trousers black against the smooth pale bedspread. Tall boots standing upright on the floor beside the bed.

But no blouse. No bra or panties or even socks.

Had she been going around with nothing on, at all, beneath her black costume?

Pete heard his heartbeat quicken its pace. His mouth felt dry. He was suddenly short of breath. As he panted for air, he felt himself getting stiff and hard.

She must've done it in the dark, he thought.

Turned out the light right away, even before starting to undress.

Did she suspect something?

Is she naked now?

Maybe just in her bra and panties.

Flimsy little things . . .

Black like the rest of . . .

Where the hell is she!

Hiding? Maybe she heard me unlocking the door.

Oh, my God.

If she's awake and knows I'm here, Pete thought, it means major trouble. Huge trouble. Disaster.

Getting fired, he realized, might be the least of his troubles.

Could he end up in jail?

I just wanted to look at her!

He dropped his hand from the front of the flashlight, and the full bright beam shot forward. He shined it on the coffin just beyond his feet. Sidestepped around the coffin. Knelt between the beds and lifted the hanging covers to make sure she wasn't hiding under either bed. Got to his feet and checked the space on the other side of the far bed. Turned in a full circle to light every corner of the room. Then entered the bathroom.

No tub, just a shower stall.

He swept aside the plastic curtain and shined his light in, ready and hoping to find Tess cowering naked on the tile floor.

She wasn't there.

Where is she?

She hasn't left. The hearse is still here. Her clothes are still here.

Outside the bathroom, Pete played his light over the scattered clothes.

She was the best, the finest. He had never in his life seen such a girl. All the others were . . . crud . . . compared to Tess.

This isn't fair! Where are you?

In despair, Pete sank down onto the corner of the bed.

I'll wait for her, he thought. She's got to show up.

What if she had spare clothes in that bag, changed into them, and walked away? Fed up, maybe, with chauffeuring stiffs.

Maybe that's it.

If that's it, she'll never come back.

No. No, she talked about responsibilities. She wouldn't even leave the coffin outside in the hearse, so she certainly wouldn't abandon the thing.

She acted as if it was her *duty* to transport this Dracuson fellow's . . .

*Dracu*son?

Pete shined his light on the coffin.

Could that really be the stiff's name – Dracuson? Maybe Tess was kidding. Thought it would be fun to tag the poor jerk with a name that sounds like Dracula.

Like I'm sure there's a vampire in there.

Like Tess is some sort of chauffeur for a fuckin' vampire, rides him around all night, maybe pulls off the road sometimes to let him fly off and suck people, and then they hole up all day long in some crummy motel. So Drac can rest up in his coffin till dark, and Tess can get her beauty sleep.

Stupid, Pete thought.

Crazy.

No such thing as vampires.

If there *is* such a thing, though, everything would make sense. Everything except Tess's disappearance.

Hell, Pete thought, that's an easy one.

She isn't just Dracuson's chauffeur. She's his lover, too. She's right there inside the coffin with him.

Yeah, right. Every day and twice on Sundays.

Pete knew that the notion was stupid, crazy, ridiculous. But he suddenly *had* to look inside the coffin.

He stood up. His legs shook as he sidestepped past the coffin. He felt as if his stomach was shivering.

She isn't going to be in there, he told himself.

If you open it up, all you'll find is crispy black Mr Dracuson.

Yeah? Then where is Tess?

Pete crouched at the foot of the coffin. He shined his light on the lid. The wood looked like mahogany, reddish brown and glossy.

He listened.

No heavy breathing came from the box. No thrashing sounds, no thumps.

If she's in there, he thought, she isn't humping any vampire. She's lying quiet and still.

Maybe she heard me, knows I'm here. What if she tries to nail me when I open the thing?

He thought, *Ha.*

He almost laughed out loud.

If Tess was inside with her vampire lover, which seemed highly unlikely, she would be face-down on top of him. She could hardly spring upon Pete from that position.

He gripped the flashlight in his right hand.

He hooked the fingertips of his left hand under the edge of the coffin lid.

Throw it off quick. Don't give her a chance to roll over.

But he imagined the noise of the heavy lid thumping the floor.

No way.

What I need here, he thought, is silence and stealth.

Instead of casting the lid to the floor, he eased it upward a few inches. He ducked his head. He shined his light inside.

And glimpsed pajama legs of pale blue fabric as shiny as silk.

A hot jolt raced through him.

He raised the lid higher, crept his light up the body.

There was only one.

It lay on its back, cushioned by the white satin of the coffin's lining.

A slim body garbed in loose, clinging pajamas that took on the curves they covered. The shirt overhung the waist of the pants. It had four big white buttons. It rose smoothly over the mounds of her breasts and jutted with the thrust of her nipples. It was spread open above the top button, showing a wedge of bare chest, the hollow of her throat.

Pete saw the underside of her chin. Though his angle was all wrong to see the face, he knew this was Tess.

Who else *could* it be?

So where's Dracuson?

Who the hell knows?

Who the hell cares?

It only mattered that he had found Tess and she still seemed to be asleep.

Pete set down the flashlight to free his right hand. Then he worked his way to the side of the coffin. Slowly, carefully, he lifted off the lid. He swung around and lowered it onto the bed.

Kneeling, he picked up his flashlight. He held it low as he changed it from his left hand to his right.

Don't shine it in her eyes, he warned himself. That'd wake her up for sure.

Why the hell is she sleeping in the coffin? Two perfectly good queen-size beds.

Must be nuts.

Seriously weird.

But, oh man! So what?

He raised the flashlight. He shined it on her chest, holding it close enough to her body so that the bright disk would stay tight and away from her face.

He gazed at her breasts.

He wanted to touch them.

He wanted to slip the big white buttons out of their holes and spread open the pajama shirt and see her breasts naked and touch them, caress them, squeeze them, try them with his mouth.

This is it. My big chance. She's zonked, dead to the world.

But she'll wake up if I try to undo any buttons. She'll wake up for sure if I touch her.

Wake up screaming.

Unless . . .

He shined his light on her face, saw her open eyes, gasped as his heart lurched, then leaned and swung, hammering her forehead with the flashlight. The first blow shattered the lens and killed the bulb. After that, he swung and pounded in darkness.

When his arm wore out, he dropped the flashlight.

He got to his feet, staggered to the wall, and flicked the switch. The chandelier came on.

He looked down at Tess.

Her face was a bloody ruin.

But the rest of her was unharmed.

Pete took a pillow off one of the beds. He covered Tess's face with it, thinking only to hide the ugly damage, but then pressing the pillow down hard just to make sure she wouldn't wake up and cause trouble.

He held the pillow down tight against her face for a very long time.

Leaving the pillow on her face, he unfastened the big white buttons of her pajama shirt. The shirt was spattered with blood. He opened it wide. Some of the blood had soaked through, staining her skin pink.

'Oh, Tess,' he whispered. 'Oh, Tess.'

Her breasts were wonderful. More than wonderful. He lingered over them, gentle and rough, savoring their weight and texture and taste.

Later, he plucked apart the snap at the waist of her pajama pants, drew the pants down her legs and tossed them onto the bed. He raised her legs, spread them, and hooked her knees over the edges of the coffin.

He stripped and climbed in.

He kissed her and caressed her, squeezed her, licked her, nipped her, probed her, and it was the best, better than anything, worth everything, worth killing her for especially when he thrust into her slick heat.

It was what he had always wanted to do, and better than he'd ever dreamed.

The cleanup went off without a hitch.

Though the sun was bright above the cornfields to the east by the time he dragged the coffin out of room ten, nobody seemed to be wandering about. Pete was pretty sure that nobody saw him.

He got the coffin into the rear of the hearse.

He drove the hearse for a while, then turned up a dirt road and parked it inside a shabby, abandoned barn.

He left the coffin in the hearse, Tess in the coffin with her various garments and overnight case. But not with the pillow, because he was afraid it could be traced back to the motel.

He spent a few minutes wiping away his fingerprints with a rag. Then he hiked back to the motel.

The hike of two miles took him half an hour.

He made one more visit to room ten for the pillow and his broken flashlight. He concealed them in the trunk of his car.

At the office, he returned both room keys to their proper nook and destroyed the registration card. He kept the cash payment for himself.

So far as anyone except Pete would ever know, Tess Hunter had never checked into the Wanderer's Rest Motel.

* * *

At 8:00 a.m. that morning, Pete was relieved by Claire Simmons. He ate breakfast at Joe's Pancake Emporium. Then he drove out to the barn where he had left the hearse.

He spent the hot, summer morning with Tess. And much of the afternoon.

Late in the afternoon, tired to the bone, he drove home to the one-room house that he rented on the far side of town. He set his alarm clock for 11:00 p.m., stripped and climbed into bed.

He closed his eyes and smiled.

Life could be so great when you just had the guts to take what you wanted.

Wow!

He wondered how long Tess would keep.

Pretty hot in that old barn, but . . .

The alarm didn't wake Pete. He was stirred from his slumber, instead, by light shining in his eyes.

He blinked at the glare of the lamp beside his bed.

He squinted at his clock. Only 10:03.

What the hell . . .?

'You slimy creep.'

He knew the voice.

Young and female, with a lilt that sounded a bit English.

Pete bolted upright.

Tess, naked, stood beyond the end of his bed, fists planted on her hips, legs apart. She was shaking her head at him. Her face was clean. Unswollen, unbroken. As if Pete had never battered her to a mess with the flashlight.

Her short, pixie hair was matted down and dark. Wet. Her skin had a rosy hue. She looked as if she had just stepped out of a shower.

But Pete didn't find himself thrilled by the sight of her.

He didn't get stiff and hard. On the contrary, he shriveled.

He peed.

He began to whimper.

'I only wanted a bit of a rest, you know,' Tess said.

'Ya . . . you're *dead*!'

A corner of her mouth tilted upward. 'Not quite, actually – in spite of your moronic efforts, you sniveling pervert. If you'd had half a brain, you would've put a stake through my heart. My God, you *had* to know what I was.'

She stepped up onto the bed.

'Don't . . . Don't hurt me. Please.'

'Oh, I fully intend to hurt you. I'll hurt you quite a lot, word of honor. Cross my heart.' She flicked a fingernail against the creamy skin between her breasts, drawing a quick invisible X. 'You'll hurt beyond your wildest dreams.'

Baring her teeth, Tess bellowed and threw herself down on Pete.

And kept her word.

Roadside Pickup

When the piano stopped, the voice came back. It was soft and friendly, like the music, and kept Colleen's thoughts from dwelling on the empty road. 'That was Michel Legrand,' it said, almost whispering, 'and this is Jerry Bonner bringing you music and talk from midnight till dawn here on easy-listening KS . . .' She rolled the knob of her car radio and the voice clicked off.

It wouldn't be smart to keep listening. Not smart at all, since there was no telling how long she might be sitting here. Maybe all night. You can't play a radio all night without running down the battery. Or can you? She would have to ask that mechanic tomorrow. Jason. He was so good at explaining things.

She sighed with weariness and pressed her fingertips against her eyelids. If only someone would come along, and stop, and offer to help her.

The way Maggie was helped?

She felt her skin tighten.

No! Not like Maggie!

As Colleen rubbed her bare arms, she started to remember it again . . . the telephone that rang in her dream until it woke her to the real ringing, the roughness of the bedroom rug under her feet, the cool slick linoleum in the kitchen. And all the time, the sickening lump of fear in her belly because the phone just doesn't ring at 3:00 a.m. unless . . .

'Cut it out,' she muttered. 'Snap out of it, okay? Think about something pleasant for a change.'

Sure, something pleasant.

Otherwise she would start remembering the cop's voice on the phone and the drive to the morgue and the way her sister had looked lying there . . .

'Shine on, shine on, harvest moon,' she started to sing. She kept on singing it. Then she began, 'Sentimental Journey.'

When they were kids, they used to sing those songs on long trips. Mother and Father would be sitting up front, she and Maggie in the back, four shadows holding off the lonely night with sweet, half-remembered lyrics.

Maggie always had lots of trouble remembering the words. Whenever she got stuck, she would listen to the others and sing out the right words a moment later, like a cheery echo.

The night her car broke down, nobody was there to sing her the right words.

Colleen caught her breath. A light! A speck of light no bigger than one of the stars high above the cornfields moved in her side mirror. A car was coming.

Would this one stop? Three, so far, had whooshed by without even slowing down. Three in almost as many hours.

Maybe one of them had stopped, somewhere farther on, and phoned the state troopers.

The headlights of the approaching car were set low and close together. Not like a patrol car, more like a sports car.

She flashed her lights on and off, on and off.

'Stop,' she whispered. 'Please stop.'

As the car bore down, Colleen squinted at the glaring slab of her mirror. It hurt to look, but she didn't take her eyes away, not even when the headlights exploded across the mirror in a final brilliant flash.

After the painful brightness, the soft glow of the tail lights felt soothing to her eyes.

When the brake lights flashed, something clutched the inside of Colleen's stomach. She hunched over to ease the pain and saw the cold, white backup lights come on.

Her hand trembled as she rolled up her window. She glanced across her shoulder. The lock button was down. Swinging her eyes to the passenger door, she saw that it too was locked.

The car stopped inches from her bumper.

Colleen filled her lungs with air and let it out slowly.

A sports car, all right – small and shiny, with the canvas top of a convertible.

The driver's door swung open.

Colleen's breath made raspy, heartbeat sounds in her throat. Her mouth was parched. Did Maggie feel this way the night she died? She must have. This way, only a lot worse.

A tall, slim man stepped out. He looked to be in his late

twenties, close to Colleen's age. His hair was fashionably long, his checkered shirt was open at the throat, his trousers flared at the cuffs.

She couldn't see his lean, dark face until he bent down and smiled in at her. She nervously returned the smile. Then the stranger raised his hand into view and made a circular cranking motion.

Colleen nodded. She lowered her window half an inch.

'What's the trouble?' he asked, speaking directly into the slit. His breath, so close to her, smelled sweet and heavy with liquor.

'It's ... I'm not sure.'

'Something the matter with your car? Your car break down?'

His breath filled her nostrils. She gripped the window crank and told herself to roll it up – roll it up *now* because he's been drinking ... and she saw the dead battered face of her sister.

'You all right?' the man asked.

She rubbed her face. 'I'm feeling kind of woozy, I guess.'

'You ought to roll down your window, get some fresh air.'

'No, thanks.'

'The fresh air'll do you good.'

'I'm all right.'

'If you say so. What's wrong with your car?'

'It overheated.'

'What?'

'Overheated,' she said into the window's gap. 'I was driving along and a red light on the dashboard came on, and then the engine started to make some kind of awful whiny noise, so I pulled over.'

'I'd better have a look.'

He walked to the front of the car and touched the hood the way a person touches something that might be hot.

Then he slipped his hands under the hood's lip. He couldn't get it open. Finally, he crouched, found the latch, and opened it.

He spent only a few moments under the hood before returning to Colleen's window. 'You've got a problem,' he said.

'What's wrong?'

'What? I can hardly hear you. If you'd just roll down your window a bit more . . .'

'Roll it down?'

'Sure.'

'No, I don't think so.'

'Hey, I don't bite,' he said, grinning and shaking his head. Colleen smiled back at him. 'Are you sure?'

'I only bite when there's a full moon. It's just a half-moon tonight.'

'A gibbous,' she corrected.

The man laughed and said, 'Either way.'

Colleen opened the window and breathed deeply. The breeze tasted wet with the freshness of the cornfields. A train, far away, was making a snickity sound. Somewhere a rooster heralded dawn three hours early.

It's a beautiful night, she thought. For a moment, she wondered if the stranger was also thinking about the peaceful sounds and smells. She looked at him. 'What's wrong with my car?'

'Fan belt.'

'Fan belt? What does that mean?'

He moved his face down closer to hers. 'It means, young lady, that it's a good thing you stopped.'

'Why's that?' she asked, and turned away fom his liquored breath.

'If you go far without a fan belt, you burn up your engine. *Kaput*, kiss your motor goodbye.'

741

'That serious?'

'That serious.'

'What could've happened to the belt?'

'It probably just broke. They do that sometimes. Me, I change mine every two years just to be on the safe side.'

'I wish *I* had.'

'I'm glad you didn't,' he said, and grinned a charming, boyish grin that frightened Colleen. 'It isn't every night,' he continued, 'that I'm lucky enough to run into a damsel in distress. Especially one as pretty as you.'

She rubbed her perspiring hands on her skirt. 'Can you . . . can you fix it?'

'Your car? Not a chance. Not unless you've got a new fan belt in your pocket.'

'What'll I do?'

'You'll let me give you a lift to the nearest service station. Or somewhere else, if you'd prefer. Where would you like to go?'

'Well, I don't think I should . . .'

'You can't stay here.'

'Well . . .'

'It would be foolish to stay here – a woman as pretty as you. I don't want to alarm you, but there've been a number of attacks on this stretch of road.'

'I know,' she said.

'Not to mention half a dozen murders. Men and women both.'

'You've alarmed me.' She smiled nervously. 'I'll come with you.'

'That's what I like to hear.' He reached into the car, unlocked the door, and opened it for her. She climbed out. When he shut the door, it made a dull thump that sounded very final.

'Do you live far from here?' he asked, taking Colleen's

elbow with cold, firm fingers and leading her toward his car.

'Thirty miles, maybe.'

'So close? Why don't you let me take you home?'

'That would be very nice. But I hate to put you to the trouble. If we can find a gas station . . .'

'No trouble. Thirty miles is nothing.' He stopped walking. His fingers tightened around her arm. 'I guess I'd be willing to drive a woman like you just about anywhere.'

She saw the way he smiled and knew it was happening.

'Let go of me,' she said, trying to sound calm.

But he didn't let go. He jerked her arm.

'Please!'

He mashed his mouth against hers.

Colleen closed her eyes. She started to remember it again – the telephone that rang her awake, the long walk to the kitchen, the rough apologetic voice of the cop.

I'm afraid that somebody assaulted your sister.

Is she . . .?

She's gone.

Gone. A funny way for a cop to put it.

She bit the stranger's lip. Her forehead snapped against his nose. She jabbed her knuckles into his throat and felt his trachea collapse. Then she ran back to her car.

By the time Colleen returned to the man, he was lying motionless on the road. Kneeling beside him, she lifted his hand and searched for a pulse. There was none.

She dropped the hand, stood up, and took a deep, deep breath. The breeze off the cornfields smelled so fresh and sweet. So peaceful. Yet there was something a little sad about the aroma, as if the cornfields, too, missed Maggie.

Colleen stifled a sob. She glanced at the luminous face of her wristwatch. Then she bent under the hood with her wrench and fan belt, and got to work.

It took her less than six minutes to complete the job.

Not bad.

Faster than ever before.

Wishbone

'Some honeymoon,' Diane muttered, stepping to the side of the trail. She squatted until a boulder took the weight of her backpack.

Scott, farther up the trail, stopped and turned around. 'What's the matter now?'

'What isn't?'

He came toward her, shaking his head. Diane knew that his pack was even heavier than hers, but he seemed just as energetic as when they had started out this morning.

She took off her hat and sunglasses. Squinting against the brightness, she unknotted her neckerchief and used it to mop her sweaty face.

'We'd better keep moving,' Scott said. 'We've only got a couple more hours before sunset.'

'Why don't we just camp here?'

'You're kidding.'

'I mean it. I'm wiped out.'

'There's no water here, for one thing.'

'Well, I'm not moving another inch.'

'For godsake . . .'

'We've got plenty of water for one night.'

'There's supposed to be a lake just on the other side of the pass.'

'Well, fine. *You* go to the lake. I'm staying.'

'Diannnnne.'

'I mean it. My blisters have blisters. Every bone in my body aches. Besides that, I've got a headache.'

'But this place really sucks.'

'*I* wanted to stop by that stream, remember? But no. "Oh, we can make it over the pass,"' she mimicked him. '"No sweat, sweetheart." You want to see sweat?' She raised her red bandanna toward Scott, balled it up with one hand, and squeezed. Sweat spilled out, fell between her boots and made dark spots on the trail dust.

'Just think how nice the lake'll be,' Scott said. 'These are glacial lakes up here. Ice cold. You can take a dip while I set up camp.'

'I'm not budging.'

'All right. Suit yourself.' He turned away and started hiking up the trail. His boots scuffed up pale puffs behind him. The gear on his backpack and belt creaked and clanked.

He isn't really going to leave me here, Diane told herself.

The bandanna felt a little chilly when she tied it around her hot neck. She slipped out of her pack straps, made sure the bundle was steady on the boulder, and stood up. Her feet felt cramped and burning. But she enjoyed the feel of standing without the awful weight of the pack. The breeze cooled the sweat on her back.

Scott was still walking away.

'I know you're just bluffing!' she called.

He acted as if he didn't hear her.

He passed a bend in the trail and disappeared behind a cluster of blocky granite.

He's just going to stop there and wait for me, Diane thought. It'll be a long wait.

Groaning, she rubbed her sore neck. She peeled the sodden shirt away from her back and fluttered it. Shoving a hand down the seat of her jeans, she plucked her wet panties out from between her buttocks.

'Scott?' she called.

He didn't answer.

'Stop playing games, okay? Come on back here.'

She heard only the wind.

What if he didn't stop?

Diane felt a squirmy coldness in her bowels.

He wouldn't leave me here. He just wouldn't.

She left her pack on the boulder, and strode up the trail.

Scott wasn't behind the outcropping. The trail ahead slanted upward, bordered by blocks and slabs of rock. About a hundred feet ahead, it bent out of sight.

She saw Scott nowhere.

Either he'd hidden, or he'd kept on going.

'You shit!' Diane yelled.

Then she hurried back to the place where she'd left her pack. She put on her hat and sunglasses. She slipped her arms through the straps, leaned forward, and felt like weeping as the weight came down on her shoulders like the hands of a giant trying to shove her into the ground.

She began trudging up the trail.

How could he go off and leave me? I'm his wife.

Shouldn't have married him, she thought. She'd known he could act like a real bastard. But that side of him had always been directed at other people, not at her.

If I'd known he might treat *me* like this . . .

What if I can't find him?

She found him nearly two hours later atop a high boulder beside the trail, perched up there in the last rays of sunlight, a corncob pipe in his teeth and a flask of rum resting on his knee. He smiled down at her. 'What took you so long, sweetheart?'

Diane gave him the finger. Staggering past the boulder, she saw their campsite surrounded by a stand of trees. The tent was already up. Pale smoke curled and drifted above a campfire. Beyond the encampment was the lake, dark blue in the shadow cast by the bleak wall of granite along its far side.

She almost made it to the tent, then yanked the straps from her shoulders and let her pack drop. She sank down in front of it. Struggling for breath, she unlaced her boots and tugged at them. Her feet made sucking sounds when they came out. Her white cotton socks were filthy and drenched. They were dappled at the heels and toes with rusty bloodstains. She peeled them off. She slumped back against her pack, gasping and trembling.

Scott loomed over her.

'I knew you could make it,' he said.

'Go to hell.'

'I tell you what. Why don't you just relax. Camp's already up, and I'll take care of tonight's supper.'

He walked away.

Diane remained where she was, her back braced up by the pack, her rump on the ground, her legs stretched out. Soon, her breathing was almost normal. But the wind was stronger now, and colder. Though the sky remained pale blue, the sun was below the ridge and gave her no heat. Something on the ground was digging into her left buttock. Her skin felt itchy because of the damp clothes.

She felt miserable, but she couldn't force herself to move.

She wished she had the strength to get up and change her clothes. Put on something warm and dry. She wished she had socks on. Warm, dry socks.

I'll never be able to move again, she thought.

They'll find me up here someday, frozen like that leopard on the western summit of Kilimanjaro. And they'll wonder what I was doing up here.

Killed by an asshole.

Who strolled by, just then, and took the corncob out of his mouth long enough to say, 'You shouldn't just lie there. You'll get hypothermia, or something.'

'Thanks for the warning,' she muttered.

'Want me to get you something?'

'Yeah. An annulment.'

He chuckled. 'I think I'll do a little exploring around the lake before I start cooking. You want to come along?'

'Gee, I don't imagine so.'

He wandered off.

Diane was glad to be rid of him. After a few minutes, she managed to sit up. She crawled to the other side of her pack. Kneeling there, she opened it. She tossed her rolled sleeping bag toward the tent, took out her coat and spread it on the ground. Soon, she managed to dig out a fresh pair of socks, sweatpants and a hooded sweatshirt.

She pulled the socks over her tender, wounded feet. Then she stood on the coat. She looked all around. No sign of Scott. Shivering, she stripped off her cold, damp clothes. She stooped, picked up her sweatpants, lowered one foot into the waist hole, lifted her foot off the ground as she sought the opening at the ankle of the pants, and lost her balance. She stumbled backward, fighting to stay up.

She landed on her back, feet in the air.

The ground felt moist and cold. Twigs and rocks dug into her bare skin.

'Great,' she muttered through her tight throat. 'Just great.'

Then she saw someone high in the branches of a nearby tree, staring down at her.

Not *someone*, exactly.

Not *staring*, exactly.

The skeleton of someone. It had a skull with empty sockets.

It seemed to be sitting up there, the gray bones of its legs straddling a limb, its back resting against the trunk, its skull tipped downward as if watching her.

Diane felt icy fingers squeezing her insides.

She thrust both feet through the sweatpants and scurried up. She brushed damp debris off her buttocks, then tugged the pants around her waist.

'Scott!' she yelled. 'Scott, get back here!'

She heard only the wind.

It's just a skeleton, she told herself. Nothing to be afraid of.

Shivering, she swung the sweatshirt behind her back. She held it by the sleeves and swept it from side to side a few times. Then she put it on. She brushed some dirt and bits of leaves and twigs off the front. She pulled up the hood. She hugged herself, clutching her breasts through the soft fabric.

Shoulders hunched, legs tight together, she stood there trembling and gazed at the skeleton.

It really did seem to be staring down at her.

Just a heap of bones, she told herself. It isn't watching me. It's dead. It's got no eyes, no brain. Nothing but bones. It's no more alive than a rock.

It doesn't even know I exist.

We've gotta get out of here.

Kneeling on her coat, Diane searched her backpack until she found her sneakers. She put them on fast, got up wincing, snatched up her coat and hobbled toward the lake.

She stepped out onto a flat shelf of rock that jutted into the water. From there, she spotted Scott roaming among the jumbled granite beyond the lake's northern tip. She shouted his name. He turned his head and waved, then gestured for her to join him.

'Come here!' she yelled. 'Quick!'

With a shrug, he started to come back.

* * *

'What's the matter now?' he asked, obviously annoyed that Diane had interrupted his exploration.

'We've got a visitor,' she said.

Scott raised his eyebrows, looked toward the campsite, and shook his head. 'What're you talking about?'

She pointed toward the high branches of the tree.

'I don't see anything.'

All that Diane could see was one bony foot. The rest of the skeleton was hidden behind limbs and leaves.

'What is it, an owl or something?'

'You'll see.' She led the way, and stopped beside her pack where she'd changed her clothes. From there, the entire skeleton was in plain sight. She pointed up at it. 'That's no owl,' she said.

She watched Scott. When he saw the thing, his eyes opened wide and his jaw dropped. After a few moments, he rearranged his face into a smile. He met Diane's eyes. 'Big deal,' he said. 'A skeleton.'

'*I'll* say it's a big deal. I'm not spending the night here. No way. Not a chance.'

Scott smirked at her.

'I mean it.'

'Don't be ridiculous.'

'It's a *dead* person, for Christsake!'

'So? It won't hurt anything.'

'Damn it, Scott.'

His smirk twisted into a scowl. 'You've been dragging your ass all day, belly-aching about how fucking *tired* you are, and now that we're finally here and the camp's all set up, you wanta get everything *alllll* packed up again and go looking for someplace *else*, just 'cause of some crummy skeleton? Right. Sure thing. Every day and twice on Sunday. Has it ever occurred to you that maybe *I'm* tired, too? I spent a fucking *hour* putting up the tent all by myself and fixing the place up for you while you're taking your sweet time back on the trail somewhere and now you wanta just keep going? Well, fuck that!'

'Fuck *you*!' she yelled.

'Fuck *me*?' He slapped her, smacking her face sideways.

Diane twisted away from him, held her cheeks and hunched over, crying.

'You don't like Ol' Bony up there, go and hide in the fucking tent. Go on, get.' He swatted the back of her head.

Whirling around, Diane smashed her fist into Scott's jaw. For a moment, he looked stunned. Then he chuckled.

Diane grabbed her sleeping bag and rushed for the tent.

She was snug inside the down-filled mummy bag when she heard the rustle of the tent flap.

'You'll come out to eat, won't you?' Scott asked. He sounded calm and caring.

Diane raised her face off her crossed arms. She looked over her shoulder. Scott was crawling over the floor of the tent. The tent was dark inside. Behind Scott, she saw the glow of the campfire, the gloomy hues of dusk.

'What can I say?' he said. 'I'm sorry. I don't know what got into me. I can't believe I really hit you.'

'Twice,' she murmured, and sniffed.

Reaching out, he gently stroked her hair.

'Are you okay?' he asked.

'What do you think?'

'I told you I'm sorry.'

'That's a big help.'

'Don't be that way, honey. I love you. I just lost my head. Come on. Why don't you get up and come out by the campfire? You'll feel much better once you've got some good hot food inside you.'

'All right.'

'That's my girl.' He patted her back.

After he was gone, Diane struggled free of her mummy bag. She put on her coat and sneakers, then crawled from the tent and stood up. She peered into the tree. The skeleton, way up there, looked as if its gray bones were melting into the darkness.

'You oughta stop worrying about that thing,' Scott told her.

'Sure.' She moved in close to the fire and sat down on a rock. The surface was rough, but fairly flat. Cold seeped through the seat of her sweatpants.

Scott, bending over the fire, ladled stew out of the pot. He filled a tin plate, added a fork, and brought it to her.

'I just wonder what Ol' Bony's doing up there,' he said.

'Watching us,' Diane muttered.

Scott laughed.

She set the plate on her thighs. It felt nice and hot. Steam rose off the stew.

'I mean, I find it intriguing. What's he doing up there, you know? Who was he? How'd he get there?' Scott filled a plate for himself and stood at the other side of the fire as he started to eat. 'Maybe he fell out of an airplane. You know? Could've been a mid-air collision. Or maybe he parachuted. Hey, maybe he's D.B. Cooper.'

'Cooper didn't even jump in this state,' Diane pointed out. 'Besides, where's the parachute?' She took a bite of the stew meat. It was stringy and tough, but hot. It tasted good. 'For that matter, where are his clothes?'

'Probably the same place as his skin and eyes.'

'Oh, very clever.'

Scott laughed, and ate some more. 'I've got it!' He pointed his fork toward the skeleton. 'Jimmy Hoffa. No, I've got it! Judge Crater!'

Diane smiled.

'All right! She's perking up!'

'That's just because God's gonna strike you dead, any second now, for being such a wise-ass.'

'You'd find that amusing, would you?'

'It'd serve you right for making fun of dead people.'

'Ol' Bony doesn't mind.' Scott turned toward the tree and tipped his head back. 'Yo! Up there! Wishbone! Yeah, you!'

'Don't,' Diane said. 'Come on.'

Laughing, ignoring her, Scott cupped a hand to the side of his mouth and called, 'You got any problem up there with what I been saying? Are you . . . taking offense at my remarks?'

'Would you shut up!' Diane snapped.

He looked at her. Grinning, he said, 'What's the matter, afraid he might answer?'

'It's just not right. Okay? That was a person once.'

'Whoop-dee-doo.'

'God, why don't you grow up.'

'Oooo, the little woman's getting testy. Again.'

She hunched low over her stew and forked some into her mouth.

'Yo, up there! Now look what you've done! You've got my bride all upset! How dare you!'

Diane kept her head down and kept on eating.

What's *wrong* with him? Maybe it's marriage. Now that he's got me, he thinks he can start dumping all over me. Now he can treat me like shit, the way he treats everyone else.

Maybe it's just being in the mountains. Maybe roughing it brings out all this nasty macho shit.

'You're really fucking up our honeymoon, Bonebrain!'

Diane raised her head.

Crouching, Scott set down his plate. He picked up a stone, and cocked back his arm to hurl it at the skeleton.

'No!'

He threw it.

The pale chuck of rock flew high and vanished into the darkness. For a moment, Diane heard only the crackle and pop of the campfire, the distant howl of the wind. Then came a faint thud as if the rock had struck the tree. Or the skeleton.

'Did I getcha?' Scott yelled. 'Huh? Want me to try again?' He squatted and searched the ground for another rock.

Diane flung her plate down. She leaped to her feet. 'Damn it, don't you dare!'

'Oh, dry up.' He found a rock. He stood up. He tossed it understand, caught it, and grinned at Diane.

Oh shit, she thought. *This one's for me.*

But she never found out for sure.

Out of the corner of her eye, she saw something sailing down from the tree. She jerked her head that way and squinted.

A big, pale rock was curving down through the darkness at Scott.

Not a *rock,* exactly.

A skull.

Just as Scott turned toward the tree, the skull crashed against his forehead. It didn't shatter. It didn't bounce off. Its teeth clamped, biting into his scalp and eyebrow. It stayed there, hanging on as Scott staggered backward and dropped his rock and fell to the ground beside the fire.

Diane stood frozen, staring and dazed.

That didn't happen, she told herself. Impossible.

This isn't happening, either, she told herself when she looked toward the tree and saw the headless skeleton on its way down.

It seemed very agile for a pile of bones.

It shinnied down the trunk to the bottom branch, some ten or twelve feet above the ground. It sat on the branch. Then it pushed itself off, dropped, and landed standing up.

It seemed to have a bounce in its step as it walked toward Scott.

Bending over him, it grabbed its skull with both hands and tugged. Its teeth ripped free of Scott's face.

He groaned.

Through the disbelief that fogged her mind, Diane realized he was still alive. He'd been knocked unconscious by the skull. Now, he was coming to. His face was bleeding horribly.

The skeleton, holding the skull in one hand, seemed to examine it for a moment. Then a fingertip of bone flicked a scrap of Scott's flesh off one of its upper teeth. With that accomplished, it raised the head and planted it atop its spinal column.

Scott, eyes still shut, squirmed a little bit.

The skeleton placed a foot on his chest. It rubbed its hands together.

Then its head slowly swiveled until its eyeless sockets seemed to fix on Diane. It raised an arm and waved.

Waving goodbye? Wants me to leave?

This can't be happening, Diane thought.

But just in case it is . . .

She staggered backward a few steps, then swung around and ran.

Diane didn't sleep.

She spent that night huddled in a crevice, hiding from the skeleton and the wind, shivering, wondering what had happened.

When dawn came, she climbed onto a boulder. From

there, she could see the northern end of the lake at the bottom of the slope. But not the campsite. Outcroppings along the shore hid that from her view. She was glad.

Soon, the sun appeared above the eastern ridge. Its rays slanted down across the valley, warming her. She took off her coat and sat on it for a while, savoring the feel of the heat.

She didn't want to return to the camp. But she knew it had to be done.

And so, with shaky legs and a sick lump of dread in her stomach, she made her way down the slope and along the lakeshore.

The campsite was just as she had left it.

But the fire was dead. And Scott no longer lay sprawled on the ground beside it.

His clothes were there. Shredded and bloody.

Diane gritted her teeth to stop them from chattering. She wrapped her arms tightly across her chest. She turned toward the tree and raised her eyes.

Scott was straddling a high limb. The skeleton, braced between his body and the tree trunk, appeared to be sitting on his lap. His face rested against its skull, his lips mashed to its teeth. His bare legs dangled. Diane could see one arm of bone wrapped around his back, one fleshless leg against his side like the thigh of an eager lover squeezing him.

Some honeymoon, she thought.

She started to giggle.

First Date

Shannon latched her seatbelt, then turned to Jeff as he started the car. 'Can we go someplace?' she asked. 'I don't really want to go home yet. Okay? It's still early, and . . . I mean, I'd like to spend more time with you.'

'Hey, fine,' Jeff said, suddenly feeling shaky. 'Great. I was thinking the same thing.' He gave her a smile, then looked over his shoulder and started to back out of the parking space.

Oh God, he thought. Is it really possible that she *likes* me?

She must. She came to the movie with me. Now she wants to *go someplace*.

Unbelievable.

Swinging forward onto the road, he asked, 'What time do you have to be home?'

'Not till midnight.'

'So we've got a couple of hours.'

'Looks that way,' she said. 'Is it all right if I roll down my window?'

'Sure, go ahead.'

As Shannon lowered her window, Jeff shut off the air conditioner and opened his own window.

'It's such a lovely, warm night,' she said.

'A night made for roving,' Jeff said.

He glanced at Shannon and saw her smile in the dim glow cast by the streetlights.

God, she's so beautiful, he thought. And she's with *me*. She's sitting right there, Shannon Ashley, *smiling* at me. And she wants to *go* someplace.

He suddenly wished he'd had the guts to hold her hand during the movie.

Maybe she would've liked it, after all.

But he'd been too afraid to try.

I should've just done it!

Why not now? he asked himself.

NO!

'Are you hungry?' he asked. 'We could go someplace . . . Pizza Hut or Jack in the—'

'I'm stuffed. Really.' She suddenly frowned. 'But if *you're* hungry . . .'

'No, no, I just thought *you* might be.'

'I'm fine.'

'So, where would you *like* to go?' he asked.

'Someplace . . . *different*.'

'Ah,' Jeff said.

'Ah,' Shannon echoed.

They looked at each other. Shannon was all blurs and shadows, dim angles and patches of darkness. She seemed to be smiling. Her teeth were as white as her blouse. Jeff found his gaze sliding down the front of her blouse, lingering on the rises formed by her breasts.

'Maybe you should keep your eyes on the road,' she said.

Jeff looked forward fast, blushing. 'Sorry,' he muttered.

'I just don't want to end up in the hospital.'

'It'd be *different*.'

'I hate hospitals,' Shannon said. 'The *morgue*, on the other hand . . .'

'Morgues are cool.'

'Ever been to one?' Shannon asked.

'No.'

'Me neither.'

'No time like the present.'

'No way!' Shannon gave his upper arm a gentle punch. It felt *wonderful*.

He was tempted to give her a nice, soft punch in return – a way to touch her – but he didn't dare.

'What was that for?' he asked.

'Being an idiot.'

'Ah.'

'I mean, it'd be crazy. Even if we could *find* a morgue and get in, we'd probably end up being arrested.'

'Jail would be different.'

'*I've got it!*'

'What?'

'That old graveyard! The one out there by the church!'

'What church?'

'You know. Out on County Line Road.'

'Oh!'

'You know?'

'Jesus. You don't want to go *there*.'

'Sure. Why not? I mean, wouldn't that be just *perfect*?'

The idea of it made Jeff feel shivery inside. 'I don't know,' he muttered.

'Scared?' Shannon asked.

'Who, me?'

'How about it?'

It seemed like a bad idea. An old cemetery behind a long-abandoned church in the middle of nowhere seemed like a *very* bad place to go, especially late at night.

But Jeff didn't want to look like a coward.

And, somehow, the idea of being in such a horrible place with Shannon made him tremble with excitement as much as dread.

'I'm game,' he said. 'If you're sure that's where you want to go . . .'

'I'm sure.'

'Okay. We'll go. It's this way, isn't it?'

'Yeah, just keep heading out of town. I'll tell you where to turn.'

'Have you been there before?' Jeff asked.

'Just driving by. I've never even gotten close enough to take a good look. But I've always thought it'd be a neat place to stop. I mean, it looks so *creepy*. I just *love* creepy stuff.'

'Me, too.'

'I know. That's how come it's so perfect, you and me going there tonight.' She reached over and put a hand on his thigh.

Jeff struggled not to moan.

Her hand felt warm through his jeans.

'We're so much alike,' she said. 'I kept waiting and waiting for you to ask me out. I *knew* we'd be perfect together. We're two of a kind.'

'What kind is that?' he asked, blushing so fiercely that he thought he might melt.

'Dark.'

'Yeah?'

'Lured by the mysteries of the night, the gallows, and the grave. I knew it from the moment I first saw you.'

'That's why you asked me out tonight?' he asked.

'We just *had* to see *Eyes of the Vampire* together. I didn't want to go alone, and everyone else I know . . . they would've *mocked* it. I *had* to see it with you. *Share* it with you.'

'*Near Dark* was better.'

'Ten times better.' Her hand moved slightly higher, and her curled fingers rubbed the side of his thigh. 'I wish we'd known each other then.'

'You and me both,' Jeff managed to say, squirming a little. Her hand remained where it was, barely moving, but caressing him.

Doesn't she know what she's doing? Jeff wondered.

She's so *close*.

'Here comes County Line Road,' Shannon said. 'You'll want to hang a left at the stop sign.'

After he made the turn, she said, 'This is going to be so exciting. I've never been to *any* graveyard at night. Have you?'

'No.'

'So it'll be the first time for both of us.'

'Guess so.'

'And a full moon.'

'Maybe we'll run into a werewolf,' Jeff said.

'I'm not real big on werewolves.'

He turned his head and smiled at her. 'You're a vampire person.'

'You bet,' she said, and squeezed his thigh. 'Wouldn't you just love to run into a vampire?' she asked.

'I think there's a pretty slim chance of that.'

'But if you *could* . . . you know?'

'I guess it'd be pretty cool.'

'What would you do?'

'Run like hell.'

She laughed and slapped his thigh and took her hand away. Where her hand had been, the leg of his jeans felt warm and slightly moist.

'What would *you* do?' he asked. 'Interview him?'

'You think he'd let me?'

'If you ask nicely.'

'I think he'd probably be a lot more interested in biting my neck.'

'More than likely,' Jeff said.

'Or she.'

'Good point. I'd *much* prefer a female, myself.'

'Not me. If a vampire's going to chomp on my neck, I want it to be a *guy*.'

'So then, I guess *ideally* we'll need to get attacked by *two* vampires – a guy for you and a gal for me.'

'And they've got to be *heterosexual* vampires,' Shannon added.

'Do they come both ways?'

'Do they come at all?'

Blushing, Jeff shook his head. 'I guess it all depends on who you read,' he said.

'What about *real* vampires?' she asked.

'What do you mean by real?'

'The kind that are really *out* there.'

Jeff smiled at her. 'I hate to break it to you, Shannon, but there ain't no such animal.'

'Think not?'

He chuckled softly. 'Hope not,' he said. 'Oh, I know there are nutcakes who like to *think* they're vampires . . . But I have some serious reservations about the existence of the genuine article. The "undead" variety? You know, going on for centuries, turning into bats and mist and stuff, scared of crosses . . . the whole nine yards.'

Shannon didn't say anything.

He looked over at her. On this stretch of road, there were no streetlights. She seemed to be made of black and a few shades of gray.

'What if I told you *I'm* one?' she asked.

Jeff suddenly felt a squirmy chill inside. 'You're not,' he said.

'Are you sure?'

'Pretty sure.'

Her hand returned to his thigh. Her fingernails dug in. He groaned and squirmed.

'*How* sure?' she asked.

'I'm sure I've seen you in daylight. And I've seen you in mirrors a couple of times. I've *definitely* seen you eat real food. Who's ever heard of vampires eating popcorn and Milk Duds?'

'Hmm. Good points. You must be right. I must *not* be a vampire.'

He said, 'You're not.'

'Apparently not.'

'Hey, come on. You're making me nervous.'

'You'd better slow down,' she said. 'The turn-off's just around the next bend.'

He took his foot off the gas pedal. 'Are you really sure you want to do this?' he asked. 'Go to a cemetery at this hour?'

'I spooked you, didn't I?'

'I *know* you're not a vampire.'

'If you say so.'

'There *isn't* any such thing.'

'Of course there isn't.'

'And even if they *do* exist, which I doubt, *you* can't possibly be one. Hell, you've got a *suntan*.'

'But is my suntan *real*?'

'Come on, cut it out.'

'Here it is.'

Jeff stepped on the brakes and swung onto the side road. The old strip of asphalt looked gray in the moonlight. Nothing remained of its center line, if there had ever been one. The surface was potted and cracked. Weeds grew in the fissures. Though Jeff drove slowly, the car shook and bounced.

'Kill the headlights,' Shannon said.

'I thought you didn't want to end up in the hospital.'

'There's plenty of moonlight.'

He shut off the headlights. 'Jesus,' he muttered, and slowed almost to a stop.

'It's all right. There's not much to hit, anyway.'

'Hope not.' He could see almost nothing in front of his car. 'This is weird.'

'I think it's neat,' Shannon said, her voice hushed.

'Well . . . it *is*, sort of.'

'It's like we're invisible.' She was a dim silhouette in the passenger seat, her features shrouded by darkness.

Jeff grinned at her and said, 'Maybe we can sneak up on the vampires.'

'Nah. They'll hear us coming.'

'We could park here and walk in.'

'What if we need to make a quick getaway?' Shannon asked.

'I thought you *wanted* to run into some vampires.'

'Vampires, yes; perverts and murderers, no.'

'Ah. Okay.'

'Let's park right up close to the graveyard,' Shannon suggested.

Jeff realized that he could now *see* it.

With his headlights off, the night had been infiltrated by moonlight.

The moonlight seemed to wash everything with a dim, pale mist: the cracked and pitted road ahead; the weeds growing through the asphalt; the thickets and scattered trees on both sides of the road; the old wooden church with its boarded windows and broken steeple; the desolate, flat, weed-cluttered landscape of the parking lot in front of the church; and the graveyard off to the right.

As he drove onto the parking lot, Jeff said, 'At least we're the only car.'

'So far, so good,' Shannon said.

He steered toward the cemetery: a field of tomb-stones, burial vaults and statues, stunted trees, thickets, and long, dry grass.

'I don't see anybody,' Shannon said.

'Me neither.'

'This is *so* cool.'

'Yeah.' Jeff's voice sounded steady, though he felt as if his entire body was being shaken by quick, tight tremors. 'I'll turn us around,' he said.

'Good idea.'

He made a U-turn, then backed up, swinging the wheel until the front of his car pointed to the entry road. Then he looked at Shannon. 'Now I suppose we have to get out.'

'Of course.'

'Fun and games.'

She reached over and rubbed his shoulder. 'It'll be great,' she said.

They unfastened their seatbelts. When Jeff opened his door, the overhead light came on. He muttered, 'Shit!' and scampered out.

Shannon hurried out the passenger side.

They both shut their doors quickly, silently. The light in the car went dark.

Standing by his door, Jeff watched Shannon stride around the front of the car. In the moonlight, her white blouse and white jeans looked as bright as a field of snow. Her blonde hair, face and hands were much darker, and hard to see.

'So much for the element of surprise,' she said. She was smiling. Her teeth were white.

'I forgot all about the interior light.'

'Well, nobody's here anyway.'

'Maybe.'

Side by side, they faced the cemetery.

Jeff saw many figures that might be people. Some were apparently statues, while others were formed by combinations of bushes, crosses, shadows . . .

'I don't see anyone,' Shannon said. 'Do you?'

'No. But there must be a thousand places to hide.'

'You aren't going to chicken out on me, are you?' As she asked, she moved slightly sideways.

Their arms touched.

'Not me,' Jeff said. Then he added, 'You wouldn't happen to have a gun?'

'No, but I've got this.' Her arm went away from his. As she turned to face him, she shoved a hand into a front pocket of her white jeans. She pulled out a folding knife. Using both hands, she pried open its blade. 'See?' The three-inch blade glinted like silver.

'Hey, cool.'

'I'm a dangerous woman.'

'So I see. You wouldn't happen to have a cross or two?'

She shook her head. 'I used to wear a cross all the time. You know, on a gold necklace? Never took it off. Not even in the shower. I figured the minute I took it off, I'd get nailed by a vampire. But then, a couple of years ago, I sort of started to think I might *like* it.'

'Getting nailed by a vampire?'

'Yeah. You know? I *wanted* it to happen, so I ditched the cross.'

'You really *are* a believer.'

'A hoper.'

'But no luck, so far?'

'Maybe tonight,' she said. 'Let's take a look around.'

'Okay.'

Shannon folded her knife shut. Instead of returning it to her pocket, she held it in her right hand.

They walked toward the cemetery.

'If there's trouble,' Jeff whispered, 'make a run for the car. The keys are in the ignition . . . in case I don't make it.'

'If there's trouble,' Shannon said, 'I'll stick with you. Like I told you, I'm a dangerous woman.' She took Jeff's hand in hers.

This was the first time they'd ever held hands.

The feel of it sapped his strength, quickened his heartbeat, numbed his mind.

It's no big deal, he told himself. It's just her hand. Calm down.

Just her hand.

He gave it a gentle squeeze. She squeezed back, and turned her head and smiled at him.

'My heart's pounding like crazy,' she whispered.

'Mine, too.'

'This is *so* creepy.'

'Me?' he asked.

'Not you, *this*. The *bone orchard*.'

'Oh. Yeah.' He saw that they were standing among the graves. It came as no great surprise. After all, this was where they'd been heading when Shannon took his hand. But he had no memory of actually *entering* the cemetery.

Must've been on automatic pilot, he told himself.

He looked over his shoulder. They hadn't gone far. The rear of his car was probably no more than twenty feet away. But they'd already waded through the tall grass past several tombstones.

Shannon whispered, 'This is better than any old movie, isn't it?'

'You can say that again.'

'This is *real*. We're actually sneaking around in a *graveyard*.'

Pulling him by the hand, she led the way. They walked slowly, trudging through the dry grass, ducking under low branches, stepping around stone monuments, sometimes pausing to stare at human figures – and to make sure they were seeing statues, not people.

They wandered deeper and deeper into the cemetery.

Soon, the car was out of sight.

They kept walking.

And found themselves in a moonlit clearing surrounded by burial vaults. The pale, stone buildings, all the same size and evenly spaced, looked as if they'd been carefully positioned to form a large circle. In the center of the circle, perhaps forty feet away from the chambers that surrounded it, was something that looked like a large block of stone.

'What is this?' Jeff asked.

'Who knows? I didn't even know it was here. You can't see it from the road.' Shannon turned her head slowly. At first, Jeff thought she was admiring the vaults. Then he realized she was counting them. 'Thirteen,' she said. 'Creepy.'

'You like creepy, right?'

'Love it,' Shannon whispered. 'Come on, let's see what this thing is.'

Still holding hands, they walked toward the strange, blocky object at the hub of the thirteen vaults. It was about the height of Jeff's shoulders, flat on top, apparently round in shape and ten or twelve feet in diameter.

'What do you think it is?' Shannon asked.

'I don't think it's fountain. Looks like nothing . . . a platform, a stage?'

'An altar?' Shannon suggested, and squeezed his hand.

'Could be.'

They stopped a few paces away from it.

'This must be where they perform their human sacrifices,' Shannon said.

'More than likely.'

She bumped against Jeff's side. He bumped back.

'There're thirteen vampires, and they all come out to watch,' she said. 'The king of the vampires actually does the killing.'

'They've got a king? What's his name?'

'Pete.'

Jeff burst out laughing.

'It's blasphemy to laugh at King Pete.'

'Oh. Okay. Sorry.'

'So then, after King Pete opens the throat of the victim . . . and drinks his fill . . . he leaves her there for the others. They swarm in and scamper up and have at her. They're ravenous. They plant their mouths everywhere on her. Thirteen mouths, all of them *sucking* on her.'

'Wow,' Jeff said. He felt shaky and a little breathless.

'She's naked, of course.'

'Of course.'

'Come on.' Shannon let go of his hand. She stuffed the knife into her pocket, then stepped forward, placed her hands on the stone, leaped and thrust herself up. She swung a knee over the edge. Jeff thought maybe he should help her. But she might take it wrong, so he kept his arms at his sides.

She crawled forward. When she was safely away from the edge, she got to her feet. She turned around. 'Hey, this is great. Come on up.'

'Okay.' Jeff placed his hands on top of the stone, then just stood there and gazed at Shannon.

She looked wonderful standing up there in the moonlight, feet parted, hands on hips.

'You know what I think this might've been?' he asked.

'You mean *really*?'

'Yeah. A pedestal for some sort of statue.'

'What makes you think so?'

'Seeing you up there.'

'Yeah?' She suddenly raised her right leg, planted an elbow on its knee, and rested her chin on her fist.

'Exactly.'

'So where'd the statue go?' she asked.

'They must've gotten rid of it.'

'Maybe because it represented hideous, unspeakable evil.

The thirteen worshipped it.' She turned around slowly, arms raised. 'Thirteen vampires. They built their tombs around the statue of their king. But the villagers grew wise to this foul sect of blood-sucking fiends and attacked in the night. They slew them all, then tore down the statue and destroyed it.'

Jeff grinned. 'That's probably just what happened.'

'But they couldn't destroy the *evil*.'

'Which is with us always.'

'Right.'

He boosted himself up, scurried over the edge, and got to his feet. 'I think it must've been a statue of King Pete.'

'Hail to King Pete!' Shannon called out.

Jeff cringed.

'The blood is the life!'

'Shhh!'

'What's wrong?'

'You don't have to yell.'

'Scared?'

'Want to get us kicked out?'

'By who?' Shannon asked.

Jeff shrugged. 'I don't know, but . . .'

'I think you're afraid I'll bring out the vampires,' she said.

'They were slain by the villagers, remember?'

'That was just a story. Don't you know a story when you hear one? Come here.' Standing in the center of the pedestal, Shannon gestured for Jeff to approach.

When he stopped in front of her, she put her hands on his hips. 'If there *are* any vampires around here . . . real ones . . . they must've heard me. Don't you think so?'

He swallowed hard. 'You were loud enough to wake the undead,' he assured her.

'So they know we're here.'

'I guess so.'

'They'll be coming for us.'

'Any moment.'

'They'll come and suck our necks,' she whispered. Easing forward, she slid her arms around Jeff and pressed herself against him. Stunned, confused, he wrapped his arms around her. He had never held a girl this way before. He could feel the warmth of her thighs. He could feel the rise and fall of her chest. And the push of her breasts. And the tickle of her breath on the side of his neck. Her hair, soft against his cheek, carried a mild scent so fresh and clean that it made him ache.

He moved his hands up and down her back. Through the cloth of her blouse, he felt smooth slopes and curves and no straps.

She kissed the side of his neck.

It gave him a sudden rush of goosebumps and made him squirm.

'That's where they'll get us,' Shannon whispered. And licked him there.

He shuddered. 'Gives me goose pimples,' he said.

'Do it to me, okay?'

Shannon released him, so he loosened his hold on her. She took a small step backward. Head down, she unfastened a button of her blouse. Then another. Then she slipped the left side of her blouse off her shoulder. It fell and hung against her upper arm. With a fling of her hand, she swept her hair out of the way.

She was bare skin from her ear down the side of her neck, bare skin along her shoulder and down her arm halfway to the elbow.

And bare down her front to where a button held the blouse together.

Her left breast was only half covered, the nipple just out of sight, shrouded by white cloth.

If that button goes . . .

Shannon curled a hand around the back of his head. Fingers in his hair, she drew his head down to the curve at the base of her neck. He kissed her gently there. Her skin felt smooth and warm.

'Harder,' she whispered.

He opened his mouth, pushed with it, slid his tongue back and forth.

She moaned and squirmed.

While her left hand clutched Jeff's head, her right hand rubbed up and down his side from his hip to his armpit. His own left hand, he realized, was gripping her shoulder as if to hold her in place. His right was locked on her upper arm – but not where it was bare.

He moved it higher.

Up to where her skin was.

Shannon didn't protest.

So he caressed the smooth, naked skin of her arm and shoulder while he licked and sucked her neck.

Shannon writhed and trembled.

Jeff thought about the half-bare breast only a few inches below his hand.

But he stayed away from it.

'Bite,' she gasped.

He pressed the edges of his teeth against her skin. It felt firm and springy. He squeezed a little harder.

'Make me bleed,' she gasped. 'Break my skin and suck my blood.'

'I don't—'

'No! Wait!' She suddenly jerked his head back by the hair. Gazing into his eyes, she shook her head and muttered, 'Wait,' again. Then, 'No good. Stupid.' She released Jeff's hair and dropped her hands away from him.

In the moonlight, Jeff saw a silvery slick of spittle on the left side of her neck.

'You all right?' he asked.

'Yeah.'

'Did I hurt you?'

'It was great,' she said. 'We've just gotta take our clothes off.'

'*What?*'

She unfastened the next button of her blouse. The left side fell and hung below her breast.

Jeff gazed at her bare breast, stunned. He'd never seen a real one before. He felt as if his breath was being sucked out. His heart thudded. His penis, growing stiff, shoved at the front of his pants.

Finished with her buttons, Shannon pulled her blouse off.

Jeff gaped at her.

She was naked above her white jeans.

'Get yours off, too,' she said, and tossed her blouse toward the edge of the pedestal.

'I . . . what's going on?'

'We don't wanta get blood on our clothes.'

'Huh?'

Balancing on one leg, she brought up the other and pulled her sneaker off.

'What blood?' Jeff asked.

'*Our* blood.' She tossed the sneaker aside. It landed near her blouse, but bounced and fell off the edge of the pedestal. 'Don't just stand there.' She tugged off her sock and gave it a fling.

Jeff began to unbutton his shirt. 'What's going on?' he asked.

'We're gonna *do* it.' She worked on her other sneaker and sock.

'Do what?'

'You see any vampires around here?' Shannon asked, and opened the button at the waist of her jeans.

773

'No.'

'Me neither.' She pulled the zipper down. 'I don't think they're coming.'

'Probably not.'

'Never a vampire around when you need one.' With that, she bent over, sliding her jeans down. She stepped out of them. Then she dropped to a crouch. Holding the jeans up between her knees, she dug into a pocket. 'We'll have to do this ourselves,' she said, and took out her knife. 'Come on, take your clothes off.'

'What's the knife for?' Jeff asked, and tossed his shirt out of the way.

'All the better to cut ourselves with.'

Shannon stood up. Turning aside, she threw her jeans. They tumbled and flapped. In midair, her panties drifted free and fell toward her blouse. Her jeans disappeared over the edge of the pedestal. 'Pooey,' she said. Then she turned toward Jeff.

Pale moonlight dusted her hair, her face, her shoulders and breasts. Each breast cast a shadow below it.

So many shadows.

So many hidden hollows.

But her belly was brushed with light. So were her hips. And a tongue of moonlight found its way to a wispy tuft of hair between her legs.

Groaning, Jeff looked away from her.

'I'll help,' Shannon said. She stepped up to him. 'Here, you hold the knife.'

She gave it to him. Then she unfastened his jeans. She crouched and tugged. His briefs went down with the jeans and his erection leaped at her face. 'Holy mackerel!' she gasped.

'Sorry.'

'Just, uh . . . keep it to yourself, okay?'

He swallowed hard. 'Sure.'

She finished pulling his pants down, then stood up and said, 'I mean, we're not here to . . . you know, screw around.'

'Maybe we should've kept our clothes on.'

'And get them all bloody? My parents'll probably be up and waiting when I get home. They'll go apeshit if I walk in drenched with blood. Sit down. We have to get these off you.'

Jeff eased himself down. The cool, stone surface of the pedestal felt rough and grainy against his buttocks. Leaning back, he stretched out his legs and braced himself with his arms.

Shannon squatted in front of him. She removed his shoes and socks, his jeans and shorts. Then she picked them up, twisted around and snatched up his shirt. Holding them all, she stood and walked toward the edge of the pedestal.

Her hips swept slightly from side to side. Her buttocks looked creamy in the moonlight. Jeff watched how they moved with each step. And he stared at the shadowed cleft between them.

Instead of avoiding her clothes and sneaker scattered in front of her, Shannon swept them together with her feet. Then swept them off the edge of the pedestal.

'What're you doing?' Jeff asked.

'Clearing the deck.' She opened her arms. Jeff's clothes and shoes fell over the side. She turned around. 'They'll be fine down there.'

'Fine,' he said.

'This way, there's no chance they'll get bloody.' She came toward him.

Look at her, look at her, look at her. My God!

Jeff was dry-mouthed, trembling, hard – and a little embarrassed about the way that his penis was sticking straight up out of his lap.

Shannon stopped at his feet. 'Maybe we should do it standing up,' she said.

Jeff licked his lips and said, 'Fine with me.'

He got to his feet.

It felt very strange to be standing up, this high above the ground, with no clothes on. In the middle of the night. In front of beautiful, naked Shannon. In a graveyard. Surrounded by thirteen burial vaults.

He turned around slowly, looking at the moonlit chambers, at the shadows between them, and at the pale, grassy clearing.

With a glance at Shannon, he saw that she was looking, too.

'Oh, my God!' she suddenly blurted. 'Who's that?'

Jeff's heart slammed. He whirled around. 'Where?'

'Gotcha!'

'Jeez!' He turned to her. 'Real nice.'

Laughing softly, she stepped over to him and put her hands on his hips. 'Did I scare you?'

'Yeah. A little.'

'I didn't really see anyone,' she said.

'I know.'

'But I *do* have this sneaky feeling we're being watched.'

'Terrific,' Jeff muttered.

'I'm all shivery.'

'You and me both.'

'Yeah?' She slid her hands behind Jeff and scraped her fingernails lightly up his back. Goosebumps scurried over him. He trembled. Her hands stopped at his shoulder blades. Holding him there, she eased forward. Her belly pushed at his penis. Her nipples touched his chest. Her wet, open lips caressed the side of his neck.

She kissed him, licked him.

Jeff moaned.

Her mouth went away. 'Let me have the knife,' she whispered.

The knife felt hot and slick in his hand. He kept his hand shut. 'I don't know.'

'You're not gonna chicken out, are you?'

'Might be dangerous.'

'Of *course* it's dangerous. But not very. Not if we're careful. It won't even *hurt* much if we use the knife.'

'What about . . . diseases?'

'What've you got?'

'Nothing, I don't think, but . . .'

'Me, neither. Come on, you want to do it, don't you?'

He didn't much care for the idea of playing vampire, but he very much wanted to have Shannon touching him again. If it meant losing a little blood, fine.

'Sure,' he said.

'You don't *sound* very sure.'

'It's just . . . what if you hit my jugular vein, or something?'

'That's why we got our clothes out of the way, silly.'

With that, she had him laughing. She laughed along with him.

Then she said, 'You're pretty nervous about this.'

'A little.'

'I tell you what. Why don't *you* go first?'

'I thought that was what we were talking about.'

'I mean, you go first and suck *me*. I loved how it felt when you were doing it before. I wanted it to keep on going, but then I started to worry about our clothes. And I remembered about the knife – so now you can get to my blood without mauling me. Just a neat little slit or two. It'll be great.'

'I don't want to *cut* you.'

'I'll do it. Let me have the knife.'

He gave the knife to her. Holding it in front of her belly, she looked down and tried to pry open the blade. She seemed to have some trouble with it. 'My hands are shaking,' she murmured.

Jeff stared at her breasts. They were only inches from his chest. The dark nipples jutted out as if reaching for him.

'There we go,' Shannon said, swinging the blade out of the handle. It locked into place with a soft click. 'You want the left side?' she asked. She tilted her head to the right.

'I guess so.'

'Good.' With her left hand, she fingered the side of her neck. 'About here?' she asked.

'That'd be fine.'

'You don't sound too thrilled.'

'I'm thrilled, all right. Just nervous. I've never . . . drunk blood before. Just my own a few times. You know, when I've had a cut. Never someone else's.'

'Same here. Now we'll find out what all the fuss is about.'

'Yeah.'

Keeping her fingers against her neck to mark the place, she brought up her right arm. Elbow high, she swung her forearm across the front of her neck and touched the point of her knife to the area in front of her middle finger.

'How's this?' she asked.

She's really going to do it!

'Fine, I guess.'

'Ready?'

Jeff lowered his gaze from her hands, from the knife poised at her neck, and stared at her left breast. She was breathing hard. The breast was lifted by her expanding ribcage, then lowered, then lifted again.

'Jeff? Are you ready?'

'When you are,' he said, and raised his eyes.

'Here goes.' Her skin dented under the point, then enveloped it. The blade went in no more than a quarter of an inch, maybe less. When she pulled it out, a dot of blood grew and began crawling downward. 'How's that?' she asked. 'Fine.'

'No, wait. One more. Gotta make it official.' She poked the point into her neck again – cutting a fresh wound an inch from the other. Then she ducked, set the knife by her feet, and rose up again in front of Jeff. 'Okay,' she said.

By then, blood from the first cut had spilled over her collar bone and was sliding down her chest.

Jeff put one hand on her right shoulder, the other on her left side – just below her ribcage.

Shannon soon had two strips of blood rolling down her chest.

Jeff stared at them.

'Are you gonna do it?

Trying to sound like Lugosi, he said, 'Your blood, it is so beautiful to watch.'

'You wanta taste it, don't you?' Shannon asked, her voice trembling.

Jeff watched the narrow, dark trails slide out onto her left breast.

Shannon squirmed. 'It tickles,' she said.

One stream curved off to the side of her breast, while the other trickled to its very tip.

Jeff crouched slightly, leaned in and licked the blood off her nipple.

Shannon flinched.

He sucked her nipple into his mouth, swirled his tongue around it and tested it with his teeth, relishing its stiff, rubbery feel.

'Hey.' She pulled his hair. 'Don't.'

He took his mouth away. 'The blood,' he gasped.

'But no funny stuff.'

'Sorry.'

She let go of his hair.

He expected her to grab it again as he lapped the blood off the side of her breast, but she didn't. He licked the side and the bottom, and up from underneath to the front, briefly running his tongue over her nipple. She stiffened and moaned, but made no attempt to stop him.

Though he ached to suck on her nipple again, he figured it might be pressing his luck.

So he abandoned her breast and licked his way up her chest, following the strips of blood.

He followed them over the smooth curve of her collar bone, followed them to their source. As he latched his mouth against the wounds, he wrapped his arms around her and drew her tightly to his body. Her breasts pushed against his chest: the right was dry and warm; the left was moist and clammy. His rigid penis shoved against her belly and glided upward on splippery juices until its whole underside was snug against her.

He squirmed, rubbing her.

And he sucked.

Sucking, he felt her blood come into his mouth.

He wondered if he could make it *squirt*.

The harder he sucked, the more blood poured into his mouth. And the more Shannon groaned and gasped and writhed against him.

She's going *nuts*, Jeff thought. She *loves* it.

Bet she won't stop me now.

Keeping his right arm clamped against her back, he brought his left arm forward, turned himself slightly to make room for his hand to fit between their bodies, then slipped it in and took hold of her right breast.

It filled his hand.

The nipple pushed against his palm.

'Don't,' she gasped, still writhing.

She loves it.

He squeezed the breast. It felt soft, firm, springy, incredible. He sucked harder on her neck. Blood flooded his mouth. Shannon shuddered and panted.

'Stop it,' she gasped.

Okay, okay. Better do what she says.

He let go of her breast and put his hand behind her. Eased it downward. When he curled it over the smooth hump of her right buttock, she whimpered and squirmed against him.

Yes! This she likes!

'Jeff!' she blurted.

He slid his other hand down. He clutched her buttocks with both hands, digging his fingers in, pulling her more tightly against his body, rubbing himself against her, digging his teeth into her neck, sucking, swallowing.

'No!' she squealed. 'Stop! It hurts!'

Of course it hurts, I'm biting your neck.

I AM biting her neck!

SHIT!

He opened his mouth and pulled his head back. Above and below the tiny knife cuts on the curve of her neck were crescent rows of tooth-holes. Deep, distinct impressions as if he'd sunk his teeth into a block of cheese.

In the blink of an eye, they filled with blood.

He yelled, 'SHIT!'

And then Shannon chomped the side of *his* neck.

Pain blasted through his body. He cried out, flinched rigid, then lost his footing as Shannon wrapped her legs around him. He stumbled backward, clutching her tight against him by her buttocks.

Then he fell.

His back slammed the stone. His head, past the pedestal's edge, hit only air. He let it hang, too stunned to raise it.

He had lost his hold on Shannon's buttocks. His arms lay by his sides.

But she hadn't lost her hold on his neck.

She was on top of him, squirming as she sucked.

Grunting as she sucked.

He could feel her teeth buried in his flesh, feel the force of her suction, feel his blood squirting out.

Hear the sloppy wet sounds as she sucked and swallowed.

Then her teeth released him. Her mouth went away.

'No. Shannon. Don't. Don't stop.'

'Like it?'

'Christ. Yes. Please.'

'No more blood. Not tonight.'

'Please!'

'No, no, no. No more blood.'

On elbows and knees, she glided backward, lightly sliding her nipples against his chest and belly and thighs.

And kissed his rigid penis.

Slid her lips around it.

Sucked it deep into the tight, wet hole of her mouth.

Squirmed and grunted, licked, sucked, stroked the hard length of it up and down with the slick O of her lips . . . and finally swallowed.

Later, they licked each other clean. Then they jumped off the pedestal and hunted for their clothes. Wearing their shoes but carrying everything else, they hiked back to Jeff's car. There, they patched their necks with gauze pads from Shannon's purse. Then they checked themselves for blood in the car's overhead light. After removing the last traces, they hurried into their clothes and sped for Shannon's home.

'I'm afraid you're going to be late,' Jeff said.

'Who cares?' Shannon asked. 'This was the greatest.'

'Not only that,' Jeff said, 'but the vampires didn't get us.'

Shannon grinned at him. 'Think not?'

Stickman

We were on a forty-mile stretch of blacktop through the cornfields after taking in a double bill bloodfest at the drive-in movies over at Darnell, the County Seat. There were four of us in Joe's old convertible.

There was Joe Yokum at the wheel, of course. Up there next to him sat Windy Sue Miller, her feet propped on the dash, her hair blowing wild in the hot wind, a Hamms in one hand.

I sat in the rear next to Jennifer Styles.

She was Windy Sue's cousin from Los Angeles. She'd been in some TV ads, and figured she was mighty hot stuff. Too hot for the likes of me. I hadn't been in the car with her more than two minutes before I was wishing I'd stayed home. Then we finally parked at the drive-in, and Joe had no sooner got the speaker box hooked over his window than she narrowed her eyes at me and said, 'You just keep to your own side of the car, Spud, and everything'll be fine.'

For one thing, my name is Dwayne, not Spud. For another, I didn't need any warning.

It turned out to be a mighty long double feature, what with Joe and Windy Sue carrying on in the front seat, me stuck in the back with Jennifer the Great.

I couldn't even enjoy the films much. All the commotion in the front seat didn't bother me much except to remind me of what I was missing. But it bothered me considerably to be sitting next to a gorgeous thing who thought I was dirt. And then, just about every time I'd manage to put her out of my mind and get into the screen action, she'd let out a long, weary sigh.

She was plainly dying of boredom, and wanted us to know it. Not that the lovers were in any shape to notice. But I sure noticed.

Just once, near the end of the second movie, I looked over at her when she let loose with one of those sighs.

'What's wrong with *you*?' she said.

I sniffed a few times. 'Is that Obsession, sweet thing? Or did you cut one?'

'Fuck you, tractor boy.'

I decided to keep my mouth shut after that. Finally, the movies ended. I sure didn't look forward to the long trip home, but Joe pulled over just past the city-limits sign. He went around to the rear, opened the trunk, and came back with a cold six-pack of beer.

'You aren't going to drink with *me* in the car,' Jennifer protested.

'It's a long walk home, honey,' Joe told her.

'Don't you "honey" me.'

'Lighten up, huh?' Windy Sue said.

'It's more for the rest of us,' I said.

'Gawd,' said Jennifer as we popped our lids.

I wished Joe had broken out the suds back at the drive-in. Would've made things go a bit easier. But us being only sixteen and in a convertible, he'd likely figured it wasn't worth the risk. Anyway, it was good to have them now.

Jennifer took to sighing all over again, but put a different spin on the things so they sounded pissed off instead of bored.

She sure was a piece of work.

She kept herself busy sighing while the rest of us worked on our beers and Joe steered us along that forty-mile stretch of blacktop. The first beer tasted great. The second one tasted even better. When it was half gone, I rested the can on my knee and settled back in the seat. I felt the hot wind blowing against me. I smelled the fresh, sweet air of the cornfields. The sky was spread out overhead, all sprinkled with stars. The full moon made the night so bright I could read the label on my beer can.

I looked over at Jennifer. She sat crooked, her knees against the door, one arm on the windowsill, the other on her lap. Maybe she sat that way to enjoy her view of the corn, but I figured it was meant to show me her back.

She did look fine, the way her hair streamed out behind her in the moonlight, the way her arm looked so dark against the white of her blouse. The blouse was sleeveless, so I could see her whole arm, all the way from her shoulder down to where her hand lay on her lap. Her shorts were white, so I couldn't tell where her blouse left off and the shorts started. The one leg I could see looked as dark and nice as her arm.

'You sure look fine from way over here,' I told her. 'A real shame you're a snot.'

Up front, Joe laughed.

Windy Sue twisted around, reached down over the seatback and gave my knee a swat. 'Dwayne, you behave.'

'It ain't easy.'

She squeezed my knee, then took back her arm and mussed Joe's hair for him.

Up ahead, the road spit into a Y. Joe steered for its right-hand branch, then killed the headlights. The blacktop pretty much disappeared.

Now *that* got Jennifer's attention. She unglued herself from the door and faced front. 'What the *hell* are you doing! Turn those lights back on. Are you crazy? We'll crash.'

'We ain't gonna crash,' Joe said.

'Put them on *this instant!*'

Windy Sue looked back at her. 'Can't just yet. Stickman might get us.'

'What?'

785

'This time of night, Jen, we sorta gotta *sneak* through this section.'

I punched the back of Joe's seat. 'Hey. Stop the car. Jennifer doesn't know about Stickman.'

I grinned as Joe hit the brakes and swung over. He parked us between the roadside and the edge of a ditch, then shut off the engine.

'What are you doing?' Jennifer asked. She didn't sound curious, just peeved.

We didn't answer, but boosted ourselves up onto our seatbacks and gazed off to the right.

'There,' Windy Sue said, and pointed.

A second later, I spotted his straw hat and head. The rest was behind the cornstalks that reached up and hid him to the shoulders.

'He don't seem to be moving,' Joe said.

'Cut it out,' Windy Sue said. 'You're gonna give me the creeps.'

'Are we just going to sit here, or what?' Jennifer asked.

'You want to see him, don't you?' Windy Sue asked.

'See who?'

'Stickman,' I told her.

'Climb on up back there and take a look,' Windy Sue said. 'You've gotta. He's famous in these parts.'

Jennifer gave off a good, loud sigh. Then she pushed herself up and sat on the back of her seat. 'So where *is* this fabulous Stickman?'

Windy Sue pointed.

'See?' I asked. 'There's his head.'

'You see him?' Joe asked.

'In the straw hat?'

'That's him.'

'Why, that's nothing but an old scarecrow.'

'Stickman,' I said. 'He's not just *any* old scarecrow. The

story has it that once a year – on what they call Stickman Night – he comes to life and wanders the fields, looking for someone to kill.'

'How terribly quaint,' Jennifer said. 'Can we go now?'

'What night's this?' I asked Joe.

'July twenty-fifth.'

'Is not,' Windy Sue said. 'It's past midnight.'

'Oh my God,' I said. 'Then this *is* Stickman Night!'

'I know that,' Joe said. 'Why do you think I killed the headlights?'

'You people are a riot.'

'Tell her about him, Dwayne,' Windy Sue said.

'Aaah, she doesn't care.'

'Right.'

'Tell her anyhow,' Joe said.

'*I* want to hear it again.' Windy Sue turned sideways to face me. She hung one leg down off the seatback and swung it. 'Go ahead. Joe, you keep your eyes on Stickman.'

'Well,' I began, 'it all started about a hundred years ago.'

'Is this *necessary*?'

'Shhhh. Let him talk.'

'Christ.'

'Like I was saying, it started about a hundred years ago. Darnell, the town we just came from, got itself a new undertaker by the name of Jethro Seer.'

'Jethro? Give me a break.'

'That was his name.'

'Keep interrupting,' Windy Sue said, 'and we'll be here all night.'

'And Stickman'll likely come after us if we hang around too long,' Joe added.

'Sure.' Jennifer turned toward me and folded her arms across her chest so she looked like she was cradling her boobs. Which were so big I judged they could use the extra support. 'Go on,' she said. 'Let's get it over with.'

It took me a minute to recall where I'd left off. 'Oh, yeah. Jethro. He was about six-three, and skinny as a rail.'

'Skinny as a skeleton,' Windy Sue added.

'And he was white. All white. An albino. With pink eyes. He always wore a black frock coat and top hat.'

'That didn't look like any top hat to me,' Jennifer said, thumbing over her shoulder toward the distant scarecrow.

'That's not Seer,' Joe explained.

'That's Stickman,' Windy Sue said.

Jennifer sighed.

'Top hat and black coat,' I went on. 'And he never went outside till after the sun was down. A real boogyman. *Everybody* was scared of him. I mean, he didn't just look so queer but he was the *undertaker*. There was talk of firing him, just to get rid of him. But nobody on the town council had the guts to do it. So he stayed on. And then people started to disappear.'

'Gals,' Joe added.

'Yeah. Just women. Young women. A few townies, but mostly they were gals who lived out on the farms around Darnell. They'd vanish in the night. Without a trace.'

'Let me guess,' Jennifer said. 'It was Jethro. Now can we go?'

'*Would* you shut up?' Windy Sue blurted at her.

She sighed. 'All right, all right. So sorry.'

'Anyway, they finally caught him one night when this gal got away from him. Mary Beth Hyde. Her folks had given her a young colt for her sixteenth birthday, and she went out to the barn by herself that night to pay it a visit. That's when he jumped her. Before she could let out a holler, he drugged her senseless with chloroform or something. She came to down in his embalming room. Flat on the table and buck naked. Jethro was up on the table, too, kneeling over her.'

'I suppose *he* was buck naked, too.'

'Yep. Except for his top hat. He had a scalpal in his hand, and was all set to open her throat, so Mary Beth hauled off and stuck her fingers in his eyes. Jabbed them right in. Glop came pouring out, and—'

'Spare me, okay?'

'Anyhow, that's how she got away. She shoved him off and ran screaming into the street. Nobody was around, it being so late. But there was plenty of action at Clancy's Bar, so she ran in there. Once they heard her story, every feller in that place raced over to the mortuary. They laid their hands on Jethro and made him talk. He confessed everything. He'd snatched every one of those missing gals, brought them to his embalming room and killed them. After they were dead, he . . . you know.'

'You're making this whole thing up.'

'It's all true,' I said.

'Right.'

'It is,' Windy Sue told her. 'Every word.'

'Anyway,' I went on, 'he'd kill them first and *then* he'd fool with them. He just wasn't interested in anything that wasn't dead. Now, he only snatched a gal when there was a funeral set for the next day. Once he got finished with her, he'd haul her pieces out to the bone orchard and plant them at the bottom of the grave that'd already been dug. Nobody ever caught on. Next day, there'd be a funeral and they'd lower the casket and cover it up.'

'Two burials for the price of one,' Joe said.

'They had to dig up fourteen caskets,' I explained, 'to recover the remains of all his victims. That happened later, though. The night the guys from Clancy's got their hands on Jethro, first they made him talk, then they lynched him.

Hustled him down Lincoln Street to the square. He was bawling and squealing the whole time, blood and goo running down his face from his eye sockets.'

'You are really disgusting.'

'He's just telling it like it was,' Windy Sue said.

'Anyhow, they got themselves a good strong rope and made a slipknot at one end.'

'That was so he'd strangle real slow,' Joe put in.

'Right,' I said. 'You take a genuine hangman's knot, it's supposed to bust a feller's neck. Like that.' I snapped my fingers. 'But they wanted Jethro to suffer for his crimes, so they used a slipknot so he'd strangle and choke.

'They didn't tie him, but just dropped that slipknot over his head, tightened it around his neck, and tossed the other end of the rope over the limb of an oak tree at the corner of the square. Then they hauled him up. Once he was off the ground, they tied off the rope on the trunk and just watched him. For a while, he danced and flapped around. He kicked and swayed and jerked. He pissed. He took a dump.'

'Lovely,' Jennifer muttered.

'Then he quit. He just dangled there, limp, and they figured he was dead. So then they started arguing. Some wanted to leave him hanging so the whole town could enjoy the view, come morning. Others said they oughta cut him down in consideration of the ladies, since he wasn't wearing a stitch of clothes.

'They hadn't quite made up their minds, though, when all of a sudden Jethro let out a roar. His arms flew up. He grabbed that rope above his head and climbed straight up it hand over hand, going for the branch they'd hung him from. Some of the guys just freaked out when he did that. But one of them, Daniel Guthrie, who'd lost his daughter to the nut, ran hellbent and leaped and caught hold of Jethro's legs. The extra weight was too much. Jethro lost his grip on the rope. They both dropped. When Jethro hit the end of the rope, his head popped clean off. Then both guys landed on the ground. Guthrie, he scrambled off the body. Before anyone could stop him, he snatched up Jethro's head and ran off with it.

'They carted the rest of Jethro off to the mortuary. When the sun came up the next morning, the hanging branch was missing from that oak tree on the town square. Somebody had sawed it off during the night. It was Guthrie, of course. The next thing you know, he had himself a new scarecrow out in his cornfield. *This* cornfield,' I added.

Jennifer glanced over her shoulder. 'That one?'

I nodded. 'Yep. It looked just like any other scarecrow, dressed up in bib overalls and an old shirt, stuffed plump with straw, a straw hat on its head. But its bones were made of the branch from the hanging tree. And its head was the head of Jethro Seer.'

Jennifer's upper lip crawled away from her teeth. 'They didn't let him keep it, did they?'

'Are you kidding? Nobody was about to mess with Guthrie. So the scarecrow stayed put, and so did Jethro's head.'

'It's still . . .?'

'Nothing left but an old skull,' I said. 'Guthrie's family still owns the farm. They tend to the scarecrow, keep it dressed and stuffed. I don't know who started calling it Stickman, but the name stuck.'

'No pun intended,' Joe said.

'And once a year – so the story goes – on the night of July twenty-sixth, the anniversary of the hanging, Stickman walks. He wanders the fields, searching for beautiful young women to kill.'

'Uh-huh.' Jennifer twisted around and peered back. 'That's actually supposed to be Jethro's *skull*?'

'It *is* his skull.'

'I'm sure.'

'Can't fool Jennifer,' Joe said.

'I'm not *blind*. That head out there's too big for a skull.'

'What you're looking at is a burlap bag,' I told her.

'There were too many complaints when you could see the skull from the road,' Windy Sue explained.

'Jethro's skull is *inside* the bag,' I said. 'But it's right where it's always been, jammed onto a stick from the hanging branch.'

'I'll just bet.'

'Go look,' I said.

'Right. What do you think I am, an idiot?'

'Scared?' Windy Sue asked her.

'Of what? An old scarecrow?'

'Stickman,' I said. 'You're scared the story's true and he'll grab you.'

'I don't *have* to go and look. I *know* it's all a big lie.'

'You don't know any such thing. Tell you what.' I hauled my wallet out of my jeans. I opened it, pulled out my twenty-dollar bill, and held it up in front of her. 'I'll bet you this twenty that you haven't got the guts to go over and *see* if there ain't a skull under that burlap.'

'Go for it,' Joe urged her.

'Hey, come on, guys,' Windy Sue said. 'If anything happens to her . . .'

'Don't worry,' I said. 'She isn't about to do it. She's great when it comes to putting us down and calling us liars, but she's gutless.'

'It has nothing to do with guts,' Jennifer protested. 'The whole thing's silly.'

I waved the bill at her. 'What's silly about this? I know it ain't much for a big TV star like you, but twenty bucks is twenty bucks. Pretty good pay for a little stroll through the corn.'

'I don't want your twenty dollars.'

'What if we go with you?' Joe asked.

'*I'm* not leaving this car,' Windy Sue said. She gave Joe the eye. 'And *you're* not leaving me alone here.'

'*I'll* go with you,' I volunteered.

'Sure thing. Just the two of us? You'd like that, wouldn't you.'

'Not much.'

'Right.' She shook her head. 'This whole thing's probably nothing but a trick to get me alone with you.'

'Nope. I'll stay right here if that's the way you want it.'

'I won't do it for your measly twenty dollars.'

'Surprise, surprise,' I said.

'But I *will* do it.'

Now, that *did* surprise me.

'Don't,' Windy Sue warned her.

'I'll do it on one condition.'

'Name it,' I said.

'I'll walk over there all by myself. And I'll just *see* if it's got a skull. Even though I already know there's nothing but straw inside that sack. I'll check anyway. Because I know your story's a lie and I'm not scared. And then, when I get back to the car, you keep your twenty dollars. But you get out and we leave you here and you have to walk the rest of the way home.'

Joe went 'Yah-ha!' and started laughing.

I figured we were about halfway between Darnell and Sackett. That would mean a twenty-mile hike.

If I lost.

But Jennifer was sure to chicken out before she ever got anywhere near Stickman.

'What do I get if you chicken out?' I asked.

'I won't.'

'Hey now. A bet's got to work both ways.'

'He's right,' Joe pointed out.

'Let's just forget this whole thing,' Windy Sue said, 'and get out of here.'

The corners of Jennifer's mouth curled up. 'I'll grab the scarecrow's hat. If I come back with it, Spud, you walk. If I come back without it, I'll let you take me to the drive-in tomorrow night. Just you and me.'

I laughed, but my heart was starting to pound a bit harder. 'Sounds like I lose, either way.'

'I'll pretend to like you.'

'That I've gotta see,' I said.

She raised her right hand. 'I swear. It'll be the best night you ever had.' She lowered her hand, and grinned. 'But it won't happen. Because I'll be back with the hat.'

'And if you chicken out, we've got a date for tomorrow night?'

'They're my witnesses.'

Joe pursed his lips and let out a low whistle.

'This is crazy,' Windy Sue said.

'Is it a bet?' Jennifer asked.

'It's a bet.'

We shook on it, and the way she squeezed my hand sent a hot current rushing all the way through my body. I could still feel her, even after she let go and scooted away and swung her legs over the side of the car.

'You shouldn't do it,' Windy Sue said as Jennifer hopped to the ground.

'Right. Stickman'll get me. Get real.'

Windy Sue's back stiffened. 'It's your funeral, hot shot.'

'Right.'

Windy Sue turned around, and the three of us sat perched

on the seatbacks watching while Jennifer rushed down to the bottom of the ditch and climbed the other side. At the top, she glanced back at us. She shook her head as if she thought we were a bunch of real losers. Then she shoved her way in between a couple of corn rows.

While the stalks were only shoulder-high on Stickman, they were taller than Jennifer's head. She didn't take more than two steps into the cornfield before she vanished.

We could hear her, though. Crackling, rustly noises as she tromped along.

Joe grinned at me. 'Hope you've got your walking shoes on, good buddy.'

'She'll be back. Without the hat.'

'Think so, huh?'

'Yep.' Actually, I didn't think so. That girl would likely do just about anything to win the bet. She was a royal pain in the ass, for sure, but there was no doubt but what she had a whole lot of nerve. 'Either way,' I said, 'at least we've gotten rid of her for a while.'

'Nothing better happen to her,' Windy Sue said.

'What could happen to her?' I asked. 'Stickman Night's still two weeks off.'

'I know that,' she muttered. 'Even so . . .'

'Two weeks off!' Joe blurted. 'Hey, let's get real. There *is* no Stickman Night.'

'You don't have to tell *me* that,' I said. 'I'm the guy that made it up. But it's *supposed* to be August 10. That's the night they lynched Seer, so it has to be the night Stickman goes hunting.'

'But he *doesn't* go hunting.'

'I know, I know.'

'Glad to hear you say so. I was starting to worry about you. About both of you.'

'I still don't like her going off like that,' Windy Sue said.

We all went quiet for a while and studied the cornfield. I couldn't see any stalks moving about to show where Jennifer was. She must've made some distance, because I couldn't hear her, either.

For no good reason, I got a cold feeling in my stomach.

'She'll be fine,' I said. 'The worst that can happen is she actually gets to Stickman and sees the skull.'

'Yeah.' Joe chuckled. 'She *knows* it ain't there.'

'I'd sure like to see the look on her face if she lifts that bag and finds old Seer gaping at her.'

'Hope she don't wet her pants,' Joe said.

'Have you got a towel you can put under her?'

'Cut it out, guys. I'm worried.'

We stopped talking again and watched the cornfield. Still, no sign of Jennifer. I saw that Stickman, off in the distance, still wore his straw hat.

'She must be almost there,' I finally said.

'I think something happened to her.'

'Nothing happened to her,' Joe said.

'There's no telling who might be out in that field,' Windy Sue said. 'Maybe some sort of pervert or killer or . . . Thelma Henderson, she vanished without a trace last month. Nobody knows what—'

'Jeez, honey, don't get yourself worked up.'

'Well where *is* she?'

'I guess she might've gotten lost,' I admitted.

So Windy Sue began to shout Jennifer's name. She called out five or six times, but never got an answer. Then she frowned at Joe. 'You *still* think nothing's happened to her?'

'She's probably just having some fun with us.'

'Trying to get us worked up,' I added.

'We've gotta go and find her,' Windy Sue said. 'Come on.' She stood on her seat, planted a foot on the door sill, and jumped down. Turning to us, she jammed her fists on her hips. 'Well?'

'Shit,' Joe muttered.

We had no choice, so we both stepped across the seats and hopped to the ground. Joe took the lead. I took the rear. We made our way to the bottom of the ditch. Windy Sue slipped going up the other side. I had to catch her by the rump and give her a push, which was about the only good thing that'd happened to me so far that night. She had a mighty fine rear end.

I wondered how things might go at the drive-in tomorrow night. If Jennifer kept her side of the bet . . .

'Who wins if we find her before she gets to Stickman?' I asked as Windy Sue pushed her way into the cornstalks.

'Forget your dumb bet,' she told me.

'That bitch wouldn't have put out for you anyhow,' Joe said.

'Maybe not, but—'

'You don't want to mess with her,' Windy Sue said. 'Why would you *want* to?'

Joe laughed. 'That's a terrible way to talk about your cousin.'

'Dwayne's a sight too nice for her.'

'Yeah?' I asked.

'Well, you are.'

That made me feel really good, coming from Windy Sue. Of course, I knew she was Joe's girl. It was nice to hear, anyhow. My night seemed to be getting better and better, and I didn't mind at all that we were shoving our way through a forest of cornstalks. I was with my best friends. We were having our own little adventure, and I figured we'd stumble onto Jennifer sooner or later and it would all turn out just fine.

I even stopped caring about the bet. Damned if I would

walk home after this, but it seemed that I would just as soon miss out on the trip to the drive-in with Jennifer.

I might get in some feels – at least if she kept her word – but they wouldn't be worth much. I've messed around before with some gals I didn't much like. Even though it was kind of exciting at the time, it left me wishing I hadn't.

So the hell with the bet. And the hell with Jennifer.

Then she screamed.

Somebody did, and it wasn't one of us.

Windy Sue gasped, 'Oh, my God,' then yelled, 'Jennifer!'

No answer.

'Guess she found the skull,' Joe said.

'Get going!' Wendy Sue snapped at him.

'Don't shove!'

'Move!'

I couldn't see what Joe was doing, but he must've put on some speed because Windy Sue started running. I rushed after her, keeping her back in sight and staying far enough behind not to trip her up. We crashed along for a while. Then Joe yelped. Windy Sue stumbled and flopped down on top of him. I couldn't stop in time, and fell sprawling onto her back. She was hot underneath me. Squirming and panting. But I couldn't enjoy it much, too worried that I'd hurt her. 'Are you okay?'

'Yeah.'

As I crawled off her, Joe gasped, 'Christ, you broke my ankle.'

'Did not,' Windy Sue said.

'You sure didn't *help* it any.'

'Why'd you slow down?'

'I didn't.'

They untangled themselves and stood up. Windy Sue bent over and held her knees and tried to catch her breath. Joe put a hand on her shoulder to steady himself, and tested his right foot. 'Guess it's okay. Just watch where you're going.'

'I didn't stomp you on purpose. Come on, let's move it.' She gave Joe a push.

We took off running again. Pretty soon, it started to seem like we'd gone too far. We'd set out on a line between the corn rows that should've led us directly from the car to Stickman, and as far as I knew we hadn't turned. So we should've gotten to him by now. But maybe we'd hurried right by him. He'd be easy to miss, even if he was just a couple of rows off to the side.

'Hey!' I called. 'Hold on.'

They stopped in front of me.

'We must've gotten off course.'

'Nah,' Joe said.

'We must've. Maybe after we fell. It wasn't this far.'

Nodding and breathless, Windy Sue grabbed Joe's arm. 'Down. Get down.' He sank to a squat. She stepped behind him and swung a leg onto one of his shoulders.

'You've gotta be kidding,' he muttered.

'You got a better idea?'

'Yeah. Let's give it up and go back to the car.'

'Not without Jennifer.' Windy Sue hooked her other leg over Joe's other shoulder. With his head clamped between her thighs, she took hold of his hair. 'Okay, all set.'

Joe sighed, then stood up, lifting Windy Sue above the tops of the cornstalks.

I thought how very much she looked like a kid perched on her father's shoulders to watch a parade go by. A large kid, but this was the only way she could see over the heads of the crowd. The crowd was cornstalks, a mob pressing tight around us so we couldn't see anything. I thought how lucky she was to be up there above it with a view.

Real lucky.

At first, she and Joe had their backs to me. She glanced this way and that.

Joe, holding her thighs, turned slowly.

I had a side view when it happened.

Way up there in the moonlight, Windy Sue looked from left to right. She shook her head. 'This is weird,' she said. 'I can't see either of them.'

'You *gotta* . . . be able to see . . . Stickman,' Joe gasped, straining under her weight.

'Maybe I gotta, but I can't.'

'Oh, for godsake. Open your eyes.'

'He's not . . .' Windy Sue's voice went still. Her back went rigid. Her mouth fell open.

Because she heard it. We all heard it. The rush of someone smashing through the cornstalks right in front of Windy Sue and Joe.

'Jennifer?' she asked.

Jennifer's arm jammed through the leafy wall of corn. I glimpsed a pointed stick – in her hand, I thought – just an instant before she punched it deep into Windy Sue's belly just above the top of Joe's head. Windy Sue grunted like she'd been slugged.

I shouted, 'No!'

In my shock, I figured Jennifer had gone mad.

Then she yanked the stick out of Windy Sue and I saw it wasn't gripped in her hand – it was where her hand *should've been*. It jutted out from the stump of her wrist.

Joe, making gaspy whines, staggered as Windy Sue slumped forward and grabbed his face.

I threw a body block against him. It bashed him aside, but put me in the way of Jennifer's next thrust. The stick only ripped through my shirt and gouged my arm. Then I slammed down on top of Joe. Even as I landed on him, I heard Jennifer shove her way through the cornstalks.

It isn't really right to call her Jennifer, I guess.

But I was still *thinking* it was Jennifer until I flipped over and saw the thing coming at us.

It was partly Jennifer, all right. But it was mostly Stickman.

I saw him plain as day in the moonlight, striding toward us. Joe must've seen him, too, because of how he shrieked.

The burlap bag was off the scarecrow's head. The eyeless skull of Jethro Seer wobbled at the top of the center stick. The shirt and bib overalls were gone, too. And all the straw stuffing.

Stickman wore nothing but Jennifer.

Parts of her.

He wore her arms and legs, just as if he'd torn them from her body, plucked off the hands and feet, and skewered the remains onto himself.

He wore her torso, too.

It was stripped naked.

His middle stick came out at the top through the stump of Jennifer's neck a few inches below Seer's skull. It came out at the bottom through her pussy. Just under there, the branch forked and ran down to where her legs were spitted on.

It was a sight to make you sick. And to make you think you'd lost your mind.

Joe and I both yelled like a couple of lunatics as Stickman lurched toward us.

What I wanted to do was run like hell.

Instead, I jumped up and tackled him. His balance wasn't that terrific, as he was only standing like someone on stilts. I tried to dive at him low enough to miss Jennifer and just knock him off his pins. But my shoulders hit her shins. I grabbed the sticks under her ankle stumps, and slammed Stickman down on his back.

Then I scurried off. Joe and I hefted Windy Sue and shoved sideways through a few corn rows to get clear of

Stickman. Joe carrying her by the shoulders, me carring her legs, we raced all the way back to the road.

We didn't look back till we got to the car.

No sign of Stickman.

We stretched Windy Sue across the backseat. I sat with her, her head on my lap, and pushed my palm against her wound to slow the bleeding while Joe sped us to the emergency room at Sacket General.

Nobody believed Joe and I, of course. I can't blame them. I couldn't really believe what'd happened, either, and I'd seen it with my own eyes.

We likely would've gotten nailed for murder, only Windy Sue pulled through. She hadn't seen much, but enough to convince the cops that she hadn't gotten stabbed by either one of us.

So they figured Jennifer must've been murdered by a stranger.

Their search didn't turn up any stranger. It turned up Stickman's overalls and shirt, his straw hat, the burlap bag with a face painted on it, and scattered clumps of straw stuffing. It turned up Jennifer's clothes, too. And her hands and feet. And her head. Nothing else.

All those things were found on the ground right where the scarecrow used to stand. Still, though, nobody would believe our story.

The county papers ran stories about the 'Cornfield Butcher'. They claimed he must've been a serial killer passing through.

Pretty soon, we gave up on trying to convince anyone otherwise. No point in making ourselves look crazy.

We never went back to the drive-in that summer, not even after Windy Sue got well. There was just no way to get there, not without driving the forty-mile stretch of road that passed through the Guthrie family's cornfield.

The search party hadn't found Stickman, but we knew he had to be out there. Somewhere. With what was left of Jennifer hanging on him and Jethro Seer's skull grinning in the moonlight.

Mop Up

Flophouse Droolers

A live one came after Mike Phipps when he shouldered open the door of 214. This kind of thing had happened plenty of times before, but it still turned his stomach to warm jelly.

The drooler hadn't been missed by the main force when it moved through. He'd been hit by something, all right. In the shimmering red fire glow from the tenement window, Mike could see that he was holding a bundle of his guts with one hand as he lurched past the end of the bed, raising a butcher knife that looked as if it had already been used on someone. '*Commmme* to papa,' the guy said, foam spraying from his mouth.

Mike groaned.

God, he hated this.

He gave the drooler a squirt.

The blast of fire from his flame-thrower filled the room with light. The drooler, suddenly ablaze from head to toe, shrieked and staggered backward, dropping his knife, dropping his guts. His intestines spilled toward the floor, sizzling and snapping like sausage on a skillet. The end of the bed knocked his legs out from under him. He flopped onto the mattress.

By the light of the burning man, Mike scanned the room. Over near the open closet was sprawled a naked woman. She'd been head shot, probably by the main force. And someone had been snacking on her.

Mike gave her a squirt, shrouding her with flames.

He looked back at the bed. The fiery body of the man seemed to be sinking into the mattress.

Backing into the corridor, he did a quick pivot to make sure there were no other live ones around. The smoky hallway fluttered with firelight from the doorways of the three other rooms where he'd already torched bodies. He ran past them, crouching low, eyes watering, the smoke bitter in his nostrils, dry in his throat.

His heart gave a sickening lurch as he started down the stairs and stepped on a drooler. He'd forgotten about this one. He'd passed it coming up, and planned to light it on the way out. But the damned thing had slipped his mind. When his boot came down on its shoulder, the body flipped onto its side, hurling Mike at the banister. The rail creaked and wobbled as his hip slammed against it. For a moment, he thought he was going over the top. But he rebounded off the banister and stumbled down several stairs, somehow missing the drooler's legs, grunting each time the fuel tank pounded his back. With a quick grab of the rail, he managed to stop himself.

When he had his breath again, he turned around and gave the corpse a quick burst.

He trotted to the bottom of the stairs. He was tempted to skip the ground-floor rooms. The last thing he needed was a run-in with another live one. Besides, the fire would take care of any leftovers down here.

You can't be sure of that, he told himself. One could get

buried under the rubble and never be touched by the flames. Might pass it on to somebody sooner or later.

So Mike rushed down the dark, narrow corridor to its far end. Then he began working his way back toward the foyer, throwing open doors, charging into rooms, checking inside closets and bathrooms, behind furniture and under beds, finding plenty of dead droolers and torching each of them.

After the last room, he paused in the foyer. The top half of the stairway was a bright pyre. Its flames had already joined the conflagration at the opening to the second-floor hallway.

Feeling shaky but relieved, Mike pushed open the front door. He rushed out into the night.

Sarge, Ray and Stinger, already done with their buildings, stood by the Land Rover in the middle of the street. Only Stinger still carried his flame-thrower. He was busy taking the tank off his back as Mike approached.

Sarge was lighting a cigar.

Ray was using the front of his open fatigue shirt to wipe the grime and sweat off his face.

Doug was missing.

Mike turned around slowly as he pulled the straps off his shoulders. The street, flanked by burning shops and flophouses, was a junkyard of charred cars, broken glass and rubble blasted from buildings. Several bodies were scattered around – black, misshapen heaps on the pavement, some still smoldering. Mike had fired a couple of them himself, during the Exterior Mop-Up Phase.

But he saw nobody moving about.

No sign of Doug.

He eased his flame thrower down, stretched, and rubbed his shoulders.

'Having fun yet?' Stinger asked.

'Take a leap,' Mike said.

Stinger's lean face grinned. 'Got me a couple of livies over at the pawn shop.'

'Made his day,' Ray muttered. Ray, a baby-faced kid of nineteen, didn't care for Stinger any more than the rest of them did.

'Yessir. They was both packin' heat. Not as much as me, though.' Chuckling, he nudged his flame thrower with a boot. 'Took out the fella, first. Gals can't shoot worth shit, anyhow. Shoulda seen the tits on this one. Out to here, y'know? Gazoombas. She's coming at me, butt naked, poppin' caps, missing by a mile, these big old headlights bobbin' around. So I let her have it, y'know? Zip, zip. A dash here, a dash there. She starts floppin' around with her tits on fire.'

'Shut up, huh?' Mike said. 'I'm getting pretty sick and tired—'

'Hey man, hang on, haven't got to the good part yet. So then I lay one right in her face.'

'Knock it off, Stinger,' Sarge said.

'Her fuckin' head explodes. *Explodes!* Can you dig it? Got some on me.' He wiped his hand across a gob of goo on his shirt and swept it at Mike's face.

Mike swatted the hand away.

'I *said* knock it off!' Sarge snapped.

Stinger laughed, shook his head, and rubbed off the mess on a leg of his fatigue pants.

'You're having such a high old time,' Sarge told him, 'suppose *you* go look for Doug.'

'Fuck that. Dickhead's a pain in the ass.'

Sarge scowled at Stinger, squinting through gray shreds of cigar smoke. Then he took a final suck on the stub, plucked it from his mouth, tapped off a load of ash, and shot the cigar at Stinger's face. Red sparks flew as the glowing tip shattered against the soldier's cheekbone.

'Hey! Ow! Shit!' Stinger cried out, slapping away the embers and ash.

'Do what I tell you,' Sarge said.

'Jesus! I was *gonna*. Jesus!'

'On the double.'

'Yessir!' Stinger hefted his fuel tank, swung it onto his back and shoved his arms through the straps. Crouching, he snatched up the squirter. 'Which way'd he go?'

'He took the Carlton Hotel.'

'Well no wonder he ain't back yet,' Stinger whined. 'Look at that place!' The hotel, at the end of the block, was a square brick structure four stories high.

Mike scanned its upper windows. He saw no trace of fire. Doug would've started at the top and worked his way down. That was SOP. If he'd made it to the fourth floor, he must've found no droolers to torch.

But maybe Doug hadn't made it that far.

Mike didn't like the way the squad was getting whittled down. If they lost Doug, they'd be down to four men. Scuttlebutt had it that they wouldn't be getting any replacements.

'Okay if I go with him?' he asked Sarge as Stinger headed for the distant street corner.

'Yeah. Go on. It'll hurry things along.'

Mike picked up his weapon.

'While you're in there, do the place.'

'Right.'

'Be careful,' Ray said.

'Bet on it.' He slapped the kid on the shoulder, then hurried to catch up with Stinger.

He joined the lanky soldier and walked beside him.

'Just don't fuck with me, Phipps.'

'I may kill you, pal, but I'll never fuck with you.'

Stinger laughed.

Mike followed him into the lobby of the hotel.

Sissy Suit

'Krugman!' Stinger yelled up the dark stairway.

'Krugman, you shit, answer up!'

'He isn't going to hear you,' Mike said.

'Oh, yeah. Worse pussy than you are.'

They turned on flashlights and started climbing the stairs.

Doug Krugman, who generally acted as if every other guy in the squad was no better than after-birth, had a fear of contagion that prompted him to continue wearing his protective gear – dubbed 'sissy suits' by Stinger – long after everyone else had tossed theirs. Mike had kept his suit longer than anyone except Doug. He didn't consider the garments to be sissy suits, but they were just too bulky and confining. And the head covering knocked out most of your vision. He'd decided he would rather take his chances with the virus than get himself blind-sided by a live one. Or fall down a flight of stairs.

Which I nearly did anyhow, he thought, remembering the last place.

Stopping at the second-floor landing, Stinger again yelled, 'Krugman!'

'Knock it off.'

'He mighta taken off the headgear, dipshit.

'Not Doug. So hold it down.'

'Scared I'll wake the dead?'

'It's not the dead I'm worried about.'

Mike heard a soft, nasal snort. 'Wouldn't be no fun, we didn't run into some livies now 'n' then. Know what I mean, sweetums?'

Mike didn't bother to answer.

As they climbed toward the third floor, Stinger said, 'Booger at twelve o'clock.'

'Hold fire.'

'Yeah yeah.'

They reached the landing and hit the drooler with their flashlight beams. He was a kid, maybe sixteen, slumped against the wall with an axe across his legs. He wore his Fruit of the Looms, and nothing else. Someone had stitched him with an M-16, poking a trail straight up his front from groin to forehead. As it for the fun of it, his eyes had been shot out.

Stinger laughed softly. 'Guess what? I'm not the only guy with a sense of humor.'

'Let's split up,' Mike said. 'You take this floor, I'll take the top.'

'Don't like my company?'

'Just don't go torching anyone till I'm down.'

'Can't make no promises. I run into a livie—'

'Use your pistol.'

'Where's the fun in that?'

'All depends where you shoot 'em,' Mike said.

'Ha! Good one!'

Mike stepped over the outstretched legs of the drooler, and shined his flashlight up the last flight of stairs. The area looked clear. He started to climb.

He felt a little guilty about his last remark to Stinger. Like stooping to the creep's level. Better that, though, than to leave him thinking it might be amusing to set the place on fire.

The bastard might do it, anyway.

Probably fire escapes up here someplace, Mike told himself.

Stinger's better pray he doesn't make me use one.

Nearing the top of the stairs, Mike switched off his flashlight. He climbed the final steps, crept across the landing, and leaned through a doorway. As he'd expected, the corridor glowed faintly – light from the burning neighborhood that came in through the room windows.

Several doors had been left open by the soldiers of the main force, so that patches of murky, rust-colored light trembled in the hallway. Not much, but enough to see by.

Mike clipped the flashlight to his web belt, glad he wouldn't need to use it.

He stepped into the hallway, took a shaky breath, and tried to decide whether to start here or at the far end. There were points in favor of both methods. If you torched them in the rooms as you went along, you took a chance of fire spreading into the corridor and blocking your escape. That was its downside. Its upside was that it pretty much removed the chance of a live one jumping you from the rear.

The first order of business is finding Doug, he reminded himself.

So he made up his mind to check each room as he went along, hold off on squirting any droolers he might find, and take care of them on the way back.

Where the hell *is* that guy?

He stepped into the first room. A female drooler lay spread-eagled on the floor at the foot of the bed, her face shot away.

Like most of them, she was naked.

All they wanted to do, once the virus nailed them, was fuck and kill and eat each other.

The damn germ must've been invented by a guy like Stinger, Mike thought.

He stepped past the sprawled body. He used his flashlight to check the bathroom and under the bed. No other droolers. No Doug.

As he headed for the door, glancing all around, the pale beam of his light swept across the body and his heart gave a kick when something moved down there. He whirled. He gazed at the corpse.

It *couldn't* have moved. The poor gal was as dead as dead

can be. What he'd seen must've been a shadow cast by her body as the light passed over it.

Nothing more.

But he stared at her chest, half expecting it to rise and fall with her breathing.

If she sits up, he thought, I'm gonna throw a heart attack.

But her chest appeared motionless.

She had a small freckle above her left nipple.

The same as Merideth.

She *looked* like Merideth.

Feeling hot and sick, Mike realized that the dead woman appeared to be in her early twenties. Her hair, spread out against the floor, was long and blonde. She had Merideth's slim build, small breasts . . . and that freckle.

With the face demolished, there was no way . . .

It's not her, Mike told himself. Impossible. She was in Sacramento when Black Widow hit.

But she's just as dead as this woman. Probably sprawled out naked and shot in her apartment . . .

He knew that. She'd had no more chance than anyone else who didn't have protective gear when the strike took place. He'd been living with the knowledge, trying to do his job, trying to keep her death hidden in a back corner of his mind.

He wished he hadn't come into this room.

He wished he hadn't taken a closer look at this corpse.

His throat tightened. The body blurred as tears filled his eyes. Switching off his flashlight, he backed away. His shoulder bumped the doorframe. He staggered into the corridor, turned away and flinched as a dark shape moved through the shadows down the hallway.

He brought up his flame thrower.

Suddenly realized the vague figure was a man in a sissy suit.

'Doug!'

A gloved hand waved a greeting at him.

'Jeez, man, what've you been doing up here? We figured they must've gotten you.'

Doug didn't answer. The lenses of his headgear shimmered golden for a moment as he strode past the doorway of the next room down. The glow of distant firelight fluttered on the camouflage pattern of his suit.

He had no flame-thrower. His gunbelt was gone.

'Where're your weapons?' Mike asked. 'What's going on?'

A muffled sound of laughter came from him.

Mike felt a chill spread up his back.

'Take that thing off and talk to me,' he said.

More laughter.

'Doug, stop being an asshole and . . .'

In a voice that sounded as if it came from inside a tight box, Doug said, 'Okay, okay.' A stride away from Mike, he halted. With gloved hands, he reached up and tore at the seal of his mask.

He lifted the hood off his head.

Grinned and laughed, slobber flowing down his chin.

Mike thought, *Quit kidding around.*

Then he thought, *He's turned into a drooler.*

Then he knew. *It's not Doug.*

A live one who just bore a vague resemblance to the guy.

He thought, *Shit!* and tried to swing up the muzzle of his flame thrower as the laughing drooler rammed the headgear into his face and shoved him. He stumbled backward. He crashed to the floor, the tank slamming into his spine. The drooler kicked the weapon from his hands. It tumbled across the hallway until the fuel hose jerked it to a stop and it dropped. Mike tried to sit up, saw a kick coming at his face, and turned his head so the blow only clipped his cheek. It was enough to knock him back.

The drooler stomped on his belly. His breath blasted out.

The infected man flopped down on him, straddling his hips, ripping open his fatigue shirt. Mike went for his pistol, but a knee blocked his way. He landed a punch that snapped the drooler's head sideways. The guy didn't seem bothered, though. Chuckling softly, he rubbed and slobbered on Mike's chest. Then he clutched Mike's shoulders and lunged toward his face, the germ-rich saliva splashing a trail up his chest and throat and chin. Clamping his lips tight, Mike punched both thumbs into the man's eyes.

The eyeballs popped, splashing warm fluid down his thumbs and wrists.

The drooler shrieked.

Thumbs deep inside the sockets, Mike clutched the sides of the drooler's face and hurled him sideways. Scrambling to his knees, he jerked out his Beretta and put three 9 mm slugs into the man's head.

Hot Spit

Mike tried not to panic. Keeping his mouth shut and panting through his nose, he threw off the straps of the fuel tank and yanked his shirt off. With the back of his shirt, he scrubbed the foamy spittle off his mouth and cheeks, his chin, his neck and chest. He wiped spit and blood and viscous fluid off his hands and forearms.

I'll be okay, he told himself.

He didn't think he had any breaks in his skin.

If the stuff doesn't get into your bloodstream . . . What do they know? Maybe it only has to get in your mouth. Nobody knows shit.

Snatching up his sidearm, Mike glanced through the doorway at the body of the woman who looked like Merideth.

He didn't want to go in there. So he ran to the next room. He fumbled the flashlight off his belt, switched it on and rushed in.

Looked empty.

He raced to the bathroom door and threw it open. A skinny, naked drooler lay sprawled over the side of the tub – feet on the floor, butt on the edge of the tub, back bent, shoulders and head resting on the bloody enamel of the tub's bottom. His arms were flung out, and a straight razor lay near his right hand. He'd been hit in the chest with something better than an M-16. Probably a 12-gauge assault shotgun.

Crouching beside the body, Mike twisted a faucet handle. Water splashed from the spout.

Works!

He grabbed the drooler by the ankles and yanked him out of the tub. The head made a nasty thump when it struck the floor. Mike dragged him from the bathroom, rushed back inside, and slammed the door. It bumped open. The doorframe was splintered, the latch plate hanging by one screw. Soldiers from the main force must've bashed the door open, coming for that guy.

Big deal, Mike thought. So you can't lock it. The bastard slobbered *all over you!*

He set his flashlight on the edge of the sink so its beam lit the partly open door. Bending over the tub, he turned the water on full force. No hot, but he didn't care. Lucky to have any water at all. He plucked up the shower knob. In seconds, a hard spray was rushing from the nozzle. He let it run to wash the drooler's blood down the drain. While he waited, he picked up the straight razor and tossed it into the sink. Then he hurled his shirt into the tub and climbed in.

The water felt icy on his hot skin. It splattered his face,

sent cold rivulets flowing down his body, soaked through his pants and made them heavy and clinging.

With a bar of soap from the dish beside the tub, he lathered his body.

He left the shower curtain open. He kept the automatic in his right hand. He watched the lighted doorway. He wondered if the soap and water would do any good.

Or was he already a walking dead man?

Yesterday, a live one bit Ringo. The little guy had kept it quiet, explaining his torn and bloody sleeve away by claiming he'd been cut on a broken window. They went about their business. Two hours later, when he didn't come out of a liquor store, Ray had gone in after him. Ray returned looking as if the blood had been drained from his usually rosy cheeks. He'd found Ringo in the back room, humping a drooler. When he shouted, Ringo had turned his head and grinned, foam gushing from his mouth. One squirt took care of Ringo and the girl.

After Ray finished telling his story, Stinger had said, 'You get all the luck, Raygun.'

I'll blow my own brains out, Mike told himself, before I end up like Ringo.

I'll know one way or the other in a couple hours.

Thinking about that, heat seemed to pulse through his body and he had a hard time catching a breath.

I'm probably all right.

Jesus, what if I've got it?

He rinsed off the suds. Watching the door, he soaped himself again.

How do you know if you've got it? he wondered. All of a sudden, you just start feeling horny for no good reason?

When Stinger starts looking good to me . . .

He heard himself laugh. It sounded a bit mad.

Maybe it's when you start laughing at shit that isn't funny.

God, he thought, I'll be like one of *them*. When it hits, maybe I'll *like* it. Maybe I won't want to kill myself, just everyone else.

Mike let the spray wash the soap off his face, then turned his back to the shower. He raised his Beretta in front of his face. He could barely see it.

Go ahead, he thought.

But what if I'm not infected?

What if you are? You want to risk it? What if it hits you and you take out Sarge or Ray?

He tipped the barrel downward to make sure it had no water in it.

What, scared it'll blow up in your hand?

He opened his mouth wide. He inserted the muzzle. He clamped it between his teeth.

Oh shit, he thought. I don't want to do this.

Merideth's dead. And Mom and Dad. The whole country's fucked. Maybe the whole world, by now. Or pretty soon. Nobody around but droolers and soldiers. Even if you get out of this mess in one piece, what's left?

Come on, find one good reason not to blow your head off. Better make it a good one.

Okay. What about Sarge and Ray? Stinger can take a leap as far as I care. But what about Sarge and Ray? They're my friends. How're they going to feel, I go AWOL on them? What if they run into some bad shit and need me?

I'll go back out there. Tell them what happened. Tell them to drop me if I turn haywire.

Mike eased the pistol out of his mouth. He slipped it into his holster and sagged beneath the cold spray, shivering and gasping for air.

The door crashed open.

Hider

Dropping to a crouch, Mike pulled his sidearm, pivoted and swung the gun toward the bathroom doorway where Stinger stood in the bright beam of the flashlight.

'It's only me from across the sea, dickbrain.'

Mike straightened up. He put away his pistol and bent under the spray to shut the water off.

'What the fuck are you doing in here?' Stinger asked.

'I got drooled on. Did you see the guy in the hallway?'

'Doug?'

'That's not Doug.'

'Could've fooled me. Course, there wasn't much face to go by.'

'Must've killed Doug and taken his suit.' Mike bent to pick up his shirt, then decided against it.

'And he gotcha, huh?'

'He didn't *get* me. It's not like Ringo. He just yucked me up, so I showered off.'

'Yeah?'

As Mike climbed out of the tub, Stinger unclipped his own flashlight and stepped the rest of the way into the bathroom.

The beam hit Mike's face. He squinted and turned away.

'Don't mind if I check you out, do you?'

'For what? Bite marks?'

'That. Broken skin.'

'What if you find something? You going to torch me?'

'Yep.' The beam swept slowly down Mike's body. 'Turn around.'

He did.

'Drop your pants.'

'Not for you, pal.' He turned around slowly and squinted against the glare of Stinger's light. The muzzle of the flame-thrower was pointing at his chest. 'Maybe the guy did get me with his spit. I don't know. I guess there's a chance of it. So how about you keep an eye on me? If I start acting weird, take me down.'

'Maybe I oughta just do it now.' In the glow of the flashlight on the sink, Mike saw a grin lift the corners of Stinger's mouth.

'Maybe you should,' he said. 'No replacements coming, though. It'll just be you, Sarge and Ray. You three and the droolers.'

For a few moments, Stinger didn't move. Then he lowered the muzzle of the flame-thrower. 'I can wait,' he said. He backed through the doorway.

Mike rinsed off his flashlight at the sink, dried it on a leg of his pants, and followed Stinger to the corridor. They made their way toward the far end, Mike checking the rooms on the left, Stinger taking those on the right.

Mike found plenty of dead droolers, but no Doug. He had two rooms to go when Stinger called, 'Got him.'

He rushed across the hallway. Stinger was standing over the body.

Doug lay on his back between the bed and an open closet. The top of his head was caved in. His shirt had been ripped open. His pants were down around his knees. Here and there, his skin was caked with white glop. Strips of his flesh had been torn off. Chunks of him were gone.

'Who says this ain't a picnic?' Stinger said.

'Shut up.'

Doug's flame thrower and gun belt were a few yards to the right of the body. They looked as if they'd been in the drooler's way, and he'd flung them.

Mike stepped over to the cast-off gear. With his flashlight, he checked for drool. Then he hefted the flame thrower, slung its tank onto his bare back, and worked his arms through the straps. He fastened Doug's web belt around his waist, just above his own belt, then slid the buckle to the rear so that the holster rested against his left hip.

'You're takin' all that stuff, go on and help yourself to his dog tags.'

'Why don't you.'

'I'm not touchin' that fucker. Be glad to torch him, though.'

'I'll do it,' Mike muttered. Stepping close to the body, he shined his light down. The dog tags were embedded in the bloody mess that was left of Doug's neck. Mike put his flashlight away and shifted the flame thrower to his left hand. Crouching, he took out his knife. He cut off a patch of Doug's shirt, sheathed the knife, and wrapped his hand in the fabric.

'What a pussy.'

With his covered hand, he fished the dog tags out of the gore and yanked, breaking the chain. He left them wrapped in the square of shirt. He shoved them into his pocket.

As he backed away, Stinger sent a stream of fire into Doug's bloody groin.

'You rotten . . .'

Laughing, Stinger hit the body with a full dose that wrapped it in flame. 'Happy trails, asshole.'

Mike, staggering backward, had his pistol halfway out of the holster when he thought, I can't shoot him for being a maggot.

He wondered if his urge to kill the son of a bitch was an early symptom. Jamming the pistol back down tight into the holster, he turned away and rushed from the room.

Seconds later, Stinger joined him in the hallway. 'You got a problem?'

Mike glared at him.

'Okay, let's move it. We got us four stories worth of droolers need squirting.'

They took care of the rooms at the end of the corridor, then made their way back toward the stairs, racing from room to room, entering those they'd already checked and torching the corpses. Mike came to the one with the body that looked like Merideth. He didn't focus on her, just fired a quick stream through the doorway.

He grabbed a strap of the flame thrower he'd discarded after nailing the drooler in the sissy suit. Hefting it beside him, he watched Stinger torch the guy. Then they rushed down the stairs.

At the third-floor landing, he dropped the spare weapon beside the dead drooler who had the axe. He raced down the hallway after Stinger. They split up and charged through the rooms, leaving fiery bodies behind. Mike lugged the extra flame thrower down the stairs to the second floor. He left it on the landing, and picked it up again after they'd flamed every body on that level of the hotel. He lugged it down to the first floor and left it near the foot of the stairs.

'You take care of the hall,' Stinger gasped. 'I'll see what we've got in the lobby.'

Mike didn't like that idea. Alone, it would take him twice as long to hit each room. Twice as long, with three stories of hotel above him. Ten to fifteen fires on each story. All of them growing.

But the lobby needed to be done. There was an area behind the registration desk. There were at least two doors that he could see at a glance. Maybe more, off in the shadows.

'Okay,' he said, and dashed for the end of the corridor.

Don't worry about the fire, he told himself. Right. Probably an inferno up there, by now.

But it won't spread downward all that fast.

You hope.

I'm on the ground floor, he reminded himself. I can always bail out through a window.

And the door at the end of the hall was probably an emergency exit.

He stopped short of that one and shouldered a room door hard so it slapped the wall behind it. Satisfied nobody was behind it, he entered. Nobody on the bed or floor. He pulled his flashlight and rushed to the bathroom. Clear. He dropped and shined the light under the bed. Clear.

He rushed across the hall and hit the next door. Male drooler slumped against the wall, one arm blown off, a pulpy chasm in the middle of his chest. Mike searched for others. None. He splashed the corpse with fire, and rushed out.

Ran to the next door. Hit it. Charged in. A pair on the bed. Still at it, obviously, when the troopers nailed them. An automatic had poked a large S into the guy's bare rump and back. Mike couldn't see much of the woman. Just her spread legs on each side of the guy and one arm stretched across the mattress.

The floor around the bed looked clear. He checked the closet and bathroom. No one. No need to check under the bed. If a drooler was down there, it would go up when he torched these two.

Mike wondered about the woman, though. If she'd been under this guy when the troopers barged in, where was she hit?

Stepping closer to the side of the bed, he checked her with his flashlight. Her head was turned the other way, the guy's face resting on top of it. She had blonde hair, very short. No head wound was visible. Mike began to wonder if she might be a male, after all. But he saw that her armpit was shaved. A woman, all right. Not much of her showed, the way she was mashed between the body and the mattress. Just her bare side. Still, he saw no evidence of wounds.

Her skin, glowing softly in the firelight from the window, looked warm and smooth.

He considered throwing the guy off her.

You want to see how she got it? he thought. Or you just want to check her out?

Come off it! She's a drooler. She's dead.

He realized he *did* want to look at her. There was a tight, growing heat in his groin.

It's kicking in, he thought. Oh, shit! The bastard got me, all right. I'm a dead man.

All of a sudden, he didn't feel horny any more.

He felt as if his genitals were shriveling with cold.

Maybe there's hope after all.

He heard himself let out a weird laugh.

He raised the flame thrower.

Someone made a faint, high whimper.

Mike gasped as the man's head lifted.

A live one!

Before he could fire, he realized that the man hadn't moved his head. The head beneath it was already facing his way.

Wisps of golden hair across the brow. Big, terrified eyes. A bruised cheekbone. Lips pressed tight together. Chin trembling.

The mouth opened. No foam spilled out.

'What're you gonna do with that thing?' she asked in a tight, shaky voice.

She looked no older than twenty. She looked beautiful. She didn't look like a drooler.

'You're alive?' Mike muttered.

'So far. No thanks to the goddamn army.'

'Sorry. I . . .'

'You gonna kill me?'

'How can you be alive?'

'I'm a good hider.' She shoved the dead man. Mike stepped back fast as the corpse tumbled off the bed and hit the floor at his feet. He watched the woman sit up and swing her legs toward him. She had a slender body. One of her breasts had a smear of dried blood on it. There was another stain on her belly, just above the gleaming curls of her pubic hair. Another on her left thigh. Mike watched the way her breasts jiggled slightly as she stood up. She pushed his flashlight aside. 'You don't have to stare.'

'Sorry,' he muttered.

Crouching, she rolled the body away from the side of the bed. She got down on her knees and reached under the bed.

Mike gazed at the sleek curves of her back and rump.

He felt a hot swelling in his groin. This time, it didn't throw him into a panic. It's not Black Widow, he thought. Just healthy lust. Besides, it's too soon. With Roger, it took a couple of hours.

The young woman dragged a small pile of clothing out from under the bed, got up and sat on the mattress. As she drew pink panties up her legs, she looked at Mike. 'Come on, do you mind?'

He suddenly remembered something.

'Oh shit, we've gotta get out of here! The whole damn building's going up in smoke.'

RIP

He grabbed her arm and yanked her off the bed. She came up clutching some clothes to her belly. 'Take it easy!' she blurted. She jerked her arm, and Mike let go. Crouching, she snatched a pair of sneakers off the floor.

Mike raced to the door. The corridor was bright with fire from the rooms to the right. Some smoke, but not much. Should be no problem making it to the lobby.

He looked back. The woman, just behind him, was bent over and pulling her shoes on.

'Come *on!*'

She rushed up to him. He gave her a shove to help her through the doorway, then took a stride toward the corpse on the floor.

A good hider, he thought. Christ, how could anyone do that? Play dead under a drooler. Both of you in the raw.

He squirted the body, then turned to the doorway.

She was in the corridor, glimmering with firelight, a skirt or something clamped between her knees while she stretched up both arms and worked a T-shirt down over her head. Her face popped through the neck hole. 'What're we waiting for?' she asked, pulling the shirt down. It was bloody, torn, and much too large for her. It hung off one shoulder. It draped her thighs like a short skirt.

Mike rushed past her, crossed to the next room and bashed its door open.

'I thought we were getting out of here.'

'I've got a job to do. Stay put.' He entered, checked the room, found no droolers, and returned to the hallway. Now, the woman had a skirt on. It looked like denim. Only a bit of it showed below her draping T-shirt.

She stayed beside him as he hurried to the next room. She waited while he went in. One drooler. He torched it. When he came out, flames were lapping out of the doorways down the hall.

'Shouldn't we get going?' she asked. 'I don't exactly look forward to getting cooked.'

'We'll be okay.' He left her and did the next room. Empty.

When he came out, the woman was gone.

He snapped his head to the left.

Spotted the faint white of her T-shirt. She was running. Almost to the lobby.

'Stop!' Mike shouted.

She kept running.

He raced after her.

So I let her have it, y'know? Zip, zip. A dash here, a dash there. She starts floppin' around with her tits on fire.

Mike ran as hard as he could, hands squeezing the flame thrower, tank pounding his back, lungs aching as he gulped the smoky air, eyes watering.

'No!' he yelled, and wondered if she could hear him over the noise of the roaring, snapping flames. 'Stop!'

Blinking his eyes clear, he saw the woman halt and turn around.

Not soon enough.

She was already beyond the start of the corridor, standing in the foyer.

Good as dead, Mike thought. If Stinger's there.

Dashing closer, he expected a burst of fire to squirt out of the darkness and engulf her.

'STINGER!' he shouted. 'DON'T HIT HER!'

Probably can't hear me, anyway.

But the woman heard. She looked away from Mike for a moment, then hurried toward him.

They met in front of the last room before the lobby.

'I told you to wait!'

'I'm sorry. But the fire . . .'

'I know, I know.'

'There's somebody else?'

'Yeah, a trigger-happy jerk. He'd zap you in a flash.'

'Oh.' She bared her teeth. A grimace as if she knew she'd done something stupid and wanted to kick herself for it.

'Get behind me and stay close.'

She nodded. Then she followed him into the lobby.

There was no sign of fire except for the glow behind them and brightness near the top of the stairs. The lobby looked just the same as when Mike had left Stinger there. Except for a door behind the registration counter. It had been shut. Now, it stood open.

'Stinger!' Mike yelled.

No answer. He heard only the roar of the fire at their backs and above them.

'Maybe he went outside,' the woman said.

Or ran into trouble, Mike thought. Doug's kind of trouble.

Then a dim shape filled the upper part of the doorway that was visible beyond the counter. Fire bloomed. In its light, Mike saw Stinger back out of the room and turn around.

He wondered what Stinger had been doing in there before torching someone just now. Must've been at it a long time.

Better if I don't know, he thought.

'It's me,' he announced. 'I've got a survivor with me, so take it easy.'

'You *what?*' The lean soldier braced a hand on the counter, swung himself up, scuttled across the top and leaped to the floor. He raised his flame-thrower.

'She's okay. She's not a drooler.'

'Step aside.'

'I told you, she's okay.'

'I'm not infected,' she said from behind Mike.

'Then you're the only one, babe.' Striding closer, he said, 'Let's see ya.'

'Don't even think about torching her, man.'

'Shut your face. Over here, hon.' He gestured with the muzzle of his flame-thrower.

The woman stepped out from behind Mike and stood beside him. Her arms were raised high as if she knew how to behave like a prisoner.

Stinger blew through his pursed lips. Holding his flame-thrower on the woman with his right hand, he used his left to unclip his flashlight.

From somewhere above them came a wrenching crash. Mike felt the floor shake under his boots. 'The place is coming down,' he said. 'Let's get out to the street and—'

'Go on and get. She stays.' The beam of his flashlight roamed up the woman's body. She squinted and turned her head away when it hit her eyes. 'A real cutie. Open up, cutie.'

She opened her mouth wide.

'Say, "Ahhh."'

'For Godsake, Stinger! You wanta play doctor, wait'll we're outa here.'

'And let Sarge spoil the fun?'

'You bastard.'

'What's your name, hon?'

'Karen.'

Fire began to lap around the doorframe behind the registration counter.

'She doesn't *look* like a drooler,' Stinger said. He sounded amused. Stepping close to her, he slipped his flashlight under the bottom of her T-shirt. Its beam seeped out through the thin fabric. He moved the flashlight upward, lifting her shirt.

'Leave her alone!' Mike snapped.

'Stay out of it.'

He could see Karen trembling as the bastard raised her shirt above her breasts. She made quiet gasping sounds.

'Just checking for open wounds,' Stinger said.

With the rim of the flashlight, he rubbed her right nipple.

Karen swept an arm down. She knocked the flashlight aside.

Stinger smashed her jaw with it.

Crying out, she stumbled backward. She fell to the floor.

Stinger pointed the muzzle of his flame-thrower at her.

Mike put a bullet in his head.

The 9 mm slug came from Doug's pistol, held low in

Mike's left hand. It punched through Stinger just above his right ear, kicked his head sideways and came out the top throwing up a tuft of hair, gobs of brain, chunks of bone, and a thick spray of blood. Stinger stood there while the mess rained down. Then his legs folded. His rump hit the floor. He flopped onto his side.

Mike gazed at him, stunned.

My God, he thought.

I didn't have any choice. He was going to torch her.

I killed one of our own.

He realized Karen was holding him, pressing her warm body tight against his, pushing her face against the side of his neck. He could feel her harsh shaking. And the racing of her heart.

'You okay?' he asked.

He felt her head nod.

Am I? he wondered.

He flinched as he saw a fiery beam crash down at the top of the stairway. With a shower of sparks, it slammed against the banister. The railing shook, but held. The heavy beam, weirdly balanced, rode it down, lopped the knob off the top of the newel post, and dropped to the lobby floor.

On top of Mike's discarded flame thrower.

He yelled, 'CHRIST!' He shoved Karen back, holstered Doug's gun to free his hand, grabbed her wrist, and ran. They raced past the beam's burning end. He threw open the front door, tugged Karen outside, and dashed with her into the street.

At the far curb was the charred husk of a station wagon.

Behind its rear fender, Mike clutched the back of Karen's neck and forced her down flat against the pavement. He sprawled on top of her.

'What're you doing?'

He didn't have the breath to answer.

'You're mashing me.'

An explosion pounded the night. A few seconds later, debris started coming down. Mike lifted his face off the back of Karen's head and saw splinters of wood and glass striking the pavement alongside the car. A few bits of something clinked against the tank on his back. But he felt no jabs.

He felt Karen shaking and flinching beneath him. Soon, the flinching stopped. But she continued to tremble.

Through the ringing in his ears, he heard her say, 'Holy cow.'

'Yeah.'

'Can we get up?'

'Not just—'

A second explosion boomed in his ears. That would be Stinger's fuel tank. Not as close to the front of the hotel. The blast wasn't quite so deafening, and none of the debris came down anywhere near Mike and Karen.

'Okay,' he said. He crawled off her, lifted his flame-thrower by its forestock, and got to his feet.

Karen stood up.

He rested a hand low on her back.

Side by side, they gazed over the roof of the car at the blazing hotel. The brick walls were still intact. Fire flapped and fluttered from the demolished doorway and most of the windows.

'I'm sorry about your friend,' Karen said.

'He was no friend.'

'I'm sorry anyhow.'

He rubbed her back, and she leaned against him.

He looked up the street. The Land Rover was gone. Sarge and Ray were nowhere in sight.

The Survivor

Mike led Karen out to the middle of the street – a canyon walled by burning buildings. The squad had been working its way through the slum from west to east. Maybe Sarge and Ray had gone on ahead to the next block. Nothing beyond the cross-street appeared to be on fire, though. Mike couldn't see the Land Rover, but it might be there, blocked from sight by the numerous abandoned vehicles.

'I was with two other guys,' he said.

Karen looked at him.

'Don't worry, they're not like Stinger.'

'Where are they?'

'Must've moved on. I don't know.' He took off his flame thrower. Crouching, he checked the tank's fuel gauge.

Still has some juice, he thought. But not much.

He stood up and faced Karen. 'About what happened back there.'

'I'll back up whatever you say,' she told him.

'Thanks. A drooler got Stinger, that's all. We didn't see it happen, just found the body.'

Gazing at him with solemn eyes, she nodded.

Mike reached behind his back and unhooked Doug's web belt. 'Put this on.'

She took the belt from him. She swung it around her waist and fastened it in front, the holster low against her right hip. Mike saw how the belt pulled the T-shirt taut over her breasts and how the wide neck hole, stretched shapeless, drooped off her right shoulder. The shirt was smudged with grime and dry blood, torn here and there. A small flap hung down, showing the smooth skin just below her collar bone. Her belly showed through a sagging rip that looked like a big, grinning mouth.

She finished adjusting the belt and looked up at Mike. 'Not much,' she said, 'but at least I've got one.'

'Huh?'

A smile turning her mouth, she reached out and patted his chest. 'A shirt.'

'Mine got wrecked,' he said.

Her smile vanished. 'Mine got taken. This one's borrowed.'

He nodded. 'Do you know how to use the pistol?'

'I'll manage. What's your name?'

He was surprised she didn't already know it. He felt as if they'd been together for a long time. 'Mike,' he said. 'Mike Phipps.'

'Karen Hadley.' She offered her hand, and he shook it.

This is strange, he thought as he said, 'Nice to meet you.'

'Same here.' Her smile returned. 'Boy, is *that* the truth. An honest-to-God human being who doesn't want to rape, murder, and gobble me up.'

'I just wanted to burn you.'

'Well, you didn't. And you saved my life.'

'Glad to be of service, ma'am.' He looked over his shoulder. 'I guess we'd better try and find the others.'

They started walking up the middle of the street. 'You're not taking your flame thrower?' Karen asked.

'It's almost empty,' he said. 'Anyway, we've got some extras in the Land Rover. If we can find it.'

'Think the guys ran off and left you?'

'Probably just on the next block. We were in there a long time.'

'*I* was in there for days.'

Mike wrinkled his nose. Unable to look at her, he asked, 'Under that guy?'

'Lord, no.' She took hold of his hand. 'He was on me for maybe ten minutes. When I heard you guys, I . . . *Ugh!* I don't like to think about it.'

'Must've been gross.'

'I've been through worse.'

'Can't imagine that.'

'Then you're lucky.'

He looked at her. She turned her face toward him. Her jaw was slightly swollen where Stinger had struck her with the flashlight. Her eyes glimmered in the glow of the nearby fires. Somehow, they looked both vulnerable and tough.

'Want to tell me about it?' Mike asked.

'Not much.'

'That's okay. I know it must've been pretty bad.'

'Yeah. If it wasn't the sickies, it was the soldiers. It's a miracle I'm still alive.'

'Why *are* you still alive?'

'Darn good at playing dead, for one thing. As you saw.'

'But the Black Widow?'

'Is that what they're calling it?'

'It's what *we* call it, anyway. Because of how it makes people act.'

'Iraq do it to us?'

'That's what we've been told. Who knows. They tell us whatever they want. But I haven't heard of any other survivors. I mean, as far as I know, the thing nailed everyone who was exposed to it. We were told there *weren't* any civilian survivors.'

Karen looked up at him with something of a smirk, her head tilted to one side. 'That's 'cause they didn't know about me.'

'You weren't exposed to it?'

'Oh, you've got to be kidding.' She turned her face away and peered straight ahead, her eyes narrow. 'For starters, the strike caught me outside. So I got . . . what do they call it? "Primary exposure." After that . . . I had some intimate contact with sickies. A *lot* of it.' She glanced at him, a fierce hurt look in her eyes, then lowered her head.

'I'm sorry, Karen.'

She squeezed his hand. 'Anyway, I've probably had enough of that virus in me to kill off the planet.'

'But you're okay?'

'Peachy,' she muttered. 'But I don't have the foaming crazies, if that's what you mean.'

'Why not?'

'It's 'cause I'm pure of heart.'

Mike felt a smile stretch his face. 'Maybe that's it.'

'Either that,' she said, 'or I've got some kind of a natural immunity.'

They stepped around the charred heap of a body. He saw Karen turn her face aside.

'If you're immune, there might be others.' He thought of Merideth. Maybe she . . .

'Won't be,' Karen said, 'by the time the army's done. They're dropping everyone in sight.'

'God,' Mike muttered. Survivors being cut down by the military. Maybe only a few here and there. But if Karen was immune, there almost had to be others. 'They think everyone's a drooler,' he said. 'We've got to let someone know . . .'

'Sure. Phone the White House.'

'The Land Rover has a transmitter. We can radio a message to—'

'But where is it?'

Mike halted, and Karen stopped beside him. They were in the middle of the intersection. On the block ahead, no fire seemed to be coming from any of the buildings. But there was plenty of light from the burning block at Mike's back to reveal corpses littering the street. Most were naked. None had yet been torched. There were some abandoned vehicles:

a taxi at the curb, its windshield shot up; an overturned clunker with a body hanging out the driver's window; a bullet-riddled VW Bug resting crooked on the center line, doors on both sides open; a few others. Halfway down the block, faint but visible in the ruddy glow, was a bus that had crashed into a parked car. The bus, angled sideways, blocked a lot of Mike's view.

He didn't see the Land Rover. He didn't see Sarge or Ray.

'Hope nothing's happened to them,' he muttered.

'Maybe they're behind the bus,' Karen said.

'Could be.' He glanced to the right and left. The cross-street didn't catch as much firelight as the area straight ahead. Not far beyond the intersection, the glow faded to moonlit darkness. From what Mike could see, however, it was no different from every other street in this section of the city. It looked desolate. He saw the dim shapes of scattered bodies. Trashed vehicles. Debris he couldn't recognize.

Nothing moved out there.

He saw no Land Rover. No Sarge or Ray.

'Let's go straight,' he said. 'I don't know why they'd take off, but that's the way we were heading.'

They started walking again. Karen held his hand tightly. They cast shadows on the reddish pavement in front of them.

Even though the night was warm, he felt a chill on his sweaty back as they left the fires behind.

Twin bright lights suddenly broke through the darkness beyond the rear of the distant bus.

Headlights!

He grinned. 'We're in business.'

He heard the faint, familiar sound of the Land Rover's engine turning over.

The headlights started to move, pushing their pale beams through the night.

'I guess they've seen us,' Karen said. She sounded a little nervous.

'Don't worry,' Mike told her. 'These guy's are okay.'

The vehicle picked up speed. It swerved to dodge the VW, but didn't bother to miss a body. A front tire bumped over the corpse, tipping the headlight up for a moment.

Somebody let out a merry whoop.

Mike said, 'Uh-oh.'

He drew his automatic.

The Charge of the Night Brigade

'Your guys?' Karen asked.

'Isn't them.'

Then the vehicle was close enough for Mike to make out the shapes of people above the glare of the headlights. A woman rode the hood, feet on the bumper, bare skin dusky in the fire glow, hair blowing, arm waving a bayonet as if she were leading a cavalry charge. A man behind the windshield. Someone in the passenger seat, mostly blocked by the gal on the hood. Two or three in the cargo bed, one standing.

The standing one, a bald man with a beard, raised a handgun as the Rover bore down.

Mike put two rounds through the windshield. One of them caught the driver's face. The vehicle swerved, throwing out the drooler with the gun. It sped by, fishtailing, tires screaming, and spun around. The one who'd fallen out stopped flipping over and lay motionless. Mike heard the engine die and watched the Rover skid until it came to rest near the far curb, some fifty feet down the street, headbeams pouring through the remains of a shop's display window.

He and Karen opened fire. Droolers leaped and scurried

from the vehicle, ducked behind it. Someone shot back at them. A bullet whined off the pavement near Karen.

Mike slapped her arm. She looked at him. 'Come on!' He whirled around.

Side by side, hunching low and weaving, they dashed across the pavement. Behind them, gunshots crashed. They leaped the curb, crunched across the glass-littered sidewalk, and lunged through a dark doorway. They crouched and leaned against the front wall. Karen was huffing loudly.

'You okay?' Mike gasped.

'Peachy.'

'Christ.'

'At least . . . you got two of them.'

He duck-walked past Karen and she followed him toward the display window.

'How many more?' he asked. 'Did you see?'

'Four, maybe. I don't know.'

'Where'd *they* come from?' The damn troops, Mike thought, were supposed to nail these fuckers. How in hell did they miss so many? And how come these droolers had bunched together instead of going at each other?

He wondered if they'd killed Sarge and Ray.

Likely.

But there were other mop-up squads around the city. The Land Rover could've been taken from one of them.

Then where's ours?

Stopping at the edge of the smashed window, Mike leaned sideways until he could see out.

Nobody coming.

There were some droolers behind the Rover, keeping low, heads backlighted by the fires on the next block.

They all there? he wondered.

'Do you see them?' Karen asked.

'They're still at the Land Rover.'

'What're we going to do?'

'Take 'em out.'

'You're not into hiding?'

He laughed softly. 'Not when I have a choice. Besides, I want to get my hands on that radio.'

'We could sneak out the back,' she said. 'There must be a rear exit.'

Karen's comment reminded him of the store at their backs. He'd been too concerned about the droolers in the street to worry about others. Unclipping his flashlight, he turned away from the window. 'Keep an eye on 'em,' he whispered.

Karen crept past him, squatted beneath the window and peered out.

Mike swept his beam across the room.

They seemed to be in a small grocery market. A checkout counter to the left of the door. Beyond that was a refrigeration unit, probably the meat section. In the middle of the room stood three rows of shelves, the floor cluttered with fallen cans and packages. Over to the right was a liquor section. There, the shelves he could see were almost bare. Some broken bottles on the floor, but he supposed that most of the booze had been taken by looters – droolers, or soldiers from the main force.

He saw no bodies.

He saw no live ones.

Karen was right, though. There had to be a delivery door at the rear.

'Mike?' she whispered.

Stowing the flashlight, he twisted around and looked out the window.

The droolers were inside the Land Rover again. Its lights had been shut off, and it was slowly backing away from the curb. It came across the street at an angle, rear first, swerving slightly from side to side but making steady progress toward the market. And picking up speed.

One drooler was driving. Two seemed to be watching, their faces pale blurs just above the tailgate.

'We got trouble,' Mike muttered. 'Tailgate's armored.'

'Does that mean we can't shoot them?'

'Not unless you're Annie Oakley. Let's try for the driver.'

Mike shuffled sideways until his shoulder met Karen's. Then they opened up, their automatics roaring, jumping in their hands, ejected brass flying. The moment the shooting started, the droolers in the back dropped out of sight. Bullets sparked off the tailgate. Others slammed through the windshield. The driver slumped out of sight.

The Rover kept coming. Faster and faster.

Karen's gun went silent.

Mike fired his last round. He jerked Karen's sleeve. 'Let's go!' he shouted as the vehicle sped across the center line.

They lurched up and staggered away from the window.

Mike expected the Rover to keep on coming and try to ram through.

But it skidded to a halt at the curb. Two faces rose above the tailgate. A third drooler stood up behind them.

Time seemed to slow down as that one came to her feet in the cargo bed, as Mike rushed backward with Karen, as his hand worked fast to release his empty magazine.

The rising drooler was the one who'd been on the hood when the vehicle first came at them. Her right side shimmered with the distant firelight, and her left side was dark. She looked magnificent standing there – tall and slim, her shoulders broad, her right breast glowing like polished gold, public curls glistening. Magnificent and awful. She had the bayonet clamped in her teeth. Slobber flowed down her chin. The shoulder Mike could see bore the dark strap of the fuel tank she wore on her back. Clamped between her arm and ribcage was the stock of the flame-thrower. Its muzzle swung toward the store window.

Mike hurled himself sideways, slamming against Karen. They hit the floor rolling as a gust of fire rushed by. He kept tumbling until he saw Karen scamper up. He thrust himself off the floor and followed her. Glancing back, he saw a path of fire that led from the windowsill across the floor to the first section of standing shelves.

The woman came through the display window like a hurdler.

Before she landed, shelving blocked Mike's view. He kept his eyes on Karen's back. She was a few strides ahead of him, her shirt a pale, jolting blur.

As he ran, he shoved a full magazine up the butt of his pistol. He slapped it home. He jacked a cartridge into the chamber.

Karen still had an empty gun. He wondered if she knew how to reload. Probably not.

They were almost to the rear of the store. He glanced back. The drooler'd had time to reach their aisle, but she wasn't there. Probably in a different aisle, planning to get them as they cut across the back. He was about to warn Karen, but she let out a small yelp and lurched to a halt. Mike dodged, missed her, and stopped.

Just in front of them was a refrigerator unit that ran along the back wall. It had sliding glass doors. Instead of soft drinks and beer, it held a drooler. Mike couldn't see much. But he saw plenty. The naked guy was spread-eagled so tight against the glass that it pressed his skin flat. His nose and erection looked mashed. He was writhing, licking the glass, gazing out at them.

One arm stretched out farther. He hooked a rim of the door with his fingertips and the glass started to slide.

Mike put a bullet in his forehead.

He stepped around Karen, holding a hand up to keep her still, and leaned past the end of the shelves. In the fluttering red light from the fire, he could see that the back aisle was clear. The rear exit ought to be just beyond the end of the refrigeration unit.

If they went for it, they'd be exposed to anyone lurking between the next two rows of shelves.

Though he heard nothing except the crackle and snap of the fire, he knew that the gal with the flame-thrower had to be nearby. And the other two or three droolers were probably in the store by now, sneaking through the aisles. One of them, at least, had a gun.

He didn't want to go out there.

Maybe sneak back to the front and try to . . .?

He heard a quiet skidding sound – the sound that a door of the cold-drink compartment might make, sliding open. The skin on his back crawled. He snapped his head around.

The body of the drooler toppled out as Karen, gripping the handle, leaped out of the way.

'What're you doing?' Mike whispered.

She didn't answer. Crouching over the feet of the body, she reached forward with both hands, lifted up on a wire shelf rack inside the refrigerator and shoved it. Mike heard a few cans tumble and roll. The rack clamored, apparently dropping to the floor behind the unit. Karen raised and pushed the next shelf up. More falling cans. Another clatter.

Mike checked the rear aisle. Still clear. He scooted backward and glanced around the way they'd come. Okay there.

Where are the fucking droolers!

As another rack rang against the floor, he crawled past the end of the shelving for a glance down the next aisle. He eased his face around the corner and looked straight at the belly of a drooler. A skinny old thing. A woman. Squatting there, grinning and slobbering. 'Hi-ya, honey,' she whispered.

Mike was on his hands and knees, his automatic pressed against the floor. As he started to bring it up, the hag dropped toward him, grabbed his hair with both hands and twisted his head, flipping him onto his back. He clamped his mouth shut tight.

Foam spilled onto his lips and chin.

Just like last time.

If the other time didn't infect me, he thought, this won't either.

Her tits slapped the side of his chest. Her hair draped his face. He jammed the muzzle of his automatic against her ribs. Her open mouth was inches above his face when a shoe shot in from the side, caught her in the eye, knocked her head sideways and Mike pulled his trigger three times.

He shoved the drooler. She tumbled off him. Karen grabbed the wrist of his gunhand and pulled as he staggered to his feet. She kept his wrist. Crouching, she guided him toward the open refrigerator. He stumbled as he stepped on the rump of the drooler who'd been in there. He fell to one knee between the guy's legs.

Something to the left.

He snapped his head that way and jerked his hand from Karen's grip as she ducked into the compartment.

Beyond the last section of shelves stood the gal with the flame-thrower.

Bayonet still in her teeth. Tawny skin shimmering. Thick suds of drool flopping off her chin and flowing like lava down between her breasts.

Mike triggered four rounds at her. The first seemed to miss. The next pounded her hip. One got her square in the chest, shaking her breasts and splashing out a thick spray of drool and blood. One punched her under the nose. She flinched as each bullet struck her. As she staggered backward, Mike knew she was dead on her feet. Her back hit the far wall. She dropped to her knees. And flame bloomed from the muzzle of her weapon. Straight at Mike.

He sprang for the darkness. His hip scraped the edge of the sliding door. The back of his head struck a wire rack. Cans above him bounced and clinked. He landed belly first on the floor of the refrigerator compartment, sliding, kicking up his feet. Karen grabbed him under the armpits and dragged him the rest of the way through.

He looked back. His boots weren't on fire, but the aisle back there was ablaze.

He stood up, Karen holding him steady as cans and wire racks teetered under him. They were in a storeroom stacked with cartons.

Apparently, the stock people loaded the shelves from back here. Karen must've known that.

It looked like the looters had missed this area.

'You okay?' she whispered.

'You're a genius,' he said.

'That's me. Used to work in a 7-Eleven.'

Things Can Only Get Better

Mike wanted to hug her, but he realized his face was still wet with the slobber of the drooler.

No shower handy, this time.

'What happened out there?' Karen asked.

'I bagged the babe with the squirter.'

'All *right*!'

'Gotta clean my face,' he muttered.

Karen put a hand on his shoulder. 'Bend down,' she whispered. 'You think we got them all?'

'One or two left, maybe.'

When he was squatting in front of her, she tugged her T-shirt free of her belt, put a hand inside it, and lifted the fabric toward his face.

'You don't want to get this on you.'

'I'm immune, remember?'

With the front of her shirt, Karen rubbed the saliva off his cheeks and lips and chin.

'Thanks,' he muttered. He straightened up. 'Give me your pistol.'

She handed it to him.

'Over here.' He stepped around a stack of cartons, and she followed. They crouched down.

'Do you think we hit the driver?' Karen asked.

Mike dropped the empty magazine into his hand. 'I don't know.'

'Me neither.'

'There ought to be one more, plus the driver if we didn't get him.' He took a fresh magazine from the pouch on his belt, slammed it up the pistol butt, and worked the slide. 'Maybe they can't get back here,' he said, giving the weapon back to her. 'That gal laid a path right across the rear. They'd have to come through it.'

'So you think we're safe?'

'Well, we might burn up.'

He heard a soft laugh come from Karen.

After reloading his own Beretta, he said, 'What we'll do is take the back way out. Work our way around to the front and get back to the Land Rover. Then head for battalion.'

'What about your friends?'

'I don't think they're alive any more. These creeps must've taken 'em out.'

Mike stood up and turned around. Most of the storeroom was in shadows. Here and there, firelight shimmered on the sides of stacked boxes. He saw no one. 'Looks okay,' he said, holstering his sidearm as Karen rose beside him.

He ripped open the top of a carton, reached in and pulled out a can. In the gloom, he couldn't see what it was. 'Thirsty?' he asked.

'You bet.'

He popped the can open and gave it to Karen. As she drank, he took out another, and shook it hard.

'Hey, that'll . . .'

'I know,' he said. Tipping the can toward his closed mouth, he flipped its tab. With a *whish*, warm soda sprayed his face. Some went up his nose, but most of the liquid splashed his lips and cheeks. It spilled down his chin, ran down his neck and chest. He rubbed it around with his left hand.

'That's a crazy way to drink Pepsi,' Karen said.

'I can't stand having that stuff on me. I know it's not supposed to give you the Black Widow, but . . .'

'No harm being careful.' Karen set her can on the box. She pulled off her T-shirt, turned it around, and used its back to mop the soda off Mike. 'You're going to be sticky.'

'You too, now.'

'I'll survive,' she muttered.

He wanted to reach out and touch her, slide his hands up her smooth sides. But one hand was wet and the other held the Pepsi can. Besides, she might not appreciate it. God knows what had been done to her by droolers before he came along.

She finished drying him, shook open her shirt, and lifted it overhead to put it on. He watched her breasts rise slightly. The ruddy light trembled on them. Her nipples were dark and jutting. Then they were out of sight beneath the filthy, torn shirt.

She picked up her can, and drank some more.

Mike rubbed his wet hand on a leg of his fatigues. He shifted the can to that hand, and drew his pistol. He took a few swallows of the Pepsi. He wished it were beer. He wished it were cold. But it tasted sweet and good. He finished off the can, and set it down inside the carton.

'Maybe we can latch onto some food,' Karen said.

'When was the last time you ate?'

'I don't know. The army came through here this afternoon. Yesterday, I . . .' She shook her head. 'Must've been day before yesterday. Didn't get much, though. I got into the kitchen of some diner, but then a couple of sickies came after me. The whole place was crawling with them before the soldiers showed up.' She made that '*Ugh!*' sound again.

'Come on,' Mike said. 'Let's see what we can find. But we'd better hurry.' Though the fire hadn't yet penetrated the storeroom, smoke was coming in and the temperature seemed to be rising fast. 'Keep your eyes sharp,' he said.

Karen took another swig of Pepsi, then set the can aside. They made their way across the floor. They passed the double doors that led into the shopping area. Tongues of flame were lapping through the crack at the bottom. Rushing by, they came to more stacks of boxes. Karen started ripping them open while Mike stood guard.

'Chicken soup,' she muttered. She tore open another box. 'Mayo. Darn.'

'Hurry.'

She ripped into another. 'Ah-ha! Oreos! Do you like Oreos?'

'Fine.'

'Double-stuffed, too.' She hugged them to her belly. 'All set.'

'That's all you want?'

'It'll do for now.'

He led the way to a large metal door at the back of the storeroom and shouldered it open. 'Wait a second,' he said. He stepped out.

An alley.

He checked both ways. Dark back here. Walled in by brick buildings. To the left, the alley stretched into darkness that seemed to have no end. To the right, the distant opening at the cross-street glowed from the block that Mike and the others had left burning. He saw trash bins here and there along the walls. Most of the buildings had rear doors. Some had loading docks. He saw no droolers.

'Looks okay,' he said.

He braced the door wide with his back and Karen came out, followed by a few shreds of smoke. He stepped away. The door swung shut with a heavy clank.

Side by side, they walked down the middle of the alley toward the ruddy light. The plastic wrapper crackled, and Mike watched Karen take out a cookie. 'Open up,' she said. He did. She pushed the cookie into his mouth. As he chewed, he peered past her at a loading dock to the right. The bay door beyond the platform was open.

We could go straight through to the street, he thought. We'd come out by the Land Rover.

But the area beyond the door looked black.

God knows what might be in there.

Here in the alley, at least he could see what was coming.

Karen used her lower teeth to pry her cookie in half. She chewed, then scraped off the white filling with her teeth and moaned softly as she savored it.

Mike switched the pistol to his left hand. He put his right hand low on Karen's back. Her shirt was damp. He thought about drooler germs, but told himself that the real slobber was on the front of her shirt. This was mostly Pepsi. So he caressed her back through the moist fabric.

She turned her head and smiled at him, the bottom half of the Oreo wedged between her teeth.

Looking at her, Mike felt warm and achy in his chest. He smiled. 'You're something else,' he said.

Karen crunched the cookie.

He moved his hand higher on her back. Up between her shoulder blades, the shirt was dry. He slid it against the smoothness of her skin.

'I came real close to blowing my brains out, earlier tonight.'

'I'm sure glad you didn't,' she said.

'I thought I might be infected,' he explained. 'And there didn't seem to be much point in going on, anyway. Everything's . . . gone.'

'Not everything. There's still Oreos.'

Mike laughed softly. 'Yeah. And there's you.'

Karen shifted the package of cookies to her other arm and eased closer. Her hip touched the side of his leg. Her arm went around his back and she caressed his side. 'I'm awfully glad we found each other,' she said. 'Things were looking pretty bleak, all right. Not that I ever considered suicide, but . . .'

'You're a survivor.'

'I just like things, you know? Food . . .'

'I noticed.'

'Sunsets, baths, friends, lovers.'

Mike curled his hand over her bare shoulder.

'You name it. There's always enough good stuff to make up for everything that's rotten. Besides, I figured things could only get better, you know? Turns out, I was right.' She squeezed his side.

Mike realized they were nearing the cross-street. And he realized he'd forgotten about their peril. He quickly looked over his shoulder. In the shadows behind them, nothing stirred.

We're doing just fine, he told himself.

But there's got to be droolers around. Don't let your guard down again.

At the mouth of the alley, he glanced from side to side. There was good light from a blazing tenement at the corner across the street. He saw debris, bodies, abandoned cars. Nobody moving.

He turned Karen toward the right, took a few steps, then stopped and faced her.

She looked up at him.

'I don't want to lose you,' he said.

She nodded slightly.

'If we join up with the main force . . . I'll be in it all again. They'll probably ship you off somewhere.'

'I wouldn't like that,' she murmured. She caught her lower lip between her teeth. She had a cookie crumb at the corner of her mouth.

'When we get to the Land Rover . . . How would you feel about heading west? I don't know what we'll find. Just dead people and ruins, probably. But there won't be any troops. We'll be on our own.'

'That sounds good to me.'

'I can radio battalion headquarters from the Rover to pass on the word that there are survivors. Then we'll just head the other way.'

'You'll be a deserter, Mike.'

'They'll just think I'm a casualty. Hell, our whole squad's bit the dust. I'll just be one more guy the droolers got.'

'Are you sure you want to do this?'

'Do you?'

'You bet your ass. Let's get to that Land Rover and head for the coast.' Breaking away from him, she hurried up the sidewalk. She had a bounce in her step. Her short hair shimmered golden in the firelight. The tail of her T-shirt, rounded over her small buttocks, shifted and swayed with each step. She looked over her shoulder and smiled at Mike. His bowels seemed to freeze.

The naked drooler that lurched around the corner of the building twenty feet in front of Karen was a fat bald man with a hard-on and an automatic.

'NO!' Mike shrieked.

The drooler fired.

Gunplay

Karen's head jerked as the slug hit her. She twirled like a clumsy ballerina, her arms swinging out, cookies flying from their package as it tumbled through the night, her legs doing a weird jig until she stumbled off the curb, tripped over her own ankles, and flopped onto the street.

Mike watched. Numb.

A bullet zipped past his ear, and he focused his mind long enough to empty his Beretta into the drooler.

He staggered toward Karen's body. She was sprawled on the pavement, her face turned away from him. One of her sneakers had come off. The bottom of her bare foot looked clean and pale. Her foot seemed very small, almost like that of a child.

Mike sank to his knees beside her.

The tail of her T-shirt had come up. It lay rumpled and crooked against the seat of her denim skirt. He holstered his pistol. Leaning forward, he rested a hand on the back of her shirt. It was damp from when she'd used it to dry the Pepsi off him in the storeroom.

A sob wrenched Mike's chest. He hunched over and clutched his face with both hands and cried.

'I'm not dead yet,' Karen muttered. 'No thanks to you, Quickdraw.'

'Oh, God!' He wiped his eyes and tried to stop crying as she rolled slowly onto her back.

The right side of her face was torn and bloody. She kept that eye shut, but it didn't look damaged. There was a pulpy furrow just in front of her ear. Her cheekbone was laid bare. A corner had been knocked off the tip of her nose.

'Won't win any more beauty contests, huh?'

Mike sniffed and wiped his nose. 'You will if I'm the judge,' he murmured. 'Does it hurt much?'

'I've hurt worse.'

He unsnapped a satchel at the side of his belt and took out his first-aid kit. As he opened it, he checked around. The area looked clear.

He remembered that he'd emptied his pistol into the drooler.

He lifted the front of Karen's T-shirt above her waist and pulled Doug's pistol from the holster. He set it down on her belly.

For the next few minutes, he worked on her face. She flinched and gritted her teeth as he fingered the wound, gently prodding some torn flesh back where it seemed to belong. The bullet had carried plenty off with it, but enough remained to fill in some of the gouge and cover most of her cheekbone. When Mike figured he could do no more to improve the situation, he bandaged her, taping down the gauze pads as firmly as he dared.

'That should hold you,' he said, 'till I can get you to a field hospital.'

'Field hospital?'

'You need real doctors.'

'We're going west, remember?'

'I can't take the chance. The wound might get infected. You could die.'

'Not me. I'm the survivor, remember?'

'Pure of heart.'

'Damn right. We're heading west, just like we planned.'

'I don't know.'

'I do.' She started to sit up, and groaned.

'I'd better carry you,' Mike said.

'Yeah, you'd better. I'll ride shotgun.' She reached down to her belly and picked up the pistol. She raised its barrel toward the reddish sky, twirled a little curlicue with it, and said, 'Let's go.'

Mike pushed one arm under her back. He slipped the other behind her knees.

'I think I'm missing a sneaker.'

'Okay.' He left her for a moment. He picked up the small shoe. She wiggled her toes as he started to put it on her. He felt his throat thicken.

'You don't have to tie it,' she said when he was done.

'Thanks.' He returned to her side, squatted low, and lifted her.

Instead of taking Karen to the sidewalk, he made his way to the middle of the street.

No more surprises, he told himself.

It felt wonderful to be holding her. To feel her warmth and movement as he walked.

He stepped past the corner, continued to the center of the intersection, and turned to the right. Some distance up the street, the Land Rover was just where he'd last seen it – stopped a few yards from the front of the market. The store was blazing. Though flames were gusting up from the display window, none reached as far as the Rover.

Karen's head was turned. She was looking, too. The pistol, tight in her grip, rested on her belly with its muzzle pointed that way.

'Spot any sickies,' she told him, 'just say the word.'

'If I spot any, I'll put you down and take the gun.'

'Don't trust me?'

'I've never seen you hit anything,' he said.

'Doesn't mean I can't.'

Mike smiled down at her.

She was cradled against his chest, the bandaged side of her face upward as she watched the area ahead. Her right arm was pressed against him. It was bent at the elbow, forearm angled across her belly, the barrel of the pistol resting on her left wrist as if ready for whatever might come at them from the front.

Her left hand lay curled between her upraised legs. The denim skirt, bunched around her hips, left her thighs bare. They gleamed in the firelight.

Mike knew he should be watching for droolers, not admiring Karen.

But she was keeping watch.

So he looked at her breasts. They were just below his face, very close. The loose T-shirt hung lightly over them. It took on their shape. He could see the way her nipples pushed the fabric out. The motion of his walking made her breasts shake and tremble just a bit.

She's so beautiful, he thought.

If he lifted her higher, he would be able to kiss her right breast. He imagined the turgid, springy feel of the nipple in his mouth. The shirt would be in the way.

'Looks like we got him,' Karen said.

Mike raised his eyes, then halted. They were only a few strides from the Land Rover. The driver was slumped forward, head against the steering wheel. The exiting bullet had splashed gore against the pocked and webby remains of the windshield.

Mike carried Karen closer to the Land Rover. A single flame thrower remained in the cargo bed. No droolers.

He leaned over the side and started to lower her.

'Hey, I want to ride up front with you.'

'You should be lying down,' he said. Gently, he set her down.

'No, I mean it. I don't want to ride back here, Mike.'

He pulled his arms out from under her. She started to sit up. With a hand on her bare right shoulder, he eased her down.

She strained against it for a moment, then seemed to relax. As if giving up, she let her legs go out straight.

'How am I going to ride shotgun for you if I'm back here?' she asked.

'Won't be for long,' he said.

'Promise?'

'Yeah.' He slid his hand away from her shoulder. He curled it over her breast. Through the T-shirt, he felt the heat of her skin, the push of her stiff nipple. Karen covered his hand and pressed it down more tightly.

Mike's heart raced. He had to swallow, but his throat felt tight. His penis felt like a hot iron bar jamming into the front of his fatigues.

He freed his hand.

He climbed over the side of the Rover, and Karen scooted sideways to make room for him.

'Mike,' she said softly. 'I don't know.'

'It'll be all right.' He crawled onto her, knelt above her.

'My face . . .'

'I know, but . . .' Shaking his head, he lifted the T-shirt above her breasts. The nearby fire felt hot and good on his back, but he wished his shadow wasn't in the way. He caressed her breasts. So smooth. They felt even more wonderful than he had imagined.

Karen writhed a little. In a low, husky voice, she said, 'We'll be in an awful fix if some sickies show up. Shouldn't we wait?'

'I can't.'

'Okay. I want you, too, but . . . Okay.'

As he gently explored her breasts, Karen set down the pistol. With both hands, she unhooked Doug's belt and spread it away from her waist. She unbuttoned her skirt, lowered the zipper.

Mike crawled backward, pulling the skirt down her legs. He slipped trembling fingers under the elastic of her panties. As he drew the flimsy garment over her sneakers, Karen sat up slightly. She crossed her arms and lifted the T-shirt over her head.

Kneeling beside her feet, Mike no longer blocked the firelight. Karen's naked body was bathed in the russet glow. As he gazed at her, she lifted a foot, gently rubbed his thigh with the sole of her sneaker, then swung her leg past him.

She was sprawled before him, open, waiting.

Mike unhooked his web belt and tossed it aside.

'Come here,' she said.

He crawled forward. Her thighs felt like warm satin under his open, fluttering hands. Between them, she was hot and slick.

Karen guided his hands to her breasts. And while he caressed them, she opened his pants. She tugged them down his thighs. She drew the band of his shorts away from his belly. She dragged the shorts down.

Suddenly free of the confining garments, he let out a shuddering breath.

He had never known such desire. His penis felt solid, huge, monstrous.

Karen's fingers slipped around it. They glided downward.

Gasping, he squeezed her breasts. She whimpered quietly, squirmed, but didn't tighten her grip. She slid her hand slowly upward. And then it was gone. Mike sank onto her. He kissed one of her breasts. He tongued the nipple. He filled his mouth with the breast, and sucked. Hard enough to make her cry out softly and flinch.

He wondered how it would be to bite it.

Karen clutched his hair with one hand. She gave it a sharp pull.

She can't take any more, either, he thought.

He scurried up her body. He licked drying blood from her lips, savoring its coppery taste, then thrust his tongue into her mouth. He pushed his erection slowly into her slippery, tight warmth.

Karen writhed under him. She raised her legs, and he felt himself sink in more deeply.

He felt buried in her.

Then he felt a cool steel ring against his temple.

He pulled his tongue from Karen's mouth. He raised his face, but the muzzle stayed tight at his head. He stared down into her eyes.

'I hope to God you don't have it, Mike.'

'Huh?'

'But I think you might.'

'No!' he blurted, panting for air. 'It's just you! I haven't got the Widow!' A string of saliva spilled from his lips and dribbled onto Karen's chin. He swallowed hard. 'It's just . . . I want you so bad!'

'I'm sorry,' she said. 'God, I'm sorry.'

He shouted, '*DON'T!*' sprayed her, and a hot blast kicked through his head.